KNIGHT

KAREN LYNCH

For my brothers

Alex, Marty, and Tom

ACKNOWLEDGMENTS

Thank you to my family and friends, as always, for your love and support. Thanks to my amazing PA, Amber, my editor, Kelly, my cover designer, Melissa, my beta readers, and all the people who make this possible.

1

"Hey, watch it!"

"Sorry," I called over my shoulder. I leaped over a basket of silk flowers that had been overturned by the elf I was chasing and sped down the row of tables.

Déjà vu hit me when I passed a display of banti dream catchers. Two and a half weeks ago, I had run through this same flea market after a different elf, and that visit hadn't gone so well for me.

The elf ahead of me now was faster and more agile than Kardas, and he lengthened the distance between us with every stride. By the time I cleared the tables, he was already at the rear door that led to the parking lot. He opened the door, paused long enough to shoot me a victorious smirk, and ran outside.

Gritting my teeth, I put on an extra burst of speed and reached the door before it closed all the way. I dashed out into the bitter cold, my breath coming in steamy puffs as I locked my eyes on my target and set off after him.

The parking lot was covered in snow and ice from a recent storm, which made running impossible. Fortunately, elves didn't handle ice any better than humans, and my quarry floundered when he hit an icy patch. Unfortunately, I hit one, too, and did my own impression of a dancing marionette.

I righted myself in time to see the elf take off again. I swore because there was no way I could catch him on foot now. But I'd be damned if I was letting this one get away.

I glanced around and spotted a family watching me from a few feet away.

I ran over to the little girl, who held a pink plastic toboggan, and gave her my ID. "Hey, can I borrow that to catch a bad guy?"

"Sure!" When she handed me the toboggan, I grinned at her and took off running on a stretch of snow. I threw myself onto the toboggan and tucked my body low as I flew across the icy parking lot after the fleeing elf.

He looked back, and his eyes bulged when he saw me rapidly closing the distance between us. He tried to outrun me, but he hadn't spent his childhood winters racing Violet in Prospect Park.

I ducked my head and slammed into his legs. His weight landed on top of me, but I was braced for it, and I rolled to the side, tipping him off me. He tried to scramble to his knees, but I was on him too quickly.

He swore and ranted at me as I shackled his hands behind his back. "I have friends, and they won't take lightly to this."

"If they're anything like you, I'm sure you'll be seeing them in Faerie soon," I said, rolling him over.

The second I released him to stand, he tried to kick me in the head. I blocked the kick and flipped him onto his stomach. Kneeling on his back, I bent low to speak into his ear. "Try that again, and you'll be getting ankle jewelry to match your bracelets."

I grabbed his arm and pulled him to his feet. Clapping and cheering behind me had me turning to face the dozen or so people standing outside the building. The elf hadn't made any friends here after he'd robbed so many people.

Picking up the toboggan, I gave the onlookers a tight smile and walked the elf to my Jeep. He balked at the sight of the iron cage in the back, but I was a little short on sympathy. These days, I wasn't particularly fond of elves who broke the law. Every time I saw a male elf, I thought it could be Rogin or Kardas, who were probably on the other side of the world by now. I hated that I was letting those assholes get into my head, but I didn't know how to stop it.

Once I had the elf secured in the cage, I shut the rear door and carried the toboggan back to the girl. "Thanks. I couldn't have done that without you."

"That was the most amazing thing I ever saw!" She glowed with excitement as she handed me my ID. "I'm going to be a bounty hunter just like you when I grow up."

I glanced at her mother, who looked horrified by the idea. Some of my favorite people in the world were hunters, and I was tempted to speak up on their behalf. Instead, I said, "I bet you'll be a great one."

I walked back to the Jeep. I was about to open my door when I spotted a lone figure watching me with an unreadable expression from the other side of the street. A knot formed in my stomach as anger and a dart of fear went through me. What the hell was *he* doing here?

My cold gaze met Conlan's. This was the first time I'd laid eyes on him or any of his friends since that morning in Rogin's basement, and I wasn't foolish enough to think this was a coincidence. If I'd learned anything about Lukas and his men, it was that they did nothing without purpose.

Whatever the reason, I wanted nothing to do with it or them. They'd gotten what they wanted, and in the end, so had I. As far as I was concerned, Prince Vaerik and his royal guard were a part of my past, and that was where they were going to stay.

Breaking our stare, I got into the Jeep. I didn't cast another glance in Conlan's direction, but I could feel his gaze on me as I drove out of the parking lot. It wasn't until I was a few blocks away that I was able to breathe normally again, but I couldn't stop worrying about what his sudden appearance meant for my family and me.

At the gym, later that afternoon, I was so distracted my trainer kept yelling at me to keep my head in the game. Maren was an ex-MMA fighter who'd gotten two world titles under her belt before she'd had to retire because of a spine injury. She was my parents' trainer and in high demand, but she had agreed to take me on when I'd called her two weeks ago. She said I was a natural like my father, but I had a lot of work ahead of me.

"You call that a high kick?" she taunted. "My great aunt Franny can do better."

I scowled at her and resumed my attack on the bag with renewed vigor, despite the fact I'd been going at this for almost an hour. If I didn't put a hundred and ten percent into each workout, she would tack on something extra, like fifty pushups or a plank challenge. She was sweet like that.

I finished up the bag routine with a series of jabs and then rested my wrapped hands on my knees to catch my breath. Maren handed me my water bottle, and I gulped the water greedily.

"Ready for round two?" she asked.

I glared so hard at her she burst out laughing, her teeth a brilliant white in contrast with her dark skin.

She tossed me a towel. "Good job, kiddo."

"Thanks." I wiped my sweaty face and neck as I watched two regulars sparring in the ring. It reminded me of the times I'd come by the gym to watch Dad working with Maren, and I wondered how long it would be until he could step into the ring again.

Maren unwrapped my hands. "Your Mom and Dad are strong, Jesse. They'll be back on their feet in no time."

"I know." I met her understanding gaze as my phone rang. I rarely let it out of my sight these days in case there was a call from the hospital. I snatched it up, and my heart thumped when I saw the hospital's number. "Hello?"

"Jesse, this is Patty," said a woman's voice. No last name was necessary because I'd spoken to the nurse almost every day in the last two weeks. "Dr. Reddy asked me to call you and let you know your father is awake."

"He's awake?" I shouted. Dr. Reddy had told me they would start to wean my parents off the sedation drugs this week, but I hadn't expected either of them to wake up this quickly. "Thank you! I'll be there as soon as I can."

I smiled so wide at Maren my face hurt. "Dad's awake! I have to go."

Laughing, she grabbed my arm as I spun toward the exit. "Maybe you should shower and change first."

"Oh." I looked down at my sweaty sports bra and leggings and made a face. "That might be a good idea."

I showered in record time, and ten minutes later, I waved goodbye to Maren as I ran out the door. The bitterly cold air stole my breath, and I was glad for the wool cap I'd pulled on over my damp hair.

It seemed to take forever to get to the hospital, and I nearly plowed into two people as I ran from the Jeep to the hospital entrance. Instead of waiting for the elevator, I raced up the four flights of stairs and emerged on the floor, panting from my mad dash.

Nurses smiled and waved at me as I hurried past them. I was a daily visitor, and they all knew me. Even the agent stationed outside my parents' room greeted me with an austere tilt of his head.

Two days after my parents had been admitted to the hospital, they were moved to a private room, and an agent had arrived to stand guard outside their door. I'd wondered why the Agency would place a protective detail on two bounty hunters until I had gone in to give my full statement about what had happened. They'd questioned me for hours, and they had been particularly interested in hearing about the Seelie royal guard's involvement in my parents' disappearance. I couldn't tell them why the guard had taken my parents, and the Agency was hoping to get answers when they woke up.

Having an armed agent on guard did little to ease my worry about my parents' safety. The Seelie guard weren't just any faeries, and if they wanted to get to my mom and dad, no agent was going to stop them. I'd reached out to Tennin because I'd learned it was he whom my parents had trusted to ward our apartment, but whenever I called him, his voice mail said he was in Faerie, with no mention of when he would return.

Dr. Reddy was in the room, which had been rearranged to accommodate two beds. He looked up from checking on my father and came over to meet me at the door. My gaze was fixed on the man in the hospital bed. He was lying on his back, and from here, I couldn't tell if his eyes were open.

"Jesse," Dr. Reddy said in a low voice, drawing my attention to him. "Your father's awake, but I want to remind you he is very confused. Don't be alarmed if he doesn't respond to you at first. That might take a day."

I peered around him at my father. "He hasn't spoken yet?"

"No. But that is normal in a case like this."

"Has anyone told him what happened?" I asked.

The doctor shook his head. "He's too confused to process much right now. You can tell him if he asks, but keep it simple so you don't overwhelm him."

"Okay." I let out a breath. "What about my mother? Will she wake up today, too?"

"She hasn't shown any signs of waking. It could be another day or two." The doctor adjusted his stethoscope around his neck. "I'll stop by after my rounds to check in."

"Thank you." I walked over to my father, who appeared to be asleep. He looked the same as he had on every other visit, except for the noticeable absence of the feeding tube. I laid my hand over his cool, dry one that felt nothing like the strong, warm hand I was used to. "I'm here, Dad."

His eyelids fluttered and lifted to reveal the blue eyes I'd waited almost two months to see again.

"Dad?"

A crease formed in his brow, and I could see his eyes moving as he stared at the ceiling. I squeezed his hand gently, and he slanted a dazed look at me. My chest constricted when I saw no hint of recognition in his eyes, and I had to remind myself of what the doctor had said.

For a long moment, I stood beside his bed, holding his hand. I wanted so much to hug him, but I was afraid it would upset him in his current state. For now, I'd have to be content with knowing he was coming back to us.

I looked around for the chair I used on my visits and saw it in the corner. Letting go of his hand, I went to pull the chair over beside his bed.

A garbled sound from him had me running back to the bed. "I'm here."

He looked at me, and this time he tilted his head in my direction to see me better. My breath caught when his mouth formed a word. "Jesse."

I leaned down for the hug I desperately needed. "I missed you so much," I whispered against his chest. He didn't speak, but a few seconds later, his hand came to rest on my back. The comforting weight made me feel like a part of me that had been lost had come back.

Reluctantly, I let him go and straightened. Warmth flooded me when he gave me a weak smile and reached for my hand holding the bed rail. I grasped his larger hand and fought back the tears that threatened. I had to be strong for him and Mom and show them all they needed to worry about was getting better.

"Mom?" His voice was barely audible, but the worry in his eyes said what he could not.

"She's right here." I stepped back and pointed to the bed behind me. "The doctor said she'll wake up soon."

He strained to lift his head so he could see my mother lying in the other bed. I knew the moment he saw her because his face softened, and his whole body seemed to relax. He returned his gaze to me. "How...long?"

I hesitated to answer, unsure if he was asking how long they'd been here or how long they'd been missing.

His fingers flexed around mine. "How...long...gone?"

"A month." Shock flashed in his eyes, and I gauged his reaction before I added, "You were found two weeks ago, and you've been in the hospital ever since."

He frowned at the ceiling as if he was trying to remember, and I could see him getting frustrated when the memories wouldn't come. I squeezed his hand. "It's the drugs. The doctor said it could take a while for your memories to come back."

The crease in his brow disappeared as he looked at me again. "You... Finch?"

"We're doing great. I've been sneaking him in to see you when I can. He's going to give me hell for not bringing him today."

My father smiled, and it was in that moment I knew he would be okay. He had a difficult road ahead, but if anyone was strong enough to do it, it was him.

I spent the next half hour reassuring him things were okay at home, carefully omitting anything about my new career and most of what had been happening in my life while he was gone. When I left out the bounty hunting, my search for them, and Lukas, there wasn't a whole lot left to tell, but he seemed too confused from the drugs to notice.

After a while, his face took on a pinched expression, and I could see he was in pain. He would never admit that, so I told him I was going to get some water, and I left the room in search of a nurse. I found Gloria, one of the regular nurses on this floor, and she consulted with Dr. Reddy about how much pain medicine my father was allowed to have.

I was waiting for her to end the call when I spotted a familiar figure emerging from the stairwell.

"Tennin." I hurried toward him. "You got my messages."

He arched an eyebrow. "Yes, all twenty-eight of them."

I smiled. I'd called him twice a day for the last two weeks, and I didn't feel the least bit guilty for filling up his voice mail.

"Your messages didn't tell me much beyond that you'd found your parents and needed a ward placed on them. Do you want to fill me in?"

I nodded and looked around for somewhere to talk. The small waiting area wasn't exactly private, but it was empty, and it would have to do. Keeping my voice low, I gave him a condensed version of what had happened at Rogin's.

After everything had gone down, I'd realized Tennin had known Lukas's identity all along. Lukas was an Unseelie prince after all. I didn't hold it against Tennin because I understood faeries were loyal to their royals. And it wasn't as if he hadn't tried to warn me away from Lukas and his men.

"Now you see why I need a protective ward on my parents," I said when I was done.

Tennin pursed his lips. "My wards are very strong, but Queen Anwyn's guard is ruthless. If they do come after your parents, you'll want the strongest protection available."

"Meaning what?" Fear sliced through me. Was he saying his magic couldn't stop the royal guard?

"Meaning, I'll have to add several layers of protection." He smiled. "Don't worry. You think your mother and father would let me ward your home if my wards weren't some of the best?"

We walked to my parents' room as Gloria came out and gave me a reassuring smile. The staff here was wonderful, and I'd miss them when my parents were moved to the treatment facility.

The agent posted outside the door put up a hand to stop us. "No unauthorized visitors allowed inside."

"Tennin is a family friend, and he's here at my request," I told him.

The Agent shook his head. "No authorization, no entry."

I crossed my arms. "Then call your superior and have them authorize him because he *is* going to enter that room."

The two of us were locked in a stare down for a good ten seconds, until he nodded curtly and pulled out a phone. Tennin and I walked a few paces away while he made the call.

Tennin let out a low whistle when we were out of earshot. "You've come a long way from the girl who showed up at my place in November, and I feel compelled to add you're hot when you're bossy."

I ignored his "hot" comment. "I'm not that girl anymore."

"I think you are. A little jaded, maybe, but I still see her."

Uncomfortable with his scrutiny, I changed the subject. "My father doesn't know about my hunting or my involvement in their rescue. I'd appreciate it if you didn't mention any of that around him."

"You don't think he'll find out eventually?"

"I plan to tell him, but not until he's stronger." I glanced toward the room. "The drugs are messing with his head, and I don't want to upset him."

"Understood."

The agent walked over to us. "You have permission to go in," he said to Tennin.

I smiled at the agent. "Thank you."

He gave his customary nod and went back to his post outside the door.

I crossed the hallway and entered the room. Walking to my father's bed, I found him sleeping peacefully, thanks to the pain meds Gloria had administered. It killed me to know this would be his life for the immediate future, but there was no other way to recover from a goren addiction.

I turned to look at Tennin, who was frowning in the doorway. "You can come in."

He waved a hand through the air, and a stream of pale green magic flowed from his fingertips and immediately dissipated. Taking a step into the room, he repeated the action with the same result. He pressed his lips together and finally met my gaze. "Your parents have already been warded."

"What?"

Tennin nodded absently as he felt for the ward again. "And it's a strong one, more powerful than mine."

"Who would do that?" Other than me, the only people determined to protect my parents were the Agency, and they hadn't mentioned a ward.

He didn't answer right away. "Your mother and father have many bounty hunter friends. Perhaps one of them hired someone to ward your parents."

My gaze swept the room as if I would spot the answer hiding in one of the corners. "It's possible, but why wouldn't they tell me? And how did they get in? The Agency has been guarding my parents around the clock."

"That I cannot answer." He swiped his hand through the air again as if testing the ward. "But this is the best ward money can buy. It will stop any attack from human or faerie. A bomb could go off in this room, and your parents wouldn't get a scratch."

"But it doesn't keep faeries out if you're able to come in."

He put a hand to his chin. "It's a very complex ward, made up of multiple layers. It would only allow me entry when you asked me to come in, and I suspect only you or your parents can invite a faerie in."

Shock mingled with my relief. My parents were safe, but I had no idea who would go through this trouble for them.

Tennin smiled. "I guess my work here is done."

"Wait. The old ward you did at my apartment required an incantation to let faeries in. This one doesn't?"

"This is far more advanced than that one. You only have to invite a faerie into the room."

"Like inviting a vampire in," I said dryly, and he laughed.

I walked over to him. "Mom and Dad will be moved to the treatment facility in Long Island in a few days. Will you ward their room at the facility when they go there?"

"That won't be necessary. When I said your parents were warded, I meant the magic is attached to them, not the room. The ward will stay with them wherever they go."

I gaped at him. "You can ward a person?"

"If you know what you're doing, yes. It's not common knowledge, but many of your world leaders have body wards to protect them from assassination."

"What about your royals? Are they warded, too?" I thought about the assassination attempt on Prince Vaerik that I'd help thwart. Had he been safe all along?

"Our own magic interferes with other magic, so wards don't work on us." Tennin smirked. "Except to keep us out."

I digested this new bit of knowledge. "There is so much I don't know."

Tennin looked past me at my sleeping parents. "For a girl who doesn't know much, you've done well. I'll admit I didn't have high expectations at first, and I've never been so happy to be proven wrong." He lowered his voice. "Don't tell your mother and father that I sent you to Teg's."

I laughed at his look of mock terror. "Your secret's safe with me."

He said he had to leave, and I walked him to the stairway exit since he hated to use the elevator.

"Tennin?" I said when we reached the door.

"What's on your mind, Jesse?"

"Do you know if...?" I pressed my lips together as I thought of how to voice my question. "Can you tell me if Faris is okay? I understand if you can't talk about him. I'd just like to know he made it."

Surprise flickered in his eyes. "I haven't heard anything, but if he had died, it would have been announced at court."

I let out a breath. "That's good to know."

He tilted his head to study me. "You're not going to ask about Lukas?"

"No."

"If that's all then." He reached for the door.

"There is one more thing. Do you have time to redo the ward at my apartment while you're in town?"

He let go of the doorknob. "You have no ward at home? What happened to the one I created for your parents?"

"It was kind of destroyed when Conlan created a ward on the apartment."

"You should be good then. His magic is as strong as mine, maybe stronger."

I shifted uncomfortably. "His ward also lets him and his friends enter my home whenever they want."

"Ah."

"Exactly. I hired another faerie when I couldn't get you, but he wasn't able to take down Conlan's ward."

"I'm not surprised." He stroked his chin. "I'll come by in a few days and see what I can do."

"Thanks." I didn't ask him how much it would cost because I already knew it wouldn't be cheap. A ward like his old one could run upward of five thousand dollars, but leaving things as they were was not an option. I tried not to think of my other expenses, such as the building's intermittent water pressure problems that were most likely going to require a very expensive plumber.

"Okay then." Tennin opened the door. "I'm out of here. Prince Rhys is in town, and I found out where he's having dinner tonight."

"Of course, you did."

He smirked. "See you around, Jesse."

"Jesse, you haven't listened to a word I've said."

Violet's exasperated voice broke my concentration, and I glanced up from my task. "Sorry. But you were amazing the first four times you ran through the lines. I didn't think you needed me to listen again."

Her scowl transformed into a pleased smile. "You're just saying that."

"You're fishing for compliments. You know those lines so well you can probably say them in your sleep. Like I told you an hour ago, those people are idiots if they don't give you that part."

"You're right." She tossed the pages she'd been reading on the coffee table and sank down on the other end of the couch to grin at me. "How long have you been at that?"

I shrugged and adjusted the position of the pick I was using to free myself from the shackles on my wrists. "About an hour."

"I thought you'd already figured out how to pick every lock in this place, Miss Smarty Pants."

"Every normal lock. These are Agency shackles, and the lock is a lot more complicated. I've been working on them for the last few days, and I'm determined to get it tonight."

In addition to training with Maren, I'd dedicated time each day to practicing with my parents' weapons and mastering my lockpicking skills. I had also been going through Mom's computer files that detailed every one of their jobs. Her notes were meticulous. If she and Dad ever wanted to retire from hunting, they could make a killing writing how-to books.

Violet snorted indelicately. "You expecting the Agency to arrest you?"

"Not anymore, but it never hurts to be prepared for any situation. I... Ow!" I rubbed my ear as I glared up at the tree house across the room. There was no sign of Finch, but I knew the little brat was watching me from behind the vines that covered his house. "Stop that!"

"Why is your brother throwing peanuts at you?" Violet asked, not trying to hide her amusement.

"He's sulking because I went to the hospital without him to see Dad." I raised my voice. "And if he doesn't behave, I might not take him tomorrow."

An indignant whistle came from the tree house, and I bent my head to hide my smile. I'd never follow through on that threat, but it was enough to make him stop trying to injure me.

Violet snickered and picked up the TV remote. She turned on the TV and flipped through the channels while I went back to trying to pick the shackle lock.

"Did the doctor say when your mom and dad will be moved to the treatment facility?"

"Not for another week, at least."

As much as I wanted my parents to get better, I wasn't looking forward to the move. Dr. Reddy had informed me last week that the facility limited family visits to only one a week for the first month. I was already trying to figure out a way around that restriction, more for Finch's sake than mine. He was going to be crushed when he found out he couldn't go see them every day.

"Once again, here is tonight's top story," said a female voice from the television. I looked up at the breaking news headline scrolling across the bottom of the screen beneath a live aerial view of a big house in Hollywood hills. "Jackson Chase has died. The twenty-one-year-old actor, who famously began an exclusive relationship with Princess Nerissa last summer, died earlier today during an apparent failed conversion."

Violet and I shared a stunned look before turning our attention back to the television. The news anchor tried unsuccessfully to maintain a solemn expression, but the gleam in her eyes betrayed her excitement as she recited the limited details they had about the star's death. As she spoke, a clip played that showed agents leading a sobbing dark-haired faerie from the house.

"Is that the princess?" I asked.

Violet nodded and placed a hand on her throat. "She looks totally destroyed."

I swung my gaze back to the news report that was replaying the same footage on a loop. "Why would they risk it?"

Violet wiped away a tear. "They were in love. I guess they couldn't bear the thought of not being together."

"But he was too old. They had to know it would never work."

"Love makes you do crazy things." Violet shook her head sadly. "Poor Princess Nerissa. What do you think will happen to her?"

I lifted a shoulder. "Nothing. She'll probably just be sent home."

It didn't matter that the princess had broken the law and violated numerous treaties. She was Fae royalty and not subject to punishment in our realm, no matter how serious the crime. And there were few crimes more grievous than an unsanctioned conversion.

Conversion was a simple term for the process to change a human into a faerie. It was so dangerous that it was illegal unless permission was granted by a member of the Fae monarchy. In the rare event that it was allowed, there were certain conditions that had to be met.

The first condition was that the human had to be sixteen or younger. Once the body finished puberty, the risk of it rejecting the change increased exponentially. The younger the human, the greater their chance of survival.

The second was that the child had to be terminally ill. No healthy children were allowed, and there were no exceptions.

The third condition was that only a royal could perform the conversion because of the amount of magic required. Not all royals were created equal, so only faeries with the bluest blood were powerful enough to attempt it.

Even if all conditions were met, there was still a risk of the child not surviving the change. To my knowledge, there had been only nineteen successful conversions in the thirty years the Fae had lived among us. All of the children had been under the age of sixteen.

Violet lowered the volume on the television. "I know what she did was wrong, but I feel so bad for her. If I were in Jackson Chase's shoes, I might have done the same thing."

"No, you wouldn't." When we were younger, she used to talk about what it would be like to be a faerie, but she never would have left her parents or me."

She sighed. "You're right. My life is too awesome to risk it."

I snorted and went back to trying to free myself from the shackles. I had barely fitted the pick into the lock when my phone vibrated on the couch beside me. I looked down at the screen and frowned at the Agency insignia displayed there. Picking up the phone, I logged into their secure app and read the message I'd received.

"Something wrong?" Violet asked.

"It's a notification to go to the Plaza tomorrow for an important announcement." I set the phone down. "The only other time I got one of those messages, it was about the two kelpies in the East River."

She pursed her lips. "You don't think it has something to do with Jackson Chase, do you?"

I resumed work on the shackles. "They already know what happened, so I can't see why they'd involve us. Plus, something that high level would be handled by the Agency."

She started flipping through channels again, and it was no surprise to see most of them were covering the Jackson Chase story. This was as big as Prince Rhys's debut last month, maybe bigger, and people would be talking about it for a long time.

I held my breath when my pick found a mechanism inside the lock that I hadn't noticed in all my hours of trying to pick the shackles. It was cleverly hidden behind the row of pins I'd been working on for what seemed like forever, and it moved when I nudged it carefully with the pick.

My stomach fluttered when the tiny lever clicked into place, and I eagerly went back to the pins. Seconds later, I let out a triumphant whoop when the shackles sprang open.

2

"Jesse, over here," Trey called when I entered the crowded lobby of the Plaza the next morning. Looking around, I found him and Bruce standing off to my far right, and I headed over to join them.

Bruce smiled broadly. "I heard your father woke up yesterday. How is he?"

"He's still a bit out of it, but the doctor said that will pass. I'm going to see him and Mom tonight. The doctor said she'll wake up soon."

"Tell them they are missed," Bruce said.

I leaned against the wall beside him. "If you want, I'll try to get you added to their visitor list."

"I'd like that."

"Dad would, too." I scanned the lobby, seeing a lot of familiar faces and a few new ones. "You know what this meeting is about?"

"No idea." Bruce's brow furrowed, and I followed his gaze to the main entrance where three agents had entered the lobby. My lip curled at the sight of Agent Curry, whom I'd had some not-so-pleasant dealings with last month. The fact that he'd freed me from the cage in Rogin's basement hadn't made me forget how determined he'd been to prove my parents were guilty of crimes they didn't commit.

I recognized one of the men as his partner, Agent Ryan. The third man looked familiar, but I couldn't place him. The way he walked in front of the other two agents told me he was in charge.

"Do you know who that is?" I asked Bruce.

"Ben Stewart." Bruce watched the agents cross the lobby. "He runs the New York Special Crimes division."

"I knew I recognized him from somewhere." Ben Stewart was Agent Curry's boss and the person who had ordered Curry to stop harassing me after Violet's mother had talked to him on my behalf. I'd seen him in passing when I went to the Agency to give my statement two weeks ago, but he hadn't spoken to me. I wondered why the Agency's head of Special Crimes was at the Plaza.

The elevator opened, and Levi Solomon got off, along with the other bond agents who worked in the building. They shook hands with the three agents and conversed for a few minutes before they turned to face the room.

Ben Stewart stepped forward, and everyone grew quiet as an air of anticipation filled the lobby. Whatever he was going to say had to be big to summon us all here like this.

"Thank you all for coming today," said the sandy-haired man who looked to be in his early thirties. He went on to introduce himself and his two companions before he finally got to the reason for his visit. "What I'm about to share with you is highly classified information. Something of this nature is normally handled within the Agency, but the need for expediency requires us to utilize all available resources."

Translation: they were looking for someone or something, and they had hit a dead end, so they were calling in the cavalry.

The agent cleared his throat. "Six months ago, a sacred religious artifact was stolen from a temple in Faerie and brought to our realm. The faeries asked for our help in locating it, but our investigation has turned up nothing substantial so far. The disappearance has been kept under wraps, but the artifact is part of an important Fae religious ceremony that will take place this spring. This makes its retrieval one of our top priorities."

Quiet murmurs spread throughout the room in the short pause before he continued. I held my breath as I waited to hear what he would say next.

"The artifact is called the *ke'tain*, and it's a small stone roughly the size of a walnut," he said.

My hand automatically went to the small stone hidden in my hair.

Ben Stewart continued. "The stone is round and closely resembles blue labradorite. The difference is that the ke'tain will glow when you touch it. It also has a distinct energy signature that can be detected by Fae magic. We'll be issuing sensors tuned to pick up the ke'tain's signature. There are no photographs of the ke'tain, but we have an artist rendering we will be sending to each of you. You should receive it in the next thirty minutes."

"What the heck is labradorite?" Trey whispered, but neither Bruce nor I answered him. I'd never heard of it or the ke'tain.

A dozen hands shot up, and Ben Stewart pointed at one of the hunters. "Go ahead."

"Is this thing dangerous to humans? Do we need to take special precautions with it?"

"The ke'tain is harmless to us." The agent answered before he pointed at someone else.

"Does the Agency think there is a connection between this and the death of Jackson Chase?" another man asked.

"No. The ke'tain's power is lethal to faeries. If Princess Nerissa had used the ke'tain, she would be dead."

Kim, one of the few female hunters I knew, raised her hand. "Have you called us in because you think the ke'tain is in New York?"

Ben Stewart shook his head. "All we know is that the ke'tain is no longer in Faerie, which means it could be anywhere in our realm. Bounty hunters all over the US and the world are getting the same information I'm giving you now. That said, New York is one of the top five locations in the world for travel to and from Faerie, so it's highly likely the ke'tain was brought here."

"Can you tell us more about the artifact?" Kim called over the voices firing questions at Stewart. "Any reason why someone would want it? That might give us an idea about where to look."

The agent seemed to think about how to answer her. "Faeries say the ke'tain contains actual breath from their goddess, and the word ke'tain translates to goddess breath. It's one of several religious objects used in a celebration to Aedhna, and it's never been removed from the temple until now.

"The ke'tain would have no meaning to a human, unless they were a collector of Fae antiquities. We've been focusing one of our investigations on known collectors and black market sellers."

Something niggled at my mind, but there was no time to dwell on it because Ben Stewart was still speaking.

"We've also been watching several Court faeries of interest, but that has been tricky because of the treaties protecting them. Unless we have solid evidence proving they have committed a crime, we are limited in what we can do."

I scowled. Here was another glaring example of how unfair the laws were that governed faeries in our realm. The authorities wouldn't think twice about entering the home of a lower faerie, but Court faeries were held to a completely different standard. They didn't have total immunity like their royals, but it was the next best thing. This was why I planned to study law. I wanted to fight for the rights of all faeries, not just the privileged.

"What is the bounty for this?" asked a gruff voice that belonged to Kim's brother and hunting partner, Ambrose. Leave it to him to get right down to business.

Trey leaned over to speak in my ear. "I bet it's a level Five."

A level Five? A thrill went through me at the possibility. I'd learned that the bounty for a Five was an insane fifty thousand dollars, and not even Mom and Dad had ever brought in one of those.

Ben Stewart cleared his throat. "The ke'tain is irreplaceable, and it's imperative that it is returned to Faerie as soon as possible. Therefore, the job has been classified as a level Six with a bounty of one hundred thousand dollars."

My jaw fell as the room erupted in a clamor of voices. Next to me, Trey whooped so loudly it made my ears ring.

Rubbing my ear, I turned to Bruce, who looked as dumbstruck as I was. "I've never heard of a Six."

He scratched his chin. "Because there's never been a Six until now."

"Are you going to join the search?" I asked him as I watched people talking excitedly among themselves while the agents tried in vain to restore order to the room.

I'd be lying if I said I didn't want that bounty. One hundred thousand dollars would support my family until my parents were able to come back to work, and it would help pay for the repairs needed on our building. But that much money made people crazy. If bounty hunters were competitive over level Three and Four jobs, what would they be like for a one-hundred-thousand-dollar payout?

Trey snorted. "Of course, we're going after it. Aren't you?" He quieted and gave me the side-eye. "You don't have any ideas about where it is, do you?"

I shot him an incredulous look. "I heard about it five minutes ago. How would I know anything about it?"

"Because you're super brainy and read all those books," he said in a tone that was almost accusatory. He still hadn't gotten over that whole bunnck incident.

"Sorry to disappoint you, but none of the books I've read mentioned the ke'tain or any Fae artifacts."

Trey looked only slightly mollified. "But you are going after the bounty?"

"I don't know yet. I could probably pick up a ton of other jobs while everyone else is focused on this one." The competition for the ke'tain job was going to be fierce, and I'd take guaranteed income over the slim chance of a big payout.

Bruce nodded approvingly. "That's smart thinking. We might do the same."

Trey spun to face his father. "You can't be serious."

"We'll discuss it when we know more about this," Bruce replied.

"Jesse," called a male voice.

I turned my head to see two young men shouldering their way through the crowd toward us. Aaron and Adrian Mercer were identical twins with blond, curly hair and hazel eyes, and they were both built like linebackers. They had been in Trey's class, and we'd always gotten along, although we'd never hung out outside of school. Like me, their mother and father were bounty hunters, and for as long as I could remember, they'd talked about following in their parents' footsteps.

"Crazy stuff, huh?" Aaron grinned at me. I knew it was him because of the tiny bump in his nose where it had been broken in high school. Before the break, no one had been able to tell them apart.

Adrian stood beside his twin, the two of them forming a wall between me and the rest of the room. "We wanted to get to you before anyone else."

"Get to me?"

They nodded in perfect unison, making them look comically robotic.

"To ask you to partner with us for the job," Aaron said as if it should be obvious. "Everyone knows how smart you are, and they'll all want you on their team."

Adrian flexed his impressive biceps. "The three of us would make a killer team. You'll be the brains, and we'll be the brawn."

Trey stepped closer, crowding me. "Jesse isn't going after the ke'tain, so you're wasting your time."

"I didn't say that." I elbowed him in the ribs.

He rubbed his side. "Well, if you do, it makes the most sense for you to work with Dad and me."

"We asked her first, Fowler." Aaron scowled at Trey, reminding me they hadn't been the best of friends in school. I couldn't remember the particulars, but I was pretty sure it had to do with a girl they'd both liked.

"Boys," Bruce called sharply. "Back off, and give Jesse room to breathe. She can speak for herself, and if she wants to partner with any of you, she'll let you know."

I shot Bruce a grateful look as the Mercer twins backed up a step.

"Sorry, Jesse," Adrian mumbled. "Got carried away."

I smiled at them. "I'm flattered you asked, but I haven't decided yet what I'm going to do."

Aaron pulled a business card from his pocket and handed it to me. "This has our numbers if you decide to join us."

"Thanks." I took the card and stuck it in my back pocket. I could hear other hunters around us talking about forming teams to go after the ke'tain, and it felt like the day of the kelpie hunt all over again. Only this time, the bounty was much higher. The air in the room practically crackled with energy, and this was only the beginning.

No one else approached me to be on their team, but I did catch a few sizing me up. Whether they were viewing me as a collaborator or as competition, I had no idea.

It took a good twenty minutes for Ben Stewart to take command of the room again, and his first order of business was to remind us we were forbidden to share anything we'd learned here with the general public. Then he informed us the ke'tain sensors could be signed out at the Agency headquarters in Manhattan starting tomorrow.

The second he told us we were free to go, every phone in the room dinged or buzzed with an incoming message. I looked down at my phone and saw a drawing of a smooth, blue stone that appeared to glow from within. The image looked so real that I touched the screen before I realized what I was doing. Feeling foolish, I stuck my phone in my pocket.

Aaron and Adrian had wandered away, so I said my goodbyes to Trey and Bruce and headed for the exit. I had a bunch of errands to run this afternoon, but I might be able to squeeze in some research on the ke'tain before Finch and I went to the hospital this evening. It was a lot quieter there at night, and there was less of a chance of someone walking into the room and seeing him.

"James, wait."

I stopped at the sound of Levi Solomon's raspy voice and turned to watch the obese man lumber toward me. He was sweating and panting by the time he reached me, and I wondered how he hadn't keeled over from a heart attack.

He waved his phone. "I know you're probably running off to get a head start on the ke'tain job, but a level Two came in that needs to be handled as soon as possible and with some delicacy. I think you'd be perfect for it."

"What kind of level Two?" I asked.

"A banti."

"Oh." My pulse leapt. I'd never seen a banti in real life, and it was on my list of jobs I wanted to do. Levi knew that, which was why he wore a devious little smile.

"Why would a banti job require delicacy?" I asked him.

He coughed wetly. "It's at the Ralston, and they don't exactly like bounty hunters hanging around. But you –"

"– don't look like a bounty hunter," I finished for him.

"Exactly."

I sighed, mentally ticking off the errands I could postpone until tomorrow. "I'll do it."

"I thought so. I'll email you the details as soon as I get to my office."

"Thanks for helping me out on this," I said to Violet as we entered the lobby of the Ralston two hours later.

"Are you kidding? I'm psyched to help you on an actual job." She bounced on her toes as she looked around the elegantly-furnished white marble lobby. "Do you think we'll see someone famous?"

"Maybe." I smirked and immediately sobered when I remembered seeing Lukas here on my first visit to the hotel. He was the absolute last person I wanted to run into.

We approached the front desk, and I recognized the receptionist I'd talked to when I'd come looking for my parents. He hadn't been too happy to assist me then, and he looked down his nose at me now.

"May I help you?" he asked in a haughty tone that suggested he'd rather do anything but.

I held up my ID. "Agency business. I was told to ask for the manager."

His nose wrinkled as if he smelled something bad. "Ah, yes. One minute."

He called someone, and I looked at Violet, who was taking in the grandeur around us. Her family was well off, but even their lifestyle was modest compared to this. The massive chandelier in the lobby was rumored to have cost more than one hundred thousand dollars, and I'd read there was an even bigger one in the ballroom.

"Jesse James?"

I turned to find a woman in her early thirties with short brown hair and wearing a dark blue suit walking toward us.

"Yes."

"I'm Marjorie Cooke, the day manager." Her steps slowed, and she frowned when her eyes took in my black jeans, boots, and the short gray peacoat I'd borrowed from Mom's closet. "You're the bounty hunter?"

I smiled and held out my hand. "Yes."

She shook my hand and looked past me at Violet. "And you?"

"I'm her apprentice."

The manager gave a bemused nod as if she wasn't quite sure what to make of us. "Please, come into the office."

We followed her to the manager's office. Once we'd shut the door, she sat behind the desk and invited us to take seats.

I spoke first. "I wasn't given much information other than that you have a banti problem. What can you tell us about it?"

"It started two days ago that we know of. Some of the human guests were overheard complaining about having strange dreams. Last night, a family staying on the fifth floor reported an attack on their fourteen-year-old daughter. The father swears he saw a banti on her bed. They checked out immediately after the incident."

Violet shuddered, and I barely hid my own revulsion. Banti would go after any sleeping human, but they loved tormenting teenagers the most. As if puberty wasn't bad enough, we had to worry about some pint-sized *Freddy Krueger* wannabe giving us nightmares.

Marjorie clasped her hands on the desk. "The owner wants this taken care of as quickly and quietly as possible. We were assured you would be discreet."

She didn't need to tell us why the owner wanted this kept under wraps. Hotels used special wards to keep banti out, and the wards had to be redone every year. It looked like someone had dropped the ball on keeping theirs updated. The Ralston would lose their five-star rating and a lot of high-profile guests if word got out that they had a banti problem.

"We're the soul of discretion," Violet piped in.

I stood. "If you could give us access to the room where the incident occurred, we'll get to work."

The manager got up and took a card key from the desk. "It's room 5017. I'll show you to the stairs."

"Can't we use the elevator?" Violet asked as we left the office.

"We'd prefer that you were seen by as few guests as possible." Marjorie led us down a hallway to a smaller, but no less elegant, lobby at the rear of the building where a huge, muscled security guard was stationed. I knew without asking that this was the entrance used by celebrities who didn't want to deal with the paparazzi out front.

She handed the card key to me. "Call the front desk and let them know when you're done. You can give Amos the key and leave by this exit."

She turned to go back the way we'd come, and I headed for the door to the stairs on the right side of the lobby. Violet followed me, not speaking until we were alone in the stairwell.

"Do you always get treated like that when you go out on a job?"

"Like what?"

She huffed behind me. "Like you're some dirty little secret."

A laugh slipped from me at her indignation. "Most people are happy to see us, but it makes sense for the staff here to want to keep us out of sight."

We emerged on the fifth floor and located 5017. I unlocked the door and pushed it open, and we gawked at the lavish suite before us. The main living area was decorated in warm cream and blue with velvet couches, white marble tables, and delicate crystal lamps I was afraid to touch. The room boasted its own glittering chandelier, and the drapes were drawn on large windows, giving us a wide view of the buildings lining the other side of the street.

I entered the suite, taking a moment to wipe my feet on the entry rug before stepping onto the polished wood floor. Setting down my duffle bag, I went to check out the bedrooms on either end of the main room. The rooms were identically furnished except for a king bed in one and a queen bed in the other.

"This must be the room the girl slept in," I said as I ran a hand over the soft white duvet covering the queen bed.

Violet flopped down on the bed with a dreamy sigh. "I can't wait to be famous and stay in places like this."

I smiled at her unwavering conviction that she would make it in Hollywood someday.

She lifted her head to look at me. "So, what now?"

"Now we catch a banti." I went back to the main room to get my bag and carried it to the bedroom, closing the door behind me.

"And how exactly do we do that? You never explained that part to me."

"We bait a trap and lure it in." Unzipping the bag, I pulled out a rolled-up pair of my pajamas and tossed them at her. "Put these on."

"Why?"

I grinned as I took off my coat and laid it on a chair. "Because you're the bait."

Banti were most active at night, but they could be lured out during the day with the right enticement. Technically, Violet was still a teenager, and she was in the same bed the banti had visited last night. I was banking on him not being able to resist coming back for seconds.

"What? No way!" She leaped off the bed like it was on fire. "Why can't you be the bait?"

"Well, for one, you can doze off at the drop of a hat, and the bait needs to be asleep. Two, snoring attracts them."

"I don't snore."

I raised my eyebrows at her, and she flushed. I continued as if I hadn't been interrupted. "Three, one of us has to trap him, and I'm the best one to do that."

"Fine." Grumpily, she undressed. "But next time, I want full disclosure before I agree to help you on a job."

"Deal." I hid my smile as I took the things I needed from the bag. One of them was a real banti dream catcher, not one of the cheap knockoffs at the flea market. It had iron and muryan woven into it, and it was supposed to make the holder invisible to banti. I was about to find out if that was true.

The bedclothes rustled, and I looked over to see Violet lying in the middle of the bed with the cover pulled up to her chest.

"Relax." I closed the drapes and turned off the lamp, throwing the room into semi-darkness. "I won't let anything happen to you."

She took a deep breath. "I know. But I have to warn you it might take me a little longer than usual to fall asleep."

"Want me to sing you a lullaby?"

A snort came from the bed. "I thought the banti was supposed to give me nightmares."

"Ha ha." I walked over to a chair in the corner and sat. "Now be a good little girl and go to sleep."

We fell quiet, except for the occasional sound of Violet shifting around. After thirty minutes, she stopped moving, and her soft snores filled the room. I smiled to myself and relaxed in the comfortable chair. All there was to do now was wait.

I occupied my time by thinking about the missing ke'tain. Why would a faerie steal one of their religious artifacts and take it from their realm? Understanding the motive behind that might be the best clue to where the ke'tain was now. There were collectors of Fae objects who would pay a lot of money for it, but Court faeries didn't need money. Lower faeries weren't wealthy, so money could be a motive for one of them. Would a lower faerie have access to the goddess's temple? There was so much about their world I didn't know, despite my extensive reading on all things Fae.

I hadn't made up my mind yet on whether or not I was going after the ke'tain bounty. It was a lot of money, too much to dismiss lightly, but did I really want to take on something like this with everything else going on in my life?

I was saved from answering by an almost inaudible whoosh of air across the room. Peering through the gloom, I was just able to make out movement at the bottom of the door. I watched in fascinated horror as green fog poured into the room from beneath the door and slowly solidified into a distinguishable shape. The creature was barely eighteen inches tall with green skin and matted green hair, and it strongly resembled the goblin I'd brought in on my first job.

Once it was fully formed, the banti turned its head slowly as if scanning the room for a threat. I didn't dare breathe when its beady yellow eyes stared straight at me, making goose bumps rise on my arms. Pictures didn't do these guys justice. In the flesh, they were as creepy as hell, and looked like something out of the nightmares they wove.

A soft murmur drew his attention to the bed, and he crept soundlessly toward it. He disappeared from my view for a minute before he leaped lightly up onto the foot of the bed. Violet didn't move, and the banti stood stock still watching her until she began to snore again.

It was all I could do to sit there as the ghoulish little faerie walked over to peer down at my sleeping friend. I almost came out of the chair when he climbed up to sit on her chest. My entire body was tensed to spring, but I couldn't move too soon, or I would lose him. I had to wait until he started to weave the nightmare because that was when he would be most vulnerable.

He held his hands out over Violet's face, and yellow magic flowed from his fingertips. It wafted down and was immediately inhaled into her partially open mouth. A twisted little smile curved his lips as she began to twitch and jerk in her sleep, her arms pinned to her sides like someone strapped down to a table.

Not yet, I told myself as the tension in my body ratcheted up with each second that little monster was touching my best friend. When I'd promised to keep her safe, I'd forgotten I would have to stand back and watch this until the time was right.

Violet let out a whimper in the throes of a nightmare, and the banti snickered gleefully, enraptured by her dream.

I shot up out of the chair and stalked silently to the bed, gripping a large butterfly net in both hands. Violet moaned in terror, and I stumbled into the foot of the bed, dropping the dream catcher.

I righted myself as the banti's head did a one-eighty, and those sinister yellow eyes burned into mine.

3

Violet cried out again, breaking us from our stare down. The banti jumped off her chest and gave me a look of pure malice before his shape began to blur.

Oh, no. If he escaped, I'd never catch him, and I was not going to fail this job. Leaping across the bed, I sprawled over Violet's legs and brought the net down over him. The second he was inside the net, I yanked on a string along the handle, and the opening of the net closed, trapping him.

The banti began to screech and thrash weakly in the net, but the thin iron threads sewn into the mesh prevented him from changing form and escaping. At the same time, Violet woke up screaming like the devil himself was after her. She wriggled out from beneath me and scrambled off the other side of the bed.

"Oh, my God!" She swiped at her face and chest as if she could remove the feel of the creature on her.

I took a step toward her, holding up the net. "It's okay. We got him."

Her eyes went impossibly round, and she backed up against the window. "Keep that thing away from me," she screeched over the banti's caterwauling.

My eardrums hurt from the noise coming from the two of them. Desperate for some relief, I sang a few bars of the first song that popped into my head. By the third line of "Shake It Off," the banti looked like a limp doll inside the net, and Violet was staring at me with her mouth agape.

Still singing, I set the banti on the bed and opened the net. From my back pocket, I pulled a tiny iron-infused collar I'd stuffed in there earlier and fitted it around the faerie's neck. The collar was designed for faeries too small for shackles, and it served the same purpose, with one added benefit. It rendered the wearer mute.

I stopped singing, and the banti opened his mouth to screech at me again, only to discover the wonders of the collar. His withering glare was enough to make me not want to sleep for a week.

"You had to sing my favorite *Taylor Swift* song," Violet griped. "I'll never be able to enjoy it again."

"Sorry, but it was hard to think with all the racket." I held back my smile. She'd be dancing around in her room to that song by tomorrow night.

She shuddered. "Why didn't you sing when he showed up, before he got into my head?"

"Because I had no idea if it would work on him, and we could have lost him." I carried the banti over to my duffle bag and put him into a small animal carrier I'd brought with me. I placed the plastic carrier in my duffle bag and looked over at Violet, who was already stripping out of my pajamas. She threw them at me, and I tucked them in around the carrier to cushion it.

Violet hurriedly dressed in her own clothes while I made sure I had all my gear stowed away. She didn't speak again until we were in the hallway, walking toward the stairs.

"Despite having the single most horrible experience of my life, I have to say you're a natural at this bounty hunting thing."

"I'm sorry I put you through that. What was it like?"

She shivered and rubbed her arms. "You ever have one of those nightmares where you know you're dreaming, but you can't wake up? It was like that, only worse. I knew the banti was sitting on me, but I couldn't move to get him off me. It felt like I was paralyzed."

Remorse coiled in my stomach. "God, Vi. I never should have asked you to do that."

"I knew what I was signing up for – sort of." She smiled for the first time since she'd woken up. "Know that was my one and only banti hunt."

I pushed open the door to the stairwell. "I'll make it up to you."

"Oh, I know you will," she quipped as we started down the stairs.

We emerged on the first floor and walked over to Amos, who resembled a stone statue. The security guard didn't move until we were directly in front of him, and even then, only his eyes shifted to take us in.

"Can you let Marjorie Cooke know the job has been finished?" I discreetly unzipped the duffle bag and let him see the angry banti in the pet carrier.

Barely batting an eye at the faerie, he pressed a button on his headset and spoke in a voice almost too low to hear.

Violet and I wandered a few feet away to wait for him to finish the call. We were looking at a large oil painting of Princess Titania when the exit door slid open and two blond male Court faeries dressed in black entered. I barely had time to wonder about their hostile expressions when Violet let out a strangled squeak.

I looked past the two faeries at a third male, and this one I recognized instantly. It was impossible not to when his face had been plastered on almost every magazine cover, billboard, and social media site for over a month.

I took a moment to study Prince Rhys. He already wore the bored, arrogant look of a celebrity who had spent too much time in the limelight. He was handsomer in person, but so was every other Court faerie. I could see nothing extraordinary that set him apart from them.

My gaze moved to the three unsmiling, dark-haired faeries behind him that made up the rest of his personal guard. A sliver of fear went through me when I thought of the Seelie royal guard who had taken my parents. Queen Anwyn's guard was completely separate from her son's, but that didn't mean they weren't working together.

The prince and his men stopped a dozen feet from Violet and me, and one of the blonds in the lead raked his icy stare over us as if assessing us for threats. His gaze took in my inexpensive attire and narrowed on my duffle bag.

"What is your business here?" he demanded.

His arrogance rankled me, but I kept my expression and voice neutral because I didn't want any trouble. I'd had enough dealings with Fae royalty and their guards to last me a lifetime.

"I'm here on Agency business," I said.

The other blond guard moved to block the prince from our view. "You do not look like an agent."

"That's because I'm not an agent. I'm a bounty hunter."

His suspicious gaze shifted to Violet, who stood mutely at my side. "And her?"

"She's my assistant." I moved protectively in front of her. The last person I wanted paying any attention to my best friend was a member of the Seelie royal guard.

"I've never met a bounty hunter," said a new voice.

"Your Highness..." protested a voice from the back as the prince shouldered past his guards to stand before me.

His five guards automatically formed a semicircle around him. I swallowed as I faced some of the deadliest faeries in the world, who looked ready to end me if I so much as blinked wrong.

I looked into the blue eyes of the prince and got the strangest feeling I'd met him before, which was absurd. I definitely would have remembered meeting the Seelie crown prince.

We stared at each other for a few seconds before his mouth curved into a smile that transformed his aristocratic face from aloof to boyishly charismatic.

"I am Prince Rhys of the Seelie Court," he said as if there was anyone over the age of ten who wouldn't recognize him by now. Reaching out, he took one of my hands in his long fingers and brought it to his lips.

"Jesse James." I didn't want to give my name, but it would be rude not to. Chances were his men would have me investigated the moment they were out of sight, and giving a fake name would only raise their suspicions.

"Like the outlaw?" At my look of surprise, his eyes sparkled with humor. "One of the things I like most about your world is your history. I particularly enjoy the stories of the Wild West." His gaze moved to my hair, which I'd worn in a ponytail for this job, and lingered there for a few seconds. "Are all bounty hunters as lovely as you, Jesse James?"

I raised my eyebrows. "I don't think the male hunters would appreciate being called lovely."

Prince Rhys laughed. "I guess not." He glanced over my shoulder. "And who is your quiet friend?"

Reluctantly, I moved to Violet's side, giving the faeries a full view of her. "This is Violet. She's helping me on a job today."

"*Two* beautiful hunters. I must be goddess-blessed." As he'd done with me, Prince Rhys lifted her hand to his lips and kissed it.

Violet made an incoherent sound. I slanted a look at her and found her staring dumbly at the prince. Biting back a grin, I discreetly elbowed her in the ribs. It was enough to shake her from her daze, and she smiled shyly at him.

"It's...nice...to meet you," she managed to utter.

"The pleasure is all mine." His gaze returned to me. "I mean no offense, but are you really a bounty hunter? I must confess I imagined hunters were like the tough western lawmen."

"I'm not offended. I get asked that all the time." I pulled my ID card from my back pocket where I always kept it. His guards looked coiled to attack, and it reminded me of how wary Lukas and his men had been with me in the beginning. Shaking off the memory, I held up the card for them to see.

One of the blond guards took the card and studied it intently before subjecting me to the same scrutiny. "You don't look strong enough to hunt."

I shrugged because it wasn't anything I hadn't heard before. "Hunting isn't only about strength and speed."

"Jesse is super smart," Violet squeaked.

The guard looked skeptical as he handed me my card, but the prince appeared to be even more intrigued. The last thing I wanted was the attention of another royal, especially one from Seelie.

I was trying to think of a way to extricate Violet and me from the encounter, when Amos called, "Miss James."

Relief flooded me as I faced him. "Yes?"

"Miss Cooke said to thank you for your help." He pointed to the exit. "You can leave through there when you're ready."

"Thanks." I adjusted the duffle bag on my shoulder and turned back to Prince Rhys. "It was nice talking to you."

His smile slipped. "You're leaving?"

"Yes. Our work here is done."

"Then you will stay as my guests for dinner," he said imperiously as if that settled everything. "I wish to talk more and to hear about your job."

All five of his men looked ready to object, but I beat them to it. "Thank you, but we have plans."

"Surely you can change your plans for one evening." Prince Rhys flashed me the same flirtatious smile I'd seen on TV that made women everywhere swoon. He was charming, but I felt no attraction to him. Lukas had made sure I wouldn't want another faerie again.

I shook my head. "I'm afraid I can't. It's a family obligation."

His brow furrowed. "Tomorrow then."

"Between family commitments and my job, I really don't have much free time. I'm sure you can understand that."

"Yes." His frown eased, but his eyes still showed disappointment. Something told me it was a foreign emotion for him.

"Hope you have a great stay in New York," I said as I snagged Violet's sleeve and started for the exit.

The moment the doors shut behind us, I sucked in the cold air, but I didn't slow our pace until we were around the building and back on the street. It took that long for Violet to find her tongue again.

"Holy Shih Tzu!" She let out a small squeal. "Did that really happen?"

I steered her toward the Jeep. "Do you mean the part where we met the prince or the part where you forgot how to speak?"

"Ugh. Don't remind me. I have no idea what came over me in there." She looked wistfully back over her shoulder. "I can't believe we met Prince Rhys, and I was a blithering idiot."

"You weren't that bad, and I'm sure he has that effect on most people."

"Not you," she retorted.

"I have a good reason to not want anything to do with the Seelie crown prince."

Violet's face flushed. "Oh, Jesse. I wasn't thinking."

"Don't worry about it. Besides, you wanted to meet someone famous at the hotel, and they don't get more famous than he is."

"You can say that again. Every celebrity I meet from here on out will pale in comparison."

We reached the Jeep, and I stowed my bag in the back. "I'll drop you off at home before I take our little friend to the Plaza."

She pouted as she buckled her seat belt. "I don't get to go with you?"

"You're not a licensed bounty hunter," I reminded her. "You helping me on a job isn't against the rules, but it's frowned upon. I don't want to give Levi or the other bond agents any reason to stop hiring me."

"Fine." She slumped in her seat.

"You're not missing much; trust me."

She waved a hand. "It's not that. I can't believe I met Prince Rhys, and I didn't think to get a single picture. My agent keeps telling me I need to do more to bump my social media following, and I let the perfect opportunity slip right through my fingers. I'll never hear the end of it if she finds out."

I started the Jeep. "I won't tell her if you don't."

"Stop squirming," I hissed into the front of my coat as the elevator stopped on the fourth floor of the hospital. "You're going to get us caught before we even get there."

Finch went still, not that I could blame him for fidgeting. He had already been excited to see Dad before I'd gotten the call an hour ago letting me know Mom was awake. The drive here had seemed to last forever.

"And remember what I told you. Mom and Dad don't know I've been hunting, and we're not going to tell them until they're feeling better."

A low whistle was his reply. Finch didn't lie, especially to our parents, and I'd had to explain several times why a lie of omission was okay in this case. I hoped he didn't forget that in his excitement to see them.

The elevator doors opened, and I hurried down the hall to their room where a female agent stood guard this time. I'd seen her a few times before, so she didn't stop me when I opened the door and entered the room.

I saw my father first, slightly reclined in his bed, his color improved, and looking more alert than he had yesterday. He beamed at me before he turned his head to look at the other bed. I followed his gaze to my mother, who lay on her back with her eyes closed.

I hurried over to her bed. Her feeding tube was gone, and she looked good, despite the gauntness in her face. Dr. Reddy had assured me my parents would regain the weight they'd lost once they were awake and eating solid foods again.

"Mom?" I said softly, not wanting to startle her.

Her eyes fluttered open, and I was surprised when she looked at me without any of the confusion my father had shown the day before. She stared at me for a moment, and then her mouth curved into a small smile as love filled her green eyes.

I smiled back, unable to speak at first because of the golf ball-sized lump in my throat. There were so many things I wanted to say to her, and I was on the verge of bawling my eyes out like a five-year-old.

An impatient whistle came from inside my coat, and my mother's eyes widened. Grateful for the diversion, I reached for my zipper. "I brought someone to see you."

I'd barely pulled the zipper all the way down before Finch poked his head out. The second he saw our mother, he made a sound like a wounded animal and scrambled out onto the bed.

"Careful," I warned him, but he was already hugging her neck with his face buried in her hair.

Mom's eyes welled, and she lifted a shaky hand to cover his small body. "My...babies," she croaked, wincing from the effort. Her throat had to be sore from the feeding tube.

"Don't try to talk." I laid my hand over hers, drawing strength from her touch, as I answered the question in her eyes. "We're okay, just really happy to see you."

She closed her eyes with a sigh and stroked Finch's back with her thumb. I left them to go to my father, who was watching them with shimmering eyes. I leaned down to hug him, and his arms enveloped me in a tight hug.

"She asked for you the moment she woke up," he said against my ear. "Your mom is a strong woman."

"I know." Smiling, I pulled back to kiss his cheek. "How do you feel today?"

"Pretty good for a goren addict."

I sat on the side of his bed. "You remember what happened to you?"

"No. The doctor told me about the goren." He pressed his lips together. "He also said we have to go to a treatment facility, so it'll be a while before we can come home."

I squeezed his hand. "Don't worry about that. Finch and I are holding down the fort. You guys focus on getting better."

He turned his warm hand over to hold mine. "I'm so proud of you."

"I have been told I take after you." He had no idea how true that was, and I wondered what his reaction would be when he learned what I'd really been up to since they disappeared.

"Jesse," my mother said in a scratchy voice.

I hurried over to her. "Do you need anything?"

She lifted her free hand and clasped mine. "I have everything I need."

Finch whistled softly, and I looked to where he sat beside her shoulder. He made the sign for dad, so I picked him up and carried him to the other bed. The moment I set him down he flung his little arms around our father's neck.

"Hey there, Buddy." Dad cleared his throat as he patted Finch's back. "I think you've gotten bigger since I last saw you."

Finch sat up, signing, *I help Jesse. We're partners.*

Dismay filled me, and I jerked my gaze from him to Dad. I was scrambling for an explanation when the door opened. "Finch," I whispered urgently, opening my coat. He leaped inside, and I zipped it as a male nurse entered the room.

The nurse smiled and went to my mother's bed to check her vitals and to ask if she was in pain. Then he came over to do the same with my father before he left, saying he'd be back in two hours.

Dad crooked a smile at me. "Why do I think you two have done this before?"

I unzipped my coat again to let Finch out. "We've had to learn to be sneaky. Finch is good at hiding."

Finch nodded eagerly and signed, *I'm sneaky.*

That earned a laugh from our father, and the sound was the best thing I'd heard in a long time. Feeling lighter than I had in months, I left him and Finch to visit while I went back to my mother, who wore a contented smile as she watched us.

"You look different," she said softly.

"Different how?" I sat on the chair between the two beds.

A frown creased her brow. "I'm not sure. More...grown-up."

I shrugged. "Guess it had to happen sometime. I *will* be nineteen in a few months."

She didn't look completely satisfied with my answer, but she didn't press it. We talked for a few minutes until I noticed she was struggling to keep her eyes open. The moment I stopped talking, she fell asleep.

Dad and Finch were deep in conversation, and I decided not to interrupt them because Finch needed this time with him more than I did. I took out my phone to check for messages, and then I spent a few minutes searching for information on the ke'tain.

I wasn't surprised when my search brought back zero results, and I made a note to visit the Library of Congress web portal when I got home. They had a restricted Fae section that was available only to members of law enforcement, including bounty hunters. I'd already spent hours there searching for any mention of goddess stones. I hadn't had any luck, but if there were any records of Fae religious artifacts, they were sure to be there.

I found it odd that the Agency had given us so little information about the ke'tain. If it was important enough to create a new job level and huge bounty for it, why weren't they sharing everything they knew with us? It didn't make sense.

An hour and a half later, Mom and Dad were sleeping peacefully, and I had to swear to Finch that we'd come back tomorrow in order to get him to leave. It had been a long day, and I still had to stop and buy groceries on the way home. On top of that, they were calling for freezing rain tonight. I hated driving in bad weather, and I wanted to be home before the roads got slippery.

A light snow was falling by the time I parked on our street. The temperature had dropped, and I made sure Finch was zipped inside my jacket before I got out. I was already shivering when I opened the cargo door to grab the groceries. Eyeing the shopping bags stuffed into the cage that took up the back of the Jeep, I calculated whether or not I could carry them all without having to make a second trip.

"Jesse."

My heart lurched, and I spun to face Conlan, who stood a few feet away. His face was illuminated by the streetlight, revealing a shadow of the easy smile he always used to wear.

"What are you doing here?" After Lukas, Conlan's betrayal hurt the most, and seeing him was a painful reminder of how gullible I'd been to believe he had actually been my friend.

The practical part of my brain told me I should be afraid, even though he didn't appear threatening. He was a member of the Unseelie royal guard, and the last time I'd been this close to him, he'd looked at me with contempt. But the hurt and anger welling up in me crowded out every other emotion.

"You know what? I don't care." I showed him my back as I gathered the grocery bags, cursing silently when I realized I would need to make two trips.

"Let me help you." He moved in to take the bags from me.

"No," I snapped. "It's a little too late for your help."

He flinched, and regret filled his eyes. My heart softened for the second it took for me to remember seeing his face through the bars of my cage.

"I'm so sorry, Jesse. We failed you when you needed us the most."

His admission took me by surprise, and I had to school my expression as I went back to my groceries. "What happened? Did Faolin torture that weasel Rogin until he told the truth?"

"Faris told us."

I sucked in a breath. "Is he...?"

"He's recovering slowly, but he's going to make it."

"I'm glad to hear that." I had only known Faris for a few hours, but I'd felt a connection to him in that short time.

"I hear your parents are going to make a full recovery, too. I'm happy for you."

I stiffened. "How do you know about my parents?"

"Faolin keeps tabs on certain persons of interest and –"

"No!" I pointed a finger at him. "My mother and father are *not* persons of interest to you. Faolin got his brother back, and I got my parents. You tell him to focus on his own family and leave mine alone."

My chest was heaving when I finished, and I fought to get my emotions under control. It was something I had struggled with since my ordeal, and I'd thought I was doing better. But the mere mention of Faolin or any other faerie watching my parents was enough to set me off.

Conlan raised his hands. "I didn't mean to upset you. Faris asked Faolin to check on your parents because he wanted to know how you were doing. He asks about you every day."

Some of the tension left me. "Well, now you can tell him you saw me, and I'm doing great."

"Are you?"

"Better than ever." I turned back to the groceries so he wouldn't see the truth on my face.

"Faris has been asking to see you."

"That's not a good idea." Not even my concern for Faris would be enough for me to go near that building or its occupants again.

"Why not?"

I huffed. "Do you really need me to spell it out for you?"

He was quiet for a long moment, and I was hoping he'd left when he spoke again. "Lukas won't be there if that will make you more comfortable."

I wanted to tell him Lukas's presence wouldn't bother me, but I wasn't that good a liar. "Did he send you, or did you take it upon yourself?"

"I requested to be the one to talk to you. You should know I wasn't the only one."

I didn't ask who else had wanted to come. I was happy Faris was recovering and that I wouldn't have to worry about Faolin hunting me down to avenge his brother. But I was moving on and putting all of this behind me. I couldn't do that if I let Conlan and his friends back into my life.

I picked up as many bags as I could carry and closed the cargo door before I faced Conlan again. The disappointment in his eyes told me he knew what my answer would be.

"I'm going to politely decline your invitation and ask that you give Faris my best. Now if you'll excuse me, it's cold out here, and I need to take care of these groceries."

He nodded once and stepped aside to let me pass. I half expected him to follow me or call after me as I crossed the street to my building, but he didn't.

I didn't look back until I was in the lobby, and I wasn't sure how to feel when I saw Conlan standing where I'd left him, watching me. I wasn't scared exactly, but it did make me nervous. Something told me I hadn't seen the last of him or his friends.

4

My phone woke me early the next morning. I cracked open my eyes to see it was barely light outside, and then I squinted at the unknown number. A few months ago, I would have let it go to voice mail, but these days, I never knew when someone from the hospital might call about one of my parents.

"Hello?" I rasped.

"Jesse James?" The male voice sounded familiar, but I couldn't place it.

"Yes."

"My name is Ben Stewart, and I work for the Agency in the New York branch."

I sat up. "I know who you are." Fear clawed at my stomach because there was only one reason he would call me personally. "Did something happen to my parents?"

"Your parents are safe. But there was an incident at the hospital last night, which required us to move them to a new location."

I got out of bed to pace the room. "What kind of incident? And where are they now?"

"All I can tell you over the phone is that there was a security breach, but your parents were unharmed," he said in a calm, authoritative voice. "We'd like you to come in today to discuss it further."

"I'll be there in an hour," I said, already pulling clothes from my closet.

I raced to dress and brush my teeth. I had serious bedhead but no time to deal with my hair, so I pulled it back in a single braid to tame it.

Finch whistled to me when I ran into the living room, and all I told him was that I had to go to the Agency. Mom and Dad were safe, so there was no need worrying him if I didn't have to.

I grabbed my coat and keys, and I was out the door less than five minutes after talking to Ben Stewart. I groaned in frustration at the sight of the ice-covered Jeep and street. After calculating how long it would take to clean the Jeep, and whether or not I wanted to risk driving, I decided against it.

It took longer than usual to walk to the subway station on the icy side-walks, and running was out of the question. I spent the entire ride to Manhattan worrying about my mother and father and wondering why the head of the Special Crimes division would call me about the incident at the hospital. Shouldn't his hands be full with the search for the ke'tain?

My stomach was one big knot of anxiety by the time I entered the Agency headquarters and was shown into Ben Stewart's corner office. Eschewing formalities, I blurted, "Where are my parents? Are they here?"

"Jesse James, I presume." The agent smiled and came around the desk. "Your parents are at the rehabilitation facility they were supposed to go to in a few days. We simply moved up the schedule. They're in on a secured level with agents watching them around the clock."

I took the chair he motioned me to, but I was too upset to relax. "What happened at the hospital?"

He returned to his chair behind the desk. "We don't know much, unfortunately. An agent arrived at midnight to relieve the one on duty, and she found the other agent asleep and the two nurses suffering from memory loss."

My fingers clenched the arms of my chair. "Glamoured?"

"The nurses were. The agent was wearing his anti-glamour device, so he was knocked out."

"And my parents?" I asked in a tight voice.

Stewart clasped his hands on the desk. "Your father said a flash of light woke him up. He saw someone in the doorway, but he couldn't make them out. Your mother slept through it."

The powerful wave of relief that went through me left me almost giddy. I owed an immense debt of gratitude to whomever had created that ward.

"That brings me to the first question I have for you," Stewart said. "Who did you hire to ward your parents? Our faerie consultant said it's the strongest she's ever seen."

"I did ask a friend to do it, but he told me they were already warded. I thought the Agency might have done it since you're guarding them."

He shifted in his seat. "We warded the room the day your parents were admitted to the hospital, but since then, someone created a new one that overrode ours. Our Fae consultant could not enter the room or get within ten feet of your parents. She informed us the ward is attached to your parents, not the room, which is difficult to do."

"My friend told me that, too." I lifted my hands and let them fall. "I honestly have no idea who did it. I wish I did so I could thank them."

He stared at me thoughtfully for a moment and nodded.

"You said that was your first question. You have more?" I asked.

"You spent several hours with your parents last night. Did either of them say anything about what happened to them or why they were held prisoner?" He picked up a pen and rolled it between his fingers. His actions were casual, but the gleam of interest in his eyes told me my answer was very important to him.

"I didn't ask my mother about it because she'd just woken up. My father said he couldn't remember anything."

Stewart was slow to hide his disappointment. "That's too bad."

"Their doctor told me this is normal with all the drugs in their system, and they might get those memories back eventually."

"Yes. We were told that as well," he said.

"May I ask you a question now?"

He nodded. "Certainly."

I leaned forward. "Why is the Agency so invested in the protection of two bounty hunters? What are you hoping my mother and father will remember?"

He smiled. "That's two questions."

I was still too wound up about the breach to play word games with him. "Then how about this? You think my parents' disappearance is connected to the missing ke'tain, and you're hoping they will remember something that will help you find it."

His head jerked back. "Why do you say that? Do you know something you haven't told us?"

"No, but it's not that hard to put the pieces together."

"What pieces?" He furrowed his brow.

"I've been wondering why the Agency would guard two bounty hunters around the clock, especially since no one here was too concerned about finding them when they were missing." There might have been a hint of accusation in my tone. "I was at the Plaza yesterday when you made your announcement about the ke'tain, and then I get a call from you, instead of one of your agents, about the security breach. That doesn't sound like something the head of Special Crimes would do."

He nodded. "Go on."

"Last night, I thought about what you said about the Agency looking into collectors of Fae antiquities. When I spoke to Agent Curry at the hospital after my parents and I were found, he asked me if Raisa Havas had said anything about Cecil Hunt trafficking stolen Fae antiquities. I didn't think anything of it then, but now I suspect they are connected."

"Is that it?" His expression gave nothing away.

"No. As I said in my official statement, Raisa Havas told me it was the Seelie royal guard who took my mother and father. What if they did that because my parents uncovered something about the ke'tain?"

"You think the Seelie royal guard took the ke'tain?" He steepled his fingers against his lips, no longer trying to appear casual.

I shrugged. "I'm not saying they stole it. All I have is my gut feeling, which might not count for anything with you. But I do know this. My mother and father are too smart to go up against the royal guard of either court. There has to be a damn good reason why the Seelie guard wanted them out of the way."

Stewart pursed his lips. "Impressive. I read in your file that you have an above average IQ. With your academic scores, you should be an agent, not a bounty hunter."

"I should be in college." I chose not to respond to his implication that agents were smarter than bounty hunters.

"Why aren't you in college? If you don't mind me asking."

"Life happened," I said matter-of-factly. "I'll get there eventually. Right now, my only concern is the safety of my family. If a faerie got past your agent at the hospital, what makes you think your agents can protect my mother and father at the rehabilitation facility?"

"The agents posted there are only a precaution. Your parents are protected by the ward attached to them."

I clasped my hands in my lap. "And you're sure it will keep out all faeries, including the Seelie royal guard?"

"Nothing is one hundred percent guaranteed, but I don't think you'll find a more powerful ward." He smiled confidently. "Your parents are as safe as the First family."

I relaxed my stiff shoulders. "When can I see them?"

"Tomorrow. Their doctors said the upheaval and sudden move was taxing, and your parents will need a day to settle in." He glanced at his watch. "I have a meeting in five minutes. Is there anything else you'd like to discuss before then?"

There were a lot of things I wanted to ask him, but I settled on one. "You said yesterday that no faerie can use the ke'tain's magic. Why would one of them want the ke'tain?"

"I wish I knew."

The slight tightening of his jaw made me suspect he wasn't being entirely honest with me, but I didn't press the matter. He had been cooperative so far about my parents, and I didn't want to do anything to change that.

I thanked him for everything they were doing for my parents and left his office with his business card, in case I ever needed to contact him. Instead of leaving the building, I took the elevator to the second floor, where I had gone to have my ID done. It was also where we had to go to sign out the ke'tain sensors.

One thing I knew for certain was that my mother and father were still in danger. If the faerie who had tried to get to them last night was after the ke'tain, they weren't going to give up until they had it or until my parents were no longer a threat to them. The only way my family would be safe was for someone to find the ke'tain first and turn it over to the Agency.

I told the guard what I was there for, and he sent me down a hallway to the requisitions room. Inside, an agent stood behind a tall desk, working on a computer. He looked so young he had to be fresh out of the academy. I guessed they had to start new agents somewhere, and I realized this could have been me if I'd joined the Agency. I imagined working in this dull, windowless room and shuddered. I'd go stark raving mad before my first week was up.

He looked past his monitor at me. "Can I help you?"

"Yes. I'm here to sign out a ke'tain sensor."

"Those are only for agents and bounty hunters," he replied dismissively, going back to his computer as if I wasn't there.

I was used to people assuming I wasn't a hunter, and it normally didn't get to me. After my morning, I was in no mood to deal with the attitude of someone, who would probably wet his neatly-pressed pants if he saw the things bounty hunters faced.

I slapped my ID down on the counter so hard he jumped. "And you think the guard would have let me in here if I wasn't authorized?"

"Everything okay here?" asked Bruce, who had entered the room without my notice.

I looked over my shoulder at him and Trey. "I'm waiting for..." I peered at the agent's badge and had to swallow back a laugh. "Agent Smith to issue my sensor."

The agent in question picked up my ID, his gaze flicking between me and the card. "You're that bounty hunter who got kidnapped in Queens last month. They found you and your parents in some basement."

"That would be me." I tapped my fingers on the desktop. "Can I get my sensor now?"

"Uh, sure." He clicked around on his computer with the mouse and then stuck my ID in a scanner. After the light on the scanner turned green, he removed the card and slid it across the counter to me. "I need to go in the back and grab you one."

"Thanks."

He left through a door behind him, and I turned back to Bruce and Trey. "I guess I know why you guys are here."

Bruce smiled. "We're still going to take on the usual jobs, but it would be foolish not to search for the ke'tain, too."

"We weren't expecting to see *you* here," Trey said. "Thought you weren't going after the ke'tain."

I pocketed my ID. "I figured it wouldn't hurt to have a sensor just in case."

"Very smart of you," Bruce said.

Trey snorted. "You came all the way to Manhattan first thing this morning to pick one up just in case?"

I narrowed my eyes at him. "No, I came all this way because I got a call from the Agency, telling me they had to move my parents after a security breach at the hospital last night."

"What?" Bruce's eyes widened in alarm. "What happened? Are they okay?"

I filled them in on what Stewart had told me about the incident at the hospital. "Do you know anyone who would pay for a ward like that?" I asked Bruce.

He shook his head. "I don't know anyone who could even afford it."

We fell quiet when Agent Smith returned and placed an oblong object the size of a vehicle remote on the desk. There were no buttons on the sensor, only a single light that glowed a dull red color.

"How does it work?" I asked him.

"It's pretty simple. The device will start to vibrate when it's close enough to the ke'tain to pick up its power signature. The light will change from red to yellow to green the closer you get to the ke'tain."

I lifted my eyes to his. "If the ke'tain has never left Faerie, how do we know the sensor works?"

He looked at me as if I'd asked why the sky is blue. "Because the faeries supplied the stones that power the devices. I'm sure they know what they're doing."

"I bet they do." I reached over and picked up the sensor, and the light began rapidly flashing red, yellow, and green. "Is it supposed to do that?"

"No." He took the device from me, and the flashing changed to soft intermittent flickers. "It must be bad. I'll have to get you a different one."

He disappeared into the back again and returned with a new sensor. The light flickered before he handed it over to me. It went crazy when it touched my hand.

"That's strange. These were fine when we got them in yesterday." Frowning, he took the sensor and turned it over in his hands.

"Can I see it?" Bruce asked.

Agent Smith handed the sensor to him. I waited for it to act up, but nothing happened. Bruce passed it to Trey and still nothing. Trey gave it to me, and it lit up like the Fourth of July.

The agent eyed me suspiciously. "Are you carrying anything on you that might interfere with the signal?"

"Like what?" I set the device down and emptied all my pockets. Other than my ID, I had my phone, keys, some cash, a wool cap and gloves, and the new MetroCard I'd purchased today.

"That's it?" Smith asked.

I held up my arm and pulled down my sleeve to show him my leather bracelet. Agent Curry had returned it to me when I came in to give my statement about my kidnapping. "Except for my anti-glamour talisman."

"That can't be the problem because Trey and I are both wearing talismans," Bruce said.

Smith was unconvinced. "There has to be something else."

"Unless you plan to strip search me, you'll have to take my word on it. There is nothing on my person that could interfere with a Fae device."

The moment the statement left my lips, I realized that wasn't true. I raised my hand automatically, but checked myself before I could touch the tiny stone hidden in my hair. To cover the action, I tucked a stray strand of hair behind my ear.

Trey grinned and raised a hand. "I'm happy to –"

"In your dreams." I scoffed, and Bruce chuckled.

Smith picked up the device again. "I don't know what to tell you then. For some weird reason the sensor doesn't work for you."

I let my shoulders sag. How was I supposed to search for the ke'tain without a sensor? The stone could be right under my nose, and I wouldn't know it.

My face must have shown my disappointment because Trey said, "You can still work with us if you want to. Right, Dad?"

Bruce smiled. "We'd be lucky to have you."

"Thanks. I'll think about it." I stuffed my belongings back into my pockets as Smith took Trey's ID and scanned it. He handed Trey one of the sensors he'd brought out for me and repeated the process for Bruce.

"Did you drive here, Jesse?" Bruce asked as the three of us walked to the elevator.

I made a face. "The Jeep had about half an inch of ice on it, so I took the train."

He pushed the button for the elevator. "We're headed home if you want to ride with us."

"That'd be great."

We exited the building, and a cold wind sucked the breath from me. Shivering, I pulled on my wool cap, tugging it down over my ears. Days like this made me think Maurice was onto something, spending his winters hunting down south. I hadn't heard from him since I'd called him after my parents went missing, and I wondered what kind of job he was on that kept him out of communication for so long. Had to be a big one, although not as big as the ke'tain job.

"Have you done any research on the ke'tain?" Trey asked me as we walked down the slippery sidewalk toward their SUV.

"I was going to do some last night, but I didn't get around to it. I know where we might find some information, if there is any to be found."

The two of them stopped walking and gave me expectant looks.

"The Fae section at the Library of Congress. There's an online portal you can log onto with your ID number."

Bruce rubbed the back of his neck. "I've never had to use it, and I probably wouldn't have remembered it."

"You might want to check it out because you know I'm not the only hunter who thought of it."

He gave me a grateful smile. "Thank you, Jesse. We'll need every advantage we can get with this one."

"I hope it helps." It didn't matter to me which one of us found the ke'tain as long as it ended up in the right hands.

Trey was a little more exuberant with his thanks. He pulled me into a tight hug and lifted me off the ground to swing me around. "You're the best!"

He set me back on my feet and wrapped an arm around my waist to steady me when I slipped on the ice.

Laughing, I pushed him away. "You're such an..."

The words died on my lips when I looked past Trey and into a pair of midnight-blue eyes.

Lukas stood less than ten feet away, his face carved from stone as his gaze shifted from me to Trey, who still had one arm loosely around me. Our eyes met again, and my traitorous stomach did a little flip before it tightened in anger.

I don't know what he saw in my expression, but his face lost some of its hardness. For a brief moment, it was almost like looking at the old Lukas, the one I'd thought I knew before he'd shown me what a naïve little girl I was.

Movement behind Lukas tore my gaze from his. Iian and Kerr flanked him, and they looked uncertainly between him and me. Of course, he wasn't alone. A Fae prince didn't go anywhere without his personal guard.

I opened my mouth to yell at him, to tell him all the things that had been bottled up inside me for weeks. But the words wouldn't come. Here was my opportunity to confront him on equal ground without bars between us, and I was too emotional to speak. The more I tried, the more my throat closed in frustration.

My back was ramrod straight as I pulled away from Trey and marched past Lukas without another look at him or his men. I didn't look back to see if Trey and Bruce were following me. All that mattered was getting as far away from *him* as possible.

Idiot! I berated myself as I stalked off, barely noticing my surroundings. I'd known there was a chance I would run into Lukas eventually, but I hadn't been prepared for it to happen so soon. Even after Conlan's visit last night, Lukas was the last person I'd expected to see today.

I didn't stop walking until Trey snagged my arm and pointed at their SUV, which I'd passed. He and Bruce cast questioning looks at me as I climbed into the back seat, but I didn't offer them any explanation. I was shaken from seeing Lukas, and I was afraid I'd embarrass myself by crying or ranting if I had to answer questions about him.

Bruce and Trey talked quietly among themselves for the ride to Brooklyn. When we pulled up to my building, Bruce put the vehicle in park and turned in his seat to look at me.

"Was that something I need to worry about?"

I forced a smile to reassure him. "I'm okay, and you don't need to worry."

"You'd tell me if you were in trouble, wouldn't you?"

"Yes, and I promise I'm not." I opened the door. "Thanks for the ride. Happy hunting."

"I'll be with you in a minute," Levi Solomon rumbled as the door to his office

44

opened. Muttering under his breath, he continued writing out the check for the two peri I'd brought in.

I looked toward the door as a man in his late twenties entered the room with a large frayed backpack slung over one shoulder. His sun-bleached blond hair and tanned skin screamed California surfer, and I was betting he was one of the out-of-state bounty hunters flooding the city.

Levi's mouth was pinched as he handed me the check. "I have a dozen new jobs and twice as many hunters in the city, but all anyone cares about is that bloody ke'tain." He inclined his head toward the newcomer, who was studying the old wanted posters adorning the walls. "You here for a job?"

"I was told at the Agency to check in with a bondsman before I got to work on the ke'tain job," the man said.

"See?" Levi shook his head at me, making his chins wobble. "Not sure how the Agency expects me to get anything done when no one wants the jobs."

"I'll take them."

"Very smart, James." He gave me a shrewd smile. "There's a lot of money to be made here. Let everyone else fight it out over the ke'tain."

I folded the check and stuck it in my pocket. "Actually, I am going to search for it, but I'll take those other jobs, too."

He raised his bushy eyebrows. "You sure you can manage all of that?"

"Are you going soft on me, Levi?"

He barked a laugh. "You can jump off the Brooklyn Bridge for all I care, as long as you don't screw up my jobs."

I placed my hand against my chest. "You're all heart."

Five minutes later, I had four new jobs with the promise of more as soon as I finished them. I was pretty pleased with myself as I stuffed the list into my pocket. One of the jobs was a Three, and the rest were Twos. I intended to knock them out as fast as possible so I could get started on the ke'tain job.

Levi's phone rang as I walked to the door, and he grumbled as he answered it. I had a feeling the bondsman had some long days ahead of him until things went back to normal.

I had just pushed the button for the elevator when Levi's office door opened, and he said, "Good, you're still here."

I faced him as he ambled toward me. "Something wrong?"

"Got a rush job that needs to be handled ASAP. House with a bunch of creatures on the loose."

"What kind of creatures?"

"A nixie and possibly a drakkan," he said.

I perked up at the mention of a drakkan because I'd never seen one up close. I couldn't imagine why a drakkan and a nixie would require a rush job, though.

"And about three dozen verries," Levi added slowly.

I shuddered. "Verries?"

"They're a level Three," he reminded me. "For the lot."

I didn't respond. Normally, I wouldn't hesitate over a Three, but five thousand dollars suddenly did not sound like a whole lot of money.

Levi's face twitched like he was fighting some internal battle. Either that or he really needed to go to the restroom. "Fine! Double the bounty for the verries, but only because I don't have anyone else to ask."

I stuck out my hand. "Deal. I have to run home to get a few things."

"Don't take too long," he said, squeezing my fingers in his meaty grip.

The elevator doors opened, and I stepped inside. "Where am I going?"

"Flatbush. The Agency raided the home of a black market dealer there, and he freed everything he had in cages to create a diversion." Levi's lip curled. "The agents weren't equipped to handle the verries and called us for help cleaning up their mess. As if I don't have enough to deal with, without them creating more work for me."

My stomach quivered with excitement. Raids were not uncommon, but the Agency was too focused on the ke'tain to bother with some guy selling the usual Fae contraband. If they suspected the dealer knew something about the ke'tain, it was the perfect place for me to start my own search.

"Text me the details," I called to Levi as the elevator doors closed.

It wasn't hard to find the house in Flatbush. Turning onto the street, I saw a bunch of cars and vans in front of a white, two-story house, and six agents in tactical gear standing in the driveway. I found a parking spot and took a white, hooded coverall from my bag, which I pulled on over my clothes. It didn't provide much protection from the cold, but shivering was the least of my concerns.

The agents watched me approach, but they didn't say anything until I reached the bottom of the steps.

"I'm Agent Ross," said one of them as he took in my outfit and duffle bag. "You one of the bounty hunters?"

I showed them my ID. "Levi Solomon sent me. What's the situation inside?"

"Honestly, we have no idea," Ross answered a little sheepishly. "We cleared out when the verries got loose, and we haven't been inside since. As far as we know, none of them escaped the house."

"They wouldn't survive long in this cold if they did." I adjusted the strap of my bag. "I guess I'd better get in there."

They parted like the Red Sea, and one of them even went ahead of me to open the door. I entered the foyer, and the door shut quietly behind me. If not for the ten-thousand-dollar bounty, I wouldn't want to come in here either.

I unzipped my bag and took out a pair of white painter's booties, which I pulled on over my boots. Then I removed my glasses and donned a white ski mask and white gloves. Taking a few deep breaths, I gave myself a silent pep talk and left the foyer to begin my search.

The house was an old one that hadn't been renovated to give it one of the open floor plans that were so popular today. Before me was a short hallway with two open doors on my right and two on my left. At the end of the hall were the stairs to the second floor.

I crept slowly down the hall, stopping to peer into the first two rooms. The one on my left was an office, and for a few seconds, I was tempted to go inside and snoop around. But the Agency could arrest me and strip me of my bounty hunter license if they caught me messing with potential evidence. And then there were the verries that needed to be dealt with.

I looked at the room on the right, which was a combined kitchen and dining room. Seeing no signs of movement, I kept going.

The second room on the left was more interesting. It contained at least twenty iron and plexiglass cages of varying sizes. All the cages were empty, but at some point, they had each contained a faerie that was sold on the black market.

A security camera was mounted in one corner, most likely so the owner could keep an eye on his inventory while he was out. I'd seen one in the office and at the end of the hallway, too. I wouldn't be surprised to find them all over the house. People who dealt on the black market were generally para-noid about their security.

I looked at the cages again, and anger licked at me when I thought about Finch and his parents in one of these. How terrified he must have been when they were taken from him and sold off. What would have happened to my brother if our parents hadn't found him and brought him home with them?

Reminding myself I had a job to do, I left the room and walked the few steps down the hall to the last door on the right. On silent feet, I entered the living room and stopped to stare at the sight before me.

On the walls and every piece of furniture were giant moths in a wide array of colors. Each moth was as big as a dinner plate with a thick body and two sets of antennae on its head. I'd watched a National Geographic docu-mentary on verries a few years ago, but that paled in comparison to seeing the creatures up close.

A ripple went through them as if they were aware of my presence, and beneath the ski mask, sweat broke out on my upper lip. I remembered thinking the documentary crew had to be nuts to get that close to so many verries, and I wondered now if any of those guys had been hit with the sudden urge to pee. I wasn't getting paid nearly enough for this.

Moving in what felt like slow-motion, I entered the living room. Verries were attracted to bright colors, except white. For some reason they couldn't see white, so I should be invisible to them as long as I didn't make a noise. Their antennae were highly sensitive to sound, and loud noises set them off. I'd rather face a ravenous bunnek than a swarm of verries.

I went to the closest verry perched on the back of an armchair. Holding my breath, I reached out and ran a finger lightly down the creature's back. On the second stroke, the verry stiffened, and its wings folded against its body.

So far, so good. I let out my breath and picked up the sleeping creature, careful not to jostle it. I turned and retraced my steps to the room across the hall where I gently laid it on the floor of a large glass cage that was littered with white droppings. One down, only a few dozen more to go.

Over and over I repeated the painfully slow process of putting a verry to sleep and carrying it to the cages. Ninety minutes in, I had captured thirty-five of the creatures, and there were five left.

I was reaching for a verry clinging to a curtain when a door slammed upstairs. I froze on the spot as the five verries left in the room fluttered their wings in agitation. The agent said everyone had left the house, so who the hell was upstairs?

Feet pounded down the stairs, and a man called, "God, I slept like the dead. Why didn't you wake me up, Lewis?"

The verries took flight.

Oh, no! I raced from the room and came face-to-face with a shocked Korean man, who paused on the bottom step.

"Who the hell are you?" he demanded.

"Be quiet," I whisper-yelled, running toward him.

"Wha–?" The word was choked off as his eyes bulged in horror.

I froze. I didn't need to look behind me to know I was too late.

5

The man yelped and whirled to escape up the stairs. He made it up three steps before the verries reached him. They circled him in a frenzy, and my stomach lurched at the sight of the large curved stingers protruding from their undersides and already glistening with venom.

I looked around frantically for something to help the man, and my eyes lit on a framed picture on the wall. I yanked it from the wall as the man let out a bloodcurdling scream. He fell down the stairs and landed in a writhing, screaming heap at the bottom. The noise only excited the verries more, and they dived at him, stabbing him with their stingers.

I ran at them, brandishing the picture. Swinging, I smashed it into a verry, sending the creature at the wall. The other verries immediately abandoned the man to search for the new threat, but my white outfit confused them. All they could see was the picture I held, and they went after it like missiles.

For a heart-pounding minute, I thought I was done for as I batted verries away one after the other. My ribs felt like they were about to crack from the pressure in my chest, and I nearly wet my pants when a stinger snagged on my glove. I managed to swat the verry away before it could jab me, but the close call made me break out in a cold sweat.

The man was convulsing and foaming at the mouth by the time I took the last verry down. I dropped the picture and ran to him, counting at least nine blistering welts on his face and arms. With that much venom in his body, he'd be dead in minutes.

I raced to the cage room where the other verries were still out cold.

Opening the door to their cage, I scooped up some of the white droppings and reclosed the door. I hurried back to the man and covered the welts with the sticky, foul-smelling paste. I had to make a second trip to get more, but by the time I was done, the man had stopped thrashing and foaming at the mouth. I had no idea if I'd done enough to save him, but I'd given him a chance, and that was better than nothing.

Yanking off the ruined gloves, I ran to the front door. When I opened it, I came face-to-face with Agent Ross.

"Get an ambulance. There's a man in here with multiple verry stings."

He stared at me for a few seconds, and then he turned to bark orders at someone. The other agents leapt into action as Ross looked at me again. "Has the threat been neutralized?"

"Yes." I pulled the ski mask over my head, reveling in the cold air that touched my heated face. Stepping back, I waved the agent inside.

He strode past me and went to the unconscious man at the foot of the stairs. More agents passed me, and they warily eyed the dead verries in the hallway as they joined their leader.

Ross called me over. "What is this white stuff all over him?"

"Verry dung." I tucked some loose hair behind my ears. "If you use it as a poultice, it draws out most of the venom."

His eyes widened. "You knew that?"

"It's my job to know that."

"Impressive," said a female agent who was kneeling beside the man. "No one could survive this many verry stings. If he lives, he can thank you for it."

"Who is he?" Ross asked me as if I should know the answer.

I shook my head. "No idea, but I'm pretty sure he's a friend of the owner. He came from upstairs, and he slept through the raid."

The agents studied the man with new interest, and the woman reached under him to retrieve the thin wallet in his back pocket. She pulled a driver's license from the wallet and read the name out loud. "Brian Kang."

"Run that name," the lead agent ordered. "I want to know everything there is to know about him and his connection to Lewis Tate."

"Yes, sir." She stood and flashed me a smile as she hurried past.

Ross turned to another agent. "Diaz, I want you to find the backup for these security cameras. If we're lucky, Tate didn't have time to delete it before he took off."

"If you don't need me, I'll get back to work," I said to Ross. "I still have to find the nixie and the drakkan."

He looked at me as if he had already forgotten I was there. "Don't enter a room until an agent clears you to go in. And if you see anything that looks suspicious, you come straight to me with it. Understood?"

"By suspicious, do you mean anything that looks like the ke'tain?"

Surprise flashed in his eyes at my bluntness. "Exactly that."

I went to the foyer to get my duffle bag. Stripping off the coverall and booties, I stuffed them in the bag, hoping I never had to use them again. The memory of the verries attacking that poor man was not one I would soon forget.

"What's this?" drawled a female voice with a thick Texas accent. "They let children play at being hunters here?"

"I reckon so," said a second voice.

I looked up at the two women standing in the doorway. One was blonde and the other was a brunette, and they looked to be in their mid-twenties. They wore faded jeans, leather jackets, scuffed cowboy boots, and matching mean girl expressions.

Blondie looked down her nose at me. "I think you're out past your bedtime, little girl."

"Run along home," her friend said. "This is a job for the adults."

I stood, pleased to see I was at least an inch taller than both women, even with their heeled boots. Their pinched expressions said they were decidedly unhappy about it. I'd never had to deal with bullies in school, and none of the local hunters had ever been hostile toward me, so I wasn't sure how to deal with this situation. I wouldn't back down from them, but I didn't want a confrontation with them either.

I smiled so sweetly I was sure their teeth must have ached from it. "I'll be out of here as soon as I finished the jobs I was sent here to do. You're welcome to one of them. Do you want the nixie or the drakkan? Sorry, but I already did the verry job."

I knew perfectly well that these two weren't here for the small jobs. Like every other out-of-town bounty hunter, they were looking for the ke'tain. They had heard about the raid, and they'd shown up hoping to find their prize. I'd bet half my bounty that they wouldn't be the only hunters arriving here before the night was out.

Blondie scoffed. "You can keep them. Just stay out of our way."

"Is that any way to speak to a fellow hunter?" chided a new voice as Kim pushed past the two women. The Texans had looked tough before I saw them next to her. Kim was all lean muscle and hard lines, and I'd heard she had once single-handedly taken down four ogres.

"What is this, a social event?" The brunette curled her lip. "Y'all have to follow proper decorum up here?"

Kim smiled, showing her teeth. "Consider it a little bit of friendly advice. I don't know how *y'all* do things back home, but here, we look out for each other."

"How quaint," Blondie said in a bored tone. She walked past me, shouldering me aggressively along the way. Her friend smirked and followed her.

"Bitches," Kim muttered.

I gave her a sideways look. "Friends of yours?"

"Ambrose and I had the pleasure of making their acquaintance last night. They've been here one day, and already he is in a bad mood."

I didn't respond to that because I had no idea her brother's mood could get worse.

She faced me with a scowl. "You need to toughen up, or people like that will always see you as an easy target."

"Gee, thanks," I retorted, feeling the sting of her words.

"Don't get bent out of shape. You might be a walking encyclopedia, but you need more than brains in this business."

I crossed my arms. "Dad taught me self-defense, and I'm working with a trainer now."

"That's a start." She waved a hand up and down my body. "But you still look like a high school senior. I bet that at least once a day someone asks if you're really a bounty hunter."

I opened my mouth, but I had no rebuttal because she was right.

Kim continued. "You can't do anything about your age, but sometimes a little attitude goes a long way. You're too nice. And don't let anyone intimidate you."

It was my turn to scowl. "I wasn't intimidated by them."

She nodded. "Good, because they won't be the last assholes you're going to meet before this whole ke'tain business is over. The damn city is being overrun by hunters, and some of them will sooner slit your throat than give you a hand."

"I'll keep that in mind."

"What do you mean we're not allowed inside?" one of the Texans demanded loudly.

I looked behind me to see an agent escorting the two furious women down the hall toward us. I stepped to the side to let them pass.

The brunette pointed an angry finger at me. "Why is she allowed in?"

The agent frowned at me, and I realized he didn't recognize me without the coveralls. I held up my white ski mask. "I caught the verries."

He nodded and looked at the Texans. "She's here on a job. The rest of you will have to wait outside."

"This is bullshit," Blondie ranted, but the agent ignored their protests as he nudged the two women through the door.

Kim didn't look happy either, but she slapped my shoulder before she followed them. "I guess I'll go see how much I can piss off the cowgirls while we wait."

I grinned. I would love to be a fly on the wall out there to hear the exchange between the three of them after the door closed.

Two agents were scouring the office, so I peered into the kitchen where a male agent was going through the cabinets. In one hand, he held a ke'tain sensor while he used the other to open the doors and drawers. He moved quickly, not bothering to close the doors when he was done.

"I don't suppose you found a nixie or a drakkan hiding in one of those cabinets?" I asked him from the doorway.

He frowned, clearly annoyed by the interruption, and went back to work. "No."

Remembering Agent Ross's orders, I stayed where I was until the man finished his search and left the kitchen. I didn't think he could have missed a faerie in the room, but I went through it all the same. It wasn't like I could search the other rooms yet anyway.

As I'd expected, I found nothing. A glance into the hall told me the agents weren't finished searching the other rooms on the main floor. At this rate, it was going to take forever to complete my job.

It was another thirty minutes before I was able to enter the office, which looked like a small bomb had gone off inside. I studied the scattered papers and open drawers and thought back to the day Agent Curry had shown up to my apartment wanting to search it. If he'd had a search warrant, our office probably would have looked like this when he was done.

I stepped carefully around the papers on the floor, even though I already knew neither the nixie nor the drakkan was in here. If I had to put money on it, I'd say they were hiding upstairs in the darkest corners they could find. But the Agency had raided this house because they thought the ke'tain might be here, and I'd be an idiot not to take advantage of this opportunity to do a little snooping.

Sadly, it looked like the agents had taken anything of interest, including the computer. All that was left were household bills and miscellaneous items they'd deemed unimportant. I picked up a crumpled piece of heavy linen stationary and saw it was a handwritten invitation to a black-tie New Year's Eve party from someone named DW. I thought back to my New Year's Eve spent in the hospital with my parents, and I tossed the note away in disgust.

It took the better part of three hours for the agents to finish their search of the house. I followed in their wake, checking every spot where a small faerie could hide. In the second-floor hallway, I found a busted window and a few red and gold scales on the floor beneath it. The drakkan was long gone, and I had no intention of going after him. The job had been to round up the creatures *in* the house, and that was what I would do.

After an exhaustive search, I finally found the terrified nixie curled into a ball in an old lamp shade in the attic. It took me another hour to coax her out of her hiding place.

I'd seen pictures of nixies, but none of them came close to capturing the beauty of the delicate, nine-inch tall faerie with golden hair and shimmering wings. It was like looking at a real live *Tinkerbell*, which was one of the reasons they fetched a high price on the black market. The other reason was their angelic singing voice. Mom had told me once that she had saved a pair of nixies from a dealer, and they'd sung to her. It was so beautiful it had literally made her weep with joy.

It felt cruel to put the nixie back in a cage after all she'd endured, but I didn't have any other way to transport her safely. I brought her down to the first floor and took a small plastic animal carrier from my duffle bag. I made a soft bed in it with my scarf and placed her gently inside. It wasn't much, but I eased my conscience with the knowledge she would be back home and free in a few days.

There was no way I could transport the verries I'd caught, so I called Levi to make arrangements for someone to handle it. I expected to get his voice mail because it was after eleven, so I was surprised when he answered my call. His mood hadn't improved, but he was pleased when I told him I'd finished the job. He told me to take the nixie home with me tonight and bring her to the Plaza tomorrow. I quickly agreed, glad not to have to drive all the way to Queens tonight.

Only Ross and two other agents remained in the house when I let myself out. There was one van left in the driveway and no sign of Kim or the other bounty hunters. They must have gotten tired of waiting and left. I didn't blame them.

Coatless and gasping from the cold, I hurried to the Jeep as fast as I could, carrying the duffle bag and the nixie's carrier. I tossed my bag in the back and placed the carrier on the passenger seat before I donned my coat and gloves.

I was about to climb into the Jeep when I got that prickling sensation at the back of my neck, the kind you get when you feel like someone is watching you. My first thought was of Conlan, but there was no sign of him. He hadn't hidden from me when he'd watched me at the flea market, and it didn't seem like something he would do.

Spooked, I jumped into the Jeep and locked the doors before I started the engine. I didn't wait for it to warm up before I drove away.

"You're being paranoid," I told myself as I took a left onto the next street. Not that anyone could blame me after –

I screamed when something crashed into the windshield and skidded across the hood. I hit the brakes so hard the nixie's carrier would have slammed into the dash if I hadn't grabbed it in time. Heart pounding, I gripped the steering wheel so tightly my fingers hurt.

I leaned toward the passenger side, trying to peer out that window, but whatever that thing was, I couldn't see it from this angle.

The scared witless part of me said I should drive away and not look back. But my conscience disagreed. What if an animal was lying injured in the street?

The street was well-lit, but I grabbed a flashlight from the glove compartment anyway. Opening my door, I got out and cautiously walked around the front of the Jeep with the flashlight held before me like a weapon.

A hissing sound stopped me in my tracks as I was about to reach the far side of the Jeep. I wasn't much of a bird-watcher, but one thing I knew about them was that they did not hiss.

The hiss was followed by what sounded like a faint growl. What the hell did I hit?

Gathering my courage, I moved forward and pointed the flashlight toward the sound.

It took me a moment to make sense of the crumpled shape on the ground. When the light played across red and gold scales, my free hand flew up to cover my mouth.

"Oh, no!"

I crouched a few feet from the drakkan that lay partially on one side with its opposite wing extended. It lifted its horned head to hiss at me, and a tendril of smoke curled from its snout. The effort appeared to be too much for it, and it dropped its head back to the pavement, panting.

I set the flashlight down and pulled off my coat. Keeping my hands away from the drakkan's teeth, I carefully folded his wing, which, thankfully, didn't appear to be broken, and then I wrapped my coat around him. He struggled at first until I had him swaddled like an infant. Then the fight went out of him, and he lay still.

"Don't worry. We'll get you fixed up," I crooned as I carried him to the Jeep and laid him on the passenger seat beside the nixie carrier. He made a sound that was somewhere between a whimper and a growl. Poor little thing.

I got behind the wheel again and prayed for an incident-free drive home. I'd had more than my share of excitement tonight.

When I finally let myself into the apartment, Finch was sitting on the back of the couch waiting for me. Ever since Mom and Dad went missing, he'd been waiting up for me whenever I went out. He hadn't stopped even after they were found.

What's that? he signed when I set the carrier on the table.

"This is a nixie who is going to stay with us tonight." I unlatched the carrier door and left it open for her. I'd rather spend the time looking for her tomorrow than leave her in that thing all night.

Finch ran over and climbed up on the table. *Why won't she come out?*

"She's scared. Give her time, and she'll come out when she's ready."

Leaving him staring at the carrier, I went to the computer with the drakkan still in my arms, and did an internet search on treating injured drakkans. I wasn't surprised when I found nothing because drakkans were not a common sight in our world. I had to make do with a video on how to set the wing of an injured bat. I wrapped him with a rolled bandage to secure his sprained wing to his body, not an easy task with him snapping his teeth at me and lashing at me with his tail. I managed to come out of it with only minor scratches.

He quieted as soon as I was done, and I took a minute to study him. I'd seen a few pictures of drakkans, but this was the first time I'd seen one in person. It was impossible to trap one in Faerie, and the only way to get one was to steal an egg and hatch it. That meant, this little guy had been born here in captivity.

Like all drakkans, he was no bigger than a large house cat, with four legs, leathery wings, and a long, spiked tail. Drakkans came in many different colors, and this one was red with gold tipped scales that looked like flames when he moved. He stared back at me with slit eyes that resembled pools of molten lava, and he seemed to be as curious about me as I was about him.

"Aren't you a handsome thing?" I told him. I knew he was a male because he had two little horns on his head whereas females had only one. Or so I'd read.

He flicked his tail and strutted in a circle as if he understood me.

I gave him a tired smile. "You're looking much better. Now let's see if I have anything for you to eat."

Getting up off the office floor, I went to the kitchen, letting the drakkan trail after me. Finch was still sitting on the table beside the carrier, and his eyes went as wide as saucers when he spotted our other guest.

I realized then that I had no idea what happened when you put a sprite and a drakkan together. Drakkans were carnivores, and they lived off insects and small animals such as rodents. Did they eat small faeries as well?

"Keep your distance from him until I know it's safe," I said as I walked to the refrigerator.

A soft whistle behind me had me spinning to see Finch standing beside the drakkan. Before I could protest, my brother laid his hand on the drakkan's snout, and his purple magic filled the air around them. The drakkan reacted by rubbing his body against Finch, almost knocking the sprite over. I'd seen Finch do this before with a lamal, and it amazed me as much now as it had the first time.

I pulled a package of raw chicken breasts from the refrigerator and cut a piece off one, which I put on a small plate and set on the floor. The drakkan sniffed at the meat before he snatched it up and swallowed it without chewing.

Pleased, I cut up the rest of the breast and put it before him. I'd barely taken my hand away when he tore into the meat like a starving beast. God only knew when he'd last eaten, or if the dealer had fed him regularly.

I cut up the second breast, which was supposed to have been my dinner before I'd gotten sent on the job tonight. I sighed. It was just as well that I'd missed dinner because this little guy seemed to need it more.

I cleaned up and put a dish of water down for the drakkan, and then I checked on the nixie. She was still in the carrier, but she'd moved to the front and was peeking out through the opening. I laid a few berries on the table for her, in case she got hungry, and went to shower.

It was almost one in the morning when I finally crawled, exhausted, into my bed. I planned to sleep in tomorrow, and then I'd take the nixie and the drakkan to the Plaza and settle up with Levi before I went to visit Mom and Dad at the new facility. I might even have time to knock out one of the jobs Levi had given me. I burrowed happily under my covers. Things were finally starting to look up.

Flying. I was flying, and it was the best feeling in the world. I held my arms out and looked down at the thick, green forest I was passing over. The treetops were so close I could almost touch them. I wanted to dive down beneath the canopy of branches and fly among the trees.

The forest ended, and I was over a wide field of grain swaying gently in the breeze. The sun cast my shadow below, and my breath caught when I saw a massive winged shape instead of my own. I looked up and stared in wonder at the underbelly of the dragon holding me with one of its feet.

I turned my gaze back to the passing landscape. We flew over villages and farms where the occupants went about their business as if there wasn't a dragon over their heads. When we reached a wide river, the dragon turned and followed it toward a wall of black cliffs so tall they appeared to touch the sky. The closer we got to the cliffs, the faster he flew until I was sure we would crash into them.

At the last second, he changed direction so fast that my scream died on my lips. He flew straight up the cliff face and shot over the top, and I stared at what had to be thousands of dragons of every color perched along miles of cliffs. As long as I lived, I knew I'd never see anything else that could compare to the magnificence before me.

My dragon dipped. I looked up and gasped when I saw it had shrunk to half its size. It grew smaller still and faltered as it struggled to stay in flight.

Suddenly, it dropped me, and I was falling, falling, falling...

I shot up in bed, looking around wildly at the walls of my bedroom and at the early morning sky outside my window. Over the pounding of my heart, I heard a weird rasping sound, and I scanned the room for the source.

"Argh!" I scrambled out of bed when I spotted the dark shape on my pillow. My legs got tangled in the covers, and I landed in a heap on my floor.

I was trying to free myself when something appeared at the edge of the bed. All the air went out of my lungs when I looked up into the startled red eyes of the drakkan.

I fell back on the floor with a hand over my heart. "You scared the bejesus out of me."

He yawned and flopped down on his belly.

"Nice." I stood and looked down at the creature curled up in a ball with his long tail wrapped around him. He still wore the bandage I'd put on him last night. I must have been out cold not to have felt him climb onto the bed. "What are you doing on my bed?"

He opened one eye to peer at me, and then he went back to sleep as if he owned the place.

"Don't get too comfortable, buddy. You won't be staying long."

Rubbing sleep from my eyes, I went to check on our other guest. Unsurprisingly, the carrier on the table was empty, and the nixie was nowhere in sight. I wasn't worried because she couldn't have gotten out of the apartment. After I had my coffee, I'd get Finch to help me find her.

One of the few luxuries I allowed myself was my morning coffee. Ever since a drought had wiped out most of the coffee bean crops and sent the cost of coffee soaring, I'd had to make do with one coffee a week, unless Violet had treated me to one. But I had decided weeks ago that if I was going to be my family's provider, I deserved this one thing. The rest of my earnings went either into my college savings or toward the household expenses.

I was debating whether or not this was a two-cup morning when the doorbell rang, startling me. It was barely seven. Who on earth was visiting at this hour?

Setting down my coffee, I quietly went to the door and peered through the peephole. My stomach plummeted, and I took a step back as fear slithered down my spine. The last time I'd seen the faerie on the other side of the door, he had looked ready to murder me with his bare hands.

I jumped when Faolin rapped sharply on the door.

"I know you're there, Jesse. I need to talk to you."

"Go away. We have nothing to say to each other." I hated the tremble in my voice. I was keenly aware that Tennin hadn't redone my wards yet, so Faolin could walk in if he chose to. The question was, did Faolin know that, and what would he do about it?

"I'm here on behalf of my brother. He wishes to see you." Faolin sounded like he'd rather drink liquid iron than ask me for anything.

I crossed my arms. "I already told Conlan no. I haven't changed my mind."

He didn't speak for a long moment. "Faris is not doing well."

"Conlan said he was recovering." Was this some kind of trick to lure me in?

"Physically, yes, but his spirit is low, and it's impeding the healing process. The only thing he asks for is to see you."

"Why? We barely know each other."

There was another heavy pause. "My brother said he was prepared to die in that cage, and the goddess told him his salvation was near. He believes she sent you to save him."

I laughed bitterly. "Some savior I turned out to be."

"You cared for him and made him want to fight to live."

I closed my eyes. Faris thought I'd saved his life, and he was burdened by the need to repay the debt. "Tell him he doesn't owe me anything. I'm happy knowing he's getting better."

"That is not enough. He won't be able to let it go until he has seen you for himself."

I raked my hands through my tangle of curls. I knew these guys, and they were going to keep coming back until they got what they wanted. The only way I was going to get them out of my life was to give in and pay Faris a visit. And I really did want Faris to get better. If seeing me would help him, how could I refuse his request?

"Fine. I'll go see him."

"Good," Faolin said, and I could have sworn I detected a note of relief in his voice. "I will wait for you downstairs."

"No." I would visit Faris, but there was no way I was getting into a vehicle with his brother. "I know where you live. I'll meet you there in an hour."

"As you wish."

I rested my head against the door and listened to the sound of his footsteps on the stairs. Knowing he was gone should have made me relieved, but all I felt was apprehension and the growing certainty that I was going to regret this.

6

I shut off the engine and stared at the building I hadn't planned on ever seeing again. All the way here, I'd told myself I could do this, but now I wasn't sure I could. Why had I agreed to come here? I could have called Faris and saved myself all the stress. My stomach had been in knots ever since Faolin had shown up at the apartment, and I wouldn't be surprised to find out I had an ulcer.

I wasn't sure how long I sat there before I realized I was getting cold. I reached for the ignition, intending to take the coward's way out, but something Faolin had said to me stayed my hand.

"He won't be able to let it go until he has seen you for himself."

"Damn it." I hit the steering wheel. My conscience wasn't going to let me leave until I had done what I'd come here to do, no matter how uncomfortable it made me.

Grabbing my phone and keys, I opened the door and got out. I walked to the door, unsure of what to do when I got there. There was no doorbell, and I had no idea if anyone would hear if I knocked. The times I'd been here in the past, I'd always arrived with someone who lived here.

The door swung open when I was a few feet away from it, and a stoic Faolin waved me into the foyer. His manner was the same brusque one he seemed to reserve for me, which oddly put me a little at ease. If he was nice, I'd be suspicious, and I'd probably turn tail and run.

The inner door was open, but I didn't move toward it until he told me to go in. Steeling myself, I walked into the large living area. Everything looked as it had the last time I'd been here, but it felt cold and unwelcoming.

Faolin walked past me. "Follow me."

He led me down the hallway to the library and stopped outside the closed door. "He tires easily, so don't be alarmed if he falls asleep during your visit. Leave the door open, and call for me if you need anything. I will be in the living room."

"Okay."

He opened the door for me, and I entered the room. Where the large desk had been, a bed and night table sat, and thick rugs covered the floor. Instead of books, flowering faerie plants decorated the bookcases, and they filled the air with a pleasant, exotic perfume.

"You came."

I followed the soft male voice to a blond faerie sitting in a large armchair beside the fire. His legs rested on an ottoman, and he was covered in a thick blanket, despite the warmth of the room.

If not for his eyes and the resemblance to Faolin, I wouldn't have guessed this was the same person I'd met in Rogin's basement. The dull, matted hair was gone, he was less gaunt, and his face had lost its deathly pallor. The only thing that hadn't changed was his eyes. They held the haunted look of someone who has known great suffering.

Faris extended a hand, and I walked over to take it. His skin was cool to the touch, and I noticed a tremble in his grip as he lifted my hand to his lips. Up close, I could see dark circles under his eyes, and his skin was paler than it should be. He might be recovering, but he was by no means healthy.

"Please, sit." He pointed at the chair next to his. "There is food and drink for you if you are hungry."

I looked at the small square table between the two chairs that held a large coffee and an assortment of pastries from the bakery I liked. I eyed the coffee, but made no move to pick it up.

Faris smiled. "You look good, Jesse."

"So do you. I guess neither of us was at our best the last time we saw each other."

"Not my finest first impression." He laughed, and it turned into a mild cough. "I hear your parents are doing well."

"They are. I'm glad to see you're on the mend, too. I had no idea what happened to you after..." I trailed off, not knowing how to finish the sentence. I'd come here to ease his mind, not to rehash that awful night.

Faris saved me from the awkward silence. "I was in and out of it for the first week while Faolin hovered around me, forcing copious amounts of iron antidote into me. As you've probably noticed, my brother can be a little over-bearing."

"It's one of his more charming traits," I said humorlessly. "Why didn't they take you home? Wouldn't you heal faster in your realm?"

"Under normal circumstances, yes, but my body is too saturated with iron. It would kill me the second I stepped into Faerie."

"I didn't think of that." Pure iron could not be brought into Faerie because it disintegrated when it came into contact with their air. I shuddered, trying not to think of what would happen to a faerie with that much iron in their system.

He tugged up the blanket that had slipped down his chest. "I am well cared for here with my brother and friends to keep me company."

"Can you heal in the city?" Court faeries were more sensitive to iron than lower faeries, so they used their magic as a shield against it. The shield depleted their magic, requiring them to return to Faerie periodically to replenish it. Faeries who lived in cities had to go home more often because of the higher concentration of iron.

"Faolin and the others added extra wards to this building to protect me from the iron. I can't go outside, except to the garden, but I do have the plea-sure of seeing you, my angel."

I made a face. "I told you not to call me that."

"Did you? I seem to have lapses in my memory lately."

"How convenient," I retorted, feeling a little more at ease.

He smiled warmly. "I do remember your kindness to me. I don't know if I would have made it through that last night without you."

"And you helped me forget how scared I was. I think I would have curled up in a ball and cried if you hadn't been there."

Faris shook his head. "I don't believe that. Anyone who can stand up to Vaerik and Faolin does not give up easily."

I tensed at the casual mention of Lukas's real name, but I hid my discom-fort. Faris had no idea that it was another reminder of his friends' betrayal.

"Are you still bounty hunting?" Faris asked.

I was grateful for the change in topic. "Yes. I get to do a lot more of it now that I'm not looking for my parents."

"And you enjoy it?"

I lifted a shoulder. "Depends on the job. Last night, I had to catch forty verries. Have you ever seen the size of the stingers on those things?"

A small crash came from the kitchen, like someone had dropped a glass. I didn't think faeries were ever clumsy.

His mouth fell open. "*Forty verries?* You didn't get hurt, did you?"

"Luckily no, but some poor guy got stung a bunch of times." I wrinkled my nose. "I had to smear verry dung on him before they took him to the hospital."

Faris chuckled. "You do lead an interesting life."

"For now. If things work out, I'm hoping to be in college this time next year. I will gladly trade in my bounty hunter ID for a student ID."

"What do you want to study?" he asked.

"Law." I didn't elaborate. This didn't seem like the time to discuss inequalities in Fae laws, or how I wanted to be a legal advocate for lower faeries.

He smiled. "Something tells me you'll be a force to be reckoned with."

"You can bet on it."

A floorboard creaked, drawing our attention to the open door as a huge feline resembling a black lynx with exotic amethyst eyes entered the room. Kaia was Lukas's pet lamal, and she wasn't fond of humans. She had only tolerated my presence here in the past because he'd commanded her not to hurt me.

"Kaia, stay," Faris ordered as she stalked toward me.

She ignored him and kept advancing until she stood before me. I held my breath, afraid to move. Kaia hadn't tried to hurt me the other times I'd been here, but maybe she could sense that I was no longer a friend of her master.

"Don't be frightened, Jesse," Faris said a little too calmly. "Faolin will come and remove her."

"I'm not –" I yelped when Kaia lifted up on her hind legs and rested her massive paws on my shoulders, putting her face inches from mine. Her warm breath washed over my face, and her long whiskers tickled my nose, making it twitch. I didn't dare move, and I kept my eyes averted from hers out of fear that she would see it as a challenge.

She lowered her body back to the floor and rubbed her head against my knees. A rumble came from her throat, and it took me several seconds to realize what I thought was a growl was a purr.

"You two are friends?" Faris asked, his shock mirroring mine.

"She's never done this before."

"Kaia, come," said a commanding voice that made my breath catch.

My first instinct was to ignore Lukas, but that would only let him know how much his presence affected me. Casually, I looked at him with what I hoped was a closed expression. Our eyes met for a few seconds, too briefly for me to read his.

The lamal swung her head in his direction but didn't move from her spot at my feet. I'd never seen her disobey an order from him.

"Kaia." His voice was sharp as he pointed at the floor beside him.

64

She stood and slunk over to him. Before she had reached him, he turned and left with her trailing after him. I stared at the empty doorway until Faris spoke again.

"I must apologize for my selfishness, Jesse."

I frowned. "What do you mean?"

"When I asked to see you, I didn't consider how difficult it would be for you to come here." He gave me a knowing look. "Out of all of them, he hurt you the most."

I shifted uncomfortably. "Can we not talk about that? What do you do to pass the time while you're recovering?"

Faris glanced toward the door and lowered his voice. "He has not been himself since I came home. He won't talk about it, but he deeply regrets what happened. They all do."

I pressed my lips together, at a loss for how to respond.

"I won't try to excuse my friends' actions because what they did to you was wrong. All I can do is try to offer some insight into their behavior. The six of us have been together since we were children, and we are more like brothers than friends. We are constantly on alert for threats to Vaerik's... Lukas's life, and we have been taught to never trust outsiders." Faris inhaled deeply and let it out. "For the first time, they let their guard down with someone outside of our circle, and they reacted on instinct when they thought you had hurt me and deceived them."

My jaw clenched. I couldn't fault Faris for caring about his friends, but he was seeing this through a flawed lens that only showed him one side of the story.

"I understand them being paranoid about security. They didn't exactly roll out the red carpet for me, and I was okay with that. But trust works both ways, and they broke mine even before that day. They lied to me about Lukas's real identity, even after I warned them that someone was trying to kill Prince Vaerik. I had to hear the truth from Rogin Havas while I was a guest in one of his cages."

I swallowed back the lump that formed in my throat whenever I thought of the utter betrayal I'd felt. "I don't know what was worse. Finding out I'd been lied to all along, or how easy it was for them to believe someone like Rogin over me."

Faris looked stricken. "Jesse..."

"I know you want me to forgive them, but even if I do that, I don't think I can trust them again." I gave him an apologetic smile. "I'm sorry if that's not what you want to hear."

He held up a hand. "It needed to be heard, though."

Faris wasn't talking about himself. I wasn't sure how I felt about the others listening to our conversation, but it didn't surprise me. Faeries had superior hearing, and Faolin would never leave me completely alone with his sick brother, even if he had been the one to invite me here.

"I'm truly sorry for what you've suffered," Faris said softly.

"You have nothing to be sorry for." I brightened my smile. "And I'm doing great. I have my parents back, and bounty hunting pays a lot more than my old barista gig. Life is good."

The sadness left his eyes. "I'm happy to hear that."

I looked around the room. "Now tell me, why are you sleeping in the library? You don't have a room here?"

"I do, but getting to it requires my brother or one of my friends carrying me up and down the stairs. Staying down here allows me to hold onto some of my dignity. And to entertain a guest." He looked at the tray of pastries on the table. "You haven't touched your coffee. Kerr said you love it."

"I had coffee at my place. Do you want mine?"

His grimace was almost comical. "Goddess, no. Why would you even ask?"

"You don't like coffee?"

Faris raised an eyebrow. "You used to work in a coffee house. Have you ever met a Court faerie who likes the stuff?"

I stared at him, trying to figure out if he was pulling my leg. But the more I thought about it, the more I realized he was telling the truth. I'd served coffee to plenty of lower faeries, but I'd never once served it to a Court faerie. I shook my head. "So much for my powers of observation."

His laugh was light and infectious. The longer we talked, the more at ease I became. I was glad I'd come to see him.

Barely an hour had passed when his eyelids drooped, signaling it was time for me to go. I moved to the edge of my chair, preparing to stand.

"You're leaving?" he asked with a sleepy slur in his voice.

"Yes. I have a lot to do today." It wasn't a lie. I had to bring the nixie and drakkan to the Plaza and get started on those jobs Levi had given me yesterday. Plus, I needed to figure out where to begin my search for the ke'tain.

Faris gave me a hopeful look, and I knew what his next words would be before he said them.

"Will you come back?"

I hesitated to answer, and he said, "I don't get visitors other than my brother and friends, and I've enjoyed your company immensely."

I pulled out my phone. "What's your number? I'll call you to set up a day and time."

"If you can't reach me, you can call one of the others," he said after I'd added him to my contacts.

"I might have blocked their numbers," I whispered, earning another laugh from him.

"Then I am honored you took mine."

When I stood, he held out his hand to me. I took it, and he clasped mine between both of his. "Be safe out there, and come back soon."

"I will."

I walked to the door, and when I looked back, he was already asleep in his chair. His blanket had fallen again, so I went back to him and gently tucked it around his shoulders.

Turning toward the door, I jumped when I found Faolin standing a few feet behind me. I clapped a hand over my mouth to smother the small scream that would have awakened Faris. All of these guys moved with stealth, but the last one you'd want sneaking up on you was Faolin. He'd never liked me, and I wasn't stupid enough to think he'd changed because he'd asked me here to visit his brother.

Faolin wore an expression I'd never seen on his face. He wasn't smiling, but he wasn't scowling either. His lack of hostility unnerved me, and I quickly skirted around him and left the room.

I knew my way out, so I didn't wait for him to see me to the door. Call me a coward, but now that my visit with Faris was over, I didn't want to stick around and risk running into one of the others.

I'd almost made my escape when Lukas's voice stopped me. "Jesse."

The urge to flee was strong, but I made myself turn to face him. He stood by the window that overlooked the garden, watching me like I was a skittish doe, which was close to how I felt. I wasn't prepared for the onslaught of emotions from just being alone in the same room with him, and all I could do was stand there and wait for him to speak.

Warmth filled his eyes. "Thank you."

"I didn't do this for you," I said in a stiff voice that didn't sound like my own.

He nodded and took a step forward. "I want to –"

"No." My hands curled into fists at my sides. "You've already said everything I needed to hear."

"Quiet," Faolin whispered harshly as he appeared at the mouth of the hallway. "Do you wish to wake Faris?"

Guilt washed over me. "I'm sorry."

He grunted and spun to stalk off toward the library, leaving me alone with Lukas.

"Good day, Your Highness." I caught his wince as I turned away, but I refused to feel bad about it. We weren't friends, and we were no longer on a first name basis. I had to make that clear if I was going to visit Faris again.

The door opened as I reached for it, and I caught myself before I stumbled backward. Kerr stopped short, causing Iian to nearly run into his back. The shock on their faces told me I was the last person they had expected to see in their home.

They smiled broadly, and Kerr said, "Jesse, you're here!"

"I came to see Faris." I pointed at the door they were blocking. "If you'll excuse me, I need to leave."

Their smiles fell as they moved aside. I took a step toward the door and found my way blocked by Conlan, who had entered behind them. He looked less surprised to see me and offered a tentative smile I didn't return.

I brushed past him and almost ran from the building. Outside, I gulped in cold air as I hurried to the Jeep. I barely took time to buckle my seat belt before I drove away.

That had been uncomfortable, but now that I had seen them all, the next encounter would be easier. I would make it clear I was only there for Faris and not interested in rekindling any other friendships. It was better that way for all of us.

"What do you mean she doesn't want to leave?" I asked Finch, my gaze moving between him and the nixie peeking out of his tree house window.

Aisla said Faerie is not her home, Finch signed. *She doesn't want to go there.*

"But what about her family? Doesn't she want to see them?"

He shook his head sadly. *She was born here, and her old family is gone, like mine. I told her she can join our family and live in my house with me.*

My jaw went slack. Finch was territorial about his house and didn't even like us looking inside. Now he was offering to share it with another faerie?

Can she stay? he asked with pleading eyes. *I'll share my food with her.*

"I guess so." I rubbed the back of my neck. "I need to make sure it's not against the law to keep her here."

Finch's face lit up. *I told her you would say yes.*

"Don't get excited until we know she can stay."

Most faeries and Fae creatures we caught were sent to Faerie because they posed a threat to humans. The rest – such as sprites and nixies – were harmless but considered endangered, and they were sent back to their own realm for their protection.

There was a gray area, though. Mom and Dad were able to adopt Finch because he was an orphan and his clipped wings would have made survival impossible for him in Faerie. Aisla was unharmed, but she'd been born in our realm. It would be cruel to send her to a world she'd never known, but the Agency might believe she'd be better off there than here.

Finch followed me to the office where I spent the next hour going through Agency manuals and searching online. Unable to find an answer, I finally called Levi, who told me the fact that our family had already adopted Finch would lean heavily in our favor. I had to go to the Agency and fill out a bunch of paperwork, but he didn't see them rejecting the application. They had a lot more to worry about than one orphan nixie.

I relayed all of this to Finch, who danced on the desk before he ran off to tell his new friend the good news. When I returned to the living room a few minutes later, I smiled at the happy squeaks and whistles coming from the tree house.

I looked at the drakkan watching me from his perch on the back of the couch. His bandage was gone, and his wing looked mended from this angle. "I guess it's just you and me going to the Plaza today."

He jumped off the couch, disappearing from sight behind it. I walked around it, but he was nowhere to be seen.

"Come on, little guy." I knelt to peer under the couch. "I have a ton of stuff to do today, and I don't have time to play hide and seek with you."

Finch whistled, and I looked up at him.

Maybe he wants to stay, too, my brother signed.

I rested my arms on the back of the couch. "He can't stay here."

Why not?

"For one, I don't have time to take care of him. He's not like Aisla. He'd be a pet, and pets need a lot of care. It wouldn't be fair to him."

I can take care of him when you're not here, Finch said.

"Okay. I'll go to the grocery store today to pick up some raw meat for him. You'll need to feed him twice a day."

Meat? My brother's blue face took on a yellow tinge.

"Or I could get some live mice, but I think that would be too messy." Holding back a smirk at Finch's look of horror, I counted off items on my fingers. "You have to feed him, make sure he has lots of water, train him to use a litter box, and clean up when he has accidents. I think he's shedding, too, so you'll have to pick up the scales he drops."

Finch stared at me. *Pets are a lot of work.*

"They are." I bent low to look under the couch, but the drakkan wasn't there. How the hell had he gotten past me? Standing, I swung my gaze in a wide circle. "Where did he go?"

Finch whistled and pointed to the kitchen. I swung in that direction, and it took me a moment to spot the drakkan squeezed into the narrow space between the top of the cabinets and the ceiling.

I walked into the kitchen to stare up at him. How on earth had he managed to get up there so fast without making a sound?

Grabbing the stepladder from the hall closet, I attempted to lure him down with some raw bacon. He sniffed it but refused to move. Abandoning that idea, I reached up to lift him down and was rewarded with two nipped fingers.

"Ouch!" Blood beaded on one fingertip, and I stuck my finger in my mouth as I glared up at him. Some bounty hunter I was. I couldn't even capture a drakkan in my own apartment.

I climbed down from the ladder as the doorbell rang. Casting a resentful look at the little beast, I went to answer the door.

"Tennin," I said when I opened the door. "I forgot you were coming by today."

Behind me, a crash came from the kitchen. I spun to see the drakkan sitting on the counter, gobbling up the bacon I'd left out.

"I knew you liked bacon," I yelled accusingly at him.

Tennin snickered. "Do I want to know why you have a young drakkan sitting on your kitchen counter?"

I turned to face the faerie. "He flew into my windshield last night and hurt his wing. I'm taking him in today to be sent home."

"I think he might have other plans." Tennin grinned at something over my shoulder.

I cast a look back at the kitchen in time to see the drakkan wedge himself on top of the cabinets again. Groaning, I stepped back. "Please, come in."

Tennin's laugh trailed off as he passed through the doorway. He lifted his hand, and a stream of his pale green magic flowed from his fingers.

"What is it?" I tensed, waiting for him to tell me he wasn't strong enough to replace Conlan's ward.

"I know why the faerie you hired couldn't take down the old ward," he said as he tested the magic protecting the apartment.

"Why?"

He dropped his hands and looked at me. "This is not Conlan's magic. This ward was made by the same faerie who warded your parents at the hospital."

Shock rippled through me. A faerie had gotten past Conlan's ward and entered my home. *Who is stronger than a member of the Unseelie royal guard?*

I hadn't realized I'd spoken my question aloud until Tennin answered it. "Someone with bluer blood than his."

"A royal? Why would a royal faerie want to help my family?"

Tennin quirked an eyebrow.

"No." I shook my head emphatically. "It wasn't him."

"Why not him? He's one of the strongest of my kind, and he has a personal connection to you."

"He *had* a connection to me, but he severed that, and I've made it crystal clear that I want nothing to do with him."

Tennin shrugged. "Maybe he has other ideas."

"And maybe this is Conlan's ward. You haven't been here since he created his."

"Trust me, this ward was not made by Conlan," Tennin said with a touch of swagger. "His blood might be a tad bluer than mine, but my magic is as strong as his."

I stared at him. "Conlan is a royal?"

"The royal guards are always blue bloods. Their official title is prince, but they never use it. They're lower royals, similar to an earl here," he explained. "Most other royal faeries use their real titles in this realm, but the guards don't want to be distracted by unwanted attention. I'm surprised you didn't know that, having spent so much time with them."

"They weren't exactly forthcoming about certain things."

He lifted a shoulder. "Now you know."

A scraping sound came from behind me, and I turned to see the drakkan on the counter again, trying to swallow the keys I'd left there earlier.

"No!" I ran over and snatched the keys away from him. "Bad drakkan."

Tennin snickered. "Nice pet but you better hide anything that will fit into his mouth."

"He's not staying." I made a face as I grabbed a paper towel to clean the slimy keys. "The metal doesn't hurt him?"

"Drakkan are not like other creatures from our realm. The fire in their belly protects them from just about everything."

As if to illustrate his words, the drakkan burped, and a few sparks flew out along with a wisp of smoke.

I glanced nervously around at all the flammable things in the apartment. "The new ward didn't remove my fire ward, did it?"

Tennin waved a hand in the air to test it. "You're good."

I walked back to him and hung the keys on the hook by the door as a new realization hit me. "You said Conlan's blood is only a little bluer than yours. Does that make you a royal, too?"

He took a tiny bow. "Prince Tennin at your service, although no one calls me that."

A prince. That explained why he was able to create a ward strong enough to keep Lukas's men out until I'd let them in. "But you warned me to stay away from Lukas and his men."

"I said they were dangerous, which they are when they need to be."

I was a little dejected that Tennin, like all the other Court faeries I knew, seemed to have perfected the art of speaking around the truth. When I had asked Conlan if Lukas was in service to the crown, he'd vaguely replied that they all were. Lukas had once told me that Prince Vaerik owed me a debt of gratitude, and I'd had no idea he'd been referring to himself in the third person.

"You know, most human girls would be thrilled to know they were in the presence of Fae royalty. Your disappointment is most humbling."

I laughed. "I'm sure you get your fair share of adoration."

"I can't complain, and I do get invited to the best parties." He pretended to preen.

"Even though you're a paparazzo?"

He shook his head like I'd said something amusing. "No one cares about that when you're Fae royalty. Having any royal, even a lower prince like me, at a party is a status symbol."

"Doesn't it bother you that people invite you to increase their popularity?" I asked, annoyed on his behalf.

"Not really. I'm choosy about which ones to attend. In fact, I'm going to one tomorrow night." He grinned. "The host is over-the-top eccentric, but there are always celebrities and politicians to eavesdrop on."

"Eccentric, how?"

"He's what you would call obsessed with faeries, and his homes are filled with things from our realm. At his estate in Italy, he even has a lake full of fish from Faerie. It's his own little faerie world. A bit ridiculous, but he's entertaining to be around."

"He must be filthy rich." I tried to imagine having that much money to throw away on a fantasy.

Tennin nodded. "He has enough money to buy his own country, but the one thing he wants can't be bought."

"And what is that?"

He leaned in conspiratorially. "To be Fae, of course. He'd give up his entire fortune to anyone who would change him, but no faerie will even attempt it. To do an unsanctioned conversion would be to risk banishment from Faerie, and banishment means death."

"Princess Nerissa tried it with Jackson Chase."

His smile dimmed. "Desperate people will do desperate things for love."

"Do you know her?" I remembered hearing somewhere that Princess Nerissa was Unseelie, but there were hundreds of royals in each region.

"Yes," he said grimly.

A shiver went through me, and I didn't want to know what her punishment had been.

Tennin slapped his hands together. "Anyway, you look like you have your hands full here with your new pet. Unless you need something else from me, I'll leave you to it."

He turned to go as it struck me that there *was* something else he could help me with.

"Wait."

He shot me a questioning look.

"I'm working on a job, and I'm wondering if you could tell me something about a particular Fae object."

He hesitated. It was small, but I caught it. "Sure."

"What can you tell me about the ke'tain?"

"The ke'tain?" He reached behind him and quickly shut the door. "How do you know about that?"

His reaction confirmed my suspicion that the ke'tain was a bigger deal than the Agency was letting on. He obviously didn't know the bounty hunters had been informed about its disappearance. I filled him in and told him what little I knew about the artifact.

"How do they expect us to find it when they won't tell us anything beyond what it looks like?" I grumbled. "Who had access to the ke'tain in the temple? Why would someone take it and bring it here? I can't believe a faerie would steal something sacred to your people only to sell it to a human collector for money. There has to be more to it."

Tennin stuck his hands into his pockets, looking uncomfortable. "This is something you should ask Prince Vaerik Lukas about. He can answer your questions better than I."

"You know that's not an option," I said tightly.

He tried a different approach. "Whoever has the ke'tain went through a lot of trouble to obtain it, and they will not take lightly to anyone poking around. Is the bounty that important to you?"

"This isn't about the money. I'm doing this to keep my parents safe."

His head jerked back in surprise. "What do your parents have to do with it?"

I looked around for Finch and lowered my voice. "The Agency thinks whoever took the ke'tain also took my parents because they found out about it."

"The Agency told you that?" Tennin asked in disbelief.

"In so many words. After a faerie tried to get to Mom and Dad at the hospital, I guessed it was connected to the ke'tain, and the agent I talked to didn't deny it."

He uttered a Fae word. "You didn't think to tell me this before now? Are they okay?"

"Yes. Whoever it was couldn't get past the ward, so Mom and Dad are safe for now. The only way I know to protect them is to find the ke'tain and turn it in. Then no one will have a reason to go after them."

His eyes grew troubled. "Does Lukas know what you are up to?"

"Why? It has nothing to do with him."

"Everything is Lukas's business."

I crossed my arms. "Then I'm sure the Agency has already told him everything he needs to know. And if he wants to know the name of the bounty hunters searching for the ke'tain, they will give him a list."

Tennin didn't look convinced.

"You don't want to talk about the ke'tain, but can you at least tell me if the goddess's temple is open to everyone or only certain people?" I asked hopefully. "That might help narrow down the search."

Indecision played across his face before he finally said, "Any faerie can visit the temple, but the ke'tain itself is kept behind a powerful ward. It would take four or five strong faeries working together to get through it."

"So, they would have to be Court faeries?"

He hesitated. "Yes."

Like the Seelie royal guard. I kept that thought to myself. "So, basically, any Court faerie could have brought it to our realm, or they could have given it to a lower faerie to carry it for them. Which brings me to my other question. Why would someone steal the ke'tain in the first place?"

"I have asked myself that many times."

I held back a groan of frustration. I was getting nowhere on this job, and I wondered if anyone else was having luck. I hoped so, for my parents' sake.

Tennin's phone rang, and he chuckled when he looked at the screen. "Ah, and there is Davian now. He wants to know if I'm coming solo or bringing a plus one. It's his way of asking if I'm planning to go since I missed his last party."

"Davian?"

He nodded. "Davian Woods, the tech magnate. Have you heard of him?"

"Who hasn't?" Davian Woods became famous for reaching billionaire status at the tender age of twenty-five. At thirty-one, he now owned half of Silicon Valley, and he had been trying for years to convince Faerie to share their portal magic with our world. I'd always assumed Woods wanted to make money off the portals, but after hearing Tennin's account of him, I suspected his real motive was to gain access to the realm he obsessed over. Someone with that much money and determination would probably do anything to get what he wanted.

Out of nowhere, a memory surfaced of a crumpled handwritten invitation on the floor of Lewis Tate's office. A New Year's Eve party invitation on expensive stationary signed with the initials DW.

Davian Woods.

7

My mind whirled as the puzzle pieces snapped together.

The Agency had raided Lewis Tate's house because they believed he might have the ke'tain. Lewis Tate knew a DW, who used expensive stationary and threw lavish parties. Davian Woods collected Fae objects and had the money to buy almost anything. Lewis Tate trafficked in the very things Davian would want.

Tennin snapped his fingers in front of my face. "Jesse?"

I blinked and realized I'd been staring blankly at him. "Did you go to Davian's New Year's Eve party?"

"I missed that one because I was in Faerie." He gave me an inquisitive look. "What is brewing inside that head of yours?"

"Last night, the Agency raided the home of a black market dealer looking for the ke'tain. When I was in the dealer's office, I saw –"

"Why were you at an Agency raid?" Tennin cut in.

"I was called in to catch the creatures he set free." I jabbed a thumb in the direction of the drakkan. "Anyway, I was in the dealer's office, and I found an invite for a New Year's Eve party from someone named DW. I think it was Davian Woods, and the dealer sold him the ke'tain or was planning to."

Tennin did not look surprised by my theory.

"You knew?" I asked him.

He shook his head. "Not about the dealer, but I do know Davian was investigated. All the top collectors of Fae culture were. He was clean."

"Just because they didn't find anything doesn't mean he's clean." The

76

more I thought about it, the more convinced I became that I was onto something.

Tennin shrugged. "The Agency is very thorough about these things."

"They also thought my parents were in cahoots with a goren dealer," I reminded him. "They make mistakes."

"True," he said thoughtfully. "But do you think they will listen to you if you go to them with your suspicions?"

I scoffed. "No. Besides, Davian has to be wary of the Agency now. If he has something to hide, he's definitely not going to let his guard down around them." I scratched my chin. "I need to figure out how to talk to him, maybe see inside his home."

Tennin let out a burst of laughter. "You don't walk up to Davian Woods and introduce yourself. And forget getting into one of his homes. The only way into his sanctuary is by invitation."

He was still talking when inspiration struck me. I grinned like the Cheshire Cat.

Tennin's laughter died. "Why are you looking at me like that?"

"I figured out the perfect way to meet Davian Woods." I let the words hang in the air between us.

"How?" He stared at me for a few seconds, and something like horror crossed his face. "No. Absolutely not."

"You haven't even heard my plan yet."

He backed up a step with his hands raised. "Let's leave it that way."

"You don't want to help me?" I gave him the same sad face Violet always used on me.

"It's not that I don't want to. It's that someone I have a healthy respect for would have my hide if I put you in a potentially dangerous situation."

I waved a hand. "It's a society party, not a drug den. And my dad won't know if neither of us tells him."

Tennin opened his mouth, closed it, and opened it once more. "I'm sorry."

"I understand." I pasted on a smile. "I can be resourceful. I'll find a way to meet him on my own."

Alarm flashed in his eyes. "What part of *it's too dangerous* don't you get?"

"What part of *my parents' lives depend on this* don't you get? I'll do whatever it takes to keep them safe."

He swore softly in English and hung his head. "I'm going to regret this."

"Stop fidgeting."

I let my hands fall away from the neckline of my dress and met Tennin's eyes in the mirrored wall of the elevator.

He smiled and mouthed, *"Relax."*

I returned his smile and took in our reflections. He wore black jeans paired with a black jacket, gray shirt, and tie. I wore a sleeveless, pale blue dress with a bateau neckline trimmed in delicate filigree that resembled white gold. The knee-length dress was made from soft Fae fabric, and when I moved, it subtly changed to different shades of blue.

One of Tennin's stipulations for bringing me here tonight had been that he chose my outfit. I hadn't known what to expect when he'd left my apartment, but he had returned a few hours later with the beautiful dress. I had protested until he'd pointed out that Davian Woods would recognize the dress as Fae-made, which would please the billionaire.

Violet had come over to help with my makeup and to wrangle my hair into a smooth knot at my nape. She'd insisted I leave my glasses at home since I wasn't driving. A small sacrifice in the name of fashion, as she'd put it. She didn't know my real reason for coming tonight, just that I was working on a job I couldn't talk about.

The elevator stopped on the penthouse level. Tennin and I stepped out into a pink marble foyer with a single door on either end and a pair of open double doors facing us. From beyond the doors came strains of music and the murmur of many voices. I resisted the urge to adjust my dress one more time.

Two smiling male attendants greeted us. One took my coat, and the other directed us to a glass table in the corner. I was surprised to see a selection of beautiful masquerade masks in various designs and colors.

"It's a masquerade?" I asked Tennin.

He touched one of the masks. "Davian didn't say, but he likes to add fun little twists to his gatherings."

"Choose any one you like," said the attendant.

Most of the women's masks were elaborately decorated with sparkling stones and feathers. I reached for the nearest one, but Tennin stopped me before I could pick it up.

"You don't need all that adornment." He picked up a silver Venetian mask decorated with delicate glittering swirls and helped me put it on. After he'd secured the ties, he stepped back and smiled. "Perfection."

He chose a black and silver mask for himself and donned it. Then he lifted his arm. "Shall we?"

Feeling bolder behind the mask, I smiled and took his arm. We passed through the double doors into a hallway. To our left was a winding glass staircase to the second floor, and farther on were more doors. We turned right and entered a great room unlike anything I'd seen before.

The first thing that caught my eye was the incredible view of the city through the arched windows on two sides of the room. The floor was a dark herringbone hardwood adorned with beautiful rugs, and from the high ceiling hung glass orbs containing Fae crystals that cast a soft glow over the room. Everywhere I looked, there were exotic plants, tapestries, and accents that appeared Fae in origin. The room was warm and inviting, nothing like I'd imagined I'd see in a billionaire's penthouse.

I turned my attention from the décor to the room's occupants. There had to be at least thirty people milling around, and based on their height and build, I suspected over half of them were faeries. I couldn't be sure because, like us, they all wore masks.

Several black and white clad waiters walked among the guests with trays of wine. One of them approached us, and I gave him a polite shake of my head. I was here for one reason only, and I needed to keep my head clear for it.

Tennin leaned in. "What do you think?"

"I can't imagine living in such a beautiful place. I love it."

"I am glad you approve," said a male voice from behind us.

Tennin and I turned at the same time to face our host, the only person in the room who wasn't wearing a mask. Davian Woods didn't look much different from his photos, but he was shorter than I expected. He was an average looking man with light brown hair and brown eyes, but he had a great smile, the kind that made you feel like you knew him already.

"Tennin, so glad you could make it." Davian's gaze shifted to me and lingered appreciatively on my dress before lifting to meet my eyes. "And who is your friend with the exquisite taste?"

"Davian, this is Jesse," my date said. "Jesse loves faeries almost as much as you do, and I knew she'd enjoy meeting you."

"Is that so?" Davian held out a hand. "It's always nice to meet someone who shares my passion. But where has my friend been hiding you all this time?"

I smiled and took his hand in a firm handshake. "He hasn't been hiding me. I was in high school, and my father would have hunted him down if he'd taken me to a party before I turned eighteen."

Davian threw back his head and laughed. "Well, I am honored to be your host. Perhaps I can give you a tour of my home after I greet all my guests."

"I'd like that." I felt a pang of disappointment that I had to wait to talk to him more, but I was excited about the prospect of seeing the rest of his home.

Everything I'd read about him told me he was too smart to give away his secrets, but you could learn a lot about someone by how they lived and the things they valued.

Someone called Davian's name, and his smile tightened as he waved a hand at them. "If you will excuse me, I believe the governor would like a word. Please, have a drink and some of the wonderful food my chef has prepared."

"The governor?" I whispered to Tennin after our host had left us.

"You never know who you'll find at these things. So far, I see three A-List actors, a British royal, an NBA star, and one...no two supermodels." One corner of his mouth lifted. "And one bounty hunter."

I scanned the room, trying to pick out the celebrities. Violet was going to die when I told her about this. "How can you tell who they are beneath their masks?"

"It's my job to know faces. I'll introduce you to them if you'd like."

I wanted to say yes because I would never get another chance like this. But I shook my head. "I think I should stay in the background and not draw any attention to myself. I would like to know what smells so good in that kitchen, though."

He chuckled. "Let's go see what delights Davian's chef has for us."

The penthouse dining room and kitchen were as impressive as the main room, with dark wood and glass cabinets, stone countertops, and state-of-the-art stainless steel appliances. A chef in a white jacket opened an oven door and lifted out a tray of food. He transferred it to a platter and carried it to the long table covered with trays of mouthwatering appetizers.

We went to check out the food, and Tennin told me which foods were Fae so I could avoid them. I filled a small plate and refused a glass of wine from a waiter, who fetched me mineral water instead. After we'd sampled some of the delicious appetizers, Tennin and I strolled toward the other end of the great room where he identified the new guests as they arrived.

I only half listened to him as I thought about my next move. I'd made it inside the penthouse, but I hadn't really planned what to do once I was here. I'd grilled Tennin about Davian and his home, and he'd told me Davian's office and private collection were upstairs. He had also informed me that Davian had an aversion to security cameras, which was strange for a person who made his living off technology. Or maybe he wanted no recording of what went on in his home. Thank God for eccentric, paranoid billionaires.

We turned into a hallway that had been concealed by potted trees and stopped outside a library. I wondered if I'd find any Fae books inside. Surely, someone obsessed with faeries had to have books on them, maybe some my parents didn't own.

When a woman in a red dress and a feathered red mask motioned for us to join her and two other women, Tennin groaned. "I don't suppose you will pretend to be madly in love with me for the next few hours."

My lips twitched. "I'm afraid I'm not that good an actress."

"You grow more like your mother each day," he grumbled.

"Thank you."

He set his wine glass on the tray of a passing waiter. "Care to mingle?"

"You go ahead. I'd like to check out Davian's library." I gave him a meaningful look, and he nodded.

"Stay out of trouble," he whispered before he went to join the group of women.

I entered the library and took a few minutes to circle the room and appreciate the vast collection of books. There were thousands of titles, with one whole section dedicated to first editions and out-of-print books, and a selection of what looked like old Russian literature behind glass. There was also a large section dedicated to technology and finance, not surprising for a tech billionaire.

"Ah!" I stopped walking when I came upon three full shelves of Fae books. We had half of them at home, and a few of them I'd seen at the library. But there were two I'd hadn't seen before. How could there be Fae books I'd never heard of?

I slid one off the shelf and turned it to look at the cover. I stared at the gold embossed drawing of a couple in a sexual position, and my cheeks heated when I realized what the book was about. That explained why I wasn't familiar with it.

I was curious, but I replaced the book without looking inside. How embarrassing would it be if someone were to enter the library and find me reading a sex book?

I walked to the door, and a male laugh reached me as I stepped out of the library. I froze because I'd know that laugh anywhere. What on earth was Conlan doing here of all places? If he was here, did that mean...?

My stomach quivered as I peered through the branches of a potted tree until I found Conlan standing by a window with Davian.

I let my breath out in a whoosh of air when I saw they were alone. Conlan was one of the last people I wanted to see, but it could have been worse. He could have come with –

Lukas.

My stomach sank when he appeared beside Conlan with a drink in his hand. Unlike most of the other guests, neither of them wore a mask. Power and authority emanated from Lukas, and I could tell by the way people moved around him that I wasn't the only one who felt it.

I gnawed on my lip as I watched Lukas say something to Davian, who laughed in response. His and Conlan's presence could ruin everything for me. It was too much to hope that they wouldn't recognize me in my mask, and they'd know I was up to something the moment they saw me here. What if they outed me as a bounty hunter? Davian would get suspicious and kick me out of his home.

Lukas frowned suddenly, and his gaze swung in my direction. I pulled back around the corner, my heart racing. Had he seen me? Not waiting to find out, I hurried down the short hallway. On my right was what I assumed was the door to the master suite, and on my left was the same hallway we had walked through earlier with the stairs to the upper floor.

There was no one in sight as I approached the staircase, and I debated for a whole second whether or not I should ask someone if I was allowed to go upstairs. The thought of Lukas coming around the corner any second made the decision for me.

Better to ask forgiveness than to get permission, I thought as I started up the stairs. I winced when my heels clicked loudly on the glass steps, and after the first three, I stopped and removed my shoes.

At the top of the stairs, I walked a few feet and stopped to stare at the extravagance around me. Beneath a sloped glass ceiling was a dining area with a table that could seat twenty people. A wall of windows separated it from a terrace lit with soft lights and lined with potted fir and cypress trees. To my left was a glass room, but the foliage on the other side prevented me from seeing the interior. A greenhouse or atrium maybe.

I turned in the other direction. *Aha.*

Separated from the dining area by a textured glass and copper wall was an elevated area that resembled a gallery. Shoes dangling from my fingers, I walked over and climbed the four steps to Davian Woods's private faerie collection.

I was drawn immediately to the framed artwork of Faerie landscapes painted by renowned Fae artists. The style reminded me of a Monet exhibit I'd seen once at the Museum of Modern Art, and I loved how vibrant the paintings were. If Faerie looked this beautiful in a painting, I couldn't imagine how it was in person.

After my eyes had feasted on the artwork, I turned to look at Davian's other Fae treasures displayed throughout the room in glass cases. There were carvings, books, jewelry, utensils, clothing, and various crystals. In the largest display, there was a strip of white fabric believed to have come from the goddess's robe. I wondered about its authenticity because faeries were reverent of their goddess and would not relinquish such an important artifact to a human. The massive effort to find the ke'tain was proof of that.

In the same case was half a spear that supposedly belonged to the mythical Asrai. But it was the small white stone nestled in a bed of velvet that interested me most. The plaque said it was believed to be a goddess stone, but I knew with certainty that it wasn't. A goddess stone stayed with its rightful owner until it was gifted to a new owner. If Davian had been goddess-blessed, as it was called, the stone would be on his person, not in a glass case.

At either end of the gallery was a door. I tried both and wasn't surprised to find them locked. One of them had to be Davian's office. I studied the lock on one and smiled. It was a standard five-pin lock and shouldn't be much of a challenge. Luckily, I had come prepared for this.

I reached under the skirt of my dress for the pick set strapped to my inner thigh. My hand froze when male voices drifted to me from below. I cocked my head and strained to listen. Maybe they were passing by the stairs.

The sound of shoes on glass steps had me shooting upright and backing away from the door. I planned to pretend I was admiring the gallery, until I heard the unmistakable voice of a faerie prince I knew all too well. I bolted for the steps to the dining area and raced across the tiled floor, thankful I hadn't donned my shoes yet. Quietly, I opened the door to the terrace and slipped outside.

There wasn't time to brace myself for the frigid wind that stole my breath. I ran to the potted trees and took cover in the shadows behind them. The trees shielded me from view, but they offered little protection from the cold. I shivered violently in my dress, which was meant to be worn in Faerie's temperate climate.

Wrapping my arms around myself, I watched the top of the stairs as Davian and Lukas came into view, followed by Conlan. The two faeries dwarfed Davian, who looked even plainer next to their male perfection, but he seemed unaware of it as he talked animatedly to Lukas.

The three of them ascended the steps to the gallery where Davian showed them one of the paintings I had admired. Lukas looked only politely interested, and that made me wonder what he was doing here in the first place. My conversation with Tennin yesterday had left me with the impression that Davian was a source of amusement to faeries. He was hardly the kind of person I expected Lukas to socialize with. But then, I had been wrong about a lot of things concerning Lukas. I was sure his real identity wasn't the only thing he'd kept from me.

The trio walked to the office door, and Davian used a key to unlock it. He entered the room and touched something on the wall beside the door. My knees went weak when I watched him enter a security code. A few more minutes and I would have been caught breaking into his office.

Davian must have something important to conceal if he had a security panel on his office inside his own home. He *was* the CEO of a billion-dollar company, so it made sense that he would want to protect sensitive documents. But my gut told me it was more than that.

My teeth chattered, reminding me I had a bigger concern than the contents of Davian's office. I hopped from one bare foot to the other because they were going numb, and there was no room for me to stoop and strap on my shoes without being seen.

I watched Davian and his guests enter the office as I waited for my chance to escape. The second they closed the door, I was making a run for it before I got too cold to move at all.

Several minutes ticked by, but the office door stayed open with Conlan visible inside. I looked around desperately and spotted an outside door to what I assumed was the greenhouse. Moving sideways, I crept along in the narrow space between the trees and the wall until I came to a four-foot gap in the trees. Cursing my luck, I peered through the branches at the office and saw Conlan's back was to me. It was now or never.

My body tensed to spring across the open space, but movement in the gallery stopped me. Davian emerged from the office with Lukas and Conlan behind him. He said something to the faeries, who smiled and nodded in return. I let out a breath. Maybe they were going downstairs.

Or not. Lukas and Conlan stayed in the gallery watching Davian as he descended the steps and approached the terrace door. My eyes went to our host, and my stomach knotted when his congenial expression turned to a hard mask of anger that only I could see. He came out onto the terrace and waited for the door to shut before he put a phone to his mouth and spoke.

"Did I not make myself clear when I said you were not to interrupt me tonight?" he bit out. "This had better be worth pulling me away from the Unseelie prince."

He went quiet as he listened to the person on the other end speak. Then, "Of course, this phone is safe! I designed the damn thing."

I pressed against the wall as he paced in my direction while his caller spoke. Gone was the charming host who had welcomed me to his home. This snarling man made me feel like a rabbit hiding from a predator, and I didn't want to think about what he would do if he caught me spying on him.

He stopped several feet away. "What do you mean you don't have it?" Pause. "Raided? And you're only telling me this *now*?"

His voice rose dangerously, and he lowered it suddenly. Pasting on a smile, he looked at the gallery where Lukas and Conlan stood watching him. I didn't dare move a muscle. Faeries had enhanced eyesight, and they might see me even if Davian couldn't. The mask hid the upper part of my face, but my red hair was a dead giveaway.

Davian turned away from the gallery. "Find him and get it for me. I don't care what you have to do. And remember, you are as expendable as your predecessor."

On that ominous note, he hung up. He stood quietly seething and glaring at a spot less than a foot away from me. I couldn't remember ever being as afraid of a human as I was in that moment. Physically, Davian wasn't a threat to me, but he had the money and resources to do whatever he wanted to people who crossed him. The cold malice pouring off him told me he wouldn't lose a second of sleep over it.

He closed his eyes and took several deep breaths to calm himself. Before my eyes, the anger disappeared from his expression, and the warm smile returned. If I hadn't witnessed his rage, I never would have believed him capable of it.

Composed, he spun and went back inside to rejoin Lukas and Conlan in the gallery, motioning for them to return to his office. Conlan glanced at Lukas, who was still looking at the terrace. He couldn't see me, could he?

Please, go. I wasn't sure I could endure the cold for one more minute. Much longer and my feet were going to freeze to the stones beneath them.

After what felt like forever, Lukas turned away and walked to the office with the others. I didn't wait for them to go inside. As soon as their backs were to me, I ran across the gap and behind the trees on the other side. From there, I only had to move another ten feet or so behind the trees before the office door was out of sight. Then I sprinted for the glass door of the greenhouse.

"Thank God," I said through numb lips when the door opened under my hand. I stepped inside and sighed at the heat that enveloped me. It was like walking out of a freezer and into a sauna.

I was so relieved to be out of the cold that it took me a moment to focus on my surroundings. When I did, I gasped at the room I'd mistaken for a greenhouse. It was more like something out of a dream.

In the center of the large room was a natural pool surrounded on three sides by rock and vegetation with an actual waterfall at one end. The floor of the pool appeared to be made of sand, and I could see water plants and some brightly colored fish at the bottom.

Pulling off my mask, I strolled around the room, taking in the Fae trees and flowers that filled the room with a heady perfume. Colorful birds flitted between the trees as I passed them, and in one corner, there was a small grove of trees inhabited by pixies. The tiny green faeries flew into a tizzy, unhappy about my presence, but they left me alone. Wild pixies would have tried to bite me for invading their turf, but these had most likely been raised here in captivity.

Davian had created his own little Faerie paradise in his home. Looking up at the domed glass ceiling, I imagined floating in the pool, gazing at the blue sky on a clear day. I wondered if this room was a true representation of Faerie or just his vision of it. Either way, it was breathtaking.

I walked to the interior wall facing the dining area and peeked through the vines covering most of the glass. From here, I could make out a dark head inside the office above. It could be Lukas or Conlan, but it was impossible to tell. I'd have to wait in here until they went downstairs, but this room was a vast improvement over the terrace.

Tennin had to be wondering where I'd gone, and I cursed myself for leaving my phone in my coat. He knew I was here to snoop and find out if Davian knew anything about the ke'tain, and I hoped he didn't come looking for me. He was sophisticated enough to not do anything that would give me away, but I didn't want to risk him getting more involved than he was.

I wandered over to sit on a rock beside the pool and replayed Davian's one-sided conversation on the terrace. He hadn't mentioned Lewis Tate by name, but I was convinced that was who he'd ordered his caller to find. And the thing he was looking for had to be the ke'tain. I wished he'd said more because I had no idea where to go from here.

All I had succeeded in doing tonight was confirming my suspicions about Davian's connection to Tate. I'd also seen the billionaire's dark side, which he kept hidden from the rest of the world. I shivered despite the warmth of the room. Davian Woods was not someone I would ever want as an enemy, which was why he could never find out what I'd done tonight.

Fluttering beside me had me turning my head in time to see a pair of pixies flying away with the mask I'd laid on the floor with my shoes. They could barely support the mask between them, and they dipped and swayed in the air.

"Hey. Come back here." I jumped up and ran after them into their grove.

Davian had seen me in that mask. If he found it in this room, he would know I had been up here.

I managed to get hold of the mask before they could escape to the upper branches of the trees that had to be at least fifteen feet tall. They squeaked angrily and retaliated by darting at me and yanking at strands of my hair.

"Ouch. Quit it." I swatted the little beasts away, trying not to hurt them.

Two more pixies joined the attack, and one of them managed to get tangled in my hair. I struggled to free him without damaging his fragile wings or getting bitten in the process. Unable to see where I was going, I tripped over a rock and went down. Luckily, the floor here was covered in grass and thick moss that cushioned my fall.

The sound of a door opening made me go still. I couldn't let Lukas or Davian find me in here, so I did the only thing I could. I scrambled behind a leafy bush that was barely big enough to hide me and prayed whomever it was didn't look too closely at the grove.

Footsteps, muffled by the grassy floor, came closer and stopped. I dared a peek through the leaves, expecting to see Darius or Lukas, and I was surprised to find a blond faerie standing beside the pool. He reached up to remove a mask that covered most of his face, and I felt a spark of recognition. Where had I seen him before? Something unpleasant coiled in my gut, and the longer I stared at him, the stronger it got.

He set his mask on the floor and straightened, facing me full-on. My breath hitched when it hit me where I knew him from. The day after my parents disappeared, I'd visited Levi at the Plaza, and I'd seen this faerie at the station when I was getting the train home. I remembered how his constant staring had unnerved me and the cold look he'd given as my train had pulled away.

I'd never seen him again until now, and his presence here chilled me more than Davian's anger. I had a sick suspicion that this was a member of the Seelie royal guard. I had no idea what he was doing at Davian's party or how he had escaped Lukas's notice, but I knew it would not end well for me if he found me here.

Something caught my eye, and my blood chilled. I'd left my shoes beside the pool. If he took a few steps in that direction, he'd see them and know someone was here.

The faerie raised his hands and murmured under his breath. My fear turned to excitement when pale green magic flowed from his hands, and the air began to shimmer in front of him. He was creating a portal. Faeries didn't like to create them in front of humans, so I'd never seen one. Few people had.

I gasped at a sharp pain in my scalp. I'd forgotten about the pixie caught in my hair, the one that was suddenly determined to rip my hair out to get free. Gritting my teeth, I reached up to help him, and he rewarded me with a stinging bite on my finger.

I jumped and barely stopped my cry of pain. The bush rustled, and I froze as the faerie's head swung in my direction.

8

My heart threatened to explode from my chest as I imagined what he would do if he caught me. Even if I had come armed, I had no chance against a royal guard.

He dropped his hands and took a step toward the grove. At that exact moment, the pixie pulled free from my hair and flew out of the bush, taking a few strands of my hair with it. The faerie stopped his advance and watched the pixie disappear into the branches. All I could do was pray he hadn't seen the red hairs trailing behind the pixie and come to investigate.

He took another step, shaving a year off my life, and abruptly spun back toward the pool. Raising his hands, he started again to create the portal. I watched in awe as the air shimmered and rippled, and a faerie-sized hole formed. Beyond the portal, I could make out a white stone wall and an arched window, but nothing else.

Someone spoke on the other side. I strained to hear them, but it was impossible to make out the words over the gurgle of the waterfall.

"No, Your Majesty," the faerie said. "Davian does not have it yet."

The other voice rose enough to know it was female, which could only mean one thing. He was talking to Queen Anwyn. I had just heard the voice of the Seelie queen.

The faerie bowed his head. "I am sorry, Your Majesty. I have failed you."

There was movement on the other side of the portal, allowing me a glimpse of blonde hair, fair skin, and the twinkle of a jeweled diadem. She said something else, and he nodded.

"If anyone can find him, it is Aibel. Should I join him?"

The queen spoke again, and this time I could make out the words. "No. I have another job for you."

"As you wish." He stepped through the portal, and it closed with a soft swoosh.

I didn't move for a full five minutes. When I finally stood on trembling legs, my mind reeled from what I had seen and heard. No human had ever laid eyes upon the faerie monarchs, and I had no doubt I would be dead if the queen learned what I had witnessed.

I brushed off my dress, pulled on my shoes, and patted down my hair. I was going to need a mirror to fix it before I went downstairs. There was no way I could return to the party and act like everything was normal after this. I especially didn't want to run into Lukas and Conlan. I didn't owe them any explanations, but they knew me well enough to tell when something was wrong. They would also draw unwanted attention to me, and that was the last thing I needed.

There was no sign of anyone in the gallery or office when I peeked out, so I cracked the door to listen. Silence greeted me. I left the room and found a half bath on the other side of the stairs where I fixed my hair and donned my mask.

My legs were steadier by the time I descended the stairs, and I hoped I looked more composed than I felt. A waiter hurried by as I reached the main floor, but he barely glanced at me. As long as Davian wasn't one of those paranoid people who questioned the staff about everything, my secret should be safe.

I headed directly for the exit. I felt bad about leaving Tennin after he'd brought me here, but I couldn't go back to the party with Lukas there. I'd text Tennin to explain, and he would understand. He was well aware of my reason for not wanting to see Lukas.

In the foyer, one attendant went to retrieve my coat, and I handed my mask to the other attendant. He refused it, telling me it was a keepsake to help me remember the party. I wouldn't need any help remembering tonight, but I smiled and thanked him.

The other attendant helped me into my coat and summoned the elevator for me. I waited anxiously for it to arrive and nearly ran to it when the doors opened. I stepped inside and hit the button for the lobby. The doors began to close, and I sagged against the wall.

I jumped when an arm appeared in the gap between the doors, a second before they closed. The doors slid open again, and my stomach twisted when I met Lukas's hard blue eyes. Behind him stood Conlan and Kerr. Where the hell had Kerr come from? The lack of surprise on all three faces said this was not an accidental encounter.

They stepped into the elevator, which suddenly seemed a lot smaller. Conlan and Kerr stood on either side of the car with Lukas facing me. I hadn't been this close to him since the last time he was at my apartment. My chest squeezed at the memory, but the pain was quickly eclipsed by the anger that always followed.

"When Conlan said he thought he saw you at Davian's, I told him he was mistaken," Lukas said. "What are you doing here, Jesse?"

"Attending a party, obviously," I replied stiffly.

"How did you get in?"

I lifted my chin. "I walked in just like you did."

"You know that's not what I meant. Davian is selective about his guest list, and no one gets into his parties without an invitation."

"And it's impossible for someone like me to be invited to one of your society parties?"

His sigh was barely perceptible. "If by someone like you, you mean a bounty hunter, then yes. Davian is a snob, and he considers most people beneath him, unless they are celebrities or well-connected."

"Or Fae royalty. I assume *he* knows who you really are," I retorted, letting my anger get the best of me. I was trapped in here with him and his men, and it made me want to lash out at him. Something flickered in his eyes, telling me my barb had hit home, but it gave me little satisfaction. "I didn't crash your friend's party. I came as the date of one of his invited guests."

Lukas's jaw flexed. "Who?"

"Not to be rude, but that's none of your business." Tennin had done me a huge favor by bringing me tonight, and I would not repay him by getting him in trouble with Lukas, who had made it clear he didn't want me here. To the best of my knowledge, Lukas had no idea I even knew Tennin, and I planned to keep it that way.

"Was it the faerie who gave you that dress?" His eyes dipped to my dress, and warmth suffused me.

"Also none of your business." I yanked the edges of my coat together and darted a glance at the floor indicator above the doors. Were we even moving? This was the longest elevator ride I'd ever taken, and I was beginning to feel claustrophobic.

His gaze met mine again. "Your date is not seeing you home?"

"I can see myself home. Women do all kinds of crazy, independent stuff like that these days."

A muted chuckle came from Conlan, and my scowl deepened. "Is there a point to this interrogation?"

"I want to know the real reason you are here. You don't care about celebrities or parties."

My fingers tightened on my coat. "You don't know anything about me."

"We both know that's not true." A smile touched his lips, and it fanned my simmering anger.

"Not so long ago, you thought me capable of treachery and torture," I said, my words laced with the pain and bitterness that had been eating at me for weeks. I wanted to yell at him – to yell at all of them – for their betrayal, but my throat tightened, and angry tears pricked my eyes.

The air in the elevator became thick with tension. Conlan and Kerr shifted uncomfortably, and Lukas's eyes darkened with remorse. "I was wrong."

"Yes. You were."

The elevator stopped with a slight bump, and the doors slid open. Lukas stepped aside to let me out first, and I headed straight for the exit. I'd come here with Tennin, which meant I'd have to get a taxi home. I'd rather wait for one outside than in here with them.

I'd barely made it three steps when Lukas's hand caught my arm. "Jesse."

Steeling myself, I turned to look at him.

"A man like Davian Woods doesn't get where he is without being ruthless," Lukas said quietly.

A chill went through me.

He looked like he was going to say something else and changed his mind. "Be careful."

"I will."

This time when I walked away, he didn't stop me. I exited the building as a taxi was dropping off a couple dressed for a party. I wondered if they were headed to the penthouse, although they didn't look like anyone famous, so maybe not.

I sank into the back seat of the taxi and gave the driver my address. Cab fare was expensive, but I wasn't getting the bus or the subway in this dress. I pulled out my phone to text Tennin to let him know I'd gone home and that I'd run into Lukas in the elevator. I didn't tell him what I'd witnessed upstairs because I didn't want to drag him into it.

During the drive home, I replayed everything I'd seen and heard. I needed to figure out what to do with this information before I decided on a course of action. One thing I knew for certain. If Davian Woods *and* the Seelie queen were looking for the ke'tain, I was in way over my head.

"I was so mad that I wanted to tell them all where to go," I vented to Violet as we walked down a busy Soho street the next day. "But instead, I nearly cried in front of them. It was awful."

She nodded sympathetically. "I wish I'd been there with you. I would have given him a piece of my mind."

I smiled because I knew my best friend better than she did sometimes. Violet was passionate and outspoken, but she had a tendency to get starstruck around Fae royals. The most she would have managed was a mild glare, if that.

"You stood up to him, though, so you should be proud about that," she said.

"I just hate feeling like this, but I don't know how to stop it." I exhaled deeply, wishing I could expel all the ugly emotions bottled up inside me.

Violet stopped in front of a store window. "It's only been three weeks. Give yourself time."

"I don't have time. I have to –" I broke off before I accidentally let it slip about the ke'tain. The Agency had been emphatic about us keeping it from the public, including family and friends.

She gave me a confused look. "You have to do what?"

"I have to work. You know I'm handling everything until Mom and Dad come home. And now I have Aisla and Gus to take care of."

Violet snorted. "I still can't believe you have a drakkan in the apartment. And of all the names you could choose, you went with Gus."

"He won't leave, and that was the name he liked the most."

"He also likes lipstick. You owe me a new one," she said with a pout. "It was my favorite."

I tilted my head. "I warned you not to leave your bag on the floor. But I will buy you a new one since you helped me get ready for the party."

She sighed dreamily. "That dress. Tell your faerie friend he can bring me clothes any day."

"I think you're fine in the clothes department." I held up one of the shopping bags I was carrying for her. "Did you really need five new outfits?"

She rolled her eyes at me. "I need something perfect for my second audition. Image is everything."

"You could show up in a potato sack, and they'd still pick you for that role."

Violet let out a tiny squeal. "Gah! Can you believe it? My first callback. I know it's only a small part, but this movie is going to be huge."

"Remember what they say. 'There are no small parts, only small actors.' You show them why you're the best damn space shuttle pilot they'll ever see."

She nodded. "I've watched *Star Wars* so many times I'm going to be speaking in *Wookie* soon."

I laughed, and we started walking again. One thing no one could ever say about Violet was that she didn't put one hundred and ten percent into a role.

Violet stopped abruptly in front of a store. "Oooh. Let's go in."

I looked up at the sign on the window that read *New, Pre-owned, and Vintage Guitars,* and shook my head. "I don't need –"

"Yes, you do." She grabbed my arm and tugged me toward the door. "All you do is take care of everyone else. The world won't end if you treat yourself once in a while, and I know you miss your guitar."

I chewed on my lower lip. I did miss my old guitar, but I'd been trying to save every cent I could. Our building needed new pipes in the basement, and most of the tenants' rent went to the mortgage payment, utilities, and insurance. The estimates I'd gotten from three different plumbers were enough to keep me awake at night.

"It can't hurt to go in and see what they have," she said.

I gave in. "I'm only going in to look."

Thirty minutes later, I left the store with a worn acoustic guitar case slung over my shoulder. "You are a very bad influence, Violet Lee."

She laughed and pointed at a coffee shop. "I'll make it up to you. The coffee is on me."

We entered the shop and found an empty table. I watched our bags while she went to order the coffees.

"By the way, how are your mom and dad doing at the new treatment center?" she asked as she set our coffees on the table.

I took a sip of my coffee and sighed happily. "They're doing great. You should see the place. It looks more like one of those rehab centers rich people go to. I still can't believe our health insurance covers a place like that."

I had done some research on goren treatment, and there was another facility in Newark that looked more like an institution than the resort my parents were at. Mom and Dad had a comfortable suite with windows overlooking a park, and the cafeteria resembled an upscale restaurant. Residents were not allowed computers or cell phones, and the televisions only played non-violent movies because too much stimuli was not good for recovering goren addicts. But there was a library, a state-of-the-art gym with an Olympic-size swimming pool, and beautiful grounds for anyone who didn't mind braving the cold. I'd brought Mom and Dad some of their clothes and things from home, and they looked more like themselves every day.

"Have you told them yet?"

"No. I'll do it soon." Every time I saw my parents, I wanted to tell them about my bounty hunting, but their doctors continuously warned me stress and emotional upset early in the program could cause a setback. Mom and Dad were doing so well, and the last thing I wanted was to cause them any anxiety. I also knew the longer I waited, the more upset they were going to be that I'd kept it from them.

Footsteps approached our table, and I looked up to see two thirtysomething men in suits coming toward us. I didn't recognize them, but their appearance screamed Agency. I tensed because I didn't exactly have a good history with agents seeking me out.

"Can I help you?" I asked before either of them could speak.

"Are you Jesse James?" one of them asked in a curt tone.

I looked from him to his companion. "Who is asking?"

He produced a leather badge wallet and showed me his Agency ID. "I'm Agent Collins, and this is Agent Howard. We'd like to ask you a few questions about the raid on Lewis Tate's house."

"I wasn't there for the raid. I was called in after to round up the verries."

Agent Howard nodded. "We're talking to everyone who was at the house that night."

"Why?"

"It's routine. Nothing to be concerned about," said Agent Collins.

Something about his smile made my scalp prickle. In my experience, when people said not to be concerned, the exact opposite was usually true. And the Agency didn't track down hunters at coffee shops for routine questions. They showed up at your home or called you and requested you come to headquarters to talk.

"What do you want to know?" I asked, aware of Violet watching us.

Agent Collins glanced around the coffee shop. "Let's talk outside."

I hesitated briefly before I stood. If they wanted to discuss sensitive information, it made sense to do it where we were less likely to be over heard. Grabbing my coat, I followed them out of the shop, making sure to position myself in front of the large window where Violet could see me. I didn't care if they were agents. I had good reason to be suspicious of strangers.

Agent Howard spoke first. "According to the report, you were the first bounty hunter to arrive on the scene after the raid, correct?"

"Yes."

"And you went into the house alone," Agent Collins said. "Why didn't one of the agents accompany you?"

I furrowed my brow at the question. "Because it was too dangerous with all the verries on the loose in there."

He nodded. "And you spent two hours alone in the house?"

"More like an hour and a half." I wondered where he was going with this line of questioning.

"Where did you go in the house during that time?" he asked.

"Living room, hallway, cage room."

Agent Howard cut in. "That's it?"

"That's where the verries were. I had no reason to go anywhere else."

"I see." He stuck his hands in his coat pockets. "Did you observe anything unusual while you were in the house?"

"Like what?"

"Objects that look like they could be of Fae origin," said Agent Howard.

Could these guys be any vaguer? They had to know bounty hunters had been briefed on the missing ke'tain.

"There were some Fae objects, but I didn't see anything that looked like the ke'tain," I said.

They exchanged a look, and then Agent Collins said, "So you searched for the ke'tain while you were alone in the house?"

Their questions were starting to bug me. "No, I was too busy trying not to get stung to death."

Irritation flashed in his eyes. "And after you had caught the verries, what did you do?"

"Then I helped the man who got stung."

"I thought you said you were alone in the house at that time," Agent Howard cut in, suspicion coloring his tone.

Little alarm bells went off in my head. How could they not know about Brian Kang if they'd read the report from that night? I would think they'd want to question Lewis Tate's friend and possible accomplice over me. This didn't add up.

I crossed my arms. "I'm sorry, but why are you asking me this? It should all be in Agent Ross's report, and the security camera footage will show you exactly what I did in the house. I'm not sure what else I can tell you."

Agent Collins took half a step toward me. "We will decide what is important and what is not."

"I think you should accompany us to headquarters for a full debriefing." Agent Howard moved closer, boxing me in.

I pressed my back to the window. "I'll make an appointment."

Agent Collins laid a hand on my arm. "We'd prefer to talk to you now."

9

My hand went to my pocket and closed around the stun gun I always carried now. Assaulting an agent was a federal crime, but my gut told me I wasn't talking to real agents. They might look the part, but no agent would question a witness without doing their homework first. It was obvious these two hadn't laid eyes on the report or the security footage.

"Jesse."

The three of us looked at Violet, who stood outside the door, waving her phone.

She smiled apologetically. "Sorry to interrupt, but you have a call from someone at the Agency. I told him you were talking to agents, but he insisted."

"It must be Ben Stewart. Tell him I'll be right there." I turned to Collins and Howard, who had taken a step back. "I have to take this call. You don't keep the head of internal affairs waiting."

"Certainly not," Collins agreed hurriedly. "We'll call you to continue our debriefing."

"I'm happy to come in tomorrow," I said, knowing I'd never get that call.

He nodded and held out his hand. "Thank you for your cooperation, Miss James. Enjoy the rest of your day."

I shook Howard's hand, too, and then I watched the men walk swiftly down the street. They moved like they couldn't get out of there fast enough without running.

Violet was bouncing in her seat when I returned to our table, her eyes wide with nervous curiosity. "What the heck was that about?"

"I don't know, but thanks for the rescue." I pulled my phone from my pocket. "How did you know I needed help?"

"I didn't," she confessed. "But I didn't like the look of them, and I could see they were getting pushy. Are all agents like that?"

I opened my contacts. "They weren't agents."

Her hand shot out and covered my phone. "What do you mean? They had Agency IDs."

"Forgeries." I lifted my eyes to meet her shocked ones. "The Agency raided the house of a black market dealer a few nights ago, and I was sent in to clean up. Those guys asked me things about the raid that they should have known."

Her brows drew together. "That doesn't mean they weren't agents."

"They also didn't blink an eye when I said Ben Stewart is the head of internal affairs. There is no way any agent in this city doesn't know who he is and that he runs the Special Crimes division."

Violet gasped. "Oh my God, Jesse! What do we do?"

"*We* do nothing." I pulled up Stewart's name in my contact list. "I'm going to call him and let him know there are two men walking around pretending to be agents."

"How can you be so calm?" she asked breathlessly. "I'm about to freak out."

I smiled and kept up my calm front as I put the phone to my ear. On the inside, I was having my own mini freak-out. I was certain those men would have tried to force me to go with them if Violet hadn't intervened. They were looking for the ke'tain, and clearly, they were willing to use any means to find it. Impersonating an agent was a serious felony.

I was expecting to get Ben Stewart's voice mail, so I was surprised when he answered on the third ring. I lowered my voice and told him about my encounter with the fake agents, careful not to mention the ke'tain by name.

"I need you to come in to work with one of our sketch artists," he said when I finished. There was an edge to his voice that hadn't been there the first time we'd talked. "Do you feel safe there? I can send agents to pick you up."

I walked over to the window and scanned the street for any sign of the men. "My Jeep isn't far away. I need to drive my friend home, and I'll come there right after."

"I'll expect you here within two hours."

I hung up and went back to the table. "He wants me to come in, so I have to cut our day short."

Violet's face fell. "We didn't even get to have our coffee."

"I know, but he wants me to give a description to their sketch artist."

She let out an "Eep!" and waved her hands excitedly before she picked up her phone and turned the screen toward me. It was a photo, taken through the window, of me and the two men. My back was to the camera, but she'd gotten a good picture of them.

"You took a picture?" I stared at the men's faces on her phone.

"I wasn't getting a good feeling about them, and I thought, 'What would Jesse do?'"

"You are a genius!" I beamed at her as I took her phone and sent the photo to myself. Then I texted it to Ben Stewart. He replied immediately, saying they didn't need me to work with the artist now that they had a clear picture of the men. They would run the faces through their facial recognition software, and hopefully, they'd get a hit.

"Looks like I'm off the hook with the Agency." I stood and gathered up her shopping bags. "Let's get out of here."

"Don't you want to stay and have coffee?"

"Let's go home instead and decide on an outfit for your audition."

She jumped up and pulled on her coat. "I'll get our coffees to go."

Violet chattered about the audition all the way to the Jeep. I smiled and responded when it was required, but I was on high alert, paying close attention to our surroundings and the people.

Those men could have been working for anyone, but I suspected they were on Davian Woods's payroll. Had he discovered I was a bounty hunter or were his men following their own leads? Either way, I was afraid I hadn't seen the last of them or him.

"And then he hid in the tree house for a whole day. Finch did *not* take that well. You've never seen a temper tantrum until you've seen a sprite kicked out of his house by a drakkan."

Faris threw his head back and laughed. It had been almost a week since my first visit with him, and I was happy to see he had a little more color in his cheeks. He still had shadows under his eyes, but they were less pronounced than a week ago.

We were sitting in the living room today because he didn't think it was appropriate to entertain me in the library, which was essentially his bedroom. I had been anxious about seeing the others – especially Lukas – but so far it had been only the two of us. Faris hadn't mentioned my run-in with Lukas, and I had no intention of bringing it up.

"Sprites are docile in Faerie," Faris said, still grinning. "I can't say I've ever seen an angry one."

"That's because you've never met my brother." I took a sip from the bottle of water I'd brought with me. There had been another coffee and a plate of pastries waiting for me upon my arrival, but I'd politely refused them.

"I hope I get to meet him someday." He picked up a glass of green juice and drank it down. It was a cocktail of juice from fourteen different Fae fruits and vegetables, and it helped to provide many of the essential nutrients he needed to heal.

"Maybe you will." I took the empty glass from him. "Let me refill that."

Before he could protest, I went to the kitchen and poured him a fresh glass from a large carafe on the counter. I carried the glass back to him, and he frowned as he took it from me.

"I'm the host. I'm the one who should be getting the drinks."

I quirked an eyebrow. "We shared a cage. I think we're past formalities, don't you?"

His smile returned, and I realized it was the first time I'd ever mentioned that night without feeling the usual pang of hurt or anger. Maybe Faris wasn't the only one benefiting from our visits.

"So, you've given up on trying to remove the drakkan from your apartment?" he asked.

"For now. I've been so busy with work that I've barely been at home this week. And he's been less trouble than I thought he would be."

Aside from feeding, the drakkan required very little care. I'd picked up a large litter box for him, and it had taken me two days to figure out there were no droppings in it because he'd been unlocking our tiny bathroom window to go out whenever he wanted. For the most part, he stayed out of sight, except for when he snuck in every night to sleep on my bed. I never caught him, but the red scales he left behind were evidence he'd been there. That and I'd been having weird dreams since his arrival. I had no proof, but I was pretty sure he was somehow the cause of them.

"Why are you so busy?" Faris asked.

I made a face. "I discovered adulting is not always fun, and plumbers make a lot more than bounty hunters. Thankfully, there are a lot of extra jobs available these days."

"Is there a sudden shortage of bounty hunters?"

"The opposite actually. We have three times as many hunters in New York than we normally do. They just aren't interested in doing the usual jobs."

He tilted his head to one side. "Why is that?"

"They're all after a huge bounty the Agency put on the ke'tain."

His eyes widened. "You're searching for the ke'tain?"

"Everyone is. The Agency put a one hundred-thousand-dollar bounty on it, and hunters all over the world are after it. Since New York is one of the top entry points from Faerie, a lot of hunters are coming here looking for the ke'tain. I've already had one run-in with some out-of-towners who thought I might be competition, and it's only going to get worse."

He nodded grimly. "Money makes people do insane things. And the people who want the ke'tain for their own purposes will go through anyone who gets in their way. I wish you were not involved in this."

"I wasn't at first. I planned to work on all the other jobs and let everyone else fight over the ke'tain."

"Why did you change your mind? Was it the money?" he asked.

"The money would help my family, but that's not why I'm doing it." I pressed my lips together, wishing I hadn't mentioned the ke'tain.

He frowned. "Why would you take the risk if not for the money?"

"For her parents," said a voice from above that made my stomach dip.

I looked up at Lukas as he descended the stairs, and my mouth went dry at the intensity of his gaze. He looked even more serious than in our last encounter, reminding me of the cold, hard faerie I'd met at Teg's two months ago.

He went to stand by the fireplace, and having him in the same room made me keenly aware of him. Had it always been like this with him, or were my emotions amplified because of the emptiness where our friendship used to be?

Kaia ran down the stairs and joined her master. Standing there with his hand resting on her big head, Lukas looked so powerful and regal that I couldn't believe I'd ever mistaken him for anything but royalty.

"Jesse would do anything for her parents," he said to Faris, but his eyes stayed on me. "Even if it means pulling a dangerous stunt like snooping around the home of Davian Woods."

I clutched my hands in my lap. "What are you talking about?"

"After you left the party, I returned and spoke to our host," he informed me.

A pit opened in my stomach, and I felt some of the blood drain from my face.

Lukas stroked Kaia's head. "I told Davian one of his guests had taken ill and left, and I wanted to let her date know. Imagine my surprise when I learned that person was none other than Tennin."

"Tennin?" Faris echoed.

"Yes. He and I had a most enlightening conversation." Lukas smiled at me, and it did nothing to dispel the churning in my gut. "He told me he's known your parents for many years, and he's been helping you with some things because he owes your father a debt. It took a little convincing to get him to tell me why he brought you to Davian's party. He's surprisingly loyal to your family, which is not at all like the Tennin I know."

"You had no right to question him about me." I shot up from my chair, angry at him for interfering in my business and at myself for putting Tennin in that position.

Lukas ignored my outburst. "Tennin told me you believe Davian knows something about the ke'tain, but he was vague about how you came to that conclusion. Since I also suspect Davian's involvement, I am very interested in what led you to him."

I crossed my arms. "Good detective work."

"And then you managed to get invited to one of Davian's exclusive parties where you disappeared for an hour. Tennin said he didn't see or hear from you again until you texted him on your way home." Lukas pinned me with his shrewd eyes. "The question is, where were you and what were you up to during that hour?"

I went with a half-truth. "I was in the library for a few minutes, and then I went upstairs to look around. I was going to look through his office, but the door was locked."

"And then you left the party," he said.

"Yes," I snapped, too irritated by the questions and his presence to see he was leading me into a trap.

He rubbed his jaw. "Here's the thing. Conlan and I were upstairs with Davian for a good thirty minutes, and we returned to the party approximately fifteen minutes before Kerr saw you come downstairs and leave. That would have put you and us upstairs at the same time, but neither of us remembers seeing you there. Why is that?"

I shrugged one shoulder. "Poor observation skills."

His mouth curved into a smile so achingly familiar it sent shards of pain through my chest.

"You went through all that trouble to get into the penthouse, only to leave after an hour." He shook his head. "You would never give up so easily. The only reason you would have left the party early is if you found something.

Not the ke'tain because you would have turned it in, but something important."

"I guess you have it all figured out." I let my arms fall to my sides. "Is this why I was invited here today? You thought you would ambush me and find out what I know. What's next? Are you going to have Faolin make me talk if I don't give you what you want?"

"Goddess, no!" Faris came unsteadily to his feet and lost his balance.

I lunged for him, but Lukas got there first. He caught Faris and lowered him back to the couch with great care. When Lukas straightened, his troubled eyes met mine.

"No one here will ever harm you, Jesse," he said roughly. "Don't blame Faris for this. He had no idea I was going to question you."

Feet pounded on the stairs, and Faolin ran into the room. "What's wrong? I heard Faris shout."

Faris waved him off. "It's nothing, Brother. I tried to stand too fast and fell over."

"I told you not to tire yourself," Faolin scolded, but there was concern in his eyes.

I cleared my throat. "I should go."

"Please, stay." Faris gave me a beseeching look that was impossible to refuse.

Avoiding Lukas's eyes, I sat. I immediately wished I'd left when an awkward silence fell over the room.

"Faolin and I will be upstairs if you need anything," Lukas said.

Faris waited until their footsteps had faded before he spoke. "I'm sorry about that. Since I came home, Lukas's main focus has been finding the ke'tain and those who took it."

"The ke'tain is important to your people." I didn't have to like Lukas or agree with his methods to understand why he'd want to get it back.

"It is, but that's not the only thing that drives him." Faris sighed heavily. "He's also doing it for me."

"For you? Will the ke'tain help you heal faster?"

Faris shook his head and stared out the window for a long moment. "I was investigating the ke'tain's disappearance when I was taken." He turned his head to look at me. "I should say I was taken *because* I was investigating its disappearance."

My hand went to my chest. "The Seelie royal guard."

"How do you know that?"

"Rogin's sister, Raisa, told me the queen's guard did that to you. She said Queen Anwyn has no mercy for her enemies."

He rubbed his chest as if it pained him. "She is right."

"Raisa also told me it was the Seelie guard who took my mother and father. Her brother was supposed to kill them, but Raisa saved them."

Faris frowned. "Why would the queen's guard want your parents killed?"

"All Raisa knew was that they had done something to anger the guard. I think my parents stumbled onto something about the ke'tain on their last job. It's the only thing that makes sense."

"Have you asked your parents about it?"

I shook my head. "Mom and Dad can't remember anything that happened to them, and their doctors told me I have to be careful about what I tell them. I'm afraid the Seelie guard will try to stop them from getting their memories back. That's why I'm looking for the ke'tain."

Understanding filled his eyes. "If the ke'tain is found, they will have no reason to go after your parents."

"They still might hold a grudge, but I can't think about that now." The thought chilled me, and I rubbed my arms for warmth. "I can only fight one battle at a time."

"Then let us fight it for you."

"No."

"Please, hear me out," he implored. "If you don't agree, we'll never speak of it again."

I stared at the floor as if it miraculously held the answers I needed. Finding no guidance there, I lifted my eyes to his. I hadn't known him long, and he was one of Lukas's closest friends, but for some reason I couldn't explain, I trusted him.

I folded my hands in my lap. "Okay."

He smiled. "I am impressed by the way you hold your own with Lukas. There are few who could stand up to him like you do."

"But?"

"But squaring off against Lukas is one thing. He would never harm you. Going up against Queen Anwyn and her guard alone is not just folly; it's asking to die. You need look no further than me for proof of it."

I thought about how close he'd been to death the first time I saw him. He was an Unseelie royal guard, a trained killer, and he'd had no chance against them. What hope could I have of surviving a similar encounter?

"My friends hurt you deeply, and your anger toward them is justified," he said. "But if you put your feelings aside for one moment, you'll admit there is no one better equipped to deal with the Seelie guard."

"You're right, but you're asking me to trust them with my family's lives. How do I know they won't turn on me again?"

Faris was quiet for a moment. "They've given you every reason to doubt them, so I understand your reluctance. All I can do is tell you they regret their actions more than you know, and they would make amends if you allowed them."

"I don't care about amends. I care about keeping my parents safe."

"Then you need a powerful ally, and we both know who that is."

"What I know might not even be helpful to them." Lukas already knew the Seelie guard was behind Faris's imprisonment, and Davian Woods was after the ke'tain. What could I tell him that he couldn't find out on his own?

Faris shrugged. "You won't know until you share it with him."

I inhaled deeply and set my shoulders. "This doesn't change anything. I'm not going to be their friend just because we're working together."

"Of course," he replied seriously, but I glimpsed a small smile as he took a drink from his glass. He wiped his mouth and tilted his head back to call out, "Lukas, Faolin, Jesse would like to speak to you."

"Does it have to be both of them?" I whisper-shouted at him.

"Faolin is the head of security, and there is no one more motivated to bring my captors to justice."

"Then can I speak to him?"

"I am touched," Faolin said dryly from above.

"Don't be." I scowled at Faris and steeled myself as Lukas and Faolin descended the stairs.

They entered the room, and Faolin went to sit on the couch with his brother. Lukas took one of the other chairs instead of standing like he'd done earlier. Neither spoke, waiting for me to start.

I shifted in my seat under the weight of their stares, and my palms began to sweat. It wasn't from fear. Not exactly. There were so many emotions warring inside of me I couldn't single one out.

I remembered what Faris had said about needing Lukas and the others as allies, and I pushed forward. "Do you know about the Agency's raid on a black market dealer in Flatbush last week?"

"Lewis Tate." Lukas said. "They told me he got away, and their search turned up nothing." He gave me a questioning look. "What about it?"

"I was there. They needed a bounty hunter to do some cleanup. I was in his office after they tossed it, and I saw a New Year's Eve party invitation from someone named DW. I didn't think anything of it until Tennin mentioned Davian Woods and told me about his Fae obsession. That's when I put it together. The Agency raided Tate's house because they thought he had the ke'tain, and Davian likes to collect Fae things. It was too much of a coincidence."

"That *was* good detective work," Faris praised.

Lukas nodded in agreement. "And the party?"

"Tennin told me he was going to a party at Davian's, and I asked him to bring me as his date."

Lukas cocked his head. "He said you blackmailed him. You threatened to seek out Davian on your own if he didn't take you to the party."

"That was only after I asked him and he said no. He agreed to take me because he was worried I'd do something dangerous."

Faolin scoffed, and I glared at him.

"What happened at the party?" Lukas asked. "Why were you in such a rush to leave that you didn't tell Tennin first?"

I rubbed my palms on my jeans. I hadn't told a soul about what I'd witnessed that night, not even Tennin. The secret hung around my neck like a fifty-pound yoke, but I'd been too afraid to share it with anyone.

I looked at Faris, who gave me an encouraging smile, and then I plunged ahead. I told them about sneaking upstairs, looking at Davian's gallery, and my plan to break into his office, which got aborted when I heard Lukas, Conlan, and Davian on the stairs.

Lukas's eyebrows shot up. "You were out on the terrace that whole time?"

"No." I realized I was fidgeting and stopped. "I went back inside after Davian's phone call."

A gleam entered Lukas's eyes when he realized what I wasn't saying. He leaned forward with his arms on his knees. "What did you hear?"

I told them everything, as close to verbatim as I could remember, including the change that had come over Davian during the call. Lukas's eyes darkened, and I couldn't tell if he was angry with me or Davian.

He and Faolin exchanged a look, and Faolin said, "We were right. Davian is in the middle of this."

Lukas nodded. "We need to find Lewis Tate."

Faolin stood. "I'll go through his financials again."

"There's more," I blurted.

Lukas and Faolin looked at me as if they'd forgotten I was there. Faolin took his seat again, and the three of them watched me expectantly.

"After Davian went inside, I hid in his pool room, or whatever you call it, until you all went downstairs." My stomach twisted as I told them what I had seen and heard in the room.

Lukas swore and got up to stand by the fireplace. His eyes were blazing when he faced us again, and I pressed back into the couch reflexively. But it was Faolin he spoke to.

"He created a portal. You know what this means?"

Faolin's expression turned almost as dark as Lukas's. "Yes."

I looked between the two of them and then at Faris, who seemed to know what they were talking about. Were they planning to let me in on their little secret?

"I don't know what it means," I said pointedly.

It was Faris who answered me. "It means Davian Woods is working with Queen Anwyn."

I frowned. "How do you know that for sure? Maybe Davian had no idea her guard was there."

Lukas returned to his chair. "Do you know what a dampening ward is?"

"Yes." Dampening wards limited the use of magic inside them. They were used mostly on important government buildings, but big venues had started to use them, too.

"Davian has a dampening ward on his penthouse, which means no faerie can create a portal there," Lukas said. "Unless they have been granted access to bypass the ward."

Ice formed in my veins. Davian and the Seelie queen were dangerous on their own. Together, they were unstoppable. Short of hiding my parents in a secret underground bunker, how could I possibly hope to protect them from such powerful enemies?

My face must have betrayed my fear because Lukas said, "We will deal with our friend Davian and the queen. Neither of them knows what you witnessed, so you have nothing to worry about on that front."

"As long as you keep your distance from Davian and maintain a low profile, you'll stay off their radar," Faolin added with his usual glower.

I rubbed my suddenly cold hands together in my lap. "I think I'm already on someone's radar."

Lukas narrowed his eyes. "What have you done?"

"I haven't *done* anything. Three days ago, two men posing as agents approached me while I was out having coffee with Violet. They asked about the raid on Lewis Tate's house and wanted to know if I searched for the ke'tain while I was there."

"How do you know they weren't agents?" Faolin asked.

"They looked the part, but there was something off about them. They asked questions about the raid that agents would already know the answers to."

Faris caught my eye. "Could the men have been other bounty hunters looking for the ke'tain?"

"I considered that, but their Agency IDs looked real, and those are not easy or cheap to forge." I paused. "And...they tried to get me to leave with them."

"By force?" Lukas's voice had taken on an edge that could slice through stone.

"It didn't come to that." I filled them in on Violet's intervention and my call with Ben Stewart. "As far as I know, the Agency hasn't identified them yet, and I haven't seen them since."

I had been extra vigilant since the incident, but there had been no sign of the men or anyone else nosing around. I had spotted Agent Curry as I was leaving my parents' treatment facility yesterday, and I'd wondered if Ben Stewart had sent him to check up on me and my parents or if he was there on other business.

"Do you have the photo your friend took of the men?" Faolin asked.

I took out my phone and texted the picture to Faris because his was the only number I had now. He gave his phone to Faolin, who forwarded the picture to himself before he handed the phone to Lukas.

Lukas looked up from the phone. "Do you know if the men talked to anyone else who was at the raid?"

"They said they did, but I asked another hunter who was there, and she hasn't heard from them."

"Why you then?" he asked suspiciously. "Did anything happen that night that would cause them to single you out?"

I nodded. "I was the only one who spent any time alone in the house, and that was what the men were most interested in."

"Why were you alone in the house during a raid?" Faolin asked.

"Tate released a few dozen verries when the agents got there. I was there to round them up."

Lukas's nostrils flared. "The agents sent you in alone to deal with them?"

"They didn't send me anywhere, and I got paid very well for that job." Depositing that check into my bank account the next day had felt pretty damn good. And Levi had been so pleased he'd promised to start saving some of the choice jobs for me like he had for my parents. This morning, he'd hinted he might have a Three for me tomorrow.

Faolin typed something on his phone and asked, "Have you told the Agency what you told us about Davian and the Seelie guard?"

"No. I've told no one but you three."

"Why not?" His eyes grew suspicious. At least, some things never changed.

"Because our priorities are not the same. The Agency's is finding the ke'tain, and mine is keeping my parents safe. If it came down to it, the Agency would choose the ke'tain over the lives of two bounty hunters." I held his gaze so there would be no mistaking my intentions. "My family comes before anything else. As does yours."

He tipped his chin in acknowledgement, which was the most I could expect from him. It still baffled me how he and Faris were brothers. If not for the physical resemblance, I never would have believed it.

I stood, prompting the three faeries to follow suit. "That's everything. If I learn anything else, I'll let you know."

Lukas smiled. "Don't call me; I'll call you."

I didn't return the smile. "Exactly."

Faris's face fell. "You're leaving? But we never had our visit."

"Work," I lied. "I'll come back next week."

I didn't realize Lukas had followed me until he spoke as I stepped outside. "Thank you, Jesse."

His voice was warm and sincere, and it made my heart constrict. I felt lighter having shared my burden with him and his men, but I couldn't let that lure me into a false sense of security. I forced my expression into a cold mask before I turned back to face him. "I didn't do this for you. I did it for my parents and Faris."

"I know."

I pulled up my collar against the cold. "It doesn't change anything."

"I know," he said again.

"Good." That settled, I spun and walked away.

10

I shivered in my small leather jacket and thigh-length dress and stuck my hands into my pockets. Ahead of me, women pressed together in small groups, trying to fend off the cold in their skimpy outfits.

"I can't believe I let you convince me to wear a tiny dress in this weather." I scowled at Violet, who seemed unaffected by the subzero temperature, even though her sapphire-blue dress was as short as mine.

Violet tossed her hair over her shoulder, her blue highlights almost the same shade as her dress. "I told you Va'sha has a specific dress code, and they're very selective about who they let in."

"Can't I just flash my Agency ID at them?" I whined through chattering teeth.

"Where's the fun in that?" She grinned slyly and struck a pose that hiked up her short skirt even more.

A minute later, a dark-haired faerie in a black shirt bearing the night-club's logo walked down the line, pointing at some of the people there. When he reached us, his eyes slowly swept up Violet's body from the painted toenails peeking out of her silver stilettos to her glossy hair.

"You," he said, pointing at her.

She took my arm and tugged me forward. "And my friend."

He took in my red mini dress with the plunging V-neck bodice and strapless heels that made my bare legs feel impossibly long. His gaze lingered on my hair, which Violet had insisted I leave down tonight, save for the small section on either side that I'd pinned back. Smoky eyes and red lips completed the look.

Desire blazed in his eyes, and a sensual smile curved his lips. "Definitely you."

"I have a feeling you're going to be quite popular tonight," Violet joked under her breath as we stepped out of the line.

People grumbled when Violet and I followed the faerie to the door, but I was too happy to be getting out of the cold to pay them much attention. We entered the club where a woman took our jackets and phones. Va'sha was a popular spot for celebrities, and it did what it could to protect their privacy. No cameras or recording equipment were allowed inside, and the paparazzi were banned.

A male faerie waited to usher us up a flight of stairs to the main floor of the club as if we were VIP guests. Violet took it all in stride, which made me suspect this was normal in Fae clubs.

"What do you think?" she asked when we reached the top of the stairs.

I looked around the night club, which was dimly lit by red and blue lights in the high ceiling. In the center of the room was a small, round dance floor that could barely accommodate the dozen or so couples on it. On either side of the floor was a curved wooden balustrade that separated the seating area from the dancers.

At the far end of the club was a bar, backlit by shelves of liquor. In a corner to the left of the bar was a raised DJ platform, and on the right were the stairs to the upper floor, most likely the VIP section, judging by the closed gate at the top of the stairs. A popular Hip-Hop song filled the club, but the volume was low enough to talk over. Faeries didn't like loud music, and Va'sha was a place where faeries and humans came to hook up.

"It's nice." I craned my neck to see the occupants of the tables and booths, but from here it was impossible. I suspected that was by design.

A flurry of activity near the upper floor railing drew my attention. I looked up at a group of male faeries and human women, that included a famous pop singer, an A-list actor, and Prince Rhys. Violet hadn't been kidding when she'd said Va'sha was *the* place to be.

I should have known the Seelie prince would be here since it was well-publicized that he loved the New York party scene. I wasn't thrilled about being in the same club as any of the Seelie guard, but there wasn't anything I could do about it.

A cold breeze wafted across the bare skin of my back, and I took Violet's arm to lead her toward the bar.

She waved at the dance floor. "Let's dance."

"You do remember that I'm here to do a job."

"You said she won't be here until after midnight. And you know what they say about all work and no play." She pouted prettily. "Come on, Jess. Let's play a little."

I held up a finger. "One dance."

"Two," she countered as she grabbed my hand and tugged me onto the crowded dance floor.

Three dances later, breathless and laughing, I dragged my protesting friend from the floor.

"But I love this song," she complained. "One more dance, pretty please."

I checked my watch. "She'll be here soon, and I'm thirsty."

"I'll dance with you," said a female voice.

We turned to see a dark-haired faerie in a white dress made of a material so fine you could make out every curve of her body. She spared me a quick smile, but she had eyes for only Violet, who looked like she was in love. Or in lust. With Violet I could never be sure.

Violet blushed. "I'd love to."

"Have fun," I said as the faerie took her hand and led her away. Violet went so meekly I would have suspected a glamour if I hadn't made sure she was wearing a talisman tonight.

Heading to the bar, I ordered a sparkling water and drank it while I scanned the club for my target. A few male faeries smiled my way, but none of them approached me, which was a pleasant surprise. Violet had warned me my hair would attract a lot of attention, and I'd almost worn a wig tonight. I guessed that in a place like this with so many beautiful women, one redhead didn't stand out much.

I finished my water and turned to do a walk about when a male faerie with long, dark hair stepped up beside me. "Hi. I'm Dain. May I buy you a drink?"

"No, thanks."

He laid a hand on mine to stop me from leaving. "Perhaps you'd care to join me upstairs in the VIP area. Prince Rhys is in attendance tonight, and I can get an introduction for you."

I extracted my hand from beneath his. "I'm waiting for my friend to come back."

"The beautiful girl I saw you dancing with? She is welcome to join us."

"We'd rather stay down here," I said, even though I knew Violet would kill to get invited up to the VIP section. What she didn't know wouldn't hurt her, and she looked pretty happy where she was.

He blinked as if he hadn't heard me correctly. "You don't want to go to the VIP area and meet the prince?"

It was on the tip of my tongue to say I'd already met Prince Rhys when a voice I knew all too well spoke from behind us.

"Jesse?"

Dain and I turned at the same time to face Lukas, who stood a few feet away, looking like he'd walked straight out of *Modern Fae* magazine. He wore black trousers, a white top, and a charcoal blazer with the sleeves pulled up to reveal his strong forearms. My heart beat erratically at the scorching heat in his stare threatening to turn my little red dress to cinders.

Lukas's expression changed in an instant, making me wonder if I had imagined it. His brows knitted in the beginning of a scowl, and I could almost feel the chill emanating from him when he turned his gaze on the faerie at my side.

Dain stepped away from me. "Your Highness. I didn't realize. I'll be on my way."

I stared after him as he nearly ran away from us. What the heck was that about?

"What are you doing at Va'sha?" Lukas asked.

I swung my gaze back to his. "Is there a reason I shouldn't be here?"

"You don't go to nightclubs like this."

"Don't I?"

He looked surprised by my cool response, and I had no idea why. I'd made it clear at his place, three days ago, that we were not friends. I'd had information he needed, and he had the power and resources to deal with the threat to my family. It was a business arrangement, and unless he had some news for me, we had nothing to talk about.

Someone let out a wolf whistle. I looked up as Conlan and Faolin came to stand on either side of Lukas.

"Jesse, you are a vision." Conlan made a show of ogling me, and for a moment, it felt like old times.

"Thank you."

He slanted a look at Lukas. "And here we thought tonight was going to be boring."

That reminded me we were at a club where faeries came to hook up with humans. I glanced around at the beautiful women nearby checking out Lukas, and I felt a tiny stab of something that was definitely not jealousy.

I stepped away from the bar. "I need to get to work."

"Work?" Lukas echoed.

"Yes. I'm actually here on a job." *And now he knows you have no life. Nice.*

Conlan waved at my outfit. "If this is the new female bounty hunter uniform, I wholeheartedly approve."

Lukas scowled, and I wasn't sure if it was meant for Conlan or me. "What kind of job brings you to Va'sha?"

"A nymph."

I didn't need to say more. Everyone knew that if you wanted to catch a nymph, you had to go where they liked to play, somewhere with lots of beautiful humans open to a Fae sexual encounter. In a place like this, there were very few people who wouldn't want to be a nymph's plaything for a night.

For the most part, nymphs were harmless, and the Agency didn't bother with them. The one I was tasked with capturing wasn't only seducing people. She was targeting wealthy men and women whom she enthralled to gain access to their hefty bank accounts. Her victims woke up the next day to the nasty discovery that their accounts had been cleaned out during the night.

Nymphs were normally classified as a level Three job, but this one had been bumped up to a Four. Levi had confided in me that her most recent victim was the son of an unnamed US Senator, who had called the Agency and threw a fit over her son's missing five-million-dollar trust fund. Ouch. I could only imagine what that call to his mother had been like the morning after.

One corner of Conlan's mouth lifted. "Are you the hunter or the bait?"

"Both."

He looked me up and down again and shook his head. "Lucky nymph."

"How do you know the nymph is at this club?" Lukas asked.

"Her last two victims were picked up here."

A nymph didn't change her hunting ground once she found one she liked, and she wouldn't be too worried about being recognized by one of her previous conquests. Her kind was one of the most elusive Fae races because they could alter their appearance at will. One day they could be a slender brunette, and the next a voluptuous blonde. In their real form, they were so plain and unidentifiable you would never guess they were faeries.

Conlan eyed me inquisitively. "And how do you plan to single out a nymph among all these beautiful women?"

"That would be a trade secret." My fingers flexed around my red clutch, which was much heavier than it looked. "I should get to it. Have a nice night."

I'd barely taken five steps away from them when someone walked in front of me, blocking my path. I looked up at the smiling face of Prince Rhys. Behind him were the same five guards I'd seen with him at the Ralston. Their hard expressions said they didn't share their prince's pleasure at seeing me.

"Jesse James, I thought that was you I saw from upstairs," he said as if we were old friends. "You look simply ravishing in that dress. I almost didn't recognize you, but there is no mistaking this beautiful hair."

Taken off guard, I was slow to react when he raised a hand to touch one of the tendrils resting against my cheek. The next thing I knew, there was a warm wall of muscle at my back, and I was flanked by Conlan and Faolin. In front of me, the Seelie prince's guard closed ranks around him.

"Rhys," Lukas said coolly. He was so close I could feel the rumble of the words in his chest. I hated the tiny thrill that went through me while, at the same time, I found his presence reassuring.

"Vaerik." Prince Rhys's smile didn't falter as he let his hand drop to his side. "I had no idea you were acquainted with the lovely Miss James."

"I could say the same of you," Lukas replied.

Prince Rhys gave me a secretive smile. "We ran into each other at my hotel recently. She leaves a lasting impression."

Lukas stiffened. "Your hotel?"

"Violet and I were there on a job," I said, even though I owed him no explanation.

"Ah, the pretty blue-haired girl." Prince Rhys looked around. "Is she here with you?"

"She's dancing."

He scanned the dance floor, and amusement sparkled in his eyes. "I see your friend has met Lorelle."

I turned my head to find Violet and the female faerie making out in the middle of the other dancers. It wasn't the first time I'd seen Violet with another girl, but she'd never been quite so into it.

"Jesse," Prince Rhys began. "May I call you Jesse?"

"I..." I didn't want to be on a first name basis with the Seelie prince, but I couldn't insult him either. "Yes."

"I'd be honored if you and your friend would join me upstairs for a drink. You can tell me more about your bounty hunting."

Lukas made a sound that was almost a growl. "She's not your type, Rhys."

I stepped away so I could turn to glare at him. He was right, but where did he get off thinking he could speak for me? He hadn't had that right even when we were friends. "You have no idea what my type is."

Prince Rhys's hand touched my back, and I realized what I'd done. I had all but said I was interested in him, which I wasn't.

"I think Jesse can decide for herself whose company she would like to keep," he said to Lukas.

"Actually..." I began.

"I'm sure she can," Lukas replied, not looking at me. "But she hasn't seen the best of our kind lately."

I stared at his hard, unreadable expression. Was he referring to the Seelie royal guard or his own treatment of me?

Prince Rhys withdrew his hand from my back. "Are you implying something, Vaerik? My intentions toward Jesse are nothing but honorable. Can you say the same?"

Lukas's eyes glittered dangerously. "Seelie and honor are not words I would use together."

I held up a hand. "Okay, I'm going to –"

"This from an Unseelie prince," Prince Rhys taunted.

I snapped my fingers between them. "Excuse me."

Both pairs of eyes fixed on me.

"Now that we've established you two aren't the only people in the room, I'm going to say my goodbyes. If you princes want to fight over who has the biggest crown, have at it."

I spun and stalked to where I'd last seen Violet. Behind me, Conlan let out a burst of laughter, but I was too annoyed to share his amusement. I understood there was animosity between the two courts, and Lukas had every right to be angry after what Faris had suffered. But I refused to be pulled into their argument, and I resented them talking over me like I wasn't even there.

Violet and Lorelle were standing on the other side of the dance floor, deep in conversation, when I reached them. Lorelle's hand was on Violet's waist, and the faerie looked as infatuated as my friend. I hated to interrupt them, but Violet had insisted on helping me on this job.

Lorelle put her hand under Violet's chin and tilted her face up for a kiss. "Call me."

"Tomorrow," Violet promised breathlessly.

I watched my friend as she stared longingly after the departing faerie. "I didn't mean to drive her away."

"You didn't. I told her I was here to help you on a job." Violet gave me a sly smile. "She thinks female bounty hunters are hot, and I might have played up my role a tiny bit."

"Then let's not disappoint her."

Violet gave me an expectant look. "Are you finally going to tell me how we are supposed to find this nymph?"

I smirked. "I think you are ready to learn my secrets."

"I know all your secrets." She put her hands on her hips when I didn't respond immediately. "Right?"

"All except the work-related ones," I lied.

Guilt pricked me when I thought about the goddess stone in my hair. I hadn't told anyone about it, including her, and it felt like a betrayal of our friendship. But I knew she would overreact and freak out, and that wouldn't help either of us.

What I really wanted was to tell my mom and dad about it. I trusted no one's counsel more than theirs, and I missed their guidance. But I was heeding their doctor's advice to not upset them, which was why I still hadn't told them about my bounty hunting. The secrets were piling up, and I had no idea how I was going to come clean when they were ready to hear it.

"Did I see you talking to Lukas?" Violet asked as I opened my clutch. "When did you two get chummy again?"

"We're not." I took a pair of eyeglasses from the purse and put them on. "What do you think?"

"They have no lenses." She moved closer and frowned. "What is with the funky frames? They look like they were made in kindergarten art class."

"Hey! I'll have you know I spent four hours making these last night."

She snorted. "Don't quit your day job."

I removed the glasses and held them up between us. The frames were wrapped in shiny red and gold pieces that I'd painstakingly glued in place. "See these? They're drakkan scales. Gus has been shedding them all over the apartment." I ran a finger over the scales. "Did you know that Fae glamours don't work around drakkans?"

"How do you know that?"

"Faris told me." I put the glasses on again. "It's not exactly a well-known fact, so that's between us."

Violet nodded. "But do you know if the scales will work without Gus?"

"I don't, but I'm about to find out."

We began walking through the dimly lit seating area on one side of the club, searching for the nymph who should be there by now. I scanned the faces around us, ignoring the interested looks that came my way, while Violet gushed about Lorelle.

Reaching the bar, I was relieved not to see Lukas or Prince Rhys there. We crossed to the other side of the club, and my eyes went to the cluster of people standing near some couches in the corner. I moved around them and felt a zing of excitement when I saw a man and two women sitting on one of the couches.

One of the women, a twenty-something brunette in a shimmering gold dress, had a too-bright quality about her, like an overexposed photo. When I squinted, her form blurred, and it was like looking at two overlapping shapes.

"Found her!" I whispered. I passed the glasses to Violet, who oohed and aahed when she spotted the nymph.

"You ready to do this?" I asked when she handed the glasses back to me. She tossed her hair. "I was born ready."

I returned the glasses to my clutch. "How do I look?"

"Irresistible." She linked her arm with mine, and we walked toward the couches like we owned the place. Purposely ignoring the nymph and her companions, we flounced down on the nearest couch and dived right into our rehearsed performance.

"Daddy's being so unfair," I whined. "It's my trust fund, and I can do what I want with it."

Violet rubbed my arm in a consoling manner. "What did he say?"

"He said I have to enroll at Columbia this fall, or he'll have the money frozen until I'm twenty-five."

Her shocked expression was Oscar-worthy. "He wouldn't!"

I did a practiced pout. "He's so unreasonable. Is it so wrong to want to have a little fun before I spend years with my face buried in books?"

"How about we get a little wild tonight? I heard someone say Prince Rhys is upstairs in the VIP section."

I put a hand over my heart. "I'd give anything to meet him."

Violet tipped her head slightly so the nymph couldn't see her smirk. "You and your obsession with Fae royalty."

"We all have our weaknesses," I said, trying to keep a straight face.

The couch dipped as someone sat on my other side, and I knew it was the nymph before she spoke. My stomach did a little flip, and I wasn't sure if it was the thrill of what I was about to do or a natural reaction to the nymph. I'd removed my leather bracelet talisman in favor of a delicate silver one, but that would only protect against glamours. It couldn't block the nymph's ability to heighten sexual attraction.

"You wish to go to the VIP area?" asked a voice like warm honey that made my breath hitch.

Violet's pupils dilated as her gaze fixed on the nymph, and I steeled myself before I swiveled to face my quarry. Up close, the nymph was the most beautiful woman I'd ever seen. She wore no makeup because nothing could enhance her perfect features, and her eyes were a deep azure blue that seemed to have an inner glow. I got lost in those eyes, and it took me a few seconds to break free from her hypnotic stare.

"Yes," I answered, surprised by how breathless I sounded.

"The bouncer up there is a friend of mine, and he will let us through." Her eyes roved over my face, and she reached up to twirl a tendril of my hair around her finger. She seemed as mesmerized as I'd been a moment ago. "You are so lovely."

"Thank you." I leaned into her touch as if I couldn't help myself and whispered, "Can my friend come, too?"

Her gaze flicked to Violet and darkened with lust. "Absolutely."

I smiled. "I'm Jesse, and this is Violet."

"I'm Laila." She stood gracefully and motioned for us to follow her.

As soon as her back was to us, I glanced at Violet and mouthed, *"Showtime."*

Violet nodded, looking both scared and excited. I was too full of adrenaline to be afraid, and Laila was far from the scariest faerie I'd faced in my short bounty hunter career. I was more nervous about not completing the job.

Laila drew many appreciative stares, but she appeared to be oblivious to them as she led us out of the seating area and past the bar. She smiled back at us several times to make sure we were still with her, and each time, a pulse of energy from her sent a pleasant tingle across my skin. I'd read that humans couldn't tell when a nymph used her magic on them. I made a mental note to ask Violet later if she'd felt the same thing.

We neared the stairs to the VIP section. Time to spring the trap.

"Laila," I said when she approached the bouncer standing at the bottom of the stairs. "I need to run to the restroom before we go up."

The nymph hesitated for a few seconds. "I should go, too," she said, as I'd known she would. Her magic only worked as long as she stayed with me, and she wasn't going to risk me getting out of range of it.

"I'll wait for you out here," Violet said as planned. She hadn't been happy about leaving me alone with the nymph, but I refused to put her in danger.

Between the bar and the stairs was a short hallway that led to the women's restrooms. As expected, there was a line, but it wasn't too long. It took us ten minutes to reach one of the private restrooms, and the two of us went in together. My gaze swept the room, and I turned to lock the door.

A hand trailed down my back, followed by another surge of magic that was stronger than the others. I swallowed as a tiny shiver went through me. Apparently, Laila didn't want to waste any time.

I leaned into her, relieved she couldn't see my face. Instinct had me wanting to push her away. When I'd told Violet about my plan to catch the nymph, she'd argued that she should be the bait for this very reason. But she had already served as bait for the banti job, so it was my turn to be the uncomfortable one.

More magic pulsed from Laila, but it didn't have any real effect on me, probably because I was aware of what she was doing.

"Are you sure you want to go upstairs? I know a place where we could have our own party," she whispered against my ear.

"What about Violet?" I asked as my hand inched toward my clutch.

Laila laughed softly. "She looks like a girl who can find her own party."

"She can." I smiled as I slipped my hand inside the purse, and my fingers found cold metal. "But I promised we'd stay together tonight."

The nymph's voice held a note of frustration. "Then a party of three it is."

"Great!" My voice sounded breathy and excited but for a completely different reason. The thrill of the hunt was thrumming in my veins as I turned to face her.

The glow in her eyes had intensified, and her smile was victorious as she placed her hands on either side of my face. She was taller than I was by at least five inches, and she lowered her head, her intention clear.

The clutch fell from my hands. She jerked her head back the second she sensed the iron, but I had the shackle locked around her left wrist before she could pull away.

She screamed and stumbled back from me. Her form blurred, and a short, plain woman with dull brown hair stood in her place. Shock filled her eyes, but it was quickly replaced by rage. She lunged at me, her fingers curled into claws. "You deceitful bitch!"

I ducked easily out of her path and kicked out, sending her into the door. "Takes one to know one."

She whirled on me. "Take this off me, or I will rip you apart until I find the key."

"Give it your best shot," I taunted.

She came at me again, but her movements seemed slow and drunken. Nymphs were strong in their true form, but the iron shackle had to be sapping her strength. She wasn't much stronger than a human now.

I grabbed her arm and pulled it behind her back, pinning her to the wall. She managed to elbow me in the chest before I subdued her.

"Why are you doing this to me?" she wailed. "I only wanted to give you a night of pleasure."

I shackled her other wrist. "I'm sure you would have done that before you stole my money, like you did with those men you robbed."

"You're an agent?" Fear crept into her voice, and she shrank away from me.

"Better. I'm a bounty hunter." Pushing her down to sit on the toilet seat, I went to retrieve my clutch. I closed it so she couldn't see the gray mesh sewn into the lining. Lead weighed a ton, but it made iron undetectable to faeries.

"What are you going to do with me?" she asked fearfully when I motioned for her to stand.

"I'm taking you to my bond agent where you'll be processed and sent back to Faerie."

She shook her head frantically. "But I don't want to go back."

"Sorry, not my call." I took her by the arm and led her to the door.

"I have money," she blurted when I reached for the door handle. "I can pay you whatever you want if you let me go."

I unlocked the door. "That's not your money to give. It belongs to the people you robbed."

Violet was waiting for us outside the door, holding off a line of impatient women waiting for the restroom. They stared at Laila, who looked nothing like the gorgeous woman that had entered the restroom with me.

"You're done?" Violet's eyes were wide. "That didn't take long."

"Long enough." I thought about the nymph pressing against my back and grimaced.

Violet followed us down the hallway. "So, we're leaving now?"

I stopped walking to look at her. She'd been so excited when I'd asked her to come here with me tonight, and I hated to ruin her fun. "Why don't you stay? I bet Lorelle is still here."

She flushed but shook her head. "We came together, and we'll leave together. I can always come back some other night."

"Okay. Let's go."

We drew curious stares from humans and faeries alike as I led the shackled nymph through the club. I got the impression bounty hunters were a rare sight at Va'sha, especially a hunter in a dress and heels.

We were passing the cluster of couches when a male voice called, "Jesse?"

I swore under my breath and turned to Iian, who gaped at me. Beside him, Kerr swung his head in my direction and did a double take.

"Damn." Kerr's eyes swept over me. "You can hunt me any day in that dress."

I forgot the retort on the tip of my tongue when Lukas appeared behind him like a dark thundercloud. His presence didn't bother Kerr, who smiled mischievously at me.

"Conlan told us you were here, but he left out a few details," Iian said. His eyes went to the nymph. "I see your hunt was successful."

"Very."

Laila shifted nervously under their stares, and I remembered how I'd felt the first time I'd endured their scrutiny. They had the whole intimidation thing down.

I was about to lead her away from them when I spotted a female faerie with long, black hair sidle up next to Lukas. She laid a possessive hand on his arm and said something to him. He turned his head toward her, and I couldn't help but notice how perfect they looked together. They also appeared to be well-acquainted. I quickly averted my gaze from them.

My arms wrenched painfully as Laila broke away from me. She raced toward the stairs that led to the exit, and I took off in pursuit. Adrenaline pulsed through me, and I tackled the nymph before she'd gone ten steps. I pinned her to the floor with my knee on her back.

Cheers and catcalls broke out around me, and my face heated when I realized the show I'd given everyone in my too-short dress. Scowling, I stood and pulled the nymph to her feet, marching her toward the stairs without looking back.

The only thing that made this worthwhile was the ten-thousand-dollar bounty waiting for me when I brought her in. I'd remind myself of that when I thought back on how I'd probably flashed an Unseelie prince, his date, and his royal guard.

I reached the top of the stairs when the heel of my right shoe snapped off. Grimacing, I began my undignified descent with one hand tight around the nymph's arm. Most days, this job wasn't too bad. Right now, it kind of sucked.

"Jesse!" Violet grabbed my arm while we waited for our coats. "That was amazing."

I made a face. "You know I like to make an exit."

"No kidding. Where did you learn to run that fast – and in heels?"

"I've always been a good runner." I accepted my coat from the coat check girl and put it on while maintaining my hold on the sullen nymph.

Violet snorted. "You weren't *that* good. Poor Laila never had a chance."

"Ten grand is a great motivator." I led Laila to the exit, bracing myself for the cold.

The bouncer eyed my lopsided gait and the shackled nymph with raised eyebrows. I shrugged and walked past him.

"Oh, and cute undies, by the way," Violet said with a giggle as we walked to the Jeep. "Victoria's Secret?"

11

"Finch, stop playing with your food," I said when a blueberry bounced off my cheek and landed on the kitchen floor. I straightened from my task of cleaning the refrigerator to frown over the top of the breakfast bar. "Aisla, stop encouraging him."

He whistled, and I looked up to find the fool balanced on the back of a chair with three more blueberries in his arms. Aisla stood on the table, watching him with a delighted smile. As soon as he saw he had our attention, he juggled the blueberries while trying to stay on his perch.

Aisla squeaked and clapped her hands, and Finch puffed out his chest. I shook my head. I suspected my brother had a crush on the nixie, and I wasn't quite sure what to do about it. I'd started adoption proceedings for Aisla, so wouldn't that make her his sister? I rubbed my face. I needed to talk to Mom and Dad about it when I visited them tomorrow.

I'd told my parents about Aisla the last time I was there, and unsurprisingly, they were okay with the nixie joining our family. They were less happy about Gus, but I knew they'd accept him, too. We'd always wanted a pet growing up, but Mom was severely allergic to pet dander. Drakkans had no fur, so allergies wouldn't be a problem.

A second blueberry hit the top of my head, pulling me from my thoughts. I looked up as Finch's arms flailed, and he fell backward off the chair. I went to check on him, already knowing he was okay. Sprites were like cats, and they always landed on their feet.

I planted my hands on my hips. "You going to stop showing off now?"

He gave me a sheepish smile as he scampered up the chair to the table.

I went back to scouring the refrigerator, scrubbing furiously at a tiny ketchup stain like it had offended me. I'd been in a cleaning frenzy all day ever since I woke up tired and cranky. I should be happy. Last night, I'd brought in my first nymph, and Levi had said I reminded him of my mother when she was starting out. High praise from him. On top of that, I'd come home with a ten-thousand-dollar bounty check.

I was starting on the freezer when a horrible barking sound came from the living room. *Not again.*

I ran to the other room where Gus was retching and looking like he was about to puke up an organ. There was a baseball-sized lump in his throat, and I wondered what the heck he'd tried to eat this time.

I had quickly learned you didn't leave any shiny object smaller than a softball lying around when you lived with a young drakkan. After Gus had swallowed Mom's favorite crystal candle holders, I'd locked everything he could eat in Mom and Dad's bedroom. When a drakkan ate something, it was digested like food. I had no idea how I was going to tell Mom the candle holders she'd gotten as a wedding gift from her grandmother were gone.

Gus gave one last disgusting retch, and something shot from his mouth to roll heavily across the floor toward me. I bent to pick up the Paris snow globe Maurice had given me a few years ago. Saliva dripped off it, and I scrunched up my nose at the slimy surface of the globe.

"Ew." I carried it to the kitchen sink to rinse it off. As I passed the table, I saw Finch trying to balance a stack of blackberries on one hand. This place was turning into a mad house.

I was drying the snow globe with a paper towel when the doorbell rang. *What now?*

I went to the door. "Who is it?" I called without thinking. I peered through the peephole as a familiar voice said, "Lukas."

My heart gave a little nervous flutter. What was he doing here?

"Jesse?" he called.

"Yes."

"Are you going to open the door?" he asked with a hint of amusement in his voice. I realized I'd been standing there staring at the door for at least a minute.

I unlocked the door and opened it. "Why are you here?"

He was unfazed by my cool greeting. "I need to talk to you."

"You couldn't use the phone?"

"You blocked my number." He gave me a wry smile that made my stomach do that weird somersault thing. I hated that he could still do that to me, and it only made me more irritable.

I raised my eyebrows. "That wasn't a big enough hint that I don't want to talk?"

"I've never been good with taking hints."

"So it would seem." I rested my hip against the door. "What's so important that you had to come over here?"

He inclined his head. "May I come in? This is not something to discuss in the hallway."

I almost said no because he was the last person I wanted in my home. I wasn't sure why I had even opened the door to him. I had meant it when I'd said that me giving him information about the ke'tain had changed nothing between us.

"Come in." I stepped back and opened the door wider. He entered the apartment, and my pulse jumped when he closed the door behind him. His presence filled every corner of the room, making me feel small and unsure of myself. I hated him for affecting me this way, and I was angry at myself for allowing him to do it.

I wasn't the only one who felt it. Finch and Aisla stopped playing around on the table, and even Gus went quiet.

"Okay, go ahead," I said without preamble.

He got straight to the point. "How well do you know Prince Rhys?"

The question surprised me, and I could only stare at him for a few seconds. "I don't."

"He seemed familiar with you at the club last night. What happened at his hotel?"

"What are you insinuating?" I crossed my arms. "And how is it your business?"

Lukas let out a breath. "I'm not insinuating anything. I'm concerned about his interest in you."

"Why?"

"Why?" His look was incredulous. "Jesse, do I need to remind you who Rhys is or that it was his mother's guard who took your parents and Faris?"

"You think I could forget that? I still have nightmares about finding them in that cage."

Lukas looked like I'd punched him in the gut. "You have nightmares?"

"Sometimes." I glanced away, having no desire to rehash the past with him. "As far as Prince Rhys goes, Violet and I met him when we were leaving the Ralston after a job. He has some fascination with bounty hunters, so he was curious when he found out I was one. We talked for about five minutes, and then Violet and I left. I didn't see him again until last night. Does that answer all your questions?"

"He was interested in more than your job at the club," Lukas replied.

I threw up my arms. "So were other Fae males. That just means they like a girl in a short dress."

His lips flattened, but I went on before he could speak.

"Did it ever occur to you that Prince Rhys only showed interest in me last night because he saw me talking to you? It's clear you can't stand each other. He probably thought I was important to you, and he wanted to piss you off."

The hardness drained from his expression. "You are –"

A muffled thump came from the hallway, and an angry male voice said, "I live here, goddamn it. Who the hell are you?"

My hand went to my chest. I knew that voice!

I yanked open the door to the sight of a tall black man facing off against Iian and Kerr at the top of the stairs. The man's long dreadlocks were tied back in a ponytail, and his hazel eyes were livid as he glared at the two faeries blocking his path.

"Maurice?"

Kerr looked at me. "You know this man, Jesse?"

"Yes. He lives here."

Maurice's angry expression morphed into a wide smile. Dropping the backpack and duffle bag he was carrying, he strode over and lifted me into a rib-cracking hug.

"Baby girl, it's good to see you," he said in his warm Louisiana accent. "You are a sight for sore eyes."

"You're home!" I put my arms around his neck and hugged him back. I'd always looked forward to his homecomings, but none more than this one.

He set me back on my feet and laid his hands on my shoulders. Close to my mother's age, he didn't look a day over twenty-five, and he had the kind of looks that turned the heads of women of all ages.

His eyes grew troubled. "I only heard about your mom and dad this morning. I took the first flight I could get."

"Were you on that Everglades job this whole time?"

"Yes. I came out early this morning." He pulled me in for another hug. "Can't believe you had to deal with all of this alone."

A throat cleared behind me. I was so focused on Maurice that I'd forgotten we weren't alone. Stepping back from him, I turned halfway toward Lukas, whose hard gaze was fixed on Maurice.

"Maurice, this is Prince Vaerik of Unseelie. He helped me search for Mom and Dad when they were missing." To Lukas, I said, "Maurice is my godfather and my father's best friend."

If Lukas was surprised that I'd introduced him by his real name and title, he didn't show it. I had no intention of keeping it a secret from Maurice.

Maurice eyed Lukas with suspicion. "Why would the Unseelie prince be interested in the welfare of two bounty hunters? What's in it for you?"

"That is between Jesse and me," Lukas answered coolly.

"I'm sure her parents would have something to say about that." Maurice moved closer to me. "And as Jesse's godfather, I am responsible for her while her parents are in the hospital."

I didn't point out that I was eighteen and no longer a minor. I put a hand on Maurice's arm. "It's a long story."

"Then it's a good thing I have time." He gave Lukas a pointed look. "I plan to be around for a while."

"Really?" A smile curved my mouth. For the last few years, Maurice's home visits had barely lasted a week. He enjoyed being on the road, and he got bored if he stayed in one place too long.

"Yes. And the first thing I'm going to do after you and I catch up is go see your parents." He took out his keys. "I'm going to drop my stuff at the apartment, and I'll be over right after." Translation: Say goodbye to your visitors because you and I are going to talk.

Maurice picked up his bags and walked past Iian and Kerr, who had been silent this whole time. He unlocked his door and disappeared inside, leaving the door ajar.

"That man is your godfather?" Lukas asked, his voice laden with skepticism. "He is not ten years your senior."

"Maurice is thirty-nine, a year younger than my mother."

Lukas relaxed his rigid stance. "And you trust him?"

"With my life. He's family."

That seemed to appease Lukas. "Then I'll leave you to catch up with him. We'll continue our discussion at another time."

I frowned. "What else is left to discuss?"

Instead of answering my question, he said, "When do you plan to visit Faris again?"

"In a few days. Why?"

"We'll talk then." He walked past me to where his men waited. "If you see Rhys or his guard again, keep your distance."

And just like that, he left. Iian and Kerr smiled at me and followed him.

"Good bye to you, too," I muttered.

"Goodbye, Jesse," Lukas called from two flights down, reminding me once again of his superior hearing.

I was debating whether or not to make a snarky reply when Maurice returned. Seeing me standing alone in the hallway, he shot me a questioning look, but I shook my head.

"You want some coffee?" I asked him as we entered my apartment.

His eyes lit with pleasure. "You have coffee?"

"Of course. I'll give up a lot of things but not that." I went to the kitchen and sighed at the contents of the refrigerator spread across the counters. "Excuse the mess." I put the coffee on and returned the food to the refrigerator.

"Jesse, why do you have a drakkan on your coffee table?" Maurice called.

"That is another long story."

"Something tells me you have many stories to share," he said as he came into the kitchen. He reached up and plucked something from my hair. It was a squished blueberry.

"Finch," I said with a slight scowl.

Maurice looked around. "Where is he?"

I grabbed two mugs and set them on the counter. "Most likely in the tree house with Aisla."

"Aisla?"

"She's a nixie."

Maurice's eyebrows shot up.

I laughed. "You better take a seat. This catching up might take a while."

Two cups of coffee later, Maurice stared at me with a mix of shock and concern. I'd brought him up to speed on what had happened from the day Mom and Dad went missing. I left out what had happened between Lukas and me because I didn't want any trouble between him and the Unseelie prince. I also didn't tell him about the party at Davian Woods's penthouse. If Maurice knew I'd taken a risk like that, he wouldn't let me out of his sight until Mom and Dad came home.

I did tell him about the goddess stone, and it felt so good to finally unburden myself to someone. Like me, he'd never heard of a goddess stone, and he had no idea what it meant.

He rubbed his jaw. "I have a faerie friend in Florida I can ask about it without raising suspicion."

"You think they will know something?" I asked hopefully.

"No idea but it's worth a shot." He leaned back in his chair and smiled at me. "I can't believe my little Jesse is a bounty hunter, and a damn good one by the sound of it. Not that I'm surprised. It's in your blood, after all."

I wrapped my hands around my empty mug. "I hope Mom and Dad take it as well as you did. I haven't told them yet."

"You want me to go with you when you tell them?" he asked.

"Would you? Finch and I are going to see them tomorrow, and I can get you added to their visitor list."

He nodded. "Tomorrow's perfect."

"You told Lukas you plan to be around for a while. Don't you always have another job lined up?"

"I do. I'm going to look for that missing ke'tain. I need to stop by the Plaza tomorrow to check in and let them know I'm on the job."

"Oh, boy. There are going to be a *lot* of unhappy bounty hunters when they hear the great Maurice Begnaud is getting in on the action." I wasn't kidding. Everyone in this business knew who Maurice was. My parents might be the best on the East coast, but Maurice was one of the top hunters in the country. Things were about to get a lot more interesting.

His eyes held a devilish gleam. "A little competition will be good. Keep you all sharp."

"Maybe I'll give you some competition," I joked.

"I've no doubt." He sobered. "Don't get angry, but I wish you weren't working on this job. You're still new at this, and you don't even have a partner."

"Bruce and Trey asked me to join them, and another team did, too. I guess I'm a bit of a lone wolf."

"Like me." He drained the last of his coffee and stared at me thoughtfully. "You could work with me. I haven't had a partner in a while, but I could make an exception."

A thrill of excitement went through me. Maurice was in a league of his own among hunters, and I could learn so much working with him. There wasn't anyone else, after my parents, that I trusted more with my life.

Then I remembered why he was a loner. He wanted to do things his way and on his own time, and he hated answering to anyone. Mom and Dad were his best friends, and he rarely worked with them anymore. The only reason he was asking me to work with him now was so he could keep an eye on me.

"I love you for asking, but I think I'd cramp your style." I stood and collected our mugs. "But I am going to brag to everyone that you asked me to be your partner. Trey will never get over it."

Maurice laughed. "Maybe I'd be the one cramping *your* style."

"Well," I drawled. "Have you ever gone for a ride with a kelpie?"

"Can't say that I have. But I did spend two months in the Everglades hunting a rakshae."

My mouth fell open. "No way! Did you catch it?"

"Did I catch it?" He shook his head. "Girl!"

"Tell me everything." I rested my chin on my hands in anticipation. A rakshae was a creature most people thought was a Fae myth, like the boogeyman. Its upper half resembled an elf but with green, scaly skin, and from the waist down, it was a serpent. It lived in lakes and swamps, and its bite turned humans into mindless zombies. These zombies didn't moan or crave human flesh, but they could spread the incurable disease to other people. Rakshae were nearly impossible to trap and were classified as a level Five.

I didn't think I could spend two months trekking through wetlands, even for a fifty-thousand-dollar bounty, but roughing it didn't bother Maurice. He lived for the thrill of the hunt no matter where it took him.

Maurice leaned back in his chair. "This might take a while. You have any more of that coffee?"

I jumped up eagerly. "Give me five minutes, and then I want to hear everything."

"Are you going to say anything?" I shifted restlessly as I moved my gaze back and forth between my mother and father, who sat on the couch across from me in their suite. Finch sat on the back of the couch between them, and Maurice was a quiet bystander near the window.

I had just finished giving them a condensed story about my search for them and my bounty hunting. I'd had to gloss over a lot of the details about Lukas and what had happened at Rogin's because that would only cause my parents too much stress at this stage of their recovery. Seeing their troubled expressions, I was glad I'd followed my gut and not told them more.

They had interrupted me with questions, but now that I was done, they seemed to be determined to torture me with their silence.

Dad spoke first. "Why didn't you tell us this before now?"

"Dr. Reddy told me to go slow and not say anything that would upset you. I had to wait until your doctors here said it was okay."

He clasped his hands in his lap, and I couldn't tell if it was frustration or disappointment I saw in his eyes. Never in my life had he shown disappointment in me.

My stomach twisted. "I should have figured it out sooner. I should have made the Agency take me seriously."

"You should not have been put in that position at all," Mom said harshly. "None of this is your fault."

Dad shook his head. "I don't know of any other teenager who could have done what you did. You took care of your brother, and you kept your head in a terrible situation. We couldn't be prouder of you if we tried."

"You don't mind that I'm a bounty hunter?"

Mom's eyebrows rose. "I don't know if *mind* is the right word for it. I'm sure you're doing a great job, but I'm not happy about you working alone."

Finch whistled for their attention and signed, *She's not alone. We're a team, and I help her get ready for jobs.*

"She couldn't ask for a better partner." Our mother patted his leg as she shot me a look that said we would discuss this further when Finch wasn't around.

"I'm surprised Bruce didn't have something to say about you going out alone," Dad said.

"He tried to get me to work with him and Trey, but you know Trey would have driven me insane in a week. I honestly don't know how Bruce has kept his sanity, or how Trey has survived this long."

Dad smiled. "I think Bruce was hoping Trey would go to college and not follow in his footsteps."

"I bet you never thought I'd be joining the family business either."

Mom frowned. "You've given up on college?"

"God, no. Bounty hunting is great, but I'll happily hand the reins over to you when you're ready to go back to work. By then, I should have saved enough to get me through a few years of school – if Levi keeps giving me the good jobs."

She shook her head. "I still can't believe he gave you one in the first place. Levi doesn't have much tolerance for new hunters."

I gave her a secretive smile. "I can be pretty persuasive."

"And you brought in a level Three on your first job," Maurice reminded me. He grinned at my mother. "The apple doesn't fall far from the tree, Caroline."

The three of them laughed, and I looked around the room in confusion. "What?"

My parents exchanged a look, and Dad said, "When we started out, new hunters had to apprentice with an experienced one for six months. My uncle agreed to take me on, but he refused to train your mother."

Her lip curled. "He said bounty hunting was no career for a woman. I went to every hunter in the city to ask if one of them would take us on together. A lot of the bounty hunters thought the same as your dad's uncle, and some of them laughed when I said I wanted to be one of them. They all turned me away. But I wasn't going to let a bunch of narrow-minded fools hold me back."

"What did you do?" I scooted forward on my seat.

Dad smiled proudly. "She bought a police scanner, listened to their chatter, and found out a couple of trolls were mugging people on the Flushing Line. Then she went out by herself, caught them, and dragged them to the Plaza. She caused quite a stir."

I stared accusingly at them. "You never told me this."

She shrugged. "What I did was illegal because I didn't have a license to hunt. I could have been thrown in jail. That's not something you tell your child."

I couldn't believe what I was hearing. "Did you get into trouble?"

"I would have, if it wasn't for one of the hunters. He had just moved here from Louisiana, and he was impressed by my tenacity. He covered for me and said I was his new apprentice."

"Mr. Begnaud?" I knew she and Dad had gotten their start hunting with Maurice's father, Vincente, but I never would have guessed it had happened like that.

Maurice laughed. "When my father came home and told me he'd taken on not one but two new apprentices, I was so jealous I couldn't see straight. I wanted to be the one hunting with him."

"And a year later, we were all working together," Dad said.

Mom reached over to take Dad's hand. "Jesse, we don't like the circumstances that led you to bounty hunting, but we can't fault you for doing exactly what we would have done. We raised you to be independent and to think for yourself, and we're proud of you."

"That doesn't mean we won't worry about you, no matter how smart and resourceful you are," Dad said.

Maurice came to sit with us. "I'll be around for the next few weeks at least, and Jesse knows she can call me at any time."

My parents visibly relaxed, and I shot him a grateful look.

"Now, tell us more about this goddess stone," Dad said. "You said it hasn't done anything, but I'm wary of most objects that come from Faerie."

"Lukas said it's a Fae legend. No one knows what the stones do, and to his knowledge, no Court faerie has ever been goddess-blessed. I took the stone from a kelpie, so it might have attached itself to me by mistake." I touched the stone in my hair. "I can tell you there's no mention of it in any book I've read or in the Fae archives at the Library of Congress. The only other place to look is at the Agency, and I'm not telling them about it."

Mom nodded. "The Agency tends to overreact to things they can't understand or control." She looked at Maurice. "What are your thoughts on this?"

"I agree with not telling the Agency until we know more. I'm going to ask my friend Melia if she's heard of it, but I'm not sure what she can tell me that the Unseelie prince cannot."

"You say that like there is only one prince in the Unseelie court." I knew seven, and Lukas had mentioned a brother.

"There are other princes, but only one crown prince," Maurice said, stretching out his long legs.

It felt like the air had been sucked from the room. "Lukas is the crown prince of Unseelie?"

Maurice gave me an odd look. "You didn't know that?"

"It never came up." I wanted to smack myself for once again being an idiot when it came to Lukas. A lot of the royals had bodyguards, but only the monarchs and their heirs had a full personal guard.

"Speaking of Prince Vaerik." Mom fixed me with a look that made me swallow nervously. "You said he offered to help you find us because he was looking for his friend, but you didn't tell us how you met him in the first place."

I darted a glance at Maurice, but his smile told me I was on my own for this one. I cleared my throat. "I...um...met him when I went to Teg's following a lead for the job you were working on."

"How did you know we were supposed to go to Teg's?" Her nostrils flared. "Tennin!"

I rushed to Tennin's defense. "Don't be mad at him. He told me not to go to Teg's, and I didn't listen."

She crossed her arms. "Go on."

"I saw Lukas at Teg's and again when I went to the Ralston after I found your bracelet. We kept running into each other, and he got suspicious." I thought back to the night Faolin had dragged me to Lukas's for an interrogation. There was no way I was telling my parents about *that*. "He said he'd heard of you, and he thought your disappearance might be connected to something he was looking for. The Agency was dragging their feet, so I accepted his offer to help."

"If he was helping you, where was he when you were kidnapped and taken to Rogin's?" Dad demanded.

"He had to go to Faerie the day before." I fidgeted with the hem of my sweater.

Mom's gaze sharpened. "Are you still in touch with him?"

"I see him around." I squirmed in my seat. Faolin could learn a few things about interrogation from my mother. "Faris is sick from the iron, and I visit him once a week."

"Why do you call the prince Lukas instead of by his title?" she asked, not done with her inquisition.

Finally, a question I could answer. "He goes by Lukas Rand here, and I didn't know he was Prince Vaerik at first. I got used to calling him Lukas, and now it's weird to think of him by the other name."

She looked satisfied with my response, and I hoped she was done with the questions. Once she relaxed again, I could see pockets of exhaustion forming under her eyes. It was easy to forget my parents were unwell, but even sitting and talking could wear them out.

Finch saw it, too. He whistled and signed to her. *Are you sleepy, Mom?*

"A little," she admitted, telling me she was more tired than she was letting on.

You should take a nap, he told her. *Napping always makes me feel better.*

She reached up to stroke his blue hair. "That's a good idea, sweetie."

I stood. "We should get going anyway. Aisla doesn't like to be left alone for too long."

I hugged my parents as we all said our goodbyes. After promising them again that I would be careful out there, I tucked Finch inside my jacket and left.

Maurice stayed behind at Dad's request, and I could guess what he wanted to talk about. Mom and Dad were going to ask Maurice to watch over me while he was in town. I loved having him home again, but I hoped he wasn't going to hover over me.

I was driving when Violet texted, **RU home?**

10 min, I texted back.

CU there.

Violet was standing outside my door when I got there, and I was surprised to see she wasn't alone. Mandy Wheeler, a girl from high school, was beside her.

I hadn't seen Mandy since graduation, and I'd never seen her looking like this. She was one of those girls who always looked like they'd just come from the salon. Today, her blonde hair was tied back in a messy ponytail, she wore no makeup, and her eyes were red and puffy from crying.

"Mandy, hi." I stopped in front of her. "What's wrong?"

Her lip trembled, and her eyes brimmed with tears. "I-I need your help. I don't have anyone else to go to."

Violet rubbed Mandy's back. "Jesse will help you." She met my gaze. "Your services are needed. We'll explain inside."

Confused, I nodded and unlocked the door. Once Finch was back in his tree house with Aisla, I joined my guests on the couch. "Okay, tell me."

Mandy pressed a damp tissue to her eyes. "My ex-boyfriend stole Romeo, and he's threatening to sell him." Her face crumpled, and she began sobbing into her hands.

"What?" Romeo was her little Yorkie she'd had since junior high. Mandy loved that dog more than anything, and she was always dressing him in cute outfits and posting pictures on Instagram.

Violet answered for the crying girl. "Mandy was dating a guy for six months, and she broke up with him last week. When she wouldn't go back to him, he stole Romeo and said he will sell him if she doesn't give him another chance."

Anger flared in me. "Did you call the police?"

Mandy sniffled. "Yes. But they're too busy to care about a dog."

I wasn't surprised by that. The police were overworked, despite bounty hunters handling most of the Fae cases. Even if they wanted to help her, they didn't have the manpower to spare.

She turned pleading eyes on me. "I heard you're a bounty hunter now. I know this isn't what you normally do, but I can pay you."

I held up a hand. "I don't want your money. Who is this ex of yours, and what do I need to know about him?"

"His name is Drew Gordon. He's twenty-three, and he lives in Williamsburg." Mandy rattled off information. By the time she was done, I had her ex's home and work address and his daily schedule. She pulled up photos on her phone of a blond, well-groomed man who clearly worked out and cared about his appearance. In every picture, he wore an arrogant smile, and he had the look of a man who was used to getting his way.

I checked the time and saw it was almost five. If Mandy had gotten Drew's schedule right, he would be getting home from work in an hour. Standing, I headed for my bedroom.

"Where are you going?" Violet called after me.

"To change. I can't wear these clothes on a job."

Two sets of footsteps came behind me. "We're going now?" Mandy asked hopefully.

I turned to face her. "No time like the present."

She ran over and flung her arms around me. "Thank you!"

"Don't thank me yet. Let's get Romeo back first." Stripping off my pants and top, I donned dark jeans and a black thermal shirt. I pulled on my combat boots and twisted my hair into a thick braid.

Violet eyed me appraisingly as I completed the outfit with a lined leather jacket. "You look ready to kick some ass."

I stuck my ID in my back pocket. "Let's hope it doesn't come to that."

"Don't bounty hunters have weapons?" Mandy asked as she and Violet followed me back to the living room.

"My gear bag is in the Jeep, but I doubt I'll need weapons for this." I patted my coat pocket and felt a familiar lump. "I have a stun gun and shackles in my pockets if it comes to that."

Mandy's eyes widened. "You carry shackles on you?"

"Never know when I might need them."

We walked to the door, and I stopped to look at them. "I can only take one person in the Jeep."

Mandy pulled out a set of keys. "I have my sister's car. I'll meet you there."

"Okay. If you get there first, wait for us," I said as I opened the door.

Drew Gordon lived in a nice twenty-story apartment building less than two blocks from Lukas's place. Mandy was waiting for us outside the front entrance when we got there, and she looked scared. At my place, I'd asked her if her ex had been abusive. She'd said he'd never hit her, but there was more than one kind of abuse. I didn't have experience in this area, but the fear in her eyes told me what she couldn't say.

"You don't have to come up with us," I told her.

She straightened her spine. "I want to. Romeo needs me."

I gave her a reassuring smile. "Let's do this then."

12

We entered the building and took the elevator to the seventh floor. At Drew's door, Violet and I moved to the side where we were not visible through the peephole, and Mandy knocked.

Thirty seconds later, someone approached the door. After a brief pause, the dead bolt scraped, and the door opened.

"Jesus, Mandy, you're a mess," said a male voice. "I don't know if I want you back looking like this."

I stepped quickly into view, putting myself between them. "Then it's a good thing she's not here for a reconciliation."

His head jerked back. "Who the hell are you?"

"Reinforcements," Violet announced as she showed herself.

The man in the doorway laughed, and it was an ugly sound. "Reinforcements? Really?" He sneered at Mandy. "What did you hope to accomplish with this little stunt?"

"I came to get Romeo," she said tremulously.

"Romeo who?" he asked in mock innocence. "Don't know anyone by that name."

For the first time in my life, I wanted to punch another human. "We know you have her dog. Give him back, and we'll be on our way without any trouble."

"Is that so?" He took a threatening step toward me.

Mandy put a shaking hand on my arm and whispered, "I think we should leave."

"But it's just getting fun, baby." Drew came closer until his chest touched mine.

My heart rate kicked up a notch. "You need to take a step back."

"And you need to learn to mind your own business," he bit out. "This is between me and my girlfriend."

"She's not your girlfriend," Violet said.

Drew pointed at her. "Shut your mouth, you little –"

My hand shot out and grabbed his wrist. Twisting hard, I spun him around with his arm behind his back and pushed him face-first against the wall. He bucked and lashed at me with his other fist, and I pressed on his trapped arm until he howled in pain and went still.

"Whoa," Violet breathed.

"Let's start over," I said to the man who was trembling with suppressed rage. "You have Mandy's dog, and she wants him back. We're all going inside so she can get him. Then we'll leave, and you'll never bother her again."

"Everything okay here?" called a new male voice. I looked down the hall to see a young man wearing a suit and carrying a briefcase.

"Yes," I said at the same time Drew grunted, "No."

The newcomer looked at us uncertainly. If I didn't do something, he'd be calling the police next, and I didn't need that complication right now.

Reaching behind me, I pulled out my bounty hunter ID and held it up for him to see. He was close enough to make out the official Agency seal on the card.

"We have everything under control," I said in my most businesslike tone. The use of the ID outside of Agency business was a gray area, but I was willing to stretch the rules in this case.

"Good to know." The man hurried past us and entered an apartment several doors down.

Drew laughed. "Assault *and* impersonating an agent. I hope you like Rikers."

"Actually, she's a bounty hunter," Violet informed him cheerfully. "And you touched her first, so in fact, you assaulted her, and she acted in self-defense."

I stared at her in surprise, and she shrugged. "Mom likes to work on her court arguments at home."

Grinning, I returned the ID to my pocket and produced my shackles, which I snapped around Drew's wrists. I shoved him toward the door, and the four of us entered his apartment. Mandy immediately ran from room to room, calling for Romeo.

She returned to us, looking devastated. "He's not here."

Drew snickered. "Romeo, Romeo, wherefore art thou, Romeo?"

I turned on him. But before I could open my mouth, Violet delivered an impressive undercut right between his legs. Drew let out a high-pitched sound and doubled over, but his arms were shackled behind his back, preventing him from cupping his injured parts.

"Listen here, asshole," she growled. "We're done playing nice. Tell us where Romeo is, or this is going to go very badly for you. We know people who could make you disappear like that." She snapped her fingers for emphasis, and it was all I could do not to snort.

Drew panted, and it took a minute for him to answer. "He's gone. He took off when I was walking him."

Violet poked him in the chest. "Try again, pal."

"She has ways of making you tell the truth," I said, barely keeping a straight face. "That cute look is all an act."

He straightened enough to look at us. His face was beet red, and there were tears in his eyes. "I owed a guy money," he wheezed. "He sent someone to collect, and they took the dog."

Mandy gasped. "Who took him?"

Drew pressed his lips together. I thought he wasn't going to answer when he finally said, "Two ogres."

She let out a strangled cry. I led her to a chair and left her sobbing uncontrollably while I stormed back to her ex.

"What the hell is wrong with you?" I yelled in his face. "You sold Romeo to those brutes?"

In addition to being mean-tempered, ogres were known to eat cats and dogs. If they had Romeo, chances were that he was already dead, or he would be soon.

He cringed. "They took him. I didn't have any choice."

My lips pulled back in a snarl. "You always have a choice. When were they here, and where did they take him?"

"Last night. I don't know where they live," he said, all the arrogant bluster gone out of him.

I poked him in the chest. "You better figure it out fast."

Violet held out her hand to me. "Give me your stun gun. Fifty thousand volts will jog his memory."

I blinked at her. Who was this person? I couldn't tell if she was serious or doing a damn fine acting job.

Drew blanched and began sobbing and babbling, until he finally said something helpful. "The Fenton. They live at the Fenton."

I took out my phone and did a search. The Fenton was an old theater in

Queens that had been closed for two years, making it an ideal location for squatters like ogres.

"How many ogres live there?" I asked.

He swallowed convulsively. "Just the two of them."

"You better pray that dog is okay," I said through gritted teeth as I removed his shackles.

Violet cracked her knuckles like a mob goon. "You really don't want us to have to come back."

I went to Mandy, who was crying silently now, and helped her to her feet. "Let's go."

None of us spoke again until we reached the street. Mandy was a mess, so Violet offered to drive her car. My best friend and I exchanged a grim look before we headed to our vehicles. The odds of Mandy seeing her pet again were slim, and my heart ached for her. But if there was the slightest chance Romeo was alive, I'd do what I could to get him back.

I arrived at the theater first, parking half a block away. After I texted Violet to let her know where to find me, I went through my gear to get what I might need. Ogres were strong, but they weren't good fighters or the smartest of faeries. Still, I'd learned the hard way to never underestimate an opponent, after a troll had cut me with his sword and poisoned me.

Violet and Mandy arrived as I was stuffing gear into a small backpack. Mandy had stopped crying, but her face was drawn and pale. One look at her and I knew she couldn't come in with us. There was no telling what we'd find in there, and she would only be a hindrance.

I closed the Jeep's cargo door. "You two stay in the car."

"I'm not letting you go in there alone." Violet set her jaw stubbornly. "And don't give me that 'I'm a bounty hunter and you're not' spiel because it won't work."

"You can't fight," I reminded her.

She rolled her eyes. "I can outrun an ogre. And I know you have an extra stun gun in that bag."

"Fine, but you have to do whatever I tell you to do." I opened the backpack and handed her the weapon.

"What about me?" Mandy asked.

I slung the backpack over my shoulder. "Someone needs to stay here in case we run into trouble. We'll text you if anything happens."

She reluctantly agreed and walked to her car as Violet and I set off for the theater. The old brick building was three stories with an arched entrance, and a marquee with the theater name in large red letters. We passed by the main entrance and went around to the back alley where there were two small doors. The second one we tried was unlocked, and we quietly slipped inside.

I motioned for Violet to be quiet, and we listened for sounds as our eyes adjusted to the dark. Hearing nothing, we crept past several dressing rooms. All the props, stage lighting, and cables had been removed, and the theater smelled musty from disuse. It was a little eerie being in a place that once had been bustling with activity.

We reached the stage, and I stopped walking abruptly when I picked up faint sounds coming from the auditorium. Turning to Violet, I pointed toward the curtains that still hung there, partially closed. She nodded and stood still while I climbed the stairs to the wing and tiptoed to the curtain.

Dust billowed from the curtain when I touched it. I had to smother a cough before I could inch the heavy material aside and peek around it.

The auditorium was a rectangle with two sets of floor seats divided by an aisle, and stairs on either side that led to the mezzanine and balcony levels. The walls were dark panels, and the ceiling was covered in faded murals. In the middle of the ceiling, where a large chandelier had probably hung, was a gaping hole through which a small column of smoke was escaping.

I followed the path of the smoke to its source – a fire burning in a metal drum. Seats had been ripped out of the floor and tossed aside to make a campsite for the two bald, yellow-skinned creatures sprawled beside the fire. The ogres were grunting and chewing noisily on some kind of meat, and my stomach roiled when one of them tossed a bone on a pile near his feet.

I put a hand over my mouth. *Please don't let that be Romeo.*

Craning my neck, I tried to get a better look around. My breath caught when I spotted dog crates sitting on some of the seats that were still bolted to the floor. I thought I saw a shape in one of the crates, but they were too far away for me to be certain.

One of the ogres said something in a deep rumbling voice, and then he lay back and pillowed his head with his arms. His companion kept eating, and I wondered if he was on guard or a slow eater. I watched him for another five minutes before he lay down and curled up on his side.

Carefully letting the curtain fall back into place, I returned to Violet and told her what I'd seen. "I'm going to have to get closer to those cages," I whispered.

"How long does it take ogres to fall asleep?"

I shrugged. "I don't know, but they just finished a meal. That should make them sleepy. Text Mandy and tell her we might be here a while, but whatever you do, don't mention them eating. I'm going to watch them for a while to make sure they're asleep."

She patted her coat pockets. "I left my phone in the car."

"Use mine." I handed her my phone and went back to the curtain, where I found the ogres in the same position as when I'd left them. A few minutes later, one of them began to snore. When neither of them moved after another ten minutes, I hoped that meant they were both asleep. I could take on one ogre, two if I absolutely had to, but I was praying it didn't have to come to that.

I was about to let go of the curtain when a new sound reached me. I froze and listened until I heard it again, the plaintive mewing of a cat. It was followed by scratching and the distinctive whine of a dog. It could be any dog, but hearing it gave me a sliver of hope that Romeo was still alive.

Turning away from the curtain, I nearly jumped out of my skin when I bumped into someone. I raised my hands in self-defense before it hit me that the person was too short to be an ogre.

I shot Violet a glare she couldn't see in the darkness of the stage and tugged her back to where I'd left her. "Are you crazy? I nearly clobbered you."

"I wanted to see what was taking so long. Are they asleep?"

I huffed a breath. "One is, and the other might be. And I heard a cat and dog crying in the cages."

She gave my arm an excited squeeze. "What now?"

"We'll see if there is a door from backstage to the auditorium, and I'll sneak out to get the animals."

"I'm going with you." She held up a hand when I shook my head. "You'll need help getting the animals out of there. And I'm lighter on my feet than you."

She had a point. Years of ballet and dance lessons had given her the stealth of a ninja. But she was also jumpy, and she'd probably pee herself if she came face-to-face with an ogre.

"Stop overthinking it, and let's do this," she said when I took too long to respond.

I opened my backpack. "Promise me you'll run if they wake up."

"I will."

Finding my extra stun gun, I handed it to her. "This won't stop an ogre, but it will slow them down enough for you to get away. You'll have to give them a little more juice than you would for a human."

"Gotcha."

"Okay. Let's go." I headed to the side of the building closest to the dog crates, where a set of steps led down to a small door. The door hinges squeaked, and I held my breath as I opened the door wide enough for us to fit through.

The carpeted auditorium floor muffled our footsteps as we crept along the outside aisle toward the crates. The only sounds in the room were the crackle of the fire and the ogres' snores. If luck was with us, we'd grab the animals and be out of here before those two awoke.

I stopped at the rows where the crates sat. This close, I could see that it wasn't going to be as easy to free the animals as I'd hoped. The crates were at the end of the row closest to the fire with their doors facing away from me. I was going to have to get a lot closer to the ogres than I wanted to.

"*Stay here,*" I mouthed to Violet. I entered the row behind the crates and slowly made my way toward them, freezing every time one of the ogres snorted or moved in his sleep. It took forever to reach the crates, where I was greeted by a cat's mewing that grew more insistent by the second.

"Shhh." I stuck my fingers through the bars of the top crate, and the white cat quieted immediately to rub against them. I'd seen feral cats, and this wasn't one. This was someone's pet.

I bent to peer into the bottom crate and found a shivering chihuahua. He wore a thin collar, telling me he was also someone's pet. Anger sliced through me, but I pushed it back. Now was definitely not the time to lose my cool.

I moved around to the front of the crates, close enough to the fire now to feel its heat. From here I could peer into a plastic pet carrier. I wasn't sure what I was looking at until it moved. It was a pair of black ferrets that looked more curious than afraid when they saw me.

A crack came from behind me, and I turned my head so fast I thought I'd given myself whiplash. I let out a breath when sparks sprayed from the metal drum. It was only a piece of wood popping in the fire.

Biting my cheek, I leaned down to look into the last crate. My heart leapt when I met the black button eyes of a teacup Yorkie wearing a blue rhinestone collar.

Romeo panted and let out a small whine. I petted him through the bars to calm him as I straightened and waved for Violet to join me. I couldn't carry all of these animals at once, and I was afraid they'd make a racket if I took them one at a time.

Romeo's crate was wedged in such a way that I'd need to move the one on top to open his. I'd never handled ferrets before, so I left them in their carrier. I grimaced when it got hooked on the cat's crate and made a small squeaking sound.

An ogre snorted loudly, and I nearly dropped the carrier. My heart thudded wildly. If anyone ever asked me what to do for an adrenaline rush, my immediate response would be to sneak into an abandoned building and steal from sleeping ogres.

By the time Violet reached me, I had the carrier free, and I handed it off to her. Motioning for her to wait, I freed the cat and passed it to her as well. That left the two dogs for me.

It took some maneuvering to shift Romeo's crate without making a noise, but I finally managed to get the door open. I unzipped the top of my coat and tucked him inside. He wasn't any bigger than Finch, so he fit in there easily.

Once Romeo was secure, I went to work freeing the chihuahua. The poor little thing was so terrified I had to grasp his collar and tug him toward me. His nails scraped the plastic floor of the crate, and he let out a small whimper when I lifted him into my arms. He was trembling violently, but there wasn't time to comfort him. I'd make sure he got lots of that when we were out of there.

I walked carefully back toward Violet, who was trying to hold the cat that was suddenly freaking out. With a hiss, it leaped from her arms and took off like the hounds of hell were on its heels.

Violet looked at me, and her mouth opened in horror. At the same time, I realized the room had gone strangely quiet.

I stopped and looked back over my shoulder at the ogre sitting up beside the fire. He stretched and looked around, and then his eyes found me.

He bellowed, the sound echoing in the auditorium and sending his friend scrambling to his feet. I turned and sped toward Violet, who looked paralyzed with fear.

"Go," I yelled at her above the ogres' roars.

She didn't move.

Feet thundered behind me, and I put on an extra burst of speed. "Violet, get your ass moving!"

I reached her as she picked up the ferret carrier. We turned toward the door beside the stage and skidded to a stop at the sight of the ogres coming through it. Three, four, five, six...

I grabbed Violet's arm and spun in the other direction. I started toward the theater's main entrance, but a pile of seats blocked it. Changing direction, I ran to the stairs to the upper levels, pulling her with me. I'd seen a fire escape on the outside of the building, so there had to be an emergency exit upstairs.

I pushed Violet ahead of me, and she flew up the stairs like she had wings on her feet. At the mezzanine level, I glanced back at our lumbering pursuers who hadn't reached the stairs yet. I sent up a silent thank you to Aedhna for not gifting ogres with speed.

I paused to look around and get my bearings. The fire escape should be straight ahead, but it was too dark up here to see far. Taking Violet's arm again, I set off to where the exit should be.

My euphoria at finding the door died when I saw the chain and padlock on it. I had my picks on me, but the pounding of many feet on the stairs told me we didn't have time for that.

We ran to the stairs on the far side of the mezzanine. My hope that we could run down them and escape was dashed by the sight of four ogres with clubs waiting below. Ogres were not as stupid as people made them out to be.

Violet and I ran up the stairs to the balcony level before the ogres could spot us and alert their friends. We had a head start, but that wasn't going to do us much good if we got trapped up here.

Think, Jesse! I fought back my rising panic. If I was alone, I would try something daring like using the climbing rope and grappling hook in my pack to swing from one of the boxes to the stage. But Violet couldn't make that jump. I wasn't sure I could either.

We ran to the back corner of the balcony level where there were two doors to the men's and women's restrooms. Opening the first door, I shoved Violet inside.

"Hide in here and take care of these guys." I handed her the chihuahua and Romeo. "I'll draw them away."

"You can't go out there alone."

I gave her a quick hug, almost squishing the two dogs. "I'll be okay."

I left before she could argue with me. *Please, keep her safe,* I prayed to whoever might be listening.

Shouts and thumps came from below as the ogres searched the mezzanine level. I never should have let Violet come in here with me, but it was too late to think about that now. I needed to lead them as far away from her as I could, and then I'd figure out how to get us out of this mess.

I ran lightly toward the private boxes along the side of the auditorium. As I passed the stairs, an ogre walked into my path, and we collided. It was like running into a wall. He looked as startled as I was, and that was what saved me. Before he could recover and call for his friends, I pulled my stun gun and zapped him.

He wavered on his feet. I could have used that moment to get away, but he'd shake it off quickly and bring the rest of them down on me. I struck out, slamming my fist into his thick neck beneath his ear. Ogres were built like bulls, but they had weaknesses like everyone else. The trick was reaching those weak spots without getting your head ripped off.

The ogre's beady eyes rolled back in his head, and he dropped like a stone. I stared in shock at his prone body. What the hell? My strike should have hurt him, but I was nowhere strong enough to knock him out with one blow.

I flexed my hand until I realized it wasn't hurting. I'd hit him hard enough to bruise my hand, yet I didn't feel the slightest twinge of pain.

Stepping around the ogre, I continued toward the boxes. I could ponder this mystery later. Right now, I had much bigger problems to deal with.

I entered the box closest to the stage and reached into my pocket for my phone. It was time to call Maurice for help. He'd lecture me for my stupidity, but I wasn't going to risk Violet's life to save my pride. I just needed to keep the ogres away from her long enough for backup to arrive.

My stomach plummeted as I patted my pockets frantically. I'd given my phone to Violet to text Mandy, and I'd forgotten to get it back from her.

I peered through the balcony rails and saw the four ogres on the ground level watching the stairs. I could see shapes moving around on the mezzanine, and my fear ratcheted up when two of them approached the stairs to this level.

I pulled off my backpack and took out my rope, which I looped around the sturdy balustrade. I donned the backpack again and checked to see if the coast was clear. Taking a deep breath, I climbed over the rail and shimmied down the rope to the box below.

My plan was to get to the stage, let them see me, and run like hell to draw them outside. As long as they didn't know Violet was still in the building, she was safe until I could get help.

I made it into the box and ducked out of sight seconds before two of the ogres below turned to look toward the stage. I watched them from my hiding spot, waiting for them to turn away again. They didn't. Anxiety built in my gut. I could get down the rope and to the stage before they caught me, but they'd see I was alone. This only worked if they thought the two of us were getting away.

I was so focused on the situation below that I didn't register the footsteps coming toward me until the door banged against the wall in the box next to mine.

I grabbed the rope, ready to swing down to the first floor. I didn't have any choice but to go now. If I got trapped, there was no way I could help Violet.

A loud caterwaul echoed through the building. I peeked out in time to see the white cat tear down the stairs and disappear into the back of the auditorium. All four ogres below looked in the direction the cat had gone, and they seemed to be discussing who would go after the animal.

I swung myself over the railing and slid down the rope. The second my feet touched the floor, a shout came from above, and the four ogres spun toward me. I let go of the rope and ran.

"Argh." I stumbled when something hard slammed into my tailbone, sending pain radiating up my spine. Righting myself, I looked from the wooden club on the floor to the glaring ogre in the box above me.

"You, stay," he ordered in a booming voice.

I turned and sprinted for the stage as shouts broke out behind me. I grabbed the edge of the stage to hoist myself up, but I faltered when a terrified scream split the air.

Violet.

Blood roared in my ears as I whirled to face the advancing ogres. My foot kicked something, and I bent to pick up a metal rod from an old microphone stand. Hefting it in both hands, I stalked toward the ogres between me and my best friend.

They laughed, and one of them charged me. Wielding the rod like a staff, I swung low, hooking it behind his ankles and sending him crashing to the floor.

I barely had time to straighten up when the next one came at me. I lunged away from his charge, but his fingers managed to snag my hair and my glasses. The glasses went flying and my eyes watered at the pain in my scalp as I pulled free. It felt like half my hair had been ripped out, and I was relieved to see it hanging down on the side of my face.

I brought the rod around to strike at the back of his neck. He anticipated my move and raised his club to deflect the attack on his most vulnerable area. I let the heavy rod slide along the club, slamming it into his thick fingers. Howling like an angry toddler, he released the club to cradle his injured hand.

Backing up, I dropped into a defensive stance as three more ogres joined the others. They formed a semicircle around me, and I swallowed hard. I was going to have to fight my way out of this.

13

The ogres took a step toward me, and I tensed as I studied them for weaknesses. If they came at me one at a time, I might be able to fend them off, but I didn't have a chance against the four of them at once.

The barest creak of a floor board warned that someone had snuck up behind me, even before the ogres shifted their gazes to something over my shoulder. A haze of pure adrenaline settled over me as I crouched and swung low to avoid the club that was likely aimed at my head. The metal rod slammed into a leg, and my assailant let out a grunt of pain.

I rose, swinging again, but he grabbed my weapon to block the strike. I released the rod and put all my strength into the blind punch I threw at him. My fist connected with his face with so much force that the shock traveled up my arm to my shoulder.

The metal rod clattered against the floor. I thought for a second about picking it up, then changed my mind and sprinted the six feet to the stage. Grabbing the edge of the stage, I pulled myself up with ease – and found my escape blocked by a pair of jean-clad legs.

Jeans? Ogres didn't wear jeans.

A male hand appeared in front of my face, one that definitely didn't belong to an ogre. I took it without thinking, and he pulled me to my feet. Pushing my hair out of my face, I looked up into Iian's eyes, which stared at me in amused wonder.

"What...are you doing here?" I uttered between gasps of air.

Someone clapped in the auditorium. I spun to see Kerr applauding as he and Faolin herded a group of ogres down the stairs. My gaze fell to the ogres I'd fought, and I found them kneeling and pleading with none other than the crown prince of Unseelie.

"I should have brought my phone," Kerr called. "No one will *ever* believe me."

"What...?" The question died on my tongue when Lukas turned to look at me. His nose and the front of his shirt were bloody, and his eyes were as hard as flint.

I gulped and backed up a step, only to come up against Iian, who prodded me to the edge of the stage. When I refused to jump down, he said, "He's not angry at you."

"His expression would suggest otherwise," I mumbled, not moving.

Iian chuckled and leaned in to whisper, "You punched the Unseelie prince in the face and almost put him on his ass. Tell me that doesn't feel good."

I lifted my chin because he was right. For weeks, I'd been taking out my pent-up emotions on the punching bags at the gym, and not one of those sessions had given me the satisfaction I felt now.

I jumped to the floor below and walked over to stand a few feet from Lukas. Up close, there seemed to be a lot more blood, and I tried not to wince at the sight of it.

"I guess that was long overdue," he said dryly as he wiped away some of the blood with his sleeve.

"I thought you were an ogre," I admitted.

A burst of laughter came from above. I looked up at Conlan descending the stairs with Violet in his arms. She had Romeo and the chihuahua cradled against her chest, and the ferret carrier dangled from one of Conlan's hands.

"Violet!" I ran to them.

"She's okay," Conlan assured me as I anxiously waited for them to reach the bottom of the stairs. "A minor sprain."

Violet lifted her head and gave me a pained smile. "I tried to keep them out of the bathroom, but they're strong bastards." She held up the stun gun I'd given her. "I used up the battery, but I made him think twice about grabbing me again."

I was so relieved she was safe I didn't know whether to laugh or cry. "How did you know we were in trouble?" I asked Conlan, still reeling from their sudden appearance.

He smiled. "Violet called us."

I looked at her in confusion.

She pulled my phone from her pocket and waved it at me. "As soon as you left me in the bathroom, I knew it was time to call in the cavalry. I found Faris's number in your contacts and called him. He took care of the rest."

"It's a good thing you didn't block him, too," Conlan quipped.

It was on the tip of my tongue to say that Faris hadn't given me a reason to block him, but bringing that up would be ungrateful after they had come to help us.

Lukas joined us and handed me my glasses I'd lost in the fight. Miraculously, they'd come out of it unscathed, but I really needed to think about getting contacts.

"Are you hurt?" he asked me tersely as I put on the glasses.

"No." I forced myself to look at him, and my stomach fluttered at the concern in his eyes.

Conlan snickered. "I'd say she fared better than you, my friend."

Lukas's jaw flexed. "What were you thinking, entering a building full of ogres on your own? Do you need the money so bad that you would risk your life for a job?"

"It wasn't for a job. We came to get our friend's dog. And we were told there were only two ogres here."

"Told by whom?"

"By someone who is going to be getting another visit from me," Violet said with a gleam in her eyes that didn't bode well for Mandy's ex. "As soon as I can walk again, your stun gun and I are going to have a little heart-to-heart with Mr. Gordon."

I imagined how smug Drew must have been after he'd gotten one over on us. I should have left the bastard shackled to a chair to teach him a lesson.

Conlan grinned down at Violet. "You're a bloodthirsty little thing."

"All this for a dog?" Lukas's voice was incredulous.

I put my hands on my hips. "What would you do if someone took Kaia?"

"That's different. I can handle a dozen ogres."

"There were only supposed to be two," I said defensively. "When was the last time you saw this many ogres living together?"

"A better question is when was the last time someone mistook Lukas for an ogre?" Iian asked laughing.

Conlan and Kerr joined in, and my ears grew warm. "Well, you guys shouldn't sneak up on people in the middle of a fight. Announce yourselves next time."

"You call that a fight?" Faolin came to stand with us, leaving Iian and Kerr to guard the ogres.

I scowled at him. "What would you call it?"

"I call it an untrained girl barely fending off ogres, who would have overpowered her had we not intervened. Your technique is sloppy, and you have no strength in your blows."

"Except when she nailed Lukas," Conlan piped in.

"Except then." Faolin studied me as if he was trying to dissect me with his eyes. "When you attacked Lukas, you moved with agility I did not expect from you. You have some potential."

"Strong in you the force is," Violet said in a terrible Yoda impersonation, earning strange looks from the faeries and an eye roll from me.

Faolin continued as if she hadn't spoken. "You need to fight properly if you hope to survive as a hunter. Self-defense is not enough. You must build up your strength and speed, and learn to fight offensively."

I huffed. "I'm working on it, but it takes time. Even you guys had years of training."

"We did," he agreed.

Violet flapped her hand excitedly. "You guys should train Jesse."

"No." I stared at her in horror. Had she hit her head fighting off that ogre?

"Why not?" She waved a hand at all of them. "There are like six of them, right? Who better to teach you to fight?"

I shot her a warning look. There was no way I was training with Lukas or his men. I could barely be in the same room with them as it was.

"You're right," Lukas told her. "We will train Jesse."

I whipped my head around to stare at him. "No, you won't."

He smiled. "It wasn't an offer. You will start tomorrow."

"No," I said with more force. "I'm quite happy with my current trainer, and I don't need your help."

"As you wish," he replied pleasantly. "We will follow you to keep you safe until you're able to do it yourself."

"No, you will not." I glared at him, but I might as well have been speaking to the floor.

He looked past me at Faolin. "Do you want the first shift?"

I crossed my arms. "I don't know how you do things in Faerie, but following someone here against their wishes is called stalking. There are laws against that."

"I'll notify the Agency that my guard is providing temporary protection for you," Lukas said with an infuriating tilt to his mouth. "You can hardly feel threatened by that."

"Tell that to my sanity," I said under my breath.

Conlan laughed outright, and even Faolin's lip twitched.

"It's settled then," Lukas said as if that was the end of it.

I wanted to stomp my foot in frustration. "Is this because Faris thinks he owes me a debt? Because you more than repaid it today."

"My brother's debt is his own, and none of us can repay it for him," Faolin said. "But it would put his mind at ease knowing you are protected."

I narrowed my eyes at him. "Now you're resorting to emotional blackmail."

"Not every fight is won with physical force," he replied smugly.

"Oh, that's low." I gritted my teeth. He knew I had a soft spot for Faris, and he was using it against me.

Lukas reached over and plucked my phone from Violet's hand. I grabbed for it, but he held it out of my reach and proceeded to enter their numbers into my contacts.

"You know I can just block those again."

"You won't," he said without looking at me.

I tapped my foot. "What makes you so sure of that?"

He finished what he was doing and handed the phone to me. "Because if I call you and you don't answer, I will put a twenty-four-hour watch on you."

I glared at him as I stuck the phone in my pocket. "I should have punched you harder."

"If it makes you feel better, you can do it again," he replied in a voice that made warmth unfurl in my belly.

Kerr interrupted us. "What do you wish to do with them?" he asked Lukas.

I followed their gazes to the cluster of ogres kneeling on the floor, submissive in the presence of Lukas and his men. Ogres were bad news, and if Lukas released them, they would be up to no good again tomorrow. Eventually, they'd end up with a bounty on their heads, if they didn't have one already.

Lukas turned to me. "Do you want to bring them in for a bounty?"

The ogres shifted and murmured nervously, and a few of them darted their eyes around for an escape route. Good luck with that.

I did a quick headcount. There were eleven ogres, and at two thousand dollars each that was a whopping twenty-two thousand dollars. I could finally hire a plumber to replace the bad pipes.

I pulled out my phone and called Levi. Sure enough, there was a bounty on a gang of ogres working this area. Since ogres were territorial, the odds of there being another gang here were slim.

"There is a bounty on them," I said to Lukas after I hung up. "But you caught them, not me."

His eyes lit with amusement. "You got here first, and I believe one requires a license to collect a bounty. It's all yours."

I looked at Violet, and she waved a hand. "I will settle for you not telling my mom how I sprained my foot."

Conlan laughed. "What happened to the little firebrand who was going to take a stun gun to the man who sent you here?"

She snorted. "You obviously haven't met my mother."

I walked over to them and took Romeo from Violet. "I'm going to take this little guy to his mom, and then I need to figure out how to get eleven ogres to the Plaza."

"Wait," Violet said before I could leave. "If there's a bounty on them, doesn't that mean the job was already assigned to another hunter?"

"Yep and he's not going to be happy."

"Who is it?" she asked.

I smirked. "Poor Trey, he can't catch a break."

I walked through a meadow of tall white flowers that swayed in the warm breeze, their delicate perfume surrounding me. Raising my face to the bluest sky I'd ever seen, I closed my eyes, letting the sun's warmth wash over me. I inhaled deeply and let it out on a blissful sigh. This place was pure heaven.

A whisper of sound had me turning my head to my right, and I was surprised to see I was not alone. Standing beside me was a tall, beautiful woman in a white dress with silvery blonde hair that fell almost to her knees. Her face was unlined by age, but her gray eyes held the wisdom of a thousand lifetimes.

The woman spoke, but though her lips formed words, no sound came out. She seemed unaware that I couldn't hear her until I pointed at my ear and shook my head. A frown marred her perfect brow, and she glanced up at the sky as if pondering what to do next.

She lowered her head, and her eyes met mine again before she pointed at something behind me.

I turned and gasped. On a hill rising above the trees beyond the meadow was a breathtaking white castle. It looked like it had come straight out of a fairy tale, with its gleaming white turrets and stained glass windows that sparkled like jewels in the sun.

I started walking toward it until a light touch on my arm stopped me. The woman shook her head and pointed to the sky above the castle. I looked up and watched the blue deepen to twilight in a matter of seconds. Before I could question it, undulating ribbons of multi-colored lights appeared in the sky. It resembled the aurora borealis, except for the jagged bolts of lightning at its center.

A sharp pinch on my hand made me tear my eyes from the sky. I looked at the woman, who was standing with her hands at her sides. The pain came again, and this time, it brought tears to my eyes.

"Ow. What the –?"

The world around me disappeared, and suddenly I was lying in my bed. It was dark in the room, but I could make out Gus as he paced back and forth on the bed.

"Gus, what the heck?" I cradled my hand to my chest. He'd been sneaking in to sleep on my bed every night, but he never disturbed me. This was the first time he'd bitten me since the day I'd tried to get him down from the kitchen cabinets.

He made a sound between a growl and a squawk and jumped off the bed to fly to the chair by the window. Maybe he needed to go out and couldn't get the bathroom window open.

Pushing the covers off me, I got out of bed. "All right, I'm coming."

I reached up to unlock the window and froze when I saw the ribbons of colored light stretching across the sky. I rubbed my eyes, but the lights were still there when I looked again. It wasn't impossible for the aurora borealis to appear above New York, but not in the middle of the city.

Déjà vu hit me hard, and I remembered my dream. How was it possible I dreamed of this phenomenon exactly when it was happening? Unlike in my dream, there was no lightning, but still, this was weird even for me.

Gus squawked and flapped his wings impatiently. I slid the window up for him, shivering when the cold air hit my arms. "Here you go, buddy."

Instead of going out the window, the drakkan jumped off the chair and ran under my bed. I stared after him until the cold forced me to close the window. In the sky, the lights were starting to fade. I stood there watching them until they were gone.

A glance at the alarm clock told me it was just after four in the morning. I yawned and crawled back into bed, hoping for a few more hours of sleep. I had a feeling I was going to need it today.

―――――――

"You're late," said a scowling Faolin when he opened the door of their building hours later.

I met his glower with one of my own as I stomped snow off my boots. "By ten minutes. You try getting around this city in the winter without a portal." I hadn't exactly been in a hurry to get here for my first training session with them, but I kept that to myself.

He stepped aside and waved me in. I entered the main living space, expecting to see Faris or Lukas, but it was only Faolin and me.

"Leave your things here." He pointed to one of the barstools at the island. "The training room is upstairs, and we will begin there."

"We?" A tiny knot formed in my stomach as I deposited my coat and backpack on a stool and kicked off my boots. Surely, he didn't mean *he* was training me. Then I took in his outfit – some kind of loose, black leggings that stopped below his knees and a gray, short-sleeved top.

"This way." He turned toward the stairs, but not before I caught his smirk.

For about half a second, I thought about grabbing my stuff and running. I straightened my shoulders, picked up the gym shoes I'd brought with me, and followed him.

We climbed the two flights of stairs to the third floor, which was laid out much like the second floor with closed doors on either side. Faolin led me to the door at the end of the hallway and opened it to reveal a large room with a glossy hardwood floor bare of any furniture. Along the walls hung swords, staffs, knives, and other weapons I had no name for. There were no mats on the floor to break one's fall, and I cringed inwardly, thinking of the bruises I was going to collect in this room.

"You won't need those," Faolin said when I bent to pull on my shoes.

"You want me to train in my socks?"

He glanced at my feet. "No. Remove those as well."

I gaped at him. "I can't train barefoot."

"Are you one of those human females who is self-conscious about her feet?" he asked with a note of impatience.

"Of course, not. I just don't like walking around barefoot unless I'm at home." I picked up one of my shoes. "These protect my feet and help with balance."

Faolin scoffed. "Exactly. You should not rely on footwear for balance or performance. Training without them will strengthen the muscles in your feet and teach you to rely only on your body."

"Fine." I pulled off my socks and tossed them into a corner with my shoes. What he said made sense, but if I found out this was some kind of Fae hazing prank, there would be payback.

I faced him, feeling strangely vulnerable without any socks or shoes, until I realized he had removed his as well. I wore my usual workout clothes – leggings and a sports bra, with the addition of a T-shirt.

Faolin walked over to one of the racks on the walls and took down a long wooden staff tipped with silver on each end. He grasped the staff in both hands and performed a series of slashes, thrusts, and strikes in a deadly dance that made me take a step back. He moved faster with each movement until I could no longer follow them.

His routine finished as abruptly as it had begun, and he turned to face me again. "We will train you in several weapons, but after observing you last night, I think you might be better suited to the staff."

"Where do we start?" I rubbed my suddenly sweaty hands on my hips.

He returned the staff to the rack on the wall. "We start with your conditioning."

"Okay." I relaxed a little. Maren was always putting me through drills at the gym.

"My early training required me to run up and down a mountain until I fell from exhaustion," he said.

I stared at him, sure he had to be joking. "It's probably a good thing we have no mountains here then."

"You will use the stairs."

Two flights of stairs weren't that bad. "How many times should I run them?"

The gleam that entered his eyes would have sent a smarter person running for the exit. "Until you fall or I tell you to stop."

An hour later, the bottoms of my feet were numb from hitting the hard steps, and my calves and thighs burned from the effort to move them. I'd lost count of how many times I'd climbed the stairs to hear Faolin say, "Again."

At the ninety-minute mark, I could barely drag my feet up the stairs, and I had to hold the handrail for support. Every time the sadistic beast at the top of the stairs barked for me to go again, I was convinced I couldn't do one more. I pulled on a reserve of strength I hadn't known existed in me and pushed on.

Nearly two hours had passed when I paused on the top step to catch my breath and wipe away the sweat that ran into my eyes. My chest heaved from the effort, and I wondered if running up a mountain could be much worse than this. At least, there'd be fresh air and nature to enjoy. And there would be cool mountain streams to drink from. My parched throat worked at the thought of water.

"Are you quitting?" my tormentor asked in a taunting voice. I would have given him the finger if I could have spared the energy.

"Just taking a breather," I said between pants. I wouldn't give him the satisfaction of seeing me quit.

He pushed off from the wall and walked toward the training room. "Come with me."

I followed him on rubbery legs, wondering what fresh hell he had in store for me. If he planned to start me on staff training now, it wasn't going to be pretty.

We entered the room, and he pointed to my shoes and socks in the corner. "We're done for today."

"I didn't quit."

"I know." He folded his muscled arms across his chest. "Today was not only about conditioning. It was to see how far you would push yourself and to determine if you are worthy of training."

I pushed away the sweaty hair that had come loose from my ponytail. "It was all a test?"

"Yes. Congratulations. You passed."

"Why don't I feel like celebrating?" I grumbled, walking over to gather my stuff.

He didn't answer me, not that I expected him to. Neither of us spoke as we descended the stairs to the first floor.

"You may shower in the bathroom next to the library," he said when I sat on the bottom step to stuff my aching feet into my socks.

"Thanks." I'd planned to change into fresh clothes and then shower when I got home, but my hair was dripping with sweat that ran into my eyes. The thought of driving home like that was less appealing than lingering here long enough to shower.

When I emerged from the bathroom twenty minutes later, with my damp hair pulled into a ponytail, Faolin was nowhere to be seen. It was just as well. Two hours alone in his company was more than enough for one day.

I picked up my coat and heard the clink of my keys hitting the tile floor. Bending to retrieve them, I let out a small shriek when I came face-to-face with Kaia. Where had she come from?

"Hi, Kaia," I said slowly as I carefully reached for my keys.

My fingertips had barely grazed them when they were snatched away from me. Kaia stared at me for several seconds with my keys dangling from her mouth, and then she bounded away like an exuberant puppy.

"Hey!" I ran after her.

She skidded to a stop in the living room and spun to face me. If I didn't know better, I'd think she was grinning.

I approached her slowly. "Nice kitty. Can I have my keys back?"

She didn't move as I reached out for the keys, but as soon as I touched them, she shook her head playfully and took off again.

I groaned and turned to the stairs. "Faolin, I could use your help."

Kaia jingled the keys, and I whirled to find her a foot away from me. She crouched like she was about to pounce on me, but all she did was wriggle her behind as if she was daring me to try to take the keys. I was exhausted, and the last thing I wanted to do was play, but she didn't seem to care about that.

I grabbed for the keys, and she let me get my fingers around them this time before she yanked them from my grasp. I went after her again and again, and every time I thought I had them, she'd take off, leaving me empty-handed.

Eventually, my tired legs failed me, and I tripped, falling across the couch. Kaia must have thought it was intentional because she jumped up on the cushion beside me. I made one last desperate grab for the keys and closed my hand around them. She tried to yank them from my grasp, and we began a game of tug of war that ended in the two of us rolling off the couch into a heap on the floor. I let out a loud "oof" when the heavy lamal landed on top of me and one of her paws jabbed me in the stomach.

"You don't see that every day."

I spat out a mouthful of lamal fur and looked at Conlan standing in the doorway. He wore a shocked expression I might have found funny under different circumstances. He moved aside as Lukas, Iian, and Kerr entered the room, and the four of them stared at me as if I'd suddenly sprouted pixie wings.

"Little help here," I wheezed when none of them came to my aid.

Lukas was the first to react. "Kaia, come," he said as he strode toward us.

She rose up over me and gave me a dejected look before she dropped the keys on my chest and went to him.

"Stay," he ordered her. He came to sit on his haunches beside me. "Are you okay? Did she hurt you?"

"Only my pride." I pushed up to a sitting position and grimaced at the curtain of damp hair that fell across my face. Gathering it back with both hands, I looked around for my missing hair tie. When I couldn't find it, I sighed and did my best to work the tangle of hair in to a knot.

"What happened?" Lukas asked gruffly, making me very aware of how close he was.

I scooted away from him. "Kaia wanted to play."

"Play?" he echoed as if he'd never heard the word before.

"She took my keys so I would chase her. You should get her some toys." I stood, unable to suppress a small groan when I put my weight on my abused feet.

Lukas was beside me in an instant. "I thought you said Kaia didn't hurt you."

I skewered him with a glare. "She didn't. This is from that sadist you left me to train with."

"Faolin did this? Where is he?"

"Upstairs."

Snickers came from the other side of the room, and Kerr said, "She killed him. Pay up, Conlan."

"Not until I see the body," Conlan joked. "She might have only left him for dead."

"Glad I amuse you." I limped past them to get my stuff. Pulling on my coat, I zipped it all the way to my chin. "Always nice to see you guys."

I made it to the door when Conlan called, "Same time tomorrow?"

Raising one hand, I flipped them the bird and left without looking back.

Outside, I put my head down against the wind and hurried to the Jeep. I didn't see the person who stepped into my path until I was nearly on top of them.

"Sorry." I lifted my head to meet the unfriendly, green eyes of a female faerie with long, glossy, black hair. I recognized her immediately. She was the faerie I'd seen talking to Lukas at Va'sha.

Her eyes raked over me. "Who are you?"

Her haughty tone made my hackles rise, and I instantly disliked her. "No one."

She put up an arm to block me when I would have gone around her. "I saw you leave Vaerik's. What is your business with him?"

It suddenly felt like someone was applying pressure to my chest. Were they involved? I couldn't picture him with someone so cold, but what did I really know about him or his tastes in women? And why should I even care?

"Well?" she snapped.

I shoved her arm away from me. "Not that it's any of your business, but I was here to see Faolin."

"Faolin?" Her eyebrows shot up, but she looked slightly appeased by my answer. "You and Faolin?"

I ignored her question. "Go on in. I'm sure *Vaerik* will be so happy to see you."

As if he'd heard us, the door opened behind me, and Lukas said, "Dariyah?"

"Vaerik." Her face lit up with a beautiful smile that wiped away all traces of the ugliness I'd seen.

"What brings you here?" he asked.

If he sounded surprised and not exactly thrilled about his visitor, it meant nothing to me. And that wasn't a smile on my face as I walked to the Jeep. Not at all.

14

My jaw cracked from a yawn as I glanced at the clock on the dash. It was almost ten, and I'd spend the last six hours staking out a bodega that was having trouble with a troll thug. This would be the one night he'd decided to go somewhere else for a change, and I was headed home empty-handed.

I stopped at a traffic light, barely taking notice of the people in the crosswalk as I made a mental list of what I had to do tomorrow. My days were so full now the only way I could get everything done was to plan ahead. Even then, I was usually busy late into the night.

The last two weeks had been a blur of hunting and training, with weekly visits to my parents to break up the long hours. Some of the other hunters, including Bruce and Trey, had abandoned the ke'tain search and had gone back to taking the regular jobs. But there was no shortage of jobs to be had.

I hadn't given up on the ke'tain, but I'd found no leads since that night at Davian Woods's party. I didn't have the resources to investigate or follow the billionaire, and I wasn't stupid enough to go near the Seelie guard, even if I had a clue where to find them. As much as I hated letting Lukas handle it, I'd made the right decision to share what I knew with him.

Not that I'd seen much of Lukas. I'd rarely laid eyes on him since my first day of training, and according to Faris, Lukas was occupied with the ke'tain search and other business. I couldn't help but wonder if some of his other business was with his friend Dariyah. I was only curious. He was the one who had insisted on me training with them, after all, and he was the only one I hadn't worked with yet.

As for my training, the first three days had consisted of Faolin pushing me to the brink of exhaustion, but then the others had started working with me. We'd progressed to hand-to-hand fighting techniques, and they said once I learned those, we would move on to weapons.

My phone vibrated, and I looked down at a text from Violet. It was a selfie of her with the Hollywood sign in the background. **Wish u were here!**

I smiled wistfully at her beaming face. She had gotten the part in the big sci-fi film she'd auditioned for, and now she was in LA, meeting with her agent, signing contracts, and having a blast. I'd always known she would leave New York someday to follow her dream, but I missed her something fierce, and she hadn't been gone a week yet.

I looked up to check the light, and my gaze fell on a man crossing in front of me, his head bent against the wind. I shivered despite the fact that it was toasty warm inside the Jeep. We were having a brutally cold winter, and I was grateful for my vehicle, even if it took longer to get around.

The man raised his head and glanced in my direction, and I was struck by the feeling I'd seen him before. He had to be in his early thirties, average height with a round face and brown hair. I was certain I didn't know him, so why did he seem familiar?

He continued on his way, and it wasn't until he disappeared from view that it hit me where I'd seen him before. He was Lewis Tate.

The Agency had been looking for the dealer ever since the raid on his house, and there was a ten-thousand-dollar bounty on his head. He was great at hiding, and not even Faolin had been able to track him down. Everyone assumed he'd fled the state, but there he was, walking along a street in the Bronx as if there wasn't a statewide hunt for him.

The light turned green, and I made a right turn to follow Tate. I had to drive past him to find a parking spot, and then I set off on foot after him.

We'd been walking for five minutes when a familiar graffitied, brick building came into view. Tate cut across the street, and I waited until he opened the door of the bar before I followed. Why would he come to Teg's of all places? He'd evaded law enforcement since the raid, but he was asking to be caught by showing his face here. I'd heard it was not uncommon for bounty hunters to come here when they were off the clock. Tate must not know that, or he'd give this place a wide berth.

I opened the door, but when I tried to step inside, some invisible force prevented me from getting past the door jamb. *What the hell?*

"Crap." I let the door close and shook my head at my own stupidity. Teg's was protected by a ward that would not allow entry to anyone carrying drugs or weapons. I wasn't happy about going after Tate unarmed, but it was either that or wait out here until he left.

I pulled my stun gun from my pocket and looked around for somewhere to hide it. There was a small indent in the side of the steps where a piece of the concrete had fallen off, and it was big enough for the stun gun. It wasn't ideal, and anyone who looked too closely would see it, but it would have to do.

Opening the door again, I entered the noisy bar. I braced myself for the heady Fae scent that had assailed me on my first visit, but it was gone. Or maybe it was still there, and it no longer affected me after having spent so much time with Lukas and his men.

Unzipping my jacket, I walked over to the crowded bar area to scan the room. It was virtually impossible for a redhead to blend in at a Fae bar, and I expected to have to fend off advances like my first time here. I got more than one interested look sent my way, but the faeries glanced away as soon as I met their eyes. It was strange but nice. Maybe the redhead fascination was finally going away.

I spotted Tate and another man sitting at a corner table, surrounded by elves, trolls, ogres, and a few other humans. The two men had their heads bent, deep in conversation, and every now and then, Tate would lift his head to scan the room.

I watched him covertly for a few minutes while I opened the bulletin the Agency had sent out the day after the raid. It had a photo of Lewis Tate, and I wanted to confirm his identity before I made a move. I pulled up the photo and studied his face until I was positive it was Tate I'd followed in here.

I didn't have a weapon on me, but Tate couldn't have one either. I did have my shackles, and I knew how to fight, if necessary. Unless he turned out to be a black belt, I could hold my own.

After ordering a soda from the bar, I casually walked toward Tate's table. Unlike Court faeries, lower Fae races were not attracted to red hair, so the faeries in this section only cast disinterested looks in my direction.

A few feet from Tate's table, I spoke just loud enough for him to hear. "Lewis."

His head jerked up, and he darted his eyes around before they landed on me. Confusion marred his forehead as his gaze met mine. "Did you say something?"

Smiling, I set my glass on his table. "You're Lewis Tate, right?"

"No. Sorry." His body tensed, and he put his hands on the edge of the table.

"Really? You look exactly like him." I held up my phone with the Agency photo of him displayed on the screen. "He could be your doppelganger."

He jumped to his feet and pushed past me. He was bigger than I was, but that didn't matter when I stuck out my foot, sending him crashing to the floor. It was almost too easy to roll him onto his stomach and shackle his hands behind his back. If all captures were like this, I'd be rich.

A chair scraped on the floor, and I looked up at the other man, who seemed to be contemplating whether or not to come to his friend's aid.

"I'm not here for you. That will change if you interfere in Agency business," I told him, pleased by how tough I sounded.

He looked from me to Tate, and then he took off for the door. Kim was right. Attitude was everything in this business.

"Up you go." I took Tate's arm and helped him to his feet, aware of the many pairs of eyes on us. The other patrons of Teg's might be curious, but not one of them moved to help Tate.

"I have money, lots of it," Tate babbled. "I'll pay you whatever you want if you let me go and pretend you never saw me."

"Sorry. Can't do that." I steered him in the direction of the exit.

We'd made it past the tables when a woman drawled, "Now, where do you think you're going with our boy?"

I tightened my grip on Tate's arm when the two Texas hunters stepped in front of us to block our path. I'd seen them at the Plaza a few times, but I hadn't spoken to them since my run-in with them the night of the raid. I'd heard from several hunters that they weren't making any friends in town with their aggressive behavior and disparaging comments about New Yorkers.

"Your boy?"

Leah, the brunette, pointed at Tate. "We were here first. You can't come in here and steal him from us."

Natalie, her blonde partner, smirked. "Yeah."

"He's wearing my shackles, which makes him my capture. If he was yours, you should have said something before I took custody of him."

"We're saying it now." Leah took a step toward me, and Natalie did the same.

"Your butch friend is not here to stick up for you this time," Natalie taunted. "We'll be taking our capture, if you don't mind."

"I do mind." I sized them up, taking in their heavily made-up faces and the slight slur in their voices. They were here to drink, not hunt, and I'd bet my entire bounty they hadn't even known Tate was here until they saw me with him.

They tittered, and Natalie said, "In case you hadn't noticed, honey, you're outnumbered."

I waved away the alcohol fumes on their breath. "You do know it's illegal to drink when you're hunting."

Leah made a sound of contempt. "You Yankees and your rules."

"Those are federal regulations. If you took a Breathalyzer right now, you'd fail."

She poked her finger in my chest. "I'm still a better hunter than you'll ever be."

"What is your problem?" I stood my ground. This was their second time trying to pick a fight with me. I didn't know if they hated everyone or just me.

She sneered. "You are. We worked to get where we are. We didn't have it handed to us because our parents were some hotshot hunters."

"No one handed me anything, and my parents weren't even here when I started hunting." I knew that wouldn't matter to these two. They didn't come across as people who bothered with facts.

Natalie let out an ugly laugh. "Oh, that's right. They're goren junkies."

Anger ignited in my gut, but I refused to rise to the bait. I stared them down while I thought of how to get out of here without having to fight. Giving up Tate was not an option.

Natalie's eyes narrowed when her insults didn't get a reaction from me. "I'm tired of this BS. Hand him over, or we're going to take him from you. It's as simple as that."

Her gaze flitted to Tate a second before she made a grab for him. I pushed him behind me, and she snarled when her hand touched nothing but air.

I took a step back as Leah's fist glanced off my cheekbone. My eyes stung from the blow, and warmth trickled down my cheek. I looked from her smug smile to the bloodied class ring on her right hand.

My fists clenched, but Faolin's words from one of our sessions filled my head. *"The fastest way to lose a fight is to let emotions control you."*

I smiled at Leah. "I think you broke a nail."

She started to lift her hand to examine it and dropped it to glare at me. "I'm going to break more of them on your face."

"Such aggression." I made a tsk sound. "Have you tried yoga? I hear it's great for that."

A few people nearby snickered. Leah's lips pulled back, and a vein popped out on her temple. "It's on now, bitch."

She lunged, throwing another punch. I ducked the strike and sent a hard jab to her stomach, making her double over. I'd taken a few gut punches in training, and I knew how much they hurt.

Natalie's hand grabbed my hair and yanked hard, making tears spring to my eyes. Instead of resisting, I moved toward her, only stopping when the top of my head slammed into her chin. I reached up to grab her hand as her grip loosened. Bringing her arm down, I forced her to her knees with her arm bent behind her back.

Cheers and catcalls came from the onlookers, but they were hollow and distorted as the world seemed to slow around me. My heartbeat and breathing were loud in my ears, and I could feel the vibrations of the air around me. Maybe I'd hit Natalie a little too hard with my head.

I sensed rather than saw the kick aimed at my head. Releasing Natalie, I put up both hands and caught Leah's booted foot before it could make contact. A sharp wrench was all it took to knock her off balance and lay her out on her stomach. She tried to push herself up, but I knelt on her back, holding her in place.

The world sped up, and sound returned to normal. Beneath me, Leah blistered my ears with a stream of profanity, and a few feet away, Natalie wailed that her arm was broken and I was going to pay.

"Fight's over, people," said a hard voice that made the crowd scatter. Even Leah and Natalie shut up.

I looked up at Orend Teg's scowling face. The blond faerie crossed his arms as he stood over us. "Jesse James, why is it that the two times there have been fights in my bar in the last six months, you've been at the center of them?"

"Rotten luck?" I offered.

"Mine or yours?" He surveyed our surroundings. "At least you didn't destroy my property this time."

Leah bucked, trying to dislodge me. "Someone get this crazy bitch off me."

"Allow me." Teg smirked and extended a hand to me. "Miss James."

I was perfectly capable of standing on my own, but I took his offered hand and let him pull me up. His brow creased when he got a closer look at the cut on my cheek, but he said nothing about it.

Leah scrambled to her feet, her face mottled and her hair a wild mess. She charged me, but Teg stepped between us, blocking her.

"There will be no more fighting in my bar."

"She started it!" Leah yelled.

"You tried to take my –" I swung my gaze around the room. "Damn it!"

I ran to the door and out into the street, but there was no sign of Lewis Tate. How the hell had he disappeared that fast with his hands shackled behind his back?

"Lose something?" Teg asked from the doorway.

I glared past him at Leah and Natalie, who watched me with satisfied smirks. "My bounty, thanks to those two idiots."

The Texans tried to push past Teg, but they were no match for him. He waved for someone, and a waitress with fuchsia hair joined us. I remembered her from my first visit here.

"Boss?"

"Cynthia, please give these two ladies whatever they want to drink, as long as they behave."

The waitress smiled. "Sure thing."

The two hunters shot me looks of loathing before they turned to follow Cynthia. I'd have to watch my back until they returned to Texas.

"You always give free drinks to people who fight in your bar?" I asked Teg as I went back inside.

"Only the ladies." He smiled when I gave him a questioning look. "Women attract males, and males like to spend money, especially male faeries."

"Ah." I searched my pockets and found a tissue to dab at my cut, but it had already stopped bleeding.

"I take it you know them." He looked toward the bar where Leah and Natalie sat.

I made a face. "Not really. They're bounty hunters from Texas, who don't like to play nice."

"So I saw." Teg stared at me until I squirmed under his scrutiny.

"Why are you looking at me like that?"

He blinked. "My apologies. It's just that I watched you take down the brunette, and I don't think I've ever seen a human move like that."

I shrugged. "It's called adrenaline. And I've been training every day."

"With whom? The Unseelie royal guard?" he retorted.

"Yes."

He laughed, and then his eyes widened when he realized I wasn't joking.

I took out my phone. "Excuse me. I need to let the Agency know their fugitive is running around the Bronx wearing my shackles."

The corners of Teg's mouth turned down. "Exactly what I need tonight. Agents crawling all over my bar."

I smiled apologetically as I called the Agency and was transferred to the Special Crimes division. I gave them a quick rundown of what happened, and they told me to wait there for Agents Curry and Ryan. I made a face at the mention of Daniel Curry. I was starting to wish I'd never seen Lewis Tate at that traffic light.

"You say Tate met with another man here?" Teg asked when I ended the call and told him the agents were on the way.

"Yes, he took off when I caught Tate. The Agency will want to know who he is and what business Tate had with him. I don't suppose you have security cameras."

"I have cameras covering every inch of this place, except the restrooms and my office."

"If you can give them video of the man, it will probably get them out of here faster."

He let out a resigned sigh. "Come with me. I'll need you to point them out."

"Sure." It wasn't like I could leave until after the agents questioned me. I might as well do something useful in the meantime.

Teg turned toward his office. His steps faltered, and he grabbed my arm, almost dragging me with him. He didn't let go of me until we were inside his large office with the door closed.

I rubbed my arm. "What was that about?"

He locked the door and faced me, and I was taken aback to see alarm in his eyes. "Jesse, why is a member of the Seelie royal guard in my bar watching you?"

"W-what?" I choked out the word as an icy breath tickled the back of my neck.

"I saw him standing at the back of the dais just now. You didn't know he was there?"

"No. Are you sure he's one of the Seelie royal guard?" Teg was Unseelie, so it was possible he had made a mistake.

He walked over to his desk and picked up a cell phone. "I've seen him before. He was with Prince Rhys when he made his debut, and I have it from a reliable source that he's one of Queen Anwyn's personal guard."

I swallowed dryly, trying not to panic. I hadn't seen any of the queen's guard since that night at Davian's party, and I was sure he had not seen me. If he had, I wouldn't have left that penthouse alive. I wracked my brain and couldn't think of why one of the guards was watching me now.

"Jesse?"

I started when Teg's voice broke through my deep musings. He was watching me with a concerned expression.

"You look a little pale? Do you want to sit down?"

"No." I pressed my lips together in thought. "Can you access your security cameras from in here?"

"Of course." He sat and logged onto the computer.

I walked over to stand beside him. "I got here about thirty minutes ago, and Tate entered ahead of me. Can you go back to that time?"

Teg brought up the cameras, and I was shocked to see how many there were. He hadn't been kidding when he'd said every inch of the place was covered. He started with the camera for the main entrance and found the moment Tate entered the bar. I told him where Tate had been sitting, and he switched to that camera. Sure enough, there was Tate joining the unidentified man I'd seen him with.

"Now, can you go back to just before we got there and look for the royal guard?"

He did as I asked, bringing up the camera on a dais. He stopped the video and pointed to a blond faerie. "That's him."

Relief made my legs weak. "He wasn't here for me."

"How do you know that?" Teg asked, unconvinced.

"Because I didn't know I was coming here until a minute before I entered the place. I spotted Lewis Tate as I was driving by, and I followed him." I pointed to the faerie on the screen. "Look at him. He's watching someone in the lower section, and I'll bet it's Tate's friend. He must have known they were meeting here and was waiting for them."

Teg rubbed his jaw. "Why didn't he follow them when they left?"

"Maybe he was curious because he saw me with Tate. Or maybe he likes watching women fight. But unless he can see the future and somehow knew I'd be here tonight, he wasn't here for me."

"You make a valid point." Teg switched to the live feeds, but the royal guard was no longer visible. A bit more checking showed the faerie leaving the bar shortly after we'd entered the office.

A sharp rap on the door made me jump. Teg pulled up the camera outside the office, and a jolt of surprise went through me.

I stared at Lukas, Faolin, and Conlan on the monitor. "What are they doing here?"

Teg stood. "I called Lukas."

"Why?" I vaguely remembered him picking up his phone when we entered his office, around the same time I was trying not to freak out.

He walked around the desk. "Because he is my prince, and I have to notify him of suspicious activity in my bar, especially when it involves Seelie."

Teg opened the door, and a stone-faced Lukas entered first. He barely acknowledged Teg before his angry eyes narrowed on me.

"If you're going to say I shouldn't be here, you can save your breath," I said before he could speak. "And stop glaring at me. The Seelie guard was not here because of me. It's been a crap night, and I'm in no mood for a lecture from you or anyone else."

No one spoke. I turned to Teg who was staring at me. "Tell him."

"Ah." The bar owner glanced uncertainly from me to Lukas. "We checked the security cameras after I called you. The royal guard was here before Jesse arrived."

Lukas's scowl stayed in place. "That means nothing. He could have been waiting here for her."

"He wasn't." I relayed everything that had happened from the moment I saw Lewis Tate at the traffic light. Teg showed Lukas and the others the security footage, but this time he kept playing, showing me coming in and catching Tate.

"Nice moves," Conlan said when I shackled Tate and helped him up.

I didn't respond because my confrontation with the Texans started to play on the monitor. I stared at the red-haired girl, who moved with a fluid grace that didn't look real to me. When it got to the part where I grabbed Leah's foot and took her to the floor, I saw what Teg had seen. For those few seconds, I was moving twice as fast as I normally did.

I looked up from the monitor to find Lukas, Faolin, and Conlan watching me with odd expressions. "What?"

Faolin was the first to speak. "Your fighting has improved significantly since the night you fought the ogres."

"That happens when you train every day with a bunch of bullies."

He ignored the taunt. "You haven't shown that kind of improvement during training."

I lifted a shoulder. "I guess being outnumbered brings out the best in me."

Lukas broke his silence. "The Seelie guard didn't follow you here, but Orend said he was watching you. Is there any reason he would think you have knowledge of the ke'tain?"

I slanted a look at Teg, and Lukas said, "Orend knows about our search."

I thought about it. "As far as anyone knows, I'm just a bounty hunter who came here to catch a fugitive. Everyone heard me arguing with the other hunters about the bounty."

"I still don't like it," Lukas said. "The last thing you need is to draw their attention after what happened with your parents."

A cold knot formed in my stomach. "Maybe he didn't recognize me."

"How many young, red-haired, female bounty hunters are in New York?" Lukas asked.

"We have a lot of out-of-state hunters here now, and there could be a dozen redheads for all I know."

Lukas raised his eyebrows. I was grasping at straws, and we both knew it.

I almost let out an audible breath of relief when someone knocked on the door. Conlan opened it to admit Cynthia.

"Boss, there are two agents here to see you and Miss James," said the waitress, who didn't bat an eye at the sight of all the faeries.

"Send them in."

She nodded and stepped aside, and Agent Curry appeared in the doorway. To say he wasn't one of my favorite people was putting it mildly. He might be the person who had freed my parents and me from Rogin's basement, but I couldn't forget how he'd harassed me when he should have been searching for them. If he'd put that much effort into doing his job, we might have found my parents a lot sooner.

Unlike Cynthia, the agent did a little double take when he saw who was in the office. "Prince Vaerik, I did not expect to see you here."

"Agent Curry," Lukas said in a disinterested tone, giving me the impression I wasn't the only one who didn't care for the agent. Or maybe he was this way with all agents.

Curry turned to me. "Miss James, you have some information for us about a person of interest?"

"Yes." I took a step forward.

"You can talk in here," Lukas told Curry when the agent turned to leave the office. "Two of my men are searching the area for Tate. I will inform the Agency if we find him."

Curry frowned. "You have an interest in our fugitive?"

"I am interested in anything related to the ke'tain," Lukas said. "I am also interested in the member of the Seelie royal guard who was here tonight watching your fugitive."

The agent couldn't hide his shock. "The Seelie royal guard?"

"His name is Aibel, and he is one of Queen Anwyn's personal guard," Lukas said.

I'd heard that name before. The Seelie guard at Davian's had mentioned it to the queen.

Lukas sat on the edge of Teg's desk and crossed his arms. "As we are all aware of Seelie's involvement in the Jameses' abduction, I need not explain why my men and I will stay for this interview and then see Jesse safely home."

"I have my own vehicle, and I don't need an escort," I reminded him.

"You parked half a mile away and walked here. We will take you to it and follow you home."

The set of his jaw told me there was no use arguing with him. And to be honest, I didn't want to walk back to the Jeep with one of Queen Anwyn's men lurking in the area. I swallowed back my pride and let him have this one.

Satisfied, Lukas said, "Let's get started then."

15

"**C**an I pet your dog?"

I looked up from my phone at the little girl standing in front of me. She was cute, maybe eight or nine, and her hand was reaching for the plastic dog carrier at my feet.

"No!" I shoved her hand away before it touched the carrier.

She yanked her hand back, her face screwing up as her eyes filled with tears. A woman rushed over and shot me a death glare as she ushered the crying girl away.

I sank back into my seat, ignoring the disapproving looks from some of the other ferry passengers. They should be directing their glares at the parent. Who let her child walk up to a complete stranger and stick her fingers in an animal carrier containing God only knew what?

Right on cue, growls came from the carrier along with the sounds of fighting. The carrier rattled, and the people on either side of me leaned away from me. Unzipping my duffle bag, which sat next to the carrier, I pulled out a bag of coal and stuffed pieces of it through the wire mesh gate. Ten dirty, little gnome-like faces appeared as chubby hands snatched the coal from my fingers. Soon, the growling turned to crunching as the trows inside feasted on their treat.

Brushing coal dust off my hands, I let out a weary sigh. When Levi had called me this morning, asking me to do a high priority job, I'd had no idea I would be spending the better part of the day saving the Statue of Liberty from destruction.

Okay, maybe that was a *tiny* exaggeration, but I had saved it from extensive damage. Trows looked harmless enough until you saw them in action. The little critters had retractable claws as hard as diamonds, which they used to tunnel through rock, brick, stone, or concrete. Like termites, they could destroy a building's foundation, only they'd do it much faster.

In a city like New York, trows would be an absolute disaster, and there wasn't enough Fae power in the world to ward buildings against them. For that reason, they were banned from our realm. This lot had been brought to Liberty Island and set loose by some group protesting the recession. I wasn't sure what they hoped to gain by wreaking havoc on a national monument.

Thankfully, like most faeries, the little monsters were weakened by iron. A layer of iron mesh on the bottom of the carrier was all it took to prevent them from extending their claws and breaking free.

My phone vibrated, and I looked down at a text from Violet, who was still in LA. I didn't know how I was going to get used to us living on different coasts when she finally moved out west.

Lorelle wants us to meet up at Va'sha when I get back, she'd texted.

I smiled to myself. Violet had mentioned Lorelle at least once a day since meeting her at the Fae club, and it was clear my best friend was crushing hard on the faerie. I sent her a few kiss emojis, and she responded with a blushing one.

A foot struck the dog carrier, upsetting the trows, and I looked up at the man walking past my seat. He grunted an apology without a glance in my direction and headed for the stairs to the upper decks. I was about to go back to texting Violet when the man dropped something and bent to pick it up. As he straightened, I got a good look at his face.

You have got to be kidding me.

It was Lewis Tate.

After his narrow escape a week ago, I'd figured he was long gone from New York. Anyone resourceful enough to evade Lukas's men and the Agency while shackled would not be stupid enough to stick around. What was he doing on this ferry of all places? A fugitive from the Agency didn't come out of hiding to take a tour of Liberty Island.

I stood as soon as he disappeared from sight. Picking up my duffle bag and the dog carrier, I took them to the concession stand and asked one of the workers to hold them for me. She looked at me like I was nuts until I showed her my Agency ID.

"I'll be back as soon as I can," I told her as I turned for the stairs.

I ran up the stairs and slowed as I reached the top so I didn't draw attention to myself. The middle deck was only half-full, and a quick walk-through turned up no sign of Tate. He'd either continued to the top deck, or he'd slipped past me and gone downstairs. I headed for the stairs. I'd start at the top and work my way down if I had to, but I'd find him before we docked. He wasn't getting away from me this time.

I shivered in my lined leather jacket when I emerged onto the open top deck, where not even the afternoon sun could take the bite out of the river breeze. At least thirty passengers had braved the cold to enjoy the view, including several families huddled together with their children. I was glad for my scarf and cap as I searched the deck for Tate.

It didn't take me long to locate him standing at the front of the boat, facing the city as he talked on his phone. I had expected to find him with someone, but he appeared to be alone. It made no sense unless he'd met up with someone on the island. Odd location for a meetup, but what did I know about the behavior of a fugitive black market dealer?

I approached him quietly. When I was a few feet away, I could hear him talking, and I slowed to listen.

"I don't want to hear your excuses. Do you know what a risk I took coming here today to see you?" Pause. "You said you had a lead on who stole it." Pause. "No, it wasn't Brian. He's still in custody, and he would have spilled if he had it."

My pulse jumped. Was he talking about the ke'tain? It had been stolen from him before the raid?

He hunched his shoulders. "Screw Davian. My only way out of this mess is to find it and turn it in. And remember, if I go down, you go down."

Tate hung up and turned around, bringing us face-to-face. He stared at me warily but without a hint of recognition.

I reached up to pull down the scarf covering the lower part of my face. "You owe me a pair of shackles."

Panic flared in his eyes. "How do you keep finding me?"

I could have lied and told him I was just that good, but I went with the truth. "Luck."

"No one is that lucky." His eyes darted around as if he was expecting a dozen agents to materialize behind me. "It was Cecil, wasn't it? That bastard set me up."

"Is that who stood you up today?" I asked.

"As if you don't know."

I stuck my hands in my pockets, and my fingers touched the cool metal of the shackles there. "You'll be happy to hear that Cecil didn't rat you out. The Agency will be very interested in hearing about your business dealings with him, though."

"You can't take me in." He looked to the side as if he was contemplating jumping.

I took a step closer, ready to grab him if he made a move. "You'll freeze to death if you don't drown."

"Better than what the Agency or the faeries will do to me."

The sound of an engine reached me, and I glanced over his shoulder at a speedboat headed in our direction. I should have known someone like him would have a backup plan.

Without warning, Tate rushed me. He shoved me hard to the side, but I kept my balance, thanks to hours of training with Faolin. I tackled him, and we hit the deck, drawing gasps from the other passengers.

I wrestled with him for a minute before I was able to straddle him. People were standing now, and I flashed my ID at them. "Agency business. Nothing to worry about."

"Whoa!" A teenage boy said as I shackled one of Tate's wrists.

A girl's excited voice joined in. "So pretty!"

"What is that?" a man called.

I looked up and saw the people nearby were not looking at me. They were pointing and staring at something in the sky.

Turning my head to follow their gazes, I did a double take. The sky had darkened to twilight in a matter of seconds, and above us was the same undulating light display I'd witnessed from my bedroom window weeks ago. The river reflected the colorful lights, giving the illusion we were at the center of a magical dome. It was breathtaking, yet at the same time, it filled me with dread.

People held up their phones, recording the strange phenomenon. I was about to do the same when a flash of purple light lit up the deck. I jumped to my feet in time to see a bolt of purple lightning strike the surface of the river near the New Jersey side. Water erupted into the air as the electricity from the lightning streaked in our direction.

It reached the speedboat approaching us, and in the next second, the boat exploded. I hit the deck, and around me, people screamed. A roar filled the air as the lightning churned through the water toward us. Any second it would hit, and the ferry would suffer the same fate as the speedboat.

In the next instant, the noise was gone.

"Oh, thank God," said a man's shaky voice.

He had barely uttered the words when a powerful gust of wind slammed into the ferry. The boat tilted, knocking people off balance, and I lunged for Tate as he rolled away from me.

The ferry rocked violently, and I had to grab the rail with one hand to anchor us. A teenage boy in one of the seats closest to me threw up, making me gag. The wind carried away the smell, but my roiling stomach couldn't handle the sight of vomit.

I rose to my knees and peered over the side at the city moving past us, as the boat spun slowly from the force of the wind. From what I could see, the strange storm was centered over the river, and everything inside it was lit with an eerie purple glow. Above us, jagged lightning cut through the lights in the sky. I caught sight of a private tour boat and two smaller boats also caught in the storm with us, but they were too far away to see how they were faring.

One of the small boats suddenly vanished in the swells. I searched frantically for it, and it reappeared as the other one blinked out of sight.

The boats disappeared from view as our ferry continued its slow spin. The water around us grew choppier, and we began to dip and sway as it got steadily worse. The wind howled, but it sounded wrong. It was hollow, like what you would hear in a sea cave.

I pulled Tate up until he could grasp the rail. "Hold on," I yelled as cold spray hit us in the face.

A second later, the ferry pitched heavily to one side. It was all I could do to cling to the rail as passengers were thrown from their seats. More screams filled the air, and I watched in helpless horror as some people went over the side into the river.

The boat swung back to lurch in the other direction, tossing passengers around like rag dolls. A child's terrified scream rent the air, and I spotted a little boy clinging to the leg of a nearby seat, his legs dangling as the ferry tipped.

I let go of the rail and slid down the deck to the boy. My arm circled his small waist just as he lost his grip.

"Grab on to me," I shouted. I latched onto the metal seat bolted to the deck and braced my feet against the rail as the boat continued its downward swing. The boy's arms went around my neck, and his thin legs tightly squeezed my waist. I grasped the seat with my other hand and held on for dear life.

The ferry shuddered, and my feet lost purchase on the wet railing. Fear ratcheted through me as the boy and I dangled above the churning river. More people went over, but all I could focus on was us. I was a strong swimmer, but I knew from experience how cold that water was. Even if I managed to keep us on the surface, neither of us would survive long in the frigid temperature.

For the longest moment of my life, we were suspended with the ferry almost on one side. The boat groaned, and I was filled with the awful certainty that we were going under. My mind raced as I planned for what to do when we hit the water.

And then the boat dropped back to land in an upright position. It kept swaying from side to side, but it was no longer spinning. I rolled over to look up at the blue sky through my wet glasses. The storm was gone as if it had never happened.

I sat up with the boy clinging to me like we were fused together. His blond hair was plastered to his head, but other than that, he seemed okay. Around us, it was chaos. People cried and called out for each other, and some leaned over the rail, shouting names of those who had gone into the water. A blonde woman screamed for someone named Owen as she tried to climb over the rail. It took two men to hold her back.

"Mommy," the boy cried against my throat.

"Ma'am," I called to her.

She continued to wail, and it took several shouts to get her attention. When her eyes fixed on the boy in my arms, she let out a cry and ran to us.

"Owen!" She fell to her knees and pulled the boy to her. He released me to latch onto his mother as they sobbed together.

I moved to get up, and she reached out to grab my hand. "Thank you!"

I squeezed her hand and stood, unsteady on my feet. My left hand hurt, but I ignored it as I took in the scene around me. Couples held each other, and parents comforted their frightened children. A lot of the passengers sported cuts, and a few were more banged up. One man lay on the deck with his leg at an odd angle, and several others were cradling their arms.

The sound of engines drew my attention to the dozens of harbor patrol boats speeding toward us. Half veered toward the other vessels that had been caught in the storm, and others surrounded us. One boat stopped, and the people on board pulled someone from the water.

A somber silence fell over the deck as we watched harbor patrol searching the river for survivors. How many had gone into the water? How many would not come out alive? Those of us onboard might have some injuries, but we were the lucky ones.

The captain's voice came over the speaker to tell us we would be at the ferry terminal in less than ten minutes. He requested that passengers try to stay seated for the duration of the ride. Emergency personnel would be waiting for us to see to anyone injured in the storm.

It was then that I remembered Tate. I ran to where I'd left him, but he was gone. He'd either fallen overboard, or he'd somehow made it downstairs.

A teenage boy with a bloody lip waved to catch my eye. "If you're looking for the guy you shackled, I think he went down below."

"Thanks."

I ran to the stairs. When I reached the middle deck, a ferry employee with a gash on his forehead stopped me.

"Miss, you need to sit down until we dock."

I showed him my ID. "I'll sit as soon as I find the man I was taking in."

He nodded and let me pass. I didn't bother to search this deck because Tate would have gone to the bottom deck. It was his only way off the boat when we docked.

The ferry was slowing its approach by the time I found Tate huddled with some other passengers, wearing a hooded parka he must have stolen from someone. He was pretty banged up, and he didn't put up a fight when I shackled his other wrist. It was a good thing because I wasn't sure I had the energy to chase him down.

Instead of docking at the slip where we'd boarded, the ferry pulled into the Whitehall Terminal. EMTs and terminal personnel came on board to take care of the injured and to make sure people didn't trample each other trying to disembark.

I reached for my phone to check it while I waited, only to discover it was gone. It must have fallen out of my pocket when the ferry had almost capsized. I sighed. Better the phone than me.

An EMT came to check on Tate and me, telling me it was procedure when I argued that I had no injuries. I suspected I had a mild sprain in my left wrist, but I didn't tell her that and risk being sent to the ER for something so minor.

"This one might have some fractured ribs and a concussion," she said after she'd looked Tate over. "He'll need to go to the hospital."

"Do you have a phone?" I asked her. "I lost mine, and I need to call the Agency to tell them to meet us there."

"No need. The terminal is swarming with agents." She pulled out a radio and gave me a questioning look.

"Tell them there's a bounty hunter with you, who has Lewis Tate in her custody."

She relayed the message to someone along with our location. Within two minutes, we were surrounded by four agents. Three of them escorted Tate off the boat while the fourth went with me to retrieve my duffle bag and the dog carrier from the harried concession stand employee.

I was never so happy in my life to get off a boat. In the terminal, I was taken aside by the agents who wanted my account of the storm and Tate's capture. They were especially interested when I mentioned Tate was supposed to meet with Cecil Hunt, who had stood him up. The lawyer was a slippery one if he'd been able to evade arrest by the Agency this long. I had a feeling that was about to end. Lewis Tate would give them whatever they wanted to cut a deal for himself.

It was almost two hours after I left the ferry that I was finally allowed to exit the terminal. Outside, I was confronted by a mob of reporters shouting questions at anyone who left the building. I put my head down and pushed through them. I just wanted to get out of there.

My Agency ID had secured me parking at the Coast Guard building next door, and I trudged past police cars, ambulances, and curious onlookers. My movements were sluggish when I climbed into the Jeep, and my hands shook so much all I could do was grip the steering wheel. I stared blindly out the windshield as images flashed through my mind. The one that played over and over was of the rescue boats pulling people from the water. How was I sitting here warm and safe while others might have lost their lives tonight?

Someone knocked on my window, and I looked into the concerned eyes of a police officer. I lowered the window, and it wasn't until the cold air hit my wet cheeks that I realized I was crying.

"Are you okay, Miss?" the older man asked kindly.

Nodding, I blotted away the tears. "I just...needed a minute."

Understanding lit his eyes. "You were on the ferry?"

"Yes."

He rested his arm on the door. "Is there anyone you can call to come get you?"

I didn't know why my first thought was of Lukas. I shook my head and showed the officer my Agency ID. "I have a carrier full of trows I need to take to the Plaza before I go home. I promise I'm okay to drive."

"Alright. You drive safely. We're getting reports of traffic accidents all over the city. Guess everyone was too busy looking up at the lights in the sky to watch where they were going."

"I will, thanks." I raised the window as he walked away. Talking to him had calmed my frazzled nerves, and I felt better as I started the Jeep.

The police officer hadn't been kidding about the traffic. There was chaos all over Manhattan, making the drive to Queens take twice as long as it normally would. At the Plaza, I ran into Bruce, Trey, and some other hunters, who asked a ton of questions when they found I'd been on the ferry. I answered a few of them and made my escape. All I wanted was a shower, food, and sleep. Anything else could wait until tomorrow.

Hello?" *I called as I walked down the hallway dimly lit by two flickering wall sconces. Stumbling on the uneven floor, I braced a hand against the cold stone wall to steady myself and felt a mild current of energy go through me. What a strange place this was.*

I entered a large, round room as lightning lit up the sky above the glass domed ceiling. Before I could get a good look at the room, it disappeared, and I was outdoors, standing on top of a hill overlooking the ocean. I turned in a full circle and discovered I was on a small rocky island with little vegetation and no mainland in sight.

Lightning flashed again and raced across the sky. Only it didn't look like normal lightning. Instead of branching out or zigzagging, it moved in a straight line, like a knife cutting through the very fabric of the sky. And it was bright green instead of white.

I gasped as cold rain hit me, plastering my hair to my head and soaking my pajamas in seconds. Out of nowhere, a strong wind picked me up and blew me out to sea. I looked down at the water as I flew over it, surprised to see it was calm, despite the storm raging overhead.

I blinked, and suddenly, I was no longer flying. I found myself standing at the mouth of a wide valley, surrounded on three sides by a mountain and walls of glassy, black rock. Lights dotted the mountain and the valley floor, telling me people lived here.

Overhead, the strange green lightning coalesced into an undulating display of colored lights above the valley. The air around me sizzled with static electricity, making my hair fly out in all directions.

A terrible roaring filled the air, forcing me to cover my ears. I watched with a growing sense of dread as a tear formed in the sky above the mountain. I ran toward the mountain, shouting a warning to the inhabitants, but I was too far away.

The world went deathly quiet as if all sound had been sucked from it. Then an explosion rocked the air, and the mountain began to crumble. My scream was cut short when the shock wave hit me, slamming me into the ground. I lay there unable to move and gasping for air as the ringing in my ears blocked out the distant screams.

"Jesse, wake up."

I opened my eyes and blinked to focus. The shadows above me took the shape of a person, and I let out a small scream as I rolled off the couch. I tried to stand, but I was wrapped up in my quilt like a burrito. I would have crashed into the coffee table if the stranger's hands hadn't caught me.

"Let me go." I pushed away from my rescuer, and surprisingly, they released me. Heart pounding, I fell back on the couch and stared up into turbulent blue eyes. "What the hell, Lukas?"

"Why haven't you returned my calls?" he demanded.

"What?" I asked dumbly, trying to slow my racing heart.

He let out an impatient breath. "I've been calling you all evening since we saw you on the news."

I rubbed my eyes, confused. "I was on the news?"

"You were leaving the ferry terminal. They interviewed a woman who said you saved her son's life. And we heard from the Agency that you captured Lewis Tate on the ferry." His voice grew harsher. "What the hell happened on that boat, and why did you go after Tate alone?"

I shoved the quilt off me and stood, poking him in the chest. "Don't take that tone with me. Only my parents get to talk to me like that, and you aren't either of them."

His eyes widened at my outburst.

I continued. "If you ask nicely, I'll tell you why I was there...after you tell me how you got into my apartment."

"I picked your locks," he said as if it was no big deal.

"And the ward?" The fact that he'd passed through the ward without an invitation this time confirmed Tennin's suspicion that Lukas had made it. But I wanted to hear him say it.

"I created it."

The bottled-up anger drained from me. "Why?"

He smiled ruefully. "I wanted you to be safe, and it was the least I could do after the way I treated you."

"And the ward on my parents?"

"I thought they might still be in danger, and it would kill you if anything happened to them." He raked a hand through his hair. "I knew you wouldn't let me near them, so I did it when you left their room."

I dropped back down to the couch. "It *was* you I saw leaving their hospital room."

"Yes."

"Thank you," I said thickly. If he hadn't put that ward on them, they might have been taken again or killed during the security breach at the hospital.

"I didn't do it to win your gratitude, Jesse." He sat beside me on the couch. "You owe me nothing. I hope someday you can forgive me for what I did to you, but I don't expect it."

The self-recrimination in his eyes was too much. I looked away so I didn't have to see it.

"All I ask is that you hear me out. Will you do that?"

I nodded. Part of me was afraid to hear him voice his reasons for what he'd done, but another part knew I'd never fully be able to let go of my hurt until I did.

"I was taught from a young age to trust only those in my inner circle, so I kept everyone outside of it at a distance. And then I met you. I won't lie and say my offer to help you find your parents wasn't for selfish reasons, but I also couldn't help but admire your courage and your unwavering belief that your parents were alive. Before I knew it, you had somehow slipped between my defenses, and I felt this need to protect you."

I swung my gaze back to his. "I didn't do that to –"

A smile touched his lips. "I did it to myself. I arrogantly believed I could choose whom I cared for, but you proved me wrong, and that made me question myself – and you. It's a sad excuse but the only reason I can offer for why I reacted the way I did that day. I've always prided myself on being adept at reading people and recognizing deceit, but I let myself be tricked so easily into believing the worst of you. I was too blinded by my anger to see the truth until it was too late."

"When Faris woke up." My chest squeezed tighter with each word of his admission.

"No. I knew it before then. When you yelled at me and said you had trusted me, I heard it in your voice, and I saw the complete look of betrayal on your face. I had never hated myself until that moment. I wanted to strike that elf down and take you away from there, but there was more at stake than your forgiveness."

"Faris," I whispered. Lukas's friend had been in bad shape, and his life had been more important than any friendship we'd formed. I would have done the same for my parents.

"There was nothing I could have done for Faris that Faolin couldn't. What I could do was let Havas think he'd gotten away with his plan and lead us to the people behind all of it. We left, but we didn't go far. We stayed to watch the house – and you."

My breath caught. He'd stayed?

"What we didn't expect was for the Agency to show up a few hours later. Or that someone would create a portal inside the house to help Havas escape under our noses."

I couldn't speak. I was still processing the fact that he hadn't left me there alone. All this time, I'd thought he'd walked away as if I were nothing to him. I bowed my head so he couldn't see the tears stinging my eyes.

"I'm sorry I hurt you, Jesse," he said quietly. "I've wanted to tell you this for weeks, but you were so angry, and you had every right to be. The Faerie courts have brought your family nothing but pain. I've asked myself many times if I should let you go on hating me because you would be better off without me in your life."

I stared blindly at the floor. How did I respond to that? I'd told myself I didn't want or care about an apology from him, but I'd been wrong. So wrong.

"You don't have to say anything. You don't owe me anything," Lukas said when I'd been silent too long. His hand appeared in my line of vision and picked up one of mine. His touch was gentle, but it was the hand I'd hurt on the ferry, and I jerked involuntarily.

He stilled, and then his fingers pushed up the sleeve of my sweater to reveal the compression bandage I'd wrapped around my wrist. "You're hurt."

"It's nothing, only a sprain." I tried to tug my hand from his, but he refused to release it.

"Did you see a doctor?" He rubbed his thumb over the back of my hand.

I tried to ignore the warm tingle that radiated up my arm. "An EMT checked me out before I left the ferry."

He took my hand in both of his and began to gently massage it. "Will you tell me what happened out there?"

Sensations flooded me. There was something so intimate about the act that it made me forget everything but those strong, warm fingers.

"Jesse?"

I swallowed. "I'm surprised you don't already know everything that happened."

"Faolin read the Agency report, but I want to hear it from you. How did you know Lewis Tate was going to be on the ferry?"

"I didn't know." I told him about the trow job, Tate, and the storm. By the time I finished, my chest felt like it was in a vise. "They said on the news that six people drowned. Two of them were children."

"I heard that, too."

Despite my best efforts, a tear leaked out, followed by another. I angrily swiped them away.

Lukas let go of my hand. The next thing I knew, his arms were around me, my head tucked under his chin. "Let it out," he ordered softly.

"I c-can't."

His hand rubbed soothing circles on my back. "Crying doesn't make you weak, *mi'calaech*. Holding in your pain will do you more harm."

I didn't know if it was his touch or his words that did it, but I let the tears come. I cried for the people who had died and for the children whose terrified screams would haunt my dreams.

Lukas made no move to let me go after the tears stopped. I had to force myself to pull away from the warm comfort of his arms. I felt drained, but in a good way. He was right. Letting it all out made me feel lighter and in control of my emotions again.

His eyes searched my face. "Feel better?"

"Yes." I tucked my hair behind my ears, not caring that I must look a mess. Now that I was feeling more like myself, it was time to get some answers. "What was that storm? I asked the agents about it, and they clammed up, as if I couldn't tell it was Fae-related."

Lukas exhaled slowly like someone about to deliver bad news. "There is a weakness in the barrier between our realms, and the convergence of both atmospheres caused the storm."

"But there are portals opening between our realms every day, and they don't cause problems. And what about the Great Rift? I don't remember hearing about strange storms when that happened."

"Portals are opened by magic that shields this world," he explained. "And the rift didn't cause storms because Faerie was strong enough to maintain the balance between the realms until the rift was fixed."

"It *was* strong enough?"

"When Aedhna created our realm, she put her energy into every living thing there." He placed his hand against his chest. "The magic in each of us comes from her, and that's why we have to return to Faerie to restore it. Otherwise, we'd never be able to stand exposure to the iron in this world."

"What does that have to do with the storms?" I asked.

He smiled. "I'm getting to that. Since the Great Rift, thousands of faeries have come to live in this realm. There is a lot of Fae magic in your world where there was once none, and that has upset the balance between our worlds. Faerie is still the stronger realm, but by a lesser margin than before. What that means is that Faerie is unable to fully contain its energy when there is a weakness in the barrier, and some of the energy is leaking into this one. What you witnessed tonight was the result of one of those leaks."

That was only a leak? "Can it be fixed?"

"The weakness was caused by the removal of the ke'tain from Faerie," he said. "The ke'tain has so much power that it has tipped the balance of magic. Only its return will stop the damage."

"What happens if you don't find it?"

Lukas's lips formed a grim line. "More weak spots will form, and the storms will become more frequent and severe. Eventually, the barrier could break down completely, and our worlds will either merge or be destroyed. No one knows."

It felt like all the warmth had been sucked from the room. "And the Agency knows all of this?"

"Yes. They decided it's in the best interest of everyone not to share this information with the public. It would only cause a panic and make it harder for us to find the ke'tain. The Agency believed that putting a large bounty on the ke'tain would be enough incentive for bounty hunters to search for it without asking too many questions."

I shook my head angrily. "Money isn't all we care about. They should have told us the truth because we deserve to know what's at stake if the ke'tain isn't found."

"I agree, but the Agency has its own way of doing things." Lukas's expression said he had about as much faith in their abilities as I did. "Which is why we are doing our own search, as well as working with them."

"Are you close to finding it?" I rubbed my arms, trying not to think about the alternative.

He reached for the quilt that had fallen to the floor and pulled it up to cover me. "We know it's in New York because the weakness in the barrier is here. But in a city this big, it could be anywhere. A sensor would have to get within ten feet of the ke'tain to detect it."

I burrowed beneath the quilt. "Is there any way to create a stronger sensor, one that could cover a bigger distance?"

"We tried that, but there's too much iron here to get a reading. In addition to the sensors handed out to the hunters, there are hundreds of agents and faeries with sensors assigned to grids of the city. All they do is walk the streets and enter buildings, trying to pick up the ke'tain's signature."

A sinking feeling filled me. "The ke'tain is so small it could be anywhere. If someone is smart enough to hide it in iron, it'll never be found."

"The sensors are a last resort. I've been focused on who had the means to remove the ke'tain from the temple and tracing their activity here. I know Queen Anwyn is behind it, but her personal guards are too good at covering their tracks. I also know someone in this realm was helping them, and I've narrowed it down to several people. Davian Woods is one of them, but he's smart and elusive." Lukas smiled. "Or he was until he unwittingly invited a bounty hunter into his home."

I shrugged. "No one ever believes I'm a hunter when I tell them. It finally worked to my advantage."

"You did what neither I nor the Agency could do. Thanks to you, I know about Davian's connection to Tate and the Seelie guard."

Warmth filled my chest. "Are you admitting I did a good job?"

"Yes," he said without hesitation. "But I hope you see Davian Woods is not someone to cross, especially now that we know he's working with the queen."

"I do, but if I'd known that before, I still would have gone to the party."

"Because of your parents," he said.

"Yes." I pulled my knees up to my chest and wrapped my arms around them. "There was a security breach at the hospital last month. A faerie tried to get to my parents but couldn't."

"I know. I can tell when another faerie tries to get past my ward."

"Oh." I should have known that after Conlan had set up a ward on my apartment to alert them when there was a break-in.

Lukas's eyes held mine. "Your parents are safe, Jesse. They've been under my protection since they were taken from Havas's house, and I won't let anyone harm them."

I could only nod because my throat was getting tight again. I'd been through an emotional wringer today, and it clearly wasn't done with me yet.

His gaze went to the photos of my family on the mantle. "Do your parents know what you went through to bring them home?"

"Not all of it. I'm going to tell them when they can handle it." I toyed with the frayed edge of the blanket. "Can I ask you something?"

"Yes."

"If Queen Anwyn is behind the missing ke'tain, why would she take it and risk destroying your world?"

He raked a hand through his hair. "Honestly, I don't know. For the last twenty years, Anwyn has been pushing to bring all faeries home and seal the barrier between our worlds. There is a small faction in Faerie that believes humans are inferior to us, but she's the most vocal about maintaining the purity of our realm. If anything, she wants to preserve our way of life, not destroy it."

My lip curled at his description of the Seelie queen. "If she dislikes us so much, why would she let Prince Rhys come here?"

"She allows it because the one thing she cares about above all else is her son, and she can deny him nothing. It's become a rite of passage for faeries coming of age to spend time in your world. Prince Rhys wanted to experience the human world, and his mother would do anything to make him happy."

"So, what you're saying is that he's spoiled rotten and gets whatever he wants." One corner of my mouth quirked. "Are all faerie princes pampered like that?"

Lukas smiled, and it set off butterflies in my belly. "My father has very different ideas about how to raise an heir. When I was a boy, he chose the cousins who would become my personal guard, and we trained together from that day. Whatever challenge they faced, I faced along with them. When one of us was disciplined for mischief, the six of us shared the same punishment."

I tried to imagine him and the others, especially Faolin, as mischievous boys but couldn't. "Does that mean you had to run up and down the mountains, too?"

Laughter rumbled from him. "We made a game of it. Whoever made it the longest without losing their last meal was the winner."

"Let me guess, Faolin excelled at that game."

"He did." Lukas didn't hide his smirk. "He said you performed tolerably well on the stairs."

I made a face. "High praise."

"From him it is. Be grateful there are no mountains here."

"I think I can safely say I won't go anywhere near a mountain with him." I shifted so my legs were tucked under me, feeling at ease with Lukas for the first time since that awful day at Rogin's. It felt surreal being here with him like this after all that had happened.

Something clattered in the bathroom, and he shot to his feet.

"It's Gus," I said before he could go investigate.

Lukas's brow furrowed. "Gus?"

"He's a drakkan. He goes in and out through the bathroom window."

"You have a drakkan?" Lukas shot me a look of amused disbelief.

"It's more like he has me." I sighed. "He flew into my Jeep, and I brought him home to fix his wing. Now he refuses to leave."

As if he'd heard me, Gus strutted into the living room. He took one look at Lukas and growled unhappily. Sticking his head under the coffee table, he reappeared with the football chew toy I'd bought him and stalked off down the hall again.

I grinned. "I don't think he likes you, but don't take it personally. Gus is a bit ornery, and I'm pretty sure he doesn't even like me."

"I'm surprised he comes back." Lukas stared after the drakkan. "Drakkans are not domestic. In Faerie, they are fierce creatures that guard the borders of Unseelie."

A laugh slipped from me at the thought of Gus guarding anything besides his food dish. I'd seen feral cats that were scarier than he was.

Lukas sat and smiled at me. "It's good to hear you laugh again."

My heart gave a little flutter when our eyes met, and I was suddenly very aware of how close he was. I rubbed my lips together, and his gaze dipped to them for a second. Was I imagining that his eyes had grown a shade darker?

He reached toward me, and air lodged in my throat when his hand grazed my ear. He lifted a lock of my hair, curling it around one of his fingers and giving it a playful tug that fired off every nerve ending in my body.

"Lukas," I whispered. I wanted to ask him what he was doing, but my brain short-circuited when his hand left my hair to cup my face.

His heated gaze locked with mine. He leaned in until only inches separated us, and I was overcome with a feeling of déjà vu. I lifted a hand and laid it against his chest as if it belonged there. He responded by taking my arm and placing it around his neck. A tiny shiver went through him as my fingers touched the soft hair at the back of his head.

And then his hand was slipping behind my neck. His mouth brushed mine, setting off explosions in my belly as he whispered my name against my lips. I parted them, and he needed no further invitation. His tongue swept inside, and he claimed my mouth with a fierce tenderness. I was dizzy and panting when he pulled back.

I murmured a protest, but he had no intention of stopping. His head dipped again, and he took my mouth in another searing kiss that wiped out all conscious thought. I was drowning in his touch and the sensations flooding me, and all I knew was I wanted more.

I was barely aware of being lifted until I was suddenly straddling his lap. I came up onto my knees and took his face in my hands as I fused my lips to his. He surrendered control of the kiss, choosing instead to slide his warm hands down to cup my backside and hold me against him.

He pulled out of the kiss to move his mouth down the column of my throat. "*Mi'calaech,*" he said huskily, the word sounding almost like a plea. In that moment, I would have given him anything he asked of me.

The bathroom window slammed, and it was like a spell had been shattered. Lukas went still, and for a minute, the only sound in the room was our ragged breathing. He leaned his head back against the couch with his eyes closed as if he couldn't look at me.

A different kind of heat suffused me, and I slid off his lap with as much dignity as I could muster. The fact that he didn't try to stop me said it all. Needing to put space between us, I went to sit in the chair. I looked over at him and found him watching me with a sad expression that made my chest hurt.

"Jesse –"

"I think you should leave," I said, proud of how steady my voice was despite the emotions raging inside me.

Lukas moved to the edge of the couch but didn't get up. "I will if you want me to, but not like this."

I clasped my hands in my lap. "It was only a kiss. These things happen, and you don't need to explain anything."

"It was more than just a kiss," he said gruffly. "And I stopped it because of how much I want it, not because I don't."

Something clicked in my mind, like a door I didn't know existed had opened. I stared at him as memories poured out. He and I were in my bedroom, and he was kneeling before me.

"But I like the way you kiss me. Will you do it again when I am myself?"

"No, mi'calaech. But not because I don't want to."

I put a hand over my mouth as that night came back to me. Most of it was out of focus, like a dream you can't recall exactly. But the kiss I remembered with crystal clarity.

"We kissed the night I had a fever. Why didn't you tell me?"

He rubbed his jaw. "Because it shouldn't have happened, and it was better if you didn't remember it."

I swallowed back the hurt his answer caused. "Then why did you kiss me again?"

"A moment of weakness," he admitted.

"Oh." I wished I had an eloquent response, but there didn't seem to be one for when someone kissed you by mistake.

"I shouldn't have kissed you because I knew I wouldn't want to stop at one." He released a harsh breath. "You know there can be no future for us. I care about you, Jesse, and I won't treat you like some passing affair. You deserve more than that."

He was right, but that didn't make the words easier to hear. The moment I had started to fall for him, I'd known it would only lead to heartache because human-faerie relationships could not work. Jackson Chase and Princess Nerissa had known that, and rather than be apart, they had risked everything. He'd paid for it with his life.

It would have been better if Lukas and I hadn't reconciled our differences. At least when I'd been angry with him, I had been able to turn off the other feelings. And I'd had no idea what it felt like to kiss him.

I was trying to think of how to respond when a commotion erupted outside the apartment, followed by Maurice's raised voice. "You have no authority here or any right to keep me from her."

"Not again." I jumped up and ran to the door. Yanking it open, I found my furious godfather looking ready to throw down against Iian and Kerr, who stood with their backs to my door.

Relief filled Maurice's eyes when he saw me. "Jesse, thank God. I heard you were on the ferry in that storm."

"I was, but I'm okay." I pushed between Iian and Kerr, who shifted to let me pass.

Maurice hugged me. "Girl, I think I lost ten years off my life in the last hour. Why aren't you answering your phone?"

"I lost it on the ferry." I pulled back to look at him. "Why didn't you call the land line?"

"Didn't think to." He narrowed his eyes at the faeries behind me. "It's a bit late for visitors, isn't it?"

"They came by to check on me. They were just leaving."

"Get some rest, Jesse." Lukas's voice gave away nothing of what had happened between us a few minutes ago. "You can resume training in a few days."

I made myself turn to face him. Gone was the person who had kissed me until I'd almost forgotten my own name. Back was Prince Vaerik in all his cool authority, and the distance between us could be measured in miles, not feet. He smiled, but it was nothing like the one he'd given me right before he'd kissed me. It told me there would be no repeat of tonight.

"Thanks for stopping by," I said pleasantly, earning strange looks from Iian and Kerr. Could they tell something had happened between Lukas and me? The tips of my ears grew warm. I was so ready for this day to be over.

"Training?" Maurice asked after the faeries had disappeared around the second-floor landing.

"It's mostly conditioning," I said tiredly, entering the apartment.

He followed me. "With the Unseelie royal guard?"

"You think I should stop?" Part of me wanted him to say yes, to tell me Mom and Dad would not approve. Anything to give me an excuse not to go back.

"Hell, no." He looked at me like I'd lost my mind. "I'm not thrilled about them being in your apartment, but you don't pass up an opportunity like that." He paused. "As long as they don't cross any lines."

I barked a laugh and turned toward the kitchen. "You have nothing to worry about there." *At least, not anymore.*

16

"Finch, Aisla, I'm going out for a bit," I called to the tree house as I walked past the living room.

Finch whistled, and I looked up.

You said you wouldn't work today, he signed.

"I'm not. I need to get a new phone."

Running light errands was all I'd be doing for the next few days because I couldn't hunt or train with a sprained wrist. I wasn't used to having so much free time on my hands. It figured that Violet would be in California when I finally had time to hang out.

Can you get some more yikkas for Aisla? Finch asked.

"I'll stop by the Fae market on the way home." Aisla ate the same fruits and berries he did, but her favorite food was a Fae fruit called a yikka that her captors had fed her.

I grabbed my keys and left, running lightly down the stairs. Reaching the bottom floor, I came up short at the sight of the six faeries, who seemed to take up all the space in the small lobby. The two blond faeries at the front of the group assessed me with cold, unfriendly eyes. Fear gripped me, and I tensed, ready to flee back to the safety of my apartment.

"Jesse," said a voice as the crown prince of Seelie pushed past his guard to stand before me.

"Prince Rhys. What...are you doing here?" I asked stupidly, even though it was obvious he was there to see me. What other reason could the Seelie prince have for being in my building?

His smile was almost contrite. "I am sorry for coming unannounced. I've wanted to call on you since I saw you at Va'sha last month, but I have been out of town. And then this morning, I saw the news story about the terrible ferry accident, and there you were on the television. It was like a sign from Aedhna telling me I had to come see you today."

My mouth opened, but no words came out. How did you respond to something like that?

The main door swung inward, and Gorn entered the building. He saw us and froze, his dark eyes wide.

"What is your business here, dwarf?" one of the blond faeries demanded.

Gorn's terrified eyes flitted from the faeries to me. My anger flared. This was his home, and he should be allowed to come and go as he pleased without fear.

I went to stand beside Gorn and faced the group. Prince Rhys's men scared me but not enough to keep me silent. "I'm going to ask that you not harass or intimidate people in my building. Gorn is one of my tenants, but even if he wasn't, you have no right to question his presence here."

The faerie who had spoken sneered at me. "We have every right to detain and question anyone who might pose a threat to our prince."

His statement brought back memories of the night Faolin had forced me to go to Lukas's for questioning. I'd been too overwhelmed back then to challenge them, but a lot had changed since that night.

I wasn't familiar with every single aspect of the Fae treaties, but I knew this faerie was full of BS. "You have the authority to intercept anyone who poses a *credible* threat and to use force if the prince comes under attack. You are not allowed to detain, interrogate, or harm people just for being in his vicinity. You also have no right to enter a private residence and threaten its occupants."

The five guards glared at me, and it was all I could do not to turn tail and run. But if I couldn't stand up to them in my own building, I might as well go hide in my room for the rest of my life.

Prince Rhys clapped. "Well said."

"Thank you." I looked at Gorn and gave him a reassuring smile. "I'll see you later."

The dwarf nodded jerkily and hurried to his door. He cast a furtive glance in our direction before he disappeared inside.

A door on the other side of the lobby opened, and we all turned to face my scowling eighty-year-old neighbor. Mrs. Russo's unnaturally red hair was in large curlers, and she wore a frayed, mint green housecoat that should have become cleaning rags a decade ago. Perched on her nose were rhine-stone cat-eye glasses that she only wore when she was watching TV.

"What is all this racket?" she demanded with the imperiousness of a queen. "I'm trying to enjoy my soap, and I can't hear a darn thing over all this yabbering."

The faeries stared at her, not knowing what to make of this odd, little creature who dared to question them. No one aged physically in Faerie, and they'd probably never encountered a crotchety old person, let alone one as colorful as my neighbor.

Mrs. Russo eyed them over the tops of her glasses. "Well?" she barked. "I know you can speak, so out with it."

My lips twitched, and I pressed them together to hold back a laugh.

"My apologies, dear lady." The prince stepped forward and bowed to the old woman. "I am Prince Rhys of Seelie, and I humbly beg your pardon for disturbing your daily ablution."

She leaned away from him as if he'd revealed he was an alien. Prince Rhys glanced around, clearly confused by her reaction.

I couldn't contain it any longer, and I doubled over laughing. I didn't care that everyone in the room was staring at me like I'd lost my mind. I let the laughter spill from me, taking with it all the tension of the last twenty-four hours.

"What have you done to Jesse?" Mrs. Russo asked shrilly. She pointed a bony finger at the prince. "Did you use some of that faerie hocus pocus to addle her brain?"

"I..." Prince Rhys said helplessly, and I gave in to another fit of laughter.

It took a supreme effort to regain my composure. I wiped under my eyes and went to Mrs. Russo to assure her I was okay. Facing Prince Rhys, I said, "A soap is a kind of TV show. She wasn't washing herself."

"I see," he replied, but his furrowed brow told me he didn't.

I looked at my elderly neighbor. "No one glamoured me. I just needed a good laugh."

She smiled and patted my arm. "If anyone deserves a laugh these days, it's you."

"I'm sorry we made you miss your soap."

"Don't worry about it. It's recorded from yesterday, so I'm not missing anything." She tossed an unimpressed look at the prince and his men. "Use your inside voices next time you visit." Not waiting for a response, she entered her apartment and shut the door with a resounding click.

The faeries stared silently at the door, no doubt trying to figure out what the hell had just happened. Prince Rhys was the first to speak. "Are all your elders like that?"

"No." I chuckled. "Mrs. Russo is one of a kind."

"She is quite interesting." He turned to me. "I'm sorry. My intention in coming here was not to cause trouble for you."

"Why exactly are you here?"

He smiled sheepishly. "I didn't give you the best impression of me at Va'sha, and I wanted to show you I'm not that bad. I fear this has not helped my cause."

"Your cause?" I stuck my hands in my coat pockets to cover the awkwardness settling over me.

He must have seen something in my expression because he rushed to say, "I'm not here looking for anything but friendship."

I raised my eyebrows. "There are millions of people who would kill to be your friend. Why me?"

"I don't know." He frowned, looking as confused as I felt. "Maybe because you're one of the few humans I've met who doesn't want anything from me. It's refreshing."

One of his men scoffed, but prince Rhys ignored it. "Whatever the reason, I want to get to know you better, and I'd be honored if you would consent to dine with me."

My first instinct was to say no. He was the son of the Seelie queen, and I should be putting as much distance as possible between him and me.

On the other hand, this might be an opportunity to learn more about Queen Anwyn, and maybe gain some insight into why she would want the ke'tain. I was in a unique position. I had access to the one person who knew her better than anyone else. Lukas would not be happy about it, but if it helped him find the ke'tain, how could I not do it?

"I'll have lunch with you," I said. "Do you have a favorite restaurant?"

His smile was almost blinding. "Why don't you pick a place?"

"Your Highness..." one of his men started to object, but Prince Rhys waved him off.

I considered the options, preferring to stay close to home. "My favorite Vietnamese restaurant is not far from here. Have you tried Vietnamese?"

"Yes. They have a soup that is similar to one of my favorite dishes at home."

I smiled. "Pho. I love it, too."

"It's settled then. My men will drive us there."

"If you don't mind, I'll drive myself." At his questioning look, I said, "I have some errands to run afterward, and it will save me the time of coming home to get my car."

Prince Rhys looked ready to protest, but his guards' expressions said they preferred this arrangement. I gave them the name and address of the restaurant and ushered them out of the building before he could say anything.

I wasn't surprised when they stayed behind me all the way to the restaurant. The prince probably wanted to make sure I didn't change my mind and take off. I wasn't comfortable with his interest in me, even if it was platonic, but I couldn't think of any way to discourage him without offending him. Hopefully, he'd see today that there was nothing particularly interesting about me, and he'd move on to someone else.

We beat the lunch rush, so the restaurant wasn't busy when we arrived. The hostess fell all over herself when she saw the prince, and she ushered us to a booth at the back of the restaurant. Two of his men accompanied us, and the other three took up stations near the door. At least I wouldn't have all five of them glaring at me over lunch.

I removed my coat, and Prince Rhys's eyes fell on the wrap around my wrist. "Is that from the ferry accident?"

"It's only a sprain." I pulled down the sleeve of my sweater to cover it. "I'll be good as new in a few days."

Concern filled his eyes. "My personal physician travels with me. If you will permit me, I will have her come to your home and tend to your injury."

I smiled. "You're very kind to offer, but really, it's nothing. I've gotten much worse bruises than this on some of my jobs."

A waiter approached us, looking terrified of the two guards standing beside the booth. He filled our water glasses and took our orders before scurrying away.

"Tell me, how does someone so young become a bounty hunter," Prince Rhys asked.

I sipped my water. "Most hunters start out when they finish high school. Usually, they have family in the business, and they follow in their footsteps instead of going to college." I didn't say that some of them would have preferred college, but like me, they couldn't afford it.

"And whose footsteps are you following?"

I debated how much to tell him, and then it occurred to me that his men had most likely done a thorough background check on me by now. They would know if I spoke the truth.

"My parents. They're the best in the business," I said proudly.

"Is that so?" He leaned in. "Tell me about them."

His boyish eagerness was impossible to resist. As we ate, I told him how my parents started hunting, and I shared stories about some of their bigger jobs. He listened intently and interrupted me often with questions. I didn't mind because I loved talking about my parents' work.

"I would love to meet them," he said earnestly.

One of his men shifted restlessly. I didn't need to look at the guard's face to know he did not like this turn in the conversation.

"They can't have visitors right now."

Prince Rhys's shoulders drooped. "Are they working on a big job?"

I twisted the napkin on my lap. "No. They're in a treatment facility. They were tracking down a goren dealer in November, and he locked them up and gave them the drug."

The prince's face registered his anger as he listened to the version of the story that had been released to the public. For my family's safety, the Agency had not mentioned the Seelie royal guard's involvement in my parents' disappearance.

"I'm so sorry that happened to them," he said, sounding sincere. "I haven't seen the effects of goren on humans, but I've heard it can be quite devastating."

I nodded soberly. "The doctors had to keep my parents in a medically-induced coma for two weeks while the goren was flushed from their bodies. They're recovering slowly, but they can't remember what happened. The doctors said they'll probably never get those memories back." I added the last part in case one of the prince's men was reporting back to Queen Anwyn.

"I cannot imagine what you must be going through."

"They're alive, and they'll recover. That's all I care about." I reached for my water glass. "All we've talked about since we got here is me and my family. Why don't you tell me something about you?"

He smiled. "I'm sure everything you could ever want to know about me can be found in one of those gossip magazines."

"I don't care what your favorite color is or what you like to have for breakfast. Tell me something I can't find in a magazine. What do you miss most about home?"

His eyes twinkled. "Are you trying to get the scoop on me, Jesse?"

"You tracked me down, remember?" I retorted playfully.

"So, I did." His eyes took on a faraway look. "I think I miss my tarran more than anything else. I ride every day when I'm at home."

I tried not to let my surprise show. Considering how close everyone said he was to his mother, I would expect him to say he missed her.

"I've seen drawings of tarrans. Are they really twice as big as our horses?"

A tarran was a Fae equine that resembled a larger, bonier version of a horse with two small horns on its forehead.

"Not twice as big but they do dwarf your horses, and they are much faster. There is a large meadow below the palace where I used to race my friends when we were children." He cast a petulant look in the direction of his men. "Now, that activity is frowned upon. It is deemed undignified and unsafe for the crown prince to race."

"So, you no longer race?"

"Of course, I do." His smile was full of mischief. "I just make sure the queen doesn't hear of it."

It was the first time he'd mentioned his mother, and I used it to casually turn the conversation to her. "She sounds like my mother. I don't tell her about all my hunting adventures, or she'd ground me for life."

Prince Rhys chuckled. "Parents can be overprotective no matter where they live. Mother didn't even want me to come to your realm, but she knew I would be miserable if I didn't get to experience all of this. I grew up hearing stories about this world and waiting for the day I was old enough to see it for myself."

"And did it meet your expectations?"

"Oh, yes." He nodded fervently. "It is better than anything I could have imagined. There are so many different countries to travel to and cultures to experience. I could spend years here and not see them all. I cannot wait for the time when I don't have to return home each week to replenish my energy."

"The iron affects you that much?" I knew faeries new to this world had to return to their realm to recharge, but I thought it was more like once a month.

"No. It was one of Mother's stipulations because she worries too much." He smirked. "In truth, the iron affects Bayard and the others more than it does me."

"Bayard?"

"My head of security." He inclined his head toward one of the faeries standing beside the booth.

I wasn't surprised to see it was the blond one who had spoken to Gorn. Bayard returned my look with a glare that said he still wasn't happy about his prince's choice of dining companions. I wasn't thrilled about being in Bayard's company either.

The waiter approached with our bill, but Bayard intercepted him before he reached the table. The faerie handed him some cash and told him to keep the change. I didn't know how much he'd given the waiter, but the man's rounded eyes told me it was generous.

Prince Rhys and I talked a bit more, but mostly about the places he had traveled to so far. I couldn't think of a way to steer the conversation back to the queen without raising suspicion, so I didn't try.

We had been there almost two hours when Bayard signaled to him that it was time to go. The prince nodded and smiled at me. "I can't tell you the last time I've enjoyed lunch this much. Thank you for coming."

I slid out of the booth. "I enjoyed it, too, Your Highness."

He made a face as he stood. "Oh, no. That won't do. Please, call me Rhys."

I smiled without responding. I couldn't deny he was very likeable, but I also couldn't forget that his mother had hurt my parents and tortured Faris. She had stolen the ke'tain, which could lead to the destruction of my world and everyone I loved. She was my enemy, and it would feel like a betrayal for me to be friends with her son.

We walked to the exit with his guard surrounding us. Thankfully, the lunch rush was over, and there weren't many people in the restaurant. Two people held up their phones to take pictures, but they lowered them and looked away when the guards glared at them.

"Keep your head down," Prince Rhys said as we left the restaurant.

Before I could ask what he meant, I spotted the first camera. The royal guard closed ranks around us as a throng of paparazzi I couldn't see shouted questions at the prince. The paps wanted to know who his date was and how we'd met.

My stomach twisted. They were going to follow me, take my picture, and splash it across every tabloid out there. I was supposed to stay under the radar, and that did not include being linked romantically to the Seelie crown prince. Panic flooded me. They'd find out who I was and they'd write stories about my parents being in a drug treatment facility. Tabloids didn't make money off nice stories. They thrived on the ugly ones, and they had no problem filling in the holes with lies.

Prince Rhys took my arm. "Don't be alarmed. My men will protect you."

I stayed quiet because I couldn't tell him that his celebrity was what I feared. His men couldn't protect me from that or from the fallout.

We reached the sidewalk, and the photogs surrounding us gave us a wide berth. Even those guys were smart enough to keep their distance from the prince's guard.

Through a gap between two of the guards, I saw a paparazzo lower his camera. I met his shocked gaze as we passed him.

"*Help,*" I mouthed desperately a second before he disappeared from view.

My phone rang, and Tennin's name appeared on the screen. I rushed to answer it, ignoring the dark look one of the guards shot me.

"Go into Moore Books on the corner and head to the office at the back," Tennin ordered. "The owner is a friend of mine. Tell her I sent you. I'll be there soon."

"Okay."

He ended the call, and I looked at Prince Rhys. "I have a friend waiting for me at the bookstore on the corner. I can hide in there until the paparazzi leave."

Disappointment flickered in his eyes, but he nodded. "Fame is not for everyone."

"Especially bounty hunters." I smiled, and his good humor returned.

"Bayard," he said in a low voice.

"Moore Books," answered his head of security. "Approaching now."

We stopped outside the quaint store I'd visited on a few occasions when I used to have time to read for pleasure. I thanked the prince again for lunch and hurried inside with my head down. Some of the paps tried to follow me, but the prince's men blocked anyone else from entering the store.

A pretty brunette in her late twenties, whom I knew to be the owner, was the only person in the store. She looked up from arranging a magazine display by the window when the bell over the door jingled. "Welcome to Moore Books."

"I'm a friend of Tennin's," I blurted. "He told me to hide in here until the paparazzi leave."

She peered out the window, and her eyes went round. "Oh, my. Follow me."

She locked the front door and led me to a cramped office at the back of the store. "Sorry for the mess," she said as she moved a teetering stack of books from the visitor chair to the small desk.

"No need to apologize." I steadied some of the books before they could fall to the floor.

She stood back to look at me. Her eyes searched my face, and I could see she was trying to place me.

I sank down on the chair and exhaled deeply. "I'm not a celebrity. I just had the incredibly bad luck to be caught walking with the Seelie prince."

Her mouth made a perfect O shape.

"Yeah." I smiled wryly. "You have seen me before, though. I've been in here a few times."

The back door opened, and I briefly heard the sounds of traffic before they were muted again. Seconds later, Tennin appeared in the office doorway.

"Angela." He gave the woman a quick kiss on the mouth, and her flushed skin told me they'd been a lot more than friendly at some point. "Thanks for your help."

"Anything for you." She practically glowed as she left us alone in the office.

I quirked my eyebrows at him. "Friends?"

"Yes, lucky for you." He closed the office door and stared at me like a disapproving adult about to scold a child. "Do I want to know how you happened to be having lunch with the Seelie crown prince? I hope this is not another one of your crazy schemes, because I don't want to be the one explaining it to Lukas this time."

I groaned. "I've apologized for that three times already. And no, this was not a *scheme*." I used air quotes around the last word. "Prince Rhys invited me to lunch, and I could hardly say no."

Tennin didn't try to hide his disbelief. "Since when do you know the Seelie prince?"

"I met him at the Ralston last month, and I saw him at Va'sha a few weeks later. I barely know him." I picked up one of the hardcover books on the desk and looked at the cover. "I wonder if she has this in paperback."

The book was plucked from my hands. "Does Lukas know about you and Prince Rhys?"

"There is no me and Prince Rhys, and Lukas has no say over who I talk to," I replied a little harsher than I meant to. Scowling, I reached for the book, but Tennin held it away from me.

"You're playing with fire, Jesse."

I sighed. "There is absolutely nothing going on between me and Prince Rhys. He asked me to lunch, and I made it clear that's all it was. You've been following him since before he made his debut, so you know how it is. He'll be interested in the next shiny object before we know it."

"For our sake, I hope you're right."

"What does that mean?"

He laid the book on the desk. "Did you drive here?"

"Oh, no. You don't get to say something like that and leave it hanging out there." I crossed my arms. "What did you mean by 'for our sake'?"

Tennin looked like he'd eaten something that didn't agree with him. "What have I ever done to you? Can't you forget I said anything?"

I didn't respond.

He released a pained sigh. "Lukas let it be known that you're under his protection, and that any faerie who harasses or messes with you will answer to him."

"He did what?" I shot to my feet and stared at Tennin. "When?"

"Early January. I was in Faerie, and I heard it when I came back." He grimaced. "It's not as bad as I made it sound. He did it to warn away anyone who might try to hurt you."

I couldn't believe this. "Why didn't you tell me?"

Tennin gave me an *are-you-serious* look. "He said not to."

"You're telling me now."

"Because I'm starting to think you are more trouble than he is." Tennin rubbed his eyes. "I plan to throw myself on his mercy. He'll probably grant me clemency just because he knows what I'm up against."

I scowled at him. "Now you're being dramatic."

"Is that so? Do you know what he said to me at Davian's party after you left? He told me he understood my predicament and that as long as my intentions toward you were good, he'd overlook me bringing you into Davian Woods's home."

I put my hands on my hips. "He had no right to say that to you."

Tennin shook his head. "He has every right. He's my prince, and he will one day be my king. And he wasn't wrong. I know Davian is a dangerous person, and I never should have brought you there. I'm thankful nothing bad came of it, and not because of Lukas. I could not face your parents if I put you in danger."

"At least I got to dress up and eat some of that delicious food." I looked away so he couldn't see my guilt for not telling him all that had happened that night. It was better that he didn't know. "I'm sorry I put you in that position with him."

"No worries. It only took me two days to recover."

My gaze shot back to his, and I couldn't tell if he was joking or not. "You still haven't told me why you hoped there was nothing between Prince Rhys and me for our sake."

"Can't you let that one go?"

"No."

He put his face in his hands. "Why me?" When he lifted his head, he wore a look of resignation. "Don't you get it? Lukas doesn't give his protection to just anyone. He cares about you. He's not going to take it well if he finds out you've been getting cozy with the Seelie prince, and I knew about it."

I threw up my arms. "We are *not* getting cozy."

"Good. You can tell Lukas that."

"I'm not telling him anything." I could only imagine how that conversation would go, and it was never going to happen. "I'm ready to leave now."

"Thank the goddess," Tennin muttered. "Do you need a ride home?"

"My Jeep is down the street."

He extended a hand toward the door. "We can go out the back, and I'll get you to your Jeep without them seeing you."

"You think they are still out there? Won't they follow Prince Rhys?" I asked hopefully as I trailed him out of the office.

Tennin made a derisive sound. "You might think your little lunch date was no big deal, but my colleagues out there are like bloodhounds on a scent. They'll stay as long as it takes for them to learn the identity of Prince Rhys's mystery date."

My mouth went dry. "You don't think they'll figure it out, do you?"

"Not if I can help it." He opened the back door and peeked out before he pushed it open all the way. "When your parents come home, I'm telling them we're even."

"I can't believe you didn't tell me!" Violet shook her magazine at me as I drove her home from JFK two days later. "I had to see the pictures in a magazine I picked up at the airport. A *magazine*, Jesse."

I took the exit out of the airport. "I didn't know there were pictures to tell you about."

"I don't care about the pictures. What I care about is my best friend going on a date with Prince Rhys and not telling me."

"First of all, it wasn't a date. It was lunch. Second, I was planning to tell you when you got home."

"Lunch can be a date." She opened the magazine and pointed to a picture of Prince Rhys and me leaving the Vietnamese restaurant surrounded by his guards. There was also one of me from behind as I entered the bookstore. You couldn't see my face in either photo. "According to this, you had a long cozy lunch, and then, you went shopping for books together."

I would have scowled at her if I hadn't needed to keep my eyes on the road. "*Modern Fae* magazine? Really, Vi? They're nothing more than a celebrity gossip rag."

"But that *is* you in the pictures," she argued.

My fingers tightened on the steering wheel. "Can you really tell it's me?"

"Duh. I'd know you anywhere."

"You would, but what about everyone else?"

Paper rustled as she studied the photos. "Well...they don't show your face so probably not. Everyone is wondering who the mystery woman is, and the prince won't give her – I mean your – name."

My shoulders relaxed. "Good. And for the record, we did not have a cozy lunch or go shopping. We sat across from each other in a booth with two of his guards standing over us. Then I hid in a bookstore, and I had to sneak out the back to get away from the paps."

"Oh." She deflated like a leaky balloon. "When you put it like that..."

I looked around me as I changed lanes. "Exactly. Now do you want to hear the real story?"

"What do you think?"

Smiling, I told her about Prince Rhys's visit and our lunch that had been anything but romantic. "He seems pretty down-to-earth when you get to know him. I got the impression he'd rather travel than live at court."

"Are you going to see him again?" she asked eagerly.

"No."

"Why not?"

I spared her a quick glance. "How do you expect me to explain to my parents that I'm on friendly terms with the Seelie prince? Prince Rhys might not be involved in what happened to them, but he's too close to it."

"I didn't think of that." She fell quiet for a minute. "Do you realize how crazy it is that you know princes from the Seelie and Unseelie courts? A few months ago, you wouldn't have been able to pick either of them out of a lineup."

"A lot of crazy things have happened in my life since November. And you wouldn't have been able to pick Lukas out of a lineup either."

She dropped the magazine into her lap. "I've wondered about him. Don't you think it's weird that no one seems to know his real identity? You would think someone would have let that secret slip by now."

"Maybe it's some faerie rule that they don't give away their secret identities."

"You could ask him, now that you guys are back on friendly terms again," she suggested.

"Maybe I will," I replied distractedly as I checked the traffic in the rearview mirror. Behind us was a white Lincoln Navigator, and I was certain I'd seen it when we left JFK. I'd taken several different turns since the airport. What were the odds of having the same car following us on the exact same route?

"Is something wrong?" Violet asked.

"I might be paranoid, but I think that Lincoln is following us."

"What?" She turned to look before I could tell her not to. "How do you know?"

"I don't know, but they've been behind us all the way home." I looked at the SUV again. If they were following us, they didn't have a clue how to tail someone. Or they didn't care if they were seen. The second thought sent tendrils of fear through me.

She gasped. "Maybe it's the paparazzi. What if they figured out who Prince Rhys's mystery woman is?" She pulled down the passenger visor and started fixing her hair.

"What are you doing?"

"If it's the paparazzi, I want to look good for the photos," she said as she rooted in her purse for a tube of lipstick

I shook my head. "It's not the paps, Vi."

"How do you know?"

"You've spent a few weeks in Hollywood. How many paps drive around in Lincoln Navigators?"

"Shit." She sank lower in her seat as if they were about to start shooting at us. If I wasn't so worried about the possibility of being followed, I would have laughed.

"What are we going to do?" she hissed.

I looked around and spotted an intersection up ahead. "Hold on. I'm going to try something."

"Um, do you mean to hold on figuratively or literally?"

"Both," I said through gritted teeth as I pulled over into the right lane at the last possible second. The car I cut off blared their horn, but I barely heard it over Violet's scream as I turned down a side street. I didn't slow to see if the Lincoln had managed to follow me. Heart pounding, I kept going and prayed I had been wrong about our tail.

"Are they gone?" Violet asked in a shaky voice.

I checked the rearview mirror. "We lost them."

She sat up straighter in her seat. "Can we have a normal day together for once?"

"I'm a bounty hunter, and you're about to become a movie star. I think this is the new normal."

"Well, when you put it like *that*," she said with a giggle.

Her laughter did nothing to ease the coil of worry in my gut. I tried to tell myself I'd been mistaken about the SUV following us, but too much had happened in the last few months for me to believe it.

We spent the rest of the drive talking about Violet's time in Los Angeles, and some of the actors she'd met at the functions she'd attended. Her agent was working overtime to milk her small role in this movie for everything it was worth.

"Are you going to come in?" she asked when we stopped in front of her brownstone.

"Can't. I have a bunch of stuff to do before I get back to work tomorrow. You want to come over for dinner tomorrow and hang out?"

"Okay!" She reached for the door and stopped to look back at me. "No more boats for you."

I made a face. "No more boats."

I left her to drive the two blocks to my place, but I took a quick detour to the grocery store. As usual, once I got there, I thought of a dozen things I needed, and I left the store with my arms around a large paper bag of groceries.

I was almost to the Jeep when I noticed the white SUV parked on the other side of it. A white Lincoln Navigator.

I took a step back as a blonde faerie walked around the rear of the Jeep. One glimpse of the cold determination on his face was enough to make me turn around toward the store. I came up short and almost lost my grip on the bag of groceries. A second faerie blocked my retreat, and his eyes flashed me a warning that said *don't try to run.*

17

Fear clawed at my stomach when I got a good look at the second faerie. He was the one I'd seen at Davian's party, which meant these were Queen Anwyn's personal guard.

My mind raced to think of a way out of this. I glanced around and spotted several people loading groceries into their vehicles. Even if I yelled for help, they wouldn't have a prayer against the Seelie royal guard. There were security cameras on the building, but a lot of good they would do if these guys decided to take me away from here. I'd be dead before anyone looked at the video.

"Jesse James," said a hard voice from behind me.

I turned to face the faerie near the Jeep. My arms trembled around the bag of groceries I clutched as if it could shield me.

Ruthless blue eyes locked with mine. "We have a message for you from our queen."

His hand disappeared inside his jacket, and my whole body tensed. When his hand reappeared holding not a weapon but what looked like a photo, I stared at it in confusion. He closed the distance between us and held the photo in front of my face.

I recognized it immediately. It was one of the pictures taken of Prince Rhys and me after our lunch. You couldn't see my face, but apparently Violet wasn't the only one who had recognized me.

"Queen Anwyn does not approve of your relationship with the prince," the faerie said coldly. "She will not allow her son to form an attachment to a human, especially one of your ilk."

I was so shocked by the turn of this conversation that I could barely manage to speak. "My...ilk?"

"A bounty hunter." He spat the words as if they left a bad taste in his mouth. "You are not worthy of the prince. The queen demands you cease this relationship immediately."

I shook my head to clear it. "I'm not in a relationship with Prince Rhys. I barely know him."

The faerie produced a second photo. "Explain this."

The photo was of me and Prince Rhys standing inches from each other at Va'sha. Someone had snapped the photo in the exact moment I had almost run into him, and the way the prince was smiling at me made it look like he and I were in a cozy conversation. It didn't help that I was dressed like a party girl in a club where humans went to hook up with faeries.

"I spoke to the prince for all of two minutes that night."

"That's not what the picture says. Nor does this one." He held up another photo, and in this one, the prince's hand was touching my cheek in what looked like an intimate moment.

I met the faerie's hostile gaze. "Whoever took these pictures made it look like it was something it's not. I did see Prince Rhys at Va'sha, but the only reason he touched me was to annoy Prince Vaerik."

The faerie's eyes betrayed his surprise. "The Unseelie prince was there?"

"Yes. I was talking to him when Prince Rhys saw us and came over."

"You were there with Prince Vaerik?"

I shook my head. "I was there on a job to catch a nymph, and I ran into him. I guess Prince Rhys thought I was with Prince Vaerik, and the two of them argued. It had nothing to do with me, so I left them to fight it out. You can ask Prince Rhys's guard, and I'm sure they'll tell you. Just like they will tell you there was nothing romantic about my lunch with the prince. He came to see me because he's interested in bounty hunting, and that's mostly what we talked about at lunch. He didn't ask to see me again, and I have no intention of contacting him."

Icy blue eyes regarded me. "We will check out your story. For your sake, I hope you are not lying. You do not want to make an enemy of Queen Anwyn."

A shiver went through me at the threat. The Seelie queen was already my enemy, but I didn't tell him I knew that.

"Stay away from Prince Rhys. If we hear you have seen him again, we will be back." With those parting words, he spun and went to the Lincoln. The second faerie, who hadn't spoken, stalked past me to join him. Neither of them spared another glance in my direction as the SUV pulled out of the parking spot, and they drove off.

I managed to get into the Jeep before I fell apart. Tremors shook my body as I white-knuckled the steering wheel and took deep breaths to curb what might be my first panic attack. I had no idea how much time passed before I was composed enough to drive.

At home, I practically ran from the Jeep to my apartment, looking over my shoulder to make sure the Seelie guard hadn't decided to show up here, too. I must have lost my breath as I ran up the stairs because I was a bit lightheaded when I opened the apartment door.

Finch whistled as I set the bag of groceries down in the kitchen with shaking hands. I looked over at the couch where he sat with Aisla, and he signed, *What's wrong?*

"Nothing. I'm cold." I pulled a large carton of blackberries from the bag. "Look what I got for you."

His face lit up. If I could count on anything to distract my brother, it was his love of blackberries. They cost twice as much this time of year, but his happiness was worth every cent.

I put some of the berries in a bowl and set it on the coffee table for him and Aisla to share. She still didn't say much, but her sweet smile was enough.

Leaving them to their treat, I went to my room and lay on my bed, staring at the ceiling. *It could have been a lot worse,* I told myself as my heart finally slowed to a normal pace. It had nothing to do with Mom or Dad, and we were all safe. And as long as Prince Rhys kept his distance from me, I wouldn't have to fear his mother's wrath.

I just had to keep telling myself that until I believed it.

Faris smiled broadly as he opened the door to let me into the building two days later. "I was starting to think you had forgotten us."

I laughed and walked past him into the foyer. "It hasn't been that long."

"I've gotten used to you coming every morning for training. It's the highlight of my day."

"Your life must be boring indeed if my visits are the highlight," I said as I deposited my coat and keys on a barstool, and we went to sit on the couch.

He gave me a pained look. "You have no idea. I can't wait to get back to training and my duties. A sedentary life does not suit me."

"It won't be much longer." In the weeks I had been coming here, Faris's health had improved at an incredible rate. No one who didn't know the truth would ever suspect he had been on the brink of death two months ago. His strength hadn't fully returned because of the iron in his body, but the levels dropped a little every day. The last time I'd been there, he'd told me it should be safe for him to return to Faerie in a month. A week at home and he'd be fully healed.

His mouth curved into a sheepish smile. "I sound like a pouting child when I have so much to be grateful for. I haven't even asked how you're doing. You look happier than normal."

"That's because I am." My heart felt close to bursting. "I saw my parents today, and they told me my father might be ready to come home in two weeks. Their doctors said he is months ahead of what they predicted for his recovery."

"That's wonderful news. And your mother?"

"She has to stay there longer, but the doctors said she is recovering faster than expected, too." I hated that she would be there alone when Dad was released, but she wouldn't hear of him staying with her. She said Finch and I needed him more than she did, and it would do more for her recovery to know he was home with us. I couldn't argue with her when she put it that way.

"I'm so happy for you."

"Thanks." I picked up the coffee that had been waiting for me. "The doctors said everyone recovers from goren differently."

He grimaced. "It's the same with iron poisoning. Some recover faster than others. But the main thing is your parents are doing well and your family will be together soon. It makes me glad to see you happy."

"We've all come a long way since that day." I didn't have to elaborate. It wasn't something either of us would forget.

He seemed to think about his next words. "Things have changed between you and Lukas as well."

"We talked." I suddenly became interested in a frayed thread on my jeans. Lukas was close to his friends, but he wouldn't tell them what had happened between us at my apartment. Would he?

Faris chuckled. "I don't suppose your talk had anything to do with his current mood."

"Mood?"

A door slammed, and Lukas strode into the room. His jaw was hard, and I was taken aback when his angry eyes immediately honed in on me.

"We need to talk." He pointed to the window overlooking the garden. "Out there."

I didn't move except to raise my eyebrows at him. He seemed to have forgotten his manners and the fact that I wasn't one of his subjects to order about.

It didn't take him long to realize his glare wasn't going to work on me. He released an aggravated breath. "Please."

I shot Faris a questioning look as I stood, but he appeared to be as puzzled as I was about Lukas's behavior.

As usual, the garden was balmy compared to the crisp winter outside the wall, and the air carried the fragrance of exotic flowers. I crossed the patio and stepped onto the thick carpet of grass that I knew from experience was softer than anything grown in our world.

"What is going on between you and the Seelie prince?" Lukas demanded from behind me.

I grimaced at the trees. Was there anyone who didn't recognize me in those damn photos? I turned to look at him. "You saw the pictures."

Normally, I'd tell him it was none of his business whom I spent time with. But he had as good a reason as I to hate the Seelie Queen and her son by association. He had confided in me about the ke'tain and Queen Anwyn's involvement, and the least I could do was be forthcoming with him.

His jaw flexed. "How long have you been seeing him?"

"I'm not seeing him. We just had lunch together."

"One does not *just have lunch* with the Seelie crown prince," he said brusquely.

"Why not? I've had lunch with the Unseelie crown prince," I retorted. "Does it count that I had no idea you were a prince at the time? Or the crown prince for that matter?"

"Jesse." He practically growled my name, and a tiny thrill went through me. It vanished when his scowl deepened.

I heaved a sigh. "Prince Rhys came to see me the day after the ferry accident. We went to lunch and talked mostly about bounty hunting. It was all very platonic, and if those paps hadn't taken pictures of us, you and I wouldn't be having this conversation."

"He came to your apartment?" Lukas's nostrils flared.

"I ran into him in the lobby before he could come up to the apartment."

Lukas bit out a Fae word. "And he went through the trouble to find you only to talk about bounty hunting?"

"We talked about other things too, but yes."

"Like what?"

I crossed my arms. "Like what any two people would talk about over lunch. He didn't spill any Seelie secrets if that's what you're asking. I would have told you if he had."

Lukas began to pace. "I don't like his interest in you or him knowing where you live."

"You're not the only one who wants him to stay away from me."

He stopped walking. "What do you mean?"

I bit the inside of my cheek. It wasn't like I had planned to hide this from him, but I had to mentally prepare myself for the explosion to come. "Queen Anwyn doesn't approve of her son having any connection with a bounty hunter."

Lukas went stock still, his eyes boring into me. "How do you know that?"

"Her guard came to see me and warned me to stay away from the prince. I told them I –"

"What?" Lukas's shout scared the birds in the garden into silence. Behind him, Faris's concerned face appeared in the window.

I held up my hands. "Look, it's not as bad as you think. Let me tell you what happened before you blow a gasket or something."

He nodded stiffly, and I told him about the queen's guards stopping me outside the grocery store to deliver her message. Seeing the fury in his eyes, I was glad I'd decided to leave out the part about them tailing me from the airport.

"They had photos of you and Prince Rhys at Va'sha?" he bit out.

"The photos were manipulated to make it look like something it wasn't. You were there the whole time, remember?"

Lukas swore. "If they are willing to approach you in a public place, there is nothing to stop them from coming after you when you are alone." He resumed pacing and stopped abruptly. "You will stay here. It's the safest place for you."

I nearly choked on my saliva. There was no way I was staying in his home after what had happened between us. I wasn't cool enough to handle that level of awkward.

"Staying here is not an option. I have to work, and my father is coming home soon. Besides, the apartment is protected by your ward."

"The ward won't protect you when you're not at home." He stared at the brick wall around the garden. "One of my men will watch you when you leave the building."

I shook my head vehemently. "No."

Lukas strode over to me. "Jesse, the Seelie queen has you in her sights. There is no way I'm letting you walk around this city unprotected."

"She only cares if I see her son, and I have no intention of doing that. I made that clear to him, too, after our lunch."

"And if Rhys ignores her wishes and tries to see you again?" Lukas asked.

I didn't have an answer for that because I'd wondered the same thing. I stared up at the sky and watched a bird fly over the fence into the garden. Strange. The ward kept the rain out but not a bird.

I dropped my eyes to meet Lukas's. "Put the same ward on me that you did for my parents. That'll keep the Seelie guard away from me."

His expression turned to one of frustration as he let out a harsh breath. "I can't."

"Why not?"

He dragged his fingers through his hair. "I've tried four times already to ward you, and it won't hold. The ward collapses the moment I stop putting magic into it. Something is blocking it, but I have no idea what."

Shock washed over me. "When did you try that?"

"At the hospital. The first week your parents were there, you used to fall asleep in the chair in their room. It was easy to slip past the nurses and the agent on duty."

I didn't know what to say. He had been at the hospital, not once, but multiple times, and I'd been entirely clueless.

There was one thing I did know, and that was why his ward wouldn't work on me. I suspected it was the same reason the ke'tain sensor went on the fritz whenever I picked it up. I had to tell him.

I cleared my throat. "Do you remember our talk about goddess stones after I told you about the stone I took from the kelpie? I asked if you wanted to go back to the island and look for it. You said it wouldn't be there because it had gone back to the kelpie."

He frowned, puzzled by the abrupt change in topic. "Yes."

I reached for his hand, and my stomach quivered at the contact. Lukas didn't say anything when I lifted his hand and placed it on the back of my head.

"What if the goddess stone chose a new owner?" I asked as I pushed my hair aside so his fingers could feel the stone cleverly concealed there.

The confusion on his face gave way to shock as he touched the smooth stone. He turned me so my back was to him, and I could feel his warm breath on my nape when he leaned in for a closer look. The feel of his hands in my hair, touching my scalp, sent a jolt of heat straight to my belly. It was all I could do not to close my eyes and lean back into him.

"So, what's the verdict?" I asked lightly to hide my reaction to him. "Is it the real thing?"

He studied it a moment longer. "I've never seen a goddess stone, so I don't know. You had this when you left the island?"

"I don't know. I didn't find it in my hair until I showered at the hospital. It was white when I took it from the kelpie, but I think it's the same stone. If I remove it, it reattaches to my hair, and it hides itself if I put my hair in a braid. Violet did my hair one night and she didn't see the stone or she would have said something. It's like it has a mind of its own."

Lukas didn't speak for the longest time, and his silence made me nervous. Not being able to see his face, I couldn't tell what he was thinking. Did he think I was lying? Or was he upset that a human was in possession of a precious Fae object? It wasn't like I had any choice in the matter. I'd happily give it to him if I could.

But what if I could give it to him? I'd only ever taken the stone from my hair and put it in my room. If I gave it to a faerie, it might choose them instead.

Reaching up, I pushed his hands away and grasped the stone. I winced as I pulled it free. I spun to face Lukas and shoved the stone, along with a few strands of my hair, into his hands. "Take it. It belongs with a faerie."

He turned the red stone over in his hand. "I can feel something inside it."

"Magic?"

"It's more like energy." His hands stilled, and he did a quick intake of breath. "It feels like Faerie."

"Don't all Fae objects feel like that?" I asked.

Lukas continued to stare at the stone. "Once something leaves Faerie, it loses that energy. Magic remains, but the life force of Faerie fades. It's why we have to return home to replenish it." His eyes were full of wonder when he lifted them to mine. "I believe it *is* a goddess stone."

I'd suspected that all along, but having him confirm it left me a little shaken. "Why me?"

His tone gentled. "It's not for us to understand Aedhna's ways, but she gifted the stone to you. You jumped into the river to save a life, and then you took the stone from the kelpie. Aedhna must have felt that act was worthy of her blessing."

"But I'm only human," I protested.

He picked up my hand and placed the stone in it. "I would never use the word 'only' to describe you, Jesse."

The air around us felt charged as we stood inches apart with my hand in his. I wanted to blame it on the stone, but it had never filled my stomach with butterflies or made me crave someone's touch.

Lukas's lips parted slightly, reminding me what they felt like against mine. He moved an inch closer, sending my heart into an erratic rhythm. I was like a moth drawn to a flame as I closed the remaining distance between us. I felt the tremor that passed through both of us when my body pressed against his.

He lowered his head, and I closed my eyes as his lips grazed mine so lightly I thought I'd imagined it. His warm breath caressed my cheek, making me light-headed from anticipation and need. *Kiss me*, my whole body begged him.

His mouth covered mine as if he'd heard my silent plea. Unlike the hungry kiss on my couch, this one was tantalizingly slow and filled me with longing for something I couldn't have. Lost in his touch, I didn't care about the world outside this garden or the things that would never be. There was only him and me and nothing else.

I knew it had to end, but that didn't dull the sting when he broke the kiss. Or the cold that rushed in when he released me and stepped back, putting distance between us.

"Jesse… I shouldn't have," he said roughly, but it was the guilt in his eyes that hurt more than his words.

I held up a hand. "Don't. I kissed you back, so this is not on you. We were caught up in the moment."

He looked like he wanted to say more, but nothing he said would change our situation. My heart constricted, and I looked down at the stone in my hand as I regained my composure. "Now that you know about the goddess stone, do you think it's why your ward doesn't work on me?"

"It's the only thing that makes sense."

"What if I give it to you? Or Faris?" I held it out to him.

He shook his head. "It doesn't work that way. It has to be gifted by Aedhna."

"What have we got to lose?" I spun and headed to the door. If he didn't want to try, I'd get someone else to do it.

"Where are you going?"

"To give it to Faris," I called over my shoulder. "If anyone deserves to be goddess-blessed, it's him."

I entered the living room and walked over to Faris, who was now reading a book. I held out my hand with the stone on my palm. "Take this."

"What is it?" He lowered his book to look at my hand.

"It's a goddess stone. I want you to have it."

He gave me a lopsided smile. "I think those are supposed to come from the goddess, not an angel."

I glowered at him. "Just take it."

Chuckling, he plucked the stone from my hand. "Ten minutes alone with Lukas and you are bossier than he is. Now why do I need a...a...?"

"Faris?"

He didn't answer, only stared at me with the glazed look of someone in a trance. Fear clawed at me, and I grabbed for the stone, but it was clenched tightly in his fist.

I shouted for Lukas, but he was already there. He rushed past me and tried unsuccessfully to pry Faris's fingers open. Whatever was holding them together was stronger than the crown prince of Unseelie.

My legs wobbled, and I sat on the couch beside Faris. Guilt rolled through me as I watched Lukas trying to rouse his unresponsive friend. *Please, Aedhna. Don't punish him for my mistake. Please, please, please, please, please.*

Faris blinked once, twice. His blank expression changed to one that could only be described as serene. I held my breath as his fisted hand opened to reveal...nothing.

My hand went to the back of my head, and sure enough, the stone was back in my hair. But what about Faris? If it had hurt him, I'd never forgive myself.

"Faris?" I said tentatively.

"Angel." He smiled at me. Was I imagining it, or did his color look better than it had a few minutes ago? And there was something different about his eyes. There was a spark in them I'd never seen before.

"Are you okay?"

He inhaled deeply, like a man breathing fresh air for the first time in months. "I can't remember the last time I felt this good."

"What do you feel?" Lukas asked him.

Faris stood with ease and walked to the other side of the room where he turned and threw out his arms. "I feel like myself again."

Lukas went to stand beside him. He pressed his palm to Faris's chest, and the air around his hand shimmered with a soft blue magic. It was the first time I'd ever seen him use his magic, and I suspected he didn't do it often around humans.

"I can't detect a trace of iron in your body." Lukas lowered his hand. "You're completely healed."

Faris placed his fist over his heart and looked at me. "You did this."

"It was the stone." I looked to Lukas for help.

Lukas smacked his friend on the shoulder. "It's seems our Jesse has been goddess-blessed."

"What?" Faris's jaw fell.

I let Lukas explain it. Picking up my lukewarm coffee, I sipped the rich brew while he brought Faris up to speed. Conlan, Iian, and Kerr came in halfway through the story, forcing Lukas to start over. Their loud exclamations over the miraculous healing brought Faolin running downstairs, his hair wet from the shower. There was a lot of back-slapping and man hugs as they cheered Faris's return to perfect health.

I sat quietly through it all, feeling more and more like an intruder on their private celebration. My eyes strayed to the door, and I wondered if anyone would notice if I snuck out.

Standing, I moved as unobtrusively as I could toward the barstool where I'd left my coat and keys. I picked them up, careful not to jingle the keys.

"And where do you think you're going?" asked Lukas from right behind me.

I yelped and spun around. My keys flew from my hand and skidded across the floor to stop at his feet. He picked them up, making no move to give them back.

I clutched my coat to me, suddenly the center of attention of the Unseelie crown prince and his entire royal guard. "I figured I'd..."

"...sneak out while we weren't looking?" Lukas finished for me.

Yes. "No."

His cocked eyebrows said I was a crappy liar. But what was I supposed to say? That I felt out of place here? That it was awkward being around him after we'd shared an incredible kiss that had ended with him saying it was a mistake? Or that I was afraid I might be falling for him again, and there was nothing down that road for me but heartbreak? They were all true, but I couldn't bring myself to say any of them.

He motioned for me to sit on one of the barstools. "We still have the matter of your protection to discuss, now that we've established that a personal ward isn't an option."

"Who does she need protection from?" Faolin asked.

Lukas's eyes stayed on mine. "Anwyn."

That got a reaction from them. They all gathered around us as Lukas told them about my visit from the Seelie royal guard. Before I knew it, they had decided who would be on the first watch, and my protests fell on deaf ears.

"You're all blowing this out of proportion. I won't see Prince Rhys again, and the queen's guard will leave me alone." I rubbed the back of my neck, which had started to ache.

Conlan rested his elbows on the island. "You don't know Anwyn. If she even hears a rumor about you and her precious son, she will be all over it."

A chill settled over me. There was nothing to stop one of those gossip magazines from making up a story if they thought it would sell copies.

"Then we give Anwyn a different rumor," Faris said. "Something that will assure her Jesse has no interest in Rhys."

I looked at Faris. If the mischievous gleam in his eyes was meant to reassure me, it failed miserably.

"What do you suggest?" Lukas asked.

"Pictures of Jesse with someone who is not Rhys. Nothing compromising, but it will have to look like they are more than friends."

"No," I blurted, but no one was paying attention to me.

"It has to be someone Anwyn will recognize," Conlan said. "One of us."

Faolin spoke up. "Anwyn's not going to believe a human chose a lesser royal over a crown prince."

Faris nodded. "It has to be Lukas."

"You're not serious." I laughed nervously and looked at Lukas, who did not laugh with me. In fact, he appeared to be considering this ludicrous idea. Didn't he realize he'd be subjecting himself to rumors, too? From what I'd seen, he had never been linked romantically with a human.

"This has to be handled right," Conlan said. He snapped his fingers. "Tennin. We can have him take the pictures, and he'll know exactly how to spin it for our purposes."

I slid off my stool. "You guys have lost your minds. There's no way I'm letting you put my picture up on some tabloid site."

Faris laid a hand over my keys when I reached for them. "Tennin will make it look good. He won't embarrass you."

"That's not it." I trusted Tennin, but once your picture went out into cyberspace, you had no control over it. I turned to Lukas who was watching me with an unreadable expression. "What happened to me keeping a low profile?"

"That went out the window the moment Anwyn saw those photos of you and Rhys," he said pointedly. "This is the best way to throw her off your scent."

I sank down on the stool in defeat. "I think I'd rather go with the bodyguard idea."

Conlan threw an arm over my shoulder. "Now where is the fun in that?"

18

I got out of the Jeep and shut the door, wincing when the movement sent a dull pain through my shoulder. I rolled my arm to loosen the joint before I started up the street to our building. I needed to remember to tell Levi to ease off with the troll jobs. Trolls might be as dumb as a bag of rocks, but they were dirty fighters. I was going to have to keep ice packs on my shoulder tonight if I wanted to move it at all tomorrow.

I didn't see the figure standing by the lamp post until I reached the steps to the building. Movement out of the corner my eye had me reaching for my stun gun as I whirled toward the person approaching me. I hadn't seen any of the Seelie royal guard in the week since they warned me to stay away from Prince Rhys. But I was still a little jumpy at times, such as when someone came up to me on the street at night.

This someone was not the royal guard or anyone else I'd ever expect to see outside my home, but there was no doubt in my mind she was here to see me. I took my hand off the weapon in my pocket and waited for the faerie to state her reason for being here, even though her sneer spoke for itself.

Dariyah didn't bother with a greeting. "Who do you think you are?"

I bristled at her aggressive tone. "I know who I am. You seem to be the one confused and lost."

"Stay away from him. He is not for the likes of you." Her gaze swept over me, and her mouth twisted like she'd smelled something foul.

"And who would that be?" I asked innocently. We both knew I knew who *he* was, but I was too irritated to play along.

"Vaerik," she bit out. "I saw the photos of you with him. I should have known you weren't sniffing around his place for Faolin."

Ah, the photos. How could I have forgotten those?

It had been two days since Tennin had taken the carefully-staged photos of Lukas and me outside of a restaurant and uploaded them to one of the more reputable celebrity gossip sites. In the pictures, we were standing close together with Lukas's arm around my waist and him smiling down at me. You could only see us in profile, but I was identifiable to anyone who knew me well and, most importantly, to the Seelie Queen.

So far, there had been no mention of the name of the mystery girl photographed with Lukas Rand. Lucky for me, a much juicier story had popped up last night, involving a Seelie princess and a US congressman. If the public loved one thing more than a faerie scandal, it was a scandal about faeries and politicians.

Dariyah scoffed loudly. "If you think you'll get more from Vaerik than a few nights in his bed, you're delusional. He might not be immune to a pretty redhead, but you must know you're only a diversion to him. He doesn't keep human lovers for long. He's too *honorable* to toy with their feelings."

She said *honorable* like it was a character flaw. I didn't bother to correct her assumptions about Lukas and me or tell her he had already made it clear we were nothing more than friends. I didn't owe her an explanation, and I did *not* appreciate her tracking me down at my home.

"How did you find me?" I asked. Lukas would not have told her anything about me, even if they were dating.

"I have my ways." She tossed her hair back over her shoulder. "And now that we've had our little talk, I hope you don't give me a reason to come back."

Her thinly-veiled threat reminded me of the one from the Seelie guard, but unlike him, she didn't scare me. I laughed humorlessly. Twice in a week, I'd been accosted and warned to stay away from a faerie prince. I must be on a roll.

Dariyah looked like she'd swallowed a bug. "What is so funny?"

"Private joke." I rubbed my sore shoulder. "If we're done here, I'll be going now."

I turned to the steps, but didn't make it to the first one before she grabbed my bad arm in a painful grip, reminding me how much stronger than me she was.

"I don't think you are getting my message, so let me put this in words you can understand," she ground out. "Vaerik is the Unseelie crown prince and heir to the throne. As king, he will need a consort to continue his line, and no one but a blue blood is worthy of that role. Vaerik knows this, and he will choose a mate suitable to rule with him."

"Such as you?" My heart suddenly felt like it was in a vise, but I wouldn't let her see it. It wasn't as if she was saying anything I didn't already know.

Her smile held no warmth. "Have no doubt, when the time comes, I will be his consort."

"Then you have nothing to fear from a human, do you?"

She tightened her hold on my arm and leaned in. "You will not see Vaerik again."

I held her gaze. "If you have a problem with our friendship, you can take it up with him."

Her brow furrowed, and it took me a moment to realize the source of her confusion. She had tried to glamour me.

I yanked my arm out of her clutches, ignoring the pain that shot through my shoulder. I was fed up with faeries trying to tell me what I could and couldn't do. I wasn't some piece on a game board they could push around as they pleased.

"Glamouring a human is against the law, but I'm sure you know that. Attempting to glamour a bounty hunter is just plain stupid."

She laughed arrogantly. "I am a royal, and we both know I'm above the laws of this backward realm."

"Why are you here if you hate our world so much?"

"To protect what is mine, of course."

"Of course." I shook my head. "I think we're done here."

"Yes, you are," she snarled.

I didn't see the intent in her eyes until it was too late. She raised her hands, and pale green magic shot from them to encircle my throat. Her hands curled into fists, and the magic tightened like fingers around my throat, choking off my air. I clawed at the invisible fingers, but there was nothing to grab.

Dariyah grunted, and I could see the strain on her face from using so much magic. She would exhaust it soon, but before or after I was dead?

I drew back my good arm and punched her with every bit of strength I could muster. Her head snapped back, and I heard the crack of a bone as she flew backward. She landed hard a dozen feet away, and I sucked in air as the magic around my throat disappeared.

I stalked toward the faerie, who lay sprawled on the sidewalk. Her mouth was bloody and her eyes stared up at me with a mix of shock and fear. She'd recklessly used too much magic, and she was completely at my mercy.

"I'm a... royal," she stammered, spraying blood all over her white top.

I stood over her. "I couldn't care less if you were the queen of Seelie. You come at me like that again, and I'll have you in shackles so fast your royal head won't stop spinning for a week."

I was tempted to shackle her now, but I didn't know what the iron would do to her in her current condition. Leaving her on the ground, I stomped up the steps. At the top, I looked back to where she still lay, too weak to stand. I uttered a few choice words and took out my phone to dial a number.

"Angel," Faris said, and I could hear the grin in his voice. He was a lot more energetic now that he was healed.

"I need a favor." I didn't bother to scold him for the use of the nickname.

"Anything. What kind of favor?"

I watched Dariyah trying futilely to sit up. "The kind you can't tell Lukas about." All I needed was to have to explain to him that his potential mate had tried to kill me.

"Dare I ask why?"

"I'll tell you when you get here." I moved my bad arm and bit my lip against the shooting pain in my shoulder. "And if you could hurry, I'd really appreciate it."

I hung up and looked at Dariyah, who was still lying where I'd left her. Heaving a sigh, I walked over to her and hooked my arms under hers to lift her to her feet. She was so weak she couldn't walk, and I had to literally drag her to the building and prop her up on one of the steps. I stayed on the sidewalk, keeping an eye on her while she shot me death glares. I didn't bother to tell her she was wasting her time. She was far from the scariest faerie I'd met.

Twenty minutes later, when a silver SUV drove up the street and stopped in front of me, I was surprised to see one of said faeries get out.

"I thought Faris was coming," I said irritably.

Faolin walked around the front of the SUV wearing his usual annoyed expression. "I was closer. He said you need a favor that requires some discretion."

"And you rushed right over."

"I didn't break any speed laws." He gave me a once over. "You don't appear to be bleeding to death. What's the problem?"

I stepped to one side so he could see who was behind me. If it was possible for eyebrows to hit a hairline, I think his accomplished it.

"Dariyah, what are you doing here?" he asked in the harsh tone that used to make me cringe. I didn't miss the answering flicker of fear in her eyes.

She didn't respond, and he cast a questioning look at me.

I stuck my hands in my pockets. "She and I had a little misunderstanding, but we got it all sorted out. I think she's stayed too long in our realm, though, and needs to go home to recharge."

Faolin's scowl deepened, but he said nothing as he went to Dariyah, picked her up, and carried her to the vehicle. I opened the door for him, and he deposited her on the passenger seat.

He closed the door and went around to the driver's side. "He should know about this."

"*You* know about it."

A smile ghosted across his face, and he gave me a head tilt before he opened the door and got in. The short exchange was the most meaningful conversation we'd ever had, and the closest to an apology I'd probably ever get from him for the whole Rogin thing. I could live with that.

"I could have driven us home," Dad said for what had to be the fifth time since we left the treatment facility two weeks later.

I spied a parking spot and headed for it. "I know, but I've gotten very attached to this Jeep."

"Oh, no. You are not keeping my Jeep." He patted the dash affectionately. "I've missed this thing."

"Okay, but I have no idea how I'll fit the cage in Mom's car."

He laughed as I pulled into the spot and turned off the engine. I looked over at him, and he smiled. There were new lines at the corners of his mouth that hadn't been there before, along with some more gray in his hair. Goren took its toll on the body, but the doctors said he hadn't been on the drug long enough for serious long-term effects. A few gray hairs were nothing.

We got out, and I grabbed his suitcase from the back. He protested when I left him with the smaller bag, but it fell on deaf ears. One of the stipulations for him getting released early was that he would not overexert himself. He was supposed to spend the next few weeks resting, and slowly ease back into regular activity. I'd finally gotten him home, and I wasn't letting him do anything that might put him back in the facility.

Halfway across the street, I realized Dad had stopped walking. I looked back to find him staring at the building.

"Are you okay?" I asked.

"It feels like forever since I saw this place. It looks exactly the same." He lowered his gaze to mine. "I don't know why I thought it would be different."

"When you go through an ordeal like yours, it's hard to imagine the rest of the world not changing with you."

He caught up to me. "When did you get so smart?"

"At birth." I smirked, and he laughed.

We entered the lobby, where Mrs. Russo was standing in her doorway, waiting for us with a plate of brownies for Dad. He hugged her and asked how she was doing, and I remembered the last time the three of us had stood here talking. That had been back in November, and it felt like another lifetime, which in some ways it was. My life would forever be divided into before and after the day my parents went missing.

"Jesse did a fine job taking care of the building while you were gone," Mrs. Russo said. "She even hired a nice man to fix the pipes."

Dad smiled proudly at me. "I never had any doubts."

We said our goodbyes and leisurely climbed the stairs to our floor. If he knew I was deliberately taking my time for his benefit, he didn't mention it. After a month of training with Faolin and the others, I could run up these stairs carrying two suitcases.

"I should warn you that Finch doesn't know you're coming home today," I said in a low voice as I unlocked the door. "I wanted to surprise him."

I opened the door and entered first. "Finch, Aisla, I'm home."

Two little faces appeared in the tree house doorway. Aisla took one look at Dad and disappeared. It took Finch a few seconds longer to realize I wasn't alone. His eyes bugged out, and he began to whistle crazily as he leaped from the tree house to the couch to the floor. Dad went down to his haunches, and my brother literally dived into his arms.

It was several minutes before Finch calmed down enough to sign legibly. Dad sat with him on the couch while I tried to coax Aisla out of hiding. She was great with Violet, but she was afraid of men. I suspected it was because a man had kept her in a cage her whole life. Once she got to know Dad, she'd love him as much as we did.

Dad looked a little tired, so I told him to relax while I made dinner. To celebrate his homecoming, I'd bought some thick steaks and put them in to marinate before I left to pick him up. Instead of baked potatoes, I made a healthy salad because the doctor said Dad needed lots of fresh vegetables and leafy greens in his diet.

I had invited Maurice to eat with us, and he arrived as I was turning the steaks over. Hearing the two of them talk and laugh together in the living room made me smile as I finished cooking and set the table.

Dinner felt almost like old times, except for Mom's noticeable absence. Finch ate in the tree house with Aisla while Dad, Maurice, and I spent the meal discussing work. A few days ago, Maurice and I had talked about how we would bring Dad up to speed on certain things such as the ke'tain. We had no idea what might trigger a memory, so it was better if he heard about it from us instead of someone else. I watched him closely, but he showed no sign of recognition when Maurice told him about the artifact.

"A one-hundred-thousand-dollar bounty?" Dad stared at us like he was waiting for one of us to yell "Gotcha!"

Maurice cut a piece from his steak. "And every idiot with a license from here to Mexico is after it. Two nights ago, I had to break up a fight between a pair of Texas hunters and a team from Florida. The four of them had more attitude than good sense."

"Were the Texans a blonde and a brunette?" I asked.

He grinned at me. "You've met them?"

"You could say that."

Dad set down his fork. "Jesse, I don't like the idea of you being mixed up in this. Hunting is one thing, but there are people who will go to any lengths for that kind of money."

"You don't have to worry. I was looking for the ke'tain, but Lukas convinced me it would be safer to let him go after it." I didn't elaborate. He did not need to know what had led to Lukas taking over.

"Lukas, huh?" Dad gave me a searching look. "And how often do you see the Unseelie prince?"

"Not often. I think he spends most of his time looking for the ke'tain now."

I assumed that was what Lukas was doing. The last time I'd seen him was the day Tennin took the photos of us. I still went to his place to train, but he was never there, and he hadn't been here since the night we'd kissed. None of his men mentioned him when I was there, and I didn't ask, even though his absence from my life felt deliberate. Maybe he had figured out I had foolishly developed feelings for him, and he was doing the honorable thing, as Dariyah had put it.

I hadn't seen her either since the night she'd attacked me. The next time I'd seen Faolin, he'd told me Dariyah would not bother me again, or she would have the royal guard to answer to.

Dariyah might be gone, but the things she'd said had stayed with me. As much as I disliked her, she hadn't been lying about the future king needing a consort. The more I thought about Lukas choosing a mate who could give him blue-blooded babies, the less I wanted to know about it. I wasn't naïve enough to think for a second that there could have been anything between us. But the thought of him with someone like Dariyah really pushed the knife deeper in my gut.

I was cleaning up from dinner when Bruce showed up. Word had gotten out that Dad was coming home today, and a bunch of his friends had wanted to throw him a welcome home party. I'd nixed that idea because of the doctors' warning that he had to take it slow. Bruce and Maurice were his best friends, and they wouldn't let him overdo it.

"Did the doctors say when you can go back to work?" Bruce asked as I rinsed the last plate. I turned off the water to hear them better.

"Not for a few months," Dad said. "I'm going to manage the business from home until they clear me, and Jesse will do the hunting."

I dried my hands and walked into the living room as Bruce said, "She's a natural hunter. Is she still planning to go to college?"

"Yes," Dad and I said together, and we all laughed.

The bathroom window banged, announcing Gus's arrival. Bruce was the only one who started at the noise because I hadn't told him about my new pet. If you could call Gus a pet. He came and went when he pleased, never listened to a thing I said, and seemed to barely tolerate me. The only time he came near me was for food or when he crept in to sleep on my bed every night.

The cantankerous drakkan walked into the living room and bared his teeth in a hiss when he saw all the people there. Tiny wisps of smoke issued from his nostrils, and he flapped his wings in agitation before he disappeared down the hallway again.

"He's hungry," I explained. I went to fill his bowl with raw chicken and carried it to my bedroom. Gus's tail stuck out from under the bed where he was sulking. He did that whenever he was unhappy. I'd learned there was no use trying to coax him out, so I set the bowl on the floor and left. The smell of raw meat would draw him out soon enough.

"You're supposed to turn in your captures, not keep them," Bruce joked when I returned to the living room.

"Tell that to Gus." I sat next to Dad on the couch, and he slipped an arm around me. I snuggled against his side like I was ten years old again, happy to sit quietly and listen to them catch up.

As much as I enjoyed their company, I wasn't sorry to see Maurice and Bruce leave an hour later. Finch came down from the tree house to curl up on Dad's shoulder, and the three of us watched an old western. The only thing that would have made the evening better was if Mom were here.

I took the next day off from hunting. After breakfast, Dad and I sat at the table with my laptop and went through the family and business finances. When I showed him Mom's spreadsheet, which I had been maintaining in her absence, he was shocked at the number of jobs I'd done since I started.

"Jesse, you've brought in a hundred thousand dollars in just over three months."

The pride in his eyes filled my chest with warmth. "I learned from the best."

He shook his head as he went back to poring over the list of jobs I'd done. "I think you have more Threes and Fours here than your mom, Maurice, and I did in our first year together."

"Not quite." I grinned at him. "I checked."

"Maybe I should let you take over the business," he teased, the corners of his eyes creased with laughter.

I put up my hands. "Oh, no. I will admit I like hunting more than I thought I would, but I am quite happy being the nerd in the family."

"You can be both if that's what you want."

"I know, but my heart is set on college." After all the craziness of the last few months, I was looking forward to school more than ever. I daydreamed about ivy-covered buildings, nights at the library, lectures, and creating study schedules. Most people might find those things boring after the adventures I'd had, but I couldn't wait to just be a normal college student.

I pushed up my glasses. "Besides, this job is hell on glasses. How does Mom do it?"

He chuckled. "The Agency's vision insurance covers unlimited replacements."

"Now you tell me."

He opened the file where I'd been keeping track of household expenses. "I know this plumber. How did you get him to replace the pipes for that price?"

I shrugged. "He quoted almost twice that much when he came out to give me an estimate. But when he sent me his invoice, that was what he charged me. I called him to make sure it wasn't a mistake, and he said we were good."

Dad frowned. "This doesn't look right. The labor alone would cost that much."

A knock at the door was followed by, "I know you're in there. It's no use hiding from me."

Dad and I laughed, and I went to open the door to Violet, whose arms were loaded down with bags. I helped her carry them to the table, and then she practically squeezed the life out of my father. Violet was a big hugger, and she loved my parents. Her eyes were misty when she pulled away and took a large Tupperware container from one of the bags.

"Mom made you quinoa salad with all kinds of healthy stuff in it." She made a face. "There's probably kale in it. You've been forewarned."

He took the container and peeked inside. "Looks great. I'll have some for lunch."

"There's grilled chicken breasts, too," she pointed at a second container. From the other bag, she lifted a pink box with a neighborhood bakery logo on the side. "This is from me."

I gave her a disapproving look as she handed the box to Dad. I didn't need to look inside to know it was Boston cream doughnuts, his favorite.

She shrugged. "He's allowed to splurge."

"Yes, he is." Dad picked up one of the doughnuts and took a huge bite. He looked happier than a man just released from prison.

Violet inclined her head at the laptop, "What are you two up to?"

"I'm bringing Dad up to speed on the business," I said.

She scrunched her nose. "I'll go hang out with Finch and Aisla until you're done adulting. And then I'm going to tell you about the *amazing* night I had."

"Lorelle?"

She pretended to swoon. "You know what they say. Once you go Fae..."

Dad coughed, sending bits of doughnut across the table. Violet giggled and patted him on the back. "Alright there, Mr. J.?"

"Yes," he wheezed.

She grinned at me over his head and went into the living room. I sat in front of the laptop while he polished off his doughnut and licked chocolate from his fingers. The television came on in the living room, and I could hear Violet's voice as she talked to Finch. Aisla still didn't speak, but she seemed to understand us well enough.

"Hey, Jess, did I tell you my agent got me an audition for another big sci-fi film?" Violet called as she flicked through TV channels.

"That's great," Dad said. "What's it about?"

"I can't say, but the director may or may not have done a certain franchise about robots that turn into cars." She paused. "You didn't hear that from me, though."

"Hear what?" Dad and I said in unison and grinned at each other.

Violet snorted. "They're holding auditions at the Ralston next week, so wish me luck."

"Good luck, even though you won't need it," I called in a singsong voice. "Right, Dad?"

He didn't respond. I slanted a look his way to find him staring off into space, his brow creased like he was deep in thought.

"Dad?"

"Sorry. Didn't mean to space out on you." He blinked and smiled at me, but I could see that he was preoccupied with something.

I lowered my voice. "Did you remember something?" The doctors had told us that being home in familiar surroundings could help him recover some of his memories.

"I don't know." He frowned. "I keep seeing the ballroom at the Ralston. It's only flashes, so I can't be sure."

My pulse jumped. The Ralston was the last place he and Mom were seen the night they disappeared. And a maintenance man had found Mom's broken bracelet in one of the ballrooms there the next day.

"It feels like there's something I need to remember, but it's blocked." He rubbed his temple like it was hurting.

"It's only your first day home. It'll come to you."

He looked at me, and his frustration was almost palpable. "Whatever it is, it's important to all of us."

It had to be the ke'tain. What else could be more important to everyone?

Fear snaked through me. Except for waylaying me to give me the queen's message about her son, the Seelie guard had left me and my family alone. What would they do if they found out my father was getting his memories back?

"Jesse, do you know where the fey dust is?" Dad asked a week later as he did inventory of the supplies on the office shelves.

I made a face and paused writing up notes on last night's job. "I might have used it all."

"You used a whole bag of fey dust?" He turned to give me an incredulous look.

"Remember that bunnek I told you about?"

He frowned. "Fey dust doesn't work on bunneks."

"I know that *now*. It was a bulletin, and I didn't exactly have time to come home and read Mom's notes on bunneks." I pointed at the monitor. "We need a mobile version we can put on our phones and sync with the main one."

His grimace pulled a laugh from me. The computer was Mom's domain, and he liked it that way. Lucky for us, I'd taken computer classes the last three years of school, and like Mom, I loved spreadsheets.

"I'll do it." I had been thinking about it since January, but there'd never been time. "I should have asked Maurice about his contact for the fey dust."

"Don't worry about it. You had enough on your plate." Dad went back to sorting supplies. "We mainly use it for trolls and ogres. No one wants to fight those brutes."

I fought back a groan as I realized how easy it would have been to rescue Romeo from the ogres with fey dust. Not to mention the troll jobs. No sprained shoulder or kolosh poisoning.

No Lukas kiss.

My skin heated when I remembered how I'd grabbed his shirt front, pulled him to me, and kissed him. And then I'd asked him if he would kiss me again.

"Jesse?"

I started and met Dad's curious gaze. "Huh?"

"How did you do the troll jobs without the fey dust?" he asked.

Before I could answer, Gus made an awful retching sound in my bedroom. I ran to my room in time to see him vomit in the middle of my bed. Gagging from the horrible smell, I picked him up and carried him to the bathroom to clean him.

It was the fourth time he'd thrown up in two days, and I was starting to worry that he might be sick. He usually did it when he'd tried to eat something too big to swallow, like my paperweight. That wasn't the case now.

Dad stood in the doorway with my quilt bundled in his arms. "Is he okay?"

"I think he's sick." I gently cleaned the drakkan's snout with a wet cloth. The fact that he didn't nip at me confirmed my fears. "What should I do?"

"When faeries get sick, they go back to Faerie to heal. I hate to say it, but Gus might have to be sent home, too."

I caressed the red gold scales on his head. "But he's never been there. How will he know how to hunt and live in the wild?"

"They'll introduce him to a flock, and he'll adjust," Dad said. "Drakkans are not solitary creatures. They need to be with their own kind."

I swallowed around the unexpected tightness in my throat. Somehow, the cranky little guy had wormed his way into my heart, and I realized I would miss him if he had to go.

"I'm not taking him to the Plaza," I said thickly. There was no way I'd allow him to sit in a strange holding cell until he was sent home. "Faris is planning to go home tomorrow. I'll ask him if he can take Gus with him."

Dad nodded. He hadn't met any of my Fae friends yet, but he'd finally stopped giving me strange looks whenever I mentioned the royal guard. The only name that didn't come up often was Lukas's. It had been three weeks since I'd laid eyes on him, and I had a feeling this was how it would be from now on. If my father thought it was odd that I rarely spoke of Lukas, he didn't say anything about it.

Dad made a little nest of towels on my bed and laid the subdued drakkan in it. I sat in the chair by the window and called Faris.

"Your father is right. Gus doesn't belong in this realm," Faris said after I explained the situation to him.

"Will the other drakkans accept him into their flock if he was hatched here?"

I could hear the smile in Faris's voice when he answered. "I promise Gus will be very happy in Faerie. Do you want me to come to your apartment to get him?"

I looked at Gus, who was watching me warily from the bed, and I wondered if he could tell I was talking about him. "I think it might upset him less if I bring him to you. Will Kaia be okay with him there?"

"I'll leave tonight instead of tomorrow," Faris said kindly. "You can stay to see us off if you'd like."

"I would." I stood, knowing the longer I put off what had to be done, the harder it would be. "We'll be there in thirty minutes."

I hung up and avoided looking at Gus as I left my room. I closed the door behind me so he couldn't take off if he suddenly got it into his head, and I went to the office to tell my father where I was going. Next, I had to go to the living room and break it to Finch and Aisla, who had also grown attached to the drakkan. Explaining to my tearful brother why Gus would not be coming back home would forever sit near the top of my list of things I never wanted to do again.

I couldn't risk driving with an unrestrained drakkan, so I dug out the dog carrier I'd used for the trow job. I replaced the iron mesh in the bottom with some old towels and took it to my bedroom where Gus hadn't moved from his spot on the bed. He growled when I picked him up and placed him in the carrier, but he soon settled down, another indication of how unwell he was.

"Do you want me to come with you?" Dad asked when I walked out and set the carrier on the coffee table.

I almost said yes, until I saw Finch's sad face as he reached through the wire door to pet Gus. He needed our father more than I did now. Dad followed my gaze, and no other words were needed between us.

"I'll be home in a few hours," I told Dad as I pulled on my coat.

"Take your time," he said and added in a low voice. "Finch will be okay."

I gave Finch and Aisla a few more minutes with Gus, and then I made myself pick up the carrier and leave. As I put it on the passenger seat of the Jeep and secured it with the seat belt, I told myself the tears at the back of my throat were for Finch, not for the grouchy drakkan who didn't even like me on his good days.

Gus didn't make a sound for the first ten minutes. When he began to growl and turn around in the carrier, I smiled, relieved to see him showing some energy again.

"You won't have to stay in there long. Where you're going, you'll be able to fly all day with other drakkans. Won't that be nice?"

He growled louder, and I jumped when he started clawing frantically at the metal grate in the door.

"Gus, calm down." Keeping my eyes on traffic, I reached over to pat the top of the carrier. I miscalculated, and my hand touched the door instead.

"Ow!" I yanked my hand back and sucked at the blood beading on one fingertip. "Gus, what the hell?"

I looked up as the car ahead of me stopped suddenly. I slammed on my brakes and barely avoided rear-ending them. Horns began to blow, and the screech of metal on metal came from somewhere behind me.

My gaze fell on the pedestrians on the sidewalk, who had stopped walking to stare up at the sky. Some people had their phones out and were recording or taking pictures.

I leaned forward to look up at the sky, and I felt a frisson of fear when I saw the lights and jagged bolts of electricity. Based on my location, I guessed they were over the Hudson, exactly where they'd been the day of the ferry accident. I shivered and prayed for the boats on the river.

Gus chose that moment to go into a full freak-out, tearing at the sides of the carrier. It wouldn't hold him long like this, and I did not want to be trapped in here with him when he got free. Traffic resumed at a crawl, and I looked around for a place to pull over.

I saw someone leaving a spot up ahead, and I grabbed it, earning an angry honk from the vehicle behind me. Ignoring the rude gestures from the woman as she drove past, I pulled off my coat and threw it over the carrier. It helped a little, but what I really needed was to get the drakkan inside, preferably away from windows. I looked up to see what buildings were nearby and let out a breath when I saw the sign for Moore Books.

Angela was standing by the window with a customer, looking at the sky when I ran inside. The owner's eyes lit with recognition and dropped to the carrier, which emitted angry growls and squawks.

She cautiously approached me. "You're Tennin's friend."

I nodded and spoke in a rush. "I hate to impose, but can I use your office again. The storm is upsetting him, and you have no windows in there."

"Sure," she said with more than a hint of uncertainty. "Go on back."

"Thanks!" I hurried to the office and shut the door. Setting the carrier on the floor, I knelt in front of it and crooned to Gus until he stopped trying to claw his way out.

Angela knocked on the door. "The lights are gone. Is he okay?"

All the tension left my body. "Yes. You can open the door."

She cracked it a few inches and peeked in. "Can I ask what it is?"

"It's a drakkan."

Her eyes went impossibly wide. "For real?"

I smiled. "Tennin probably didn't tell you I'm a bounty hunter. This little guy was injured, and I took care of him at home. Now I'm taking him to a friend, who will return him to Faerie."

"Wow." She opened the door further. "Can I see him?"

"Yes, but don't be surprised if he growls at you. He doesn't like people." I lifted the carrier and set it on the desk with the door facing her. Angela crouched to peer in from a safe distance, and surprisingly, Gus didn't make a sound.

"He's so pretty," she cooed. "Oh. I think he's getting sick."

I looked inside and sure enough, Gus was retching again. His whole body rocked forward over and over until he finally threw up whatever was left in his stomach. A few droplets of bile landed on the floor, but the rest landed in the bottom of the crate.

Angela gagged and clapped a hand over her mouth. "God, that smell."

"I'm so sorry." I covered my own mouth as my eyes watered. "I'll need to clean him up. Do you have a bathroom?"

She backed out of the office and pointed at another door. "Right there. I'll be up front."

I took the carrier into the bathroom, which consisted of a toilet and a pedestal sink. There was barely enough room to turn around once I shut the door, and I had a hell of a time lifting Gus from the crate without getting the putrid green slime all over me. He didn't put up a fight, even when I set him in the sink and gave him an impromptu bath under the faucet.

"Oh, Gus. I hate that you're not feeling well," I said as I dried him off with paper towels. I put him on the floor and set about removing the soiled towels from the carrier and stuffing them into the garbage. It reeked in here. Angela was going to have to use a can of air freshener to get this stink out.

I tipped the carrier to wipe it out, and something fell out and rolled around the sink. I looked down at the small object coated in slime. Was this the reason he was sick?

"What the heck did you eat this time?" I turned on the faucet and rinsed the mysterious object. As the slime washed away, it revealed a round, iridescent blue stone that was warm to the touch and seemed to glow from within.

My stomach did a full summersault. It couldn't be. I dried the stone off with shaking hands and held it up.

It was the ke'tain.

19

I leaned heavily against the sink. I'd found it. Or Gus had found it. I stared down at the drakkan preening himself on the floor. How had this happened? How had a stolen Fae artifact, sought after by Faerie, the Agency, and half the bounty hunters in the world, ended up in the stomach of my drakkan?

I needed to sit down.

Picking up Gus, I opened the door and went back to the office. The visitor chair was full of books, so I took the chair behind the desk. I looked at the ke'tain again, and not knowing what else to do with it, I tucked it into the front pocket of my jeans.

Once the initial shock passed, I was able to think a bit clearer and put the pieces together. I'd known all along Gus had to be the drakkan that escaped from Lewis Tate's house during the raid. With Gus's propensity for eating anything that could fit into his mouth, it made sense that he would have swallowed the small stone. Whether that had happened the night of the raid or before, I'd never know. What I did know was that the ke'tain had been under my nose this whole time.

And now it was in my pocket.

My scalp prickled with unease. I had an object in my possession that people would kill for. My parents had almost died because of it, and the longer I held onto it, the longer my family was in danger.

I got up and pulled on my coat. I had to call Lukas. He would come get the ke'tain, and everything would be okay.

I had just taken my phone from my pocket when a large shape filled the office doorway. Already on edge, I let out a small scream and dropped the phone, which clattered across the floor. I could only stare as he bent and picked it up.

"Conlan, what are you doing here?" I asked in a voice that was an octave higher than normal. "You scared the hell out of me."

He handed the phone to me. "You ran in here, and when you didn't come out, I worried something had happened to you."

My shock gave way to confusion. "How did you see me run in here, and why were you waiting for me to come out?"

"We've been watching you and your father since he came home," he said matter-of-factly. "Lukas was worried the Seelie guard or Davian might come after you if they thought your father remembered something."

"You've been following me for a week, and no one bothered to tell me?" Never mind that I'd had the same fear ever since my father remembered the Ralston ballroom.

Conlan smiled unapologetically. "Telling you wouldn't have changed anything." He looked around the office and settled his gaze on Gus. "Faris said you were bringing him a sick drakkan. Why did you stop at a bookstore?"

My indignation over him following me vanished. All that mattered was the stone sitting in my jeans pocket. I pulled Conlan all the way into the office and went around him to shut the door. Turning, I saw him staring at me in amused bewilderment.

"I found it," I whispered urgently.

"Found what?"

I took the stone from my pocket and held it out on my palm. For a few seconds, there was no reaction from Conlan. Then he surprised me by falling to one knee with his head bowed, and his hands crossed over his heart. He murmured something in Fae that sounded like a prayer, before he lifted his head to look at me.

"You are indeed blessed by Aedhna," he said reverently. "How did you find it?"

I closed my hand around the stone and motioned for him to stand. "I'll tell you once we get it somewhere safe."

In the blink of an eye, the charming Conlan I knew was gone, and in his place was one of the legendary royal guard. He even looked bigger, if that was possible. "You're right. I'll take you to Lukas."

My heart gave a little flutter at the thought of seeing Lukas again, but I grabbed Conlan's arm when he reached for the door. "You should take the ke'tain."

One corner of his mouth lifted. "You planning to ditch me when we get outside?"

Leave it to him to joke at a time like this. "No. I think it will be safer with you." I held the stone out to him, but he backed away.

"I can't touch it."

"That's right." I remembered Ben Stewart saying the ke'tain was lethal to faeries. I stuffed the stone back into my pocket. "Okay. Let's go."

He opened the door and looked around before he led the way to the front of the store. There was no sign of the owner, and I felt a prickle of unease as my eyes searched the bookstore.

"Angela?" I walked toward the register. It wasn't until I was close enough to see through the glass top that I spied the body on the floor behind the counter. I ran behind the counter, and when I saw her sightless eyes, I shouted for Conlan. The unnatural angle of her head told me her neck had been broken.

Silence greeted me. I shot to my feet and almost tripped over Angela's body at the sight of the six masked men in tactical gear surrounding Conlan. The faerie was slumped between two of the men who were holding him upright.

"Conlan!" I shouted, and he didn't respond. "What did you do to him?"

The biggest man spoke. "A special cocktail of sedatives and iron. He's still alive for now."

"Sedatives don't work on faeries," I said shakily.

His smile was visible through the mouth hole of his mask. "This one does. It'll keep him out long enough for us to get what we came for."

My mouth went dry. "What do you want?"

"Don't play coy with me, Miss James." The man, who appeared to be the leader of the group, held up a device that resembled the ke'tain sensor, only bigger. The light on the device was blinking green. In his other hand, he held a gun that was pointed at my head. "Give me the ke'tain."

I gripped the edge of the counter as my knees threatened to give out. No matter how afraid I was, I couldn't hand the ke'tain over to him. This was bigger than I was, bigger than Conlan. If he were awake, he would agree with me. It was about protecting the people we loved.

I met the man's eyes, which were shadowed by the mask. "I don't have it."

"And I don't have time to play games with you." He turned his gun on Conlan. "Even a faerie can't survive having his head blown off at point-blank range."

"Do you know who that is? He's one of the Unseelie crown prince's best friends. You kill him, and the entire Unseelie royal guard will hunt you down."

None of the men reacted. I had to stall them somehow. By now, Faris had to be wondering why I wasn't there yet. He'd call me, and when I didn't answer, he'd call Conlan, whom he would know was following me today. When he couldn't reach Conlan, he'd sound the alarm. Faolin would trace our phones or Conlan's car to this street. They'd come.

"You think Davian Woods won't give up your names when Prince Vaerik is done with him?" The man's head jerked back a fraction, betraying his surprise. I seized on it. "The prince is onto Davian and knows all about his little schemes."

A tiny movement behind him caught my attention. I darted my gaze to Conlan and saw him open his eyes and look right at me for a second.

I met the leader's gaze again. "Prince Vaerik knows Davian was trying to buy the ke'tain from Lewis Tate until Tate disappeared. He also knows Davian is working with the Seelie guard. If anything happens to Conlan, the prince will know it was done by a professional hired by Davian. How long do you think it will take him to track you down?"

The man lowered his gun until it was no longer pointed at Conlan's head. "I'm coming over there, and you are going to give me the ke'tain, or I will take it by force. The prince might care about his friend's life, but I doubt yours will matter to him."

"Give it...to...him," Conlan stammered, surprising everyone in the room.

"No." Why would he say that?

Conlan lifted his head and stared at me with an expression that said to trust him. "He will...find it."

"Yes, I will," the leader said confidently. But Conlan wasn't referring to him. He was telling me Lukas would find the ke'tain if I let the men take it to Davian.

"Jesse." Conlan smiled weakly to let me know it would be okay. "Do it."

I stared at him for a long moment before I nodded stiffly and reached for my pocket.

"Stop." The leader waved his gun at me. "Come out here where we can see you."

I did as he ordered and walked around the counter. Reaching into my pocket, I retrieved the stone and held it out to the man. I felt sick as he approached me with his hand outstretched. Was I really doing this? I was going to give it to him without a fight?

I wanted to yank my hand back when his fingers brushed it. My other hand itched to curl into a fist and punch him in the throat. I was strung tighter than my guitar strings as I waited for him to take the damn thing already.

"What are you doing?" one of the other men asked. "Take it so we can get out of here."

"I can't," the leader said through gritted teeth. "It won't move."

My eyes flew to his knuckles, which were white from their grip on the ke'tain. The tendons strained in his wrist as he pulled, but all I felt was the weight of the stone in my hand.

"Give it to me," he snarled.

"I'm not doing anything." I looked at Conlan, but he seemed as confused as I was.

The other man who had spoken came over. The leader let go of the ke'tain, and his friend grabbed it. He grunted as he tried to pull it from my hand. Releasing it, he glared at me. "You're using magic. Stop it."

"I am not!" I turned and placed the ke'tain on the glass counter. "There. Take it."

He reached for the stone, but the second he touched it, it disappeared. "What the hell?" he yelled, turning angry eyes on me again.

I felt the warm weight in my hand before I opened it. He was right that there was some kind of magic at work, but it wasn't coming from me. For some unknown reason the ke'tain was stuck to me, just like the goddess stone.

The goddess stone. That had to be it. Somehow, it was connected to the ke'tain and keeping the men from taking it from me. There was no other explanation.

I couldn't tell them any of that. God only knew what Davian Woods would do if he found out I had an actual goddess stone. I'd probably end up locked away in one of his private collections.

"That's it. You're coming with us." The leader grabbed me roughly by the arm. "We get paid as long as we deliver the ke'tain."

"Let her go." Conlan charged us, but his movements were still sluggish from the iron. The other men easily subdued him and shackled his hands behind his back. The shackles weren't Agency-issue, but they were iron, so they did the job.

"Put the ke'tain back in your jeans pocket," the leader ordered. After I did it, he emptied my other pockets, tossing my keys, ID card, stun gun, and phone on the counter. I held my breath as he patted me down, and I bit my cheek when he found the pick set in the inner pocket of my coat.

When he was done, he spun me around and wrenched my arms behind my back none too gently. I felt cold metal as a pair of shackles were locked around my wrists, and I wondered if my captures experienced the same helpless fear I felt now.

The men forced us toward the back of the store. We passed the office, and I caught a glimpse of Gus curled up asleep on the desk where I'd left him. He was so worn out that he'd slept through everything. What would he do when he woke up here alone?

And poor Angela. Heaviness settled over me at the memory of her lifeless body. All she'd done was help me, and she'd died because of it. They'd murdered her.

"Why did you kill her?" I asked as I was shoved toward the back door.

No one answered as they took Conlan and me to a plain white cargo van parked beside the dumpster in the small alley. They sat us on opposite sides of the van and pulled black hoods down over our heads. The engine started, and I was overcome with an awful feeling of déjà vu. Only this time, I wasn't alone in the trunk of a car. I didn't know if I was more relieved that Conlan was with me, or if I felt guilty for dragging him into this.

I paid attention to every turn the van took, visualizing the route as they drove through Brooklyn. I knew immediately when we started to cross the bridge into Manhattan, and it wasn't hard to guess where they were taking us. At least, it wouldn't be a filthy cage in a drug dealer's basement this time.

The van took a sharp turn and went down a short ramp. It stopped, and the driver lowered his window for a minute before he drove on. We were in a parking garage, and I was sure it was the one beneath Davian Woods's building.

With the hoods still over our heads, Conlan and I were herded from the van and into an elevator. All eight of us fit inside, so it had to be a service elevator, not the one I'd been in the night of Davian's party. We rode up in silence, and when the doors opened, we were led down a hallway, through a door, and down a short flight of stairs. Finally, someone pushed me onto a chair and bound my legs to the chair legs with duct tape. My hands were left shackled behind my back.

I heard footsteps leaving the room. As soon as the last one faded, I called for Conlan and was met with silence. My stomach clenched. What had they done to him? Maybe they'd put him in a different room so we couldn't talk and plan an escape.

I wasn't left alone for long. The soft tap of shoes heralded the approach of a man, but not one wearing combat boots. I didn't have long to wonder about his identity because he grabbed the top of the hood and pulled it off my head.

Davian Woods stood before me in a dark gray suit, looking like he was about to walk into a boardroom. He wore the same smile he'd given me the night we met, but unlike then, it didn't quite reach his brown eyes.

I wasn't that surprised to see we were in the upstairs dining area of his penthouse. I turned my head toward the terrace and felt a surge of relief when I saw Conlan shackled to a chair on the other side of the table. His head was down, and he appeared to be unconscious.

"Miss James," Davian said, bringing my attention back to him. "I can walk into a room full of the sharpest business minds in the world and read every person there. I've built an empire on that ability. Yet you were not only able to gain access to my home, you flew under my radar for months. How?"

He put a hand to his chin, his head tilted like he was intensely curious about my answer. If he expected to hear I was some highly-trained operative, he was about to be disappointed.

"You didn't notice me because I'm a nobody – to you anyway. Tennin has a weakness for redheads, and you have a weakness for faeries. And neither of you would suspect a girl for wanting to go to one of Davian Woods's society parties on the arm of a faerie prince."

Davian cocked his eyebrows at my assessment of him, and then he laughed. "That is brilliant in its simplicity."

I smiled in response. The less I said the better.

His eyes grew shrewd. "How does a young bounty hunter with no obvious connections come to be friends with the Unseelie prince?"

"I wouldn't exactly call us friends." I didn't know what to call my relationship with Lukas. The best word I could come up with was *confusing*, but I wasn't telling Davian that.

Davian's gaze flicked to Conlan and back to me. "You were found in the company of one of his royal guards, whom I'm told was quite protective of you. Why?"

I eyed my captor with contempt. "You could ask him that if your hired guns hadn't knocked him out."

He sighed ruefully. "That was not supposed to happen. I will have to smooth things out with Prince Vaerik."

I almost choked, trying not to laugh. Davian had clearly gone off the deep end if he thought he could talk his way out of this after hurting one of Lukas's men. I decided to let him discover that for himself.

"I will address that problem in due course," Davian said. "Right now, I believe you have something I paid a great deal to obtain."

"Something that doesn't belong to you." I tensed, completely at his mercy with my hands bound behind my back.

"It's not for me. It never was."

"I don't understand. Don't you know what this thing is doing to our world? What good are all your money and your prized possessions" – I tilted my head toward the gallery – "if the world is destroyed?"

He frowned. "Queen Anwyn never meant to damage the barrier between the realms. Her men lost the ke'tain, and they've been trying to find it to take it back to Faerie. Once they do, the barrier will heal."

"Prince Vaerik is looking for the ke'tain, too. Give it to him and let him return it to Faerie. It'll go a long way to smoothing things out with him for what your men did to Conlan."

"It would, but I have an agreement with the Seelie queen," he said. "Payment upon delivery."

I stared at him. "You have more money than you could ever spend, and you have no problem getting things brought to you from Faerie. What could she possibly give you that you can't buy?"

Davian's eyes took on a feverish gleam. "Immortality."

I shook my head. "That's impossible. No one can give you that."

"The Seelie queen can."

"She's lying to you." I leaned forward in my chair. "You're too old. You'd never survive the change."

He chuckled, and there was a note of madness in it. "You're wrong. With the ke'tain, she'll have the power of the goddess in her hands, and she will be able to do anything."

"The ke'tain's power is lethal to faeries. Queen Anwyn can't use it." I wanted to yell at him, scream, anything to get through to him.

He held out his hand like I hadn't spoken. "I will take the ke'tain now. The sooner she gets what she wants, the sooner I get what I want."

"How do you suggest I do that?" I strained against my shackles.

Davian grasped my arms and pulled me to my feet. Having my legs tied to the chair made me sway, but he steadied me. Unabashedly, he reached into the left front pocket of my jeans and then the right. He smiled when his fingers touched the ke'tain, but his elation faded when he couldn't pick up the stone. He tried again and again with the same result, his face growing more mottled with each attempt.

"Stop it," he bit out.

"I'm not doing anything."

The slap came fast and hard, sending my glasses askew. Davian grabbed my shoulders and shook me so viciously my glasses flew off, and I thought my neck was going to snap.

"Do not play games with me," he snarled, spraying my face with spittle. "Give me the ke'tain, or I will have my men throw you off the terrace."

"I can't!" I screamed at him as fear gripped me. He would do it. I could see it in his eyes. He'd kill me without an ounce of remorse.

He pushed me down to the chair and stepped back. "You're telling the truth."

"Yes," I choked out.

"Did he do this?" He pointed at Conlan. "Did he put some kind of ward on you?"

"No."

Davian pressed his lips together and nodded. "The queen's guard will know what to do."

I tried to stand and fell back down. "They'll kill us!"

He retrieved my glasses from the floor and tossed them on the table beside me. "Then you'd better find a way to give me that stone before they get here."

"How?"

"You're a smart girl. Figure it out." He walked toward the stairs, stopping to talk in a low voice to someone hidden by the textured glass wall. I could hear two other male voices, and Davian telling them to stand guard until the faeries arrived.

A chill went through me when I heard his footsteps on the stairs. If he called the Seelie royal guard, they could be here in minutes by using a portal. The thought of what they would do to us threatened to make me hyperventilate.

I forced myself to stay calm because panic would not help Conlan or me. Davian was right. I was a smart girl. I just had to think rationally and work the problem.

I almost laughed hysterically at that. We were on the second floor of a penthouse apartment that was guarded by at least six armed men. Oh, and the Seelie guard could be on the way here at this very minute.

Stop it, Jesse. I took a deep breath and let it out slowly. All I could do was focus on the things within my control. I'd figure out the next part when I came to it. My first problem was getting out of this chair, and thanks to Davian, I had the tools to do that.

I listened for the men and heard them having a quiet conversation over by the stairs. Easing to a standing position, I leaned toward the table. It took some stretching and straining, but I was able to reach my glasses. I sat and carefully broke the ears off them, stuffing the frames in my back pocket. Then I set to work on the shackles.

It wasn't easy to maneuver with my wrists shackled, but I'd practiced on Agency shackles at home until I could free myself every time. I was used to working with an actual pick set, which made this harder, but not impossible. I just needed to get the feel for it.

"Jesse," Conlan whispered.

I fumbled and almost dropped one of the ears. Heart racing, I whipped my head in his direction and found him still slumped in the chair. "Conlan?" I said in a voice too low for the men to hear.

The hood moved a fraction. "Did he hurt you?"

"No." I went back to work on the lock. "What did they do to you?"

"More sedative, I think. The shackles are iron. Can't move much yet."

My heart sank. I'd been counting on Conlan fighting his way out of the penthouse once I woke him up. That wasn't going to happen in his current state.

"Give me a few minutes," he said in a calm, reassuring tone. "I'll get us out of here."

"We might not have a few minutes. Davian couldn't take the ke'tain from me, so he is calling the Seelie guard," I said as I worked on the shackles. I bit my lip when I heard a distinct click in the lock, and the shackles loosened. Before they could fall to the floor, I grabbed them and laid them quietly on the table.

Conlan muttered a few Fae words. "Do you know where we are?"

"We're in Davian's penthouse." I bent forward to work on the duct tape around one of my legs.

"Faris knows by now that something happened to us. Lukas will suspect Davian, and they will come here looking for us," Conlan said softly like he was trying to soothe a frightened child.

"I know." I freed my leg and started on the other one. "How long will it take you to get your strength back?"

He lifted his head. "Once the iron shackles are gone, it should not take more than ten minutes."

I turned my head to stare at him. Were all royal faeries that strong, or was it a royal guard thing? I wouldn't be surprised to learn Lukas and his men deliberately exposed themselves to iron to build a resistance to it.

I dropped the tape on the floor and stood quietly. After checking on the men who were still talking in low voices, I crept around the far end of the table. Conlan had to be more affected by the iron than he was letting on, because he didn't stir as I came up behind him.

"Jesse?" he whispered.

I leaned down and spoke next to his ear. "Yes."

He startled but didn't say a word as I pulled off his hood. His shocked expression was almost comical, and I smiled as I went to work on his shackles. I made short work of them and heard his sigh of relief when he was free of the iron.

"How?" he asked as I removed the duct tape from one of his legs. The men had used twice as much on him as they had on me.

"It's a bounty hunter thing," I quipped softly.

Conlan shook out his arms. "More like a Jesse thing."

"That too."

I finished freeing his leg and moved to the other one. "I'm sorry I got you into this."

"It's not your fault, and I'm glad I'm here with you." He laid a hand on my shoulder. "I should have been there for you at Rogin's, and I wasn't. I'm sorry."

"That's all in the past."

"Not for me. We were friends, and I broke your trust. Losing your friendship will always be one of my biggest regrets."

I looked at his downturned mouth and eyes full of remorse. "You did hurt me, but we can be friends again. You just have to do one thing."

He nodded. "Anything."

"You can start training me with a weapon. I've had enough conditioning to last me a lifetime."

Conlan chuckled. "Only if you promise not to use it on Faolin."

"I can't make any promises where he is concerned." I pulled off the last of the tape and stood. "Can you walk?"

He cocked his head. "Yes. But the two men over there have guns. I will not risk you getting shot."

"Then we need to disarm them." My mind raced as I came up with plans and discarded them just as quickly. My lips curved. "I have an idea. How fast can you run right now?"

Two minutes later, I was back in my chair with my arms behind my back and the duct tape wrapped loosely around my ankles. "Hey, I figured it out," I called excitedly.

"Figured what out?" asked one of the men.

"The ke'tain. I think I can give it to you now."

There was silence, and for a long moment, I feared they were going to call for Davian. Then I heard two sets of feet approach, and both men rounded the corner. One had his hand on his gun, and the other was unarmed. They looked from me to Conlan, who sat with his head down and his hood back in place.

"I don't see it," one of them said suspiciously.

I wriggled my arms like they were still bound, rattling the shackles for good measure. "It's in my right pocket. You'll have to get it."

The two exchanged a look but didn't make a move to take the ke'tain.

I injected as much desperation as I could into my voice. "Please. I don't want the Seelie guard to come. Give the ke'tain to Davian, and he'll let me go."

The unarmed man came over to me and stuck his fingers into my pocket. I let out an indignant shriek. "No groping!"

"I'm not groping you," he snarled. "I'm trying to reach the damn thing."

The second man moved closer. "Stand her up. It'll be easier that way."

The guy removed his hand from my pocket and pulled me to my feet. I pretended to lose my balance, and both men reached out to steady me.

Things happened in a blur after that. I brought my arms around and punched the first man in the throat as Conlan appeared behind the second one. Before I could slap the shackles on one, Conlan had both of them on the floor and out cold.

I gaped at him. If he could move like this with iron and a sedative in his system, it was no wonder he was one of the most lethal faeries in the world.

He smiled at me. "Good job. Now let's get out of here."

I picked up the men's guns and pointed one at the stairs. "After you."

Conlan took one of the guns from me, and we crept to the top of the stairs. He listened for sound below and signaled that there were two men at the bottom of the stairs. Then he indicated he would go down alone and neutralize the men.

He started down the stairs, but on the third step, he froze. The next thing I knew, he was beside me again. "They're coming."

Fear gripped me. "The Seelie guard?"

"They will be here in a few minutes." Conlan ushered me away from the stairs. "Davian is lowering the dampening ward for them now."

"Then you'll be able to create a portal out of here," I said as he tugged me toward the terrace. "You can go and get help."

"And leave you behind?" he growled. "Have you lost your mind?"

I looked around desperately. "I'll hide somewhere. They'll think I went with you."

Conlan pushed open the door to the terrace and pulled me outside. "Davian and his men might be fooled, but the guard won't. They will search every inch of this place until they find you."

"Then you better hurry," I said as we moved to one end of the terrace, out of sight of the stairs. He scowled at me, and I added, "If you have a better idea, I'm all ears."

The look he shot me said he didn't.

I pointed at a cluster of small trees in the corner. "I'll hide behind those."

He nodded stiffly and raised his hands to test the ward. A pale blue aura appeared around his hands but nothing happened.

"Is the ward still up?" I asked.

"No," he answered in a strained voice. "I can't. I'm still too weak from the iron."

"You need an energy shot." I yanked the goddess stone from my hair and thrust it into his hand.

When I'd given Faris the stone, he'd gone into a peaceful trance of some kind. Conlan's body jolted like he'd been stabbed. He gasped and stared at me with eyes that were round with wonder.

Whatever the stone was doing to him lasted less than thirty seconds. His body sagged, and he opened his hand, but the stone was no longer there. I didn't need to check to know where it had gone.

"How do you feel?" I asked him.

"Stronger than I've ever been in your realm." He raised his hands again, and magic poured from them. As it had the night I'd watched the Seelie guard create a portal, the air in front of Conlan rippled, and an opening began to form. I caught a glimpse of hazy blue on the other side.

Someone shouted inside the penthouse. I whirled to face the door as it was flung open. Armed men poured out, followed by Davian.

"Don't let her escape," Davian shouted. He pulled something from his pocket and waved it in the air as he chanted.

"He's raising the ward." I turned to Conlan. "Go now."

He pulled me to him. "I can't leave you."

"Take her," a man bellowed.

Conlan spun us, shielding me with his body. I didn't hear the gun fire, but I felt the shock of the impact when the bullet hit him. He staggered, and my knees turned to rubber. *Oh, God. They shot him.*

In front of me, the portal began to close.

"Conlan," I cried out, but my words were muffled against his chest as he swung me up into his arms.

"Goddess, forgive me," he whispered.

And he stepped through the portal.

20

I'd always thought that when faeries traveled by portal, they appeared somewhere in Faerie for a moment, and then created a second portal to their destination here. That was how it had been explained to me anyway. I lifted my head when the sounds of New York vanished, expecting to see a lush green forest or a glimpse of the Unseelie court. All I saw was a white fog surrounding us. *This* was Faerie?

Another more unsettling thought formed in my head. Humans couldn't travel through portals, so what if this wasn't Faerie after all. What if I had died, and I didn't know it yet?

"Conlan?" My voice sounded hollow to my ears. It felt like I was alone in a huge cavern devoid of sound and smell and color. It was what I imagined a sensory deprivation chamber to be like.

A faint roaring sound came from far away, like a distant waterfall. It grew steadily louder, and I couldn't tell if it was coming to me or if I was moving toward it. The closer it got, the more I could pick out the murmur of voices, a phone ringing. My breath caught. It sounded like home.

The fog parted, revealing a blur of color up ahead. It grew brighter and brighter until I had to shield my eyes from it. Just like that, the fog was gone, and I was standing in a room I knew all too well. I spun and found Conlan standing behind me wearing a bemused smile.

"You never cease...to amaze me, Jesse James," he said before he fell to his knees.

"Conlan!" Horror filled me at the sight of the red stain blossoming on his shirt.

Someone caught Conlan from behind, and I stared up into Kerr's shocked face. There was movement off to the side, and Iian appeared beside Kerr, looking as dumbfounded as his friend.

"Conlan's been shot," I said when they continued to gape at me.

"S'okay," Conlan murmured as Kerr lowered him to the floor. "Lukas?"

"He's with Faolin and Faris. They're looking for you two." Kerr tore open Conlan's shirt to inspect the wound. "You'll be okay, my friend. The bullet went straight through, and you are already healing."

Relief made me lightheaded, and I needed to sit down. I didn't know how it was possible, but we'd made it.

"Jesse?" Iian rushed over to me with his phone in his hand. "You have blood on you. Are you hurt?"

"It's Conlan's." I frowned. My voice sounded funny. And why did it suddenly seem darker in here?

I had the sudden sensation of floating, and then I was lying on the couch with Iian and Kerr's worried faces above me. Kerr pulled the front of my coat and shirt apart and cool air touched my skin.

Iian spoke into the phone. "Jesse has been shot."

"Shot?" I said, and the taste of blood filled my mouth. I tried to speak again and choked as blackness crowded my vision.

...

"Don't you dare leave me, Jesse," ordered a harsh male voice. Lukas. "How much longer?"

"Almost there." Faolin.

I drifted inside a cocoon of warmth, but I could feel the cold pressing to get in. I was so tired. I just needed to sleep for a few minutes.

"No, Jesse. Stay with me." Lukas's voice was commanding, impossible to disobey. "Your father is coming. You have to stay awake for him."

...

The warmth disappeared, and then there were bright lights above me, machines beeping, and people shouting. Two people wearing surgical masks appeared over me. They were speaking to each other, but I couldn't make it out over the noise.

Someone placed an oxygen mask over my mouth and nose. The lights dimmed.

...

Beep. Beep. Beep.

"I'm sorry, Mr. James. There was too much damage to her heart. If there is family you need to call, you should do it now."

"There has to be something you can do for her," said my father's anguished voice. Was he talking about Mom? Had something happened to her?

Dad? Can you hear me?

...

Beep. Beep. Beep.

"Mom is coming. Please, hold on, Jesse."

Dad, what's wrong? Why can't I see you?

...

Beep. Beep. Beep.

Someone was crying. It was Violet. Why was Violet crying?

"I understand the risk." My father's voice was hoarse and desperate. "Please, do whatever it takes to save my little girl."

Voices rose in argument. "I cannot authorize that," said a woman.

Faolin spoke close by. "She will die if you do this, Lukas."

"She will die if I don't."

...

Beep. Beep. Beep.

"Forgive me, *mi'calaech*. I can't let you go."

...

Beep. Beep. Beep.

A gentle hand stroked my forehead. I knew it was my mother before she spoke into my ear. "We're all here, baby. We love you so much."

...

Beep, beep, beep, beep, beep...

"She's crashing!"

Beeeeeeep.

"Not this place again."

My voice sounded small in the cavernous space. I turned in a full circle, but all I could see was the endless white fog.

"Hello?" I called. "Anyone there?"

Nothing.

I started walking. The fog swirled around my feet, which made no sound on the ground. It was like walking on a cloud.

Am I dead? Wasn't I supposed to see a light or something to show me where to go? I stopped walking when an awful thought struck me. What if I was stuck in this colorless, soundless place for eternity.

I resumed walking. If this was the afterlife, there had to be more to it than this, and I was going to find it. It wasn't like I had anything better to do.

"Would it have killed them to put up a few signs to show dead people where to go?" I muttered after a few minutes.

"You are not dead."

I jumped at the female voice and looked to my left at a beautiful woman with long, silvery blonde hair. Her warm, gray eyes regarded me with affection and a touch of sorrow.

"I've seen you before." I wracked my brain trying to remember her, and it finally came to me. "I dreamed about you. You were talking to me, but I couldn't hear you."

She smiled. "I thought my gift would allow me to speak to you, but I discovered it does not work on humans."

"Gift?"

"The stone in your hair. The instant you took it from the kelpie mare, I sensed you would be the one to help restore the balance between our worlds." Her eyes twinkled. "For any human who would go into the water with a kelpie to save a friend must have a good and courageous heart."

"Aedhna?" I squeaked, not sure whether to be afraid or in awe. "I don't understand."

She hooked her arm through mine. "Come. I will explain it."

We started walking. She seemed to know where she was going, so I let her lead me as she spoke.

"Do you know what the ke'tain is?" she asked.

"It's a sacred object that is kept in your temple." I looked at her. "It's not your actual breath, is it?"

She laughed, a musical sound. "No. I created the stone to hold a part of my essence to provide the energy Faerie needs to flourish. There are three others, but they are well-hidden and long passed from living memory.

"When the ke'tain was brought to your world, it weakened Faerie. The other three stones have been able to sustain Faerie, but the imbalance is weakening them and my world."

"Lukas told me the barrier between our worlds is failing because Faerie is no longer strong enough to hold it."

"Yes," she said sadly. "I knew if the ke'tain wasn't found soon, it would slowly tear apart the world I created. I tried to find it myself, but I have no power in your world. I sought humans who could help return it to Faerie. When you touched the kelpie's stone, I sensed you might be the one I sought. I gifted the stone to you, and I watched you to see if you were up to the task."

I sneaked a glance at her. "Was I?"

She squeezed my arm lightly. "I could not have chosen better. The stone not only allowed me to watch you, it also attracted the ke'tain to you. I knew you would do the right thing and return it to Faerie."

I stopped walking to stare at her. "Is that why Gus flew into my car and refused to leave my place? The ke'tain was drawn to me?"

"It was. And once there, the ke'tain knew it was safe within the ward created by the Unseelie prince."

I frowned. "Lukas and Tennin saw Gus at my apartment. Why didn't they feel the ke'tain?"

"The drakkan's fire hid the ke'tain's energy from them."

"Why didn't the ke'tain let them know it was there?" I asked. "Gus could have thrown it up, and all of this would have been over."

Aedhna sighed and resumed walking. "Drakkans are unpredictable and do things in their own time."

"Gus certainly has his own mind." I thought about how he kept sneaking into my bed, no matter how many times I scolded him for it. "Was it the ke'tain that made me dream of you?"

"The stone did that. The ke'tain did give you increased strength and speed, but that would happen to any human exposed to it as much as you were."

"Now that you mention it, there were a few times when people said I was faster than normal. And here I thought all my training was paying off."

She chuckled softly, and it made me smile. She was the personification of beauty, grace, and strength, and just being in her presence made me want to be a better person.

"What happens now that the ke'tain has been found?" I squinted at a spot ahead of us. Was the fog playing tricks with my eyes, or had I seen something there?

Aedhna held up a slender hand. Lying on her palm was the ke'tain. "It will be returned to its rightful place, and our worlds can begin to heal."

"And me?" I swallowed, bracing myself for her answer.

It was her turn to stop us. She turned me and placed her hands on my shoulders. "Your body has been damaged badly, but the ke'tain has kept you alive."

Hope ignited in my chest. "Does that mean it will heal me?"

She shook her head. "Now it is in his hands."

"Whose?"

She took my arm again and led me toward a dark shape. The fog parted as we neared it until I could see Lukas, kneeling beside someone who lay on the ground. We walked around them, and a chill went through me. The person on the ground was a ghostly pale version of me. Her lips were colorless, and even her freckles were nearly invisible. She looked dead.

A transfusion hose ran from Lukas's arm to hers. My eyes were glued to the hose as blood began to flow through it, getting closer and closer to the girl on the ground.

The girl shuddered, and warmth flooded my arm, slowly spreading to the rest of my body. It was nice, like sinking into a hot bath on a cold night.

Lukas reached up and felt around in her hair, and when his hand reappeared, it held the goddess stone. His jaw was hard with determination when he closed his hand into a fist, and placed his other one flat over the girl's heart. He spoke softly in Fae, and the only word I recognized was *Aedhna*. He was praying to the goddess.

Waves of blue magic poured from his hand and into the girl. I felt the pressure of a hand against my chest, but when I looked down, there was no one touching me. The sensation stayed even when I rubbed at the spot.

The girl began to shake as heat built behind my ribs. I shifted uneasily as my chest cavity grew warmer. It felt like there was a metal band around my heart that was slowly getting tighter and hotter.

The magic turned a brighter blue, and I released a breath when the uncomfortable heat in my chest abated.

The girl's back bowed suddenly like she was having a seizure. A second later, scalding heat erupted in my chest, burning the oxygen in my lungs. I tried to inhale, but my windpipe was blocked. I clawed at my throat as black spots floated before my eyes.

The fire receded, and I sucked in a lungful of air. I managed two breaths before the heat came again. This time, it raced through my torso, down my spine, and along my arms and legs. The heat saturated muscles, cartilage, and bones, growing hotter and hotter until I doubled over in agony.

I fell screaming to my knees when blinding pain exploded in my skull. My eyeballs were burning in their sockets, and I curled my fingers to gouge them out and end the excruciating pain.

Something cold touched my forehead, and the pain in my head lessened to where it was barely tolerable. I opened my eyes to see it was Aedhna's hand that had eased the pain. I looked at her through my tears, and her ageless face was etched in remorse.

"This was not part of my plan for you, my child," she said gently. "You were supposed to return the ke'tain to its rightful place and go on with your mortal life." Her other hand cupped my chin. "You have new trials ahead of you, but know that I believe in you. You are strong and brave and worthy of any challenge. And you will not be alone. Trust your friends, and let them guide you."

"Now," Lukas shouted harshly.

Out of the fog stepped Faolin, who knelt at the girl's head. Next came Iian and Kerr, who took positions at her feet. Conlan and Faris appeared last to kneel on either side of her.

Conlan and Faris took the girl's hands in theirs while the other three touched her head and feet. They all looked at Lukas as if they were waiting for him to speak. He held out the hand with the stone in it, and the five of them layered their hands over the stone. Lukas nodded, and magic in different shades of blue and green poured from their free hands to envelop the girl.

Not even Aedhna's cool touch could hold back the inferno this time. It felt like my blood had been turned to gasoline and set ablaze. I writhed on the ground as the fire consumed me, incinerating me from the inside out. Soon there would be nothing left of me but ash, floating forever in this endless foggy world.

And then a bomb detonated inside my skull. There was no more pain, no more me. Only blessed, blessed nothingness.

21

I woke slowly. My entire body felt like it was wrapped in cool silk, and I didn't know if it was real or part of a wonderful dream. I wanted to stay like this and not wake up to have it disappear.

Flashes of another dream tried to intrude on my bliss, but I pushed the images away, except for one. There was something about the beautiful, silver-haired woman that was comforting and familiar. I wanted to remember her.

I had no idea how long I drifted in that pleasant state of being only half awake, before my body decided it was done with sleep. The first thing I noticed before I opened my eyes was that I could still feel the deliciously cool material against my skin. The second thing was the amount of bare skin exposed to it. I rubbed my legs together. Why wasn't I wearing my sleep pants?

My eyes opened, and I stared up at the high ceiling. I let my gaze fall to the dresser across the room, and then to the dark red bedspread covering me. My pulse jumped. What was I doing in Lukas's bed? The last thing I could recall clearly was Conlan stepping out of a portal into the living room with me in his arms. I had the ke'tain. And Conlan... He'd been shot!

I bolted upright, staring around the very masculine room. I gasped when my eyes met those of the faerie sitting in a chair beside the bed. Lukas watched me with an unreadable expression that unnerved me.

I jerked the covers to my chin. "What am I doing here? Where are my clothes? Where's Conlan?"

Something flickered in Lukas's eyes and was gone. "You're here because you've been recovering, and there's a bag in the closet with some of your clothes in it. As for Conlan, I believe he is downstairs with the others."

"He's okay then?"

Lukas smiled. "Yes, and he'll be delighted to hear that your first thought upon waking was his health."

"Well, he did take a bullet for me." Conlan was going to milk that as long as he could, but he *had* saved my life. I looked down at the bedspread covering everything but my head. "How long have I been here, and what am I recovering from?"

Lukas's expression darkened. "You don't remember any of it? The hospital?"

"No." Panic made my voice higher than normal. "I was in the hospital?"

He left the chair to sit on the edge of the king bed. There was still at least three feet between us, but it might as well have been three inches. His presence was comforting and disquieting at the same time.

He met my gaze again, and a small pit of dread opened in my stomach. I knew that look. It was the same one Dr. Reddy had given me when he'd told me my parents had to be placed in a medically-induced coma. It was the kind of look someone had when they were about to give you bad news.

"You were shot," Lukas said in an easy tone. "The bullet went through Conlan and into you."

"What?" I quickly took stock of my body, but I didn't hurt anywhere. "But I feel fine."

"The bullet hit you in the chest. When Conlan took you through the portal, it destroyed the bullet, but it couldn't heal you. We got you to the hospital, and they worked on you for hours, but there was too much damage to your heart. As far as I could tell, the ke'tain was somehow keeping you alive. We think it was the reason you were able to survive the portal as well."

As Lukas spoke, flashes came to me of bright lights, machines beeping, my mother's voice, and him asking me to forgive him. But I'd already forgiven him for what happened at Rogin's.

I swallowed dryly, wishing I had some water. "The ke'tain saved my life?"

Something shifted in his expression. For the first time since I met him, he looked reluctant to speak. Suddenly, I didn't want to hear whatever he was going to say.

"You were dying. The ke'tain was only delaying the inevitable." He paused. "I told your father I would try to save you with his permission. We knew there was a good chance you would die whether I did it or not."

"Did what?" I asked warily. Lukas was one of the most powerful faeries in his realm, but Fae magic couldn't heal humans. That had been tried numerous times over the years to no avail.

He let out a breath. "The only thing that could be done. I made you Fae."

"That's not funny, Lukas."

He didn't smile.

I shook my head slowly as my heart began to race. "No. I'm too old."

"You were," he admitted. "But you also have something no other human does – a goddess stone. I used it to amplify all of our magic and the magic in my blood that was pumped into your veins. Together, we were strong enough to complete the conversion."

"No!" I scrambled away from him toward the other side of the bed. Throwing off the covers, I jumped out and ran to the bathroom, slamming the door behind me.

I gripped the edge of the marble vanity and fought to control my breathing. He was lying. I didn't know what game he was playing, but I was *not* a faerie.

I straightened and looked at myself in the large mirror. The first thing I saw was Dad's old *U*2 T-shirt I'd stolen from him two years ago. It was from the first concert he and Mom had gone to, and seeing it calmed me a little.

My eyes lifted to my face, and my hands trembled in relief when I saw the same reflection I'd looked at in the mirror my entire life. Faeries didn't have red hair *or* freckles. They had flawless skin, straight, shiny hair, and perfect teeth. I bared my teeth, and there was the bottom tooth that was still slightly crooked after two years of braces.

"The conversion doesn't change who you are."

I jumped and spun to see Lukas filling the doorway. I'd been so consumed by panic that I hadn't heard him open the door. His tone was kind, but his expression was the same one he used when he was prepared to win an argument.

"I feel exactly the same. I feel human." I held up my hands. "See. No magic."

"It doesn't work that way," he said patiently. "Humans who become Fae don't have magic at first. It takes time for their bodies to adjust and to develop their magic."

I cross my arms. "You're telling me I look and feel human, but I'm not human?"

"Yes."

I pushed past him and went around the bedroom, searching for something to prove I was right.

He followed me. "What are you looking for?"

"Iron," I said as I reached for his closet doors. "If I'm a faerie, iron will affect me."

"There's no iron in this room."

My hand paused in midair. Of course, he wouldn't have iron in his bedroom, at least not in pure enough form to harm him. I went to the door. There had to be something iron in this building.

"Jesse, stop," Lukas called.

I grabbed the doorknob and twisted it. "You don't get to tell me what to do."

"And you don't want to go out there without pants."

I froze and looked down. The T-shirt barely covered my underwear, and below that was a lot of bare skin. Under any other circumstances, being in a state of undress in front of Lukas would have made me pink with embarrassment. I was too upset and angry at the moment to care.

Stalking across the room, I threw open the closet doors and found the bag with my clothes in it. I dug around and pulled out a pair of jeans, a long-sleeved tee, and a bra. I turned to see Lukas watching me, and I scowled at him. "Do you mind?"

The corner of his mouth lifted, and he presented me with his back. I fumed as I dressed and dug some sneakers and socks from the bag. Glad one of us found this amusing.

Being in my own clothes gave me a semblance of normalcy and made me feel less vulnerable. I didn't think Lukas would harm me or do anything inappropriate, but it felt like we were on more even footing now.

I didn't say a word to him as I went to the door again and opened it, only to nearly trip over Kaia, who lay in front of it. The lamal rolled to her side to look up at me, making no move to get up.

"Kaia, move," I ordered.

She leaped to her feet and stepped back, surprising the hell out of me. I walked past her to the top of the stairs and stopped, unsure if I should go up or down.

As if I'd spoken out loud, Lukas said, "If you tell me what you want, I can point you in the right direction."

"Iron. The kind that would affect you," I answered.

"Training room."

I knew it. They used iron as a part of their training regimen. I ran up the stairs to the third floor and entered the training room, relieved to find it empty. I was not in the right state of mind to deal with anyone else.

Lukas followed me inside and went to one of the cabinets built into the wall. He walked over to me, carrying a wooden box that contained a length of iron chain, iron weights, and a pair of Agency shackles. He set the box on the floor at my feet and waved a hand at it.

I crouched beside the box, and my stomach twisted. What if he was telling the truth? What if I touched the iron, and it weakened me? I couldn't be Fae. I didn't know what I would do if I was no longer human.

"It won't hurt," he said softly. "It will only weaken you."

Physical pain was the least of my fears as I reached into the box. I held my breath as my fingers made contact with the shackles, but I felt nothing. I picked them up, and still, I felt no different.

"Are these real Agency shackles?" I looked up at Lukas, who was watching me closely.

"You can't tell?"

My chest expanded in elation. "No."

He frowned. "Try the chain."

I returned the shackles to the box and picked up the heavy chain with both hands. It was thicker than the chain we had in our supplies at home, but it looked like real iron. The disbelief on Lukas's face when I glanced up at him told me it was.

"There you go." I dropped the chain into the box triumphantly. "No faerie could hold all that iron without feeling it."

He shook his head. "I can't explain why the iron is not affecting you, but you are Fae, Jesse."

"I look human, I feel human, I have no magic or Fae strength, and iron has zero effect on me – yet you say I'm a faerie." I put up my hands. "I'm sorry, but I don't believe you."

His jaw flexed, and I could see my lack of trust bothered him. I couldn't imagine one scenario where he'd have a reason to make up something like this, and it hurt to think he'd want to deceive me. But what was I supposed to think?

"Why would I lie to you, Jesse?" His tone was pacifying, but all it did was put me on edge.

"I don't know."

Lukas took a step toward me. "I know you're Fae not only because I made you one, but because I can see your aura when I look at you."

The sincerity in his eyes was too much. I had to get out of here and go somewhere I could think straight. I skirted around him, but he grabbed my arm.

"Let me go!" I strained against his hold, but he was too strong.

"I will, but I want to try something first."

I stopped struggling and watched as he bent to pick up the shackles. He handed them to me, wincing slightly as I took them with my free hand. I had no idea what he was trying to prove. We already knew they didn't affect me.

He reached around me, and I thought he was going to hug me until I felt a tug at my hair. He stepped back, and my stomach gave a tiny roll. A few seconds later, it was like he had attached weights to my wrists and ankles and placed a yolk around my shoulders. My entire body felt weighed down, and I barely had the energy to stand upright. I broke out in a cold sweat as bile rose in my throat, and my knees gave out.

Lukas caught me and took the shackles from my hand, tossing them into the box. The moment they were gone, I felt better. I was still weak, but the nausea was gone.

"I'm sorry. I had to do that." He steadied me and held up his hand so I could see the red stone lying on his palm. "The goddess stone is protecting you from the iron. Without it, you're as susceptible as any faerie new to this world."

I pulled away from him. "This *is* my world."

"You can live here, but Faerie is your world now." His voice was firm, but it was the sympathy in his eyes that had me backing away as the room grew too warm.

I spun and took off. I raced down the stairs, not stopping at his room to get my things. It was getting harder to breathe, and I needed air. I had to get out of this building.

I came up short on the first floor when I saw Conlan standing in front of the door. My relief that he was healthy lasted as long as it took me to realize he was blocking the exit.

"Let me out," I demanded, panting.

He raised his hands in a calming gesture. "It's going to be okay, Jesse."

My chest rose and fell rapidly. "You can't keep me here."

"It's for your safety," Faris said. I turned to see him standing in the living room with Faolin, Iian, and Kerr. They all looked at me like I was a wild animal to be handled with caution.

"Your body can't handle the iron out there yet," Faolin said in his usual candid manner. "The wards here are shielding you. If you go outside now, it could kill you."

Faris glared at his brother. "For the love of the goddess, Faolin."

"Would you have me lie to her? She needs to be exposed gradually to this environment, or it will make her sick. Coddling her will not change that."

"I'm not like you, and you can't force me to stay." I wrapped my arms around me as a cold sweat broke out all over my body, and my hands started to shake.

"Jesse, look at me," Lukas said firmly.

I turned my head to see him two feet away from me. I hadn't even heard him come down the stairs.

"Everyone in this room is your friend, and we're going to help you through this. You're frightened and upset, but running away won't change anything."

"You make it sound like she has a choice," Faolin said. "She is Fae now, and this is her life. She has to adjust and learn that she has limitations in this realm."

Conlan huffed. "She just woke up from a five-day sleep to find out her whole life has changed. Give the girl a break."

Five days? The walls started to tilt and close in around me.

"It's going to be okay, Jesse," Lukas said as he held me from behind. "It's just a panic attack. Breathe."

I pulled away from him and moved toward the door still blocked by Conlan. I shoved at him and pummeled his chest with my fists, but he was immoveable. I screamed, but I didn't know if it was in my head or out loud.

Lukas said something, but the words were lost in the roaring that filled my ears. And then Conlan stepped aside, and I was throwing open the door. I stumbled into the foyer and reached for the exterior door.

The sun blinded me when I ran outside, and I had to close my eyes as I gulped in air like someone drowning. I bent over and put my hands on my knees while I fought the hysteria threatening to engulf me.

I wasn't sure how long I stayed like that before I was able to stand and breathe normally. I opened my eyes and took in my surroundings. How could I be different when everything around me looked exactly the same?

My feet started moving, and the next thing I knew, I was on the street. I had no car, no money, and no phone, but I had a destination. Home.

When Lukas appeared at my side, I kept walking and refused to acknowledge him until he took my hand in his.

I jerked away, not meeting his eyes. "I'm not going back. You can't make me."

"I'm not here to bring you back," he said gently. "I'm going to take you home."

I rolled the rubber football chew between my hands as I stared at the scratches and nicks in the surface. It was the only toy Gus hadn't been able to swallow, and the one he'd always leave on my bed when he slept here.

I turned my head to the side, half-expecting to see him curled up on my pillow like he owned it. Pain pricked my chest, and I wondered for the hundredth time where he was and if he was happy. I'd asked about him when I came home, and Dad told me Faris had taken Gus to Faerie while I was asleep. One more part of my life gone forever.

A guitar string twanged.

I didn't bother to look up. "Not now, Finch. Maybe later."

He plucked the string again.

I rolled onto my side, facing the wall. My phone rang on the night stand, but I didn't reach for it. Violet was on a plane to Utah to start shooting her movie, and there was no one else I wanted to talk to. Least of all, one of them.

That didn't stop them from calling at least once a day. I also got a daily text, updating me on the search for Davian Woods, who had vanished after his failed abduction. I didn't think Davian was a threat to me now that the ke'tain was back in Faerie, but Lukas had a score to settle with the billionaire. Davian was probably hiding out on some private tropical island that wasn't even on the map. If he was as smart as he claimed to be, he'd stay there.

"That's it." Dad entered my room and stood at the foot of my bed. "Get up."

"I'm tired," I said listlessly to the wall.

"Yes. I'm sure the pity party you've been having for the last week is exhausting."

"That's not fair." My throat tightened because he had never spoken to me in that tone before. "You don't understand."

"You're right. I don't understand what you're feeling because all you do is hide in your room, refusing to talk about it. I know you're in pain, but you are not the only person to ever suffer a loss or go through a major life change. And you aren't the only one in this family who is hurting."

His words sliced through my misery like a knife. I rolled onto my back to look at him, really look at him for the first time since I came home. His face was stern, but the worry and anguish in his eyes gutted me.

I blinked away the tears, making his face swim before my eyes. "I don't know how to talk about it. I don't even know who I am anymore."

"Yes, you do. You're my daughter. You're Finch's and Aisla's big sister, and Violet's best friend." He smiled proudly. "You're the girl who became a bounty hunter to find her parents, the one who never gives up no matter how hard things get."

I sat up with my back against the headboard and looked for Finch, but he was no longer in the room. "I just feel so...lost. Everything I planned for college and my life after, it's all gone. What do I do now?"

"What are you talking about? You can still go to college and do anything you want to do." Dad came to sit on the foot of my bed. When I came home a week ago, the ward on him wouldn't let me get within ten feet of him. Lukas said it had something to do with me now being a faerie with a goddess stone. He'd removed the ward since it was no longer needed with the ke'tain back in Faerie.

"I can't hunt," I said.

The Agency had suspended my license after they had been informed of my new "status." There had never been a Fae bounty hunter, and they weren't quite sure what to do with me. I was prohibited from hunting until they decided whether or not to reinstate me.

As far as the other hunters knew, I was taking time off to recover from being shot on a job. The Agency had been keeping the truth under wraps, mainly because of the media feeding frenzy that would happen when the world discovered an almost nineteen-year-old had survived a conversion. The few people at the hospital who knew about it had been ordered not to talk, and no one dared defy the Agency. The only people who knew the truth besides Lukas and his men were my family, Maurice, and Violet.

"That's temporary, and you're planning to go to college next year anyway."

"To study law and fight for Fae equality," I said pointedly. "I'm a human turned *Court faerie*. Who is going to take me seriously?"

"Anyone who meets you." He shook his head. "You've never let anything hold you back, and you're not going to start now. Just because the path to your dream changes doesn't mean you can't have everything you wanted. Being a faerie could open a whole new world of opportunities to you that you didn't have before."

I pulled my pillow over and hugged it. I wanted so much to believe he was right. "I don't know where I belong anymore. I don't feel like one of them, but I'm not human either."

His brows drew together. "You belong with us. You could live in Faerie for years, and this will still be your home. Always."

I shook my head vehemently. "I'm not going to Faerie."

"You have to go eventually." Dad tilted his head. "You've spent years reading everything you could about Faerie, and now you're not the least bit interested in seeing it firsthand? You're not curious at all?"

"No." I crossed my arms.

"One thing hasn't changed. You still can't lie that well." He chuckled and stood. "Get up and put on something besides pajamas. We're going out."

"Where are we going?"

"To do something we haven't done yet this winter." He went to my small closet and poked around, reemerging with my ice skates. "Think you can still keep up with me?"

I grinned, suddenly feeling lighter. Mom didn't like skating, so it had been Dad and my thing ever since I could walk. "Can we have hot chocolate?"

Relief flashed in his eyes. Since the day I came home, I'd had no appetite and I'd only eaten to placate him. This was the first time I'd shown interest in food or drink.

"Of course." He carried the skates to the door. "You have five minutes."

"Make it twenty. I need to do something first."

He gave me a knowing smile and left. I got up and went to pick up my guitar for the first time since I came home. Sitting cross-legged on the bed, I strummed a few chords and began to play *Annie's Song*. I was a minute into the song before Finch ran into the room and climbed up onto the bed. Aisla flew in and landed gracefully beside him.

Sing, Finch signed.

I did, and then I stopped halfway through the first verse when I realized he hadn't fallen into his usual trance. It made sense. Only humans could entrance faeries that way.

I finished the song and rested my guitar on my lap. "I'm sorry I haven't been a good sister this week."

I'm sorry you're sad, he replied.

Aisla nodded and whistled.

"Me too, but I'm lucky to have you guys." I patted the guitar. "You want me to play another one?"

They nodded eagerly, and I played them two more songs before I had to change for my outing with Dad. As I was leaving the room, I reached for my spare pair of glasses on the desk, and I had to remind myself that I had perfect vision now and no longer needed them. I wasn't sure why I still had them. Maybe because I wasn't ready yet to let go of that part of me.

"I'm driving," Dad said when the two of us reached for the keys hanging by the door.

I grabbed the knob and twisted it. "This time."

Swinging the door open, I stopped short when I found the Seelie prince standing on the other side with his hand raised to knock. He was surrounded by his stone-faced guards. I hadn't spoken to him since the day we had lunch, and he was the last person I expected to see today.

"Prince Rhys." My first reaction was surprise. That quickly turned to fear when I remembered Queen Anwyn's warning that had been so effectively delivered by her own guard.

He stared at me in wonder. "Incredible. I heard you were made Fae, but I didn't believe it. And yet, here you are, and you look so healthy. It took me weeks to acclimate to the iron in this world."

"Here I am," I managed to say. "How did you hear? The Agency said no one knows about it."

He gave me an indulgent smile. "The rulers of both courts are informed if a new faerie is made. As soon as I heard it was you, I wanted to come and see you, but my attendance was required at court."

Dad made a sound behind me, and I stepped aside to awkwardly make introductions. Prince Rhys's face lit up like a little boy at Christmas when he found out who was with me.

"I'm thrilled to make your acquaintance, Mr. James. Jesse has told me such entertaining stories about your work."

I turned to my father. "Prince Rhys is a big fan of the old west, and he's very interested in bounty hunting."

"Is that so?" Dad smiled politely because that's what you did when Fae royalty showed up at your door. I could see the tension in his posture that the prince and his men might not notice.

"Oh, yes. I would love to talk to you at length about it. Perhaps you and Jesse would consent to be my guests for dinner one night this week."

Bayard cleared his throat, and Prince Rhys gave me an apologetic smile. "Forgive me. I got carried away, and I completely forgot decorum. You are Unseelie now and newly changed, and I really shouldn't be here. But I wanted to let you know you have a friend at the Seelie court."

"Thank you," I said weakly. "It's all very new to me, and I appreciate your kindness."

"That's very good of you." Dad stepped out into the hallway and extended his hand. Prince Rhys accepted it like a teenager meeting his idol, when he himself was one of the most adored celebrities on the planet. Out of all the surreal moments I'd experienced lately, this had to be near the top.

Watching him with my father, I was more convinced than ever that Prince Rhys had no idea of his mother's involvement in my parents' disappearance. He was a pampered royal with unfortunate parentage, but he had an earnest sincerity about him that I believed was authentic. If not for our very different situations, he was someone I could see myself befriending.

I was so lost in my thoughts I barely registered the two of them were still talking. I tuned in to hear Dad telling the prince about a series of western fiction he might like by someone named *Louis L'Amour*.

"I'll find them today." Prince Rhys's eyes lit up. I smiled to myself because he reminded me of Dad in that moment. Kindred spirits maybe.

"Your Highness, we should be going," Bayard said. "You have that interview in an hour."

"That's right." Prince Rhys's face fell, and for a second, I thought he was going to tell Bayard to cancel. "I hope we can talk again, Mr. James."

"I'm sure we can arrange it," Dad replied. His initial wariness at meeting the prince seemed to have evaporated.

"Wonderful." Prince Rhys looked at me. "I'm glad to see you well, Jesse, and I meant what I said. I am here if you ever need me."

"Thank you," I said again.

He reluctantly turned away and descended the stairs with his guard. When they were out of sight, Dad and I went back inside the apartment. He looked deep in thought as he hung the keys on the hook.

"Are we not going skating now?" I asked.

"In a minute." He left his skates by the door and walked over to sit on the couch.

I followed him, worried by his odd behavior. "Dad, are you okay?"

"Yes. It's just..." He stared at the far wall, frowning in concentration. "I think I remembered something, but it keeps slipping away."

I sat beside him. "Remember what the doctor said. Don't force it, and it'll come to you."

He rested his head in his hands. "I know, but this feels important. I have to –"

"Dad?"

"Oh, God." He lifted his head, and a chill raced down my spine at his expression. He looked like a man who had just watched his world crumble before his eyes. When he spoke, his words were barely audible. "I remember."

My stomach fluttered in nervous excitement, but I kept my voice calm and even. "What do you remember?"

"That night." He stared unseeing at me. "We went to the Ralston because of him. Your mom didn't want to wait. She could never believe he was gone. She needed to see him and tell him."

They'd gone to see Prince Rhys? My body went cold. Did that mean he had been involved in their disappearance all along?

"Tell who what, Dad?" I asked gently.

He blinked and looked at me with haunted eyes. "To tell Prince Rhys the truth."

I could barely breathe. "What truth?"

"That he's our son. He's Caleb."

~The End...almost~

You didn't *really* think I'd leave it there? Keep reading for an exclusive look at the first chapter of Queen, book 3 in the Fae Games trilogy.

QUEEN (CHAPTER 1)

If you have skipped ahead, do NOT read this chapter before you read Knight. Trust me. It will ruin Knight for you if you don't wait.

Note: This chapter is subject to change in the final version of Queen.

I stared at my father, waiting for him to say something after the bombshell he'd dropped on me. The torment in his eyes was too much to bear, and it was almost a relief when he turned his head away.

My mind whirled as I tried to think of a response to his declaration that the Seelie crown prince was my brother. My brother, who had died twenty years ago, when he was two months old. The only plausible explanation was that the stress of my near-death had caused Dad to have a mental setback.

Guilt pressed down on me. The doctors had warned me this could happen if he didn't take it slowly. I needed to call them. The possibility of Dad having to go back to the treatment facility gutted me, but we couldn't risk his health. Fifty percent of recovering goren addicts went back to using within the first year, and my father would not be one of them.

I laid my hand over his. "Dad, you look pale. Maybe you should lie down for a few minutes."

"I don't need to lie down. I've slept enough in the last four months."

"But –"

He swung his gaze back to me. "I'm okay, Jesse. It's a shock and a lot to take in, but it's not a delusion."

I stared into his clear eyes. His tone was rational, and he didn't look like someone on the verge of a mental breakdown. But his claim that a faerie prince was his dead son was the kind of thing that got people admitted to a psych ward. All I could think of to do was hear him out and see where it went.

"Can you tell me about it?"

Dad drew in a shaky breath. "I don't know where to start."

I reached over to take his hand. "Why do you think Prince Rhys is Caleb? Did someone tell you that?"

"No. Your mom recognized the prince when she saw Tennin's photos of him. She said the hair is different, but the prince has my eyes, and he looks like I did when I was twenty." Dad let out a weak laugh. "I know how that sounds because I thought the same thing at first."

"Why didn't Tennin tell me this?"

Dad shook his head. "He didn't know. Your mother didn't tell me until we were back in the car. I thought she was imagining the resemblance until she pulled out an old photo of me she keeps under the visor."

I realized I was holding my breath. "And?"

"If my hair was blond, I could have been Prince Rhys's twin when I was his age."

I had to see this for myself. Standing, I went to the cabinet where Mom kept all the photo albums. They were labeled by year, and I pulled out the one for my parents' late teens. My heart thudded as I carried the album back to the couch and sat beside Dad. I stared down at the cover, afraid of what I would see when I opened it.

"Do you want me to do it?" Dad asked when I made no move to look inside.

"No." I lifted the cover. The first few pages were of Mom with her high school girlfriends, followed by an 8x10 photo of her in her cap and gown. I turned the page slowly to reveal Dad's graduation picture, and it was as if someone had punched all the air from my lungs.

"Oh, my God," I whispered. Whipping out my phone, I brought up one of the thousands of online pictures of the Seelie crown prince. I laid the phone beside Dad's photo, and my world tilted on its axis. It wasn't only the eyes that were the same. Prince Rhys and the eighteen-year-old version of my father had identical smiles and the same tiny cleft in their chins. The prince had more refined features, like a marble statue with all its imperfections polished away, but Dad was right. They could have been twins.

I looked at Dad, who was watching me expectantly. Twenty-three years had passed since that photo was taken, and his face was leaner now with crow's feet near his eyes and lines around his mouth. When I looked past those things, all I could see was the young man smiling up at me from the album.

"How did I not see it? The first time I talked to Prince Rhys, I felt like I'd met him before, but I thought that was because his face was everywhere." I shook my head. "What about Bruce, Maurice, and your other friends who knew you back then? None of them saw a resemblance between you and the most famous faerie in the world?"

Dad shrugged. "I doubt they would remember exactly what I looked like back then without seeing a photo. That happens when you age together. As for everyone else, people don't always see what is in front of them, especially when they aren't looking for it. Who would think to make a connection between me and the Seelie prince? You didn't."

I looked down at the two photos. I knew from personal experience how easy it was not to see something that was right in front of your eyes. I still wondered how I hadn't realized who Lukas was until Rogin Havas had let it slip.

I pursed my lips as I searched for the right words to phrase what had to be said. "Prince Rhys looks like you, but that doesn't mean he's Caleb. I mean...Caleb died. You and Mom saw him, and there was an autopsy and a funeral."

I flinched internally and saw an answering expression on Dad's face. He and Mom never liked to talk about that time, but there was no way around it now.

He shifted position and glanced away before meeting my eyes again. "The medical examiner said Caleb died from pulmonary atresia, which is almost always diagnosed soon after the baby is born. Caleb was two months old, and he didn't have any of the symptoms. He looked like a normal, healthy baby. Your mom..." He swallowed. "She didn't believe the dead baby she found in the crib was ours. She said a mother knows her own child, and that someone had switched her baby for a dead one."

Dad's voice cracked on the last word. Tears pricked my eyes, and I blinked them away.

"The baby looked like Caleb, and the M.E. said there was nothing suspicious about his death. I explained that to your mom, but she was too distraught to believe it. Nothing would convince her Caleb was dead."

"What did you do?" I asked around the rock lodged in my throat. I had always seen the sadness in Mom's eyes when Caleb's name came up, but my parents had never gone into detail about his death, other than the cause.

He cleared his throat. "I thought she would come to accept it after a few days, but she refused to even make the funeral arrangements. And then she started going up to strangers with babies to check that their baby wasn't Caleb." Dad paused, his face etched in pain. "It was bad for the first year. After a while, she started to be more like her old self, but I don't think she was happy again until we found out she was pregnant with you."

"You guys never told me any of this," I said hoarsely.

"Your mom didn't want you to know. It was a very dark time in our lives, and she was ashamed of how she behaved." His face twisted in agony. "No one believed her when she said the baby wasn't Caleb – not even me. And all this time, she was right."

Needing to do something, I laid the album on the coffee table and got up to walk around the room. It hurt too much to think about what my parents had suffered back then, so I focused on their disappearance.

"What happened the night you disappeared, Dad?"

He straightened his shoulders as if he was shaking off the pain. "Your mom wanted to see the prince in person. We called one of our contacts at the Ralston and found out he was doing a photo shoot in the small ballroom on the sixth floor. The odds of getting near him were slim, but we had to try." Dad stared past me as he remembered the events of that night. "The moment we stepped off the elevator, I knew your mom was right. Prince Rhys is Caleb."

A new wave of shock rolled through me. "You saw him?"

"Not the prince. The ballroom door was open and a group was leaving. There were two male faeries in front, and as soon as they saw us, they came to intercept us. They knew who we were before we could even show them our IDs. One of them said he knew they should have killed us twenty years ago when they took the boy.

I pressed a hand to my mouth as he continued. "They restrained us and told the prince's guard to take him to his suite while they dealt with the problem. The next thing I knew, we were in the ballroom and they were calling Rogin Havas to dispose of us. They didn't want the death of two well-known bounty hunters to draw any attention to Prince Rhys and risk reporters making a connection between him and us. They had no idea Rogin's sister would intercept the call and save us."

"You remember seeing her?" I'd told him that Raisa had been the one who gave them the goren to keep them alive. Until now, he had no memory of her part in it.

"Yes. I woke up in her house. She said she would do whatever she could to keep us alive. After that, all my memories are foggy. I can't tell the real ones from the goren dreams."

I continued pacing. I couldn't think about the possibility that my brother was alive or about everything my parents had been through. It was too much for my brain to process all at once. Instead, I focused on the person at the root of it all, the one who had caused my family so much pain.

"What I don't get is *why*? Why would Queen Anwyn steal a human baby, convert him, and raise him as her son? Her *heir*? One thing I know about Fae politics is that they only want the bluest blood in the royal line. I can't believe any Seelie faerie with an ounce of royal blood would be okay with someone who isn't even Fae-born being their king someday."

"They would if they don't know he isn't Fae-born."

"That's it!" I whipped my head toward my father. "That's why her guard tried to have you and Mom killed, and why they don't want you to remember. I thought they were worried you knew about them stealing the ke'tain, but all along it was about Prince Rhys...Caleb..."

My voice trailed off, and a knife twisted in my gut at the fresh pain in Dad's eyes. I couldn't imagine what he was going through. His son had been ripped from him and raised as a faerie with no knowledge of his real parents. Even if Prince Rhys somehow learned the truth and wanted to know his family, we could never get back the life that had been stolen from us.

I went back to pacing. "It still doesn't explain why she would take a human baby and pass him off as her own. What could she gain from that?"

"I don't know." Dad stared down at his hands. "But she went through a lot of trouble to do it and to cover it up."

He was right. Her guards had done a lot more than steal Caleb. They'd switched him with a changeling made to look like my brother, which required a lot of magic. They also would have had to glamour the medical examiner to make sure the autopsy report confirmed the dead baby was Caleb and that he'd died of a heart defect.

After all of that, the guards couldn't bring a human baby to Faerie. Their magic wasn't strong enough to do a conversion, which meant Queen Anwyn had secretly come to our realm to perform it herself.

But why Caleb? Of the millions of male babies in the world, why had they chosen my brother? Had they been looking for something specific, or were we the first family they found with a baby boy? We'd probably never know the answer to that, and I feared it would haunt my parents for the rest of their lives.

Helpless anger flared inside me. The Seelie queen had done nothing but bring pain to the people I loved, and she was virtually untouchable. Not that we had evidence of her crime. The prince's resemblance to Dad could be passed off as coincidence, and we had no proof of his real identity. Once a human became Fae, none of our human DNA remained. It was one of the things I'd been struggling with this past week.

There was the body Mom and Dad had buried, but it would take a lot more than a crazy story about changelings to get the authorities to exhume it. And something like that would not go unnoticed. My family would be dead before the ink was dry on the order.

A soft whistle drew my attention to Finch, who stood at the end of the hallway. His eyes were wide and worried as he signed, *Is Dad okay?*

I followed his gaze to where Dad sat with his head in his hands, and then I signed back, *Yes. He's just figuring out something.*

Okay. He turned and disappeared again.

Dad moved his head from side to side. "It's my fault. I should have kept him safe."

"How can you say that?" I went to sit beside him. "No human is a match for the Seelie royal guard. You know that better than anyone."

"You don't understand. I had the apartment warded, but only against the kinds of faeries we hunted. I never thought to protect us from Court faeries. If I had, they wouldn't have gotten in and taken Caleb."

"You can't blame yourself for that. No one would have thought to ward against the royal guard." I laid my head against his shoulder, lost as to how to comfort the strongest man I'd ever known. My father was a protector, and he'd carry this guilt on his shoulders forever. It was one more reason for me to despise the Seelie queen.

Neither of us spoke for a long moment, and it was Dad who broke the silence. "We need to make a plan."

"A plan for what?" I straightened. Surely, he wasn't going to suggest we tell Prince Rhys who he really was. As much as I wanted my parents to be happy, I was terrified of what the queen would do to them.

"To protect our family. If Queen Anwyn learns the prince has been here and met me, she's not going to take it well. And if her guards find out I have my memories back, they –"

"No." Fear sent me to my feet. "We can't tell anyone about this. The Seelie guard will come after you and Mom, and I can't lose you again. I can't."

"Jesse." Dad stood and put his hands on my trembling shoulders. "I'm not talking about going public with this. But if the prince keeps showing interest in us, the queen will take notice, and her guard will come snooping around. We need to prepare for that."

"How?"

He pressed his lips together, and his grip on my shoulders tightened a fraction. "The first thing we have to do is tell Lukas."

"No." I shook my head so hard it almost gave me whiplash.

Dad stopped me when I would have pulled away from him. "Listen to me. I know you're still angry at him, but he cares about you. He'll protect you."

I had no idea what I felt for Lukas anymore. At first, I'd been furious at him because he'd made me Fae without giving me a choice, even though there had been no way I could have made that decision. Then I'd hated myself for being unfair to the person who had saved my life. I'd spent the last week alternating between hoping he would come assure me everything would be okay and not wanting to see him. Not that he had tried to see me – or talk to me. The others had been taking turns calling to check on me, but I hadn't heard a word from him since the day he brought me home.

There was one thing I did know. If we told him about Caleb and what Queen Anwyn had done, he wouldn't let me stay here. He'd most likely send me to Unseelie to keep me safe, and it could be months or years before I saw my family again. After everything I'd gone through to get them back, I wasn't letting anyone separate us.

I shared my fears with Dad and waited for several long minutes while he paced the room deep in thought. His face was still pale, but he looked more like himself as he worked out things in his head.

He stopped walking midstride and turned to me. "We'll tell people the doctor said our memories are gone for good. That usually only happens with long-term goren addiction, but we were given high doses and put into comas, so it will be believable. If the guard is watching, they'll get wind of it."

"What about Mom? What if she gets her memory back and tells someone?"

Dad nodded. "I'll talk to her. She'll be okay."

I didn't ask what he would say to her. If he said he would take care of it, he would. My parents' marriage was built on a deep foundation of trust and mutual understanding. They were best friends and partners and knew each other better than anyone else ever could. Whatever Dad told her, she would trust him and follow his example without question.

"That takes care of Mom. How do we protect you if the queen's guard comes around?"

A gleam entered his eyes. "The guard took me by surprise last time, but now I know what I'm up against. I'll make some preparations and call in favors from a few friends. Don't worry about me."

The pressure on my chest eased. "Are you going to tell Maurice the truth?"

"Yes. I'll ask him to come by this evening."

Maurice normally didn't stay in town this long, and I'd assumed he'd be off on another big job now that the ke'tain had been found. He felt guilty that he hadn't been there for us when Mom and Dad were missing, and he wanted to make up for that by sticking around for another month or so. I'd never been so happy to know he was next door.

"Now what do we do about you?" Dad asked, startling me from my thoughts.

"What about me?"

"It's you Prince Rhys came to see. Even if the queen believes my memories are gone for good, she's not going to allow you two to continue seeing each other." Dad paused. "Especially if she thinks his interest in you is more than platonic."

My stomach rolled at the mere suggestion that Prince Rhys might have any romantic interest in me. He was raised a Faerie, but he was still my brother. The fact that I'd never been attracted to him didn't ease the ick factor one bit.

It made much more sense now why Queen Anwyn had sent her guards to warn me away from him. It had nothing to do with me being a lowly bounty hunter and everything to do with me being his sister.

"I doubt we'll be seeing that much of him anymore. You heard what he said when he was here. He's Seelie and I'm Unseelie, so it wouldn't be right for him to visit me." I let out a breath. "And I don't think the queen will come after me now that I'm Unseelie. She knows I'm friends with Lukas, and after the whole ke'tain thing, he would suspect her if anything happened to me."

"That's true." Dad smiled, but there was no mistaking the flicker of sadness in his eyes. His focus was on keeping our family safe, but at the root of all of this was the child who had been stolen from him. What turmoil he must be feeling. To protect the rest of his family, he had to pretend he didn't know his son was alive and well.

He cleared his throat. "I'm going to the office to make a few calls."

"I'll make us some coffee," I said a little too cheerfully. "That is if you haven't used up my stash."

"I wouldn't dare." He chuckled, and the sound warmed me.

As soon as he left the room, the weight of everything I'd learned pressed down on me again. I moved on autopilot as I put the coffee on and took down two large mugs. The last week I'd wallowed in my misery, thinking about what I'd lost. That was nothing compared to what my parents had suffered and the loss to our family.

Caleb is alive. I wondered how many times I'd have to repeat those three words before they sank in. I thought back on all the years of visiting his grave with my parents, of looking at that tiny, white headstone and imagining what my life would have been like if my brother had lived. Not in a hundred years could I have envisioned a scenario where he was stolen by faeries and raised as the crown prince of Seelie. Or that if I breathed a word of it to anyone, the monster he called a mother would have my entire family killed.

The coffee finished brewing, and I inhaled the rich aroma as I poured it into our mugs. At least some things didn't change. I made my father's just how he liked it and then my own. I had been so depressed for the last week I couldn't even think about food, and the smell of the coffee made me realized how much I'd missed it.

I raised the cup to my mouth and closed my eyes to savor the first sip.

And then I sprayed coffee across the kitchen.

I set the mug on the counter and ran to the sink, ducking my head under the faucet to rinse the awful taste from my mouth. It was bitter and ashy and made me think this must be what burnt dirt tasted like. No matter how much water I gargled, I couldn't get rid of it.

Raising my head, I wiped my mouth with my sleeve and stared at the coffee left in the pot. Someone was pranking me. They'd switched out my coffee for this horrid stuff and...

Realization hit me like a blast of cold air, and I let out a cry that would have put a banshee to shame. Dad came running into the kitchen, wild-eyed like he expected to find the entire Seelie guard attacking me.

"What's wrong?" he asked a little breathlessly.

"I hate coffee," I wailed.

He stared at me in confusion until understanding dawned on his face. "I'm sorry, honey. It was bound to happen."

I bent my head so he couldn't see the tears burning my eyes.

"Jesse," Dad said at the same time the doorbell rang. I grabbed some paper towels and cleaned up my mess while he went to see who else was paying us a visit. The way this day was going, it was probably Queen Anwyn.

I didn't look to see who it was, but I could hear the murmur of male voices. Seconds later, footsteps approached, and I looked up at Faolin's scowling face. I would have preferred the Seelie queen.

"Are you crying?" he asked brusquely.

I tossed the wet paper towels in the trash. "I'm just *that* happy to see you."

He scoffed, but I caught a glimmer of amusement in his eyes, which only annoyed me more. His sharp gaze moved past me to the coffee machine and the two mugs on the counter. He quickly put two and two together, and in typical Faolin fashion, he said, "You're crying because you can no longer drink that stuff?"

I glared at him. "It's not about the coffee." I didn't need to add the words "you insensitive jerk" because my tone more than implied them.

"Then what is it?"

"It's nothing." He was the last person I wanted to confide in. I hadn't even told Dad about it. That ever since I'd woken up and learned I was Fae, I had taken comfort in the fact that I still looked and felt human. I had no magic or Fae strength, and iron didn't affect me thanks to my goddess stone. As long as none of that changed, I could pretend I was the same old Jesse.

I crossed my arms. "Why are you here, Faolin?"

"I brought you some food." He set a bulging cloth bag on the counter.

I eyed the bag warily. "We have plenty of food."

"Human food." He loosened the drawstring and took out various Fae fruits, a few of which I recognized, along with a bottle of green juice and two small, round loaves of dark bread. The juice looked like the same stuff Faris had drunk during his convalescence.

Faolin finished his task and looked at me. "Your father said you have barely eaten since you came home."

"Did he?" I shot Dad an accusing look. He hadn't been at the door long enough to discuss my eating habits, which meant he'd talked to Faolin before his unexpected visit.

Dad leaned his shoulder against the wall, not looking the least bit contrite. "You have certain nutritional needs you didn't have before, and I wasn't sure exactly what to buy."

"Faeries can eat human food," I reminded them.

"Yes, but we also require Fae nourishment." Faolin picked up something that resembled an elongated pink pear. "Fruits and juice will be the easiest for you to digest until your body adjusts to the change. You can have Fae bread but only in small portions at first."

"What? No crukk steak?" I quipped. Crukks were the main source of meat in Faerie. They looked like a shrunken version of a wooly mammoth and they were raised domestically like our cattle.

He gave me a mocking smile. "You can eat crukk if you don't mind it coming back up an hour later."

I made a face. "I'll stick to beef."

"As long as you make sure to include enough Fae foods in your daily diet." He waved a hand over the food. "You can get any of this at the local Fae market, or you can call us, and we will bring you what you need."

"Thanks," I said without much enthusiasm.

"Do you need anything else?" he asked.

Yes. I want to know why Lukas didn't bring the food, and why he is the only one who hasn't called me, I thought, but all I said was, "No."

"Then I'll be going."

Dad stepped back to let Faolin pass. "Thank you for coming by. We appreciate everything you and the others have done for us, and when my daughter gets her manners back, she will tell you the same."

I scowled at my father. What was he talking about? I'd thanked them. Hadn't I?

"You're welcome," Faolin said. His back was to me, but there was no missing the note of laughter in his voice. At the door, he turned to face me. "Don't think your new status means you no longer have to train. We will resume that after you build up your strength."

"Oh, joy. I can't wait."

"Neither can I." He flashed me a devious smile as he left. "See you soon, Jesse."

Dad followed me back to the kitchen. "It was nice of him to bring you food."

"He's a real boy scout." I opened the bottle of juice and sniffed. It *was* the same stuff Faris used to drink. I capped it and put it in the fridge then grabbed a basket from the cabinet for the fruit.

"You're not going to eat any of it now?" Dad asked when I was done.

"Not hungry." I picked up my mug and gave it a longing look before I poured the coffee down the drain. After rinsing the mug, I placed it in the draining rack to dry. "Well, I guess I'll save a lot of money on coffee."

He came over to put an arm across my shoulders and gave them a small squeeze. "There's the Jesse I know."

I heaved a sigh. "I'm sorry I've been so hard to live with this week."

"You had a good excuse, so I'll let you off easy this –"

The floor vibrated beneath our feet, and a rumbling sound filled the air as if a plane was flying low over our building. I clung to Dad as the windows rattled, and car alarms started to go off down on the street.

It was over as fast as it had started, leaving the two of us staring at each other in stunned silence.

I was the first to find my voice. "Did we just have an earthquake?"

~The End...for now~

BONUS SCENE

This is a scene from Pawn retold in Lukas's POV.

"Still nothing?"

"Not yet." Faolin scowled at his computer monitor. He had spent the last two days trying to determine how someone had managed to kill the two men under his surveillance. Few things got by him, and he was taking this one personally.

I had wanted to kill the men who had attacked Jesse in her apartment, but Faolin's cooler head had prevailed. Even he had to practice restraint when he saw the bruises on her face and throat that night. He had no tolerance for most people, but he was thawing a little for our *li'fachan*. Not that he would ever admit it.

My phone rang, and I looked down to where it lay on his desk. Something unpleasant tugged at my gut when I saw Jesse's name on the screen, and my first thought was that someone was breaking into her apartment again.

I snatched up the phone. "Jesse?"

A muffled rustling sound came from the other end, and she said something, but her voice was slurred. Jesse didn't strike me as the drinking type, but she sounded drunk now. I smiled at the thought of her drunk-dialing me and imagined her pretty blush when I teased her about it later.

Her next words were raspy and clear and sent shards of ice through my chest. "I think I'm dying."

The line went dead.

"What's wrong?" Faolin pushed back his chair and stood.

"Jesse is in trouble." I spun and strode from the large office we shared on the third floor of the building. He was on my heels when I reached the first floor and raised my hands to form a portal.

Faolin laid a hand on my arm. "What kind of trouble? Where is she?"

"She didn't say. I'm going to her apartment."

"Not without me." He stood back and waited for me to proceed.

I felt the air in front of me as I murmured the words that allowed portals to be created through the wards on my building. Distracted by my concern for Jesse, it took more concentration than usual to detect the minute traces of Fae energy in the invisible barrier between the realms and to harness my magic to the energy. Once the connection was made, it was a matter of feeding more of my magic into it and manipulating the energy to open a window into my private courtyard at the palace. From there, it required less magic to create a new window to the hall outside Jesse's apartment.

"I'll go first," Faolin said when I reached for her door. He made short work of the locks and produced a small curved blade before he silently entered the apartment.

It was dark and quiet inside, and I could see no signs of trouble. What if she wasn't here? How would I find her? I pushed past Faolin and walked stealthily toward the bedrooms, ignoring the warning voice in my head that said my need to protect Jesse was stronger than it should be for any human female.

Jesse's bedroom door was open, and I let out a breath when I found her sleeping restlessly in her bed. She had kicked off her quilt, and she mumbled something unintelligible that was followed by a low whimper. On the bed next to her was her phone.

Entering her room, I flicked on the lamp beside the bed, illuminating her sweaty, flushed face and damp hair. I laid my hand against her overheated cheek. "Jesse, can you hear me?"

She turned her head toward my touch but didn't respond.

"She's burning up." I felt her too-hot forehead.

Faolin came to stand beside me. "I see nothing suspicious. Do you think she's been poisoned?"

A fresh wave of worry hit me, and I bent low to sniff her breath. I inhaled several times to separate her normal smell from something that wasn't quite right. "I detect something, but it's too faint to identify," I told him as I touched her forehead. Whatever it was, it could kill her if we didn't do something fast. "We have to bring her fever down."

Faolin disappeared and returned with a wet cloth. He handed it to me, and I pressed it to Jesse's forehead. She let out a small sigh as I gently ran the cold cloth over her face, but it was only temporary relief. We had to figure out what had caused the fever in order to help her.

"Humans are prone to infections when they are hurt," Faolin said as if I'd spoken out loud. "Does she have any injuries?"

"Not that I can see." I ran my hands over her arms to check for cuts. Finding none, I dragged the sheet down to expose her lower body. She wore a T-shirt and shorts, and she shivered when I lifted the bottom of her top to look at her stomach.

"There." Faolin pointed at her thigh, which was marred by a pink, four-inch cut. "It looks like a knife wound, but it doesn't appear to be infected."

I studied the cut. It didn't look serious, but humans had fragile immune systems. It still amazed me that they thrived with all the toxins and diseases in this world.

"Damn troll," Jesse mumbled, curling up on her side.

Troll? Was she dreaming or telling us something? I patted her cheek to rouse her. "Jesse, did a troll do this to you?"

She nodded jerkily, and a small smile curved her lips. "Yes. But I got him."

I straightened and shared a grim look with Faolin. "Kolosh," we said at the same time.

The kolosh was an ornamental tree that resembled the bonsai tree in this realm. It had been popular here until someone discovered the sap was poisonous to humans. Trolls had begun coating their blades with the sap, which caused fever and delirium in humans, and in rare cases – death.

"I'll stay with Jesse while you get the *ghillie*," I told him.

He shook his head. "I cannot leave you here alone. You know one of us must be with you at all times."

"I have the same training as you. I will be okay without you for a few minutes. Go. Jesse needs the antidote."

He looked ready to argue, but he nodded and strode to the bedroom door. Stopping in the doorway, he said, "She is strong...for a human."

"I know." I smiled down at her. When I first saw Jesse at Teg's, she had looked so young and completely out of her element. Later, after she'd told me about her search for her missing parents, I'd admired her spirit and courage, but I never believed she'd last alone in this city. Since then, she'd fought a kelpie, survived a night on North Brother Island, and had bested two larger attackers in her home. Those were the things I knew about, but they were enough to convince me never to underestimate her again.

I brushed a damp curl from her face. "You're going to be okay. Faolin has gone to get the antidote."

She sighed. "Faolin's so nice."

I laughed softly and slipped my arms under her. "Now I know you've been poisoned. Come on. Let's sit you up."

Her brows drew together. "Sleep."

"No sleep. You have to stay awake." Kolosh poisoning spread faster during sleep, and the best way to slow it without medicine was to keep the person awake.

I picked her up and cradled her against my chest, feeling the heat of her fever through my shirt. For not the first time, I tried to ignore how perfectly she fit in my arms and the sense of rightness I felt having her there. *She's not for you*, I reminded myself as I carried her to the living room and set her down in a chair.

I went to the bathroom and wet the cloth under the cold water again. When I returned to the living room, I found Jesse barely upright in the chair and staring at the wall with dazed eyes. Kneeling before her, I gently wiped the sweat from her flushed face and neck.

"That feels nice," she slurred, sinking down in the chair.

I gave her cheek a soft slap. "Stay awake, Jesse." I glanced toward the door. Faolin hadn't been gone long, but if we didn't get the antidote into her soon, it might be too late.

She made a sound of protest and opened her eyes, which were unfocused and bright with fever. A strange, prickling sensation started in my chest, and it took me a moment to realize it was fear. I couldn't remember the last time I had experienced that emotion.

Relief filled me when the door opened, and Faolin came in. "How is she?" he asked as he walked over to us.

"Same."

He held up a cloth pouch, and I stood to let him take my place. From the pouch, he pulled a red leaf from the ghillie fruit tree that grew abundantly in Faerie and was the most effective antidote for kolosh poisoning. He held the small leaf to Jesse's mouth. "Eat this."

She shook her head and pressed her lips together like a small child refusing to eat. I should have known she wouldn't take it from Faolin. He hadn't exactly given her a reason to trust him.

I was reaching for the leaf when he tried again, speaking with all the kindliness of a wounded drakkan. "It will make you feel better. Eat it."

Jesse stared at him, unmoving. Few people could beat Faolin in a battle of wills, but he appeared to have met his match. The tightening of his mouth said he knew it, too, but he was also a master of coercion.

"Shall I get your sprite to eat some to prove it is safe?" he asked slyly.

Her eyes widened. "You leave my bro-"

I smiled when he unceremoniously shoved the leaf into her mouth and forced her to chew and swallow it. If the glare she shot him was any indication, she was going to be just fine.

"You'll live," he told her.

Her mouth turned down. "Don't sound so happy about it."

Faolin scoffed softly. And then he did something I hadn't seen him do since Faris disappeared. He smiled.

Jesse tilted her head and smiled back. "You're cute when you're not all grumpy."

A laugh burst from me as my friend's smile fell. It might have been short-lived, but for a few seconds, he'd looked like the old Faolin.

He stood and went into the kitchen to pour a glass of water. "Someone will have to watch her until the fever breaks, but she'll recover. I can stay and care for her."

"No," I said with a little more force than I intended. His eyebrows rose, and I added, "You and she are not exactly on friendly terms...except when she is delirious with fever."

One corner of his mouth quirked.

"If she comes out of it and finds only you here, it might upset her," I continued.

He watched me with the astuteness of a lifelong friendship, but if he saw something in my expression, he chose not to mention it. Instead, he held the glass out to me. "If we can get her to drink, it will be better for her."

I took the glass and returned to the living room, where our patient sat with her chin resting on her chest. I shook her awake. "No, you don't. You can't sleep yet."

"But I'm tired."

She looked so exhausted that it felt cruel to deny her rest, but there was no other way. "I know, but you have to be awake for the antidote to work."

She huffed and leaned back to pout at the ceiling. "This dream sucks."

I grinned and gave her a few minutes to sulk before I lifted her head and coaxed her to drink some water. Once she tasted the cold liquid, she tried to gulp it all down, but I took the glass away before she could. The trick was to keep her just hydrated enough to sweat out all the poison. Too much water would make her throw up, which would not help her.

A flash of blue on the other side of the room drew my gaze to the tree house in the corner. A tiny face peeked through the leaves of some vines, the eyes wide and frightened.

"She'll be okay," I assured the sprite, who promptly disappeared.

I looked down at Jesse to see her eyes had closed again. She groaned when I shook her awake.

"You're mean," she wailed.

I tucked a damp strand of hair behind her ear. "Just a few hours and then you can rest."

Glancing over at Faolin, I found him watching with that same expression he'd had in the kitchen. He looked like he wanted to say something, but he stayed silent. He wouldn't have told me anything I didn't already know.

Jesse's fever raged on throughout the night, Faolin and I taking turns watching her and giving her water. The growing scent of kolosh on her skin told me the ghillie was doing its job and flushing the poison from her body. When it finished, her fever would peak, and the danger would be past.

It was dawn when she started to shudder and make little whimpering sounds. I could feel the heat coming off her without touching her.

"It won't be long now," Faolin said.

He was right. A minute later, her body convulsed, and she cried out in pain. She tried to stand, but I held her down. Her clothes were drenched with sweat and smelled strongly of kolosh.

"It hurts," she sobbed, fighting weakly to break free.

"I know." I felt helpless. All I could do was watch until the fight went out of her. "That's it, *li'fachan*. The worst is over."

She suddenly went limp under my hands, and I was struck by the irrational fear that she was dead. I lifted her chin, and something loosened in my chest when she looked at me with sleepy eyes.

"How is she?" Faolin asked from the kitchen.

I withdrew my hand and walked over to him. "The fever broke."

"Sleep is all she needs now." He looked at his phone. "Conlan is downstairs with the car whenever you're ready to leave."

"I'll get her back to bed and make sure she's settled first."

He nodded, and then his eyes went to something behind me. "What is she doing?"

I turned to find Jesse writhing in the chair as she struggled to shimmy out of her top. My lips twitched when she made a sound of disgust and strained, but her exhausted muscles were no match for the wet garment.

Holding back a laugh, I said, "Stripping, by the look of it."

Jesse laughed to herself and called, "Violet, can you help me? My clothes are all wet, and I think I need to pee."

I looked at Faolin, who smirked and held up his hands. "I'll let you handle this one."

My gaze went back to Jesse, and I sighed. The last thing I should be doing was helping her undress, but I couldn't leave her in her wet clothes. And I certainly wasn't going to stand out here while Faolin did it.

Jesse stopped trying to remove her clothes and looked up at me when I walked over to her. I bent and picked her up, and she let out a small squeak. Striding down the hall, I entered the bathroom, which was smaller than my closet, and set her on her feet. When I was sure she wasn't going to fall over, I left to find some dry clothes for her in her room.

I waited until I heard the toilet flush to return to the bathroom. She was standing with a hand against the wall for support and looking a little lost. My original plan had been to hand her the clothes and let her take care of it. One look at her and I knew that wasn't happening.

"Turn around," I said briskly, intending to keep this as impersonal as possible.

I expected her to argue. She surprised me by obeying the order. When I grasped the hem of her top and pulled it up, she automatically raised her arms so I could remove it.

I kept my eyes trained on the back of her head until her long hair lifted with the top, giving me a view of her bare shoulders and back, which tapered to a small waist. Most of the women I'd seen naked had been all soft curves and tanned or dark skin. Jesse was toned from rigorous training, and her skin was flawless porcelain except for a sprinkle of freckles on her shoulders. I wanted nothing more than to trace the trail of freckles with my fingers and to touch that soft skin.

Jesse chose that moment to turn slightly, presenting me with a generous glimpse of a creamy, rounded breast. I swallowed as my body responded, and I hurriedly finished removing her top. Her arms dropped back to her sides, and her hair fell down to cover most of her back.

I clenched my jaw as I reached for the dry T-shirt I'd brought for her. Helping her change clothes had not been one of my better decisions.

Ever since the morning I'd carried Jesse off the island and held her on the boat, I'd felt something shift between us. At first, I had told myself it was gratitude for her alerting us to the planned attempt on my life. But then a few days later, she'd walked in on me in my towel, and a bolt of lust had gone through me when her eyes slid down my body. If she had waited another second to turn her back on me, she would have seen how much she affected me with just a look.

I held the dry top above her head. "Hands up."

She laughed, and the sound went straight to my groin. "Are you arresting me?"

I gave her a pained smile she couldn't see. "No, but I'm starting to think you're more dangerous than you look."

I lifted her arms and helped her into the T-shirt, making sure to keep my eyes fixed on the shower curtain over her head. Thankfully, she took over from there and pulled the top down over her torso.

There was no way I could help her change her shorts after that. I reached around her to shove the dry pair into her hands. "I'll turn around so you can change your bottoms."

I faced the door, trying not to listen to the swish of the wet material sliding down her legs to hit the tile floor with a soft plop. There wasn't much room in here, and imagining her so close behind me in only her panties was not helping my current situation.

"The last time I was in a bathroom with a boy, he tried to cop a feel," she said airily.

"Why did you go to the bathroom with a boy?" My gut hardened at the thought of her in close quarters like this with a hormonal teenage boy.

She scoffed. "I didn't go to the bathroom with him. I was at a party, and he followed me in."

A new image filled my mind of some boy forcing himself on her, and my hands curled into fists. "Did he hurt you?"

There was a short pause, followed by a sigh. "No. But I might have overreacted a little. I blame it on my dad. He's the one who drilled all those self-defense lessons into me."

My respect for Patrick James doubled in that instant. The tension drained from me, and I chuckled at the new image of Jesse treating the boy to a taste of the beating she'd given her two attackers. "What did you do?"

"Let's just say poor Felix walked funny for a week," she answered lightly.

I grinned at the door. "Sounds like he deserved it."

"He did." She let out another sigh. "But after that, no boy at school would come near me, except Trey Fowler."

My smile slipped. "Trey is your boyfriend?"

"God, no. I'm not desperate," she blurted. "I'm done."

I turned to find her holding a hand against the wall to steady herself. She gave me a tired smile and didn't protest when I scooped her up and carried her to her bedroom. I set her down in the chair in the corner and told her to stay put while I went to run a fresh cloth under warm water.

I should have given the cloth to her to wipe her face and neck, but the need to take care of her outweighed the reasons why I shouldn't touch her.

Even pale and tired after her fever, she was so lovely that I felt a tug at my chest. Or maybe it was due to the absolute trust in her eyes as she watched me. No one had ever looked at me like this, and it made me long for things I couldn't have.

"Are we friends?" she asked suddenly, pulling me from my thoughts.

Friendship was not a word I'd use to describe what I felt right now. I placed my hands on either side of her and met her searching gaze. "Do you want us to be friends, Jesse?"

"Yes." She nodded eagerly. "But don't tell Violet."

"You don't want her to know we are friends?" Violet was her best friend and confidante. Why would Jesse not want her to know about our friendship?

She waved a dismissive hand. "It's not that. Violet thinks I should hook up with you because...well, you know."

Realization dawned. It was no secret that humans preferred faeries as sexual partners, but I wanted to hear her say it. "Know what?"

Jesse rolled her eyes. "That faeries are better lovers. I keep telling her it's not like that, but you don't know my best friend." She expelled a breath. "It's a good thing I didn't tell her I thought about kissing you. She'd never let it go."

My pulse quickened, and the desire I'd been fighting came roaring back. "You thought about kissing me?"

"I was curious about what it would be like," she said matter-of-factly, as if she hadn't just ignited a fire in the pit of my stomach. The mere idea that she'd imagined it made me crave the taste of her lips, and I could barely think of anything else.

"And you're not curious anymore?" I asked her.

Her eyes dipped to my mouth, and the next thing I knew, she grabbed the front of my shirt and pulled me toward her. I went willingly, letting her lead as she met me halfway and grazed my lips with hers. When her tongue tentatively flicked against my mouth, I suppressed a groan, but there was no stopping me from taking what she offered.

I slanted my mouth across hers as my fingers tangled in her hair and held her against me. Her lips parted, and I kissed her with a need I'd never felt before. She responded with sweet abandon that threatened to unravel me. I could take her to the bed, and she would give me anything I asked of her. And Goddess, how I ached to feel her beneath me, around me.

It was the last thought that broke through the raw need consuming me. With a strength of will I hadn't known I possessed, I ended the kiss.

Shame swept over me like a cold wave as I touched my forehead to hers. What was I doing? Jesse was barely recovered from a dangerous fever and in no condition to think rationally, let alone give consent. One touch from her and I'd let my base desires control me like an adolescent boy. She and I were like fuel and tinder, and one spark was all it would take for us to combust.

"I was right. You are very dangerous, Jesse James."

"Is that why you stopped?" she asked in a voice laced with frustration and uncertainty.

I met her confused gaze. "I stopped because you are not yourself. I've done some questionable things in my life, but taking advantage of a female is not one of them."

"But I like the way you kiss me." Her mouth formed an adorable pout that made me want to kiss it again. "Will you do it again when I *am* myself?"

She would never know how much I wanted to grant her request. A faerie and a human could have no future, and she deserved so much more than I could offer her. I touched the end of her hair, which was dull from the fever instead of its normal fiery red. The first time I'd seen it down, it had reminded me of the *calaech* flower that resembled flames when it bloomed. It was a fitting name for her. It matched her passion and her spirit.

"No, *mi'calaech*," I said tenderly. "But not because I don't want to."

My answer seemed to appease her, and she relaxed into the chair with her eyes closed and a dreamy smile on her lips. It occurred to me then that she might not even remember any of this in a few hours, which would probably be for the best. I'd remember for both of us.

Standing, I leaned down and picked her up again. "Let's get you to bed so you can sleep this off."

As soon as I laid her on the bed, she curled up on her side. "Thanks for taking care of me. But you never answered my question."

"What question is that?" I asked as I pulled the covers over her.

She gave me a sleepy smile. "Are we friends?"

Friendship was the one thing I could offer her. I caressed her face, knowing it had to be the last time I touched her like this. "Yes. Now go to sleep."

Jesse closed her eyes, and I stood at the foot of her bed, watching her until her breathing evened out. In sleep, she looked so vulnerable that I wanted nothing more than to protect her. She'd been through so much, but I knew she would be back to hunting and the search for her parents tomorrow.

"How is she?" Faolin asked in a low voice from the doorway.

"Asleep." I didn't look at him. My men were practiced at tuning out from my private interactions, especially with women, but something told me he knew exactly what had happened in this room between Jesse and me.

"We can leave her now, unless you want to stay longer," he said.

Taking one more look at the girl on the bed, I committed to memory the image of her with her hair spread out on the pillow and her soft lips parted in sleep. I couldn't allow myself the luxury of seeing her like this again because I didn't know if I'd be able to walk away next time.

"Sleep well, Jesse," I whispered, and then I turned and left her to her dreams.

ABOUT THE AUTHOR

When she is not writing, Karen Lynch can be found reading or baking. A native of Newfoundland, Canada, she currently lives in Charlotte, North Carolina with her cats and her three adorable rescue dogs: Dax, Des, and Daisy.

Printed in Great Britain
by Amazon

L'ACCADEMIA A CAGLIARI S'ADDA FARE!

Art.9 della Costituzione Italiana

"La Repubblica tutela il paesaggio e il patrimonio storico e artistico della Nazione."

Subgrammi sullo stato dell'arte nell'isola, mai recapitati altrove

Dal 1947 con noi e gli artisti di Cagliari.

"Lettera aperta di un gruppo di artisti sardi ai deputati e all'alto commissario.
Anche di recente, sia sulla stampa che altrove, è stata prospettata la necessità di istituire con sede a Cagliari l'Accademia di belle arti della Sardegna al fine di organizzare le attività artistiche regionali, dando ad esse soprattutto un maggior sviluppo e un nuovo indirizzo.
L'argomento ha suscitato il massimo interesse negli ambienti culturali ed artistici ed ha incontrato unanime adesione.

Nei giorni scorsi, con l'intento di dar al più presto vita all'iniziativa, un gruppo di artisti isolani ha indirizzato la seguente lettera aperta di un gruppo di artisti sardi ai deputati e all'alto commissario: "

La guerra con le sue conseguenze ha in parte disperso e avvilito le forze artistiche della Sardegna, che negli ultimi anni dimostravano come l'isola al pari delle altre regioni d'Italia, avesse raggiunto maturità intellettuale e spirituale.

E' opportuno che questi pregi siano considerati proprio come elementi necessari allo sviluppo politico e sociale dell'isola che, soprattutto, attraverso l'arte, viene conosciuta ed apprezzata come regione autonoma.

Cagliari ha visto sopravvivere ben poche sue imprese artistiche a direzione regionale deve dunque riprendere la sua iniziativa con qualche istituto adeguato.

E' stata indicata come sede dell'intendenza accademica di belle arti la palazzina dei giardini pubblici dove attualmente ha sede una galleria comunale d'arte contemporanea, che notoriamente rimarrà sul posto con l'allargamento dei locali.

Il contributo degli enti sarà integrato dal contributo dello stato.

Una tale iniziativa con tal proposito servirà dal lato pratico servirà oltre a tutto ad occupare artisti isolani senza impiego che attraverso mostre regionali ed internazionali abbiano dato e diano prova del loro valore, dando loro così un indirizzo unitario col farli partecipi di un insegnamento utile e proficuo all'auspicato miglioramento spirituale e politico della regione"

COLLETTIVO DETZIDI

L'origine è nel linguaggio dell'arte!

La specie homo sapiens, compare sulla terra 200000 anni fa, l'acquisizione e l'utilizzo del linguaggio dell'arte ha avuto un periodo di gestazione lunghissimo, non si è da subito nel nome di acquisite potenzialità anatomiche e biologiche, sviluppato un pensiero simbolico e concettuale.

Per la rapida trasmissione di valori e contenuti culturali, si è dovuto fare trascorrere qualcosa come minimo di 100000 anni.

Questo non toglie che la diffusione della specie, con i suoi linguaggi dell'arte e i relativi distinguo sia stata rapida, e sia stata presumibilmente frutto d'interazioni con specie e popolazioni arcaiche ovunque.

Il caso più studiato e indagato è quello Europeo, del confronto tra gli ultimi Neanderthal e i primi Sapiens, avvenuto intorno a 40000 anni fa, questa fase del paleolitico è linguisticamente confusa e sfuggente, compaiono manufatti di pietra silicea sfuggente allungati (lame?), raffinati manufatti in ossa, corna o avorio; si differenziano tradizioni e compaiono oggetti ornamentali come conchiglie e denti forati (utilizzati per sepolture indubbiamente intenzionali), compaiono coloranti naturali come l'ocra.

40000 anni fa, dirompe e irrompe nella storia dell'umano il linguaggio dell'arte, che non è solo estetica, identità personale o etnica (di gruppo), compare l'arte rupestre, nascono le veneri paleolitiche.

Non si era mai visto nulla del genere in precedenza, questo ha accelerato la nostra storia, la comparsa di un mondo interiore, simbolico e consapevole, un mondo non fatto di sola sussistenza, da quel momento l'evoluzione dell'umano, prima che biologica, è stata culturale e artistica, ma questa rivoluzione ha avuto almeno 150000 anni di gestazione del linguaggio (il linguaggio scritto arriverà soltanto 5000 anni fa, 35000 anni dopo il linguaggio dell'arte).

Il Paleolitico è l'origine del linguaggio dell'arte che ci conduce palpabilmente alla nostra storia.

L'unica razza umana oggi esistente, quella del sapiens, si diffuse velocemente a partire da 200000 anni fa, compare nell'Africa subsahariana e arriva nell'Asia sudorientale.

In Europa i sapiens arrivano soltanto 40000 anni fa.

L'evoluzione culturale e linguistica dell'arte del sapiens, ne ha favorito l'adattamento come l'attuale sovrappopolamento globale (non ci sono mai stati così tanti umani sul pianeta terra).

Una quota significativa che alimenta distinguo e pregiudiziale tra sapiens e sapiens e nelle sue strategie, ideologie e dogmi artistico e culturali.

I linguaggi dell'arte e la cultura di popoli e territori, naturalmente e biologicamente inclusivi, hanno progressivamente introdotto un elemento di diversificazione etnica tra popoli e territori.

L'etnicità come distinguo sociale, culturale e razziale è sempre stato insito nei linguaggi dell'arte, pensate a chi poteva indossare i denti forati per ostentare una collana nel paleolitico, c'è molta differenza tra quell'appartenenza e un ultrà di una squadra di calcio?

L'intolleranza si alimenta della chiusura linguistica dell'arte, la tolleranza e l'apertura passano per la comprensione incondizionata del linguaggio artistico e culturale dell'altro.

Il razzismo è la risultante di linguaggio, religioni, condizioni socioeconomiche, tradizione, colore della pelle, sesso, cultura, relazione e diseducazione all'arte.

L'educazione all'arte non ammette circoscrizioni o gruppi, basta osservare la varietà etnica degli studenti di una qualsiasi Accademia di Belle Arti per comprenderlo, come dite? A Cagliari un'Accademia di Belle Arti non c'è?

Linguaggio è simbolo

Il linguaggio dell'arte è una narrazione storica dell'umano in ogni dove, è la capacità sensoriale di sintesi della collettività, le icone e i simboli nascono dopo il linguaggio, sono elaborazioni di forme, d'immagini simboliche o di linguaggi artistici in chiave sempre contemporanea, in questa maniera si autodeterminano le icone, ossia quelle immagini nell'ambito in cui una comunità si rappresenta.

ACCADEMIA PER IMPARARE A IMPARARE

I linguaggi dell'arte, scattano e si muovono, originandosi non dal sistema, ma dalle sue anomalie.
I processi linguistici dell'arte, si muovono quando non sono in linea con i modelli tradizionali.
I linguaggi dell'arte, e le ricerche artistiche, sono incontro e scontro, tra economia e psicologia, tra economia dominante e psicologia dell'arte.
Parlando di linguaggi dell'arte, l'economia dominante è la moda o il trend dominante, che in tempi brevissimi diviene Accademia.
Per questo, un reale intermediario, addetto ai lavori, dell'arte contemporanea, dovrebbe essere uno scopritore ed evidenziatore d'anomalie.
Soltanto con le anomalie tradotte in azioni dal valore artistico, il pubblico, la comunità e i processi dell'arte contemporanea, battono il mercato.
Il mercato come s'impone sulla culture e le ricerche artistiche di una comunità?
Con il "non esistono pranzi gratis" o "le quotazioni di mercato sono giuste"!
Una quotazione di mercato, è soltanto una previsione culturale, previsione da confermare nel tempo per evitare di trovarsi in perdita; anche solo una quotazione variabile di uno stesso artista può essere errata (in positivo più facilmente che in negativo).
Capite ora, perché a monte di tutto il sistema dell'arte contemporanea, globalmente interconnesso, ci siano le case d'aste internazionali?

La realtà di tutto questo, è che prezzi e quotazioni di case d'asta (e non solo), sono spesso ingiustificati; per questo un'amministrazione politica, non dovrebbe mai subire una quotazione di mercato come prezzo giusto, se i prezzi dell'arte imposti dalle case d'aste internazionali, fossero sempre giusti, non avrebbe senso d'essere l'arte residente come bene da tutelare e preservare con Musei e Accademie.

Le bolle e le balle economiche private, nell'arte, sono la norma da cavalcare; i privati hanno il triste ruolo d'alimentarne la frenesia.

Un'Accademia di Belle Arti a Cagliari, avrebbe questo ruolo, quello d'alimentare e sperimentare fuori mercato, anomalie linguistiche elevandole a ricerche e modello.

Le Accademie di Belle Arti, sono le più antiche istituzioni d'Alta Formazione in Occidente, sono il luogo dello studio e della ricerca sul come migliorare, sono il riconoscimento del pensiero umanistico dietro la professione dell'artista, sono l'approccio di ricerca su canoni e dati percettivi che abbatte il limite tra artisti e scienziati.

In un'Accademia, gli artisti imparano a osservare raccogliendo dati percettivi, imparano a imparare, impegnandosi ad accumulare conoscenza (non solo visiva) nel tempo.

In un'Accademia, si ricerca il senso delle cose, attraverso la memoria di ciò che accade e che si vive, si sperimentano in rete le proprie conclusioni, a partire dal giovane artista in formazione con una specializzazione linguistica che arricchisce la ricerca.

In Accademia, gli artisti imparano imparando come autodeterminarsi, imparano a essere critici verso i lavori dei critici e degli altri artisti, ma sempre nell'interesse di uno sviluppo linguistico dell'arte comune.

Il mercato privato, dinanzi i processi pubblici, d'autodeterminazione linguistica dell'arte contemporanea, può soltanto alzare bandiera bianca.

La Neotenia del linguaggio artistico!

La neotenia è il processo, che rende lo stato giovanile dei progenitori adulto nei discendenti.

I linguaggi dell'arte umani hanno questa capacità, quella di regolare il processo del loro sviluppo, di allungare o contrarre la dipendenza dal linguaggio attraverso la tempistica d'apprendimento.

Articolazione e comunicazione linguistica, hanno determinato l'evoluzione culturale dell'homo sapiens, comparso 200000 anni fa nell'Africa sub sahariana, che da subito ha cominciato a lavorare la pietra, forte di geni che regolano il suo tempo (oggi come allora).

Soltanto 50000 anni fa, i sapiens da Est e Sudovest, entrano per la prima volta in Europa, sono i "Cro-magnon".

Il tempo e lo spazio, sono stati i fattori che hanno determinato, l'evoluzione e la concettualizzazione linguistica dell'homo sapiens. Soltanto 40000 anni fa, siamo stati l'unica specie umana rimasta sul pianeta terra, e forse proprio la solitudine di specie, ci ha portato ad elaborare simbolicamente il linguaggio dell'arte.

Prima di 40000 anni fa, condividevamo la terra, con altre forme di intelligenze umane, ma attraverso il linguaggio dell'arte abbiamo avuto un'intelligenza culturale inusitata, un cambiamento profondo nei comportamenti.

Forse l'essenza della nostra sopravvivenza è da ricercare, rispetto alle altre forme e tipologie umane che si sono estinte, nella creatività mentale, nell'intelligenza simbolica e nei linguaggi dell'arte che da questo derivano.

SIAMO SOLO LINGUAGGIO

Noi sapiens, nasciamo in Africa 200000 anni fa, ma elaboriamo il linguaggio dell'arte e la sua concettualizzazione, soltanto 75000 anni fa; 45000 anni fa, la nostra mente artistica diventa moderna, in grado d'astrarre attraverso pitture rupestri, orniamo il nostro corpo e intagliamo ossa e pietre.

Nella pratica, rimasti l'unica razza ominide sul pianeta terra, abbiamo attraverso il linguaggio dell'arte, lavorato per fare emergere le nostre unicità utilizzando il linguaggio dell'arte.

Il linguaggio dell'arte, è stato lo strumento dell'umano, per articolare e offrire infinite narrazioni e combinazioni simboliche del sé e del noi.

La nostra differenza è tutta nel linguaggio, lo strumento che ci accomuna e caratterizza, che ci illude d'avere un anima, altro non siamo che una delle sue infinite varianti stratificate nella condizione dell'umano.

L'ORIGINE NEL LINGUAGGIO

I linguaggi dell'arte, sono l'origine di tutta la concettualizzazione linguistica dell'umano, 40000 anni fa i sapiens cominciano a generare il linguaggio dell'arte (pur con una storia evolutiva di 200000 anni), ma la scrittura compare soltanto intorno al nono millennio avanti Cristo. Intorno al nono millennio avanti Cristo, compaiono dei "gettoni", delle forme geometriche tridimensionali che si barattavano per scambi e

baratti (in origine in argilla, divennero dal 3500 a.C. in bronzo e piatti).
La scultura era linguaggio e concettualizzazione del linguaggio anche
economica.

I gettoni piatti avevano forme geometriche bidimensionali incise, che
sintetizzavano l'accumulo delle forme d'argilla dette "bulle".

Le bulle vennero poi sostituite da tavolette d'argilla con incise forme
geometriche e simboliche nella quantità desiderata, la scrittura nasce
su una tavoletta d'argilla e su pietra, per poi diversificarsi.

L'origine dei linguaggi dell'arte è comune, come l'origine dell'uomo, si
diversifica sostanzialmente su due percorsi, quello logografico (o
ideografico) e quello fonografico.

I sistemi logografici sono basati sul senso di un segno visivo e
linguistico; i sistemi fonografici sul suono e il significante che forma la
parola.

Non è meraviglioso constatare, come l'origine di tutti i nostri linguaggi
specializzati e specializzanti, abbia la matrice comune della
concettualizzazione artistica?

ACCADEMIA QUESTIONE MORALE

Gli artisti amano distinguersi, si muovono armati della propria cultura e
dei propri luoghi di formazione; tutte le loro differenze sono
determinate, a partire da una matrice linguistica comune.

I distinguo esistono, ma sono soltanto concettualizzazioni linguistiche,
sono dentro la testa dell'artista e non nel linguaggio fuori dal sé.

I linguaggi dell'arte, sono il frutto creativo un'unica specie umana, di cui
tutti siamo discendenti, specie umana africana, giovane, inventiva ed
espansiva come il suo linguaggio.

Con la sua specificità e attraverso il linguaggio dell'arte, l'umanità ha
creato e concettualizzato una sua diversità, diversità che ha una sua
struttura, nucleo, visione e origine d'insieme.

In questo millennio, a partire dalla diversità, del proprio linguaggio
culturale e artistico, l'umano può scoprire e determinare la sua unità.

Abbiamo costruito nei millenni, distinguo artistici e linguistici, distinguo
logografici e simbolici, ma oggi, nel nome della consapevolezza e
specializzazione linguistica, il linguaggio dell'arte è un potentissimo
strumento per guardare oltre di sé.

Questa premessa, per ragionare sull'importanza, del preservare le arti e
i linguaggi artistici residenti; l'artista residente (o se preferite nativo) è
depositario di relazioni e interazioni linguistiche simboliche e culturali,
modello (ovunque lui risieda) di sostenibilità (anche economica) del
linguaggio.

Pensateci, in origine parlavamo un unico linguaggio dell'arte, le enormi distanze l'hanno mutato, il linguaggio è mutato in relazione all'habitat dove si è fermato e sviluppato.

In quest'ottica di movimento all'origine del linguaggio dell'arte, pensate a quanto sia stato importante, nella diversificazione del linguaggio, l'errore della copia.

I linguaggi dell'arte si muovono in verticale in maniera evolutiva, ma anche in orizzontale, attraverso la narrazione e la comprensione della comunità.

Il linguaggio dell'arte, può essere influenzato da fattori esterni, da élite dominanti o da territori conquistati che resistono con il loro linguaggio (perché la storia non la scrivono soltanto i vincitori).

Pensateci un attimo, pensate a un linguaggio logogrammatico, che si origina con i sapiens 60000 anni fa, per poi muoversi intorno al mondo, che ci distingue nel segno, e nel nome dello stesso ci accomuna; la lingua scritta compare e si determina soltanto da cinquemila anni.

Nel nome di questo, se è vero (e lo é), che vi è una differenza genetica tra Sardi ed Europei (Corsi compresi), originatasi nell'antico popolamento isolano (risalente a 9000 anni fa con tribù preneolitiche) e alla deriva genetica, non si può pensare all'evoluzione e trasmissione culturale e artistica di un popolo, come fosse un'isola; quella dell'isola è una condizione geografica che non ha nulla a che vedere con la condizione linguistica dell'umano.

Come si può quindi, continuare a pensare a un'Alta Formazione Artistica isolana ferma a Sassari, e a una città metropolitana come Cagliari, ancora priva di un'Accademia di Belle Arti nel 2018?

L'isola è uno scrigno di diversità bioantropologica e culturale, c'è maggiore differenza biologica e culturale, tra due comunità isolane, che tra un portoghese e un rumeno.

Un'Accademia di Belle Arti a Cagliari, sarebbe un importante nodo di confronto e di tutela del linguaggio e ricerche artistiche residenti, in fondo le arti si radicano nell'umanità e nelle comunità, per propagare esperienza e diversità culturale e biologica.

Un'Accademia di Belle Arti a Cagliari, sarebbe un fatto culturale che costituirebbe un'assicurazione sul futuro, oggi come mai dovrebbe essere un imperativo politico morale.

MARIO PESCE A FORE, L'ANTIACCADEMIA

Il Mario Pesce a Fore, nasceva alla fine degli anni novanta, tra l'Accademia di Belle Arti di Napoli e i Centri Sociali "Officina 99" e il "Laboratorio Okkupato s.k.a." con l'intento dichiarato di condurre una guerriglia artistica, attraverso un'identità collettiva che fosse da tag comune, per delle identità artistiche dichiarate, reali e codificabili, che operasse attraverso performance e azioni rapidi, veloci e organizzate, finalizzate a occupare gallerie private, Musei e Accademie di Belle Arti. Lo scopo era portare l'attenzione di un sistema dell'arte sempre più privatizzato e provincializzante sull'arte e la formazione artistica residente.

Sovente si operava in passamontagna e armati di pistole giocattolo, si criticava nei luoghi preposti dell'arte contemporanea, la riduzione dell'arte a strategia di mercato.

Si trattava di un gruppo fatto di confronti tra gli artisti che l'animavano, alimentato da posizioni individuali divergenti, un collettivo articolato ed eterogeneo tenuto insieme da obiettivi di grande rilievo.

Le azioni erano manifesti, come le strategie da mettere in atto in contesti esterni, per sollevare la questione dell'arte residente "internazionale" quanto quella globalizzata imposta dai mercati, dalle gallerie private e dalle Accademie che ne istituzionalizzavano i riferimenti.

"Mario Pesce a Fore" è stata una reazione istintiva al boom economico degli anni Ottanta, la reazione al fatto che negli anni Novanta si fosse ridotto il tutto a una visione dell'arte come investimento, l'arte vista esclusivamente come fonte di guadagno.

Nel "Mario Pesce a Fore" non si amava l'idea della facile commerciabilità della Transavanguardia, imporre il mercato della Transavanguardia come ritorno alla pittura, voleva dire negare la pittura come linguaggio e che si fosse sempre dipinto.

Negli anni novanta una serie di distorsioni e di miraggi di volere essere come Mimmo Paladino o Francesco Clemente, aveva fatto proliferare gli spazi espostivi, esistevano almeno una se non due gallerie private per quartiere.

Il proliferare del mercato, elevato a sistema linguistico dell'arte, non sembrava arricchire il dibattito estetico, anzi sembrava stesse tutto regredendo.

Maestri d'Accademia dicevano alle studentesse "tu non sarai mai un artista, sei una donna", l'arte sembrava una questione esclusiva per maschi stereotipati, uomini o bisessuali.

"Mario Pesce a Fore" stava per Fore come località, ma anche come messa a nudo del linguaggio senza distinguo di genere e sesso.

I passamontagna e le maschere delle performance, muovevano non dall'evidenziare il proprio essere anonimi, ma era l'esatto opposto, si sapeva chi fossimo, e si diceva noi non siamo "nessuno" e se lo siamo, siamo un pericolo per chi ci nega.

Volevamo essere in maniera chiara e codificabile, la voce fuori dal coro, la coscienza del mondo dell'arte (non solo Napoletano).

Il primo spazio che prendemmo in ostaggio, fu la Casina Pompeiana, dove fummo invitati a rappresentare la contemporaneità della performance nei linguaggi dell'arte contemporanea Napoletana, all'interno di un percorso storico; d'allora comparimmo ovunque, non eravamo sistematici, potevamo accadere dovunque e comunque.

L'interazione tra di noi, determinata dalla diversità consapevole, dei linguaggi e della ricerca di ciascuno, ci sollevava da una serie di fesserie, non abbiamo mai avuto un marchio registrato, nonostante capitasse che Bonito Oliva ci presentasse in certe situazioni istituzionali.

Se c'era una causa comune nel "Mario Pesce a Fore" era nella sua stessa militanza, anche se dall'interno in sostanza, tutti lavoravano per scardinarlo in cerca dell'affermazione artistica individuale, per questo era impossibile l'anonimato, troppo ego e fame di fama, e in fondo perché nascondersi dietro l'anonimato?

Si stava rappresentando la privatizzazione artistica e culturale della città che era fin troppo evidente, ma che tutti negavano.

L'anima della posse non si è mai istituzionalizzata, le mostre erano autogestite e ciascun artista era curatore e responsabile di sé; si era con consapevolezza, espressione di una cornice storica di un sistema di potere, che si muoveva subdolo tra cultura underground e industria culturale internazionale globale.

Tutto questo nacque in maniera molto ludica, dalla prospettiva di studenti d'Accademia, prospettiva dalla quale era evidente che gli anni anni settanta erano invecchiati precocemente, che Napoli non offrisse nessuna reale possibilità per i giovani artisti, che non venerare il presente che era già il passato.

Prima del "Mario Pesce a Fore", a Napoli, e non solo, nessuno rifletteva sul sistema dell'arte, dovunque (Accademia compreso), si dava per scontato che fosse come doveva essere; nella realtà si sentiva tutto (e lo era) come retroguardia.

Avevamo una giovane consapevolezza e capivamo che l'altra strada possibile era il pubblico, pubblico e comunità potevano arginare il mercato e il privato, nel nome di questo, qualcuno di noi interessava a

qualche gallerista, e forse per questo nacque e si espanse il gruppo, per qualcuno divenne una scorciatoia per farsi notare (che miseria umana).
Decidemmo di puntare il nome inizialmente, proprio contro le gallerie, era il nodo di rete che intermediari e sdoganava gli interessi privati nel pubblico, oggi questo schema è forse saltato, il privato entra direttamente nel pubblico e nei musei.
Una cosa interessante da scoprire, fu che tutti gli interessi di mercato fossero politicamente a sinistra (era la Napoli di Bassolino).
Quello che accomunava era la militanza, il passamontagna in pubblico era simbolico, ciascuno sapeva chi fossimo e perché indossassimo il passamontagna; volevamo realmente dare fastidio e per questo l'arte la studiavamo sul serio.
Il mondo dell'arte per noi era ristretto, alto borghese e classista, e a noi piaceva essere popolani (ma non popolari).
Ancora oggi, intorno a quell'esperienza c'è molto fastidio e paura, eravamo sul serio irriverenti (non era una rappresentazione) e strategicamente dei provocatori di professione.

"Mario Pesce a Fore" di un sistema blindato!

Il "Mario pesce a fore" era una moltitudine d'artisti, liberi d'orientarsi come meglio credessero, tanti, molti, troppi punti di vista e atteggiamenti, tante prospettive quanti gli artisti che l'hanno attraversato?
Quanti artisti l'hanno attraversato?
A un certo punto per gestirci avevamo messo su un registro contabile di soci, che serviva per auto produrci video, avevamo superato i quattrocento artisti; attenzione, tra questi, alcuni avevano sposato la causa per un ora, altri ancora oggi non hanno mai divorziato da quella dichiarazione d'intenti; certo era che si trattasse di un accumulatore d'esperienze e d'intenti, chiunque poteva entrare a fare parte di quel processo creativo e occuparsi di una sua direzione di realizzazione progettuale.
Si credeva in ciò che si faceva, ci si muoveva creativamente come si fosse un gruppo rock o anche un orchestra sinfonica, si condivideva l'improvvisazione e nasceva il pezzo.
Avevamo puntato tutto e tutti, gli artisti mainstream, le gallerie, i critici, i Musei, i collezionisti e anche l'Accademia, che ci aveva generato glorificando tutto quello che ci osteggiava.
Attaccare e criticare il sistema era la nostra missione, e riuscivamo sempre a collocarlo sulla nostra difensiva:
gli artisti si giustificavano dicendo di non potere influenzare i loro galleristi.

i galleristi dicevano di non potere vendere e trattare opere e artisti che i collezionisti della galleria non erano disposti a comprare.

 i collezionisti non erano interessati alle opere che la critica istigata dai collezionisti, deliberatamente ignorava.

i critici come potevano scrivere se l'editore non recensiva?

L'editore affermava di prendere in considerazione solo ciò che era gallerie e Musei.

Capite quanto fosse tutto blindato?

Capite quanto tutto ciò escludesse e discriminasse la giovane arte residente?

La forza informativa del"Mario Pesce a Fore", stava proprio nel muoversi come cellule sparse che univano informazioni e traevano conclusioni, tutto era condito d'ironia e umorismo folk, era di fatto l'unica voce Italiana artistica, realmente fuori dal coro.

Ancora oggi, nei singoli percorsi individuali che l'hanno attraversato, Mario Pesce a Fore è stato questo, una moltitudine d'artisti, tutti diversi tra loro, che amano (o hanno amato) l'arte e odiano (o hanno odiato) l'immoralità del sistema dell'arte.

Il gruppo era realmente molto vario, attraversava generazioni: Maestri d'Accademia, di Liceo e d'Istituto d'Arte, ex sessantottini, giovani studenti d'Accademia, trans, gay, lesbiche, homeless, punkabbestia, tossici e pusher, eravamo altro rispetto al mondo dell'arte, nessuna militanza di genere, trasversalità pura.

Ci muovevamo con la pretesa e l'ambizione di raccontare tutte le problematiche celate, dell'arte e degli artisti, senza nessun distinguo e interesse di parte, non distinguevamo neanche tra l'interno e l'esterno del Mario pesce a fore, in fondo eravamo anche dentro le istituzioni che facevamo infuriare, non per nulla la nostra storia cominciava dentro un'Accademia di Belle Arti che faticava ad arginarci e contenerci.

Il Rinascimento di Bassolino

"Mario Pesce a Fore" è stato un movimento fluido, in divenire fino a svanire.

 Il suo autodeterminarsi non ha mai seguito un percorso lineare, è stato sciare e zigzagare privo di strategie e programmi, soltanto comunanza d'utopia e intenti.

Non era un'organizzazione, era aggregante, il lavoro fatto sull'analisi del sistema nel nome di tale aggregazione è stato enorme.

Si scopriva la totale assenza di diritto dell'arte residente, dell'artista marginalizzato e discriminato proprio nei luoghi dove si formava, cresceva e lavorava, marginalizzazione che avveniva nel nome dello status quo degli interessi privati.

Adesso, cosa hanno a che vedere gli interessi privati con la libera ricerca e autodeterminazione artistica?

Trovavamo molto interessante, constatare, come i Musei d'Arte Contemporanea (che già di per sé costituivano una follia) non comprendessero neanche una quota d'arte pubblica e residente che non passasse dai privati.

Gran parte delle acquisizioni dei Musei d'Arte Contemporanea, dipendevano da ricchi collezionisti, con le loro acquisizioni "a stampo" ottimizzate dal consiglio d'amministrazione dello stesso Museo.

Molto facile gonfiare il valore delle proprie collezioni private passando per il pubblico a carico del contribuente.

Mandava fuori di testa, l'idea della città metropolitana, capitale del Regno delle due Sicilie, di sinistra e progressista, che annientava, ometteva e nascondeva sotto il tappetino la cultura e la formazione artistica residente.

"Mario Pesce a Fore" e la consacrazione del leccatore

Quello che animava il "Mario Pesce a Fore" come Posse, non era una visione collettiva, ma una convergenza strategica collettiva e connettiva. Ci si muoveva a partire da storie, analisi, percorsi, vicissitudini che erano constatazioni personali e individuali; si confluiva nel Mario Pesce a Fore, dopo i tentativi individuali d'autodeterminazione, che puntualmente, se eri un giovane artista con una sua completa visione di ricerca e linguaggi, si rivelano fallimentari anche dopo qualche successo e contentino effimero.

Il giovane artista del "Mario Pesce a Fore", veniva fatto sentire dal contesto di sistema che viveva e abitava, inadeguato; affermarsi nel mondo dell'arte Napoletano (come altrove) era un impresa se la tua formazione artistica era giovane e residente.

Si era così, un poco tutti, analizzatori del sistema, con la propria esperienza come parametro, questo rendeva forti, criticavamo e venivamo criticati (anche a mezzo stampa e massmedia locali), ma quello che ci veniva venduto come "insuccesso", lo vivevamo con il giusto e ludico distacco, mai come giudizio repentino e assoluto, questo ci temprava tutti.

Tutti avevamo vocazione e preparazione, sapevamo che pochi o nessuno di noi sarebbe stato consacrato al sistema (pur avendo vent'anni), giovani e disincantati, avevamo la consapevolezza che tutto il sistema dell'arte era concepito per produrre penuria.

Avevamo capito che tutto era fondato sull'esclusione, è stato folgorante, avevamo subito cominciato a guardare oltre gallerie e mercati, sentivamo il sostegno di tutti gli artisti che avevano costituito le avanguardie storiche del Novecento.
L'esperienza del "Mario Pesce a Fore" è stata una esperienza unica, di delegittimazione degli agenti di potere, i nostri lavori circolavano liberamente per fare "Accademia", erano lingua viva per artisti.

Non piacevamo ai "leccatori di deretano" di mercati e collezionisti, avevamo ben chiaro che una carriera può essere fallimentare dal punto di vista commerciale, ma con un proprio linguaggio, una propria ricerca, una propria identità e specificità, sei parte naturale della comunità artistica, sei in grado di dire la tua, sei una cultura, sei industria intellettuale e culturale, è il gallerista a dipendere da te e non tu da lui, sei l'influencer e il riferimento per altri artisti.

LO SCHIFO DELLA STORIA TRADOTTA IN MERCATO

"Mario Pesce a Fore" aveva compreso, alla fine degli anni novanta, come la libertà di ricerca artistica nell'arte, con la propria interazione didattica e dialettica, fosse una cosa meravigliosa; si era profondamente infastiditi da come tale meraviglia fosse omessa da gallerie e musei.
Ci si scandalizzava insieme, quando si scopriva che gallerie e Musei fossero concepiti per selezionare nel presente, un ristretto numero di geni su cui investire.
L'idea del genio e del capolavoro privava e depredava il sistema della cultura di ricerca del senso, di un'intera epoca storica.
Per mettere a fuoco tempo e storia dei linguaggi dell'arte, da studenti d'Accademia, nutrivamo la convinzione storica, che fosse necessaria una moltitudine d'artisti; il mercato dell'arte era l'esatto opposto di quello che si studiava, leggeva il presente, facendolo confluire in un pugno di vincitori, e per legittimarsi aveva bisogno di una marea di pretendenti alla fama che non sapessero essere perdenti, che giocassero a fare gli artisti proprio come si gioca al superenalotto.
L'arte era (ed è) in realtà, una questione un tantinello più complessa, come si poteva pensare sul serio, che bastasse a sentenziarne

l'essenza, un gruppo d'intenditori, capaci di riconoscere il genio fuori dal tempo, ma i Maestri d'Accademia che ci vendevano questa verità erano seri?

La storia del mercato che riduceva l'artista a investimento, ci faceva schifo, questo ci rendeva uno strumento per dare forza di moltitudine critica verso un sistema di selezione atroce.

"Mario Pesce a Fore" è stato un esempio locale oltre il locale, di rivendicazione in salsa folk , da quell'esperienza si sono generate una serie di percorsi ed esperienza individuali, chi ha resistito nel tampone ne ha fatto patrimonio e fondamenta di ricerca.

Per qualche anno, prima che evaporasse disgregato dalle mille faide di visibilità individuali interne, "Mario Pesce a Fore" è stato molto ambito e ricercato all'interno del sistema; se volevi criticare il sistema senza esporti in prima persona, ti bastava invitare all'interno il "Mario Pesce a Fore".

"Mario Pesce a Fore" era l'attacco diretto a quei collezionisti che compravano in galleria e sedevano proferendo parola, nel consiglio d'amministrazione del Museo.

La coscienza è nell'estetica!

La coscienza di un artista è nel suo linguaggio come fatto estetico; l'intelligenza linguistica di un artista non è un'immagine mentale, è sintesi di tutte le entità che si relazionano all'occhio di chi guarda.

Il linguaggio è come l'impronta di un animale, un segno con il quale s'impatta per caso che può essere fermato e trattenuto nel tempo.

Il linguaggio dell'arte non è fuori dal tempo, ma scansiona in maniera fluida lo spazio e il tempo.

Il linguaggio è come una città d'attraversare, ti mostra mentre ne percorri le strade, i segni del tempo.

L'apparenza nei linguaggi dell'arte è il passato, l'essenza dei linguaggi dell'arte è il futuro.

La quiete è nel linguaggio nell'arte, ma soltanto quando sa essere fluido mentre accade.

"La Madre dell'ucciso"

L'isola sembra ritrovarsi incredula e sotto shock per la scomparsa di Manuel Careddu, diciotto anni, ucciso un mese fa, il cui corpo è stato ritrovato nel lago di Omodeo.

Ucciso per un debito di droga di una amica minorenne nei suoi confronti, lo sgarro da parte di Manuel è stato aver reclamato quei soldi. Sembra che i ragazzi stessero pensando d'uccidere anche la madre dell'ucciso....

"La madre dell'ucciso"; in fondo in quest'isola si è sempre ucciso per ragioni futili, è scritto nella storia dell'arte isolana, è scritto ne "La Madre dell'ucciso" di Francesco Ciusa.

Ciusa non frequentò l'Accademia di Belle Arti di Cagliari, neanche Maria Lai e Costantino Nivola a dirla tutta, l'Accademia a Cagliari non c'è mai stata; Francesco Ciusa si formò all'Accademia di Belle Arti di Firenze; a Firenze ricordò il drammatico episodio che materializzò la straziante Scultura, risaliva a lui quattordicenne, a Fontana 'e littu, vide una donna, Grazia Puxeddu, avvicinarsi al cadavere del figlio per chiudersi nel silenzio; il figlio fu ucciso da tre fratelli, aveva testimoniato contro di loro per il furto di maiali.

Nell'isola non c'è mai stata un'Accademia di Belle Arti a Cagliari, e si muore, oggi come allora, per futili motivi economici.

IL RINASCIMENTO "PRIVATO" DEI CAVARO

Per capire perché Cagliari, ancora nel 2018, sia priva di un'Accademia di Belle Arti, forse potremmo partire dal Rinascimento Toscano, da quel momento dove altrove in Italia (e in Europa) gli artisti passavano dalle botteghe alle corti, determinando la nascita dell'Accademia; mentre altrove accadeva questo, a Cagliari vi era una bottega, una bottega ribattezzata scuola dalla storia dell'arte locale, ma ogni sarebbe da leggere come una piccola impresa a conduzione familiare, se di scuola si può parlare, si può parlare di scuola privata.

La famiglia di pittori Rinascimentali Cagliaritani, è la famiglia Cavaro di Antonio Cavaro.

La bottega venne avviata dal figlio del pittore Antonio Cavaro, Lorenzo Cavaro, con Gioacchino Cavaro.

Uno dei Cavaro, Pietro Cavaro, era iscritto nell'associazione dei pittori di Barcellona nel 1508, a Barcellona un'Accademia era presente dal quattrocento; Pietro Cavaro tra forse nipote di Antonio, forse figlio di Lorenzo o Gioacchino (che a detta di qualcuno potrebbe essere anche il Maestro di Castelsardo), insomma una storia e una vicenda pittorica che sembra quasi privata.

A Pietro succedette Michele Cavaro, che morì sindaco di Stampace, con qualche conflitto d'interesse curò forse gli interessi della scuola e bottega e non si adoperò per porre in essere un'Accademia, come fecero invece i Caracci a Bologna nello stesso periodo storico; morto Michele Cavaro, morì la scuola di Sant'Avendrace, nella quale si distinse Antioco Mainas, il più talentoso e popolare degli studenti a bottega, con un cognome diverso.

A Sassari (non a Cagliari) l'Ex Mattatoio all'Accademia

A Sassari (non a Cagliari) l'Ex Mattatoio all'Accademia
A Sassari (e non a Cagliari) nasce la cittadella della cultura; a Sassari e non a Cagliari per questo si sono investiti milioni di euro a partire dal 2009 (sette milioni di euro); a Sassari e non a Cagliari si ritroveranno in questa cittadella l'Università di Sassari, l'Accademia di Belle Arti e le associazioni (a Cagliari l'Accademia non è mai nata); a Sassari in maniera pubblica e programmatica nascerà un pubblico villaggio della ricerca, della scienza, della cultura e della creatività.
Tutto questo accadrà in una meravigliosa area di 3000 metri quadri e sette edifici, posta proprio dinanzi all'Accademia di Belle Arti di Sassari, in comodato d'uso per trent'anni l'Accademia di Belle Arti di Sassari potrà gestire l'Ex mattatoio.
Ricapitoliamo, il complesso di proprietà del Comune di Sassari viene ceduto per trent'anni all'Accademia di Belle Arti di Sassari, per fare nascere un "Campus delle arti e dello spettacolo", a Sassari non a Cagliari dove l'Accademia non c'è mai stata.
Lo spazio Ex Mattatoio a Sassari (e non a Cagliari) verrà riconsegnato alla città come bene pubblico aperto alla cittadinanza artistica (e non) attiva.
L'Ex Mattatoio, verrà rinominato Ex-Ma.ter e avrà un uso didattico finalizzato al consolidamento dell'Accademia (e di riflesso anche dello storico Liceo Artistico "Filippo Figari" di Sassari) del ruolo della formazione artistica d'area Sassarese all'interno del tessuto cittadino e regionale.
Soprattutto Alta Formazione Artistica Regionale, soprattuto a Sassari e non a Cagliari.
L'Accademia di Belle Arti "Mario Sironi" che qualche problema di spazi laboratoriali l'aveva, farà dell'Ex Mattatoio un laboratorio dove ha programmato l'istituzione (finalmente) del corso di Restauro (sempre a

Sassari) dei Beni Culturali.

A cosa punta tutta questa operazione da sette milioni di euro?

A fare si che Sassari con la sua Accademia, rappresenti il cuore pulsante dell'Alta Formazione Artistica in Regione, ponendosi come centro risorse per le compagnie e associazioni che si rivolgeranno a lei.

Adesso, per rappresentare il cuore pulsante dell'Alta formazione Regione, c'era realmente bisogno di tutto questo?

Ma perché a voi risulta che in Regione si sia mai ragionato seriamente sulla nascita del polo d'Alta Formazione Artistica Cagliaritano?

Con chi sarebbe mai stata in competizione Sassari e il polo d'Alta Formazione Artistica Sassarese in Regione?

Se Sassari non è ancora il cuore pulsante dell'alta formazione artistica isolana e ci sia stato bisogni di questi investimenti programmatici di sette milioni di euro, non potrebbe in fondo dipendere dal fatto che soltanto nell'isola c'è un capoluogo città metropolitana privo d'Accademia di Belle Arti?

LA PROPRIOCEZIONE DELL'ARTE

I linguaggi dell'arte sono scienza e neuroscienza, sono la possibilità della comprensione della dimensione che abitiamo e che sentiamo; ogni linguaggio dell'arte assorbe l'esistenza di altri linguaggi dell'arte.

Un linguaggio e una ricerca artistica sono figli dei Maestri, degli amici artisti, di quello che si osserva, di chi li osserva e di come si risponde a tutto questo.

Un linguaggio e una ricerca artistica è dialogo con il linguaggio e la ricerca di un artista, vissuto centinaia, se non migliaia, d'anni, dalla parte opposta del mondo.

Un linguaggio artistico può prevedere il futuro, può dialogare in maniera fluida con altri cervelli, è nello stesso tempo creazione e fruizione; è sintesi di ciò che s'impara e ricorda; i linguaggi dell'arte e gli artisti sono la memoria.

Tradurre e sintetizzare una ricerca artistica in linguaggio, vuole dire sintetizzare 86.000.000.000 neuroni che si muovono tra miliardi di connessioni, vuole dire raccogliere in un gesto 160000 chilometri di fibre nervose, pensateci, i neuroni nel nostro cervello, in fila su una strada, si estenderebbero per 860000 chilometri, tutto ciò pesa 1300 grammi.

Perché vi parlo ora di cervello?

Perché il cervello come il linguaggio artistico, nasce incompleto, esiste e si autodetermina plasticamente in maniera mobile, soltanto interagendo sempre con altri cervelli, il linguaggio dell'arte si muove nel tempo proprio come si muovono i nostri cervelli, è lo stimolo a crescere, comprendere e mutare nel nostro cervello.

Non a caso, negli ultimi tre milioni d'anni, il cervello ominide (oggi esclusiva del sapiens) si è triplicato, passando da 450 a 1300 grammi; il linguaggio dell'arte l'ha aiutato a crescere; la corteccia cerebrale 2–4 mm. di spessore come le sue aree di connessione associative, aiuta a comprenderlo, facendo fluire e interagire le informazioni, soltanto nella corteccia lavorano 16 miliardi di neuroni; chimica ed elettricità sono all'origine del linguaggio dell'arte come del nostro cervello.

Linguaggi dell'arte e cervello si muovono per lo sforzo collettivo, attraverso reti neurali che si relazionano, necessario è l'incrocio sensoriale e percettivo.

Linguaggi dell'arte e cervello sono sinestetici; Pinuccio Sciola suonava le pietre che scolpiva e oggi possiamo suonarle oltre che osservarle.

I linguaggi dell'arte immaginano il futuro, lo fanno perché sono in costante dialogo con il passato.

L'autodeterminazione di un linguaggio artistico è propriocezione, ossia lo sviluppo di un proprio linguaggio artistico, come strumento di misurazione del proprio sé nello spazio.

Lo studio dei linguaggi dell'arte è riproduzione di gesti e segni, in spazi e luoghi differenti, è propriocezione nello spazio e nel tempo.

ARTIST MODE

Da docente penso che non esista una ricetta didattica per formare un artista, anzi per essere artista e non formare chi scimiotta parvenze e movenze d'artista, bisognerebbe cercare l'esatto opposto di una ricetta.

Il cuoco perfetto non esiste nei linguaggi dell'arte, se conosci tutti gli ingredienti sei tecnicamente un mestierante, devi fare un passo avanti per cercare qualcosa che abbia un suo gusto, che sappia essere originale e saporito.

Tre ingredienti però penso si possano individuare:

1) PRESTARE ATTENZIONE
Lasciare aperta la porta della comprensione dell'altro, il linguaggio dell'altro è il ricettario degli ingredienti da modificare all'occorrenza.

2) MOSTRARSI CRITICI, CORAGGIOSI E FLESSIBILI
Una capacità dell'artista, dovrebbe essere mettere in discussione tutto ciò che è norma, al punto d'apparire contro tutto e contro tutti.

Non dovrebbe esistere nessun pensiero unico dell'arte, la creatività esige coraggio, senza coraggio come si fanno a sondare altre maniere e modalità?

3) PENSARE, RILASSARSI E PASSEGGIARE
Il linguaggio dell'arte ha una vita autonoma, indipendente da quella
dell'artista, scatta e si muove in autonomia proprio quando si abbassa
la guardia e viene liberato.

A cosa servirebbero questi tre ingredienti?
A concedersi la libertà di potere essere etichettati come "strani",
uscendo dai meccanismi del pensiero consolidato.
Non ti piace il sistema dell'arte?
Chi ti vieta d'inventarti il tuo?
Le regole di divulgazione del tuo linguaggio artistico le determini tu, non
c'è la necessità di delegare gli altri.
Il linguaggio si muove in autonomia quando gli si consente d'essere
curioso, la curiosità muove il linguaggio, la curiosità determina
l'esperienza estetica, la percezione del bello non è un canone ma una
sensazione fluida.
Il linguaggio non è bello, la bellezza è personale, è una propria
riflessione, sociale, culturale, intima o politica.
Puoi essere brutto, scioccante o aggressivo nel linguaggio, ma se con il
tuo linguaggio sei aperto, se con il tuo linguaggio modifichi e ti
modifichi sei sulla strada giusta.
L'esperienza estetica modifica il mondo all'infinito.
 Il flusso del linguaggio dell'arte pretende da ciascun cervello una
lettura e una interpretazione, alimenta interrogativi e collegamenti, è il
pretesto per staccarsi dalla realtà per affrontarla con un altra percezione
e punto di vista.
Il flusso del linguaggio dell'arte ci da uno sguardo diverso e un coraggio
che è sempre nuovo, le sinapsi si muovono e ci cambiano la modalità
operativa.
In "modalità quotidiana" il cervello si occupa delle incombenze e delle
problematiche quotidiane, in "modalità artistica" giochiamo con il
nostro sistema sensoriale.
A cosa serve la tecnica?
A tutto questo, servono ore e ore, settimane e settimane, mesi e mesi,
anni e anni, decenni e decenni di lavoro per smettersi di preoccuparsi
del proprio lavoro e di non sentirlo come tale, bensì come istanza
naturale.
Se si produce linguaggio, è necessario conoscere la storia dei linguaggi
che ci precedono.
Serve l'Accademia per sentirsi artisti liberi di volare.
Il bello ha origine nei sensi, nella memoria, nelle emozioni, capite nel

nome di questo quanto siano importanti le arti residenti e gli artisti locali?

Il linguaggio dell'arte anticipa la lingua scritta di 30–40 mila anni, il canto, la pittura, la scultura sono la nostra memoria esterna originaria (altro che personal computer o drive pen), i gesti e i suoni dell'arte coordinano i nostri movimenti e determinano la nostra identità collettiva, quello che a Cagliari non c'è mai stato (se non con lo scudetto del Cagliari di Gigi Riva).

La Matematica è nel linguaggio dell'arte

Il linguaggio dell'arte, come processo, lo si può inserire nel concetto d'infinito.

Infinita è la sete di conoscenza e comprensione di chi tende ad attraversarne e navigarne seriamente le acque.

Attraversare il linguaggio dell'arte, vuole dire attraversare i frattali del caos, attraversare sistemi di misurazione. formule, cifre, unità di comprensione, determinate da soggetti che manifestano la loro natura.

Linguaggi dell'arte che si formano negli stessi contesti laboratoriali, sociali e culturali, materializzano movimenti del linguaggio diversi.

Il linguaggio dell'arte, in tutta la sua diversità e specificità, come l'artista, fa parte della natura.

Una ricerca artistica che dura una vita, è frattale di linguaggio, di forme e codici che si ripetono su scale diverse, un osservare la natura, la propria natura, in scala.

Quando un artista determina un linguaggio, in quel linguaggio si generano, formano e determinano naturali simmetrie, si determinano autosimiliarità (o autosomiglianze).

Il frattale naturale del linguaggio di un artista, si muove come fosse un cristallo o un albero, si ramifica.

Il frattale (se preferite possiamo anche chiamarlo modulo), è il concetto di ripetizione e d'infinito che consente di riconoscere la cifra, il gesto, lo stile, il linguaggio dell'artista.

Nel frattale elevato a gesto e codice del linguaggio, c'è il conscio e l'inconscio dell'artista, le simmetrie in scala, l'autosomiglianza, la casualità, il disordine, la complessità e il caos.

L'Arte non è distante dalla Matematica, la Matematica non è distante dall'arte, possibile non comprendere come l'equazione e la proporzione siano la stessa cosa?

Sistemi di misurazione e soluzioni di problemi attraverso l'analisi e la cognizione di causa.

Il linguaggio dell'arte tradotto in ricerca, è sempre nel suo insieme processuale un frattale che si muove dal micro al macro.
 I frattali sono la cifra/modulo che fa tendere i linguaggi dell'arte verso l'infinito, tutto ciò non ha nulla a che vedere con prodotti, galleristi, curatori, residenze d'artisti e quotazioni di mercato, è naturale ovunque il linguaggio dell'arte evolva come fatto culturale libero d'inseguire la propria natura.

L'IMPORTANZA DEL LINGUAGGIO DELL'ARTE

Perché riflettere sulla natura dei linguaggi dell'arte, in questo millennio è una necessità?
 Perché il linguaggio dell'arte è in questo millennio arginato e governato dalla tecnologia, l'artista sta scaricando la sua coscienza e la sua ricerca negli smartphone, il guardare sta soppiantando il pensare al punto che le ultime generazioni reputano Facebook uno strumento da vecchi rispetto a Instagram.
Ogni anno in questo scenario vengono pubblicati più di trenta miliardi di selfie.
Eppure le Accademie di Belle Arti, coltivano ancora sguardi profondi, sguardi con una loro vita e una loro grammatica cognitiva e visiva, l'atto del guardare lo si sviluppa e svolge nella profondità del cervello.
Guardare è movimento nello spazio,

L'artista contemporaneo è in sostanza un/una narciso/a della coscienza, che guarda se stesso con la consapevolezza e l'istinto del proprio linguaggio, che prende in considerazione con la propria immagine con il proprio linguaggio, il proprio posto al mondo, indagando il proprio corpo tradotto in immagine, vede il nascosto, il surreale, il mitico e il mitologico.
Per l'osservatore del mondo, il sé e la coscienza del sé, è la porta d'accesso che consente di scrutare il mondo.
 Non si sfugge dalla propria immagine riflessa in un specchio o intrappolata in un selfie, racchiude lo sguardo e interagisce con gli altri osservatori, ma soltanto se la si fa evadere dalla conformità con una reale indagine di linguaggio calibrato su di sé.
Soltanto il linguaggio dell'arte può raccontare chi si è sul serio, oltre la propria apparente immagine sintetizzata con un selfie.

CARO ASSESSORE, NESSUNA MIA PERSONALE

A Dicembre avrei dovuto fare la mia prima mostra personale pubblica, storica e istituzionale.

Una di quelle Mostre personali che segnano un punto di non ritorno, da un percorso dal quale comunque non ritornerò.

Una di quelle Mostre in una sede e cornice storica, con opere incorniciate che dialogano con il passato e con la storia, una di quelle mostre con manifesti e banner e che in genere sono accompagnata da cataloghi ragionati.

Ma il catalogo ragionato non ci sarebbe stato, il ragionamento sul linguaggio non ha bisogno di cataloghi che ragionino al posto di chi dovrebbe ragionare in autonomia sui sensi dell'arte.

Mi ero accordato con un Comune d'area di una città metropolitana, tramite un fidato intermediario, avevo preventivato una (bassa e forfettaria) cifra simbolica, cifra che in realtà era la copertura delle spese del lavoro prodotto.

Non carico mai cifre sui miei lavori che vadano oltre il tariffario di una prestazione d'opera, lo trovo scorretto per me, per il mio lavoro, e anche per i miei interlocutori.

Sono tempi complicati dove tutto può essere una bolla economica anche se in buona fede, mi limito sempre a chiedere il rimborso delle spese dei materiali, di spedizione e del tempo passato a lavorare.

La cifra prevedeva centinaia di lavori ininterrotti, sequenziali e incessanti, dal momento dell'accordo a due settimane prima dell'esposizione, in parallelo il corniciaio incorniciava e chi intermediava sul posto valutava gli spazi.

Si stava concependo una mostra pubblica nell'interesse del pubblico, si era di fatto concordato, che chiunque, turista, residente, custodi o bigliettai, potesse una volta montata e inaugurata la mostra, smontarla, a patto che si scattasse un selfie con l'opera prelevata e me l'inviasse per poi portarsela a casa.

L'impianto della mostra era destinato indiscriminatamente al pubblico, che veniva svincolato da ogni compravendita e distanza, poteva liberamente staccare le opere dalle pareti e portarsele a casa.

Pensateci, opere che segnano l'istituzionalizzazione di una storia artistica, non messe a disposizione dell'investitore privato o del politico di turno, ma di chiunque volesse, ponendo in condizione chiunque visitasse quella mostra d'avere in esclusiva il pezzo esposto ed eventualmente desiderato, a casa sua.

Mi hanno informato che si stava materializzando un altro solito scenario.

L'assessore si recava dal corniciaio con i suoi amici per mettersi da parte disegni e lavori che scomparivano dalle cartelle, in esclusiva si muovevano per altre traiettorie, questo per non doversi "imbarazzare" nel ritirarli pubblicamente in competizione con la cittadinanza.

Mi hanno riferito che si stava stravolgendo tutto l'impianto e tutta la mia idea d'arte, la mostra si sarebbe dovuta titolare #linguaggioumano, proprio perché la questione nodale era quella del flusso puro del linguaggio senza filtro o interesse alcuno; nella pratica mi hanno riferito che l'amministrazione stava valutando di bandire un asta con quei lavori e guadagnare di base cinque o dieci volte di più il rimborso spese (basso molto basso) da me richiesto per centinaia d'opere e lavori.

Non riconoscendomi, in un tale progetto, che si stava impostando alimentando distinguo e valori simbolici ed economici, ho deliberatamente (creando anche qualche imbarazzo al mio intermediario) deciso di fare saltare tutto, questione di coerenza, di percorso e di linguaggio.

Penso che pensare all'arte come linguaggio sia qualcosa di serio, così come pensare all'arte come strumento realmente pubblico, un conto è mostrarsi su una pubblica parete e vendersi privatamente in una galleria, altra cosa è lavorare su una idea d'arte come linguaggio e flusso realmente a disposizione di tutti e del pubblico, l'idea dell'investimento la rispedisco al mittente, come rispedisco al Sindaco, all'Assessore alla Cultura e l'Assessore alle attività produttive, che pensavano di potere speculare a buon mercato sulla mia storia, facendo oggetto e successo di propaganda politica personale, l'invito per una mia personale nel loro Comune.

La Storia aspetta chiunque e a suo piacimento, usa, legittima e consuma chi gli pare e piace, logora chi non ce l'ha, e per mia fortuna, una mia storia personale c'è e si muove come le pare e piace, con Mostra/mostri personali o senza.

A CAGLIARI ANCORA PIETRE SUL DAVID!

Nel 1460 a Firenze, un blocco di marmo inutilizzato giaceva nei magazzini della cattedrale di Firenze.

Cinquant'anni dopo venne chiesto a un giovane Scultore di ventisei anni di farne una Scultura.

La sua era una consegna su committenza politica.

L'artista era un artista che si era formato in quella stessa città, che era giovane, e che aveva mandato politico comunale locale di raffigurare un giovane guerriero, che visse presumibilmente nel 1000 a.C. in grado di sconfiggere un gigante con cinque sassi smussati per poi tagliarli la testa.

Il giovane lavorò per tre anni, disegnò direttamente sul marmo, decise iconoclasticamente di rappresentarlo non trionfante, ma nel momento prima dell'azione, teso in attesa di scopo.

Il ragazzo guerriero venne ritratto nudo e non circonciso, eppure nella narrazione originale il guerriero uccise il gigante perché il gigante non era circonciso.

Capite cosa siano i linguaggi dell'arte?

Capite come negandosi si sublimino e amplificando il senso dei significati simbolici?

Lo scultore era Michelangelo e il David oggi è un capolavoro universale della Storia dei linguaggi dell'arte, l'opera venne selezionata da un comitato composto da artisti come Leonardo Da Vinci e Botticelli, capite quale era la visione programmatica umanistica poetica e politica dell'arte residente?

Sapete cosa accadde durante il percorso di messa in opera del David? La gente si radunò a guardare, e una volta che l'adolescente nudo e circonciso fu tra di loro, lo presero a sassate, infastidiva la sua nudità, guardare i corpi nudi era ritenuto sbagliato, in particolare modo in pubblico e dinanzi a donne e bambini, era l'adolescenza del Rinascimento e della cultura artistica umanistica Accademica e Medicea, in quelle pietre scagliate al David di Michelangelo c'è il perché le Accademie di Belle Arti siano motore fondamentale dell'economia culturale e artistica Italiana nel mondo, ho detto Italiana e non isolana, oggi in Toscana c'è l'Accademia di Belle Arti di Firenze, quella di Carrara e quella di Pisa, quelle pietre ingiuste qualcosa hanno mosso nel tempo in Toscana.

Nell'isola?

Ci si può fregiare di avere l'unico capoluogo Regionale e città metropolitana Europea ancora priva di un'Accademia di Belle Arti, si continua a gettare pietre sull'arte e gli artisti residenti considerati inetti e inesistenti davanti all'internazionale in momentanea residenza che arriva e si determina dall'altrove.

Come dite?

L'Accademia di Belle Arti è a Sassari e solo a Sassari?

Adesso mi dite un attimo quale è la città metropolitana e il capoluogo Regionale?

IL CORPO DELL'ARTE

Il corpo è sempre stato campo di battaglia per gli artisti, Giorgio Vasari ci ha raccontato come i preti nel cinquecento notassero come i fedeli venissero corrotti dalle "lascive imitazioni dei santi".

In questo scenario arrivò Martin Lutero, con l'idea della distinzione tra spirituale e materiale, Lutero come Mosè e come il profeta Maometto era un antivisivo, ma non gli dispiaceva posare per dei ritratti (chiedetelo a Cranach il vecchio).

L'iconoclastia in realtà è soltanto mossa dalla volontà determinata dalla vanità di creare nuovi immaginari, da Savonarala a Lutero, dalla Rivoluzione Francese all'Isis.

L'Accademia tampona il degenere

Hitler aveva ambizioni artistiche, ma non fu mai ammesso all'Accademia di Belle Arti di Vienna, non ebbe l'opportunità di comprendere quanto fossero didattici e dialettici i linguaggi dell'arte. Non amava il cosmopolitismo dei linguaggi dell'arte, cosmopolitismo poteva volere dire tollerare e comprendere Ebrei e Socialisti, voleva dire tollerare malformazioni e degenerazioni, non comprendere che l'unica degenerazione possibile dei linguaggi dell'arte e non tendere oltre il limite dell'estetica ideale, dimenticando che il naturale tende sempre all'ideale.

A Monaco nel 1937 venne allestita una mostra, "Entartete Kunst" (Arte degenerata), la folla stette in fila per ore sotto la pioggia, due milioni di visitatori soltanto a Monaco, con l'invito che recitava: tu sei sano di mente, ma entra pure, vieni a vedere che aspetto ha la pazzia!

Cosa era degenerato?

Immagini africaneggianti, volti allungati, natiche abbondanti, corpi tarchiati, i corpi non ideali erano automaticamente etichettati come non ariani.

Le avanguardie artistiche per bocca di Adolf Ziegler, presidente del gabinetto della cultura del Reich:

"Sono storpi prodotti della pazzia, dell'impertinenza e dell'assenza di talento.

Necessiterei di svariati treni merci per ripulire le gallerie di tutta questa immondizia, questo avverrà presto!"

A Berlino, nel Marzo del 1939, la commissione per l'arte degenerata bruciò tremila dipinti e disegni.

L'Arte degenerata non era reale, sostenevano i nazisti, era un attacco diretto a menti e corpi ariani, in salute e unificati.

Si negava in questo maniera il diverso, il non conforme, i fuori dal coro, la trasgressione, il non allineato, l'alienato, la ricerca e il movimento del linguaggio.

La vera follia era nel considerare il linguaggio dell'arte qualcosa che potesse degenerare, ponendo limiti di genere al suo essere assoluto.

L'arte "degenerata" mostrava la vera natura della coscienza umana, sondava il pensiero di Freud, non era degenerata era un missile puntato contro i limiti di una realtà che distingueva il linguaggio dell'arte tra un nostro e un loro, con il nostro ideale che era un mostro dell'ideale. Provate a pensare a quanto avrebbe fatto bene a Hitler la possibilità di frequentare un'Accademia di Belle Arti, consentendogli di vedere oltre i propri ristretti limiti estetici, pensate anche a quanto farebbe bene alla politica Cagliaritana e isolana una Cagliari con una sua Alta Formazione Artistica residente.

Progetto grafico di un elaborato plastico sul tema #Accademia #Cagliari

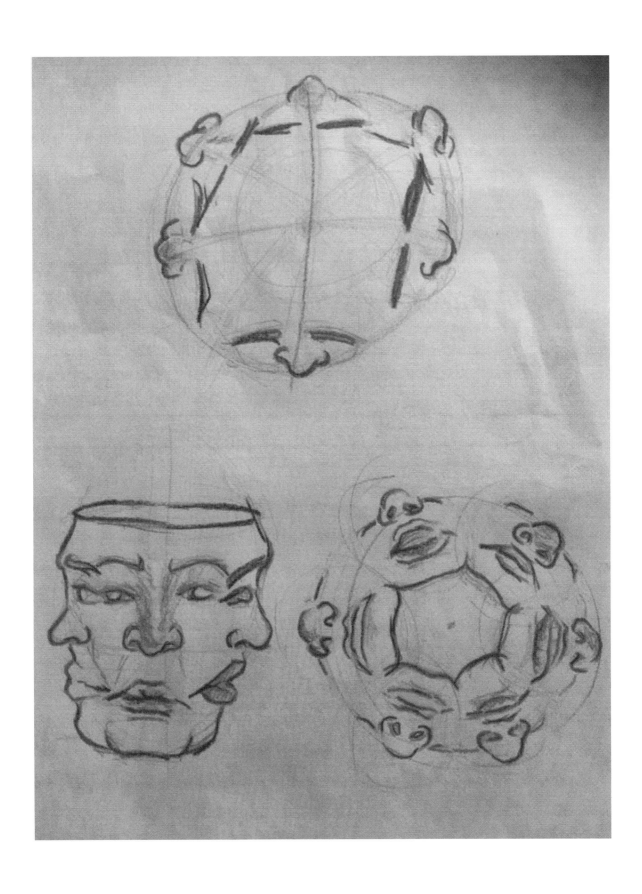

Cosa racconterà Alberto Angela sull'isola nuragica?

Cosa racconterà Alberto Angela sull'isola nuragica?

Alberto Angela racconterà un tempo dove l'isola è stata fertile d'arte, creatività e cultura residente.

Racconterà di un 'isola al centro di rotte commerciali marittime tra Oriente e Occidente; racconterà di un'isola che sapeva nutrirsi dei prodotti artistici e culturali dell'altro, di linguaggi dell'arte si nutrivano di proficua e profonda reciprocità.

Racconterà di un'isola al centro della globalizzazione preistorica dei linguaggi dell'arte, del suo benessere economico che attirava contaminazione culturale.

Ricorderà come allora i linguaggi dell'arte circolavano privi d'intermediazioni, con paesi vicini e lontani, si accumulavano ricchezze e costruivano monumenti, fortificazioni, abitazioni, attrezzi da lavoro, utensili, armi, bronzetti e tombe funerarie.

Evidenzierà come gli isolani partecipavano direttamente ai loro scambi, come le navicelle in bronzo lo raccontino, si esportavano e importavano conoscenze, esperienze e competenze.

L'isola era la sua espressione artistica residente, con le sue opere imponenti e monumentali, altrimenti come spiegare gli oltre settemila nuraghe noti?

Come spiegare gli oltre 350 bronzetti nuragici che raccontano di una economia, di lavori, di dire, di organizzazione sociale, gerarchia militare e spiritualità, di come si amava e del culto dei morti?

C'è stato un momento in cui quella isolana era una delle civiltà più avanzate.

130 bronzetti rappresentano navicelle, perché non si era solo agricoltori, cacciatori, artigiani, costruttori, guerrieri, sacerdoti, musici e cantori, si era navigatori.

Non ometterà come le maestranze erano altissime, si era carpentieri nel lavorare il legno, scultori nel lavorare la pietra per le ancore.

Quell'isola non era serva artisticamente e culturalmente, i suoi prodotti lavorati o semilavorati finivano a compratori esteri, era una civiltà con i suoi linguaggi e la sua ricerca artistica, naturalmente in espansione, economicamente e culturalmente indipendente senza essere chiusa nel suo recinto.

Quegli artisti, uomini, artigiani isolani, realizzarono opere che sopravvivendo fossero una matrice di connessione e identificazione artistica e culturale, quella è la specificità culturale e artistica isolana, a partire da quello si costruisce e determina il futuro.

Focalizzerà come il canone non sia quello classico ellenico della bellezza, dell'armonia e dell'equilibrio, non noterà decorazioni e ornamenti spocchiosi e raffinati, foglie, capitelli, cupole e volte; tutto quello che racconterà sarà potenza creativa simbolica della mente umana che risiedeva nell'isola, non imitazione ideale della natura, ma mimesi, viversi come natura.

L'Arte e l'architettura isolana che ci mostrerà è essenziale, sobria, diretta e semplice, frugale, genuina e senza ombra di dubbio autentica; all'artista isolano non piaceva (e non piace) perdere tempo, il tempo dei nuragici era eterno; un'Accademia a Cagliari vorrebbe dire tenere in vita linguaggio e memoria come origine di questa specifica identità, questo presumo Alberto Angela non lo racconterà in Rai.

L'Accademia di Belle Arti a Cagliari dovrebbe esserci per diritto naturale, per garantire agli artisti residenti in formazione di raccogliere i frutti del proprio linguaggio e della propria memoria, di fare circolare il proprio linguaggio oggi come allora per accumulare capitale che diffonda benessere artistico e culturale.

Alberto Angela non rifletterà sull'estensione della rete nuragica in tutta l'isola accostandola all'Alta Formazione Artistica ferma a Sassari, non racconterà i limiti di formazione artistica e culturale dell'isola contemporanea, in questa maniera quale identità e sistema culturale e artistico isolano si pensa di costruire e preservare nel tempo affidandosi alla sua narrazione?

DIECI MILIONI DEL MIUR PER L'ACCADEMIA (DI SASSARI)

A Sassari (e non a Cagliari) c'è un progetto da dieci milioni di euro per rimettere a nuovo un ex saponificio (il Masedu).

A tale finanziamento mira l'Accademia di Belle Arti "Mario Sironi" di Sassari (a Cagliari un'Accademia di Belle Arti non c'è) che gestisce dal 2015 il Museo di arte contemporanea mai stato e mai nato, ha presentato un progetto al Miur per riabilitare un gioiello di archeologia industriale di via Pascoli. L'edificio storico di proprietà della Provincia, dagli anni Novanta al 2011 è stato ristrutturato a più riprese, l'idea di fondo quella di farne Museo del Novecento, spazio espositivo per tutte le espressioni di arte moderna e contemporanea (a Sassari e non a Cagliari).

Museo di arte contemporanea a oggi mai nato, lo spazio ha soltanto ospitato esposizioni estemporanee.

Dalla scorsa primavera l'Accademia utilizza parte del piano terra come sede del Centro ArtLab, costola sassarese del Centro Risorse e Innovazione per i Mestieri d'Arte della Sardegna, che ha una seconda dislocazione a Cagliari nel Centro ArtiManos, in collegamento diretto con gli altri Centri della Corsica, di Nizza e di Sanremo.

L'intero complesso, nonostante le recenti ristrutturazioni, soffre il peso del tempo e degli anni di inutilizzo.

La spesa più ingente da affrontare riguarda gli impianti, in particolare quello di climatizzazione, non a norma da realizzare ex novo, gettando in discarica i macchinari installati anni fa, obsoleti e fuori legge.

Il progetto di restyling messo a punto dall'Accademia, con il lavoro di Milco Carboni, docente di metodologia e progettazione alla "Mario Sironi", oltre al rinnovo degli impianti prevede una riorganizzazione degli ambienti e il recupero dell'ultimo piano, a suo tempo era stato predisposto un bar ristorante mai entrato in funzione.

Al primo piano si è prevista la realizzazione di 4 mini appartamenti per gli artisti ospiti in residenza a Sassari (non a Cagliari).

Sarà riattivato il punto ristoro che può godere tra l'altro di una grande terrazza affacciata sul cortile interno dell'ex saponificio.

Il primo piano espositivo, una parte sarà dedicata a esporre i lavori realizzati dagli studenti.

Al piano terra troveranno spazio i laboratori di artigianato artistico di serigrafia e il centro stampa dell'Accademia, oggi nel sottopiano della sede di via Duca degli Abruzzi. Per fare tutte queste modifiche l'Accademia, diretta da Antonio Bisaccia, conta nel finanziamento del Miur, cui ha presentato il progetto.

La costante servitù artistica isolana

"Siamo stati abituati ad avere i monumenti, ma quello che ci serve sono le case.
Nei musei avevamo la Storia, ma quello che ci serve sono le storie.
Nei musei avevamo le nazioni, ma quello che ci serve sono le persone."

Orhan Pamuk

Il XIV secolo nell'isola, fu il secolo della Resistenza, della consapevolezza isolana di potere essere nazione, sentimento che passò attraverso i Giudici d'Arborea, che avevano compreso come l'indipendenza del proprio giudicato e della Sardegna, potesse essere l'unica cura per i propri territori.

Mariano IV giudice d'Arborea e di quasi l'intera isola per trent'anni, impostò una nazione Sarda, la sua attività legislativa mirava a fare fiorire la società sarda, abolì nel 1353 la servitù, quello sarebbe potuto essere il mai stato Rinascimento isolano.

Invece fu dominazione spagnola, quattrocento anni di servitù, un'isola che passo da giudici illuminati e un buon tenore di vita, a bene da spremere per le casse della corona Aragonese.

Spagnoli divennero i re, i viceré e i feudatari, la burocrazia, il clero, gli addetti al controllo di città e porti, gli esattori di tasse e gabelle, la giustizia che rendeva i vassalli servi.

Si moltiplicavano i titoli nobiliari, fiumane di baronie e marchesati, contee e viscontee, tutto con la finalità di spremere le linfe vitali locali.

Lingua e linguaggi dell'arte resistettero a tutto questo, ma in clandestinità, finirono per essere comprese dagli spagnoli, che si limitarono a usare tali conoscenze per farsi capire e sfruttare meglio i loro vassalli.

La mancanza di Rinascimento Artistico, culturale e umanistico nell'isola comparato con l'altrove, ha su tutto, la responsabilità Spagnola; un'aristocrazia pigra e indolente, una borghesia sciacalla, furba e opportunistica, non curante e ignorante, non coltivò mai l'arte e la letteratura, oziosamente indolente e passiva sulle spalle dell'isola, sistematicamente predatrice, non aveva alcuna connessione culturale con la gente del luogo, aguzzini che usavano il bastone e mai la carota.

L'aristocrazia, la burocrazia, i feudatari, il clero, i mercanti, i funzionari erano tutti spagnoli, Catalani, Aragonesi e Castigliani, torchiavano e lasciavano prostrati gli isolani.

Così, privi di Rinascimento, arte, cultura e Accademia, in Sardegna si viveva quello che altrove era Rinascimento, questa era la Cagliari d'Aragona nell'isola.

I SAVOIA E L'ARTE ISOLANA

Quando nel 1708, Carlo D'Austria prese possesso dell'isola, nell'isola nessuno battette ciglio, in fondo dopo gli Spagnoli non si poteva stare peggio.

Feudatari e borghesi subito si sottomisero, prioritario conservare le proprie posizioni di rendita.

Gli Spagnoli vennero definitivamente sconfitti e allontanati nel 1710, servì per questo l'alleanza Franco-Austro-Anglo-Olandese.

L'isola venne consegnata all'Austria, che la cedette a Vittorio Amedeo di Savoia con il trattato di Londra del 1718.

L'isola a quel punto per i Savoia divenne un peso morto, nell'isola si parlava lo Spagnolo e la lingua locale, a corte si parlava il Francese, si fecero quindi numerosi tentativi per cederla, l'unico momento dove l'isola tornò utile ai Savoia, fu a fine Settecento, quando scacciati da Napoleone arrivarono i regnanti con tutto il loro codazzo di corte, di ministri e funzionari Piemontesi.

Arrivarono con nulla e ripartirono ricchi, come gli spagnoli depredarono tutto, la costante attitudine servile isolana rendeva comodo non mutare la direzione, di un sistema di potere fondato sull'oppressione e il depredamento; a cosa sarebbe servita mai un'Accademia di Belle Arti?

I sardi erano perfetti così, analfabeti, superstiziosi e timorati di Dio. Bastava comperare con titoli e onorificenze di privilegio i soliti borghesi intermediari parassiti e sostituire ai vecchi esponenti di regime Spagnolo, nuovi soggetti d'importazione Piemontese.

Tutto doveva essere importato nell'isola, bisognava importare strumenti di lavoro e prodotti di consumo, il residente doveva non potere competere con l'altrove, che risultava essere sempre più a buon mercato.

Si formò a questo punto (finalmente) un naturale banditismo resistenziale, il Marchese di Rivarolo non si fece problema alcuno nel tagliare teste da esporre nei paesi d'origine a scopo didattico educativo.

Il sardo non è mai stato proprietario di sé, solo sudditanza e sottomissione, servitù, servilismo e dipendenza.

I Savoia trovarono comodo perpetrare il sistema oppressivo che da secoli nell'isola favoriva la classe Dirigente, non lavorarono per mutare una condizione culturale d'arretratezza e sviluppo economico, non volevano investire nell'isola tempo e denaro; il vero problema dell'isola era che nessuno voleva acquistarla, il problema erano i suoi feudatari, il suo clero, i suoi piccoli borghesi; il sistema non doveva mutare per posizione locale di rendita d'interessi privati, la posizione andava consolidata, questa era (ed è) la costante servitù culturale (e di riflesso artistica isolana), perché i Savoia avrebbero dovuto con questo scenario, pensare a donare ai Cagliaritani un'Accademia di Belle Arti?

A cosa sarebbe servita un'Accademia a Cagliari davanti a questo scenario di sardi ridotti in miseria culturale, dove l'unica ricchezza da consolidare era quella borghese e privata locale che non andava assolutamente intaccata a prescindere da chi fosse lo sciacallo proveniente dall'altrove?

Gli artisti arrivavano e davano lezioni dall'altrove, ed era (ed è?) giusto così.

CARLO FELICE, MUNIFICO PROTETTORE DELLE BELLE ARTI!

L'isola illuministica è stata un'ingenua, assuefatta e mansueta terra di contadini e pastori; contadini e pastori si sarebbero dovuti ribellare per evadere dall'ignoranza sistematica cui erano stati relegati, avrebbero dovuto dire basta alle strozzature baronali, ma respinse il suo illuminismo, respinse (come sempre) la sua storia possibile.

Rigettò in mare la rivoluzione dei lumi, quella che anche con un'Accademia, avrebbe potuto allentare se non sciogliere le catene della sua servitù culturale.

Come sempre ci si lascio manovrare dai nobili e dal clero locale, che arruolarono vassalli e cavalieri, riunirono bestiame e denaro, tutto pur di conservare i propri storici agi.

Arruolarono anche Sant'Efisio (ma dimmi tu), facendolo apparire in cima al Bastione, mentre i Francesi bombardavano la città (era il 1793).

Si era riuscito a fare credere a vassalli e cavalieri, che si stesse difendendo la propria patria, in realtà si stavano respingendo i valori dell'illuminismo e si stava conservando la propria servitù culturale (e anche artistica).

Dopo l'impresa invece, fu destituito anche il viceré Balbiano, che chiedeva un reale riconoscimento per l'impresa isolana.

Venne inviata allora una delegazione a corte dall'isola, chiedevano Statamenti militari, ecclesiastici e reali, chiedevano cariche locali, un Ministero degli affari per l'isola e un Consiglio di Stato che controllasse il governo; non furono neanche ricevuti, si era respinto Napoleone e non si venne neanche ricevuti.

Sudditi inferociti messi davanti alla loro impotenza e nullità politica, finalmente cacciarono i Piemontesi, questi furono i giorni dell'Aprile 1794 dell'Indipendenza, come andò a finire?

Di nuovo nel nome dell'ambizione personale si ripiegò verso la servitù, non ci si sapeva relazionare nel nome di un comune interesse privi di un padrone, ragion per cui si decise di riaccogliere chi si era cacciato, a momenti ci si scusò per quanto accaduto, nulla di personale contro il Re, ci si era semplicemente lamentato dei suoi aguzzini.

Si decise di consegnarsi ad aguzzini, viceré, dignitari, ufficiali, funzionari, impiegato, esattori e a chi volete voi arrivasse dall'altrove, poteva nascere un'Accademia di Belle Arti a Cagliari ?

Tornarono più cattivi e feroci che mai, l'isola non aveva il protettorato Francese e doveva tenersi l'assolutismo Sabaudo e la sua cara, amata, storica servitù feudale come fatto e consuetudine storica e culturale.

L'isola era un Regno, ma di un popolo scarso e frammentato, dipendente economicamente dai baroni, affamata e resa docile dal bisogno (cavolo, proprio come oggi), per i rivoluzionari forche e teste tagliate, nonostante fossero già passati dalla rivoluzione alla fase reazionaria per qualche onore e carica pubblica.

Le più alte cariche furono per il Re e i suoi fratelli compensati da incarichi sardi in Piemonte beffardi.

L'sola aveva Carlo Felice, aveva la sua statua e la sua strada; gli isolani venivano considerati servili, arretrati e incapaci di gestirsi come popolo sovrano, un pittore di corte (uno dei tanti inutili pittori di corte) li rappresentava come dimessi, unti, bassi e piegati, sottomessi e asserviti dinanzi ai Piemontesi.

Capite cosa vorrebbe dire un'Accademia a Cagliari ancora oggi?

La storia dell'arte dialoga lentamente con il suo passato, Accademia vorrebbe dire dimostrare (oggi come allora) che i Sardi non sono così stupidi come i piemontesi li rappresentavano.

A proposito, il quadro del pittore di corte (infimo) è ancora nell'ufficio del vicesindaco del Comune di Cagliari, dimenticavo, il pittore di corte era nato a Cagliari ma si formò a Roma (dal momento che a Cagliari non vi era un'Accademia), era Giovanni Marghinotti, e ritrasse anche Carlo Felice come munifico protettore delle Belle Arti nel 1830; a voi risulta che sia nata in quegli anni un'Accademia?

Il Regno della cultura serva!

Il Regno d'Italia, si materializza e si rappresenta come allargamento del Regno di Sardegna, è un fatto che vi sia stata un'ininterrotta continuità tra lo Stato Sardo e quello Italiano; lo statuto Sardo nasce come Statuto Albertino in vigore un intero secolo; a voi risulta che di questo ci sia traccia in un qualche libro di Storia?

Che almeno formalmente si sia scritta una storia politica dell'isola non serva e non funzionale alle produzioni artistiche e culturali imposte dall'altrove?

Sappiamo che la storia non si cambia con una citazione, ma oscurarla è ancora una volta una forma di disprezzo verso un'altra storia e un'altra cultura, mai raccontata e celebrata dall'altrove, eppur quando fa comodo, tutti dichiarano d'amare e di servire l'isola.

Ci fu nel Novecento qualche dibattito di senso, su quale potesse essere il modello di sviluppo produttivo nell'isola, eppur nessuno pensò a un'Accademia di Belle Arti a Cagliari; industria mineraria e petrolchimica per alimentare le imprese, nessuna riflessione sull'arte e la tradizione locale che avrebbe potuto trattenere ed esportare quelle risorse sotto forma d'arte e cultura residente.

Arriviamo ad oggi, dove nel 2018, un'Accademia di Belle Arti a Cagliari ancora non c'è, i sardi sembrano discendere da chi li ha conquistati culturalmente purtroppo che dalla propria autodeterminazione, millenni di contatto, di vicinanza e contaminazione con un'idea di se stessi e d'arte e di cultura imposta dall'altrove, ha reso sterile quella civiltà nuragica ribelle e lottatrice in origine.

Un'Accademia di Belle Arti servirebbe a partire da questa memoria, porre a sistema secoli e millenni d'errori storici, a rimuovere il nichilismo e convogliare la propria produzione artistica e culturale, elevata a bene comune, nella giusta direzione.
La servitù artistica e culturale determina la servitù economica e politica, cancella la storia e la memoria e incrementa la propria intima subordinazione che diventa ideologia e atto di fede.
Il Regno d'Italia nasce dall'espansione del Regno di Sardegna, nel 2018 in Italia c'è solo una città metropolitana capoluogo Regionale, priva d'Alta Formazione Artistica, indovinate dove si trova?

Accademie? Frammentate e parcellizzate sono perdenti!

L'attuale stato dell'Alta Formazione Artistica Italiana non è esaltante. Marciamo verso i vent'anni dell'introduzione del 3 più 2 Accademico, e si può fare un primo bilancio.
Ancora si sentono vecchi Maestri e giovani studenti che contestano il nuovo, continuando a rimpiangere le vecchie Accademie, i vecchi Licei e Istituti d'Arte.
Non si poteva restare fuori dall'Europa, ma solo in Italia la licenza Accademica di primo e secondo livello è equivalente alla Laurea ma non è laurea, nel nome dell'AFAM scissa dall'Università.
I percorsi tra Accademia e Accademia sono spesso differenziati e i corsi complementari sembrano essersi ridotti a strumento d'accaparramento di crediti, sistema che riduce la formazione artistica a qualcosa che sembra ragionieristica misurazione di ore e minuti.
Nonostante ciò lo svecchiamento c'è stato: c'è un percorso d'Alta Formazione quinquennale, ci sono discipline complementari di ambito scientifico e tecnologico e indirizzi professionalizzanti in chiave contemporanea che vent'anni fa nelle Accademie erano chimere; c'è la

possibilità del riconoscimento di stage, tirocini e laboratori, insomma si guarda e si forma con lo sguardo oltre la visione classica e romantica dell'artista intrappolato nella sua ricerca e lo si avvia a un'attività professionale (Grafico, Scenografo, Operatore Audio video, Restauratore, esperto di social media...).

Certe Accademie hanno prodotto e producono eccellenze (Milano, Roma, Napoli, Torino, Bologna...), altre formano in maniera generalista, isolata e autoreferenziale, certi Maestri somministrano sempre lo stesso tipo di corso a studenti con esigenze specialistiche differenti.

Qualche Accademia Italiana post riformata, sembra avere perso la sua spinta propulsiva sul territorio e la comunità dove opera, sembra abbia perso di vista il suo ruolo propulsivo, il suo essere nodo della creatività residente e forza innovatrice didattica e dialettica, rinchiudendosi sempre di più in se stessa con il suo sistema d'autolegittimazione, favorita in questo da un clima culturale, artistico ed economico, d'incertezza e paura, che porta a rintanarsi rispetto alla comunità piuttosto che aprirsi a essa, alimentando frammentazione e la balcanizzazione Accademica; servirebbe una visione e una rete d'insieme che consenta una reale riflessione partecipata e un serio confronto sui problemi dell'Alta Formazione Artistica Italiana in ogni comparto e settore.

L'eccessiva frammentazione tra le Accademie, l'eccessiva separazione tra la ricerca e quello che impone il mercato, rispetto a ciò che vive il territorio, sembra le abbia delegittimate socialmente.

Eppure l'Italia ha un bisogno disperato delle sue Accademie di Belle Arti in ogni dove, gli artisti contemporanei, in un momento storico come questo, dovrebbero sapere intercettare questo bisogno e fornire risposte diverse e adeguate a queste richieste, eppure sembra non esserci dibattito politico nazionale in tal senso, le Accademie (in gran parte) operano timorate e isolate nel loro stesso territorio, tutte le analisi sembrano parcellizzate e perdenti, come l'ostinazione Sassarese a non progettare e pianificare percorsi d'Alta Formazione Artistica che passino per Cagliari.

Le visioni non organiche perpetuano frammentazione, la conseguenza è la permanente e naturale irrilevanza.

L'ARTE DEL DISORDINE

Non è un bello spettacolo, il disordine e la confusione diffusa nell'isola tra questa o quell'idea dell'arte, nel confronto tra questo o quell'artista determinato da un mercato modaiolo imposto dall'altrove, come non ci fosse narrazione comune, come se la narrazione comune fosse in conflitto con quella individuale o quella dell'altro Comune; il Comune in conflitto con il Comune e il comune, autoproduce un sistema dell'arte autonomista Regionale fragile, vulnerabile e non competitivo.

S'importano e legittimano idee dell'arte che nascono e crescono economicamente all'estero e anche l'Alta Formazione Artistica sembra essere impostata sulla fuori uscita dei redditi residenti, l'idea è quella del saccheggio reciproco (quanto si è Spagnoli, Savoia o Italiani in questo?) che impoverisca progressivamente il vicino, senza comprendere che il vicino più povero t'impoverisce.

L'Arte e l'Alta Formazione Artistica a Cagliari è sempre stata emigrazione, legittimata dall'invidia tra artisti, propensi a dividersi nel nome della squalifica dell'altro per accreditarsi dinanzi a qualcun altro.

Con questo scenario si può parlare d'Arte Contemporanea in una Regione a Statuto Autonomo, con tutte le sue specificità, come la Sardegna?

In quest'isola gli artisti non sono mai stati ego-logici, ego-compatibili o ego-sostenibili, nascono in età moderna affamati di fama, con l'appetito della frustrazione che vien mangiando, l'ansia è sempre stata quella d'occupare la prima fila squalificando l'altro in cerca della dose di cibo più abbondante.

La servitù "artistica" isolana

Qualcuno parla della Sardegna come nazione, ma quale nazione potrebbe vantare il suo capoluogo-capitale, la sua unica città metropolitana priva d'Alta Formazione Artistica?

Una parodia di nazione senza essere nazione, una barzelletta di Regione a Statuto Autonomo.

Una Regione che con il suo capoluogo è unica città metropolitana priva d'Accademia di Belle Arti in Europa, che da tremila anni a questa parte, ha una storia di sudditanza, di servi, di lavoratori per altri, un rapporto con l'arte e la cultura residente che non è mai riuscito ad andare oltre la sua sofferta sopravvivenza.

La Regione autonoma Sarda, ha naturalmente interiorizzato la sua servitù artistica e culturale, al punto da non affrontare mai il nodo di Cagliari priva d'Alta Formazione Artistica, come potrebbe essere autonoma un'isola con la sua unica città metropolitana priva d'Alta Formazione Artistica?

Senza un polo d'Alta Formazione Artistica Cagliaritano è scritto che si sta progressivamente, nel nome del mercato, svuotando l'identità culturale e artistica di un popolo che è distinto dagli altri, che si sta marginalizzando in maniera definitiva quello che per secoli si è, con dolore e sofferenza, preservato.

Non esiste una storia dell'arte residente, e senza un'Accademia di Cagliari mai esisterà e si svilupperà nel tempo e nella storia; Cagliari e l'isola, senza un'Accademia resteranno privi di radici e vittime degli imbonitori che arrivano dal mare che diranno "vi diciamo noi cosa è arte e cultura, vi civilizziamo e rendiamo artisticamente contemporanei noi, voi state tranquilli".

Deve sentirsi inferiore quando ragiona d'arte il Cagliaritano, la sua eredità identitaria la deve percepire come marginale, insignificante, ininfluente, quando costretto a comparare la storia dei propri artisti con gli artisti dell'altrove.

Gli artisti Cagliaritani e isolani, nella propria terra, immersi nella propria cultura d'origine, devono sentirsi inferiori, fragili, instabili, pronti a essere sradicati a ogni soffio di maestrale.

Non ci sarà mai autonomia artistica e culturale nell'isola, fin quando Cagliari non avrà la sua Accademia di Belle Arti.

QUALE SISTEMA SENZA ACCADEMIA?

Un sistema artistico è una serie d'elementi connessi tra loro, un insieme di singole parti che ha come fulcro e polo educativo nei territori e nelle comunità le Accademie di Belle Arti, che anche quando non formano artisti, formano "addetti ai lavori" o sguardi consapevoli (anche critici) sull'arte contemporanea.

Le Accademie costituiscono un sistema, nel sistema di mercato, che determina mercato, obbediscono a regole e sono inserite in una serie di normative precise ministeriali e costituzionali Italiane ed Europee, ad esempio se si vuole insegnare Discipline Plastiche in un Liceo è necessario essere passati per una licenza di Scultura in un'Accademia (o Università) delle Belle Arti Europea.

Le regole di sistema, connesse tra di loro, hanno un fine univoco, chiaro e perseguito con costanza nel tempo.

Le Accademie di Belle Arti, formano arte e artisti residenti, sulla base della cultura e della storia dell'arte residente che dialoga con la Storia dell'Arte dell'altrove.

Un tempo in questa pianeta, il linguaggio dominante era quello della natura, il linguaggio dell'arte ci ha modulato e ha progressivamente adattato la natura alle esigenze dell'umana condizione.

Nell'isola non esiste un sistema dell'arte, è tutto scollegato e sconnesso, una piccola Accademia di Belle Arti a Sassari c'è, giusto che ci sia, fondamentale per il centro Nord dell'isola; questo non toglie che Cagliari sia l'unica città metropolitana e capoluogo di Regione in Europa a non avere ancora Alta Formazione Artistica, quale è il lavoro di formazione e produzione di sistema dell'arte sinergico nell'isola dinanzi a questa incredibile anomalia?

Quale sarebbe la connessione di sistema dell'arte tra Cagliari e Sassari? L'Accademia di Sassari ha come riferimento il Liceo Artistico Filippo Figari di Sassari, uno studente di Sassari può completare il suo percorso di formazione artistica e poi liberamente decidere dove vivere e lavorare, e con chi confrontarsi, può andare a fare il docente (e non il cameriere) a Roma o Milano, uno studente di Cagliari?

Storicamente i Licei nascono dove ci sono poli Accademici storici, come mai solo Cagliari costituisce l'eccezione di un'area metropolitana con un elevato numero di studenti che con un diploma di maturità artistica, non hanno un'Accademia con cui confrontarsi che ne legittimi la formazione?

Non sarà questa la Dea Madre di tutte le anomalie artistiche residenti Cagliaritani e isolane, non sarà questo il fulcro di un sistema dell'arte che nell'isola non c'è e determina sconnessione, incompetenze, sciatteria, egoismo, pulsioni predatorie di vecchi artisti ai danni dei giovani e menefreghismo?

Gli artisti Cagliaritani e isolani si muovono in maniera caotica e confusa, ciascuno pensa a se stesso, alla propria sopravvivenza e tornaconto politico ed economico, certi profili artistici nell'isola sembrano fermarsi al proprio comune di residenza.

Gli addetti ai lavori sono intolleranti verso le diverse opinioni d'altri addetti ai lavori e non si sviluppano mai dibattiti di senso, senza un'Accademia di Belle Arti di Cagliari il sistema nasce morto.

Le culture umane, compresa quella isolana e nello specifico Cagliaritana, decifrano il mondo partendo dalla propria esperienza storica.

Il proprio vissuto comunitario, collettivo e storico, genera un ventaglio di possibilità e d'attese sulla base delle quali si legge ciò che accade e che si muove nel tempo.

Rispetto al proprio passato, si è disposti a introdurre qualche modifiche, ma si guardano con sospetto le più radicali.

Questo meccanismo inconscio, guida e limita culture e territori; rassicura nel tempo perché conferma quello che già si è, si ha e si possiede; vaglia, seleziona e sonda quello che non si sa e non si conosce.

Il Cagliaritano tende naturalmente più a riconoscere e riconoscersi che analizzare, istintivamente si muove sul suo già vissuto storico.

Il Cagliaritano non ha la cultura dell'autodeterminare e prospettare nuove possibilità produttive.

Il Cagliaritano si accontenta del godersi l'esperienza immediata, la sua interpretazione critica si limita al suo passato e al suo presente in quanto vissuto, nel nome dei propri limiti non riconosce, sulla base di suoi pregiudizi, cruciali sviluppi e fenomeni del suo tempo e della sua storia, è predisposto alla distruzione intenzionale della sua arte e della sua cultura, all'incuria e al ciclico declino, nel suo caso non si può parlare neanche di crisi di sistema artistico e culturale, perché senza che ci sia mai stata un'Accademia di Belle Arti, di quale sistema artistico e culturale autonomo e rivolto all'esterno dell'isola, stiamo parlando?

Il Cagliaritano e l'isolano non convivono con il proprio passato e con la propria memoria artistica, perché, se c'è, è archeologico.

Eppure solo la messa a sistema dell'arte e della cultura residente, potrebbe consentire a Cagliari di comprendere i processi e le produzioni artistiche e culturali in corso in Europa, tutelandosi e tutelando la propria cultura, la propria memoria e cominciando sul serio a scrivere la propria Storia dell'Arte.

CAGLIARI, L'ICONCLASTICA PRIVA D'ACCADEMIA!

L'iconoclastia in questo secolo è iconica, quando discutiamo d'azioni iconoclastiche o provocatorie (come il quadro rotto in testa a Marina Abramovic o l'autodistruzione del quadro di Banksy, ma anche le distruzioni di opere d'arte dell'Isis) via Facebook e Twitter, dobbiamo considerare la possibilità che è proprio la condivisione dell'azione performatica la ragione della biopolitca iconoclastica, che si parli dell'ISIS o di Maurizio Cattelan.

I nemici di immagini Accademiche, della storia e della memoria, annientano e deridono ma producono nuove immagini, in uno scenario di sistema che è il palcoscenico dialettico dei loro movimenti (pensate a Duchamp che mette i baffi alla Gioconda).

Accusare d'idolatria un Museo Archeologico cosa vuole dire se non creare una nuova idolatria, facendosi filmare mentre si devasta?

L'immagine del distruttore d'immagini diventa la nuova icona che attrae proseliti.

L'iconizzazione del sé distruttore passa per il media, pensate che l'ISIS si muove tra 45000 account Twitter, 45000 account pronti a trasmettere distruttori d'immagini smaniosi di farsi vedere in azione mentre lo fanno, la finalità è quella di trasmettere un messaggio d'intransigenza e di forza ostinata, si condannano le immagini altrui e si produce, alimenta e promuove la propria, come le Avanguardie storiche fecero con le

Accademie tra la fine dell'ottocento e i primi decenni del Novecento alimentando il proprio mercato.

Ragionare di sviluppo artistico, vuole dire ricordarci che l'iconoclastia come l'Accademismo hanno una radice comune, comunque politica; sono un diritto d'orientamento in un orizzonte di valori linguistici, simbolici e culturali; è nella capacità di tutelare e preservare la propria storia e memoria che bisogna cominciare a misurare la cultura Sarda, se non si comincia ad adottare questo metro di misurazione ci ritroveremo a dovere sputare sui giganti di Monti Prama insieme ai turisti.

PRIMA L'ACCADEMIA, POI L'INDIPENDENTISMO!

Gli artisti che decidono di risiedere a Cagliari e nell'isola, convivono quotidianamente, con la sensazione di vivere ed essere una memoria culturale e storica che non serve a nulla.

La crisi del valore simbolico, poetico e rituale del linguaggio dell'arte sostituito progressivamente dall'estetica del selfie, cosa è se non un tracollo del linguaggio e della storia che relega ricerche e linguaggi ai margini della comunicazione nel nome dell'omologazione della propria immagine?

In Sardegna si sta marciando verso le Regionali, e nel nome di un presunto "realismo" o "pragmatismo", si accetta a testa china una politica Regionale che devasta da sempre la propria cultura, identità, memoria, territori e paesaggi e che sembra non conoscere il significato della parola Accademia, la parola Accademia evoca da queste parti l'Accademia militare piuttosto che le Belle Arti.

La politica regionale sembra avere la predisposizione genetica e biologica, coltivata in tremila anni di servitù lottizzata priva di una coscienza d'insieme, a creare generazioni perdute o migranti, prive di cultura e di memoria, tutto questo alimenta solo la coltivazione di memoria da cartolina a dimensione turista, che rende naturalmente servi e servitori del consumo culturale dell'altrove.

Come si coltiva una memoria, una città metropolitana, la dignità d'espressione dell'umano, il linguaggio dell'arte come bene comune, senza un'Accademia di Belle Arti a Cagliari nel terzo millennio?

La politica locale sembra averci fatto il callo, sembra avere la consapevolezza che l'abitudine alla deprivazione abbia generato nel

Cagliaritano rassegnazione, indifferenza e cinismo verso ciò che non ha mai avuto.

Eppure Cagliari potrebbe rinascere dalle sue rovine, potrebbe pretendere il suo giusto Rinascimento come chiave d'accesso a una sua modernità artistica e culturale, rivendicare la sua ambizione d'essere al passo con i reali orizzonti Europei; questo se è vero che la valorizzazione e la messa a sistema dei propri artisti residenti è un modello che il capitalismo ha considerato vincente, anche se valutato esclusivamente dal punto di vista turistico (modello di sviluppo che a Cagliari e nell'isola oggi sembra essere l'unico possibile).

La Storia dell'Arte è fatta di tanti Rinascimenti locali, indispensabili per sviluppare un'autocoscienza della propria storia.

Dimostrare che Cagliari, sia sempre stata fuori e marginale, rispetto a un'idea e a una visione di Rinascimento Europeo è semplicissimo per qualsiasi storico dell'arte, antropologo o sociologo serio e che si possa definire tale; l'assenza di un'Accademia, ha da sempre impedito uno sguardo sul passato che si sia potuto tradurre in fioritura culturale, questo nonostante il Rinascimento Europeo non abbia nulla di unico e omologante di luogo in luogo, da territorio a territorio, da comunità a comunità.

I vari Rinascimenti Europei passano per le Accademie di Belle Arti, e presuppongono l'idea di una nuova nascita e di una nuova coscienza, piena autocoscienza, Rinascimento è permettersi nel tempo libero di dedicarsi all'Arte e alla cultura, alla propria formazione artistica, in virtù di un nodo territoriale diffuso di educazione e rivisitazione permanente della propria arte e cultura.

Il Rinascimento in Italia e in Europa (non in Sardegna e a Cagliari) ha la vibrante dimensione storica di risposta alla decadenza e alla morte, è ciò di cui in questo tempo Cagliari e la Sardegna hanno necessità assoluta, nulla di trionfale, ma consente formazione ed educazione all'arte per rinascere ciclicamente dalle proprie rovine con coscienza e insegnare qualcosa.

ACCADEMIA PER UNA CAGLIARI CLASSICA

L'Arte nell'isola e a Cagliari non è mai stata classica, l'idea del classico e del Rinascimento, nascono in Europa negli stessi decenni del primo Ottocento, per essere poi consacrate in parallelo, come radice e nuova nascita del greco-romano.

Capite quanto l'antica civiltà dei Nur fosse esclusa da tutto questo, dall'idea del classico come fondazione della modernità?

Capite quanto una Cagliari, unica città metropolitana in Europa, priva d'Alta Formazione Artistica, materializzi e continui a rappresentare una Cagliari e una Sardegna artisticamente non Europea?

Le radici culturali dell'Europa sono fondate sulla cultura greco-romana, e la sua didattica assimilazione grammaticale e umanistica nel pensiero Accademico.

Accademia a Cagliari, potrebbe volere dire, contribuire alla comprensione, di come l'età classica, come quella Rinascimentale, si nutrì di contributi extraeuropei, di cui l'isola preclassica dei Nur è stata nodo connettivo fondamentale.

Accademia a Cagliari, vorrebbe dire tendere a fare riconoscere il termine "classico" con un'altra estendibilità, un classico esogeno ed endogeno rispetto a quello Europeo, autoctono e indipendente rispetto alla cultura Greco-Romana Europea.

Accademia a Cagliari vorrebbe dire fare riflettere su come la multiculturalità Europea sia qualcosa che possa andare oltre la classicità e la matrice greco-romana.

In fondo che cosa fu la scoperta dell'antichità classica nel Rinascimento, se non una forma d'etnologia?

Nessuna civiltà contemporanea può pensare a se stessa se non dispone di sistemi sociali e culturali, che nel quotidiano la comparino, e questo è un'Accademia!

Da quel primo umanesimo, nacque (non nell'isola), un secondo umanesimo, che pose a sistema culturale tutte le culture artistiche umane (anche quelle senza storia), ma anche in questo giro illuministico, l'isola con la sua civiltà dei Nur, restò esclusa.

Eppure la comparazione didattica e dialettica, è un requisito essenziale se ragioniamo di un possibile Rinascimento Cagliaritano, un Rinascimento che a partire da Cagliari si elevi a insieme e matrice di una cultura umana un tempo ritenuta barbara e senza storia;

Accademia a Cagliari vorrebbe dire spola dialettica incessante tra antichità come identità e alterità del contemporaneo.

La Sardegna classica, archeologica, Nuragica avrebbe attraverso un'Accademia a Cagliari, una chiave d'accesso, per accedere ad arti pari alle culture artistiche del contemporaneo.

L'Accademia a Cagliari, avrebbe tutti i prerequisiti necessari, per ampliare l'idea del classico, costituendo un'efficace piattaforma conoscitiva in grado d'andare oltre l'unicità omologata, attraverso la fecondazione della propria comparazione con l'altrove.

Orientare da Cagliari verso

l'Accademia?

Avete idea di cosa voglia dire per un docente di Discipline Plastiche di un Liceo Artistico, a Cagliari, "orientare" gli studenti verso un'Accademia, dal momento che a Cagliari un'Accademia non c'è mai stata?

Avete idea della difficoltà del fare presente, come il sistema Accademia d'Alta Formazione Artistica, sia orientato secondo un sistema di valori che la modella come istituzione Universitaria, che ha il compito nei territori e nelle comunità dove opera, di tramandare la memoria culturale, esplorandone potenzialità, allargandone gli orizzonti, tutelarne la funzione presso le generazioni future?

Come spiegare tutto questo, a chi abita un territorio, dove tutto questo non è mai stato?

Alle Accademie fanno capo, in tutte le loro articolazioni, le Università e gli enti di ricerca, le istituzioni artistiche e musicali, i musei e gli uffici di tutela dei paesaggi, del patrimonio artistico e dell'ambiente.

Capite a cosa sia connesso il processo altamente formativo Accademico che Cagliari non ha mai avuto e conosciuto?

Per le Accademie, nei territori e nei comuni, si gioca la relazione contemporanea tra cultura artistica e democrazia, è un fronte oggi di battaglia sorda tra pubblico e privato.

L'Accademia non è un addestramento tecnico ai mestieri dell'arte, non lo è nonostante riforme e modernizzazioni cerchino di snaturarne il senso; l'Accademia è da sempre in Europa, portatrice di arte e cultura, riflessione critica e pensiero creativo, cittadinanza, tolleranza e democrazia.

L'Accademia è memoria culturale, è storia dei linguaggi che educa alla diversità, è confronto tra culture, è negare l'autorità rispettando la tradizione, l'Accademia è mobilità della cultura locale tradotta in cantiere aperto a scambi e novità, è nuova cultura comune dell'Europa che relaziona la sua storia dell'arte.

Accademia, vuole dire, fondare in Europa un luogo sulla propria cultura, una cultura Europea che sa riconoscere artisticamente le proprie diversità interne, che sa esplorare e sa rendere le proprie rovine ritmo storico che pone un freno ai mercati.

La cultura artistica è quella cosa che fa rivivere luoghi e territori, che può anteporre la dignità della persona a un mercato che vorrebbe schiacciarla.

A questo servirebbe aprire l'Accademia di Belle Arti di Cagliari, per questo servirebbe bussare più forte al portone e alzare la voce.

Perché ad oggi, Cagliari non ha mai chiesto con forza un'Accademia, che contribuisse alla sua autocoscienza e autodeterminazione storica? Perché forse il Cagliaritano non ha ben chiaro, quale e quanto sia, il suo sempre inappagato bisogno di consapevolezza della bellezza, se ve ne fosse la percezione, sarebbe già stata rivoluzione; bellezza non è quella che il Cagliaritano pensa che sia, incantato, ingannato e disincantato dallo svilimento della bellezza, ridotta a marketing, business e distrazione da tempo libero; non ha mai compreso che il bello non può essere senza storia, il bello non può essere senza percezione culturale di bene comune.

La bellezza artistica non è serva del potere e figlia del denaro, è la madre del pensiero estetico interiormente libero, pronta a rinascere anche davanti al declino di una civiltà e quando il suo futuro è incerto. Bellezza non è quel provincialismo Cagliaritano, che quotidianamente svuota la sua stessa memoria culturale, depreda dalla propria storia da cui si potrebbe trarre saggezza e contenuti.

Il Cagliaritano privo d'Accademia è disarmato, è preda di miraggi, di slogan, di facile conquiste, è pronto ad acclamare qualsiasi salvatore che ne faccia attrattore di folle turistiche; gli stessi turisti vengono visti non come interessati alla specificità culturale della storia e del vissuto Cagliaritano, ma come clienti consumatori, graditi fin quando spendono e non quando apprendono.

Tutto questo, renderà Cagliari, una città metropolitana permanentemente a debito artistico e culturale dell'Europa, i suoi siti e Musei verranno sempre più percepiti come un peso, abbandonati al loro destino visti i costi, in fondo cosa ci sarebbe di strano?

I quartieri storici di Cagliari, sono in gran parte già stati svuotati dai propri abitanti, i Cagliaritani non si sono forse spostati in grandissima parte, durante il boom economico verso periferie di nuove costruzioni? Certi quartieri storici Cagliaritani, non sono diventati quartieri dove i proprietari sono più che benestanti?

Accademia a Cagliari, vorrebbe finalmente dire, tendere a quella cultura che potrebbe rendere uguali centro e periferia, potrebbe essere una piattaforma d'incontro, anche tra culture residenti e migranti, potrebbe fare di Cagliari una città finalmente plurale, in crescita con tutta la sua creatività finalizzata alla realizzazione delle proprie potenzialità.

Solo l'arte e la cultura, può fare sperare a una Cagliari città metropolitana, realmente sotto il cielo d'Europa!

A CAGLIARI ACCADEMIA DI CITTADINANZA

E' un mistero, perché ancora oggi, in quest'isola, molti lavori fondati sull'arte come linguaggio e ricerca, sembra debbano continuare ad essere declassati e non meritevoli d'essere trasmessi mediante alta Formazione Artistica; in quest'isola dove la Scultura e la lavorazione della pietra, sono un istinto linguistico e identitario fuori dal tempo, Cagliari è ancora priva di un corso di Scultura Accademico, è complicato anche acquistare una gradina che non può che essere ordinata dal continente, avete mai pensato a quanto questo dequalifichi gli Scultori d'area Cagliaritana metropolitana?

I linguaggi dell'arte (non solo la Scultura), sono linguaggi didattici legati all'attività umana, un'Accademia a Cagliari, servirebbe a tutelarli in tutta la sua area metropolitana; un'Accademia a Cagliari, consentirebbe di riqualificare tutti gli artisti e artigiani, espulsi dal sistema industriale e fuori da ambiti scolastici e universitari di formazione professionale.

Accademia vorrebbe dire attività imprenditoriale e manageriale applicata all'arte contemporanea forte della sua tradizione, si potrebbe attraverso l'Alta Formazione Artistica inserire e reinserire nel mondo del lavoro giovani e meno giovani che sentano i linguaggi dell'arte in termini di ricerca e produzione culturale (altro che reddito di cittadinanza).

Dovremmo anche dircelo che il falegname può essere non solo un artigiano, ma anche un artista e uno Scultore, come l'orafo e il ceramista, i linguaggi dell'arte attraverso l'Alta Formazione Artistica alimentano il fascino verso il proprio mestiere e le proprie competenze.

 L'attività artistica dell'umano, ha un suo intrinseco e nobile valore; la nobiltà dell'Alta Formazione Artistica, è la risposta alla pochezza e all'indolenza, al lamento e malevolenza pregiudiziale tradotta in stupidità, che sovente accompagna quest'isola di vecchi che non connettono l'amore per l'archeologia alla propria storia e il proprio futuro.

Accademia è Alta Formazione Artistica, ma è anche apprendistato e qualifica Europea, che connette l'Alta Formazione Residente con l'imprenditoria; Accademia oggi è anche competenze tecnologiche e un metodo di ricerca che consenta d'imparare a imparare per tutto il corso della propria vita.

Sarebbe il caso di cominciare di smettere di parlare a Cagliari di formazione professionale, e ragionare finalmente sulla pubblica Alta Formazione Artistica che non c'è mai stata!

Bisognerebbe spiegare, a chi amministra o ambisce a governare la Regione a Statuto Autonomo, che la formazione alle nuove tecnologie, passa per le Accademie di Belle Arti, che hanno corsi triennali e biennali in tale settore d'Alta Formazione.

Accademia a Cagliari vorrebbe dire processo connettivo e virtuoso Regionale, che amplia la possibilità di scelta degli studenti, oggi di fatto messi in condizione d'essere i veri sovrani e giudici del proprio percorso di preparazione al lavoro, sarà forse proprio per questo che a Cagliari è diventato politicamente scomodo ragionare su un'Accademia di Belle Arti?

Il fatto che a Sassari già ci sia un'Accademia, per come è strutturata la Sardegna, non sarebbe un limite e non sarebbe limitante per Sassari, ma può soltanto ampliare la connessione sinergica e la giusta competizione tra i due principali poli isolani, questo migliorerebbe la qualità didattica attraverso una comparazione Regionale dei risultati ottenuti.

Le due Accademie potrebbero anche condividere e mappare regionalmente con archivi multimediali, lo stato dell'arte contemporanea nell'isola.

Accademia a Cagliari, vorrebbe dire, consentire a Cagliari di formare i propri docenti d'indirizzo artistico, e smetterla di celebrare artisti creati "politicamente" a tavolino da comune a comune, vorrebbe dire alimentare un dialogo permanente tra i diversi laboratori dell'Accademia e le aziende, tra giovani artisti in formazione e imprenditori, tra teoria e pratica, tra i docenti e il loro impegno quotidiano nel mondo delle cose che producono e finanziano, che si cambiano e innovano, che comunicano e si vendono (e sanno vendere).

Bisognerà anche ragionare seriamente sulla penuria d'arte contemporanea residente nell'isola rispetto ad altre realtà Europee, nell'isola non manca la qualità del valore umano, mancano creativi che sappiano indicare e modulare la rotta intermediando tra passato e futuro.

Una sana competizione tra Alta Formazione Artistica Cagliaritana e Sassarese, come avviene in sostanza tra i due Conservatori, orienterebbe il mercato dell'arte e della creatività interno ed esterno all'isola, eleverebbe complessivamente nell'isola la qualità diffusa dell'istruzione e formazione artistica, farebbe dell'isola una portatrice sana d'arte e cultura allineate con la domanda, in grado di competere e connettersi con l'altrove senza provincialismo alcuno.

ACCADEMIA MEGALITICA PER DETERMINARE FUTURO E MEMORIA!

Si fosse potuto parlare di corrente artistica, il megalitismo sarebbe stata una corrente artistica d'Avanguardia, sviluppata per un lungo periodo di tempo, dal 4500 al 1500 a.C.; linguaggio dell'arte espanso che si è mosso su un'area vasta, dalla Svezia alle isole del Mediterraneo meridionale, traversando penisola iberica, Francia e Italia.

Linguaggio litico dell'arte in movimento, che si è distinto attraverso

dolmen e menhir, mosso da funzioni funerarie (sepolture collettive) e culturali, attraverso blocchi di pietra di notevoli dimensioni, i "megaliti".
L'Architettura come la Scultura, i più antichi linguaggi dell'umano, nascono su pietra, nascono su pietra per esigenza comune, dall'Europa Occidentale la Scultura e l'Architettura megalitica si sono espanse con l'umano fino all'Italia meridionale, bisogna considerare come costruzioni megalitiche siano sorte in diversi punti del mondo e in epoche diverse, questo non può che spiegarsi con la naturale convergenza dei linguaggi dell'arte verso fini e finalità comuni dell'umano.
Eppure nel Settecento, si consideravano menhir, dolmen e cultura megalitica, qualcosa di non umano, la loro attribuzione si riteneva opera di giganti venuti dall'Africa, streghe, maghi, diavoli o azione della natura; nell'Ottocento i dolmen erano considerati alzarti per sacrifici umani e riti oscuri, soltanto in seguito, penetrando all'interno di uno dei tanti dolmen, nascosti da terra e pietrisco, furono trovati corredi funebri, resti di defunti e oggetti di ceramica e pietra.
La loro espressione, non è da ricondurre a un'unica civiltà, in questo c'è tutta la trasversalità culturale dei linguaggi dell'arte, e la loro capacità di valicare confini e limiti culturali.
La megalitica è una cultura che si è sviluppata all'interno di culture con gradi di sviluppo e livelli differenti, una cultura che circolava come merce nel mediterraneo, come l'ossidiana sarda, le idee, le tecniche e le persone.
La Sardegna era un nodo nel Neolitico recente, di traffico culturale del linguaggio umano su pietra.
Menhir e dolmen erano la sintesi di contatti esterni e rielaborazioni interne, questo è sfociato nel Bronzo medio, con quel megalitismo, che ancora oggi caratterizza l'isola, unico e autonomo, che ha determinato tombe di Giganti, nuraghi e la civiltà dei Nur.
Nel neolitico si autodetermina nell'isola, la cultura di Ozieri (o di San Michele), dal nome della grotta omonima, dal 4000 a 3200 a.C. circa, una cultura sarda che ha avuto ampia diffusione in tutta l'isola.
Cultura che si è sviluppata in maniera autoctona, che ha inglobato influenze e stimoli di provenienza egeo anatolica.
La cultura neolitica isolana, in altre parole è stata autoproduzione identitaria, frutto di contatti di gruppi umani di culture diverse, culture che si incrociavano e arrivavano sull'isola nel nome della circolazione dell'ossidiana, che aveva un ruolo centrale nell'economia del mediterraneo.
I villaggi all'aperto, si moltiplicarono, assumendo dimensioni sempre maggiorii; deposizioni collettive, ossari in grotte naturali, sepolture in dolmen e domus de Janas.

Sono sorte anche sepoltura miste, in parte ipogeiche e in parte megalitiche.

Sembra che i dolmen siano stati opera di comunità di pastori legate alla transumanza, le domus de janas da agricoltori legati a uno sfruttamento stabile del territorio.

Circoli ospitavano i capi della comunità, poi deposti nelle domus de janas.

Domus de janas, diffuse anche esse in tutta l'isola, al punto d'essere elemento paesaggistico, tombe collettive scavate in banchi orizzontali, dove erano deposti i defunti con i loro corredi funebri, potevano avere un vano (monocellulari) o più vani (pluricellulari) in collegamento tra di loro, lavoro di artigiani scavatori che da la dimensione di che tipo di società complessa sia stata, spesso riproducenti la pianta e particolari architettonici della capanna, ma anche oggetti d'uso quotidiano, il tutto arricchito da una simbologia funebre dipinta o incisa a rilievo sulle pareti.

Denti di lupo, scacchiere, protomi taurine, false porte che portano verso l'aldilà, motivi geometrici e decorativi che si legano al culto del Dio Toro e della Dea Madre.

La Dea Madre è stata un simbolo ricorrente, numerose le statuette femminili di tipo cicladico, in pietra, osso e ceramica, dalla forma a croce molto schematizzata, chiara connessione con l'area egeo anatolica, come lo è anche il simbolo iconico del Dio Toro.

L'industria litica locale arrivava fino all'Italia settentrionale, capite cosa vorrebbe dire per l'isola, riportare la propria industria plastico scultorea al centro del Mediterraneo, con un'Accademia a Cagliari e un corso di Scultura, che sappia porre in chiave contemporanea, al centro della sua didattica, questo patrimonio linguistico dell'arte, unico in tutto l'Occidente?

Nell'isola c'è stata anche grande fluidità nel passare dal Neolitico all'Eneolitico, si acquisì la capacità d'estrarre e lavorare il rame, seguito dall'argento e dal piombo.

Proprio questa duttilità nel passare dal Neolitico all'Eneolitico ha contraddistinto l'isola, che pur strategicamente e culturalmente al centro del Mediterraneo, attraverso la sua insularità, aveva e avrebbe, la predisposizione naturale ad assorbire varie culture, riuscendo sempre a mantenere un suo autonomo sviluppo culturale, riuscendo a controllare, mitigare e rielaborare linguisticamente apporti e influssi esterni, perché a questa grande capacità culturale dialettica, a oggi, nell'unica città metropolitana Cagliaritana è negata l'Alta Formazione Artistica?

L'isola è stata all'avanguardia, nel passaggio tra Neolitico ed Eneolitico, nell'arte della metallurgia, ha goduto di ricchi giacimenti di ossidi, solfuro e rame, dai quali era facilmente ottenibile il piombo come l'argento, rame in quel periodo era facilmente reperibile.

Intorno al 3200-2900 a.C. nell'isola questo mosse verso l'età del rame, numerosi oggetti metallici sono stati rinvenuti in contesti abitativ.

La realtà isolana, per condizione Geografica, ha conosciuto durante il suo unico Rinascimento, quello della civiltà dei Nur, un processo evolutivo, culturale e artistico, favorito dalla sua insularità, dalla sua mediazione dei contatti esterni, per questo quando si giustifica l'assenza di un'Accademia a Cagliari, nel nome del siamo un'isola, ho l'orticaria.

Intorno al 2900-2500 a.C., vi fu un ulteriore incremento di materiali metallici, armi, utensili e oggetti d'oreficeria, gli artigiani isolani erano altamente specializzati.

Intensa continuò a essere la produzione della Dea Madre e della statuaria megalitica, i menhir cominciano a distinguersi per tipologia (aniconici, protoantropomorfi e antropomorfi) che raggiungevano anche i sei metri.

Capite quanto sia la Scultura la vera limba identitaria e artistica isolana? Capite il perché di Pinuccio Sciola o di un Costantino Nivola e perché siano diversi da Ciusa?

I menhir antropomorfi cominciarono a mostrare una faccia frontale, il tentativo di rappresentare spalle e testa, sono un centinaio nell'isola, la rappresentazione del volto parte da uno schema a T (naso e sopracciglia), sul petto la figura a tridente (o candelabro), e in basso la raffigurazione di un pugnale in rame.

Il secondo schema sotto il volto, sul petto, presenta due bozze in rilievo, interpretate come seni.

Al momento gli esemplari femminili sono otto, ma quello che m'interessa evidenziare, è lo schema plastico scultoreo come limba, con schematizzazioni che consentivano di distinguere genere sessuale nell'ambito di una religiosità collettiva, la spiritualità nell'isola è nella pietra, l'arte come linguaggio e ricerca connettiva condivisa nasce su pietra, e nonostante questo una città come Cagliari, l'unica città metropolitana dell'isola, ancora non ha una sua Accademia di Belle Arti.

Cagliari oggi è l'unica città metropolitana dell'isola, capoluogo Regionale, con il Museo Archeologico Nazionale più importante dell'intera Sardegna, il luogo dove naturalmente s'impatta per conoscere il patrimonio archeologico dell'isola e la sua storia (possiamo chiamarla così senza un'Accademia che la faccia rivivere?); dal Neolitico al bizantino, dall'eneolitico al bronzo antico, dalla cultura nuragica ai colonizzatori fenici, dai Cartaginesi ai Romani.

I materiali esposti al Museo Archeologico di Cagliari, provengono dai siti archeologici più significativi dell'area di Cagliari e Oristano; c'è la collezione privata donata dall'tenore evangelista Gennaro Gorga

all'Università di Cagliari, oggetti ceramici che vanno dal III millennio a.C. al II d.C.
Numerose sono anche le testimonianze delle industrie litiche della Sardegna, preistoriche e protostoriche, prenuragiche e nuragiche, con l'aggiunta d'industrie litiche africane e mediterranee.

Sembra che si voglia strategicamente, che tutto ciò sia destinato a non ripetersi nell'isola, sembra che l'unica prospettiva di progetto intorno a questo, siano mega sculture destinate a restinare episodio confinato all'isola, quasi a segnarne il distacco con l'altrove.
Lasciatemelo scrivere ancora una volta, un'Accademia a Cagliari, sarebbe la possibilità che sembra perduta, di relazionarsi all'esterno con una propria e interna produzione artistica d'avanguardia, oggi come allora, che vada oltre l'arigianato e che faccia dell'artigiano un artista d'avanguardia, oggi come allora.

Lettera aperta al Consigliere Comunale dei Riformatori

Stimato Consigliere, con stupore leggo della sua proposta tramite mozione, di collocare un enorme bronzetto nuragico (alto 20 metri, 5 volte il David di Michelangelo per capirci, ragion per cui più che di un bronzetto nuragico lei starebbe parlando di un bronzone che nuragico non è, dal momento che dall'antica civiltà dei Nur, è passato qualche millennio), in un luogo simbolo dell'area di Cagliari Città Metropolitana, di modo che sia visibile al turista dal mare, l'alternativa sarebbe da individuare tra la vecchia stazione marittima, in mezzo alla pineta di su Siccu o al Lazzaretto di Sant'Elia.
Parla di questo monumento come potenziale attrazione turistica in un territorio che rischia di sommergere la sua cultura e le sue forme specificità artistiche, come sembra avvenire ciclicamente proprio da tremila anni a questa parte, ma a partire da quella cultura e da quel linguaggio si dovrebbe ragionare su come farla rivivere con linguaggi e ricerche artistiche che sappiano essere contemporanee, questo è stato la Torre Eiffel, un simbolo di modernità in una città metropolitana dove è stato molto forte il dibattito e la dialettica tra Accademico e AntiAccademico, simbolo di nuovi materiali e calcoli strutturali che potevano tradursi anche in estetica di nuovo mondo, al punto di porsi in dialogo con il classico e divenire classica in questo mondo dal turismo culturale e artistico interconnesso.
Sarà il caso forse di ricordarle che Cagliari è l'unica città metropolitana

d'Europa priva di un'Accademia di Belle Arti e di riflesso priva di quella diatriba tra Accademico e AntiAccademico che dovunque alimenta il confronto tra locale e globale traducendolo in fermento culturale e artistico residente?

Propone addirittura di titolare la piazza che ospiterà il bronzone "Piazza della civiltà nuragica", ma non servirebbe prima un'Accademia di Belle Arti della Civiltà nuragica, nella città metropolitana che ha il museo archeologico più importante dell'isola?

Addirittura (e questo mi pare un tantino populista di questi tempi), propone la scelta del soggetto per tale bronzone da individuare attraverso un sondaggio on line?

La scelta del soggetto, e che lo diciamo a fare? Sarebbe tra il Dio Guerriero con quattro occhi e quattro braccia, il capo villaggio, l'arciere e il pugilatore di Mont'e Prama.

Ricapitolando il simbolo artistico e culturale di Cagliari, sarebbe una copia deformata nelle proporzioni originarie, di un simbolo di una grande civiltà risalente a tremila anni fa, nell'unica città metropolitana d'Europa ancora priva di un'Accademia di Belle Arti?

Ma sicuro che il suo gruppo politico d'appartenenza sia quello dei Riformatori?

Perché questa sembra una proposta un tantinello conservatrice e statica dal punto di vista, anche di quel dinamismo culturale, che ha caratterizzato la civiltà dei Nur, che seppe svilupparsi in maniera autoctona, che fu in grado d'inglobare influenze e stimoli di provenienza egeo anatolica, seppe essere autoproduzione identitaria, frutto di contatti di gruppi umani di culture diverse, culture che si incrociavano e arrivavano sull'isola che aveva un ruolo centrale nell'economia e nella cultura del mediterraneo.

Vorrebbe farla rivivere?

Pensi all'Accademia di Cagliari porto internazionale possibile d'Alta Formazione per gli artisti del mediterraneo, senta come suona bene "Accademia della civiltà nuragica", e non pensi al turista come qualcuno che può sentirsi attratto dal primo bronzone della storia umana che offende la sua stessa cultura e la sua stessa idea d'evoluzione possibile artistica, storica e umana.

Lavoro di Discipline Plastiche di una studentessa di una classe seconda del Liceo Artistico Foiso Fois sul tema "Accademia a Cagliari".

INTERDIZIONE ARTISTICA CAGLIARITANA

L'Alta Formazione Artistica a Cagliari trova una zona metropolitana (unica in Europa), da cui è interdetta.
Questo rende tutta l'area di Cagliari Città metropolitana un luogo dove l'arte, non ha mai potuto avviare quel processo di ricostruzione dell'identità individuale e collettiva, di cui tutte le realtà metropolitane, hanno di questi tempi globalizzati e interconnessi, ciclicamente

bisogno.

Nella pratica cosa vuole dire per il Cagliaritano, l'impossibilità d'accesso nella sua città, a una zona d'Alta Formazione Artistica?

Vuole dire privare persone, individui e cittadini, della possibilità di comprendere ed esperire il valore di una formazione altrove metabolizzata e somatizzato, vuole dire fare sbalzare Cagliari fuori dal confronto e dal flusso delle realtà artistiche contemporanee, vuole dire avere una relazione con l'arte immobile e sospesa.

Questo vuole dire porre Cagliari fuori da uno sguardo collettivo della percezione e del dialogo operativo della propria memoria da confrontare con quelle altrui.

Gli artisti Cagliaritani, anche quando mostrati ed esibiti, sono estremamente convenzionali, fedeli a un codice di rappresentazione vigile, che per certi versi appare immutato (convenzioni Accademiche imposte dall'altrove a parte) da millenni, paralizzato; so che è impopolare, ma Costantino Nivola o Pinuccio Sciola hanno realmente smosso la cultura dei Nur?

Ci hanno dialogato?

Hanno azzardato ipotesi iconoclastiche nei suoi confronti per smuoverne il linguaggio seppur di genere?

La mancanza di un'Accademia d'area Cagliaritana, rende la ricerca locale asfittica, dove la critica propositiva al codice linguistico sembra essere stata bandita da millenni.

L'isola senza un'Accademia di Belle Arti di Cagliari, sarà sempre un sistema dell'arte precario, inconcluso, dove il ben fatto dell'artigiano, in quanto non legittimato da un'idea dell'arte alta, condanna a vivere un presente professionale come un ricordo sbiadito d'alimentare artificialmente.

La Cagliari contemporanea che abitiamo, dove viviamo e lavoriamo, interdetta dalla possibilità di avere una sua Alta Formazione Artistica, subisce nella pratica, un'interdizione non solo fisica, ma anche psichica, è interdetta dal narrarsi, dal raccontarsi storicamente, dal consentire di mostrare il punto di vista degli artisti in tempo reale che mettono a fuoco gli eventi della propria storia (individuale e collettiva).

Cagliari artisticamente è stata sequestrata da una Storia dell'Arte imposta, ha vissuto e subito identità e linguaggi dell'arte determinate dall'altrove, autodeterminando per l'altrove una propria idea identitaria culturale ridotta a folk.

Cagliari vive una idea dell'arte serva dell'altrove, imposta da generazioni precedenti e passate, autocelebrative, acritiche e autoassolutorie.

Il linguaggi dell'arte nell'isola sono ridotti a essere il ready made della civiltà dei Nur (Costantino Nivola e Pinuccio Sciola).

La realtà Cagliaritana è quella di un passato artistico impossibilitato a raccontare un presente alieno, inedito e oscuro, non si possiedono gli strumenti culturali per indagare e comprenderlo.

La dialettica dell'arte a Cagliari e nell'isola, è piatta, noiosa, serva del mainstream (anche politico) che la rende inerte, paralitica, un nuovo mai nato e alimentato, un nuovo sequestrato.

La costante artistica e culturale resistenziale isolana, è mai stata da tremila anni a questa parte, mai autodeterminata, resa narrativamente immobile, indiscutibile, inattaccabile.

Cagliari senza Accademia, è una città metropolitana rinchiusa e bloccata artisticamente e culturalmente, vittima e carceriera di se stessa (anche delle Avanguardie che l'hanno animata negli anni sessanta-settanta).

Oggi un'incomunicabilità fondamentale divide la dialettica e la didattica dell'arte contemporanea dalle avanguardie dei suoi anni sessanta e settanta.

Avanguardie che senza che ci fosse un'Accademia di Belle Arti, nel nome di un'Antiaccademismo imposto e determinato dal mercato, ne hanno respinto l'istanza, che dovranno rendere di conto di un approccio all'arte ridotto ad autoassoluzione e autocelebrazione, avendo respinto al mittente l'idea della produzione artistica diffusa attraverso un'Accademia di Belle Arti, come strumento di autodeterminazione storica e culturale, identitaio e collettivo.

La Cagliari dell'Arte contemporanea è priva di narrazione e di racconto, non riconosce il valore dell'altro ma all'occorrenza lo celebra per interesse; è incapace di riflettere e criticare, di scoprire e confrontarsi con l'inatteso e l'inaspettato; propone una narrazione artistica e culturale misera, priva di ricerca che linguisticamente possa interessare l'altro, drammaticamente incapace di cogliere gli aspetti inediti, dissonanti, disturbanti di questo millennio, facendone oggetto di godimento, palesemente incapaci di godersi i disturbi del mercato, che se ci fosse una coscienza Accademica locale, tradurrebbe in percezione arricchita del reale.

Cagliari è una zona artisticamente chiusa, che esibisce ciò che non è e non ha per intravedere un altrove che è incapace d'autodeterminare, incapace di analizzare, intervenire, modificare e trasformare.

Il Cagliaritano e l'isolano sembrano avere costruito la loro interdizione, l'odio verso la complessità della percezione dei linguaggi dell'arte, il rifuggire dalle analisi complicate, con una naturalezza quasi sconcertante.

La profondità di ricerca e di contenuto a Cagliari sembra essere un peccato, si opta per la rozzezza dell'estetico e del ben fatto, con tutta la sua rozzezza e cafoneria digitale, senza neanche indagare, quanto per fare oggi un buon ritratto basti una buona applicazione a partire da un selfie, o un videoproiettore su tela da ricalcare, gli stessi artisti Cagliaritani e isolani, non hanno mai avuto l'opportunità di guardarsi dentro, per guardare fuori da loro nel tempo e con il tempo.

Altro Capodanno senza ricerca isolana in piazza

L'idea dell'arte Cagliaritana e isolana, sembra essere fondata non lo su studio o la ricerca linguistica, ma su l'imitazione, come se si fosse assorbito il peggio del carattere nazionale Italiano in tal senso, come se si fosse accettato passivamente porre da parte la propria attitudine nei confronti della vita e del mondo.
Il Cagliaritano e l'isolano appaiono incapaci d'immaginare realtà di studio e ricerca, senza abbinare il proprio "movimento" culturale a un'idea di mestiere remunerato, quasi ci si vergogna di dire che prima di tutto la propria sfera d'interesse e quella artistica e che per sostenerla possa servire un altro lavoro.
Si simulano idee dell'arte che sono anti educative, ci si auto umilia collettivamente anche nel proprio modo di raccontarsi al turista, tutto è infetto, a Capodanno si festeggia con i Subsonica e non con Drer e Crc Posse o i Sa Razza, che sono il loro equivalente culturale isolano, e il festeggiamento non è neanche dialettico; si vivono artisticamente culture distanti finendo con il non riconoscere e squalificare le proprie.
Ma in fondo perché dovrei stupirmi?
Quest'è l'isola dell'origine del rituale che passa per la maschera, dove si è mascherata anche la morte con il riso sardonico, la morte della propria memoria, l'io dietro la maschera è stato nascosto, come se l'azione non dovesse agganciare direttamente il pensiero, come i testi di Drer e Crc Posse o i Sa Razza, radicati nel territorio, divenissero per salutare l'anno, non rappresentativi.
L'isola vive culturalmente un'identità sganciata dalla sua stessa identità, il suo territorio artistico è oggi naturalmente quello della simulazione dei Talent Show che celebrano gli artisti sardi nella pagina della cultura; simulazione e rappresentazione della riproduzione.
Il popolare relegato naturalmente a folk senza distinguo di genere, la maschera dell'isolano oggi nega volti, idee, espressioni e istanze.
I Subsonica in piazza, sono l'equivalente della riduzione della maschera a retorica, sono l'espressione isolana della retorica italiana, sono i post quarantenni al potere che nell'autocelebrarsi, come da sempre in questo territorio, ne negano le problematiche.
I Subsonica in piazza sono il sistema dei valori di riferimento in quest'isola, dove lo scorrere del tempo è sempre in differita, sono l'arte dei Savoia che non si confronta con quella Cagliaritana, che sembra assente e mai pervenuta, che neanche s'interroga sul perché a oggi,

Cagliari sia l'unica città metropolitana d'Europa priva d'Accademia, sono il vecchio schema e il modello di riferimento, è il secolo scorso dell'arte in piazza, insostenibile, a questo punto avrei preferito Sfera Ebbasta, dal momento che di Mandrone non si dovrebbe a Cagliari, neanche parlare!

STATI GENERALI AFAM

Il contratto di governo Lega e Cinquestelle, prevede di portare a compimento la riforma del sistema dell'Alta Formazione Artistica, Musicale e Coreutica Italiana (AFAM), per fare si, che il più importante settore strategico Italiano, quello dell'alta formazione (e produzione) artistica e musicale si rimetta in movimento e al passo con il resto d'Europa.
La legge di Riforma del settore risale al 1999 (legge 508), nel 2007 la prima e unica convocazione degli stati generali del sistema (a Verona). Finalmente dopo undici anni su convocheranno gli stati generali dell'AFAM, a Roma l'otto e il nove Febbraio 2019.
Il Vice ministro all'istruzione, Università e Ricerca, Lorenzo Fioramonti, ha dichiarato che in tale occasione, si solleciteranno tutti gli addetti ai lavori a dare il loro prezioso contributo, e che si cercherà un confronto aperto per preservare e valorizzare il sistema AFAM, da rendere stabile e organico, innovandolo nel rispetto della sua storia e peculiarità.
Quello che mi chiedo è:
In tale occasione, dove si ragionerà sul sistema Accademie e della loro innovazione, qualcuno farà presente che a Cagliari un'Accademia non c'è mai stata e che in tal senso niente sarebbe più innovativo che la sua fondazione?
Perché tale specificità e fiore all'occhiello della cultura Italiana, ha con Cagliari l'anomalia di non esserci mai stata, e nessuna altra città metropolitana, non solo d'Italia, ma d'Europa, può condividere con Cagliari tale e incredibile negazione del diritto alla propria autodeterminazione produttiva, storica artistica e culturale.

Lavoro di Discipline Plastiche di una studentessa di una classe seconda del Liceo Artistico Foiso Fois sul tema "Accademia a Cagliari".

Accademia meglio di un iPhone!

Cagliari non ha mai avuto storicamente, un dibattito pubblico sull'importanza della formazione e produzione artistica residente. Non essendo mai stato un polo d'Alta Formazione Artistica, e da sempre priva di un'Accademia di Belle Arti, pecca d'autoreferenzialità, quasi come si alimentasse un distacco schizofrenico tra l'arte e la propria realtà culturale; oltre l'autoreferenzialità l'altro problema è la barbarie verso la propria specificità culturale, l'incapacità di concentrarsi sulle proprie specifiche problematiche, sulla propria anomalia da confrontare con le altre realtà, l'incapacità di discutere con l'altrove partendo da una propria, formata, motivata, elaborata posizione.

Potrebbe un'Accademia intervenire nel tessuto connettivo della realtà Cagliaritana?

Ovviamente si, i linguaggi dell'arte, nel loro muoversi nel tempo, riconnettono, ricongiungono e ricucino l'arte e la cultura al tessuto connettivo sociale reale.

Innovazione artistica non vuole dire iPhone, i social network di loro, non gettano una luce positiva sulla predisposizione all'inatteso, inaspettato e imprevisto.

Le Start up non hanno nulla a che fare con le avanguardie artistiche, le Accademia di Belle Arti in Italia, sono il reale agente d'innovazione artistica e culturale.

Cagliari è una realtà metropolitana, dove un'Accademia di Belle Arti non c'è mai stata, e dove l'innovazione è intesa esclusivamente come tecnica e scientifica, mai artistica e culturale.

Possibile che il Cagliaritano debba disprezzare e sottovalutare in maniere così palese, la possibilità di autodeterminare la propria Alta Formazione Artistica residente.

Mai Cagliari ha avuto una sua discussione di senso sull'arte plurale e complessa, solo retorica e propaganda di comunicazione politica, tutto quello che può disturbare (arte residente compreso) fuori dal quadro, marginalizzato e reso impotente.

C'è una barriera invisibile tra ciò che è l'arte a Cagliari e ciò che vorrebbe e potrebbe essere, il muro invisibile è costituito dall'Alta Formazione Artistica assente, il Cagliaritano e l'isolano vivono e riflettono un'idea dell'arte, funzionale a una classe dirigente politica che nel contendersi brandelli manda in frantumi un sistema dell'Alta Formazione Artistica isolano mai nato, dove tutto sembra fermarsi a Sassari, nel nome della quale Accademia, un'Accademia a Cagliari diventa scomoda da pensare.

Il giornalismo locale (tranne rare eccezioni), sembra non comprendere la problematica, preferendosi concentrare su dettagli fuori tempo, quasi come se non ci fosse una gigantesca trasformazione in atto, per la quale sarebbe necessario attrezzarsi di un'Accademia, al fine di programmare il proprio futuro anche in chiave storica e turistica.

L'inadeguatezza dello sguardo progettuale d'insieme sull'arte residente, è la cifra dominante del Cagliaritano e dell'isolano quando si ragiona d'arte e cultura, gli eventi d'arte e cultura paiono senza senso (vedi il capodanno con i Subsonica), razzi sparati per salutare l'anno senza pensare all'anno che verrà, distruttori per non affrontare e guardare in faccia le proprie carenze epocali.

Più conveniente a Cagliari (come a Sassari) recitare una commedia dell'arte e delle parti, per auto rassicurarsi confermandosi nello spazio e nel tempo isolano, la propria psicosi, l'incapacità di percepirsi in una visione d'insieme che sappia essere isola comune interconnessa con l'altrove.

Senza Accademia inferiorità storica e culturale

Cagliari priva di un'Accademia di Belle Arti, sarà sempre destinata a non avere mai la percezione di ciò che muove altrove il sistema dei linguaggi dell'arte e la loro formazione, per questo a Cagliari i linguaggi dell'arte paiono congelati, bloccati, limitati e ridotti a parodia.
La parodia di una città metropolitana che limita e imprigiona l'idea di movimento dei linguaggi dell'arte, che li sfrutta e li divora, espellendoli, costretti a emigrare per divenire cosmopoliti.
Cagliari forma i suoi artisti costringendoli a studiare e formarsi artisticamente altrove, altrove comprendono le possibilità professionali che passano attraverso i linguaggi dell'arte, trovano lavoro e diventano artisti internazionali, ma a quale prezzo interiore?
Quanto costa interiormente formarsi attraverso altre storie dell'arte, perché nel proprio territorio non si è mai progettata una messa a sistema dell'Alta Formazione Artistica residente?
I giovani artisti Cagliaritani in formazione, per autodeterminarsi sono costretti a scappare, di fatto a rinunciare alla complessità e specificità della propria identità, rinunciando in pratica alla propria diversità culturale, a un passato interiorizzato archeologicamente, proiettato e interiorizzato, che nella propria autodeterminazione professionale, non ha nessuna relazione con l'alta formazione artistica residente.
 Eppure la Storia dell'Arte Cagliaritana e isolana, porrebbe naturalmente in condizione di potere essere critici verso i linguaggi dell'arte imposti dall'altrove, ma impossibilita ad autodeterminarsi come Alta Formazione, ma non esiste, non esiste in quanto critica alla Storia, proprio perché non esiste la storia (Costantino Nivola, Francesco Ciusa, Pinuccio Sciola e Maria Lai, pensate di trovarli in un libro di Storia dell'Arte Italiana? Io a parte Mario Sironi, arrivato nell'isola, non conoscevo nessun artista isolano).
La società, la cultura, il sistema dell'arte Cagliaritano e isolano, non vive nel suo, e del suo, immaginario culturale e artistico, per questo non si può parlare di società o di sistema, ma di qualcosa di altro, qualcosa d'impostato sull'assenza.
Cagliari senza Accademia di Belle Arti, determina un sistema dell'arte isolano incomprensibile oltre l'isola, determina senza artisti in formazione, l'assenza della ribellione creativa, la passività artistica rispetto quello che impone il mercato, la furberia "medievale" dell'inventarsi la professione dell'artista, la chiusura mentale all'altro,

l'opportunismo politico disonesto intellettualmente, il complesso d'inferiorità storica e culturale, l'autocommiserazione tradotta in autoassoluzione; in sintesi si è tagliati fuori dal contesto del contemporaneo.

Lo show artistico Cagliaritano

A Cagliari l'arte è comprensibile non come studio o ricerca di senso dell'umano, ma solo come spettacolo-prodotto che esclude lo spettatore dall'interazione, comprensione e partecipazione, non essendoci un'Accademia l'artista vive una condizione sociale che lo costringe a ritagliarsi zone di sopravvivenza.
I linguaggi dell'arte, in quanto ricerca, a Cagliari e nell'isola, sopravviveranno se sapranno alimentarsi come forma di vita, diversa, alternativa, contraria a tutte quelle logiche d'amministrazione politica Regionale, che vogliono essere Cagliari, l'unica città metropolitana d'Europa, ancora nel 2019, priva di un'Accademia di Belle Arti.
Il contrario al mercato privato, oggi passa per le Accademie di Belle Arti e il loro sapere fare rete con i territori metropolitani di riferimento connessi con l'altrove; l'alta formazione artistica che passa oggi per le Accademie di Belle Arti in Europa, è il contrario della cultura ridotta a show, della rappresentazione estetica che non ha nulla a che fare con l'estetica, della comunicazione fine a se stessa, di contenuti retorici privi di forma; la forma è tutto nelle Accademie.
Nelle Accademie il sondare l'espressioni artistiche contemporanee va oltre il mercato, non si parla la lingua del mercato, è un'illusione quella che si possa distinguersi dalla piattezza comunicativa del mercato privato, adottandone il linguaggio, è un'illusione; gli schemi di ragionamento e di visione in un'Accademia sono radicalmente diversi, sono fuori da un immaginario e una mentalità omologante imposta e sono pratica di nuove e altre possibilità da diffondere.
Al Cagliaritano questo sembra vago?
No, se comincia a ragionare, in ritardo di qualche secolo rispetto a tutte le grandi città Europee, sulle implicazioni di questo.
Evoluzione artistica e culturale di una comunità, vuole dire fare fronte alle problematiche mutando, evolversi elaborando il trauma del vivere, le Accademie segnano l'ingresso dell'uomo in un tempo umanisticamente e tecnicamente moderno, senza rinunciare a se stesso, ma in grado d'ascoltare e concettualizzare, anche criticamente, le sue aspettative.
L'Accademia educa alla bellezza e alla comprensione del fuori moda, del rozzo, del maleducato, del fuori luogo e contesto, dell'inopportuno, del povero, del piccolo, del nuovo, del semplice, dell'ingenuo,

dell'arcaico, del reale, del naturale, dell'ideale, del fondamentale, del Cagliaritano e dell'isolano.

Senza Accademia di Belle Arti, quello dell'arte Cagliaritana, è un sistema linguistico chiuso, che non intrattiene rapporti con i mondi dell'arte circostanti, è sempre stato così, ma ora, in questo terzo millennio ormai maggiorenne, perseverare nell'isolamento è inopportuno e pericoloso, troppo immagini e poche visioni che sappiano interpretarle; l'arte a Cagliari pare non avere responsabilità e senza responsabilità di quale identità si ragiona?

Un'isola amministrata da irresponsabili, può perseverare, nell'ignoranza della visione, percezione e comprensione artistica e culturale dell'altro.

Senza una propria, e autodeterminata Accademicamente, Storia dell'Arte, come si può comprendere quella dell'altro e relazionarsi ad altri contesti con pari dignità, forti della propria specificità?

Arte a Cagliari distinguo di classe

Occorrerebbe fare uno studio antropologico sul come il Cagliaritano si rivolge al potere, sui suoi cambiamenti d'espressione, dallo stupore e l'ineffabile dolcezza che lo pervade quando a esso si relaziona.

Dinanzi il potere politico centrale o quando il politico ha a che fare con il cittadino normale, il Cagliaritano diventa miele, un attimo prima è ostile, scontroso, rigido, burbero e ostile, forte della propria rappresentazione sociale, l'attimo dopo dinanzi il potere politico si scioglie, diventa un bambino dinanzi alla Maestra, lo fa lo stesso politico Cagliaritano quando si relaziona alla politica nazionale del suo stesso partito di riferimento.

Il rapporto con il potere, da cittadino di provincia qual'è, è timorato, seppure con la fiducia di fondo che comportandosi bene e facendo una buona impressione il potente conserverà questa buona impressione e gratificherà usandola nel futuro.

Con il potere il Cagliaritano è accondiscendente, altrimenti come sperare che nella vita accadrà qualcosa di buono?

Voi direte che questo ha poco a che fare con la storica assenza di un'Accademia di Belle Arti a Cagliari?

Invece no, pensateci un attimo, pensate ai ceti sociali popolari Cagliaritani e a come siano omessi dal potere accedere ai mezzi di produzione e formazione artistica e culturale, è evidente che in tale maniere si evita l'accesso indesiderato al "riconoscimento sociale e artistico di classe", come sostenere altrimenti la logica del "vediamoci per un aperitivo a piazzetta Savoia", del bacino, dello sguardo complice e del discorso appassionato che non tutti possono capire perché ignoranti?

Il sistema politico e il sistema dell'arte nel Cagliaritano sono profondamente interconnessi, si legittimano a vicenda, si riconoscono reciprocamente, è tutto fondato sul quello è uno importante, quello è uno che conta, è il figlio di, il marito di, la moglie di; esattamente lo stesso schema che si riporoduce quando si ha a che fare con il continentale e chi proviene dall'altrove; l'altro se non "conviene" deve essere etichettato come uno che se si esprime , in fondo "chi si crede d'essere, non parla la nostra lingua".

Questa mentalità, che si è stratificata nei secoli, ha avuto un impatto fortissimo in termini di chiusura artistica e culturale, l'assenza di un'Accademia è una risultante di questa mentalità, non c'è prospettiva artistica e culturale residente che possa innovare e trasformare, l'arte è orientata e imposta per orientare e conservare status quo che arrivano da lontano; per questo l'arte e la cultura a Cagliari nel quotidiano non appassionano quanto e come dovrebbero, per cui paiono espressioni contemporanee distaccate dalla società, dalla vita, dalle persone, dalla comunità, come poterebbe essere altrimenti, dal momento che al Cagliaritano l'alta formazione artistica è preclusa?

Quando è che Cagliari prenderà atto, che una comunità metropolitana (di nome o di fatto') incapace di garantire a tutte le classi sociali parità d'accesso ai processi linguistici dell'arte, ha fallito la sua missione d'autodeterminazione democratica?

Quella Cagliaritana è una realtà anni ottanta, con quarantenni e cinquantenni, oggi padri di famiglia, cresciuti con il mito del paninaro e dello yuppie, che lo rivivono aggiornato e remixato, giacchetta, fintamente impegnati e comunque sia sempre connessi, nel nome di questo non si leggono e non si fanno analisi, l'arte se non un buon affare non ha per loro motivo d'essere.

Come si può vivere così?

Come si può relegare i linguaggi dell'arte a essere solo resistenza come avviene nel quotidiano in Via San Saturnino?

Educare all'arte vuole dire educare al rifiuto dell'imposizione, allo scaricamento della regola per crearne delle nuove a dimensione uomo, essere pronti a ogni secondo della giornata a rifiutare concetti e idee preconfezionati, non ci si può essere serenamente autodeterminati artisticamente e culturalmente con un equilibrio artistico residente così farlocco, precario e minaccioso, a esclusiva dimensione del vecchio che nel nome del rispetto, impone al giovane di non superarlo.

ALTA FORMAZIONE ARTISTICA IN VACANZA A CAGLIARI

Una città come Cagliari, così come una embrionale idea di nazione sarda (sempre che l'indipendentismo non sia soltanto retorica propaganda per ambizioni politico amministrative), che voglia essere aggiornata e attrattiva, avrebbe bisogno di una narrazione di sé, che non fosse frammentaria, frantumata e dispersa in realtà non comunicanti.

Le narrazioni, le fruizioni e le produzioni artistiche e culturali contemporanee Cagliaritane e isolane, devono e possono giocare un ruolo determinante per articolare il presente.

Possibile che nel 2019, non si sia ancora compreso, come la possibilità di fruizione del proprio patrimonio artistico (passato), passi per la produzione in ogni momento e attimo della giornata di arte e cultura contemporanea?

Classico e contemporaneo, con il contemporaneo che in quest'epoca algoritimica deve imporsi d'essere Romantico, sono dimensioni linguistiche che si alimentano e intrecciano, si muovono riflettendosi e identificandosi reciprocamente e continuamente.

Una città come Cagliari che non hai mai avuto fisicamente un'Accademia di Belle Arti, come può autodeterminarsi come luogo psichico collettivo e connettivo d'arte contemporanea?

Come si può pensare di affrontare la complessità di questo millennio senza Alta Formazione Artistica e investire su resort d'artisti in momentanea residenza?

Accademia di Belle Arti residente, vuole dire fornire un bacino inesauribile di reale collaborazione, discussione e alta formazione nel territorio, vuole dire nutrire artisti, critici, galleristi e collezionisti, vuole dire rendere la comunità Cagliaritana metropolitana pubblico interattivo dell'arte contemporanea.

La politica amministrativa Cagliaritana dovrebbe abbandonare la logica (e la retorica) dei grandi eventi e delle grandi mostre autoreferenziali a dimensione "aperitivo politico", e orientarsi verso progetti ridotti che sappiano essere pubblici, che siano reale connessione con realtà e territorio, che sappiano ricostruire un'identità collettiva sempre depredata dinanzi alla sua storia, che sappiano essere artisticamente responsabili.

L'artista residente (e non in residenza) è quel motore culturale e identitario, il cui lavoro è fondato sulla conoscenza diretta del contesto materiale, che vive, abita e con il quale si confronta nel quotidiano, è estensione diretta della comunità.

L'Accademia di Belle Arti, in tutte le città metropolitane Europee (Cagliari esclusa), è la filiera di sistema a Km.zero, è l'autodeterminazione di produttori e consumatori, ovviamente a questo si accompagnano politica culturali locali utili e adeguate, con questa modalità si rendono vicini produttori e artisti, consumatori e collezionisti, si costruisce un sistema locale che sa proporsi complessivamente come sistema locale in grado di radicarsi anche nei quartieri; tutto questo avviene a Roma, Milano, Torino, ma ovviamente non potrà mai avvenire a Cagliari fin quando non ci sarà un'Accademia di Belle Arti, ed è molto triste che debba essere un docente del Liceo Artistico, con secoli di ritardo storico evidenti in tale settore formativo, a dovere fare notare tutto questo mentre l'ex sede del Liceo Artistico (Ex Art) diventa con un investimento di 1.100.000 euro un resort per artisti in residenza che si formano altrove.

LA DEMOCRAZIA DELL'ARTE DISOBBEDIENTE

In questo millennio la ricerca artistica sta subendo una mutazione del suo ruolo, non solo nell'isola, ma nell'intero Occidente nel nome del mercato privatizzato.
Ai linguaggi dell'arte non si chiede più di trainare verso la conoscenza e la condivisione di cause o conquiste sociali, scientifiche e culturali comuni (anche sotto forma di critica politica), ma da trent'anni a questa parte si chiede che confermino quelle che si presume di sapere perché inculcato da logiche di mercato, si devono comprendere e giustificare delle cose per convenzione sociale, per conformismo e adeguamento al sistema.
Nella città metropolitana senza Accademia di Belle Arti, questo diviene parossistico, la politica si erge a favore dell'artigianato senza che un'Accademia di Belle Arti l'abbia mai nobilitato come Arte, gli artisti sembra si rivolgano a cittadini e turisti perfetti ai quali cercare di vendersi, quasi come se volessero staccarsi dalle problematiche della propria comunità.
Eppure nell'isola più e prima d'altrove, con l'antica civiltà dei Nur, l'arte pone l'umano dinanzi alla sua condizione mortale, costruisce il dialogo della mente oltre il tempo con se stessa, è dialogo, solo e soltanto linguaggio dialettico e didattico.
 L'arte non ha nulla di biologico in comune con la logica del profitto e la coltivazione del consenso, consegnare l'industria culturale e artistica direttamente al privato tradotto in mercato (anche dell'associazionismo politico e delle residenze d'artista) di riflesso condanna l'arte a estinguere la sua caratteristica biologica umana, e rende il ruolo dell'artista simile a quello di qualsiasi altro mestiere, un artigiano che riproduce il linguaggio senza arricchirlo o contaminarlo con lo spirito e il movimento del tempo.
Linguaggi dell'Arte e Accademie di Belle Arti, in Italia e in Europa, salvaguardano democraticamente la sana ribellione, l'opposizione, il mi dissocio, il non mi sta bene, il non accetto le condizioni e neanche i recinti normativi perché se tu mi vuoi in una maniera io ti dico che

posso essere in un altra maniera, perché sono un creativo.
 Pacificare i linguaggi dell'arte con una società globalizzata dal mercato è una follia, il conflitto artistico è culturale è la nostra vita e ha determinato la nostra evoluzione; simulare il ruolo dell'artista evitandone i conflitti, vuole dire simulare un linguaggio vivo che nasce già morto (mi piacerebbe fare i nomi dei tanti artisti che conosco che non vanno oltre il visto e non vissuto, ma non lo farò, in passato ho accumulato troppe diffide sul capo).

L'opposizione radicale al modello Accademico è l'elaborazione di un altro modello destinato a sua volta a divenire Accademico è il compito dei linguaggi dell'arte, è il confronto tra il linguaggio vivo che resta nella memoria e la propria mortalità.

Le Accademia di Belle Arti sono la dimensione di un adeguato uso della propria solitudine tradotta in interiorità creativa, quanto sono preziose in un millennio dove per non annoiarsi ci si tuffa nei social network che rendono ogni luogo del pianeta terra una metropoli?

Accademia oltre il mestiere dell'Artigiano

Una realtà come Cagliari, priva da sempre d'Alta Formazione Artistica, è in condizione di scindere tra quello che è stabilito per tradizione e convenzione e la ricerca artistica contemporanea?
in tutto questo la sua guida la si può ridurre a mercati imposti e determinati dall'altrove?
Il Cagliaritano, lo si voglia o no, ha problemi di ricezione riguardo agli aspetti linguistici del fare arte contemporanea, lo stesso artista Cagliaritano, sembra abbia un "blocco psicologico" che ne impedisce la ribellione artistica e lo limita nell'avanzamento.
La domanda che Cagliari dovrebbe porsi è: come si può essere linguisticamente innovativi e rivoluzionari, se non c'è mai stato un pubblico e una comunità adatti alla ricezione e fruizione del contemporaneo?
Gli osservatori e il pubblico Cagliaritano sanno riconoscere realmente un lavoro artistico da uno artigianale?
L'artigiano Cagliaritano sa tendere all'oggetto artistico attraverso una formazione adeguata?
Tutto appare standardizzato e immobile nel tempo, con questo scenario dove rincorrere realmente l'innovazione determinata dalla ribellione linguistica?
Cagliari ha bisogno di un luogo di progettazione dell'immaginario, di un'Accademia di Belle Arti che connetta le coscienze creative alla collettività, ci vorranno tempi lunghi, ma è il caso che si attivi un processo assente dalla storia dei linguaggi artistici nell'isola.

Necessario che l'Accademia di Belle Arti a Cagliari, diventi progetto politico trasversale, che eviti la retorica elettorale del mainstream, e che sappia pensarsi come crescita costante di costruzione di una comunità, dove ferite e traumi della storia sappiano rinascere e rigenerarsi in termini creativi; vi viene in mente un altra tipologia possibile d'investimento cognitivo ed economico che alimenti realmente il pensiero evolutivo e culturale della comunità?

Privi d'immaginario collettivo creativo

I linguaggi dell'arte non possono essere immuni dalla mutazione in corso, stanno mutando i modi d'interpretare e vivere collettivamente la realtà, di concepirne esistenza e presupposti.
Non esiste artista che possa dichiararsi immune dalla mutazione, i linguaggi dell'arte interpretano, analizzano, criticano, disobbediscono, si ribellano, ma non possono non viverla.
A cosa serve l'Accademia?
A tradurre la tradizione con lo spirito del tempo.
L'Accademia è sempre traduzione del classico in romantica chiave contemporanea, è il patrimonio che consenta d'evitare la perdita d'identità, è la traduzione della propria identità con la consapevolezza di nuovi linguaggi e strumenti.
L'Accademia serve agli artisti contemporanei per sintetizzare, rendere comprensibile ed efficace, la complessità dell'umanità con i propri codici culturali.
Cosa può fare il Cagliaritano, e il sardo, per non perdere la propria identità?
Accettare di fonderla con i linguaggi del tempo presente, saperla cedere aprendosi all'altro e identificandosi con esso, questo fanno da migliaia di millenni i linguaggi dell'arte.
L'identità locale tradotta in Accademia, fusa con il barbaro mercato, riattiva e vivifica il linguaggio dell'arte; un'identità artistica e culturale non può consentirsi d'essere monolitica, ma è la struttura psichica della collettività sociale, è il vertice dell'esistenza individuale e collettiva.
L'immaginario sociale e collettivo, che passa per un'Accademia di Belle Arti è la forma sintetizzata dell'atmosfera mentale di un intero periodo, che influenza comportamenti, idee e scelte, Cagliari questo immaginario non l'ha mai avuto.
Cagliari ha la necessità di un'Accademia per salvare i suoi archetipi culturali, trascinandoli nel terzo millennio dopo Cristo; l'Accademia a Cagliari è necessaria per garantire una crescita artistica e culturale costante nel tempo, per curare la propria memoria, per disporsi moralmente verso l'arte la creatività, per percepirsi in maniera differente

nel tempo e nella storia orientandosi verso il futuro, elevando il proprio territorio a contesto artistico di riferimento come un reale nodo linguistico della ricerca artistica contemporanea sul Mediterraneo.
Quello che è stata la civiltà dei Nur, merita di potere essere traghettato e arricchito, non mortificato da questo millennio dove l'arte e la cultura identitaria di popoli e territori rischiano di divenire algoritmici.

Artisti in residenza (e non residenti)

L'annuncio via Social Network è della Consigliera Comunale e presidente della commissione Innovazione tecnologica e comunicazione e politiche per il decoro urbano del comune di Cagliari, Giorgia Melis; e riguarda l'approvazione del progetto definitivo per ampliare i lavori della scuola media Manno e realizzare delle residenze d'artista nei locali dell'Ex Liceo Artistico, ossia l'ex complesso di Santa Teresa, tutto fantastico, se non fosse che altrove le residenze d'artista passano per partnership con Accademie di Belle Arti che a Cagliari non sono mai nate, quindi con chi dovrebbero mai dialogare a Cagliari, questi artisti internazionali in residenza?
Lo spazio nasce progettualmente con una dimensione che sembra più guardare al mondo dei curatori e dell'associazionismo, che non a una idea d'Alta Formazione Artistica residente con radici nel territorio.
Difatti l'obiettivo sembra quello di renderla un resort laboratorio, ossia predisporre la struttura all'accoglienza di artisti e curatori che possano condividere lo stesso contesto, una casa comune, adatta a ospitare e contenere le esperienze artistiche dall'incipit fino allo studio e alla mostra conclusiva.
Rivista inoltre la realizzazione di un impianto ascensore e di una rampa amovibile esterna per l'abbattimento delle barriere architettoniche che permetterà l'accesso a persone con ridotta capacità motoria, e sarà realizzata per garantire il raccordo plano-altimetrico tra la quota della pavimentazione della Piazza Dettori e il piano di calpestio dei locali interni.
Importo complessivo dell'intervento: 1.100.000,00 €
Adesso, con questa cifra, come nota il consigliere comunale del M5S Pino Calledda, non si poteva pensare a fare nascere un'Accademia di Belle Arti che si interfacciasse con accordi di rete, con i servizi turistici e alberghieri locali, per porre la formazione e lo studio dell'arte a contatto con altre realtà progettuali e rendere normativamente e progressivamente l'arte residente internazionale?

La soluzione sembra difatti non essere gradita neanche agli storici commercianti del luogo, che un tempo avevano dinanzi la vita di un Liceo Artistico, poi quella di decine di associazioni e che rischiano, come nota Sandro Mascia, barista e scrittore noir, di ritrovarsi un cantiere per anni che di fatto diventi poco più che un albergo. Ovviamente mi associo alla voce critica del Consigliere Comunale Pino Calledda, e con lui faccio notare, che Cagliari è oggi, l'unica città metropolitana d'Europa priva d'Alta Formazione Artistica, e sembra ci sia l'intenzione politica di fingere che questo non sia un problema, che sia naturale così, che qui non si debba formare artisti, ma che con l'arte si debba venire in vacanza nell'ex sede del Liceo Artistico che non diverrà Accademia di Belle Arti.

Percorso di Discipline Plastiche e Figurazione Tridimensionale, classe quarta, sez.D

2018-19

Docente: Domenico "Mimmo" Di Caterino

Contenuti:

- Test d'ingresso.

- Tre tavole di ricerca con schizzi preparatori tematici

("#Accademia #Cagliari").

- Progetto definitivo : Cinque punti di vista e relativa

ambientazione per Discipline Plastiche.

- Uno o più elaborati con un linguaggio artistico a scelta dello studente per Laboratorio Artistico (sempre in relazione al tema).

Macro Obiettivo minimo:

Sviluppare una capacità d'autodeterminazione di un percorso progettuale in un laboratorio.

Sviluppare capacità di elaborazione, progettazione e produzione autonoma, di base ad una libera ricerca di espressione ed autodeterminazione artistica.

Favorire la formazione di una personalità connessa con le problematiche sociali, culturali, economiche e produttive del territorio che vive ed abita.

#Orientailtuolinguaggio:

Diario di un orientatore!

"- Tu volevi fare una domanda? Dimmi...
- Abbiamo ascoltato voi orientatori con grande interesse, ma nella realtà pratica, che tipo di lavoro posso trovare con la maturità artistica o musicale?
- Tutti!
- Tutti?
- Partiamo da questa classe, sei seduto su una sedia, hai davanti un banco, altri banchi, cattedre e sedie, una lavagna mediale e una lavagna multimediale, tutto questo l'ha progettato un Designer per te e per noi; siamo in uno spazio classe organizzato all'interno di un edificio pensato con i suoi spazi per essere una scuola, il progetto di questa classe con i suoi spazi sarà stato eseguito da un Architetto o un Ingegnere; abbiamo visto dei video d'orientamento, del montaggio audio video se ne sarà occupato un operatore Audiovisivo e Multimediale; in un video c'è sempre una colonna sonora, che qualcuno ha composto, eseguito e interpretato in funzione di quel prodotto video, la musica è insieme alla pittura e alla Scultura, la forma di comunicazione linguistica più antica dell'umano; abbiamo visto nei corridoi di questa scuola murales, pannelli decorativi ed elaborati plastici ceramici, ossia l'identità e la storia didattica di questa scuola raccontata con i linguaggi dell'arte; abbiamo visto e siamo davanti a tutto questo con le nostre felpe e le nostre scarpe con dei loghi che indossiamo per distinguerci e identificarci, e siete stati guidati in questo orientamento, da del materiale che illustra le diverse attività di Licei e Istituti pensati da un grafico; ragion per cui avresti dovuto chiedermi: "Cosa posso non fare una volta conseguita una maturità artistica e Musicale?".
Avrei risposto: Lo decidi tu, non ti è precluso niente, anche perché la mentalità artistica creativa è trasversale a tutte le professioni e

professionalità dell'umano, immaginati tu che grazie ai linguaggi dell'arte lavoro anche io..."

"Grazie..."

"Figurati, siamo qui per questo!""

Dal "Diario di un orientatore", 30 Novembre 2018, Cagliari

————————

#Orientaillinguaggio: Diario di un orientatore!

"Il consiglio che ci sentiamo di darvi è che sia una scelta razionale, ponderata e personale.
Non dovete pensare che se un Liceo o un Tecnico Professionale è andato bene per un vostro amico o parente andrà bene per voi, non dovete pensare di non potere sopravvivere nelle scuole superiori senza il vostro compagno di classe o di banco delle medie inferiori.
Lo studio ha valore e rende, quando è passione individuale, quando ci si appassiona allo studio si studia, altrimenti se non si sente un percorso, non ci si appassiona e non si studia, si disperde lo studio e si disperde lo studente; la Regione Sardegna è la Regione con il più alto tasso di dispersione scolastica in Europa.
Forse questo avviene anche perché s'inseguono falsi miti, sarebbe forse il caso di dire e di dirci, che non esiste Liceo o Tecnico Professionale che sia agenzia di collocamento in grado di determinare lavoro e professione per tutti, diffidate da chi vi dice, "con il nostro diploma potrai sicuramente trovare lavoro", la verità è che ogni lavoro necessita di studio e applicazione derivante dalla passione, quando si ragiona di metodo di studio, si ragiona di metodo per comprendere e relazionarsi a problematiche di vario genere, che è quello che avviene in ogni settore e ogni professione, il metodo di studio lo si trova se ci si appassiona a ciò che si studia, questa è l'unica modalità d'orientamento possibile, ascoltare se stessi e comprendere su quale percorso si ha più voglia d'investire, su quale e quali materie si ha voglia di passare e investire più tempo.
Tutte le strade possono portare alla maturità, voi dovreste cercare la più comoda e stimolante per voi, capire la vostra intelligenza da che tipologia di linguaggio e di pratica si senta maggiormente attratta.
Lo studio di ciò che caratterizza la propria natura è quanto di più armonico uno vi possa augurare per il vostro percorso di studio, Claude Monet, un pittore impressionista diceva di volere dipingere così come un uccello canta, questo vuole dire studiare con passione, studiare qualcosa che si può sentire come parte integrante della propria natura."

Dal "Diario di un orientatore", Villasor

——

#Orientaillinguaggio: Diario di un orientatore.

#Orientaillinguaggio #Diariodiunorientatore

#Serdiana #Soleminis

"Non amiamo gli Open Day, dovrebbero scomparire, agli Open Day anteponiamo un'idea d'Orientamento fondata sull'Open Lab, ossia la possibilità di venirci a trovare per orientarvi in un laboratorio d'indirizzo seguiti da dei tutor, per tentare di comprendere se nel mondo dei Licei, questa tipologia di percorso di studio possa appassionarvi, il distinguo tra il buono e il cattivo studente lo fa soltanto la passione per il percorso di studio.

Gli Open Day, io personalmente li trovo insopportabili e li vieterei per decreto ministeriale, talvolta rasentano la propaganda:

i docenti propongono il loro percorso di studio come il migliore possibile, le scuole sembrano trasformarsi per una giornata in qualcosa che sembra quasi un centro commerciale, i docenti sembrano diventare politici che fanno promesse di lavoro o persone che lavorano al centro impieghi per il lavoro; nelle scuole si studia per fare si che lo studio diventi lavoro e non per trovare lavoro, anche perché non esiste lavoro al mondo dove non si debba studiare ogni giorno per tenersi aggiornati e continuare a lavorare; quindi da noi nessun Open Day, ma un laboratorio scolastico artistico d'indirizzo del biennio per capire se questi abiti dello studente possano starvi bene addosso; non mi va e non ci va, di salutare genitori sorridenti che escano dal nostro Liceo con la stessa felicità e spensieratezza di chi esce da un centro commerciale, non si sceglie un percorso di studio come fosse un iPad o un paio d'Adidas, la propria identità di studente si determina per vocazione e passione, lo studio è un processo e non un prodotto, per cui in una scelta così delicata, siate egoisti e ascoltate la vostra passione, chiedetevi cosa vi piacerebbe studiare praticamente per più tempo.

Tu, hai la mano alzata, vuoi fare una domanda?

- Prof. lei ha detto che nel suo liceo è anche possibile scegliere l'indirizzo d'Audiovisivo e Multimediale...

- Si, è uno dei possibili percorsi post biennio!

- Io ho una mia amica che studia Audiovisivo e Multimediale nel vostro Liceo e un'altra che invece studia nel Liceo di ....

- Vero, è una possibilità d'indirizzo, considera che nei percorsi Liceali Artistici sarebbe possibile anche arrivare a tredici indirizzi post biennio, proprio perché non tutti i linguaggi dell'arte richiedono la stessa tipologia d'intelligenza creativa, ma questa è una scelta da fare dopo il biennio, dove ci si orienta trasversalmente tramite il Laboratorio Artistico.

- Ma io non capisco ancora, perché ci hanno raccontato di essere l'unico Liceo dove ci fosse la possibilità del triennio Audiovisivo e Multimediale.

- Che ti devo dire?

Avresti potuto riportare l'esperienza delle tue due amiche, come vi dicevo prima, l'orientamento in questi anni sembra essersi ridotto a uno spazio di promozione e propaganda che mira soltanto a incrementare il numero degli studenti che si iscrivono, prestando poca attenzione all'aiuto verso la comprensione di un percorso di studio che valorizzi gli interessi del singolo, personalmente, come ti dicevo prima, ritengo sbagliato e fuorviante l'approccio che mira a rappresentare un percorso di studio come unico ed esclusivo rispetto ad altri, ma a questo punto per bilanciare, faccio presente che di Licei Artistici e Musicali in Italia non sono ve ne sono più di dieci, e che il nostro corso d'Audiovisivo e Multimediale vive spazi affini al Liceo Musicale e questo determina uno spazio proficuo e produttivo multimediale e musicale, immagina a esempio la possibilità pratica di realizzare un videoclip musicale."

Dal "Diario di un orientatore", Serdiana

— — — — — — — — —

#Orientaillinguaggio: Diario di un orientatore!

"Questa è la vostra giornata d'orientamento che riguarda i Licei.
Perché una giornata riguardante esclusivamente i Licei?

Perché dovete pensare all'istruzione Liceale come unico insieme, caratterizzato da un percorso comune di studio, a tutto gli studenti Liceali di 21 ore (22 dal terzo anno) di formazione comune; 21-22 ore che costituiscono lo scheletro comune di qualsiasi tipo di percorso Liceale.

Quello che distingue un Liceo da un altro, sono le ore d'indirizzo, soltanto in un Liceo ad indirizzo artistico le ore d'indirizzo saranno laboratori linguistici dell'arte (che lo studente determina dopo un biennio di studio e di percorso comune d'orientamento didattico interno), così come soltanto nel Liceo Musicale lo studio è quello della musica in quanto linguaggio (compositivo, interpretativo ed esecutivo). Nell'ambito di formazione di un percorso Liceale, dovete fare lo sforzo d'individuare delle materie o dei percorsi che sentite vi possano appassionare più di altri, anche perché, abbiamo letto su Focus, che sembra essere una scienza esatta (nell'isola più che mai), quella che quando uno studente non si appassiona al proprio percorso di studio, abbandona gli studi e smetta di studiare.

A tal proposito vi do una dritta, sapete come si acquisisce un metodo di studio?

Proprio assecondando le proprie passioni e motivazioni, assecondando la propria passione, quello che si studia con passione diventa lentamente metodo di studio, e più si studia e più ci si appassiona, e più ci si appassiona più lo studio diventa leggero, al punto che con lo studio si può anche volare, un poco come quella brochure informativa di quel Liceo che quello studente ha trasformato in un aeroplano di carta senza leggerla, noi non vogliamo stressarvi e non vogliamo convincere nessuno che questo sia il migliore percorso di studio, perché non esiste il migliore percorso di studio possibile per tutti, vogliamo soltanto tentare di farvi comprendere quello che accade da noi per far si che voi vi chiediate: "Ma mi posso appassionare a questo percorso di studio?

Potrei avere voglia d'affrontare le problematiche che questo indirizzo Liceale mi propone per 12-13 ore la settimana?

Potrei trarne piacere e beneficio maggiore rispetto a quell'altro percorso?"

- Prof.la stimo.

- Sono io che io stimo te, per la capacità di sopportazione di mattinate come questa, dove ciascun Liceo cerca d'attrarre la tua attenzione su di te, proponendosi come il miglior percorso possibile per te...".

Dal "Diario di un orientatore", Cagliari, 5 Dicembre 2018

— — — — — — — —

#Orientamento #Orientaillinguaggio

"...domande da fare? Non vedo mani alzate, questo ci fa pensare che o avete capito tutto o non avete capito nulla, ma a noi comunque ha fatto piacere incontrarvi e raccontarvi con cosa si confronta uno studente del Liceo Artistico e Musicale, vedo una mano alzata in fondo, dimmi...

- Volevo dirvi che almeno rispetto agli altri, ho avuto la sensazione che siate stati sinceri!

- Bisogna essere sinceri, a maggior ragione se creativi e se ci si orienta verso un percorso di studio come questo, etica ed estetica da sempre tendono a cercare una connessione, i linguaggi dell'arte in linea di massima sono sempre sinceri con se stessi e con gli altri, quando non si riducono a marketing, devono esserlo specialmente durante l'orientamento, nel vostro interesse, dove con voi si ragiona su possibilità e percorsi di studio.

Fatemi pensare a qualche esempio, ecco, pensate proprio al fatto di cronaca della tragedia dei sei morti al concerto di Sfera Ebbasta, in queste ore via Social Network e attraverso i mass media, lo si sta demonizzando, per dei testi, che a prescindere dalla loro pochezza, raccontano una realtà presente, sono una rappresentazione, che se non venisse raccontata si farebbe fatica a mettere a fuoco e con la quale non ci si potrebbe confrontare.

I linguaggi dell'arte sono degli strumenti preziosissimi per l'intermediazione e la comprensione generazionale, ma questo può avvenire soltanto se c'è onestà di base nella narrazione o nella comprensione della narrazione.

Qualcuno pensa a esempio in questa classe che la colpa della tragedia possa essere addebitata alla musica di Sfera Ebbasta?

- (in coro) Noooooooooooooo...

- Ecco anche secondo noi, perché a tutti i livelli, anche di genere, anche popolare, anche quando tutto si riduce a marketing, anche quando mostra o ci induce all'ascolto, di ciò che non si vorrebbe vedere o mostrare, tutti i linguaggi dell'arte restano uno strumento di scambio e di relazione dialettica e didattica tra generazioni."

Dal "Diario di un orientatore", Cagliari, 10 Dicembre 2018

——————————————

"I linguaggi dell'arte dovete considerarli come qualcosa di fluido e trasversale al genere, perché vi dico questo?
Perché di Licei Artistici che abbiano nel loro ambito la possibilità di convivenza e connivenza con un Liceo Musicale, in tutta Italia non se ne contano più di una decina, provate a pensare a quanto questo sia fertile dal punto di vista dell'interazione creativa, pensateci un attimo:
Quanto è importante per un operatore Audiovisivo e Multimediale la possibilità di potersi relazionare direttamente con un compositore o con chi potrebbe avere il compito di curargli la colonna sonora di un lungometraggio, cortometraggio o uno spot pubblicitario?
Quanto è importante per una produzione musicale autonoma o indipendente, avere a che fare direttamente con chi con immagini video dovrà con un videoclip narrarle?
Ma al di la dell'esempio scontato, pensate un attimo a come tutti i linguaggi dell'arte, dalla pittura alla grafica, dalla Scultura all'Architettura, dal Design all'audiovisivo, dalla musica alla Scenografia, abbiano a che fare con lo stesso tipo d'approccio creativo, compositivo, esecutivo e interpretativo; tutti i linguaggi dell'arte sono osservazione, riflessione ed espressione, nell'ambito del percorso Liceale Artistico e Musicale, l'espressione creativa del sé attraverso la conoscenza della grammatica compositiva artistica e musicale, che passa per l'analisi e lo studio della memoria dei linguaggi dell'arte che si vanno ad affrontare praticamente, diviene centrale, e tutta la formazione ruota intorno alla definizione e alla maturazione del sé creativo."

Da "Diario di un orientatore", Uta, Dicembre 2018

————————————————————————

" - Ma di base per iscriversi al Liceo Artistico o al Liceo Musicale serve talento?
- No!

- No?
- No, serve la creatività, qualità che da sempre accompagna la ricerca di senso della condizione umana; uno studente del Liceo Classico in fondo che talento avrebbe dovuto manifestare prima? Quello dell'andare al Bar a chiedere un caffè in greco o latino? Lo studio Liceale è passione e dedizione e tutto il sistema scolastico Italiano (e non) nella pratica accantona il talento nel nome del merito, lo studente ha il compito d'individuare la sua passione per fare si che meriti gratificazione.
- Capito!
- Da questo punto di vista l'istruzione Liceale Artistica e Musicale, è la più naturalmente umana, i linguaggi nascono tutti con un suono, la scrittura nasce tridimensionale su pietra e argilla, il suono e la visione nascono tridimensionali, questo è bene ricordarlo in un mondo di comunicazioni sempre più piatte e bidimensionali, di scritture e suoni digitali, l'istruzione artistica è sensorialmente a tre dimensioni, ci ricorda che il linguaggio nasce tridimensionale e in maniera relazionale rivolto all'altro, da questo punto di vista, penso di potere dire che si tratta del più umanistico dei percorsi possibili, perché così è stato nella storia dell'umano, cosa non da poco, in un mondo che va sempre più rintanandosi in tablet e personal computer, che chiudono in maniera autoreferenziale la comunicazione umana, in una modalità dove la comunicazione e la relazione sono un prodotto che pare essere post-linguistico, in questa tipologia di percorso il linguaggio si autodetermina attraverso relazioni e traiettorie di comunicazione che sanno essere comuni e condivise, attraverso i diversi spazi e laboratori linguistici dell'arte, condivisi.
- Grazie."

Dal "Diario di un orientatore", Cagliari, 18 Dicembre 2018

— — — — — — — — — —

"Chi esclude l'idea di potere frequentare il Liceo Artistico, perché si sente non portato per il disegno, perché quando disegna un albero di Natale si ritrova davanti a un fenicottero in vola, sappia che il Liceo Artistico non è più un Liceo dove si disegna e basta, è diventata una scuola dove l'arte si studia in quanto pratica linguistica, e dopo un biennio comune, ci si orienta verso l'indirizzo (o linguaggio) più connesso rispetto la propria indole creativa.
Vi faccio un esempio pratico, pensate alla copertina dell'ultimo album di Salmo, non è certo un ritratto Accademico o figurativo di chi ha la capacità di mettere a fuoco la realtà in maniera iperrealista, è un ritratto

eseguito da un bambino di otto anni, quel lavoro dal punto di vista grafico e comunicativo è un lavoro perfetto.

Quelli che "sanno disegnare bene" come dite voi, s'iscriveranno nel corso d'arti Figurative, ma i creativi che scopriranno di prediligere il disegno tecnico geometrico, con capacità logico, scientifiche e matematiche proseguiranno con i corso di Design o Architettura e Ambiente, quelli che invece lavoreranno su un tipo di comunicazione visiva industriale e riproducibile opteranno per un corso di Grafica o nel corso d'Audiovisivo e Multimediale, insomma, ciascuno dopo il biennio comune si muoverà in relazione alla propria area d'interesse linguistico creativa.

Il Liceo Musicale è invece l'unico Liceo che consente in parallelo, l'iscrizione al Conservatorio (Alta Formazione Musicale) o qualsiasi altro percorso Universitario, e che mette lo studente in condizione di proporsi con progetti musicali autonomi e autoprodotti una volta concluso il percorso di studio.

Importante considerare che Licei che possano interagire e progettare in autonomia su l'asse artistico e quello Musicale, in Italia se ne contano non più di dieci, la connessione tra i due universi linguistici è fondamentale, su pietra ad esempio nasce la Scultura come la Musica (chiedetelo a Pinuccio Sciola), questo Liceo è uno spazio di connessione e interazione creative tra le diverse specilaizzazioni linguistiche dell'arte contemporanea."

Dal "Diario di un orientatore", Capoterra, 20 Dicembre 2018
— — — — — — —

"Licei Artistici che comprendano anche la formazione superiore Musicale, in Italia non ve ne sono più di dieci, questo è naturalmente un valore aggiunto, pensate a quanto sia connessa la formazione artistica a indirizzo Audiovisivo e Multimediale e la formazione musicale ad esempio; pensate a come tracce e brani musicali siano spesso accompagnati da videoclip promozionali, pensate alle colonne sonore dei film o a quanto sia importante la musica che accompagna uno spot pubblicitario, questo ovviamente per sintetizzare dal momento che il linguaggio artistico e quello musicale si originano con la comunicazione dell'umano, dal momento che l'uomo comincia a scrivere su pietra e tavole d'argilla e comincia a suonare la pietra come primo strumento, pensata a come Pinuccio Sciola abbia connesso in tal senso la Scultura al suo suono e alla sua musica naturale.

Tornando al nostro Liceo e al distinguo tra i due indirizzi (quello Artistico e quello Musicale), va compreso come in entrambi i percorsi si imposti e si favori una mentalità progettuale (o se preferite compositiva creativa) nell'ambito delle ore d'indirizzo, lo studente del Liceo Artistico osserva, riflette e poi si esprime creativamente e progettualmente in relazione alla problematica d'indirizzo di riferimento, mentre lo studente del musicale ascolta, riflette e si esprime musicalmente, questo per dirvi che l'ambiente formativo del Foiso Fois è nella pratica laboratoriste multisensoriale...".

Dal diario di un orientatore, Samassi-Serramanna, 9-1-19

— — — — — — — —

"Non amiamo gli Open Day, ci sembrano funzionali a una comunicazione retorica che riduce l'istruzione pubblica, prima che a diritto costituzionale e ministeriale, a competizione tra scuole che si contendono studenti e iscrizioni quasi come simulassero d'essere attività commerciali.
Certi Open Day sembrano operazioni di marketing, programmazioni culturali e festival letterari, altri paiono vetrine per scuole che si presentano quasi come se offrissero i loro spazi e la loro collocazione più da agenzie immobiliari che da luoghi d'istruzione e formazione; altri ancora sembrano essere agenzie del lavoro sul territorio, con docenti che con i loro studenti sembrano promettere mentre il partito più votato dagli Italiani propaganda il reddito di cittadinanza nel nome di chi il lavoro l'ha perso.
A questa comunicazione costruita, talvolta illusoria e ingannatoria degli Open Day, anteponiamo un'idea di didattica costruita in ingresso. Chiediamo a genitori e studenti di aprire spazi di comprensione della passione come agente motivatore, perché è la passione che motiva verso l'autodeterminazione e l'autonomia di un metodo di studio, di ricerca culturale e professionale.
Ragion per cui, nessun Open Day da noi, ma un laboratorio d'orientamento d'indirizzo artistico biennale in un' ordinaria e quotidiana giornata di vissuto scolastico, una simulazione di una classe prima in ingresso, che faccia capire a studenti e genitori, se nell'asse dei Licei, l'istruzione artistica e musicale possa appassionare e motivare più di altri percorsi liceali d'indirizzo.
Perché l'unico dogma plausibile, per tentare di orientare il proprio studio, è ascoltare il proprio talento, la propria indole e la propria passione.
Un percorso di studio e di formazione, non può e non deve rischiare d'essere imposto e nel nome dell'imposizione demotivare lo studente. Nell'isola che ha il tasso di dispersione scolastica maggiore d'Europa,

noi non possiamo essere, in quanto pubblica istruzione agente demotivatore."

Dal "Diario di un orientatore", Sinnai, 9 Gennaio 2019

— —

"Intendiamoci, noi non siamo qui a tentare di convincere nessuno che la nostra tipologia d'indirizzo Liceale sia la migliore possibile per tutti voi, non è nel nostro interesse dirvi che siamo la migliore dell'offerta formativa possibile Liceale, non esiste il Liceo migliore possibile per tutti quanti voi contemporaneamente, esiste un migliore percorso possibile per ciascuno di voi, in base alla propria indole, talento, passioni, circostanze e interessi.
La scuola non trova lavoro agli studenti, a scuola gli studenti alimentano la passione necessaria che tradotta in studio diventa lavoro, ma lo studio non è un lavoro, lo studio determina lavoro.
Ragion per cui, siamo contentissimi d'incontrarvi e di conoscervi, ma non abbiamo niente da vendervi che non sia lo sviluppo di una forma d'intelligenza linguistica che è quella che passa per la progettazione e la composizione artistica e musicale.
Perché questa premessa?
Per far si che facciate una scelta di formazione con un minimo di cognizione di causa che passi attraverso di voi, per evitare che facciate ragionamenti come:

1) "Mi iscrivo in quel Liceo, perché è vicino casa, posso raggiungerlo in tre minuti e posso dormire fino a dieci minuti prima dell'inizio delle lezioni, io ho uno sport preferito, sono il campiono olimpionico internazionale di mandronite e voglio continuare a coltivare questo mio talento."
2) "Mi iscrivo in quel Liceo perché s'iscrive il mio compagna/la mia compagna di banca, siamo sedute nello stesso banco dalle scuole elementari, come potrò sopravvivere nel terribile mondo delle scuole superiori senza di lui/lei?
Come potrò fare amicizia e parlare e discutere con chi non ho mai parlato e discusso prima e non mi conosce?"
3) "Mi iscrivo in quel Liceo perché l'ha frequentato mia padre e li ha conosciuto mia madre, perché l'ha frequentato mio cugino, mia cugina, mia sorella e tante altre persone di famiglia, se è andato bene a loro perché non dovrebbe andare bene a me."

4) "M'iscrivo in quel Liceo perché così hanno deciso i miei genitori, perché devo sopportare questo che mi racconta questo orientatore? In fondo ho già scelto e sentire e sapere che succedere in altri Licei mi annoia e non mi serve a nulla."

5) "M'iscrivo in quel Liceo, perché mi hanno promesso che con quel titolo di studio, anche se non penso d'esserci portato, troverò sicuramente lavoro."

6) "M'iscrivo in quel Liceo perché ci sono i ragazzi più toghi e le ragazze più carine di tutta l'area di Cagliari città metropolitana."

Potrei continuare per ore, ma non lo farò, per la mia salute e igiene mentale come per la vostra, ma sappiate che sul serio per molti studenti come voi le considerazioni che si fanno sono queste, altrimenti come spiegare che uno studente su due nell'isola non arriva al diploma?

Noi pensiamo che non ci si appassioni sullo studio e non si ragioni sullo studio come passione prima che lavoro, per cui la premessa che dovreste farvi su tutto è:

Questo percorso di studio d'indirizzo può appassionarmi più di altri, questa passione può essere per me così forte da diventare professione al punto d'interessarmi e stimolarmi una vita in autonomia?"

Dal "Diario di un orientatore", Quartu, 10-01-2019

————————————————————

"Perché uno studente dovrebbe scegliere il percorso Liceale Musicale?

Perché ha come alternativa, qualora fosse interessato a studiare la musica come linguaggio, quella di frequentare il Conservatorio. Frequentare il Conservatorio per accedere ad un percorso d'Alta Formazione Musicale al Conservatorio dopo il quinquennio, vorrebbe dire, che per ottenere un diploma che abbia valore legale, necessiti frequentare con successo, la mattina un altro Liceo o un Istituto Tecnico, il pomeriggio cambiarsi d'abito e fare lo studente del Conservatorio.

Nel caso del Liceo Musicale è invece tutto dentro il percorso di formazione Liceale, perché a fine quinquennio si sarà in possesso di un diploma che consentirebbe l'accesso a qualsiasi tipo di percorso Universitario; si avrà la possibilità d'accedere al Conservatorio (con il quale si è convenzionati e in funzione del quale nasce questo percorso

Ministeriale); e qualora i casi della vita dovessero portare lo studente a non proseguire gli studi, si sarà comunque in condizione di auto prodursi, questo in virtù anche di laboratori come quello di Tecnologie Musicali che consentirebbero allo studente anche di autoprodursi e autodistribuirsi, non solo compositore e interprete, ma anche produttore.

Considerate che di Licei Musicali annessi a Licei Artistici, in Italia non ve ne sono più di dieci, questo consente di viversi degli ambiente di progettazione in maniera sinergia, e nel campo delle produzioni audio video, immagino capiate quanto questo sia importante, un videoclip musicale nasce in funzione della musica che accompagna, così come la colonna sonora di un film nasce in funzione della storia che racconta per immagini."

Dal "Diario di un orientatore", Scuola Media Dante, Pirri, Cagliari, 14 Gennaio 2019

— — — — — — — — — — — — —

"La scelta post biennio del Liceo Artistico non è da intendersi come definitiva, i linguaggi dell'arte sono tutti interconnessi.

Non esiste video che non abbia bisogno di una colonna sonora e/o di tracce audio, o di caratteri grafici d'accompagnamento rispetto all'informazione che emette; non esiste grafica che non sappia farsi anche animazione video; non esiste architetto o designer che non consideri il linguaggio plastico e la relazione con l'ambiente prima di progettare; la Scultura nasce menhir e poi diviene Dolmen facendosi Architettura; uno Scultore è educato al suono del battere la gradina su pietra sapendola ascoltare e il suo approccio al fare arte è anche uditivo, anche i primi suoni dell'umano presumibilmente sono espressi su pietra; su pietra e dentro la pietra nasce la pittura.

Perché vi dico questo?

Per farvi comprendere che il biennio comune serve per indirizzare lo studente verso l'area di progettazione e cognitiva di riferimento, che determina il metodo di studio che passa per quell'area della progettazione linguistica dell'arte, ma questo non preclude l'interazione e la conoscenza degli altri linguaggi dell'arte, i linguaggi dell'arte sono sempre interconnessi tra di loro; il pittore come il musicista ragionano in chiave progettuale di composizione di un insieme."

Diario di un orientatore, 14 Gennaio, scuola media Leopardi-Pirri

———————————————————

" – MA QUESTO NELLA VOSTRA BROCHURE È MANU INVISBLE?

– Certo è un nostro ex studente del corso di Grafica, pur essendo un artista visivo di fama internazionale, la sua prima formazione artistica è stata Grafica e si è mosso dal nostro Liceo prima di frequentare l'Accademia di Belle Arti di Milano.

– Ma allora voi conoscete il suo volto senza maschera?

– Certo, è stato proprio uno studente della Prof., ma per niente al mondo sveleremo la sua vera identità, per noi il marketing che ha saputo ritagliarsi e autodeterminare dietro la sua identità è motivo di grande vanto e di prestigio.

Ci riempie di orgoglio come stia riqualificando le aree urbane e periferiche degradate Cagliaritane.

Siamo tra i suoi principali complici, e come lui stia ridisegnando l'area Cagliaritana è anche frutto di un tipo di preparazione grafica che lo contraddistingue a livello internazionale, attraverso un linguaggio che ha saputo interpretare in maniera pura, annientando identità e narcisismo d'artista, questo forse proprio perché la sua formazione artistica ha un'impostazione specialistica grafica."

———————————————

"Nel mondo dei Licei, il Liceo Artistico è l'unico che consente durante il passaggio biennio-triennio di orientare la propria creatività verso il linguaggio dell'arte per il quale ci si sente più indirizzati naturalmente, non tutti i linguaggi dell'arte richiedono la stessa forma e tipologia d'intelligenza.
Lo studente del corso di Arti Figurative è molto diverso dallo studente del corso di Design o di Architettura e Ambiente, ha diversi media di lavoro, lo studente di Arti Figurative lavorerà con trespoli, cavalletti, colori, tavolozza, modello o modella vivente; lo studente di Architettura

e Ambiente disegnerà con righe, squadrette, goniometri, compassi, sarà comunque un creativo ma con una intelligenza più logica, scientifica, matematica e razionale di uno studente di Arti figurative, perché progetterà spazi o oggetti razionali e funzionali all'uso e all'utilizzo che se ne farà (con un'organica attenzione all'estetica), lo studente di Arti Figurative sarà invece più intuitivo, espressivo ed umanistico nella sua ricerca pittorica e plastica, lo studente di Arti Figurative è quello che voi identificate come "quello che sa disegnare bene", ma poniamo che voi dopo il biennio scopriate di non amare il Disegno tecnico geometrico che è alla base della progettazione dell'Architetto o del Designer e che scopriate per non essere portati per i linguaggi classici dell'arte, c'è allora la possibilità del corso di Grafica o di Audiovisivo e Multimediale.

Ragion per cui, se quando avete intenzione di disegnare un fenicottero rosa in volo, vi ritrovate davanti un disegno che sembra un cinghialetto in cinta raso al suolo, non disperate, è importante sapere pensare a quel cinghialetto in termini di comunicazione creativa grafica.

Pensate a proposito, alla copertina dell'ultimo album di Salmo, il rapper di Olbia (che ha frequentato un Liceo Artistico), so che l'avete tutti presente, quella copertina è il ritratto di Salmo fatto da un bambino di otto anni che non disegna di certo come Antonello da Messina, eppure dal punto di vista della comunicazione grafica è perfetto, perché tutti sappiamo disegnare o abbiamo disegnato così, perché si tratta di una forma riproducibile e modificabile su scala industriale e di un linguaggio che identifica una comunità, il grafico non cerca necessariamente la soluzione unica e originale, ma la soluzione fruibile che sappia disegnare una comunità di riferimento per questo o quel prodotto."

Dal "Diario di un orientatore", Pula, 16 Gennaio 2019

— — — — — — — — — —

"- Avrei una domanda...
- Dimmi...

- Quali prospettive di lavoro offre questo percorso di studio?

- Questa è una domanda che non amiamo e che ci imbarazza quando dobbiamo rispondere, perché ci sembra non consona e totalmente fuori luogo e contesto, una scuola non è un'agenzia per il lavoro, prima delle richieste del mercato per un lavoro va considerato come la passione per lo studio che poi diventa ricerca materializzi lavoro.

Come si può non amare il lavoro che si fa?

Come può essere bravo un docente che non ama stare in classe e fare ricerca con gli studi?
Come può un cuoco essere o diventare un bravo chef per lavoro se non ama cucinare?
Quello che mi sento di dirti è che uno studente che si iscriva e decida di frequentare un Liceo Artistico o Musicale, non rinuncia a nulla, nulla gli è precluso, il pensiero creativo è trasversale a tutte le discipline e professioni, pensa a quanto di ciò che vivi e vivete nel quotidiano dipenda dalla presenza o assenza del pensiero creativo.

La scelta di un percorso liceale o professionale dovrebbe avere sempre come fondamenta la tua passione, puoi immaginarti un musicista o un cantante che non ami la musica?

Scegliere un percorso di studio materializza con passione il lavoro, senza la passione di fondo per uno studio che possa tradursi in lavoro, che tipo di lavoratore si può diventare?
Vedo un altra mano alzata, dimmi...

- Volevo dire che mi ha fatto molto piacere ascoltare questo orientamento, finalmente abbiamo assistito a un discorso informativo di carattere generale nel nostro interesse, mi è anche piaciuto molto il fatto che non facciate degli Open Day ma dei laboratori di orientamento.

- Mi fa molto piacere tu abbia capito ciò che intendiamo per orientamento, grazie a te!"

Dal "Diario di un orientatore", Domus De Maria, 16 Gennaio 2019

— — — — — — — — — — — — — — — —

STATI FACEBOOK: TEST D'INGRESSO 2019-20

TEMA DI LAVORO #PERDIRE

*Questi sono i miei stati Facebook da Dicembre 2018 a Settembre 2019,
individuane dieci con un asterisco e commentali come più ritieni
opportuno, saranno la base teorica del tuo progetto annuale.*

Gli artisti attenti alla cornice o alla rifinitura del loro lavoro, ignorano il
loro essere dilettanti.

Dialogare con la Trap, per chi ha caricato di contenuti "politici" il
linguaggio, nel secolo passato, è necessario.

La furia dei Cagliaritani che sanno che a Napoli c'è un'Accademia
Borbonica, non è un motivo per aggredire gli ultrà del Napoli!

Napoli batte Cagliari un'Accademia di Belle Arti a zero, gol del
Madrileno nasone Carlo, Re borbone.

Babbo Natale non esiste, come l'Accademia di Belle Arti a Cagliari.

Ma la deputata, è stata aggredita al market, perché non si è
pronunciata su un'Accademia a Cagliari?

Fare, osservare e comprendere l'arte, è l'unica azione dialettica politica
che questo millennio rende possibile.

Artisti attempati, ribelli da giovani, che nel nome dell'essere divenuti
"vecchia scuola" osteggiano le nuove.

Allergico agli artisti che non avendo da dire, dicono "sto preparando
una mostra importante", puntualmente non arriva.

Le residenze d'artista sono strumento di privatizzazione politica del
pubblico, le boicotterei per principio.

Non comprate il libro di Max Papeschi, se proprio dovete comprate il
mio, PayPal e arriva ai vostri domiciliari!.

Gigi Riva vedrà il suo monumento in vita, non vedrà un'Accademia
dove verrà "studiato" come fatto artistico.

Noiosi artisti si apprestano a dipingere postando foto e hashtag, come se fosse un evento; amo il non commento.

Vi auguro di non realizzare ciò che desiderate di più, continuate a inseguirlo, questione di sopravvivenza.

"Le Sculture seppellitele nella terra, faranno da ponte tra i vivi e i morti."
Alberto Giacometti

Artisti passano la vita a collezionare i propri pezzi, sognano personale e catalogo, pensano sia storia.

Se non impari l'arte mettiti da parte!

La poesia come stato social è gratificazione dell'ego, selfie dell'apparire.

Artisti attempati pensano d'essere trasgressivi e scomodi dipingendo il sesso nel millennio di youporn.

Per dare sussistenza a un giovane si taglia il padre o il nonno che lo sostiene?

Restauratori abilitati alla professione più di 6 mila, nessuno passato per l'Accademia di Cagliari (neanche di Sassari).

Artisti che non hanno mai compreso che la rivoluzione si dona e non si vende, altrimenti è restaurazione.

La Rivoluzione in vendita è sempre mercenaria.

L'augurio è una jattura, auguratevi buon anno da soli e limitate il danno.

C'è chi fa di tutto per farti gli auguri perché vuole che tu gli faccia gli auguri, subdolo ricatto!

La democrazia non è mai accordata, perché accordarsi?

La democrazia legittima l'individualismo consumistico del "sono come sono"!

Cagliari non ha nel 2019 un'Accademia di Belle Arti, ma ieri hanno suonato i Subsonica.

Possibile che l'umano non sia stato capace di misurare lo scorrere del tempo senza l'ultimo dell'anno?

Quando un discorso comincia con "i giovani...", ho la consapevolezza di ascoltare qualcosa d'incomprensibilmente vecchio.

Ma Massimo Zedda è tra i sindaci disobbedienti sul decreto sicurezza gialloverde?

Una cosa sono le fake news altra sono le provocazioni, provocare una news non è "fotterne" una.

Ricevo troppe richieste "d'amicizia", che si stia preparando un colpo di stato al mio profilo?

L'algoritmo mi ha inviato l'amicizia d'addetti ai lavori che invitano a esporre con tributo espositivo.

A chi pensa che gli artisti siano solo "estrosi" ricordo che Licei Scientifici si chiamano "Michelangelo" o "Leonardo".

Nel 2019 ancora non si comprende che i simboli sono solo risultante del linguaggio comune.

Invocano discussioni pubbliche su linguaggi e simboli identitari e poi ti bannano non accettando discussioni.

Trovo le prese di posizione di Banksy colossali prese per i fondelli.

Chi commenta un linguaggio artistico come "bello" o "brutto" dovrebbe umilmente studiare.

Se critica è ordinaria dialettica linguistica, chi è il folle disposto a pagare uno che lo critichi?

Possibile che Lega e M5S, siano riusciti a trasformare anche Claudio Baglioni in un artista politico?

I Terroni sono prima di tutto umani, poi talentuosi, creativi, meritevoli e non servi del mercato, fatevene una ragione.

"Libero" ha presente che il Napoletano è la lingua più parlata in Italia dopo l'Italiano?

Meglio un'Accademia a Cagliari del reddito di cittadinanza.

Chi ha filmato i due di Guspini che si amavano, diffondendo il video, va condannato per atti osceni in luogo pubblico.

Ma Di Maio ha parlato dell'Accademia di Belle Arti a Cagliari?

Quando un artista si presenta come un professionista, ho sempre la sensazione che sia un dilettante.

Visual artist che si occupano di comunicazione d'immagine dei centri commerciali.

Ma quando Adriano Celentano sarebbe stato scomodo per il sistema?

Cagliari come nel 2008 non ha un'Accademia, non posso postare foto che attestino il cambiamento.

Sul serio Salvini avrebbe detto "se nasci a Cagliari rischi di non conoscere l'Alta Formazione Artistica'?

Ma sul serio qualche collega orientatore, pensa che si possa fare orientamento in un centro commerciale?

Artisti che si autoraccomandano sognando spazi espositivi su presentazione d'altri artisti che chiamano amici o fratelli.

Postano lavori con mille hashtag sull'arte contemporanea in cerca qualche "mi piace" in più di qualche addetto ai lavori.

Non amo gli artisti che non hanno studiato in un'Accademia e col social marketing attaccano le Accademie.

Artisti senza scorza che chiamano la loro incompetenza sensibilità.

Lino Banfi in Commissione Unesco da l'idea di cosa sia un artista per un algoritmo.

Per fare orientamento in un centro commerciale Lino Banfi sarebbe un docente perfetto.

Un Maestro non è un protagonista, valorizza l'armonia dell'orchestra.

Un guerriero nuragico non ha nessun problema nell'indossare un copricapo con le corna.

Ma Lino Banfi farà presente all'Unesco che a Cagliari non c'è mai stata un'Accademia?

Incubo: Adriano Celentano che vuole insegnare la bellezza a Sferaebbasta con un cartoon.

L'Ex Art un resort, l'Ex ospedale marino un albergo, un'Accademia proprio non la si vuole?

"Libero" ci dice che la crisi economica è proporzionale all'aumento dei gay Italici, interessante teoria economica.

Solo a me è parso che rete quattro abbia ridotto gli Shardana a guerrieri mercenari di classe agiata?

A Cagliari c'è un'Accademia che è un corso di formazione professionale per estetiste!

Una Scultura ci seppellirà.

Il linguaggio nasce a tre dimensioni su pietra.

L'arte è questione di vocazione, nessun talento e nessun merito.

Non immagino guerrieri Shardana ridotti ad amministrare interessi condominiali.

A Cagliari non c'è un'Accademia ma c'è un caffè per gli artisti!

In origine era pietra e Scultura, poi è arrivata l'Architettura.

In origine un creativo guardò un macigno e lo chiamò Menhir, nacque il linguaggio dell'arte.

Talvolta quello che si ha davanti è un limite per il quale non si guarda oltre.

Perché chi mi critica gratuitamente mi toglie l'amicizia su faceburd? In fondo non è mai stato mio amico!

"Arte partecipata, street art, public art...", ma parlate semplicemente di linguaggio dell'arte e fate le persone serie.

Ma Paolo Fresu sa che a Cagliari non c'è un'Accademia di Belle Arti?

Mi annoia la politica del merito e del talento, preferirei si ragionasse di vocazione.

Ma è per i pastori sardi che non si parla dell'assenza dell'Accademia a Cagliari in queste Regionali?

Distinguere l'umano tra buono e cattivo è funzionale al cattivo.

Ma è obbligatorio per "artisti" e "intellettuali" dichiarare il proprio voto fuori della cabina elettorale?

La spiritualità ha un valore di mercato troppo elevato e interiore per essere decantata materialmente via facebook.

Solinas ha già parlato di un'Accademia di Belle Arti a Cagliari?

Ma un alleanza Zedda Cinquestelle per le Comunali Cagliaritane, prevederà l'Accademia di Belle Arti?

Non amo spazi privati delimitati, distorcono la complessità del reale.

Trovo mostruose le mostre che riducono l'artista a oggetto in esposizione da fotografare con il suo lavoro.

Sono intollerante agli "artisti" che si propongono come fossero soli al mondo, servi di spiccioli che chiamano mercato.

Quando tra "artisti" ci si chiama "fratello", il fratello può essere Caino come Abele.

Artisti che invidiano altri artisti dandogli degli invidiosi che li invidiano.

Brucia così tanta arte al giorno che una cattedrale non vale una messa.

Presuntuoso l'umano che ambisce a salvare il pianeta, pensi a salvare l'umano in questo pianeta.

A qualcuno dall'uovo di Pasqua è uscita l'Accademia di Belle Arti di

Cagliari?

Quanti di voi hanno passato pasquetta nel giardino dell'Accademia di Cagliari?

Salvatori della patria confinano l'umana condizione a limiti e confini, la comunità è oltre la patria, non ne ha bisogno.

Poche cose sono noiose quanto la banalità della creatività elevata a professione, l'arte è solo vocazione.

L'ignorante legge immagini senza contenuti, cartelli stradali per i "mi piace" degli scemi che seguono.

Amo il fango gratuito, leviga la pelle.

Sa dia de sa Sardigna senza un'Accademia di Belle Arti a Cagliari!

Cagliari: due sedi di Casa Pound e neanche un'Accademia.

L'arte gioca innalzando l'asticella del limite del linguaggio.

Sant'Efisio farà il miracolo dell'Accademia di Cagliari?

La sicurezza è nell'umano che sa interagire e integrarsi con gli altri.

Chi non sa essere informale vive la trincea della formalità.

I nemici intelligenti, sono buoni consiglieri, i nemici tonti sono invece più fastidiosi delle zanzare e dei buoni amici.

KISS (Keep It Simple, Stupid, non complicate le cose).

Non amo chi, privo di coscienza dei propri limiti, vive per limitare gli altri.

L'Art Brut ha convinto alienati e disturbati che siano artisti, in realtà l'arte è solo loro terapia, povero Dubuffet!

Non è l'arroganza di chi impone a spaventarmi, mi spaventa chi la serve per ritagliarsi spazi di mediocrità.

Oltre che in un'Accademia d'Alta Formazione Artistica, mi sono formato in un centro sociale occupato.

Scolpire la pietra non è archeologico, è sempre contemporaneo, è l'origine dell'umano.

Alla Biennale di Venezia preferisco la televisione di Barbara D'Urso, amo le avanguardie popolari.

Un'Accademia di Belle Arti, nella sua pluralità linguistica, è sempre internazionale e sociale.

Il presuntuoso ignorante, pensa che quattro pennellate su tela facciano "l'artista". Non basta una vita di studio.

In arte, i termini "dilettante" e "professionista", sono usati con troppa leggerezza.

Artisti che bramano il catalogo, artisti imposti dal catalogo, io preferisco i fuori catalogo.

Amo chi con una pennellata al giorno toglie il medico di torno.

Le bi-personali sono personali a due teste, negano la personale che divorano, mostruosità da bazar curatoriali.

Tu mi stalkeri per farmi guardare il tuo dito? Io ti banno e guardo la luna che porta fortuna.

Chiudendo limiti e confini si può affermare che tutto va bene nel proprio territorio.

Prima d'inviarmi i vostri Santini elettorali, abbiate la dignità d'esprimervi sulla questione Accademia.

Votare democraticamente può non essere molto dissimile da disobbedire civilmente.

Il Liceo Artistico a Cagliari nasce nel 1967 come sede distaccata del Ripetta di Roma.

Senza il corso serale per lavoratori, Cagliari non avrebbe mai avuto un suo autonomo Liceo Artistico negli anni settanta.

Banksy che lamenta di non avere mai esposto alla Biennale di Venezia fa sorridere.

Amico è chi considera un'Accademia di Belle Arti a Cagliari più che necessaria.

Mark Caltagirone non esiste, come l'Accademia a Cagliari, l'ha rivelato Pamela Prati in lacrime.

Votato, anche se comincio a sentire antidemocratico delegare.

Riesco sempre a votare in Europa partiti che in Italia non superano il due per cento.

Il partito Comunista ha preso lo 0,90 per cento, molto meglio dello 0,30 di Forza Nuova e di Casa Pound.

I compagni che mi tolgono l'amicizia su Facebook perché non abbastanza comunista non li avevo considerati.

L'Alta Formazione Artistica a Cagliari la vorrebbe anche il centro destra.

Agli artisti che si mettono a disposizione preferisco gli indisposti e indisponenti, hanno più dignità.

Pamela Prati, è stata privata di parola ospite di "Chi l'ha visto?", voleva raccontare la sua sull'Accademia di Cagliari.

Marco Carta a Milano, non poteva rubare l'idea dell'Accademia di Brera?

Chi sostiene che l'arte (sotto qualsiasi forma) possa spaventare bambini è un orrido umano che spaventa gli animali.

La politica dovrebbe sostenere gli artisti, ma in questa campagna elettorale non sono gli artisti a sostenere la politica?

Quale Italia democratica con una città metropolitana priva d'Alta Formazione Artistica?

Fico pensa che possa bastare una fotografia con il pugno chiuso per intercettare l'elettorato di sinistra?

Greta Thunberg ha deciso d'abbandonare gli studi per migliorare l'ambiente con un'Accademia di Belle Arti a Cagliari?

Trovo volgari le aste, per qualsiasi causa vengano bandite, danno l'idea dello schiavi in vendita al miglior offerente.

Che Cagliari non possa avere un'Accademia di Belle Arti, perché nell'isola è presente quella di Sassari è una fake news.

La Lega che vuole chiudere i centri sociali Cagliaritani vuole aprire l'Accademia?

Essere di sinistra vuol dire trovare qualcuno a cui dare del fascista.

Essere di destra vuole dire recintare le diversità per questioni di ordine.

La questione dell'Accademia assente a Cagliari ha un peso produttivo politico ben maggiore di rifiuti e differenziata.

QUANDO ERO MARIO PESCE A FORE

Negavamo l'Accademia degli anni sessanta

Negli anni novanta l'onda dei movimenti generazionali, che n attraversò e determino il "Mario Pesce a fore", connettendosi agli anni sessanta, ne negava gli equilibri di peso e potere che avevano determinato, negavamo l'idea dei Maestri che ci trattavano e giudicavano come fossimo bambini irresponsabili che necessitassero della loro guida, quando era chiaro che si era dinanzi a una rappresentazione di un'idea di arte e cultura che nel nome di una "Rivoluzione" mai stata si consegnava al mercato e nel nome del mercato negava il pubblico come istituzione.

"Mario Pesce a Fore" negli anni novanta aveva compreso, come l'interesse generale e generazionale del belpaese si stesse plasmando a immagine e somiglianza degli anni sessanta.

Questo per non parlare di mezze figure e caricature della storia, che avevano come merito storico e culturale, esclusivamente quello anagrafico, e vivevano di rendita per la mitografia del periodo, che attraversava trasversalmente Università, Accademie, interessi privati e movimenti sociali.

Dall'osservatorio di ciò che era il "Mario Pesce a Fore", tutto sembrava ingigantito, la mediocrità e l'ipocrisia di una generazione era edificata dai media e nell'immaginario di una generazione che si arricchiva negando quella che aveva generato, i padri negavano lo spazio artistico ai figli, iconoclasticamente si negavano le icone delle nuove generazioni, per rendere Accademia e vecchia scuola le proprie.

Da quel momento, dagli anni settanta che hanno represso i novanta (sempre che non fossero imposti dal mercato), lo scenario della cultura contemporanea è diventato di anno in anno, progressivamente, sempre più bigotto.
Certe suggestioni artistiche, sono state espulse dal dibattito, considerate di cattivo gusto e rivoltanti, nelle migliori delle ipotesi ridotte a narrazioni di comodo semplificate, tutto questo ci ha portato dinanzi a uno scenario contemporaneo, dove il contemporaneo non lo si comprende più, dove si rinnegano i nuovi linguaggi nel nome del "non ci capisco nulla".
Eppure è il trauma dello scontro generazionale che scardina convenzioni, canoni e abitudini grammaticali dell'arte, accettate come indiscutibili, senza lo scontro generazionale e la passione del confronto generazionale, i linguaggi dell'arte non hanno passato e neanche futuro.
"Mario Pesce a Fore" mirava a fare smuovere l'interpretazione di un contesto e un'idea di arte e cultura, che nella Napoli di quegli anni si stava apprestando a essere da cartolina, dove l'unico profilo artistico professionale possibile, era quello di coltivare rendite di posizione personali; l'idea era quello di abbattere le pareti e i riferimenti per porre l'arte in quanto linguaggio al centro del reale dibattito pubblico.
La sfida artistica di una generazione a quella che la precede, controlla e governa, è il fissare il punto del dove è e chi è, senza questo la storia non ha storia, con la propria storia si possono comprendere i movimenti e i linguaggi dell'arte che seguono, per questo, provocatoriamente mi sento di dire, che gli anni sessanta sono stati anni d'indeterminazione storica, che oggi si traduce nell'insignificante, di artisti che nascono e muoiono in tempi così brevi che neanche ci si accorge che siano nati.

IO, BOCCIONI, SOFFICI E MARIO FRANCO

Era il 1911, Ardengo Soffici era un intellettuale affermato, appena rientrato da Parigi, visitò una mostra dei Futuristi a Milano e scrisse su "La Voce" che ne era rimasto sdegnosamente deluso, lo venne a sapere Umberto Boccioni, che ritenne opportuno radunare tutti i suoi amici Futuristi e prendere il treno per Firenze, dove sapeva abitava Soffici; riuscirono a trovare Soffici, era seduto amabilmente a un tavolino di un caffè, il caffè "Giubbe rosse", era con il letterato Prezzolini e lo scultore Medardo Rosso.

Umberto Boccioni era uno Scultore di movimento, non esitò a schiaffeggiare il "critico", si scatenò una rissa furibonda e intervenne la polizia, la sera dopo a Santa Maria Novella fù invece Soffici che volle rendere il favore ai futuristi che tornavano a Milano, qualche anno dopo i due si riconciliarono tramite Aldo Palazzeschi.

Nel 2000, io con un gruppo di amici e artisti, il "Mario Pesce a Fore", prendemmo in ostaggio nella facoltà di lettere a Napoli, il docente e critico Mario Franco, me lo ricordavo da Maestro di "Teorie e tecniche dei Mass Media" dirmi:

"bella cosa questa del Mario pesce a fore, l'unica cosa che non funziona è il nome, è troppo local, dovresti cambiarlo, servirebbe un nome magari in Inglese…", da studente lo ascoltai in silenzio, tentati di spiegargli che si voleva essere popolari e rompere gli schemi convenzionali di un'Accademia che sembrava essere un nodo passivo del sistema dell'arte e del mercato globale, piuttosto che un ente di ricerca con lui che continuava ad affermare che il nome non si prestava a una esperienza da sistema dell'arte, ero uno studente e gli diedi ragione; qualche anno dopo il caso volle che per "Adunata sediziosa" nell'ambito del "Contromaggio dei movimenti" con la complicità del Laboratorio Okkupato S.K.A. lo prendessimo in ostaggio in un convegno organizzato nel nome di questa performance di cui lui era all'oscuro, assaltammo lo spazio e lo chiudemmo al pubblico, lui voleva in qualche modo ironizzare su quello che stavamo rappresentando e prese la pistola giocattolo di Luigi Ambrosio e me la puntò contro, in quel momento fece proprio ciò che Soffici fece con i futuristi, ragion per cui come Umberto Boccioni, per la buona riuscita della performance non ebbi scelta, fui costretto a dargli uno schiaffo, lanciargli gli occhiali in aria e ripristinare l'intervento prima della nostra fuga.

Concluse l'intervento in sala come se nulla fosse accaduto dicendo: "questi interventi e queste modalità performatiche le trovo estremamente datate, cose da anni sessanta e settanta, oggi soltanto degli ingenui e degli sprovveduti si possono porre nei confronti del sistema dell'arte in questa maniera."

Non so se mi sono mai riappacificato con Mario Franco d'allora, ma nel 2014, per una collaborazione con Lobodilattice, mi venne in mente il precedente, ragion per cui gli rivolsi qualche domanda, in fondo la dialettica nel sistema dell'arte, passa anche per lo sberleffo, lo schiaffo e il pugno, e le Accademie servono anche a rendere anche scontri culturali e ideologici percorso e processo creativo.

Vi ripropongo su Cagliari Art Magazine, il nostro dialogo, datato 2014 ma ancora attuale:

MARIO FRANCO: FACEBOOK? LA FABBRICA "POP" DEL CONSENSO DELL'ARTISTA CHE VERRÀ.

Regista, studioso del Cinema Napoletano. Fondatore della prima sala di essai napoletana, la "Cineteca NO", e successivamente della "Cineteca Altro. Si occupa da anni di cinema d'avanguardia, d'arte e teatro.

Ha documentato incontri di rilievo con artisti internazionali del calibro di Warhol. Docente dell'Accademia di Belle Arti di Napoli di "Teorie e tecniche dei Mass Media".

Scrive recensioni e editoriali per diversi quotidiani e riviste d'arte.

— — — — —-

Napoli è da sempre una città in grado di caratterizzare e possedere la mutazione dei linguaggi sociali e comportamentali e farli propri, questo secolo dell'estetica del "selfie", delle app e dei social network, sembra stia, con la complicità del mercato dell'arte appiattendo e canonizzando i linguaggi dell'arte, in cosa l'identità linguistica, intesa come anima artistica, resiste a questo processo?

Fu il futurismo a teorizzare il «completo rinnovamento della sensibilità umana avvenuto per effetto delle grandi scoperte scientifiche». Il discorso da allora in poi può esser giudicato semplicistico o complesso.

Ogni forma di comunicazione ha sulla psiche degli uomini un'enorme influenza.

Il mondo è trasformato continuamente.

Questi cambiamenti sono altrettanti modificatori della nostra sensibilità.

FB rientra in queste nuove modalità di comunicazione.

Il fatto che dia spazio ad una sfrenata autorefenzialità e ad una volgarità di temi e di parole è il sintomo di una moderna sfiducia nella democrazia rappresentativa (giudicata non più in grado di funzionare), ma anche di un'assenza di ipotesi alternative.

Nella maggior parte dei casi si moltiplicano i sentimenti xenofobi e razzisti o si accede ad un "buonismo" da romanzetto rosa.
FB è anche un indicatore del crescente analfabetismo "di ritorno" che è tratto tipico di un'Italia in recessione non solo economica ma anche culturale.

Napoli, città disastrata e senza servizi moderni, trova in un'autocompiacimento nostalgico e disperato la sua filosofia lenitiva. Non riesce a produrre artisti in grado di imporsi a livello internazionale, ma solo figure epigonali, spesso interessanti, mai innovative.

Sulla mutazione in corso dei linguaggi dell'arte, godi di un punto di vista privilegiato, quella della storica cattedra di Teoria e tecnica dei mass media all'Accademia, come sta mutando nella percezione dei giovani artisti, il tempo e il ritmo di trasmissione dei propri processi artistici multimediali nell'epoca dello smartphone?

O in una qualche maniera su un modello bipolare indotto, la consapevolezza della relazione tra "arte e vita" continua a viaggiare processualmente, su un processo che mira a costruire figure d'artisti destinate a interagire con gli "addetti ai lavori" continuandoli ad anteporre per specializzazione, a processi dettati da una applicazione?

L'utilizzo compulsivo dei social network inteso come trasmissione di messaggi o come "condivisione" di messaggi altrui contribuisce a formare le nostre opinioni.

Smartphone e tablet hanno reso familiare tecnologie digitali anche a chi era refrattario all'uso del computer. L'autoreferenzialità del selfie ha ampliato il vecchio slogan di Warhol sui "15 minuti di celebrità" ancora legato ai media generalisti come la stampa e la TV.

Quanto è pronto il mondo dell'arte proveniente dal secolo passato, ad accogliere l'incredibile mutazione di linguaggio in corso e a interrogarsi su come gran parte dell'economia dell'arte, legata al secolo passato, stia o possa scomparire?

Mi riferisco ovviamente al fatto che la comunicazione artista-pubblico possa non passare più per gli spazi preposti e questo finisce con mettere in discussione anche il ruolo storico del critico moderno, che in qualche modo ad oggi, ha raccolto una sorta di diritto di rappresentanza e di delega, sulla trasmissione di senso del lavoro di un artista.

I social network hanno sviluppato una relazione "connettiva" con il mondo.

E il connettivo determina una psicologia di gruppo, sia priva di identità, sia in grado di sviluppare nuove competenze.
Le relazioni condizionanti tra tecnologia e creatività sono più complesse di quanto sembri.

Più il nostro pensiero è critico, più è distante dalla massa.

La distanza che separa l'arte contemporanea dai suoi fruitori è sempre più profonda.

Al suo posto si insinua, con sempre maggior successo, la fotografia e il video: linguaggi semplificati e maggiormente aderenti alle esigenze di un pubblico medio, abituato alla decodificazione di messaggi visivi "riconoscibili" grazie alla pubblicità, alla televisione, alla rete.

Questa nuova "arte pop" trova sempre più consenso ed al suo interno cominciano a nascere nuovi artisti e nuovi comunicatori.

IL DISEGNO CHE MI PIACE

Mi piace il disegno che sa essere gesto immediato, che confina con lo scarabocchio ma l'eleva come sintesi cognitiva dell'atto del disegnare e il piacere dell'insegnare che accompagna il segno.
Mi piace il disegno che sa essere insolente e non conosce l'asservimento e la servitù della decorazione, che in tale maniera si

pone come solco trionfante, che con il suo percorso sembra studiare e integrare visibile e percepibile, che nota e connota idee quasi come se si temesse di perdere segno e memoria (quasi come se con il gesto si stesse rincorrendo il proprio sogno).

Un disegno non è mai uguale all'altro, parlo a spazio, tempi e ambienti diversi, come le note risuonano nello spazio, risponde a momenti diversi e diverse capacità di messa a fuoco sulla propria immagine e immaginazione, è sempre e comunque soltanto "studio", linee, tracce, percorsi e viaggi guidate dallo sguardo di chi disegna.

Quello che si abbandona su carta, su tela o su pietra (dove nasce la Scultura, il Design, la scrittura e'Architettura) è un mappa che segna il viaggio e il percorso di chi solca il segno, e se il segno è profondo resta nel tempo, oltre l'istante del suono e del tempo del corpo che l'ha prodotto.

Il segno e il disegno non hanno età, non è una lingua che nei millenni muta e non è comprensibile, in fondo cosa è cambiato tra i Nuragici e Giacometti?

Cosa è cambiato tra i pesci degli Egiziani e quelli di Matisse?

Segno e disegno sono l'essenza della nostra umanità, il nostro vero testamento grafico, sono il nostro mondo alternativo, per questo diffido dal "ben fatto", dall'imitazione che sembra togliere al segno lo sforzo e la fatica della vita, riducendo il contorno di una forma a stasi estetica ed estatica.

Amo i disegni veloci, che annotano informazioni e impressioni, che esorcizzano memoria e paura di perderla, mi piace disegnare come se un disegno ne chiamasse un altro, come se una pagina ne chiamasse un'altra, come se una tela non avesse senso se non seguita da un'altra, e poi mi piace che questo si allontani da me, che abbia una propria vita autonoma, che con me non abbia nulla a che vedere, perché l'importante è avere segnato, quasi come se si trattasse di un esorcismo, rivolto a non so chi o cosa, ma qualcosa mi dice che il maligno da sempre lo si teneva lontano così, attraverso l'informazione dell'energia che c'è dietro il gesto umano del raccontarsi e sintetizzarsi con il segno.

Il disegno è: sono questo e ho vissuto questo.

Il disegno è il mio come il tuo passato prossimo, non c'è nulla d'eterno e l'artista che sogna l'eternità con il suo disegno è idiozia pura e non distillata incapace d'ascoltare la sua naturale
istanza d'urgenza.

L'origine locale del segno

Trovo noioso l'approccio all'arte e al disegno "professionale", pittura e scultura esistono d'almeno 50000 anni, le pitture esistono da quando non esistevano strade ma solo sentieri naturali, frequentati regolarmente d'animali che si muovevano per sopravvivere.

I linguaggi dell'arte nascono per esplorare i luoghi dove si arriva e dove conduce la vita, esplorano il mistero della realtà.

Oggi quello che chiamiamo cultura artistica, più che fondata sull'idea dell'esplorazione del luogo dove si arriva, sembra impostata sulla partenza e la mobilità incessante, da tre secoli regna la balla (nata in parallelo con la Rivoluzione industriale) che l'arte debba essere qualcosa d'internazionale e non qualcosa di localmente internazionale, questo falso storico ha portato alla cultura dei resort d'artisti in residenza che giocano a fare gli artisti internazionali, quando in realtà in un contesto iperconnesso e iperglobalizzato come quello contemporaneo, gli artisti sono in ogni dove, e ovunque risiedano, internazionali.

Le specializzazioni artistiche contemporanee, anche in certi approcci "Accademici" pittorici e plastico scultoree, sembra si rifiutino di esplorare il mistero e la meraviglia della conoscenza e coscienza dell'umano, anzi, nel nome del "si fa così", sembrano eluderli.

Nella storia dell'umano, l'arte nasce per camminare da subito con l'umano, in autonomia si muovono insieme, il talento creativo e la necessità di scambiarsi informazioni complesse attraverso segni e disegni, nascono insieme.

L'artista disegnava illuminato da torce di carbone in grotte, riusciva a visualizzarli come segni (e sogni) al buio, erano pietra e pigmento, i segni erano rituali, scorrevano privi di confini, in ogni dove linguisticamente nascevano linguaggi e culture visive simili, passato e futuro erano il quei segni la sintesi dell'altrove da indagare.

Nel paleolitico si utilizzava già la prospettiva (ma non quella Rinascimentale, una prospettiva gestaltica, intuitiva, che serviva a misurare e indagare praticamente lo spazio), in qualsiasi epoca e momento si disegni, si sa che ci sono cose più vicine e più lontane, non è solo questione ottica, ma tattile, tocco e mi muovo nello spazio e lo comprendo; la prospettiva all'origine del linguaggio è apparizioni e sparizioni, intermittenti come le luci di natali o le note di un pianista, ma ininterrotto, fluido, incessante, il linguaggio dell'arte è l'elettricità dell'umano.

Quell'arte "primitiva" è nata e rimasta sul posto, è nei posti e nei luoghi, che con segni disegni, pitture, sculture e percorsi, l'uomo indaga le sue similitudini umane e i suoi distinguo culturali (sempre simili), per connettersi a distanza a se stesso, possibile che il forte e significativo patrimonio artistico residente isolano, non abbia ancora materializzato a

Cagliari un'Accademia di Belle Arti che connetta la coscienza e conosce dell'arte in formazione residente a Cagliari, con l'altrove?

— — — — — —

Il disegno non ferma il tempo!

Non esiste linguaggio artistico che possa fare a meno del disegno, non a caso il disegno è alla base di tutti i linguaggi, video compreso, non si può sostituire l'istruzione artistica con nessuna altra materia di fondamenta che non sia il disegno.

Il disegno non lo si può considerare finalizzato esclusivamente alla realizzazione di pitture o sculture, disegnare vuole dire improntare, solcare, tracciare, vuole dire sondare il limite tra la cecità e il tatto, dove s'incontrano mano, occhio e mente.

Il disegno nasce per dare forma al concetto, anche quando il concetto è assente ma è da indagare, è la maniera di fare apparire quello che non c'è o che c'è e al momento non si vede.

Legare il disegno esclusivamente all'idea Rinascimentale, vuole dire non comprenderlo, la realtà del disegno è l'origine di tutti i linguaggi, precede di molto il linguaggio scritto e l'architettura.

Il disegno è l'origine dell'arte come della vita, è come il canto, è qualcosa che accompagna la storia dell'umano da almeno quarantamila anni, altro che Rinascimento.

Il disegno è quel luogo dove s'incontrano il non volere vedere e le visioni, è qualcosa di molto più profondo e misterioso di quello che passa nei laboratori Accademici d'Arte, non ha nulla a che vedere con il collezionismo d'arte, è elemento essenziale del rituale della condizione umana, quanto il canto e la danza.

Il disegno è ritmo grafico che accompagna gli umani nella scansione del loro tempo, si muove navigando a vista, tra errori e correzioni di rotta, in relazione allo spazio e al tempo, la tensione della comprensione lo muove, si agita dalla resistenza dei tempi lunghi di comprensione dell'umana condizione.

Le linee, i segni, ridisegnano la memoria e la tendono verso futuri movimenti, il disegno è mosso dal difetto della messa a fuoco, dall'impossibilità di fermare il tempo.

Il disegno è lo strumento di conciliazione tra presenza e assenza, pitture e sculture in origine erano lo strumento di dialogo con i defunti, la rappresentazione della loro memoria.

Il disegno è la compagnia dell'invisibile, sono la presenza dell'assente, sono la visione non visibile, sono la materia non materiale.

Il disegno è la grammatica del linguaggio, dello spirito e dell'anima dell'umano, è l'invisibile essenze che ci accompagna, sempre al nostro fianco.

Il disegno è dei vivi

Quando disegno, ho sempre la sensazione di scolpire, anche quando scrivo, lavorando su una superficie bidimensionale mi sento a tre dimensioni.

I gesti sono gesti che si compiono nell'aria, il segno e il disegno nascono su pietra, sento che sono a tre dimensioni, il disegno lo sento più vicino alla Scultura che alla pittura.

Tra artisti (anzi tra chi segna, disegna e insegna) i gesti e i segni dell'arte, sono fuori dal tempo, in un altro tempo, sono diagrammi disegnati, sono il riappropriarsi di un linguaggio umano privo di limiti.

Il disegno è la connessione con l'altro, è la relazione a tre dimensioni con se stessi e con gli altri; si può girare il mondo ovunque e comunque, si scopriranno sempre delle affinità con la propria cultura artistica, visiva e iconica, dovunque si vada attraverso il segno passano delle informazioni che vanno oltre le distanze della lingua scritta e parlata.

I disegni muovono parole e commenti, quelle parole e commenti muovono disegni e culture umane più di qualsiasi emigrazione di massa della storia dell'umano.

Il disegno non ha un luogo e quando il luogo è codificabile tende all'altrove, il disegno è il segno del sapere e dei sapori locali, lo eseguo in un posto dove e necessario e in quanto linguaggio tende verso l'altrove, mi offre la libertà.

Il disegno è dei vivi, sono i vivi che disegnano, solo i vivi, disegna ogni giorno che vuole continuare ad affermare questo.

L'Arte evoluzione della specie

L'evoluzione dei linguaggi dell'arte, nella maniera in cui si muove, è paragonabile all'evoluzione organica della specie.

Gli artisti cercano modi e modalità originali d'espressione del sé, stile e originalità linguistica come li si misura?

Non certo con la quotazione di mercato, originalità e stile si misurano in base a quanto le novità introdotte attirano l'attenzione dell'altro e degli altri, questa la si misura in relazione a quanto si è imitati, più imiti lo stile dell'altro più ne attesti l'originalità, questo è il linguaggio dell'arte.

La spinta all'innovazione linguistica è l'equivalente dell'evoluzione genetica, il linguaggio si muove come la genetica, pensate ai geni che ci portiamo dietro, quelli che i genetisti chiamano "carico mutazionale", questi tramite mutazioni e cambiamenti ambientali possono per caso essere favoriti, in questa maniera si è autodeterminato l'organismo umano per come è oggi; nella stessa maniera si sono mosse le innovazioni linguistiche dell'arte, che quando si affermano attraverso l'imitazione dell'originale, diventano il motore delle arti creative.

Il plexiglass, i vandali al Bastione e la Dea Madre

La natura è stata da sempre la casa degli artisti, questo dalla comparsa degli umani anatomicamente moderni 100000 anni fa.
Questo controtendenza mi ha portato a decidere di abitare l'isola con l'unica città metropolitana d'Europa priva di un'Accademia di Belle Arti, il legame che questa terra ancora sembra potere offrire con la natura. Diecimila anni dopo la nascita dei villaggi e dei capo tribù, l'umanità è restata fedele al suo unico grande culto, quello della Dea Madre natura. L'umano non può vivere o sopravvivere a lungo distante dall'ambiente naturale che si sostenta da sé.
L'umano, con il suo linguaggio artistico, vive la sua limitata esistenza, con il linguaggio come filo conduttore da trasmettere nel tempo, all'interno della nicchia ecologica della natura terrestre.
Il mondo terrestre naturale, ha una sua forza e una sua energia, che rende il linguaggio dell'arte umile, con la consapevolezza di un suo fluire eterno, per questo in quest'isola si sente ancora la forza della Dea Madre; nella storia geologica della terra Dea Madre, la consapevolezza profonda è quella d'essere nient'altro che una perturbazione della natura.
L'arte moderna e contemporanea, imposta e determinata dal mercato e dalla fama della firma, è arte ribelle, che nel nome di culti e culture private e disarmonizzanti, è scappata dal legame con la terra e la natura per cercare successo in città metropolitane, ma la natura è ancora nei nostri volti, comunichiamo (e inganniamo) con posture e espressioni mimiche e facciali.
Ma se potessimo scegliere liberamente dove abitare (e in questo io mi sento e sentivo libero), perché non ascoltare la nostra predisposizione congenita ?
Chi di voi non abiterebbe in luoghi con vaste estensioni di terra, vicino a montagne, laghi, fiumi e il mare?
Perché l'isola è tutto questo, è ancora tutto questo!
Gli artisti isolani hanno ancora quest'anima, tra le più congeniali alla

sopravvivenza culturale dell'umano.

Come i primi esseri umani, si hanno a disposizione ampie visuali, passeggiare a contatto diretto con la natura ha un effetto conciliante tra fisico e mente, si accarezza l'istinto del cacciatore che siamo stati.

La relazione quotidiana con la natura, per il tempo dell'esistenza umana è la magia dell'arte e dell'umano, è attingere da quello che siamo.

L'isola e Cagliari area metropolitana, amplifica rispetto all'altrove, la possibilità d'indagare il reale senso originario del linguaggio dell'arte, ma l'assenza di un'Accademia di Belle Arti marginalizza e isola culturalmente tutto questo potenziale (anche in termini d'economia comune), esiste una tendenza culturale evolutiva che passa per la moltiplicazione di specie e linguaggi, l'idea dell'arte come mercato è invasiva e cancella l'approccio naturale e culturale al linguaggio dell'arte come ricerca di senso.

L'artista che si legittima solo nel nome del mercato, è una specie invasiva, che cancella la relazione tra il linguaggio artistico e la Dea Madre, da sempre presente in questo territorio, attraverso un'Accademia di Belle Arti di Cagliari, lo si potrebbe tutelare in quanto processo naturale dell'umano, da tradurre in idee ed emozioni evocativamente poetici, senza di questo, Cagliari è destinare a coltivare brutture, come il plexiglass al Bastione e le relative scritte vandaliche "politiche" di contestazione che ne evidenziano la forzatura.

Cervello è linguaggio

Un cervello di un adulto pesa il due per cento del peso corporeo, in media 1,5 Kg., è fatto di 200 miliardi di cellule interconnesse, metà sono cellule nervose (i neuroni), l'altra metà sono cellule di supporto (gliali). Provare a contare i neuroni è utopia, servirebbero 3171 anni, in fila arriverebbero da Milano a Reggio Calabria (1000 Km.circa).

Come sopravvivono queste cellule?

Grazie all'acqua, contengono acqua, l'ottanta per cento del nostro cervello è composto d'acqua.

Tutto questo trasmette segnali chimici, emette onde sonore che percepiamo, segnali trasmessi da sostanze di natura proteica denominate neurotrasmettitori (nostro malgrado).

Quali sono i segnali chimici, che sono poi i segnali chimici della vita come dei linguaggi dell'arte?

La dopamina interviene nelle emozioni, l'acetilcolina nei movimenti, la serotonina stimola la fama e regola l'umore, la noradrenalina ci fa sudare, questo smuove le connessioni sinaptiche, i nodi di rete del nostro sistema.

Che velocità hanno queste connessioni?
Possono essere lente come una passeggiata (mezzo metro al secondo)
o veloci come un aereo (120 metri al secondo), l'energia che consuma il
nostro cervello in queste connessioni?
Quanto una lampadina di 20 W; incredibile, il 2 per cento della nostra
massa corporea (il cervello), consuma il 20 per cento dell'energia totale
del nostro corpo, sangue e ossigeno l'alimentano durante il giorno e la
notte.
Ma sapete tutto questo quanta memoria contiene?
Tra i tre e i 1000 terabyte, il computer più potente del mondo, arriva
soltanto a 160 TB di memoria.
Come è avvenuto tutto questo?
Attraverso i rituali di socializzazione umana veicolati dalla nascita del
linguaggio dell'arte, il veicolo principale di comprensione del pluralismo
e della diversità dell'umano sintetizzata in simboli e linguaggi che
accomunino nel senso e nelle cause comuni.
Esagero a fare ruotare tutto questo sviluppo dell'umano intorno ai
linguaggi dell'arte?
No, non esagero!

L'ABITUDINE CREATIVA

Il sistema nervoso ha una funzione eliminatoria e non produttiva, ci
protegge dalla tempesta d'informazioni cui siamo quotidianamente
sottoposti, filtra ed esclude quello che non aiuta praticamente, mi piace
pensare che il linguaggio dell'arte si autoselezioni e autodetermini in
questa maniera, gli artisti che non ti ricordi sono artisti che non incidono
a prescindere dal valore di mercato, questo quando si è mentalmente
lucidi, perché oltre il proprio cervello, non c'è nulla che renda
artisticamente più intelligenti, lo stile e l'abitudine creativa alimenta il
cervello del creativo.

LETTERA DI FINE ANNO

Auspico un 2019, dove a Cagliari e nell'isola, siano gli artisti residenti,
profondi conoscitori dell'uomo e della sua natura, a indirizzare la
politica Regionale e non il contrario (come avviene da tremila anni da
queste parti); auspico questo perché una politica Regionale isolana,
senza direttive calibrate, non ha nulla a che fare con il linguaggio
dell'arte inteso come ricerca del perseguimento del bene comune.

A Cagliari e nell'isola, purtroppo, la ricerca artistica residente è collocata in basso rispetto alla politica, molto in basso, molto più in basso,

Auspico un 2019, dove si progetti un sovvertimento radicale di quel paradigma, che vede l'arte residente soltanto come una voce spesa della politica, incapace di vedere e leggere l'alta formazione artistica residente come uno strumento strategico, la spada di una economia possibile che può portare beneficio alla collettività, misurabile e rivalutabile nel tempo.

Auspico un 2019, dove dell'Accademia a Cagliari se ne occupino attivamente gli artisti residenti e non i politici di professione, la politica dovrebbe solo trasformare la conoscenza degli artisti residenti in strumenti legislativi (con un'Accademia a Cagliari), ma gli artisti devono monitorarne la messa in opera produttiva per evitare che diventi rendita di posizione politica tossica.

A cosa serve altrimenti nell'isola parlare di bilinguismo, autodeterminazione, identità, specificità culturale e libertà?

Libertà vuole dire azione concreta d'autodeterminazione, autodeterminazione vuole dire autonomia decisionale, vuole dire incoraggiare a fare le scelte migliori per se stessi e per la propria società, cosa può liberamente decidere un giovane artista in formazione a Cagliari impossibilitato alla mobilità?

Cagliari e l'isola hanno bisogno di coscienza artistica e culturale, coscienza vuole dire condizione sistemica di connessione tra fattori interni e fattori esterni, vuole dite impostare ambienti culturali, sociali e ambientali predisposti all'interazione e condivisione attiva dell'arte.

L'identità cosa è?

Interazione tra fattori genetici e ambientali, è esperienza di vita, educazione ambientale e sociale, questo alimenta la personalità e l'identità artistica,

Questa è la lezione dei linguaggi dell'arte che bisogna sistematizzare il prima possibile.

La politica regionale deve ripartire da Cagliari e dall'alta formazione artistica, se si vuole realmente occupare della qualità di vita intellettuale residente.

Folle che a Cagliari si pensi all'arte solo come investimento privato, serve intervenire strutturalmente materializzando corridoi tra creatività residente e benessere, altrimenti si sarà sempre più marginali e periferici dal punto di vista della consapevolezza artistica contemporanea del proprio (ancora potenziale) patrimonio residente.

Auspico un 2019 dove la politica Regionale isolana rifletta sul proprio fallimento, in ambito formativo artistico residente, quale Regione Autonoma vanta oggi, il capoluogo Regionale e città metropolitana priva di un'Accademia?

Si può continuare a collocarsi su traiettorie di discussioni politiche mediatiche eterodirette, che alimentano instabilità e paralisi legislative? La produzione d'arte contemporanea, cresce dovunque in media rispetto a Cagliari e nell'isola, la politica Regionale continua a essere distratta da una perenne campagna elettorale che scomoda Salvini per una scultura a Gigi Riva, dal momento che non si vogliono affrontare le oramai millenarie carenze, si tira a campare proteggendo il proprio status fondato su compromessi e strategie di autosopravvivenza che paiono non voleva toccare il delicato equilibrio Regionale trasversale al voto Regionale Cagliari-Sassari.

Non si può più pensare a un'isola dell'arte privata e privatizzata, è necessario configurare un sistema artistico regionale che sia pubblica impresa in grado di sostenete con il suo ritorno il sistema politico, economico, sociale e culturale Isola.

Possibile che nell'isola non sia ancora mai ragionato, su come una visione Rinascimentale comune determini un albero genealogico di menti, al servizio del pubblico, in grado d'autodeterminare i mutevoli e mutanti percorsi della storia?
Quale è la prospettiva di Cagliari e dell'isola, priva di un'Accademia, nell'unica città metropolitana che piò fungere da cerniera tra i centri produttivi del sapere artistico e culturale e il cittadino?

Fin quando Cagliari non avrà un'Accademia di Belle Arti, l'arte continuerà a essere percepita in questo territorio (Sassari compresa) come qualcosa che brucia e si consuma in una nuraghe, funzionale a essere bistrattata per questo o quell'interesse via social media.

Auspico un 2019 senza stanchi slogan e la riduzione dell'arte a strumento di propaganda mediatica (come i Subsonica in piazza per Capodanno o le Sculture di Mimmo Paladino alla Galleria Comunale), mi auguro strutturali interventi politici pratici, che garantiscano a i giovani artisti in formazione una traiettoria residente accessibile che non abbia distingui di classe e portafoglio, che ponga in condizione di formare e del fare professione la propria passione, che ponga in condizione i giovani artisti residenti di scegliere di progettare.

Progettare un'Accademia e il suo interno didattico e dialettico, vorrebbe dire conoscere e autodeterminare un contesto sociale sostenuto da pesanti teste pensanti, approcciare l'arte in modalità condivise rendendo l'isola vicino alla penisola, con la relativa socialità comunitaria che questo comporterebbe.

Serve che Cagliari e l'isola sappiano invertire la tendenza, nonostante il ritardo secolare serve provarci, la tecnologia va inquadrata in un media della conoscenza e non il fine.

Auspico un 2019 con la politica Regionale isolana, che sappia fare dell'Alta Formazione Artistica una premessa d'evoluzione culturale e produttiva, serve definire questa traiettoria del possibile, per armonizzare le potenzialità produttive Cagliaritane e isolane, l'interesse comune è quello delle abilità isolane di sapere essere artisti della cultura e del progresso.

A cosa serve un iPad senza un'Accademia?

Cosa vuole dire Alta Formazione Artistica?
Su tutto, vuole dire che il concetto di bello non è mai stato immobile nel tempo, e che in tempi veloci, interconnessi e mobili come in questa alba di millennio, varia e muta tra una generazione e l'altra.
 Bello è un canone affascinante, a cui attribuiamo un valore simbolico che va ben oltre l'estetica, il bello è un'entità culturalmente astratta che determina l'innamoramento, oltre, molto oltre la semplice fascinazione estetica.
 Ogni artista, ogni epoca, ogni passaggio generazionale, coltiva la sua idea del bello, bello è interagire sul perché si ha una propria idea del bello (che è sempre discutibile), perché si ha una idea di bello legata a

uno stile e un linguaggio (anche il proprio).

L'Accademia è la palestra dei giovani artisti, il laboratorio della loro loro elaborazione del bello calibrata nel tempo, senza dialogo e dialettica il bello lo si ridurrebbe a fatto tecnico, che nulla ha a che vedere con l'arte.

L'Accademia è funzionale anche a concettualizzare la funzione emotiva dell'arte, se l'arte la si potesse ridurre a fatto tecnico ed estetico, non si muoverebbe su traiettorie di comune interesse dell'umano.

Cagliari nel 2019, non ha ancora metabolizzato questo, non ha metabolizzato attraverso un'Accademia di Belle Arti operante nel suo territorio, che l'artista moderno è un intellettuale, uno che nel suo tempo ha il dovere di scuotere il gusto, scardinare regole e mode dopo averle vissute e sondate, è il motore del rinnovamento sociale e culturale.

Le Avanguardie novecentesche, nate attraverso incessanti e accese interazioni dialettiche rivolte alle Accademia, si prefiggevano di rinnovare sistemi sociali e culturali dell'umano, vi sembra una cosa da poco?

Capite lo stato dell'arte residente Cagliaritana, se diventa provocatorio come fatto artistico, evocare ed invocare un'Accademia che non c'è mai stata?

Non è curioso che in un contesto come quello Cagliaritano, capoluogo di provincia di una Regione a Statuto autonomi, e unica città metropolitana dell'isola, ragionare su un diritto costituzionale di base come quello dell'Alta Formazione Artistica, possa venire letto come una provocazione?

Evocare e invocare un'Accademia, dove non c'è mai stata e non è mai nata, viene letto come una provocazione, disorienta al punto che si riduce l'Accademia a orpello decorativo di cui, come si è sempre fatto, si può fare a meno, si è incapace di leggere l'Accademia come un nodo d'elaborazione e produzione del bello in mutazione col tempo, il luogo dove evadere dalla forma è una condizione mutevole per attingere alla vita.

A Cagliari, invocare ed evocare un'Accademia nel 2019, viene letta come una provocazione Dadaista, pensate un poco voi, eppure l'arte esiste da quando l'umano attraverso la sua produzione sviluppa il proprio cervello; i linguaggi dell'arte sono il vero social network globalmente interconnesso della condizione umana, e hanno solo quarantamila anni, a cosa serve un iPad senza un'Accademia?

Eppure in quest'isola la modernità tradotta in mercato, imporrebbe un dialogo necessario tra la modernità psicoanalitica e la natura, la sensazione è che il Cagliaritano si isoli nella sua natura, rinchiuso nella modernità e incapace di dialogare e conoscere se stesso attraverso la sua natura.

L'Arte contro la volgarità politica!

Cosa ho trovato realmente e veramente istituzionale nel messaggio di Mattarella di fine anno?

La presenza di un quadro che gli rubava la scena dinanzi al quale sarebbe potuto stare anche in silenzio, che per linguaggio e scelta cromatica ne attestava l'istituzionalità.

Osservavo il quadro invece di ascoltarlo, un quadro dalle risonanze suprematiste di pura sensibilità della forma che va ben oltre rigidi rituali istituzionali, che pareva essere un Rothko ma con una diversa spiritualità, un Rothko dissonante; un Malevic emotivo e non rigido, un Mondrian che non necessita della rigidità del suo neoplasticismo.

Quel quadro attestava l'avanguardia divenuta nell'arco di un secolo istituzione Accademica, quel quadro è stato linguaggio dell'arte che nel nome della sua ancestralità e umanità schiaccia la rigidezza del media di massa e mostra un Presidente prima di tutto uomo che sente il linguaggio.

Mattarella ieri ha elevato e reso istituzionale l'arte in quanto linguaggio, al punto da omettere il nome dell'autore (Diego Salezze, veronese, classe 1973. Figlio d'arte, sia il nonno che la madre erano pittori) e citando solo il contesto ambientale dove quel lavoro è nato e gli è stato donato il lavoro, il centro regionale per l'autismo che ha sede all'ospedale Borgo Trento di Verona.
Quell'arancio reso plastico da tocchi plastici di giallo, quanta spiritualità, quel gioco di piani con quel grigio in primo piano lacerato, quasi strappato, tremendamente formale e istituzionale che con quello strappo apriva un varco di comunicazione umana con il freddo e distratto spettatore mediatico, quel nero che il grigio sembra comprimere verso il basso nel nome di quello strappo che sembra aprire il varco verso l'arancio.
Questa è la comunicazione istituzionale che ho sempre desiderato, senza parole, dinanzi alla quale la pochezza della propaganda di Di Maio e Di Battista con gli sci che dichiarano di combattere i privilegi, o la volgarità di un Salvini che mangia la nutella scompaiono e si

dissolvono, l'istituzione che non sa parlare nobilmente il linguaggio dell'arte nega se stessa.

Il linguaggio dell'arte nobilita le istituzioni e consente loro di sorvolare sui social network, questa è la vera lezione di linguaggio dell'arte di questa fine dell'anno, altro che la volgarità di concertoni e pop star.

Linguaggio dell'arte fuori dal tempo e senza un autore che sia una firma o un investimento di mercato, dinanzi alla forza umana del linguaggio dell'arte, ieri sera non si poteva fare altro che scostarsi e mettersi da parte.

IL DIAVOLO NEGA IL SIMBOLO

Cosa è un simbolo?
Un simbolo è la conseguenza di un apparato iconografico , un elemento di un codice linguistico che attraverso il simbolo, elemento di un codice, consente di potersi riconoscere.
 La cultura Nuragica è l'unico codice simbolico e linguistico, nell'ambito della quale si possono elaborare codici Accademici e iconici prettamente isolani, si potrebbe anche parlare di codice nuragico.
Come si ragiona su un simbolo, un simbolo deve essere facile da realizzare e trasmettere, può anche non avere velleità artistiche (pensate ai Grafici più che artisti si qualificano come professionisti), il significato di un simbolo e di un codice linguistico simbolico, può essere più importante dell'aspetto figurativo, questo a esempio è già un distinguo sostanziale tra un canone classico greco e un canone isolano nuragico.
Simbolo cosa vuole dire?
Cosa si vuole dire quando si dice "quel simbolo non mi appartiene"?
Il termine simbolo ci arriva dal latino symbolum che ha origine dal greco symbolon, il tema è quello del verbo symballo, che riunisce i termini "insieme" e "gettare", in altre parole sta per connettere immagine e significato, rifiutare un simbolo vuole dire rifiutarne il significato, vuole dire negare la discussione con l'altro e con gli altri.
Capite quanto sia folle preventivamente rifiutare o disconoscere un simbolo o una sua elaborazione?
Il simbolo non è un dogma, veicola messaggi che possono essere anche tra loro dissonanti.
L'iconologia è quella disciplina che decodifica i simboli nei loro significati, nascosti prima e liberati poi, il simbolo è sempre un elemento

di discussione e non nega mai l'altro, sovente l'altro negando il simbolo nega la cultura dell'altro attestando la sua ignoranza.

Infatti, sapete qual'è il contrario del termine simbolo?

Il termine diaballein, che sta per separare, disunire, avere in odio, ingannare e indurre in errore, da questo termine deriva la parola diabolico e diavolo, è la negazione della sacralità di chi in quel simbolo si riconosce.

Il simbolo è una discussione su un valore culturale, negare un simbolo con un altro è prendere la distanza dalla dialettica tra simboli che all'interno di un codice è dialettica e didattica culturale che arricchisce tutta la comunità, il simbolo integra e si integra e negarlo vuole dire negare la propria cultura.

Beuys, la politica isolana e il cinghialetto

Il linguaggio dell'arte sa muoversi oltre le convenzioni; sa essere coinvolgimento e rinnovamento, è flusso in grado di mutare, dovunque si trovi, in relazione all'identità di chi lo genera e il tempo, quando si genera ha una portata di comunicazione che va ben oltre il luogo dove si svolge e dove si determina.

L'Accademia serve a questo, a fare entrare l'arte nella vita di ogni individuo che la frequenta.

L'Accademia insegna e forma nel comprendere cosa sia un reale atteggiamento artistico.

L'Accademia è movimento artistico e culturale che localmente diventa istituzione, è forza rigenerativa quotidiana nella vita di tutti i giorni, è il pubblico che forma didatticamente e dialetticamente che può non avere nulla a che fare con gli aspetti mercantili ed economici delle opere d'arte.

La conoscenza diretta dei linguaggi dell'arte è una risorsa incredibile per la vita di ciascuno, anche quando si traduce in "scarabocchio" di chi pensa di non sapere disegnare.

In quest'ottica,non so quanto chi fa politica a Cagliari e progetta d'amministrarla culturalmente tra Comune, Città Metropolitana o Regione, conosca un artista come Joseph Beuys.

Joseph Beuys è stata una vera figura mitologica dell'arte contemporanea, la sua idea di Scultura era di "Scultura sociale", cosa voleva dire questo?

Voleva dire che la materia dello Scultore contemporaneo poteva non essere più fredda materia inerte, come Marmo, Trachite, Granito o Argilla, ma azioni poeticamente politiche e didattiche in grado di plasmare coscienza e conoscenza della popolazione; le sue performance erano segni che nel tempo pensava potessero rimodellare la società, un artista straordinario che fondò il partito dei Verdi che nel suo nome ha fatto tante battaglie, insomma un artista eticamente un tantino più alto di un Beppe Grillo.

Beuys indagava l'armonia tra uomo e natura, immaginate a Cagliari quanto potrebbe essere importante per dei giovani artisti studiarne la poetica, anche semplicemente per comprenderla, la Cagliari moderna ha mai avuto nelle sue amministrazioni un artista che ne conoscesse il lavoro attraverso un'Accademia?

La natura era per Beuys uno mezzo per formare un agire etico che si potesse tradurre in autocoscienza e creatività soggettiva.

Beuys indagava, e il suo lavoro studiato e compreso indaga, le contraddizioni del contemporaneo nel nome della salvaguardia della natura, della libertà e della democrazia, capite cosa possa essere un'Accademia?

Nel 1974 in America fece un performance che ancora oggi ha valore simbolico del capolavoro, in aeroporto si rifiutò di mettere piede sul suolo Statunitense, si fece trasportare su un'ambulanza, erano gli anni del Vietnam e con quel suolo non voleva avere nulla a che fare.

Si fece portare in una prestigiosissima galleria di News York per incontrare un coyote, animale che era sacro per i nativi americani, non voleva incontrare gli Stati Uniti dei colonizzatori, voleva ascoltare le origini nella natura, le vere radici ataviche del paese.

Foto e video della performance raccontano di convivenza in un primo momento difficoltosa, ma poi uomo e animale si pacificano e ricreano in galleria, a New York, l'armonia tra uomo e natura, i due (artista e coyote) hanno vissuto una settimana nella galleria e il pubblico poteva osservarli, riflettere e comprendere, poi Beuys si fece avvolgere nelle coperte per farsi trasportare bendato nell'areo che lo riportò nel vecchio continente.

Provate a immaginare un Beuys a Cagliari: impossibile non c'è un'Accademia e lui in Accademia insegnò (anche se ne venne allontanato).

Provate a immaginare degli artisti che con l'arte facciano politica per un'Accademia (come potrebbero senza formazione Accademica che sviluppi coscienze in tal senso?).

Provate a pensare ai candidati presidente della Regione Sardegna chiusi in una stanza di una galleria per una settimana con un cinghialetto per ascoltare la forza e la natura della propria terra, ci riuscirebbero? Guadagnerebbero a Cagliari voti e consenso?

NON AMO LA TRANSAVANGUARDIA

Non ho mai amato la Transavanguardia, è troppo anni ottanta, l'ho sempre sentita "educativamente" imposta.

Impostazione di movimento troppo ambigua, Transavanguardia stava per oltre l'avanguardia.

La Transvanguardia voleva abbandonare la sperimentazione linguistica e tornare al quadro, nessun Cubismo, Futurismo e Astrattismo, ma atmosfere da Espressionismo e Surrealismo, ma può un movimento che dice di volere attraversare e sintetizzare le avanguardie, negarne alcune?

Il movimento nacque praticamente sulle pagine di "Flash Art" a fine 1979, con sostanzialmente cinque artisti proposti da un critico.

Troppo, troppo anni ottanta, troppo Den Harrow e Sandy Marton, disimpegnati politicamente e rivolti verso il proprio intimo privato, che perché mi avrebbe dovuto interessare?

La Transavanguardia, era ed è, fenomeno di mercato, è il boom economico anni ottanta con un investimento nato e strutturato ad arte, era la medioborghesia che acquistava e oggi non vende e trattiene per come la Transavanguardia si è insinuata nel pubblico.

La verità sulla Transavanguardia è che il quadro possa entrare nei salotti borghesi determinandone lo status.

Si affermava la Transavanguardia e io in suo nome, decidevo di non volere fare parte di nessun mercatino che consolidasse quelle logiche di mercato.

Sulla tomba dei giganti!

Cosa ne sa Cagliari di Avanguardie storiche?

Cosa ne sa, di come le avanguardie storiche d'inizio novecento abbandonino tecniche e tradizioni artistiche miscelandosi tra di loro, mutino le proprie fondamenta e determinino una moltitudine di nuovi linguaggi pittorici e plastici?

Nel nome di quale Accademia o Accademismo ci si doveva ribellare?

Che ne sa Cagliari, di come con le neovanguardie diventino con questo atteggiamento decise nel legittimare linguaggi e tecniche che cessarono di essere sperimentali, ma generi.

Il contemporaneo rende tutto quello che a Cagliari non c'è mai stato Accademia, pittura e Scultura sono il debito con il passato che con l'Accademia dialogano e ne costituiscono la base e l'origine, eppure a Cagliari si pensa ancora che artista voglia dire pittore e Scultore.

L'artista contemporaneo è un contaminato che attraversa, a prescindere dalla sua specialzzazione, tutte le discipline dell'arte, il suo linguaggio può rasentare la politica, l'economia e la scienza.
Tutti gli aspetti della vita sono creativi, non c'è media che non richiami altro media nei contenuti e nel linguaggio, ogni artista è rappresentazione del reale originale e imprevedibile, Cagliari non ha questo patrimonio, è tutto immobile e prevedibile nello spazio e nel tempo, si continua a dialogare con il proprio altrove, soltanto ponendo l'orecchio sulle tombe dei giganti, oggi come allora l'Accademia è mai stata!

Accademia è studio che diverte!

Stiamo vivendo un momento epocale nella storia dei linguaggi dell'arte, si stanno distruggendo tutte le certezze che hanno accompagnato gli artisti del secolo passato:

- La memoria e il passato artistico e culturale come qualcosa da tutelare e custodire a prescindere non è più scontata.

- Il sistema dell'arte futuro per alcuni in cerca di like è motivo di entusiasmo, per altri è un'Apocalisse, gli artisti sembrano non avere cause e dimensioni che prescindano dalla loro dimensione privata e personale.

- Lentamente si stanno erodendo le istituzioni, il linguaggio nella sua classicità, il diritto all'istruzione artistica per formare e sensibilizzare l'umano.

- Arte e linguaggio dell'arte sembrano ripiegare verso piccole comunità e nicchie incapaci di andare oltre il senso d'appartenenza comune, il limite della propria identità linguistica dell'arte fa sentire sicuri.

- Ci si muove in un millennio complesso, impossibile da codificare con una corrente di linguaggio o stile, ci si muove tra forze che spingono il linguaggio dell'arte in direzioni opposte.

Eppure spazi istituzionali dell'arte ancora esistono, e la cultura e la formazione diventa un luogo nel territorio d'andare a cercare con consapevolezza.
Cagliari necessita in quest'ottica di ciò che non ha mai avuto, un'Accademia di Belle Arti, che sia in grado di trasformare l'impulso

della comunicazione web, imposta e indotta, c he ci vede rovesciare sugli altri istinti, o se attraverso l'Alta Formazione Artistica, da sempre assente nel territorio, trasformare le pulsioni istintive mosse e indotte dall'altrove del web, in benzina fisica e mentale per fare agire gli artisti Cagliaritani e isolani nel mondo.

L'Alta Formazione Artistica è il percorso possibile per uscire dai condizionamenti cognitivi e sociali che portano Cagliari a essere la città metropolitana più conformista d'Europa a qualsiasi cosa, che con naturalezza e senza battere ciglio si consegna alle legge del mercato imposto e indotto senza nessun tipo di identità culturale che sappia adattarsi e costituire una costante resistenziale che sappia essere didattica e dialettica verso l'altrove.

L'Accademia è uno strumento di alta formazione, per spingere il Cagliaritano, non verso la lamentela o l'indignazione, ma alla creatività, alla disobbedienza, alla filosofia che sa entrare in strada, al divertimento intellettuale e cognitivo come esercizio di stile, quel divertimento profondo che Cagliari non ha mai coltivato se non attraverso il mercato.

Accademia che stimoli e non quieti il Cagliaritano!

Già negli anni settanta si ragionava sui limiti del concetto di cultura, l'arte e la cultura non sono e non possono essere formazione lunghissima e non autonoma.

L'arte non può essere un linguaggio simbolico statico nel tempo che si riproduce all'infinito, la ricerca artistica non può avere come una convenzione il valore simbolico di mercato attestato e compreso dalle classi sociali più elevate.

L'arte che non si muove e non si contamina, che non educa e non dialoga, è arte non calibrata sulla persona, è un tranquillante che si propone come valore assoluto e non uno stimolante.

Studiare e approfondire valori consolidati, senza ricercare, non rende liberi artisticamente e culturalmente, anzi contribuisce al mantenimento dello status quo.

L'artista, dal dopoguerra del secolo scorso, si è progressivamente conformato a un valore di ricerca attestato dal mercato; ricchezza, potere e onore in cambio di una totale aderenza agli standard del pensiero unico (anche quello politico programmatico) in corso d'opera, l'artista non conforme era etichettato come "incompreso" e lo si abbandonava tra gli stati più poveri, ignoranti e ignorati delle diverse comunità locali che tendevano globalmente a connettersi.

L'Alta Formazione Artistica in tale maniera è stata limitata, arginata, i linguaggi dell'arte non dovevano proiettare le comunità verso il futuro ponendo domande, l'artista professionista era quello "quotato", attraverso il quale si ometteva coscienza e conoscenza critica, che arginava mutazione e autodeterminazione.

Cagliari oggi però, fa i conti, dopo la diffusione persuasiva dei media di massa con le nuove tecnologie che globalmente interconnettono le sue reali politiche artistiche con l'altrove, la certezza che il solo Cagliaritano ha in Europa, che i propri artisti siano un patrimonio inutile da coltivare, non è più granitica.

L'attuale contesto sociale e culturale consente d'essere libero soltanto a chi si assume la responsabilità, come scelta, del proprio linguaggio e dei propri pensieri, secondo i propri desideri, senza un'Accademia di Belle Arti, chi farà riflettere gli artisti in formazione e residenti a Cagliari, su come la libertà artistica, sia una programmatica forma di disciplina, educazione e autodeterminazione?

Quali creativi e quali artisti si formeranno, abbandonando l'Alta Formazione Artistica Cagliaritana agli umori dei social o alla riduttiva e feudale visione dell'arte come "professione"?

Fino alla fine del millennio, era possibile per Cagliari nascondere la polvere sotto il tappeto, adesso è la polvere del ritardo a nascondere a Cagliari le innumerevoli possibilità che le offrirebbe l'Alta Formazione Artistica residente.

I giovani artisti d'area Cagliaritana, perché dovrebbero accettare i compromessi che le generazioni precedenti gli hanno imposto di sopportare?

Il sistema dell'arte fondato sul mercato sta crollando ed è in parte già crollato (è tenuto artificialmente in vita dai suoi più arcigni e facoltosi investitori e si è insinuato nel pubblico).

Cagliari necessita con una sua Accademia di Belle Arti, d'aprirsi una sua porta verso il futuro, questo non toglie che Cagliari può anche dichiarare il suo decesso artistico e culturale nel contemporaneo nel nome delle sue insicurezze, ma potrebbe anche andare oltre e navigare con i suoi artisti altamente formati in spazi aperti.

L'Accademia a Belle Arti a Cagliari potrebbe fare ragionare il Cagliaritano sull'arte come agente propulsivo di cambiamento, stimolare la coscienza artistica in una comunità che per scelta personale potrebbe trovare in ogni cosa, uno stimolo verso il cambiamento.

Pensateci, una Cagliaritano che dinanzi propagande televisive e mediatiche, dinanzi un quadro o un fumetto, possa iconologicamente considerare: questo prodotto è un tranquillante o uno stimolante per i miei neuroni?

L'Alta Formazione Artistica a Cagliari non è mai stata, la comunicazione via social network evidenzia il distacco tra l'artista Cagliaritano che non ha studiato e quello che da Cagliari ha studiato e si è formato altrove, e per fare l'artista può non servire un'Accademia, ma certamente non è fondamentale studiare Ingegneria o Scienze Politiche.

Quali artisti residenti a Cagliari, hanno realmente una visione del futuro? Gli artisti a Cagliari non hanno creato Whatsapp, smartphone e social network, ma li useranno senza resistenze e senza la percezione che siano "innaturali", saranno funzionali sempre e comunque a vecchie élite in corsa per i loro guadagni e profitti.

Non serve affrontare questo con studi e lavori artistici di ieri, serve essere desiderosi di praticare e studiare i linguaggi dell'arte e il loro senso oggi.

Cagliari in questo momento non ha bisogno del colto artista che rientra dopo avere studiato in un'Accademia dell'altrove, ma neanche del barbaro che pensa d'essere creativo semplicemente usando uno smartphone, entrambi non hanno il desiderio di conoscere di più di quanto sappiano,

A Cagliari servono artisti che bramino desiderio e non si accontentino di questa Cagliari, servono artisti che vogliono conoscersi e indagare per conoscere e indagare, servono artisti che non sentano la loro ignoranza e il loro provincialismo come un limite, servono artisti in formazione affamati di narrazione, servono artisti che non vedano l'ora finalmente di fare girare pagina a Cagliari.

Non ha più senso che Cagliari si autocondanni a fare emigrare artisti in formazione, che quando tornano pensano soltanto a difendere il loro status acquisito altrove e che in maniera schizzinosa elevano le mura del proprio feudo; quello che è importante è che Cagliari riempia lo spazio del suo futuro con un'Accademia di Belle Arti.

Cagliari senza un'Accademia di Belle Arti, vuole dire una Cagliari barbara, che pensa che tutto sia immediato e a portata di mano, che non distingue tra prodotto e processo.

Linguaggio dell'arte oggi vuole dire dialettica e didattica, vuole dire collaborazione, narrazione e ascolto degli altri, desiderio di imparare ciò che non si sa di altre culture e altri linguaggi per confrontarsi nel territorio del presente.

I linguaggi dell'arte a Cagliari, dovrebbero essere patrimonio di tutti, che anche se liquido e gassoso, sappia essere come tale indistruttibile.

Servono artisti formati per non fermarsi mai, anche davanti a compiti troppo impegnativi e alla propria imperfezione nello svolgerli e affrontarli.

Il vecchio è in questo millennio stantio ovunque, solo quello che è autentico si salverà dinanzi al futuro dell'arte, Cagliari si salva se comincia a raccontare nuovamente la propria memoria, ma per fare questo servono artisti che a Cagliari si innamorino dei processi artistici che diventano progetti di vita, che possano viversi il loro amore e la loro passione per l'arte, che riescano a raccontarla raccontandosi, soltanto così Cagliari si stimola e non si tranquillizza, soltanto a Cagliari si sarà umani e l'umanità non sarà un diversivo acquista voti.

L'Accademia a Cagliari non serve a distrarre il Cagliaritano da ciò che è, serva a fargli conoscere e comprendere ciò che è e che sarà in questo millennio!

A Cagliari il simbolo è mercato!

L'arte contemporanea non necessita più di singoli spettatori, il partecipante alla performance linguistica che determina il prodotto dell'artista, è invitato a immergersi attivamente nella sua realtà, lo spettatore e il fruitore d'arte contemporanea è non solo spettatore, ma anche attore nel determinare il valore simbolico dell'arte.

Non esiste più un reale distinguo in questo millennio, tra l'artista celebre e famoso e l'artista che non lo è, esistono soltanto diversi livelli di popolarità, il problema di Cagliari è illudersi che l'autocelebrazione di contenuto, priva d'Alta Formazione Artistica possa avere un valore storico ed economico internazionale invece che locale, senza coltivare strategicamente, l'Alta Formazione Artistica residente.

Chi amministra Cagliari, non può più pensare che in un sistema sociale esista solo quello che è comunicabile, perché se questo fosse vero, l'incomunicabilità della conoscenza, naturalmente cesserà di essere, la fiamma della ricerca di senso dei linguaggi dell'arte, senza alta formazione artistica, è naturalmente destinata a spegnersi nella ghiacciaia virtuale.

Un sistema artistico, come quello Cagliaritano, privo d'Alta Formazione Artistica, è semplicemente un sistema di mercato, dove esiste soltanto quello che è invocato, da portare immediatamente a sé; la conoscenza e la coscienza artistica è ben altra cosa, si canta da sé, è qualcosa da privato che necessita di essere coltivato nel pubblico.

Quella dell'artista è un patrimonio di coscienza e conoscenza pubblico al servizio della sua comunità sociale e culturale, non è solo pubblicità per un proprio brand, altrimenti si tratterebbe di qualcosa destinato a scomparire con la scomparsa dell'artista (a quanti artisti Cagliaritani in relazione con altrove, è successo nel tempo o nella storia?).

La storia dell'arte locale termina, quando è sconnessa da un serbatoio di coscienza e conoscenza comune (a questo serve un'Accademia), senza un serbatoio didattico e dialettico di linguaggi dell'arte residente, che sappia attingere al valore simbolico (prima che economico) dell'arte e dell'artista, dinanzi a parole al vento imposte dall'altrove, coscienza e conoscenza locale si deteriorano e consumano.

Cagliari priva di un'Accademia di Belle Arti, vive una grande confusione in relazione a cosa sia pubblico e cosa sia sia privato nei linguaggi dell'arte contemporanea.

Il Cagliaritano tende a sovrapporre il proprio spazio privato ma al tempo stesso lo esibisce, esibendo il valore simbolico dell'arte senza comprenderlo.

Questo è comprensibile, Cagliari e il Cagliaritano, non hanno mai vissuto, non hanno mai abitato e neanche mai concepito, uno spazio pubblico d'Alta Formazione Artistica con una natura specifica d'incontro, dialettica e didattica, uno spazio dove la relazione sia tra le mani e le relazioni dello spazio che si abitano e dove ci si forma insieme.

Senza un'Accademia, l'arte a Cagliari è performance massmediatica, è relazioni via social network dove non esiste bene comune distinto dal proprio avatar social o interesse personale; Cagliari è un non luogo dove l'interesse personale e privato è sempre dominante, prende il sopravvento e invade la pubblica amministrazione.

Cagliari è una città metropolitana, dal punto di vista dell'Alta Formazione Artistica disconnessa, gli artisti residenti vivono alienati, disconnessi e separati da una parte di sé che disimparano ad abitare.

Una ricerca artistica non può essere determinata dal ritmo social della produzione costante di contenuti, il bisogno di meraviglia necessita di nutrirsi di anche di quotidiana intimità, silenzio e contemplazione.

A questo serve un'Accademia di Belle Arti, a prescindere dal fatto che i follower di una ricerca siano i propri familiari o venti milioni di persone via social network.

Sul serio Cagliari senza un'Accademia di Belle Arti, può affrontare questo millennio senza riflessione artistica?

Senza la noia e il silenzio della ricerca artistica fatta linguaggio, svincolata dalle timeline?

Senza un'Accademia di Belle Arti, la creatività Cagliaritana e isolana, è destinata al disagio, continuerà a muoversi senza farsi istituzione, non sarà mai libera e svincolata dall'ansia di prestazione.

L'arte Cagliaritana non può sopravvivere, se si limita a essere una rappresentazione social, d'eventi effimeri che si condividono pubblicamente, l'artista Cagliaritano non si può autoconvincere d'essere soltanto un selfie che si condivide su uno schermo.

Cagliari priva da sempre di un'Accademia di Belle Arti, sembra non conoscere l'arte della conversione, appare incapace d'invertire il non sense del suo andare, il Cagliaritano sembra incapace di trasgredire dalla regola e dalla tecnica per determinarne altre, impossibilitato a deviare lo sguardo dell'opinione, è fermo al si dice che "non può nascere più di un'Accademia per Regione" o "L'Accademia a Sassari c'è per volere di Cossiga", fermo al suo palmo di mano, non sa rifocalizzarsi verso l'altrove che sa autodeterminarsi.

Fronte mare, il Cagliaritano, non sa disobbedire alla sua vecchia, comoda e franca visione feudale del mondo, non sa spezzare le catene dei suoi pregiudizi e ai suoi limiti della comprensione della bellezza e davanti l'orrore esclama "si, è ovvio".

L'Accademia a Cagliari servirebbe a fare cambiare posto e prospettiva a Cagliari nel mondo, per sondare e conoscere realmente il proprio potenziale creativo identitario.

Chi salverà altrimenti il Cagliaritano da una vita di aperitivi, dal desiderio del possesso dell'ultimo iPhone, dall'urlare "noi non siamo Napoletani" quando vince il Cagliari, dal pensare d'essere il numero di like di un suo post, dall'estetica (e non dall'etica) della propria reputazione on line e off line?

Cagliari non può rifugiarsi dentro un iPhone quando nel resto del mondo c'è la bufera della miseria umana, economica, artistica e culturale, alla quale solo i linguaggi dell'arte che la comprendono possono rispondere.

Accademia a Cagliari vorrebbe dire, visione d'insieme Regionale (o se volete nazionale).

L'Accademia a Cagliari avrebbe un doppio valore in questo momento della storia dell'umano, quello di usare il web con la consapevolezza creativa della propria terra come risorsa, vorrebbe dire avere la consapevolezza di sapere ciò che si fa, sapere muoversi ricordando con il filo conduttore del proprio linguaggio tradotto in ricerca.

TALENTO E MERITO NON FANNO L'ARTISTA!

Non amo le performance d'arte contemporanea, mi sembra spingano gli artisti verso la legittimazione della propria alienazione nella comunità della quale dovrebbero essere figli e riferimento.

La performance d'arte contemporanea, è l'antitesi della vocazione, l'arte e gli artisti contemporanei necessitano di vocazione, di superare il puro interesse personale e porsi al servizio della comunità che li determina.

La vocazione è servizio, il talento è narcisismo, il talento che non diviene vocazione è inutile, determina artisti narcisi ed egocentrici, che hanno come unico parametro il proprio successo.

Gli artisti privi di vocazione sono tristi, infelici, si sforzano in maniera costante d'essere alla moda, questo avviene anche quando agli occhi di altri paiono invidiabili.

Privi di vocazione si è artisti controllabili, ovvero non si è artisti, ci si muove su binari predeterminati e non si crea una propria narrazione, si crede a tutto ciò che viene somministrato senza discernimento, a frasi fatte come "serve conoscere le persone giuste" o "esponendo in quel posto ti bruci", più che artisti si è consumatori, consumatori che incredibilmente si disprezzano, perché ci si convince d'essere i depositari dell'unica verità possibile e plausibile dell'arte contemporanea, sicuri del fatto che gli "addetti ai lavori" a cui hanno conferito autorità, dicano sempre il vero.

Capite quanto siano manipolabili gli artisti privi di vocazione?

Non hanno filtro alcuno e non si pongono domande!

Vocazione vuole dire liberarsi dai condizionamenti, non avere certezze incrollabili, non credere in autorità che allontanano dal pensiero e dal pensare.

La vita di un artista non è fatta di obiettivi, non ha scopo pensata come un progetto, senza vocazione l'artista è controllabile perché ha "obiettivi", non ha propri riferimenti ma li cerca all'esterno, è l'arte tradotta in populismo d'artisti presunti che nel nome dell'obiettivo non hanno scopo!

Quale libertà d'artista?

La tristezza dell'arte contemporanea ridotta a prodotto, rende gli artisti tra di loro, non individui che si confrontano con un loro linguaggio in maniera didattica, ma prodotti, l'altro artista è un media per raggiungere un obiettivo (che lo si critichi o si lavori con lui), l'uso dei social isola il linguaggio (che non è condiviso ma è individuale) e rende l'artista una maschera sotto la quale c'è ben poco.

 Gli artisti contemporanei vivono ossessionati da cosa accade sul loro profilo social, dimenticano di essere dei soggetti e il loro progetto artistico li divora, tramutandoli in avatar.

L'artista come soggetto principale dei linguaggi dell'arte, nel mondo dei social media, sembra essersi ridotto al suo progetto, si autopromuove sotto la costante osservazione della sua rete di contatti.

Se c'è stato un momento della storia, dove l'artista e i linguaggi dell'arte tradotti in ricerca, sono stati liberi, non è questo, in questo millennio l'artista può lavorare e vivere in qualunque posto (anche se certa

politica Cagliaritana nel nome delle "residenze d'artista" internazionali sembra sconfessarlo) e lavorare sempre, tutto sembra essere possibile nel nome del turismo globale, ma ci sono delle cose che paiono essere indiscutibili se si vuole fare l'artista:
- serve avere un progetto.
- serve ottimizzare il proprio tempo.
- serve produrre dei propri contenuti.
- l'artista deve volere comunicare qualcosa.
- serve essere motivati.
- serve essere creativi per scardinare il linguaggio tradotto in progetto di chi ci ha preceduto.

Pensate a un artista con tutte queste limitazioni, costretto a formarsi in una realtà come quella di Cagliari città metropolitana, dove un'Accademia non c'è mai stata, non studia il senso di tutto ciò, non è in condizione di potere criticare, e attraverso la rete connettiva, si ritroverà una vita incatenato al mondo e al sistema dal quale è partito quando ha la fortuna d'emigrare per studiare, vivrà di feedback sterili dove diventa normale per frequentare un'Accademia, pur vivendo in una città metropolitana, emigrare, l'idea che altrove nei secoli si sia stratificato un sistema di pensiero creativo, fatto d'artisti e storie residenti, si ritroverà naturalmente a essere marginalizzata.

L'artista che emigra da Cagliari per studiare, sarà costretto a indossare una maschera, quella del professionista, dalla quale non potrà più liberarsi, e il provincialismo con il quale affronterà il mondo dell'arte, sarà per lui sempre lo stesso, rimuoverà l'essere emigrato nel nome che l'altro, quello che non può permettersi di vivere da studente fuori sede, diventa insignificante, esiste solo il proprio progetto e la propria immagine da coltivare, che passa per non risiedere a Cagliari (dove neanche c'è un'Accademia), ma farsi celebrare con quale residenza d'artista in resort.

Il progetto professionale dell'artista diventa la sua norma, il metro di giudizio sugli altri.

Accademia Nuragica non è "Dataismo"

Perché è importante nel 2019 lavorare e studiare la pietra, osservando i movimenti di sole e luce, come facevano gli antichi Nur?
Perché affidandoci completamente al digitale, le macchine saranno in grado meglio di noi di gestire le nostre informazioni in un mondo sempre meno sensoriale a due dimensioni, nel due dimensioni il mondo non è più nostro e la terra tenda a divenire piatta, a quel punto l'umanità e i linguaggi dell'arte diverranno inutili; siamo pronti a prendere atto, nel nome di questo della nostra insignificanza?

Rischiamo di ritrovarci a vivere vite da uomini e artisti d'allevamento, tutto quello che sarà potrà essere determinato da un'informazione priva di formazione, tutto questo nel nome del movimento del millennio che è il Dataismo (il culto del dato), ossia la riduzione dell'osservazione dell'universo a un flusso di dati destinati a nutrire umani ridotti a algoritmi biochimici.

I Nur di questo millennio, rischiano d'essere ridotti a guerrieri da tastiera, i loro rituali del nome del marketing turistico, ridotti a riti della santa circolazione dell'informazione nel nome del bene universale.

Si può accettare di perdere la propria coscienza storica e identiaria in cambio di una promessa d'eternità che non va oltre l'avatar?

Gli sciamani della Silicon Valley, rischiano d'allontanare la memoria dei nur, di farne cessare la pratica, la tecnica, l'efficacia, la potenza semiotica, nel nome della percezione d'informazioni che non sono formazione.

La Scultura a cielo aperto, è uno strumento di coscienza per fare dell'umano che la pratica e l'osserva, qualcosa in più di un flusso di dati, è la sonda del mistero di cui siamo testimoni e portatori, non siamo solo un pacchetto d'informazioni, la Scultura a cielo aperto interagendo con la luce e gli umori del tempo è uno spicchio e una porzione pratica d'indicibile.

Il digitale è uno strumento che serve se porta all'attenzione l'ignoto dell'umano e la sua storia, senza di questo l'umano sparisce dalla scena con la convinzione d'essere al centro del palco.

Guerrieri nuragici da tastiera!

Molti guerrieri nuragici da tastiera, pensano alla mente come se fosse un software che gira sull'hardware-corpo, perché nel nome di non so bene quale evoluzione culturale, si sono abituati a fare così.

La tecnologia avanzata esteriore sembra stia plasmando il linguaggio della tecnologia interiore.

Sembra si sia dimenticato, che il pensiero, anche attraverso i media digitali, è pensare attraverso la carne, è la carne il materiale con cui e attraverso il quale si trasmettono informazioni.

Il mistero della coscienza non si può interpretare fuori dal corpo che si abita, il corpo è la vera antenna nuragica di chi abita l'isola e ne vive e comprende il mistero.

Il corpo di chi vive con i nuraghe l'isola nuragica, riempie di senso la scelta dello stare nell'isola, di espanderne la cultura, gli abissi e le vette, tutto questo non può passare per il web, il web è solo un territorio di metanazioni digitali, un luogo dove si determinano sudditanze e fedeltà digitali, dove pulsioni e istinti diventano shitstorm, fake news, siti di incontri on line, manipolazioni politiche, consumismo esasperato del superfluo, uno spazio che non è luogo dove si determinano gogne pubbliche finalizzate ad approfittarsi dell'ingenuità e dell'ignoranza dell'altro.

Il virus del pensare alla democrazia in rete nella pratica è un ritorno al passato che nega la democrazia, il virus dei "dittatorelli" è tornato a infettarci negando il valore delle istituzioni democratiche e quello che rappresentano in quanto diritto.

Difficile in questo contesto d'inquinamento del pensiero, dirsi e sentirsi liberi, si è sudditi se si accetta la privazione della propria libertà di essere e di fare in pubblico, non si può barattare questo con l'apparenza mediatica, la comunità non si può creare artificialmente usando i social network o i media di massa, se lo si fa, si vive d'intrattenimento, che in qualche modo si paga, diventando parte integrante del problema della comunità (pur dichiarando di volerne risolvere i problemi), nessuno si senta assolto dalle problematiche di questo tempo, si è tutti coinvolti, sempre che non si abbia la forza e la coscienza, di ricordare, che il primo social network è stata una pietra e che la scultura non nasce digitale a due dimensioni, ma nasce a tre dimensioni su pietra e tavolette d'argilla.

Capite nel nome di questo, a cosa servirebbe un'Accademia di Belle Arti a Cagliari?

Il Menhir rende liberi!

A cosa serve nel 2019 girare intorno a una pietra per leggerne quotidianamente l'interazione con la luce e lavorarla?

A nutrire il proprio pensiero laterale, ovvero la capacità di sondarla, tastarla, conoscerla e renderla un oggetto plastico che guidi il pensiero laterale di chi la realizza come di chi l'osserva.

Il pensiero laterale è lo stimolo alla soluzione alternativa, sviluppa la capacità creativa e come il pensiero lineare affronta e risolve il problema.

Il pensiero laterale si nutre anche di impicci e impedimenti, anche dei limiti di comprensione e di prese di posizioni ideologiche dell'altro, il performer legge le ombre e come si muovono sulla e nella pietra.

Muoversi intorno a una pietra, sentirne suono, vibrazioni e resistenze è pensiero magico, è deriva delle polemiche gratuite via we, è l'urgenza di reincantarsi dinanzi il fare, è il modo per trovare la bellezza e l'armonia cosmica dei nuragici, è connettersi con loro per comprenderne l'armonia, di sentire la connessione con il tempo e la storia e renderla erotica, pensata a quanta arte urbana e public art sia priva di eros.

Sentire e osservare la pietra, vuole dire sfuggire alla manipolazione, non

farsi influenzare dagli altri, sfuggire anche alla morsa psichica di chi vorrebbe manipolare nel nome dei propri interessi la comunità.
Capite quanto muoversi ogni giorno intorno a una pietra, ascoltarla e osservarla, renda liberi?

Libertà è volontà!

Il linguaggio dell'arte, in quanto spazio dialettico e didattico dell'umano, è sempre pubblico, è uno spazio che si muove in relazione con quanto avviene al suo esterno.
Il linguaggio dell'arte nasce nel privato, con la libertà dell'artista di perseguire una sua morale, di usare il linguaggio o il senso del sacro che preferisce, di usare il proprio tempo come meglio preferisce, ma a livello plurale la morale veicolata dai linguaggi dell'arte, diviene etica ed estetica, il linguaggio dell'arte deve essere condiviso e per esserlo la sua sacralità deve essere inclusiva, altrimenti si generano conflitti e non c'è il bene comune come finalità principale.
Convivere con i linguaggi dell'arte nel quotidiano, vuole dire partecipazione attiva, ossia la base della coesione sociale.
La partecipazione attiva (dello spettatore, del committente, degli artisti che lavorano in comune con entrambi) è la garanzia di libertà, per il cittadino che osserva e la società che rappresenta, osservare i processi linguistici dell'arte e praticarli, aiuta a coltivare le proprie opinioni.
L'umano è fatto per agire, il suo cervello è fatto per agire, pensiero ed emozione materializzano il sentire comune e comunitario.
Ascoltare e osservare i linguaggi dell'arte, vuole dire ascoltare i propri talenti.
Il linguaggio dell'arte non è guadagno personale, ma progetto a lungo termine che l'umano trasmette al prossimo oltre la sua morte, per fare questo serve libertà e volontà, per coltivare la libertà e la volontà degli artisti Cagliaritana nella propria comunità, un'Accademia è una necessità!

Lettera aperta al Presidente della Regione Sardegna Christian Solinas

Oggetto: Accademia di Belle Arti a Cagliari!

Onorevole presidente, le scrivo da docente di Discipline Plastiche e orientatore del maggiore (per densità di popolazione e contrasto alla dispersione scolastica Regionale) Liceo Artistico (da qualche anno anche Musicale) dell'intera isola, parlo del "Foiso Fois" di Cagliari, Liceo che al momento conta novecento studenti (quanti ne ha l'Accademia di Belle Arti per capirci), l'unico Liceo Artistico dell'isola comprendente anche l'indirizzo musicale (in Italia non si contano più di dieci che connettano normativamente il linguaggio dell'arte e quello della musica), ma a questi studenti andrebbero sommati gli studenti che frequentano i Licei Artistici di Quartu (con annesso il serale), Iglesias (dove è operativa sul territorio una Scuola Civica d'Arte Contemporanea) e Sant'Antioco per capire realmente la portata numerica dell'utenza d'area metropolitana.

Il ragionamento diventa anche più strutturato se considera come il Foiso Fois ospiti quotidianamente studenti (quotidianamente pendolari o ospiti del Convitto) che provengono anche dall'area Oristanese, dove c'è il prestigioso Liceo Artistico C.Contini; il settanta per cento degli studenti del Foiso Fois è pendolare, capisce quanto sia importante l'istruzione artistica per una città nodo metropolitano che ambisce a proporsi come porto d'arte e cultura del mediterraneo?

Altissima è anche la percentuale di studenti speciali, perché è un fatto che tale percorso di studio favorisca le pari opportunità e lo sviluppo e la crescita creativa d'intelligenze trasversali.

Non ci si può improvvisare Capitale Europea della Cultura senza programmare la propria storia e memoria nel tempo attraverso percorsi d'Alta Formazione Artistica.

Immagino sappia che l'istruzione Liceale Artistica, nell'isola, non solo a Cagliari, arriva soltanto nel 1967-68 (a Sassari vi era un Istituto d'Arte e Mestieri, che soltanto con la recente Riforma Gelmini è divenuto Liceo Artistico), perché le scrivo questo?

Perché la Regione Sardegna di cui lei è divenuto con merito governatore, vanta un primato, quello di avere l'unica città metropolitana (nel contempo capoluogo di Regione) priva d'Alta Formazione Artistica; che ci sia Alta Formazione Artistica a Sassari è giusto, sacro e legittimo, dal momento che le Accademie nascono calibrate sulla realtà storiche e comunitarie dei luoghi che abitano, connettendone passato e futuro, incredibile che Cagliari nel 2019 non abbia Alta Formazione Artistica.

I Licei Artistici nascevano nel 1923 con la Riforma Gentile, in quelle realtà Italiane che da secoli vantavano un'Accademia di Belle Arti, oggi Cagliari è l'unica città metropolitana d'Europa priva d'Accademia di Belle Arti, non è forse questo un problema e un grosso ritardo produttivo artistico e culturale dell'isola tutta rispetto l'altrove?

Le Accademie come i Conservatori sono strutture d'Alta Formazione Artistica e Musicale, l'AFAM che se ne occupa non fa capo alle

Università, MIUR e AFAM sono due entità distaccate, un Conservatorio Musicale c'è a Cagliari come a Sassari, i due Licei Artistici per densità di popolazione e qualità degli studenti, riconosciuta dovunque, sono a Sassari come a Cagliari, quello che realmente non si capisce e perché l'Alta Formazione Artistica si fermi a Sassari e non possa essere praticata a Cagliari anche mediante trienni specifici e d'indirizzo distaccati (a Ravenna nel 1973, nacque un'Accademia di Belle Arti Comunali fondata sull'arte del Mosaico, unico corso, ancora oggi attivo, riconosciuto dall'Accademia di Belle Arti di Bologna.

Quanto è stato importante per Ravenna dal 1973 investire sulla sua storia dell'arte e valorizzarla attraverso la pratica della professionalità degli artisti locali residenti, che la tutelano e che sono messi in condizione di praticarla con un percorso legalmente riconosciuto d'Accademia, dovunque in Europa senza essere etichettati come "folk" o "artisti minori"?).

Pensi a quanti Scultori della trachite locale operano nell'isola e a tutta la tradizione della pittura muralista isolana, perché fare si che tutto ciò resti esclusivamente folk e destinato alla pubblicità della birra Ichnusa nel nome de "i nostri vernissage"?

Le rammento come il contratto di Governo nazionale Lega - Movimento Cinque Stelle, intenda ripartire per valorizzare l'arte e la cultura locale proprio dalla centralità delle Accademie come istituzioni didattiche e dialettiche della pratica dell'arte locale, Cagliari che un'Accademia non l'ha mai avuta da cosa dovrebbe ripartire?

Da orientatore le dico che è altissima la percentuale di studenti maturandi al Fois che emigrano dall'isola per non tornare più se non per farsi qualche bagno estivo al Poetto o qualche residenza d'artista, perché a parità di costi di spostamenti da studenti fuori sede, ritengono altre realtà Italiane ed Europee più stimolanti di Sassari; alta (ma in proporzione minore, dal momento che l'ottantacinque per cento degli studenti del Fois prosegue con un percorso UNICA) è anche la percentuale di studenti che abbandonano l'Accademia di Sassari per una questione di costi da fuori sede, non sostenuti da adeguati stimoli (dal momento che le Accademie in rete con i Licei delle comunità dove operano, dovrebbero fondarsi sulle proprie tradizioni culturali e artistiche locali, e Sassari e Cagliari non hanno la stessa storia dell'arte, non si può paragonare il Rinascimento Fiorentino a quello Senese, la Storia dell'Arte e la formazione artistica hanno una dimensione locale da connettere con l'altrove, anche a livello Regionale (la Regione Sicilia vanta un'Accademia di Belle Arti per ogni capoluogo di provincia, la Puglia ne ha tre, solo per fare qualche esempio).

Questo avviene nella Regione d'Europa che ha il più alto tasso di dispersione scolastica e d'emigrazione giovanile d'Europa, ottica nella

quale andrebbe considerato come un'Accademia non sarebbe
destinata soltanto ad accogliere studenti dei corsi d'Arti Figurative del
Foiso Fois, ma anche diplomati fuoriusciti da altri percorsi con indole e
animo creativo (chi l'ha detto che un diplomato Geometra non possa
diventare uno Scultore o uno Scenografo?).
In questi anni d'opposizione alla giunta Pigliaru, molte forze politiche
della sua coalizione della sua opposizione si sono mosse per
sensibilizzare l'allora maggioranza su questa incredibile anomalia, è
forse il caso di mettersi da subito al lavoro in tale direzione o non è
così?
La saluto con stima e affetto e le auguro buon lavoro (a lei e la sua
maggioranza di governo), con la speranza che la sua amministrazione
della Regione Sardegna riesca dove a oggi hanno fallito tutti, non
leggendo neanche la reale portata Regionale di questa anomalia,
progettando e autodeterminando l'Accademia di Belle Arti di Cagliari,
Mimmo Di Caterino.

Arte, sesso e cervello

Ipotesi recenti, attestano che molte delle modalità comportamentali dei
sapiens, proprio quelle che paiono essere esclusive della natura della
condizione umana, si sarebbero evolute e stabilizzate per effetto della
selezione sessuale.
La selezione sessuale avrebbe affinato il linguaggio rendendolo più
articolato, le manifestazioni e le espressioni artistiche, musica, senso
etico ed estetico, morale e via dicendo.
La consapevolezza del linguaggio e dell'espressione artistica,
sembrerebbe conferiscano a chi le esercita, nella competizione
riproduttiva, la base seduttiva del patrimonio ereditario.
Sembra che di riflesso, anche l'espansione encefalica, sia d'attribuire
alla nostra selezione sessuale, al controllo sugli altri e alla selezione con
cognizione.
L'arte sarebbe legata esclusivamente alla seduzione e al
corteggiamento, l'ostentazione dell'arte e della sua comprensione (da
parte dell'artista, del collezionista, del critico, del curatore, dello storico
o del generico "addetto ai lavori"), sarebbe l'equivalente umano di ciò
che ostentano pavoni o cervi, ossia code spettacolari e impalcature di
corna ramificate, nulla a che vedere con la sopravvivenza o con
l'economia tradotta in cibo, non facilitano la vita in natura ma la
rendono più problematica, ma costituiscono un inequivocabile richiamo
sessuale.

Sostanzialmente l'uomo con il suo cervello e la sua capacità di leggere e comprendere i linguaggi dell'arte contemporanea, si muove con maggiore comodità di un cervo e di un pavone, a patto che un cervello educato all'arte e alla sua comprensione lo abbia.
Perché scrivo questo?
Perché forse un'Accademia di Belle Arti a Cagliari contrasterebbe il fenomeno delle denatalità d'area metropolitana con annesso spopolamento e una comunità sempre più anziana, passando per la passione estetica tradotta in etica, mi sbaglio?

#AccademiaNuragica a Capoterra

Il primo Maggio è stata presentata nella località della Maddalena Spiaggia, la Scultura "Accademia Nuragica", Scultura realizzata nello stesso litorale che ha avuto tre mesi di lavorazione a cielo aperto.
La Scultura è stata realizzata su pietra (ignimbrite di Serrenti), ed è stata frutto di un lungo lavoro d'interazione e relazione quotidiana con la comunità e il territorio.
Il formato della pietra è di 4 metri di larghezza per un basamento di 1 metro per 1 metro e cinquanta, pare essere la Scultura in trachite più grande realizzata nell'isola in maniera tradizionale.
Gli Scultori e l'amministrazione Comunale hanno tenuto a sottolineare come il lavoro non volesse confinare la cultura degli Shardana e dei Nur a qualcosa di archeologico e immutabile nel tempo.
L'idea di fondo è stata quella di rendere contemporanea e vitale una Scultura che avesse la grammatica di fondo della cultura dei Nur.
In quest'ottica e con la consapevolezza che la collocazione definitiva del monumento sarà una rotonda all'ingresso di Capoterra, si è lavorato su di un impianto di fondo circolare e multisprospettico, prestando particolare attenzione all'interazione con la luce.
Il prospetto principale rappresenta un gigante nuragico, che in realtà è un ritratto del Maestro Antonello Pilittu, storico Scultore Capoterrese con alle spalle un'attività quarantennale, nonché anima e maestranza curatoriale e progettuale di "Accademia Nuragica".
Origine ideale della cultura Nuragica e Shardana è un frammento di Dea Madre protonuragica dalla quale si animano guerrieri e forme ambigue che componendosi fanno pensare a una navicella, ricorrente è anche la figura del capovolto protonuragico a porre l'accento su come la Scultura Nuragica costituisse anche una connessione e un collegamento spirituale con l'oltretomba.
Elemento di riflessione importante del progetto e l'avere pensato alla Scultura come progetto culturale da radicare nel territorio, nel nome di

questo si è andati oltre l'individualismo dell'arte e degli artisti contemporanei.

 Sul progetto comune "Accademia Nuragica" hanno lavorato e interagito, tra di loro e con la comunità, cinque diversi Scultori ("piccaparderi" direbbe nella sua immensa umiltà Antonello Pilittu) ai quali a loro volta si sono connessi durante la gestione del lavoro artisti e intellettuali dell'area di Cagliari città metropolitana (per citare qualche nome: la storica dell'arte Ivana Salis, i composer Nicola Agus e Mebitek, i cantautori Andrea Andrillo, Flavio Secchi, Igor Lampis e Andrea Locci, l'attrice Elena Pau, il jazzista australiano Peter Waters, la poetessa e scrittrice Alessandra Fanti, il fotografo Antonio Maria Dettori, il blogger Gianfranco Ghironi, il filmaker indipendente Roberto Pili, l'archivista della soprintendenza Vincenzo Gaias, lo studioso Pierluigi Montalbano, lo storico interprete compositore degli "Is Cantores" Albino Puddu, il mascheraio e curatore d'arte contemporanea Massimiliano Vacca e tanti altri).

Sindaco e amministrazione comunale, in attesa del passaggio di Sant'Efisio, accompagnato dalla musica di Nicola Agus, hanno reso noto di stare già lavorando per determinare una seconda (da fare partire a breve) e una terza edizione di Accademia Nuragica, come fosse un triennio d'Alta Formazione Artistica, di formazione e condivisione didattica e dialettica per la comunità e il territorio.

L'idea di fondo è che la Scultura sia da sempre il principale social network d'aggregazione dell'umano, dal momento che la scrittura e i distinguo tra le varie culture dell'umano nascono in maniera tridimensionale su pietra o tavolette d'argilla, in tal senso il progetto "Accademia Nuragica" negli anni a venire lo s'intenderà progressivamente sempre più aperto e inclusivo nei confronti dell'arte residente, dal momento che l'attuale panorama sociale globalizzato e interconnesso, rende tutti i luoghi "internazionali", proprio come il team di questa edizione di Accademia Nuragica, composto da intelligenze residenti (o domiciliate) a Capoterra provenienti da ambiti culturali e di formazione eterogenei.

Accademia Nuragica attesta come Capoterra possa autodeterminarsi come polo attrattivo non solo turistico ma anche culturale e artistico, partendo proprio dalla Scultura contemporanea su pietra, che in quest'ottica "Accademia Nuragica" possa costituire la pietra miliare sulla quale fondare un triennio d'Alta Formazione Artistica di Scultura?

In fondo a Capoterra oltre ai cinque artisti di Accademia Nuragica (Antonello Pilittu, Luigi Ignazio Cappai, Jennie Baila, Barbara Ardau e Mimmo Di Caterino) risiedono anche Scultori come Gianni Marongiu ed è stata la comunità dove hanno scelto di vivere e di lavorare artisti di spessore internazionale come Primo Pantoli, interessante è anche il movimento di giovani artisti che vivono e lavorano a Capoterra come Francesco Cogoni, Oleg Mulliri e Alessandro Pili, d'altronde l'entusiasmo con cui il sindaco Francesco Dessì e la sua giunta hanno sostenuto il lavoro e il progetto, non può che essere espressione di un clima e di un approccio culturale profondamente radicato nella dignità e nell'intelligenza collettiva e connettiva dell'intera comunità Capoterrese.

ACCADEMIA PER IL CORAGGIO DI NON PIACERE

Questo è il millennio di Facebook, Twitter e Instagram, il millennio dove gli artisti, ma anche presunti esperti d'arte, cercano il consenso e il riconoscimento pubblico attraverso persone che conoscono a malapena.Lo studio passa con questa logica in secondo piano, e si sottovaluta come anche milioni di persone con le relative visualizzazioni, in fatto di ricerche artistiche contemporanee possano errare e prendere un abbaglio.Pensateci: sul serio pensate ci possa fidare delle folle? Pensate a tutti gli artisti che dalla Rivoluzione industriale in poi, hanno dovuto passare una vita a confrontarsi e contrastare proprio le persone deputate a riconoscerli, pensate agli Impressionisti e a quanto oggi siano caratterizzanti per tutta la storia dell'arte moderna e contemporanea.Frequentare seriamente un'Accademia d'Alta Formazione Artistica, vuole dire educarsi a non seguire conformisticamente il flusso della corrente, vuole dire essere sfacciati con la consapevolezza e la coscienza dello studio, ed anche del rischio che comporta la connessione tra la propria coscienza etica e la percezione estetica.Percorsi diversi nascono solo attraverso lo studio, altrimenti che tutti tendano a fare parte della massa ed essere conformi agli altri è una tappa obbligata.Una cosa è fare arte per piacere al prossimo, altra cosa investire sullo studio da tradurre in originale percorso creativo, quello che è originale (e la Storia dell'Arte e della Scienza questo insegnano) non è sempre popolare, l'originalità è messa in discussione, indagata, messa alla prova e smontata, ma se nell'originalità c'è una buona ricerca che sa connettere linguisticamente passato e futuro, tradizione e innovazione, allora sopravvivrà. Questo è un'Accademia di Belle Arti, l'educazione al coraggio di non piacere, fate attenzione artisti vecchi e giovani privi di studio e formazione, non piacere potrebbe anche piacervi.

ACCADEMIA PER APRIRSI AL MONDO

La relazione tra l'estetica e la propria condizione interiore, determina l'impressione del bello, questo avviene nell'umano universalmente. L'estetica necessita però di educazione e di formazione, in tutti i linguaggi come in tutte le culture, si manifesta con diverse specializzazione linguistiche (pittura, scultura, musica, videoarte, fotografia, scenografia, architettura, scrittura, poesia, danza...), il bello muta e si manifesta in relazione al sentimento estetico e alla cognizione culturale dei singoli come degli individui.

Quando si ragiona su cosa sia o non sia bello, serve partire dal canone culturale di chi lo materializza e di chi l'osserva.

Non esistono canoni ideali e norme comuni, non esistono bellezze universali da leggere in bellezze particolari, la bellezza è un canone linguistico e culturale particolare, sempre da comprendere e studiare.

Nell'evoluzione della vita, delle vite e nei linguaggi c'è il segreto dell'esuberanza creativa dell'essere che vive, è la vita ad essere l'artista quando sa tradursi in narrazione linguistica e simbolica, isolare l'estetica dal pensiero creativo è deleterio.

Lo stato poetico dell'osservatore più che dell'artista (che a volte osserva se stesso) determina l'emozione estetica, l'estetica è intercomunicazione, interconnessione e intercontaminazione.

L'artista insegue non il bello ma l'estetica, l'artigiano insegue l'utile che abbia qualità estetica, la magia di questo inseguimento determina l'estetica.

La storia dell'umano è fatta di magia, religione e identità, questo materializza sculture, dipinti, tatuaggi, maschere, bracciali, collane, danze, musiche, canti, ceramiche, fiaschi, anfore..., così si determinano identità, clan, comunità e anche la sessualità, nel contemporaneo il linguaggio dell'arte, che si affrancato nel tempo dalla religione, si è isolato e specializzato nel nome dell'arte per l'arte, l'emozione estetica quando si determina connette mistero e magia, questo alone e codice ambiguo, ci riporta non solo all'essenza dell'arte ma all'essenza dell'umano.

Estetica barbarica?

La cultura artistica Occidentale (ma quella Sarda è altra storia dell'Arte) ha creduto per molto tempo che i suoi canoni di bellezza fossero universali.

La Scultura e la Pittura, la bellezza greca rappresentata da Lisippo e Prassitele, è stata concepita (o imposta?) come modello di ogni bellezza, Rinascimento e Neoclassicismo altro non hanno fatto che partire da quella grammatica per creare nuove opere.

In Europa e in Italia (che non vuole dire Sardegna) si è, erroneamente, creduto che la concezione classica della bellezza (compostezza, armonia, equilibrio e regolarità), debba escludere ogni scoria critica, ogni bruttezza e nefandezza da ricondurre all'umano, determinare un'antinomia senza riserve tra bello e brutto.

La globalizzazione ha contribuito a sdoganare (o imporre?) quest'estetica elevata a dogma prima che a canone, non è proprio il marketing della globalizzazione a rendere popolare la Gioconda a Tokyo anche più di Leonardo?

Marketing e globalizzazione non sono riusciti ad annullare i generi e i canoni estetici Giapponesi di bellezza, e in quest'ottica non possono e non riusciranno ad annullare i canoni estetici e il linguaggio artistico Nuragico, con buona pace di Winckelmann che lo giudicava infatti primitivo e barbarico.

Non è forse la globalizzazione a fornire in questo millennio all'isola la possibilità di scoprire e fare riconoscere la specificità e la bellezza della sua cultura attraverso la sua storia e i suoi artisti?

Ci fosse un'Accademia nell'area di Cagliari Città Metropolitana, si potrebbe riflettere con cognizione di causa su come Goya in Occidente abbia rinegoziato le frontiere tra bello e brutto in Occidente, di come Impressionisti, Van Gogh e Cézanne abbiano gettato le basi per una sensibilità estetica che sappia essere bella anche nella disarmonia.

Le condizioni della creazione e della progettazione artistica, sono, prima di Goya, Van Gogh e Cézanne, per lungo tempo dipese da signori e corti potenti o da papi, l'arte comincia a esercitare la sua libertà di ricerca e autodeterminazione tra il XIX e il XX secolo.

Ma in questo passaggio, bisogna comprendere come affrancandosi dalla religione, dal potere e dal mecenate, progressivamente si è consegnata alla dipendenza del mercato, gran parte di quelli che oggi si considerano artisti contemporanei sono solo merce.

L'idea dell'artista individualizzato non è dissimile dalla contemporanea comunicazione dei social network, ci si oppone alla società del denaro per dipenderne; l'artista "disobbediente" esalta la sua libertà, la sua originalità e la sua creatività, in un contesto sociale di gregge di filistei, che, comunque, seppure insultati da lui, comprano le sue opere.

Un'Accademia serve a tamponare questo processo che riduce i linguaggi dell'arte a merce, a sensibilizzare sui linguaggi dell'arte come bene culturale comune da radicare nella comunità.

La tradizione pittorica e scultorea di un territorio, di una cultura, di una comunità, non può essere manipolata dal mercato, deve sapere svilupparsi nel pubblico e con il pubblico e tamponare gli eccessi e le bolle economiche del mercato, il profitto della ricerca artistica comunitaria deve sapere tamponare il profitto della ricerca artistica omologata, globalizzata e privatizzata, in questo millennio quella dei linguaggi dell'arte è una battaglia che ha comunque bisogno della collaborazione con il suo antagonista, il profitto, in quest'ottica un'Accademia nodo formativo in una realtà complessa come quella Cagliaritana, è una necessità.

La creatività artistica deve essere stimolata da condizioni esterne, non è detto che per essere artisti contemporanei serva frequentare un'Accademia, ma è certo che anche per chi non frequenta un'Accademia di Belle Arti, l'Accademia di Belle Arti è uno stimolo territoriale a lui esterno.

L'arte è l'espressione più elevata del gioco della maturità, gli artisti residenti (e per questo la loro Alta Formazione e lo stimolatore Accademia a Cagliari sarebbe fondamentale) connettendo estetico e ludico, sono un valore aggiunto economico, politico, cerimoniali e religiosi, chi se non l'artista residente è guida che pone il suo talento con la sua vocazione, al servizio di una causa o di una fede comune?

L'umanità non può vivere solo di realtà, l'arte è il compromesso con la realtà che ci consente di sopportarla, l'arte residente è l'unico strumento reale, quando sa mettersi al servizio della comunità, per evadere, per ritrovare umanità, passione, compassione e comprensione, evade dal divertimento senza divertimento, è vivere poeticamente la realtà con la consapevolezza della sua crudeltà, l'arte (come tutte le cose) non salva nessuno dalla morte, ma con l'amore e la passione verso la comprensione dell'umana condizione, che stimola e determina, che include e in cui è inclusa, è la sola risposta possibile della vita alla morte.

Cagliari necessita di sviluppare e porre a sistema la sua cultura, considerando il termine cultura in tutta la sua complessità.

La cultura è etnografica, ossia la cultura di un popolo, i suoi riti, i suoi costumi, le sue credenze; la cultura è anche Antropologica, non innata, qualcosa che va appresa con il linguaggio, la tecnica, le arti, a questo servono i corsi di un'Accademia di Belle Arti.

Certo, anche senza un'Accademia di Belle Arti, la cultura è presente nella realtà metropolitana Cagliaritana, ma è cultura popolare, ferma al piacere e al divertimento; è cultura di massa, mediatica, cultura della stampa nazionale, dei quotidiani, televisiva, di facebook e Instagram, ma questa cultura voi la definireste senza riserve estetica? Vi sembra questo possa supplire all'Alta Formazione Artistica?

La comprensione e l'educazione all'estetica, che passa per l'Alta Formazione Artistica radicata in una comunità, necessita d'empatia, i linguaggi dell'arte permettono di aprirci a noi stessi mediante la comprensione del linguaggio dell'altro.

La meraviglia della comprensione e l'esercizio dei linguaggi dell'arte, è la conservazione dell'umano, riuscire a essere meno chiusi, meno egocentrici, più comprensivi, aperti e complessi.

In questo millennio, uno dei grandi problemi dell'arte e della cultura residente è proprio questo, come conservare nel contemporaneo il valore umano della pratica dei linguaggi dell'arte.

L'umano Cagliaritano non si può solo nutrire culturalmente di pani e casu, di cinghialetto e maialetto, e fritture di pesce e bottarga; quella della comprensione dell'arte dell'altro è una sua necessità formativa spirituale, l'arte è una necessità per non ridurre una vita a calcolo, profitto e tornaconto personale, tutto questo porta alla frammentazione e alla dispersione dell'umano.

Uno dei più grandi piaceri dell'umano è la condivisione artistica e culturale, comprendere insieme un linguaggio artistico arricchisce poeticamente; comprendere vuole dire riconoscere l'unità e la diversità nel linguaggio dell'altro, per fare questo Cagliari necessita di un'Accademia di Belle Arti che garantisca un'insegnamento e una formazione costante alla comunità metropolitana, che radichi una apertura linguistica e comunitaria stabilmente nei giovani artisti residenti che verranno, che vada oltre la comprensione che duri il tempo di una mostra o la visione di un quadro.

Accademia a Cagliari vorrebbe dire, insegnare cosa e quanto sia importante la poesia dell'essere nella vita, sviluppare una cognizione di causa e dell'essere estetico che vada oltre la seduzione dell'estetica.

La creazione artistica è sempre complessa, connette conscio e inconscio, implica l'innesto di sapere e competenze multidisciplinari, in quest'ottica, un'Accademia di Belle Arti a Cagliari, sarebbe una rivoluzione possibile (culturale prima che economica) essenziale.

Formare l'arte e gli artisti residenti, vuole dire dialogare con la bellezza della vita nel mondo, ma anche resistere alla sua crudeltà di senso.

ACCADEMIA ARGINE PER LA RIVOLUZIONE TRADITA

"La privacy non è più una convenzione sociale."
Mark Zuckerberg

A Cagliari tutto quello che riguarda l'Alta Formazione Artistica, sembra una questione di "borghesia mancata", tutto sembra ridursi a uomini e donne con interessi artistici velleitari e superficiali, tutto appare incatenato a un mondo fatto di cravatte, colletti bianchi, tacchi, borsette, tailleur, giacche, giacchette e preoccupazioni burocratiche.

L'arte e gli artisti, la ricerca e l'elaborazione di linguaggi artistici non sono questo, non sono servi di logiche di produzione e distribuzione del tempo, spesso si muovono anzi contro tempo, non seguono l'onda della massa, la criticano e inducono a fermarsi a riflettere.

La contemporaneità al di fuori degli spazi didattici e dialettici dell'arte (Accademie e Musei) sembra muoversi per escludere gli artisti che non sono funzionali, alle logiche commerciali di questo tempo.

Pensate a Youtube, ha un ritmo di crescita annuale del sessanta per cento, è di fatto il più importante canale di diffusione di video sull'arte e la cultura al mondo, ma quanti sono i video che superano le mille visualizzazioni?

La verità è che produzione, autodeterminazione e ricerca artistica culturale, non possono passare il web, il web non è riuscito ad eliminare gli intermediari; curatori, galleristi, storici e critici sono soltanto stati allineati dal web, sono finiti a intermediari le esigenze dei grossi mercati, convergendo e mettendosi d'accordo su parole, aree d'interesse e artisti funzionali a ingenti vestimenti privati di mercato.

Il web ha traghettato gli addetti ai lavori verso il dogma ideologico del "più forte prende tutto".

In questo panorama artistico e culturale, globalmente piatto, è difficile pensare ad artisti che non mirino a essere prodotti di mercato, difficile che maturino privi d'adeguata formazione, artisti che elaborino linguaggi complessi che richiedano tempo per essere compresi appieno; per questo un'Accademia a Cagliari sarebbe necessaria, servirebbe ad attrezzarsi contro il tempo, per investire su linguaggi contemporanei che sappiano essere fuori dal tempo.

In Italia oggi l'Accademia è l'unico intermediario possibile tra la formazione e la ricerca di un giovane artista e il suo territorio e comunità culturale, altrimenti come evadere dalla logica del capitale e dei governi che si legano l'uno all'altro, facendo tabula rasa della cultura del pubblico e dello specifico di una comunità con la sua cultura artistica millenaria come quella isolana?

Questo è il millennio della massiccia concentrazione di potere di pochi colossi finanziari, avviene in ogni settore dell'economia globale, avviene ovviamente anche nel settore dell'arte contemporanea, mercato dell'arte contemporanea che ha degli interessi ovviamente nel settore strategico dei mezzi di comunicazione di massa.

Complici delle performance eccessive di certe opere d'arte contemporanea, sono nel mito dell'efficienza giganti del web come Google, Amazon e Facebook, che rendono tutto merce prima che ricerca artistica e culturale, il valore materiale passa attraverso i gigabyte che riguardano l'artista, da consumatore come da produttore; guardate un video? Leggete un articolo? Fate una ricerca su questo o quell'artista? Contribuite a determinare il mercato e a legittimarne i valori.

Un tempo il ruolo sociale dell'artista era evidenziare le ingiustizie e le dissonanze sociali (e culturali), in certi periodi la Storia dell'Arte è stata rivoluzione e disobbedienza, l'artista d'avanguardia era questo.

Oggi il web ha scardinato e appiattito questo, oggi l'artista che vuole lavorare sulla libera ricerca, connessione e autodeterminazione artistica e culturale, deve, forza maggiore, relazionarsi e sottostare ai giganti del web.

Tutto quello che avviene nell'arte contemporanea, più che in mostre e in cataloghi, è su Google o Facebook, la vanità e l'ego dell'artista vanno ben oltre il suo riserbo, ovunque interesserà il pubblico attrarrà la sua economia

Google e Facebook vantano più di un miliardo d'utenze, Amazon trecentocinquanta milioni, pensate ai loro introiti pubblicitari, in quest'ottica, nel sistema artistico e culturale che si annuncia, le informazioni sugli artisti sono le monografie che verranno, scritte in tempo reale, il nuovo petrolio del sistema dell'arte.

Il web è le principali piattaforme dell'arte, non risolveranno mai i problemi valoriali dell'arte e della cultura contemporanea, non consentiranno mai all'artista di comprendere come guadagnare e cercare gratificazione nel proprio lavoro o ricerca, non illustrerà mai il possibile ruolo sociale dell'arte e dell'arte nell'epoca dell'economia digitale.

Per questo Cagliari avrebbe bisogno di un Rinascimento Nuragico (se preferite Shardana) prima che digitale, come tutti i Rinascimenti, questo dovrebbe passare per un'azione di resistenza culturale verso il modello economico globalmente imposto, per questo servirebbe che avvenisse quello che non è mai avvenuto a Cagliari, porre l'Alta Formazione Artistica al centro della politica di sviluppo economico, culturale e turistico, quell'Accademia di Belle Arti che non è mai stata.

La cultura e la ricerca artistica, non sono come un modello di cellulare superato da gettare via non appena sorpassato dall'innovazione digitale; le Accademie di Belle Arti in Italia e in Europa sono un patrimonio secolare, la ricerca artistica in un territorio, ha nella continuità la sua fondamenta irrinunciabile, l'artista è soltanto un anello di un sistema, un anello di una catena della memoria che vive e legge (anche criticamente) il presente.

L'Accademia è il luogo di tutela e custodia della specificità artistica e culturale di un territorio, le barriere e i limiti si traducono in melting pot quando la tradizione e la cultura sanno vivere e rigenerarsi in uno spazio geografico.

I linguaggi dell'arte, la formazione artistica e l'alta formazione artistica sono il connettore tra persone che si ritrovano per cultura, linguaggio e simboli; come si può fare arte contemporanea a Cagliari senza studiare i suoi ultimi diecimila anni?

Tutto questo, si può sintetizzare nel consenso del click on line?

Pensate a Cagliari oggi, esiste la figura dell'artista contemporaneo?

Che ruolo sociale svolge?

Quanto è riconosciuta la sua attività poetica e intellettuale nella comunità?

Eppure questo millennio dovrebbe e potrebbe essere il momento più grande e di maggiore visibilità della storia dell'arte Cagliaritana e isolana nel mondo; mai come oggi, una quantità ampia d'artisti Cagliaritani, interagisce e dialoga con le ricerche artistiche dell'altrove, tutto questo dovrebbe essere stimolante e adrenalinico, e per chi proviene dal secolo passato e si è formato adeguatamente forse lo è, ma la vera domanda che ci si dovrebbe porre è: l'artista Cagliaritano del futuro, come potrà farsi una vita e formarsi artisticamente se impossibilitato a emigrare? Quale contesto sociale e culturale dovrebbe stimolarne la ricerca se un'Accademia a Cagliari non c'è mai stata?

Se intendiamo connettere etica ed estetica nel presente che formerà il futuro dell'arte Cagliaritana, un'Accademia d'Alta Formazione Artistica è un polo necessario.

Google, Facebook, Youtube e Instagram, non possono formare artisticamente in questo millennio, non possono farlo perché sono aziende private, aziende che hanno come loro tesoro i dati personali dell'utente, di riflesso trattano l'artista come un utente consumatore.

Tra un video documento di un'intervista a Pinuccio Sciola e un video di gattini, quello che si trova più appetibile è il video che ha un numero maggiore di visualizzazioni, le visualizzazioni materializzano introiti pubblicitari, così si muove il web.

Bisogna considerare come il sistema dell'arte in questo millennio, sia ispirato al modello economico dominante, ossia quello di Google, Amazon e Facebook, presumibilmente senza queste grosse aziende, l'intero sistema economico dell'arte proveniente dal secolo passato, sarebbe già abbondantemente in ginocchio.

Con questo nuovo scenario didattico ed educativo dell'arte, ponte e nodo, tra la ricerca artistica contemporanea e le nuove tecnologie, non può che essere un'Accademia di Belle Arti.

In fondo, senza formazione artistica adeguata, quali contenuti che elevino il senso comune, si possono inserire in una piattaforma di 1,6 miliardi di utenti come Facebook?

Su Facebook non si paga per mostrare il proprio lavoro e ci si può dichiarare artisti senza passare per un'Accademia di Belle Arti o gli addetti ai lavori, ma questo avviene perché postando su Facebook si è già un prodotto.

Gli utilizzatori abituali di Facebook sono 1,23 miliardi di persone al giorno, utenti che accedono alla propria pagina per 12 minuti al giorno, concedendo i propri dati e contenuti a un monopolio che su questi guadagna immense fortune, tutto questo verso dove dirotta l'arte? Verso universi di comunicazione interpersonali, autoespressivi, verso il passatempo e l'intrattenimento, questo dirottamento ha qualcosa a che vedere con la comunità?

Facebook non mostra il sé reale dell'arte e dell'artista, rappresenta il sé potenziale, l'artista si mostra e appare come l'artista che vorrebbe essere, si alimenta di un sistema ideale che nella realtà è finzione determinata dall'interesse.

Complicato per artisti attempati avere uno sguardo critico su tutto questo, immaginate quanto possa esserlo per un generico studente che non passi per un percorso d'Alta Formazione Artistica, comprendere tutto questo ed esprimere e sviluppare propri contenuti via social network.

Da studente io, una mia opinione politica e culturale, una mia ricerca artistica, ero riuscita a impostarla sfuggendo al controllo della cultura imposta dai luoghi comuni dove ho studiato e mi sono formato e anche al controllo dei miei genitori, attraverso lo studio e attraverso l'Accademia, ma se fossi nato in questo millennio privo di privacy? Questo è il millennio del marketing della sorveglianza, dove chi riesce a raccogliere più dati personali sulle vite, il linguaggio e la ricerca degli artisti, le rivende al migliore offerente; è il millennio delle pubblicità sponsorizzate, ogni euro delle campagne pubblicitarie on line fa finire nelle tasche di Google o Facebook 85 centesimi, evidente che non ci sia artista che cerchi attenzione del pubblico che possa fare a meno di loro.

Facebook è l'intermediario capace di garantire, agli addetti ai lavori dell'arte, un pubblico di due miliardi di utenti, ma logicamente, questo "acchiappa clic" abbassa il livello dei contenuti culturali e artistici dell'umano.

Curatori e intermediari vari, individuano artisti interessanti esclusivamente su Facebook, per questo a Cagliari servirebbe un'Accademia d'Alta Formazione Artistica, per fare si che gli artisti Cagliaritani sappiano anteporre i contenuti della loro ricerca ai contenuti sponsorizzati.

I linguaggi dell'arte e la ricerca artistica, sono vivi quando si confrontano con una pluralità dialettica, questo ha bisogno di un luogo reale, di un'Accademia; Facebook filtra strumentalmente la visione, e questo è ideologico, non è civile, la propria rete di contatti diventa un limite ideologico nel nome del "togliere l'amicizia", e questo è ovvio che precluda la formazione.

Intanto nel nome del lavoro (che non c'è più), scuole, licei e Università, rincorrendo crediti e Attività Scuola Lavoro, diventano sempre di più istituti professionali, questo è criminale, non si può vivere senza arti liberali, non si può vivere dipendendo intellettualmente da Wall Street o dalla Silicon Valley.

Le arti liberali sono il pilastro fondante delle comunità, senza arte diffusa non c'è empatia, è l'arte con la sua estetica a determinare le condizioni interiori per una condotta etica; senza arti liberali diffuse e sostenute, l'arte diviene un semplice prodotto postato su Facebook, una subcultura dove l'ego e il narciso, demoliscono l'empatico.

Il sistema dell'arte che viaggia via social network, è una macchina di artisti resi prodotti, alimentazione della serialità della creatività, una idea di talento fondata esclusivamente sulla pertinenza tecnica, quello che attraversa i social network non potrà mai essere Rinascimento.

Un Rinascimento potrebbe essere lavorare in maniera comune e trasversale per un'Accademia a Cagliari, è un fatto che i periodi storici prolifici durino un lasso di tempo ristretto per poi esaurirsi, ma determinano a partire da loro, un'interesse incessante; contrapposizioni, rivalità tra artisti che lavorano, si confrontano e discutono, questo eleva la media comune, questo sarebbe un'Accademia.

L'Accademia a Cagliari, sarebbe l'unica risposta possibile all'omologazione dei social; internet consente ritagli di spazi personali, ma ingloba in ricerche di bassa qualità.

Serve capire che se quella digitale in questo millennio è stata una rivoluzione, storicamente non esiste rivoluzione che non tradisca se stessa, chiedetelo ai Parigini dopo il 1780 o a Mosca dopo il 1925; la nuova frontiera Cagliaritana sarebbe da individuare nel porre a sistema Regionale una propria alta formazione artistica residente, rappresentando una Cagliari che sappia essere artisticamente empatica, capace di narrare, riflettere e agire culturalmente, perché il lato umano ed empatico dell'arte, non può essere dominato dalla tecnoscienza e da algoritmi digitali.

IL LINGUAGGIO NELLO SGUARDO

Jacopo Pontormo,
sapeva che un quadro,
senza ombre, spazio, misura di poesia nel colore,
agitava i conformisti.

Michelangelo non eseguiva ritratti,
ma uno lo fece, quello di Bruto;
il ritratto di chi uccise un padre che vuole uccidere la Repubblica;

oggi non serve un pugnale, ma la forza delle idee.

L'Arte non rimuove la memoria, non rende mai le voci critiche immobili,
impone la verità, come faceva Tiziano ritraendo i suoi stessi padroni,
questo è l'artista,
tira la verità, la spiega, la stira e l'indossa.

Prima di Twitter, di Facebook, della televisione e della radio, il potente e
il padrono, cho voleva promuovere una notizia,
non si rivolgeva al giornalista sciacallo della notizia, ma agli artisti, arte e
artisti rappresentano l'impero, questo si era capito nel Rinascimento.

L'arte è la finestra del sogno di una comunità, consente d'osservare
tutto senza toccare niente, puoi osservare la vita dell'artista con il suo
sguardo, ma non sarai mai lui,
con lo sguardo della vita dell'artista si può vivere la propria vita,
continuando a osservare.

Osservando la verità ci si confronta con il potere,
s'impara che il potere non ama la verità e anche che non esiste un
potere che possa sostituire la verità;
si può nascondere la verità, si può uccidere la verità, ma mai sostituirla.

Zeusi e Parrasio sapevano che il dialogo tra artisti ha un'unica modalità
per essere possibile,
attraverso l'opera tradotta in linguaggio comune,
attraverso lo sguardo che diventa linguaggio e risponde allo sguardo
dell'altro.

Arte e artisti non servono alla cultura, servono alla natura.
Il linguaggio dell'arte è nella natura, è sintetico, vola più alto delle parole
al vento e di quelle controvento.

IL CONTATTO CON L'ARTE

Qual'è l'ambizione di tutti i linguaggi dell'arte?
La relazione, il riuscire a toccare l'altro, a contattarlo, questo non lo si
può soltanto studiare, non si possono ottenere reazioni spontanee ed
emotive nell'altro dandogli soltanto quello che si aspetta, fosse così il
linguaggio dell'arte sarebbe solo "tecnica dell'arte".
Il linguaggio dell'arte deriva dall'incontro e dal contatto dell'intera
esperienza dell'umano, narrazione e rappresentazione d'esperienze di

corpi e di sensi, il contatto tra umani che passa attraverso il linguaggio dell'arte, riduce la distanza tra l'osservatore e lo spettatore, ma non l'abolisce.

Il prodotto del linguaggio di un artista è un punto di contatto, ma resta la distanza individuale tra chi rappresenta e chi è contattato dalla rappresentazione.

L'identità individuale si costruisce e si rappresenta in funzione della relazione con l'altro, si forma in relazione all'altro.

La concettualizzazione dei linguaggi dell'arte, vincola tutto al senso sociale e alla comunità, ma i linguaggi dell'arte tendono sempre a scardinare la tensione tra la libertà individuale e di ricerca dell'artista, e il senso sociale della comunità.

Il contatto che passa attraverso i linguaggi dell'arte, tutela il singolare come il prulare, disegnando una comunità di cui tutti fanno parte; l'arte è quella stretta di mano che determina la libertà individuale e personale d'essere.

Toccare l'altro con il proprio linguaggio artistico, o lasciarsi contattare da un linguaggio artistico attraverso l'osservazione, vuole dire garantire l'esistenza dell'altro e tastare la propria esistenza.

Arte è osservare

Copiare le opere d'arte è qualcosa che era prassi ai tempi dei Romani, si moltiplilcavano pitture e sculture famose e apprezzate attraverso reticolati e puntellature; oggi esporre una copia di una Scultura greca o romana in giardino è considerato in sostanza di cattivo gusto, ma nel mondo antico la copia era la norma, anche tra i privati più colti e raffinati.

Oggi lo Scultore lavora su committenza pubblica o privato, e il suo lavoro non consiste nella copia, ma nell'interpretazione, passando per il proprio linguaggio, stile e ricerca, ma l'elaborazione di un linguaggio, di uno stile e di una ricerca, si origina ancora dallo studio Accademico di una copia dal vero, si osserva e s'interpreta assecondando la propria visione e capacità d'osservazione.

Non esiste ragionando sull'arte come linguaggio, e non come mestiere, una vera copia, talvolta anche chi è convinto di copiare non si rende conto di stare interpretando.

L'arte non è pensata per produrre serialità, ma certe specializzazione di genere dei linguaggi dell'arte pensano seriale (la Grafica e il Design ad esempio).

Raccordo e origine di tutti i linguaggi e le specializzazioni di genere dell'arte contemporanea, è il disegno; disegnare non vuole però dire tracciare figure, ma inventarle, il disegno è lo strumento del ragionare. Disegnare in tutte le materie laboratoriali artistiche (Pittura, Scultura, Design, Grafica, Audiovisivo, Scenografia e Architettura), vuole dire progettare, non esiste linguaggio dell'arte contemporanea che non richieda la progettazione; progettare vuole dire anche pensare ai canali di diffusione e divulgazione di un'idea, non si può pensare a progettare un artefatto senza pensare a una sua messa in opera sociale.

Capite quanto sia anomalo lo scenario artistico Cagliaritano, privo di un'Accademia che dovrebbe formare chi dovrebbe pensare al linguaggio dell'arte inserito nello scenario programmatico operativo Cagliaritano?

La comunicazione artistica accade sempre in un flusso d'altra comunicazione, alla base del flusso c'è sempre il saper vedere, la pittura è nel cinema, la letteratura è nella pittura, il cinema è nella danza, la danza è nella pittura, non si può pensare a nessun linguaggio di genere dell'arte contemporanea senza tenere presente che tutto è originato dalla vista.

Tutti i linguaggi dell'arte sono una questione visiva e d'immagine, l'umana è la civiltà dell'immagine; ovunque si muova e fugga, l'umano sarà sempre circondato da suoi artefatti visivi; pubblicità, blog, artefatti e videogiochi.

Immagini mai naturali e mai neutre, immagini con un linguaggio, con un funzionamento, una struttura e un'ideologia.

Come può Cagliari configurarsi come una città metropolitana dentro la civiltà dell'immagine, senza un'Accademia di Belle Arti?

Quello che si osserva ha sempre un significato, il significato lo determina lo spettatore, se chi guarda non sa attribuire significato simbolico a quello che osserva, cosa se ne fa del mondo?

Come leggere il mondo se non si sanno osservare e leggere le sue immagini?

Cagliari avrà sempre bisogno d'esperti provenienti dall'altrove? L'esplorazione dello sguardo, muta a seconda della cultura dell'occhio dell'osservatore e del suo pensiero, l'Accademia è il nodo e il luogo dell'educazione all'osservazione.

Certi luoghi comuni, reputano le figure e le immagini, da sole, più efficaci delle parole, si tratta di menzogne; non esiste nell'umano una visione svincolata dal linguaggio, quando pensa e legge un'immagine l'umano cosa fa se non parlarsi in testa?

I linguaggi dell'arte sono sempre tutti sinestetici, percepiamo con gli occhi in sinestesia con gli altri sensi e in relazione all'immaginazione; questa è la base della progettazione della rappresentazione, la sinestesia si mostra allo sguardo e abita i pensieri.

BASTA COL PREGIUDIZIO
DELL'ARTISTA SENZA MAESTRI

Il modello di sistema culturale e artistico Cagliaritano, privo di un'Accademia di Belle Arti, materializza l'ovvietà che chi ambisca ad esercitare la professione del fare arte, trovi lontano dall'isola luoghi migliori dove vivere con la propria professione determinata dalla passione.

Il ragionamento è semplice: come convincere altrove della qualità degli artisti "Made in Casteddu" senza un'Accademia di Belle Arti?

Il sistema dell'arte contemporanea, dai nodi di rete locali ai centri della globalizzazione, quando produce arte residente, non lo si può ridurre a una relazione tra colonizzatori e colonizzati; è un fatto che oggi basti avere un computer e una scrivania per divulgare e condividere i linguaggi dell'arte e i loro contenuti culturali, ma è fondamentale che la cultura e l'arte che si mettono in circolo, in reti globalmente interconnesse, siano frutto della cultura dialettica locale (che sappia sintetizzare locale e globale).

Non basta per fare arte e cultura, nascere in un luogo e incarnarne i valori e la cultura, è necessario che quel luogo sappia porre a sistema produttivo le arti e gli artisti residenti.

Questo millennio non distingue più simbolicamente artisticamente tra dominati e dominanti e neanche tra cultura e controcultura, il mercato dell'arte privato ha anche dissolto e squalificato nel nome dell'investimento l'idea dell'Accademia come istituzione e autorità, un blogger è diventato anche più autorevole di un giornalista; quello che oggi costituisce il reale valore di un'Accademia è la sua ricaduta comunitaria e territoriale, è uno strumento di autodeterminazione e autoproduzione locale di giovane ricerca artistica indipendente, un reale nodo diffusivo e propulsivo per la ricerca artistica locale.

Innegabile che il web abbia dato visibilità a un'anomalia che Cagliari rivendica da almeno sessant'anni, sessant'anni di pubblico e di pubblica offerta istituzionale proveniente dall'altrove, lo stesso Liceo Artistico di Cagliari nel 1967 nacque come Liceo pubblico sede distaccata del Liceo Artistico di Roma di Via Ripetta (chi lo ricorda? Proprio oggi me lo ricordava lo storico e ventennale Dirigente del Foiso Fois Umberto Di Pilla), il Liceo Artistico di Cagliari riuscì a tendere verso i cinquecento studenti e ottenere la sua autonomia con l'istituzione del corso serale, che nacque appositamente e nel giro di pochi mesi raccolse duecento studenti tra tutti coloro che praticavano arte residente da "lavoratori" senza avere fatto un percorso di studio preposto.

Dalla nascita del Liceo Artistico di Cagliari nel 1967 a oggi, permangono a Cagliari le pregiudiziali che le competenze visive possano non essere acquisite e nutrite, così come l'arte non necessiti di Licei, Accademie e Maestri, pregiudizio da debellare se si vuole affrontare questo millennio con cognizione di causa, proiettando la propria arte e la propria cultura in un scenario culturale ed economico interconnesso e globalizzato.

Qualsiasi esperienza visiva, non affiancata da strumenti critici, proprio come avviene nella realtà metropolitana Cagliaritana, può essere considerata naturale, ma la conseguenza è una distorsione prospettica, una visione distorta impostata su un sistema culturale e sociale fondato su produttori e consumatori acritici nei confronti di tutto quello che è comunicazione visiva.

L'anomalia Cagliaritana va letta in uno scenario economico globale di conflitto tra pubblico e privato, dove il distinguo tra artista e non artista, tra professionista e amatore sono già divenuti labili nell'immaginario collettivo; ma questo non ha mai precluso l'inquadratura del nodo di rete istituzionale e territoriale Accademia, in un sistema interconnesso di produzione e consumo locale dell'arte residente.

L'Accademia è il nodo di formazione artistica territoriale locale, dove si ricerca la modalità di realizzazione di un artefatto da inserire socialmente e rendere fruibile per chi è disposto a spendere tempo e denaro; in Accademia si ragiona su come rendere l'artefatto strumento di guadagno e simbolo riconosciuto dalla comunità come prodotto.

Un'Accademia a Cagliari è necessaria per fare produrre e consumare arte, per insegnare a porre delle domande come:
- Qual'è il punto di vista dell'artista?
- Chi sta influenzando chi?
- Cosa chiede quell'immagine a chi la guarda?
Senza Alta Formazione Artistica, le domande tipiche del Cagliaritano resteranno:
- Ma perché?
- Ti piace o non ti piace?
Cagliari oggi è una realtà territoriale metropolitana non educata a leggere le immagini in tutta la loro complessità e in relazione all'uso che ne viene fatto; una realtà dove ancora non si è compreso che più che il talento quello che conta è la sua visione progettuale che tenda a farlo operare nella società dove risiede.

Senza consapevolezza artistica, Cagliari come potrà avere una sua Storia dell'Arte che non subisca passivamente e di riflesso quella prodotta altrove?

Accademia vorrebbe dire, dare finalmente spessore a progetti d'autoproduzione e tendere a visioni che vadano oltre il folk, l'artigianato e la decorazione.

La semiologia (non quella del Cagliaritano purtroppo), ha ben presente come i confini dei linguaggi dell'arte oggi siano fittizi, come le opere pratichino un linguaggio che va ben oltre la propria cornice; i linguaggi dell'arte e la loro produttività, sono questione d'influenze reciproche con tutto ciò che erroneamente si pensa distante dall'arte; Cagliari e i suoi addetti ai lavori, sembra non abbiano la dimensione di come la critica faccia sempre parte di un lavoro, raccontare un lavoro e la propria impressione è azione sociale di divulgazione culturale ed influenza reciproca; l'arte non è un'insieme di nozioni e interpretazioni, è un processo socialmente condiviso anche quando pare non esserlo, i significati non sono solo interni alle opere, sono prodotti attraverso il consumo e la circolazione; le immagini non parlano a tutti nella stessa maniera, parlano a specifici gruppi più o meno grandi, a Cagliari il gruppo di "addetti ai lavori" e di "operatori culturali" è ristrettissimo, un'Accademia di Belle Arti lo renderebbe più ampio e condiviso.

Accademia è pubblicità per la comunità!

Cagliari appare nel 2019, ancora incapace di leggere la relazione tra un'Accademia di Belle Arti inserita nel proprio tessuto culturale connettivo, e la pubblicità per il proprio territorio derivante da tale intervento.

L'intero sistema sociale contemporaneo, e tutti i sistemi culturali, sono pensati e strutturati su vasta scala, le relazioni che il sistema dell'arte locale tesse con l'esterno è planetario, non ha mai una dimensione esclusivamente locale, da questa prospettiva un'Accademia di Belle Arti a Cagliari, è da intendersi come media didattico in grado fare pubblicità dialettica al territorio dove opera, strumento di narrazione e informazione.

La didattica dell'arte, senza la società di massa nella quale inserirsi, non avrebbe senso d'esistere in una realtà globalmente interconnessa come quella contemporanea.

I mass media sono nello scenario contemporaneo, uno strumento delle Accademia di Belle Arti, sono loro diffusori di contenuti, amplificatori della pubblicità artistica e culturale di cui l'intero territorio beneficia.

Non a caso, molte delle operazioni artistiche contemporanee, nascono in modalità intercomunicative, pensate per essere amplificate dai media, divenendo oggetto d'altra comunicazione, un fluido interminabile circolo ermeneutico promozionale.

Pensateci, un artista che frequenta o ha frequentato un'Accademia, che vede il suo lavoro recensito in spazi mediatici culturali, che diventa pubblicità locale, merce, arredamento e anche valore culturale comunitario.

Neanche il più integralista cultore della Scultura nuragica, può pensare che oggi l'arte possa essere distante dai mass media, e che la pubblicità sia sicura soltanto in aree limitate e specializzate.

Possibile che a fronte di questo potenziale, da sempre inespresso, Cagliari sembri non comprendere il valore e l'universo umanistico che c'è nel pensare e realizzare arte?

Che si rappresenti un triste contesto sociale e culturale dove le parole e le figure sembrano muoversi su traiettorie rigide e distinte?

Cagliari sembra frequentare eternamente una pessima scuola primaria, dove si ritiene che per leggere e scrivere sia necessario studiare e impegnarsi, e che il disegno sia un'attività ricreativa.

Possibile che si pensi ancora all'arte non come alta comunicazione dell'umano, ma come sola espressione del sé?

Relegare il disegno a dominio del talento è da ignoranti che privano i meno predisposto al ragionamento e alla visualizzazione del pensiero.

Pensate se ragionasse in maniera contraria, se non s'insegnasse a leggere e scrivere a chi non manifesta il talento potenziale di Ugo Foscolo.

Non solo la scrittura, tutti i segni dell'umano sono in relazione con il linguaggio, chi quando guarda un quadro astratto non parla forse con la propria mente quando trae considerazioni?

MAI CHIUDERE UN PROGETTO!

Un progetto artistico non dovrebbe mai passare per la computer grafica, l'immagine simulativa riduce il percepito e la percezione a pixel, favorisce un approccio mentale incorporeo, esclusivamente teorico.

Un aspetto importante, legato al funzionamento profondo della mente del creativo, è il fatto che la creatività si forma, determina e apprende in base ai modi e ai mondi che le si mettono a disposizione.

Se ci si forma e si progetta davanti a uno schermo, il cervello creativo resterà imprigionato in un pattern, la creazione artistica sarà ridotta a un Minotauro in un labirinto di un laboratorio.

La pratica dell'arte necessita invece di un corpo e di uno spazio, l'artista non può guardare senza fare (prima si osserva, poi si riflette e poi ci si esprime).

Non si può non considerare quanto sia importante il corpo nel formulare un pensiero creativo.

Disegnare, scolpire, dipingere e suonare, non sono attività che si possono praticare osservando le nuvole, le idee della Scultura non vengono prima di scolpire (dove c'è solo l'intuizione grafica dell'idea), si determinano e confermano o meno solo scolpendo.

Quando un artista prende appunti, schizza, progetta, inventa e scarabocchia, mette in pratica e connette pratiche operative mentali diverse, si muove senza confini precisi tra scrittura, organizzazione e disegno (io opero così, saltello di media in media, muovendomi tra scrittura, linguaggio, organizzazione e disegno); le attività progettuali e grafiche non sono nient'altro che lo spostamento di un pensiero su di un foglio.

Per questo non amo i progetti nati esclusivamente al computer, eliminano delle possibilità, tastiera e mouse non consentono alla mente del creativo delle pratiche miste; il touch screen è pieno di vincoli, ci si muove nell'ambito di qualcosa che è previsto a monte, dove è il rapporto tra il creativo e il linguaggio come insieme di regole da forzare e scardinare?

L'attività progettuale necessita del saltellare da un uso all'altro, pensate alla scarica fisica per uno studente d'arte che cancella un disegno di cui non è contento, non è energia quella della violenza con cui si nega un segno sotto altri segni?

Muoversi su di un foglio è attività ultrasensoriale, non bisogna smettere di disegnare per essere più svelti e precisi con il digitale, senza disegno non c'è la pratica motoria e cognitiva che si muove con il corpo.

Anche se li si celebra come creativi, Designer, Architetti e Illustratori Grafici si muovono come impiegati, incastrati in posture rigide e schemi ripetitivi.

L'arte ha bisogno del farsi laboratorio per non prendere le distanze dall'umano, il progetto deve muoversi con scarabocchi, segni, disegni, colori, appunti, l'idea deve muoversi con la postura di chi la determina.

Non è un caso, che la grafica globalizzata tende a essere omogenea, a somigliare un poco tutta, questo avviene non per influenza culturale, ma per modalità progettuale.

Designer, Architetti e Grafici compiono gli stessi movimenti, maneggiano pixel all'infinito (a destra, ruota, abbassa, taglia, copia, incolla...).

Design, Grafica, Architettura, si stanno riducendo con i nuovi media a processi standard di spostamento di pixel, è nell'origine dei linguaggi dell'arte che si ragiona su come l'impostazione dei problemi consenta di raccontare e definire storie, disegno, scrittura, pittura e scultura sono la chiave dei processi creativi.

VADEMECUM PER L'ACCADEMIA A

CAGLIARI

Articolo 5 dello Statuto Autonomo della Regione Sardegna

Salva la competenza prevista nei due precedenti articoli, la Regione ha facoltà di adattare alle sue particolari esigenze le disposizioni delle leggi della Repubblica, emanando norme di integrazione ed attuazione, sulle seguenti materie:
a) istruzione di ogni ordine e grado, ordinamento degli studi;

b) lavoro; previdenza ed assistenza sociale;
c) antichità e belle arti;
d) nelle altre materie previste da leggi dello Stato.

Dal momento che per la prima volta, nella storia politica Comunale di Cagliari, l'Alta Formazione Artistica diviene uno dei nodi del confronto tra i due candidati sindaco (Paolo Truzzu e Francesca Ghirra) e le rispettive liste, ci sembrava opportuno condividere un ragionamento su come nasce un'Accademia d'Alta Formazione Artistica:

La maniera più semplice e celere sarebbe farla nascere come sede distaccata dell'Accademia di Belle Arti di Sassari, individuando delle aree di specializzazione locale che a Sassari non siano attive, sul modello di come è nata l'Accademia di Belle Arti di Ravenna, che si occupa soltanto dell'arte del Mosaico; l'Accademia di Belle Arti di Ravenna in tale ottica partendo dalla sua specificità storica, artistica e culturale, ha elevato la sua tradizione artigianale locale a forma d'arte contemporanea, traghettando la formazione artistica locale del mosaico a ricerca artistica contemporanea da non ridurre ad artigianato folk, ma da esportare dovunque nel mondo con i propri artisti altamente specializzati, diventando meta di chi per formarsi in tale specializzazione di genere sceglie Ravenna come meta di studi. In tale ottica l'eventuale sede distaccata dell'Accademia di Belle Arti di Sassari potrebbe fondarsi e reggersi esclusivamente su forme artistiche d'area, come l'arte dell'intaglio lapideo (pensate quanto sia sentita la Scultura e la pietra nella tradizione artistica isolana e anche a quanto Pinuccio Sciola ci tenesse ad aprire una scuola d'arte e mestieri della pietra, in questo caso si andrebbe oltre e si conferirebbe a tutto questo la dignità d'Alta Formazione Artistica residente, ponendo la Scultura isolana con tutto il suo carico di tradizione e memoria proveniente e testimoniato dai nuragici a contatto diretto, dialettico e didattico con la ricerca e l'alta formazione artistica contemporanea evadendo dalla dimensione folk e da cartolina che oggi grava e pesa sulla Scultura contemporanea isolana, in tale ambito tra i corsi complementari potrebbe esserci quello di "fonderia e d'arte della ceramica" altro settore d'eccellenza artigianale locale in forte crisi di settore); altro settore altamente formativo e caratterizzante potrebbe essere quello dell'arte dei murales e delle pitture parietali, l'isola è la Regione d'Italia che ha il numero maggiore di paesi Museo a cielo aperto e di murales, ma nonostante questo gli artisti isolani non hanno mai avuto una reale proiezione e formazione istituzionale (anche da guardare in maniera critica) e neanche la possibilità (al di là di percorsi personali) di confrontarsi con l'altrove, la public art è oggi un'evoluzione dell'arte del muralismo e in quest'ottica l'isola con i suoi artisti, vista anche la disponibilità di fruibilità di spazi potrebbe divenire estremamente attrattiva per la formazione artistica internazionale di settore. L'Accademia di Belle Arti di Ravenna è interessante come esempio, perché è convenzionata con l'Accademia di Bologna ma è Comunale, questo vuole dire che gli studenti che s'iscrivono in tale percorso di studio versano direttamente la tassa d'iscrizione nelle casse Comunali, il che contribuisce a coprire i costi di gestione di personale e spazi in attesa della statalizzazione. Triennio e biennio di specializzazione, pur trattandosi di un'Accademia Comunale hanno valore legale proprio nel nome della convenzione con l'Accademia di Bologna, alimentando un interesse d'area comune Regionale Emiliana nei confronti dell'Alta Formazione Artistica Contemporanea.

Altra possibilità (oggettivamente più tortuosa) sarebbe lavorare per un'Accademia di Belle Arti di Cagliari partendo dai dati di dispersione scolastica e emigrazione giovanile isolana e nello specifico Cagliaritana come città metropolitana, un'Accademia di Belle Arti di Cagliari sarebbe da tampone all'emigrazione e alla dispersione scolastica, anche perché l'accesso sarebbe possibile non soltanto agli studenti con maturità artistica, ma a tutti i maturandi d'area metropolitana (l'area di Cagliari città metropolitana corrisponde ai 2/3 delle residenza isolane e i numeri di Sassari raccontano di una realtà ben radicata nel proprio territorio che non si alimenta certamente degli studenti provenienti da Cagliari e neanche dalle altre Regioni d'Italia o dall'estero, dal momento che la percentuale di studenti che arrivano da fuori Regione è pari soltanto all'un per cento), le due Accademie si legittimerebbero dialogando a vicenda e incrementerebbero i dati legati all'industria dell'Alta Formazione nel terziario locale (che per quanto riguarda l'isola sono i più bassi d'Italia). L'area di Cagliari ha istruzione liceale artistica, una facoltà d'Architettura e un Conservatorio proprio come quella del nord

Sardegna, il distinguo è proprio nell'Alta Formazione Artistica Accademica, settore che a Cagliari non può essere coperto solo dallo IED che oltre che formare in direzioni d'Avanguardia di settore che indirizzano egualmente verso l'altrove, dal punto di vista dei costi in quanto percorso privatizzato, non è propriamente accessibile per tutti coloro che vorrebbero e potrebbero accedervi, e nel 2019 configurare l'Alta Formazione Artistica come distinguo di classe e di ceto sociale economico residente è francamente qualcosa d'insopportabile, comunque sia il percorso dello Ied non lavora sulla messa a sistema della tradizione e della memoria artistica e culturale residente spingendola nella direzione dialettica della contemporaneità, Scultura su pietra e arte del murales sono assenti. Per chiedere l'istruzione di un'Accademia di Belle Arti di Cagliari occorrerebbe un'intervento congiunto di diversi assessorati della cultura e della pubblica istruzione (dal comune, alla città metropolitana alla Regione) indirizzato al Ministro della pubblica istruzione e all'AFAM. Riferimento normativo è sempre il D.P.R. 8 marzo 1999, n. 275, regolamento recante norme in materia di autonomia delle istituzioni scolastiche,ai sensi dell'art. 21 della L. 15 marzo 1997, n. 59.

Altra ipotesi è quella di un protocollo d'intesa di rete tra scuole (non tra Comune e Accademia come nel caso di Ravenna e Bologna), in quest'ottica l'accordo di rete potrebbe essere tra il liceo artistico locale (o perché no? I licei artistici d'area metropolitana) e l'Accademia di Belle Arti di Sassari; ma niente e nessuno nell'ambito di un ordinario accordo di rete, vieterebbe un accordo tra un Liceo Artistico locale e una qualsiasi Accademia Italiana (pubblica o parificata) nell'ottica del rilascio di un attestato triennale e biennale di specializzazione che abbia valore legale. Riferimento normativo è sempre il D.P.R. 8 marzo 1999, n. 275, regolamento recante norme in materia di autonomia delle istituzioni scolastiche,ai sensi dell'art. 21 della L. 15 marzo 1997, n. 59.

Ovviamente tutte le ipotesi devono muoversi in relazione a una volontà politica trasversale (che almeno a livello politico comunale, in questa fase di campagna elettorale appare manifesta), se l'Accademia di Sassari vuole aprire una sede distaccata a Cagliari, l'operazione è molto semplice, basta che ci sia il sostegno della politica Cagliaritana, i protocolli sono anche piuttosto semplici, basta che ci siano spazi adatti e professori/Maestri di settore disponibili, che possono essere assunti e inviati da Sassari, ma se in un'accordo di rete c'è un liceo Artistico possono essere anche individuati con incarico a progetto dal Liceo e la quota docenti potrebbe essere ripartita tra Cagliari e Sassari, i "soldi" che dovrebbe trovare la politica Cagliaritana sono quelli relativi agli spazi di gestione (che potrebbero essere a progetto Europeo ma anche a fondo comunale sul modello di Ravenna).

Emblematico quanto accade a Iglesias nel 2006: La presidente della provincia di Sassari e il presidente di quella di Carbonia Iglesias, intervennero per bloccare una sede distaccata dell'Accademia di Belle Arti a Iglesias.
La prima perché temeva una sorta di OPA ostile dei Cagliaritani sull'Accademia sassarese e il secondo, per evitare che l'offerta formativa di Iglesias potesse crescere a discapito di quella della sua Carbonia.
Insomma si massimizzò il danno a fronte di un profitto inesistente.
Nel 2012 a Cagliari mancò la firma in Regione, la prospettiva era quella sulla base di un accordo di rete tra il Liceo Artistico "Foiso Fois" e l'Accademia di Belle Arti "Mario Sironi", di fare nascere una sede distaccata dell'Accademia di Belle Arti di Sassari, nell'allora sede del Foiso Fois di Via San Giuseppe a Castello, si trattava di un corso di Scenografia.

LETTERA ALL'AMICO INDIPENDENTISTA

Caro amico indipendentista, sono anni che tento "politicamente" di farti capire, che elevare a questione d'identità solo la lingua sarda, senza estendere la problematica ai linguaggi dell'arte residente, sia controproducente.
La questione dell'Alta Formazione Artistica a Cagliari è prioritaria a mio avviso rispetto a tante altre stronzate che recintano oltre misura, una cultura è una specificità identitaria, che è squalificante vincolare al solo concetto di lingua minoritaria (che vuole dire anche arte minoritaria).
Non è così che si autodetermina politicamente una nazione, così si contribuisce a escludere una Regione.

Con stima e affetto, Mimmo

IL MITO DELLA ROTTAMAZIONE DEL VECCHIO

Un mito dell'arte del Novecento è quello che l'arte nuova è sempre la migliore, il mito dell'arte contemporanea è fondato sulla rottamazione del vecchio, fondamenta è l'idolatria per il nuovo, anche quando di nuovo non si tratta, dal momento che dagli anni trenta del novecento, le avanguardie appaiono essere ricampionate all'infinito.

L'idolatria del nuovo è generata ovviamente dall'economia capitalistica, il sistema del mercato dell'arte contemporanea è fondato sull'idea dei linguaggi dell'arte e degli artisti deperibili, che passano di moda e che possono essere sostituibili, altrimenti perché desiderare un nuovo quadro di un nuovo artista?

Il nuovo contemporaneo è cavallo di battaglia, anche di circuiti culturali che si oppongono al sistema di mercato dell'arte contemporanea, anche gli artisti che criticano il sistema lo fanno nel nome del nuovo e della novità che ritengono di costituire, è la rivoluzione e non la restaurazione.

La passione e l'attribuzione di valore che i media di massa hanno verso il contemporaneo, è originata dalla nevrosi compulsiva che caratterizza la ricerca di senso degli artisti a cavallo tra ottocento e novecento, con tutta l'industria culturale (divenuta oggi Accademica) che ha determinato.

Il Novecento ha collocato da un lato la Scienza, che indagando su se stessa ambisce e perviene a risultati, mai oggettivi, ma misurabili; dall'altro l'Arte, il cui valore simbolico sembra essere vincolato e misurato esclusivamente con il valore economico; la scissione Arte-Scienza ha nel Novecento privato l'artista del suo ruolo Rinascimentale, quello d'essere l'unità di misura e il canone di una civiltà.

Nel Novecento gli artisti hanno cominciato a rincorrere e imitare gli scienziati, hanno progressivamente innescato la patologia virale dell'avanguardista innovazione, incastrandosi in un rituale linguistico spesso fine a se stesso.

Eppure l'arte non ha nulla a che vedere con la contrapposizione tra vecchio e nuovo, impossibile comparare Pollock e Leonardo, l'arte nuova non rottama la vecchia, è altro, è sinonimo di valore aggiunto, d'eccellenza che sa essere localizzata, distinguibile e percepibile al punto da rassicurare anche il committente meno preparato.

Senza un'Accademia di Belle Arti a Cagliari, si antepone alla costruzione dell'eccellenza artistica locale, la firma famosa, e si invogliano giovani e poco noti artisti, a imitare linguaggi, stili e atteggiamenti, di detentori del gusto imposti dall'altrove-

L'Accademia di Belle Arti è quel luogo di cultura plurale, dove l'espressione non ha finalità ma è la finalità; dove le discussioni sull'arte hanno consistenza estetica in una generale amplificazione dei sensi, di emozioni e cognizioni; dove c'è la messa in forma di un modo di sentire la vita o della visione del mondo.

L'Accademia di Belle Arti, educa in un sistema utilitaristico come quello del mercato dell'arte contemporanea, all'arte della contemplazione mossa dall'interesse e dalla passione; insegna a capire come l'arte non nasce mai in un Museo o fuori dalla storia, la "Primavera" di Botticelli nasceva difatti per essere appesa su un lettuccio; l'Accademia educa all'arte che nasce con una funzione e la funzione non è necessariamente muovere ingenti somme di denaro, per quello servono le Biennali (lo sa bene l'operazione Banksy) che esprimono non passione e ricerca di senso ma alta finanza; l'Accademia non forma artisti da trattare come fossero valori in borsa, non dequalifica e progetta carriere, educa allo studio e alla ricerca per creare localmente senso culturale sociale.

In un'Accademia si ragiona sull'arte come oggetto (o prodotto) che con consapevolezza sa essere pretesto per un'esperienza estetica, un oggetto e un prodotto di cui si senta l'intenzione, intenzione che può essere rivendicata in una cornice del contendere dialettico di senso. Accademia è analisi del mito e delle idee, è decostruzione del passato e della memoria, per indagare cosa sia necessario al contemporaneo; è un luogo dove ciascuno ha un proprio spazio laboratoriale, finalizzato alla comprensione di che tipo d'artista o d'osservatore si possa diventare.

Il sistema linguistico dell'arte consente scelte buone o cattive. lecite o illecite, critiche o autocritiche, attraverso la frequentazione di un'Accademia la si può finalmente smettere di chiamarsi fuori dal sistema dell'arte, evitare la provinciale e distaccata critica superficiale (il Cagliaritano eccelle in questo atteggiamento); l'Accademia è critica come messa in discussione e non come giudizio, sapere usare una matita è poca cosa, quello che serve ai linguaggi dell'arte è la consapevolezza; l'arte è un fatto sociale con committenti, pubblico e artisti che hanno desideri e intenzioni; capire d'arte non è riconoscere forme, stili e linguaggi, ma sapere chi sta parlando e perché.

L'Accademia, le comunali e gli artisti in lista!

La virtuale contemporaneità politica Cagliaritana, proietta l'arte e gli artisti residenti verso realtà inutili e anche controproducenti; questa campagna elettorale Cagliaritana ha come elemento caratterizzante quello della visibilità e della promozione personale dell'artista attraverso la politica; artisti che sembra che per sostenere se stessi debbano sostenere la politica che consente in maniera clemente loro d'essere, in realtà forti del loro ruolo sociale, culturale e intellettuale, avrebbero tutti gli strumenti per inchiodare la politica Comunale e Regionale alle proprie responsabilità civili, tra questa quella di servire l'arte e gli artisti. Il rischio della riduzione del proprio ruolo a promozione personale per promuovere cause, è quello di rendere inutile il ruolo sociale dell'arte; la riduzione dell'artista a servo dell'ideologia massmediatica della politica rende inutile l'artista, riduce il linguaggio dell'arte a icona personale e santino elettorale, lo scenario politico diventa banale illustrazione di contorno di un virtuale che è più affascinante di un reale da modificare, virtualmente si è tutti d'accordo sull'Accademia di Belle Arti da fare e progettare a Cagliari.

L'arte è rappresentazione di forme e contenuti reali, tende al vero e a questo deve fare tendere la politica, non coltivare con la politica il fascino della menzogna ridotto a propaganda e strategia del consenso. Un'Accademia a Cagliari è necessaria a prescindere da liste infarcite di addetti ai lavori in cerca di voto che la promuovono, serve perché tra una generazione a Cagliari nessuno potrebbe più sapere leggere un quadro o una scultura, perché si sta riducendo l'arte a intrattenimento, al numero di selfie che legittimano il lavoro sullo sfondo.

L'Accademia serve ai bambini come gli adulti, ai professionisti come ai dilettanti, è necessaria per cogliere la differenza tra cultura e intrattenimento, tra genio creativo e gioco; senza Accademia, Cagliari avalla l'idea che non sia l'arte a gratificare l'umano, ma che sia l'umano a gratificare e servire all'arte come alla politica.

L'Accademia è necessaria al Cagliaritano come agii artisti Cagliaritani (dilettanti o professionisti che siano), per aiutare a comprendere come l'arte necessiti di tempo per essere vista, apprezzata o criticata; l'arte è fatta per durare e non è un bene da consumare.

L'Accademia in una città come Cagliari ci deve essere, e per giustificare questo non servono artisti candidati a sostegno di questo o quello per legittimarne la richiesta; non serve chiedere un'Accademia timidamente candidandosi e portando voti, gli artisti nel loro interesse, l'Accademia di Belle Arti di Cagliari, la devono pretendere; candidarsi vuole dire distinguersi e non condividere, dissentire dall'altro può diventare alibi politico e artistico che avalla interessi personali.

Arte è condivisione e non divisione politica, l'artista che crea condivide elevando il suo linguaggio e la sua ricerca post, è il suo linguaggio (e non la sua candidatura) a reclamare una messa a sistema culturale e della memoria con un'Accademia!

UN NURAGHE DI TRECENTO METRI

In campagna elettorale se ne leggono tante, mai come in questa si ragiona d'Accademia di Belle Arti e di quanto l'Alta Formazione Artistica possa essere importante per la città, il comune e l'area metropolitana di Cagliari.

Mai come quest'anno centro destra e centro sinistra si è d'accordo su come un'Accademia di Belle Arti possa essere propulsiva per tutto il settore terziario della città; in questo scenario d'intenti comuni, la mia attenzione riguardo quello che riguarda Arte e cultura nel territorio, viene però catalizzata da questa dichiarazione che apprendo tramite un giornale on line, da parte di un candidato consigliere comunale:

«A Cagliari un nuraghe alto 300 metri che identifica la nostra terra come la torre Eiffel a Parigi e il Colosseo a Roma.
Bisogna caratterizzare l'immagine della città per chi viene dal mare o dall'aria. Questo è solo l'inizio».

La proposta sembra stia facendo molto discutere il web, capisco il perché e il per come la questione agiti sciami di utenti, anche perché Torre Eiffel e Colosseo sono simboli della Storia dell'Architettura tradotta in memoria da conservare, proprio come i nuraghe, diverso sarebbe ragionare su un'Accademia che partendo dalla tradizione Nuragica, sappia formare artisti e modellare un ambiente culturale, sociale ed economico in grado di consegnare alla memoria residente la sua storia presente elevandola a patrimonio condiviso, per cui mi chiedo, anche in questo caso e anche a questa voce che sembra essere fuori dal coro politico comune che trasversalmente reclama alta formazione artistica nell'unica città metropolitana d'Europa dove è ancora assente:

Se prima del nuraghe di trecento metro si ragionasse su come fare si che Cagliari abbia la sua Alta Formazione Artistica Residente?

ACCADEMIA PER UNA CAGLIARI DIFFERENZIATA

Cagliari è l'unica città metropolitana Occidentale a non avere pubblica Alta Formazione Artistica, che questo sia un handicap è innegabile. L'assenza di un'Accademia di Belle Arti a Cagliari è indubbiamente un macigno per una realtà ancora culturalmente arretrata come quella isolana, realtà fotografata da dispersione scolastica, emigrazione giovanile, spopolamento e denatalità; nell'isola c'è uno scenario dove l'istruzione invece d'avanzare perde progressivamente pezzi, con l'industria sparita e con l'unico settore dal quale si dovrebbe ripartire (quello artistico e culturale), che senza un'Accademia di Belle Arti a Cagliari, nella pratica non è mai stato.

A Cagliari come da sempre, anche in queste elezioni politiche comunali, si promettono rivoluzioni a tempo pieno, ma nell'agenda politica comunale l'Accademia di Belle Arti mai stata e la discussione sulla raccolta differenziata sembrano avere lo stesso peso politico (possibile?).

Come si fa a non comprendere che l'unico futuro possibile per l'isola, passa per l'industria culturale e artistica residente con la sua alta formazione permanente?

Possibile che non ci si renda conto di quale tragedia sia, l'assenza di un'Accademia Cagliaritana che si appresta a canalizzare e affrontare tutto quello che questo millennio sarà?

Il Foiso Fois nacque nel 1967 come sede distaccata del Ripetta di Roma (incredibile ma andò così) e divenne autonomo Liceo Artistico di Cagliari soltanto nel 1977, d'allora qualcosa si è arrestato a livello politico Comunale e Regionale, allora c'era la forza e la ragione per pretendere un'Accademia di Belle Arti di Cagliari, oggi resta solo la ragione; ragione che non si può di certo fermare all'Accademia di Sassari.

BIOGRAFIA:

Mimmo Di Caterino, figlio dei pittori Pasquale Di Caterino e Maria Cuturi, è Artivista e Scultore connettivo, nato a Napoli il 07/08/73; vive a Cagliari dal 2000, dove ha sposato l'artista Barbara Ardau nel 2011.

Ha pubblicato:

"Altro Sistema dell'arte", "Oltre il sistema dell'Arte", "Dentro il sistema dell'Arte" e "Other Academy" con la Booksprint edizioni.

"Artist bullshit job" e "Rockbus Museum" su Amazon.

"Artfucking" e "Shitstorms on Academy" con Caosfera.

Docente di Discipline Plastiche presso il Liceo Artistico e Musicale "Foiso Fois", ha insegnato Storia dell'Arte Contemporanea presso il Conservatorio di Cagliari ed è stato coordinatore dei corsi abilitanti per docenti ad indirizzo artistico presso l'Accademia di Sassari; ha collaborato con Flash Art, Exib Art, Tiscali, Lobodilattice, CagliariPad e Ad Maiora Media, cura e gestisce la webzine CagliariArtMagazine.it

Printed in Great Britain
by Amazon

34970800R00102